JUDGEMENT OF THE SIX

Books 1-3

Hope(less)
(Mis)fortune
(Un)wise

Melissa Haag

Hope(less)

As a human, Gabby is determined to leave the supernatural world behind. However, she doesn't count on meeting a silent, ruggedly-handsome werewolf with a single-minded determination to make her his mate. When she tries to run, he's not the only one to follow. Something truly dangerous is after her, and Gabby must turn to Clay for help if she ever hopes to discover who is hunting her for the secrets she's spent her whole life protecting.

(Mis)Fortune

Kept prisoner by a man who changes into a wolf and used for the predictions that tormented her, Michelle meekly follows orders to keep her bothers safe. She knows she needs to escape but there's nowhere she can hide forever, and no one who can protect her. Unless she can find someone stronger than her captor.

(Un)wise

When the dreams start, Bethi's very normal life goes down the toilet. Every past life she relives has Dog-men and her eventual tormented death at their hands. This time she's determined to find a way to live. While the dreams hint at an answer, they're also clear about the risk, and it's not only her life that hangs in the balance. She, and the other five women like her, need to figure out how to live...or everyone will die.

HOPELESS

JUDGEMENT

OF THE SIX

BOOK 1

MELISSA HAAG

CHAPTER ONE

I KNEW THE LOCATIONS OF THE PEOPLE AROUND ME AS IF MY HEAD came equipped with a giant fish finder. When I focused, a vast darkness opened in my mind. Instead of blips on a radar, tiny sparks of light shimmered, matching the location of people in the area immediately around me. The colors of the lights, always a yellow center and dark-green halo, never varied. Except for me. My spark had a vibrant orange halo, making me unique and alone. Always alone...

I STOOD at the entrance of the park while the bus pulled away with a screech of hydraulics. Dusk had already settled, casting shadows. Before walking my usual path through the park, I opened my senses to make sure it was as deserted as it seemed.

Though no sparks decorated the darkness in the area around me, I kept my senses open. The void was endless, but my sight did have a maximum distance. So I monitored the area around me as I walked the path and started thinking of the homework I still needed to do.

Distracted, I didn't at first notice the pale blue light with a bright green halo lingering near the pond. There had never been a color variation before. My steps slowed. Perhaps this new color meant I could see something other than humans, maybe animals. As interesting as that would be, the idea of my sight suddenly changing worried me. What if it wasn't an animal? What if it was someone like me? I could keep walking, and whatever the spark was would never know I saw it. But, I was too curious and hungry for answers to walk away. I stepped off the path to investigate.

The lawn muffled the sound of my approach. Near the edge of the pond, I spotted a shadow moving. It was much too large for an animal. I moved closer. The shadow continued to move, and in an instant, I identified the shape. A man. I froze in shock. He stood close to the water's edge.

His presence didn't freak me out as much as the lack of the normal yellow-green life-spark. In its place shimmered the oddly tinted spark. I'd actually found someone like me–a person who had a uniquely colored life-spark. Excitement built even as caution reined me in. What could this odd coloring mean? I'd never run into any variations before. Stay or run? Investigating a color I thought could be an animal was one thing, but approaching a strange man in a dark park? Not the best idea...yet my curiosity won.

As I edged closer to the grove of trees, I recognized the older man. I'd bumped into him, literally, a few days ago at the hospital. The man, who had kind brown eyes, a friendly smile, and grey hair, had apologized for bumping into me and continued on his way. That's why I remembered him.

Typically, men didn't just continue on their way after seeing me because, along with the ability to see those life-sparks, I also had a certain pull. Just on men. From adolescent to grandparent, I unwillingly drew them to me. The degree in which I affected them varied. Some just studied me like a puzzle that needed solving, but forgot about me as soon as I disappeared from sight. For others, I became an obsession.

I crept forward as I watched the man sit and remove his shoes and socks. But, I stopped when he began unbuttoning his shirt. What was he doing stripping down in the park? Given his apparent age, perhaps he suffered from some type of dementia. Maybe he thought it a good place to take a swim.

When he stepped behind the trees for a moment and reemerged completely naked, I began to think he might have more serious issues than dementia.

Still debating whether I should call out to him, I gasped when his silhouette collapsed. I automatically moved forward, thinking he had fallen. My feet covered some of the distance between us before I saw he had dropped into a low crouch with his fingers touching the ground. I skidded to a stop so abruptly the grass tore up beneath my feet.

His skin rippled like sand in a current. Immobilized, I watched his body contort and fold in on itself in some places while it stretched in others. What would make him move like that? Was he sick? Something contagious? I couldn't make myself move away. If he was hurt or sick, he needed help.

Then the sounds started. His knuckles cracked and popped, and his thumbs shrank from the rest of his fingers. I took a step back and then another. Other joints began popping in earnest. It sounded painful. Through it all, he remained silent. My pulse pounded, and I eased another step back.

His skull grew larger, longer than it was high, and his nose and mouth extended with it. I forgot to keep moving. His ears shifted higher. A grey down emerged from his exposed skin, and grew into thick fur. He shook it out when his slow transformation from human to large canine completed.

My mind screamed *werewolf* even as it denied the possibility. Werewolves were legend, myth.

His head swung in my direction. His eyes glowed eerily from the distant lights. My paralyzing shock left me, and I ran. The park entrance beckoned in the distance, but I knew I would never make it. Thanks to my second sight, I saw him rapidly closing in on me.

Rather than being attacked from behind, I spun to confront the big, grey beast bearing down on me. One well-placed kick to its throat, that's all I needed to get in before it mauled me to death. Yeah, I was going to die. I braced myself.

As soon as I turned, the beast slowed to a trot. Within ten feet, it slowed to a walk. My breath still tore through my throat in ragged, terrified gasps.

A yard away, it sat on its haunches. I stared at the creature, poised to run again. Intelligent blue eyes watched me. For several long moments, neither of us moved, and a debate raged within me. What did it want? Should I run, or should I wait to find out?

Holding its gaze, I slid a foot back. It stood. I froze, heart hammering.

The creature began to circle me. I pivoted, following its progress. Finally, we stopped when it had positioned itself between me and the north side of the park —the way home. Then it began to stalk forward, backing me toward the pond. My breathing spiked again. I didn't want to go back to the darker area of the park. Yet, I moved backward fearing what would happen if I didn't.

Just as I considered making another run for it, the creature sat down. What was he waiting for? Suddenly, it yipped. The sound scared the breath right out of me. As if that breath had been the signal he'd waited for, he trotted around me to his pile of clothes. There he morphed back to the man he'd been before; the transformation took less than two heartbeats.

Without perversion, I watched him dress, still too stunned and afraid to look away. I thought about running, but couldn't ignore the fact that he and I shared a connection. Unique life-sparks. I feared what that meant for me.

While buttoning his shirt slowly, he looked up and met my wide gaze. I tried to calm down. Was he like a real canine? If he smelled my fear, would he attack? I'd been afraid since he'd changed into his fur, and he hadn't attacked me then, so I supposed he wouldn't now either.

My rational thoughts fled when he paced toward me with his hands in the pockets of his khakis. I tensed to bolt.

He removed one hand from a pocket and held it up, palm out, signaling I should wait. Right...

"My name is Samuel Riedel, but calling me Sam suits me just fine. I'm sorry for the scare, but showing you was the only way for you to believe."

Believe I'm crazy? Done. I took a few steadying breaths before talking.

"Why did you show me? What do you want?" I fought hard to keep my breathing under control. My mind continued to race.

Sam smiled, turned, and walked toward a bench near the edge of the water. He sat and motioned for me to join him. A small noise of disbelief escaped me. He'd just changed into a dog large enough to pass for a pony. I stayed in the not yet dark shadows of the evergreens.

"You're different, but not as different as I am," he said, keeping himself turned so he could watch me.

He knew something about me? I fidgeted with the strap of my dark brown messenger bag. He could have the answers I needed to explain why I saw the lights in my head or why men acted so differently around me. The temptation of learning something, anything, rooted me. Yet there was also the possibility that he knew nothing of my gifts, that what he knew was something completely different from what I already knew.

"What do you mean I'm different?" I decided I had to be sure we were talking about the same thing before I could reveal anything more.

"You smell different. You're not exactly human, but you're not a werewolf either."

Having him say "werewolf" aloud made everything I'd just witnessed surreal. How could werewolves be possible? How could I be possible? At least, I now knew I wasn't a werewolf like him.

I still stood exactly where I'd been, yet I felt like the entire world had just changed while the crickets continued their night song.

"For clarification...no, I don't need a full moon. No, I don't eat raw meat, although I do enjoy medium-rare steak on occasion. And, no, silver bullets won't kill me any better than regular ones will." Sam chuckled while he moved over on the bench, making plenty of room, and patted the empty space invitingly. "You, dear, are not a werewolf," he repeated.

I blinked at the absurdity of his invitation to sit with him.

"What do you want from me?" I asked, not bothering to acknowledge his invitation. I still didn't understand why he'd shown me at all.

"You may not be a werewolf, but you are still special. How old are you?"

At five feet five inches, with a slight build and few curves to speak of, I looked young. The freckles sprinkling my nose didn't help me look any older either.

"Sixteen," I answered absently. "How exactly am I special?" I shifted my bag to the other shoulder.

"I was drawn to you. You have a certain scent that calls to my kind. I couldn't name the smell for you other than to say it's interesting, unlike anything else you've ever smelled."

"Is that why guys don't leave me alone?" What if I'd been born with more pheromones than the average person? I'd learned about them in biology. Pheromones attracted the opposite sex. It would explain the pull I had on men and why it'd grown stronger as I'd matured.

I couldn't pin it on anything about me physically. I had straight, shoulder length ash blonde hair, a medium complexion, and hazel eyes like a million other girls. My nose fit my face well enough, neither too wide nor too long, and my mouth wasn't so generous it'd give a guy dirty thoughts. No, it had nothing to do with my looks. Something else pulled them, and I wanted to understand what. Having extra pheromones didn't explain the lights though.

"What do you mean? What guys?" He sat forward too quickly for my comfort.

I flinched back a step and eyed him warily. When he moved like that, he looked a lot younger than his grey hair and weathered skin indicated. So, although he kept his tone light, I remained cautious.

"Guys under sixty and boys over ten."

"Well, you're young and pretty, so I'm sure it's not unusual for men to be attracted to you, dear." He settled back with a laugh.

He'd said it easily and without inflection as if he'd made an observation and stated a fact, reaffirming the pull I had on men didn't seem to affect him. Did that mean he didn't know about my gift and might not understand? Part of me deflated a little. Should I try to explain it? If I smelled different to his kind, it might still relate to my gifts. Confiding in him might be worth the risk. Besides, he could hardly run around telling people that I had special abilities when he'd just turned into a wolf in front of me.

I took a step closer, partially forgetting caution.

"No, it's more than that... A boy in school, extremely shy, picked on by jocks to the point of physical cruelty, nudged past those same jocks to wait by my locker to ask me on a date. A man shopping with two kids stopped me in the grocery store to ask if I'd consider dating an older man once I turned eighteen. The eighteen bit he threw in after my foster mom gasped in shock." I inched closer, becoming more animated as I spoke, trying to make him understand. "When I turned him down, he went back by his kids, red-faced and told them that he'd just been asking for grandpa who wanted to date again. I knew that wasn't true." I paused a moment then added, "Those are just examples of what happens to me every day."

Sam studied me for a moment.

"What's your name, dear?"

"Gabrielle Winters. I prefer Gabby."

"Well, Gabby, I don't know why men act the way they do around you, but I'd like to help you figure it out. Few people would believe what I've shown you tonight, and I ask that you not try talking anyone into believing. I revealed myself to you because you're special and worth the risk."

He stood and approached me. With the pond reflecting dimly behind him and the warm breeze ruffling our hair, I knew that memories of this night would stay with me for a long time.

"There is so much about werewolves that you need to know. The first is that I'm not the only one."

My heart sank. I didn't like the sound of that.

"I'd like to meet your foster parents, and I'd like to get to know you better. I want to be there for you if you ever need anything." He stuffed his hands into his pockets and rocked back on the heels of his brown-laced shoes while I considered his words.

"You said that I smelled good to your kind. Does that mean I'm going to be run down by other werewolves?" The prospect scared me, but I managed to keep any tremor from my voice.

"It's unlikely, but precisely why I would like to be involved in your life. I can help guide your introduction to our world, so it's not as scary as tonight."

He waited quietly while I thought it over. I watched him closely. I liked that he maintained eye contact. It was a refreshing change since the majority of conversations with men occurred while they tried to discover, visually, what about me attracted them.

He offered me an opportunity. With his help, maybe I could find out the reason behind my abilities. And given his condition, I felt certain he'd be able to keep my secret if I decided to tell him about the lights. Could I trust him? Not blindly, but I could start small.

"I'm willing to get to know you better, but I'm not ready for you to meet my foster parents." I wasn't sure if I ever would be.

I wanted to protect Tim and Barb Newton from what could be a monster. They were the first set of foster parents I actually liked. But, if I wasn't willing to bring him home, then just where would we get to know each other better? Dark nights in the park were out, and I had more brains than to suggest his place. He still scared me. Did I think he was going to hurt me? No...he had plenty of time to try to hurt me tonight and hadn't, but I barely knew the man so anything was possible. Safety in numbers. Somewhere public. Then, I remembered he already knew I volunteered at the hospital thanks to our run in.

"Let's meet Wednesday nights at the hospital café. Around six?"

"That sounds good. I look forward to seeing you next week and am truly sorry for scaring you tonight." He held out his hand for a handshake.

I looked at him closely and ignored his hand. Instead, I decided to go for blunt. "You're not going to turn creepy uncle on me, are you, Sam?" I honestly didn't expect him to admit it if he did have that planned. I just wanted to see his reaction to the question.

He barked out a laugh and dropped his hand back to his side. When he saw I remained serious, he sobered.

"I suppose that's a fair question, given what you've just told me. With me, you're safe. Honey, I'm older than I look. Heck, I'm probably old enough to be your great grandfather." He looked at me for a moment. I mean really looked at me, studying my face as if he could read all my secrets there.

"When I look at you, I see a young girl I want to help. I see a grandchild I could have had if only I'd met my one and only. And I see hope."

Fair enough. I'd wait until next week to pass any further judgments.

"All right, then. I've got to get home. See you next week."

He nodded his goodbye.

Reluctantly, I turned my back on him. Fear skittered along my spine as I walked away. My feet whispered through the grass until I reached the paved walk. When I looked back, he no longer stood by the pond, but I monitored his progress with my other sight as he left the park.

My already complicated life had just gotten more so. I took a huge risk meeting with a complete stranger, but how could I refuse? Learning about him and his kind might give me more insight, if not actual answers about my abilities–abilities that had caused me so much grief over the years. I really wanted an explanation.

When I got home, it was later than I thought. Barb and Tim waited for me in the kitchen. They fed me dinner and sat with me at the table while I explained what kept me. I didn't mention a werewolf, just an old friend of my grandfather's I'd bumped into.

I mentioned my plans to meet up with him at the hospital the next week to talk some more. Barb looked at Tim with worry a moment before Tim asked when they'd get to meet him. I asked for their patience and said I wanted to get to know Sam—again—first.

THREE WEEKS LATER, I exited the sliding glass hospital doors with Sam. We both eyed the dark clouds. The imminent downpour had cleared the usually bustling sidewalks, but the charged air filled me with anticipation.

I turned to Sam. "What do you think? Still want to go? We will probably get wet."

Sam, dressed in his unusually trendy attire for an old guy, continued to study the sky as we walked toward the bus stop.

He had been kind and informative during the first two meetings, telling me as much as he could in such a public place about his "relatives" in the hour I allotted for our meetings. Wary of outsiders, many of his kind chose to live in a closed community across the Canadian border. It had plenty of land, and the rural population of the surrounding area allowed them more space to roam freely. It also had a few old buildings that, up until twenty years ago, had been more for show than living.

After the marriage of their leader, things changed. The leader's new wife helped the community see they'd slipped too far from society and that their only chance to survive was to adapt.

A few people agreed and left to help reintegrate. A few more stayed in the buildings and started making small improvements. However, several of the structures needed larger-scale remodeling and, collectively, Sam's "relatives" just didn't have the money for it. Although remote, a few of the community's members ventured out to find work in nearby towns and supplemented the income needed to support their not yet fully self-sufficient way of life.

Gradually, those who'd denied the need for change started seeing the reality of what they'd become...a dying species...and more of the men not yet married went out looking for work. When the leader's sons were old enough, they too left.

Sam had been sent even further from the community to get the lay of the land in a more urban setting. Trying to blend, he'd decided he needed to dress more like the people of the area. At that point in his narrative, I'd wondered what he'd been wearing. Furs? When he'd gone shopping, he'd asked a sales clerk's advice regarding what to buy. The sales clerk had been about my age, which explained Sam's trendy choice of clothes.

It amazed me how much I'd learned about the man walking next to me. The compassion for his people's plight impressed upon me his selflessness, and watching him interact with other people around us, showed he had a sense of humor. Those defining characteristics had decided it for me—it was time to introduce him to Tim and Barb.

We'd reached the bus stop without a drop of rain.

"A little rain never hurt anyone," he said answering my earlier question.

Another thing I liked about Sam. He sensed when I was lost in my own thoughts and let me be.

"Okay, I'll text Barb and let her know you'll be coming over. They've been asking about you every week." He looked at me questioningly.

"I mentioned you that first night we met in the park. They wanted to know why I was late. I said I ran into an old acquaintance, a friend of my grandfather's."

A city bus drew to a halt in front of the sheltered bus stop. Sam and I waited for the other passengers to board. He surprised me by pulling out his own city bus pass to pay. The familiar driver looked at me curiously when I took my normal place behind him and slid over on the worn grey vinyl seat to make room for Sam.

Sam and I didn't talk much on the bus ride. Instead, I watched out the window, waiting expectantly for the rain.

At our stop, Sam stood and exited. He didn't offer me his hand. After only knowing me a short while, he knew I didn't like to be touched. It wasn't that I didn't like being touched. I didn't like growing attached. When you touched people, you developed attachments. Then, when they left, it made it harder to say goodbye.

He waited for me to hop down from the last step then fell in beside me as we made our way down the paved park path. Although we still had an hour of daylight left, the dark storm clouds writhing in the sky above cast the city into an early dusk. Ever since Sam had revealed himself to me, tension drove me to walk quickly through the park. Particularly in the dark. I liked having someone to walk home with me, even if that someone had started the whole thing. In Sam's company, I didn't worry as much.

"You're certain I won't disrupt things at home just popping in like this?"

"I don't think you can disrupt it any more than it's been," I said. "Barb, my foster mom is pregnant, which really is a good thing. Barb and Tim have been trying to get pregnant for years. Thinking they'd never have kids of their own, they decided to foster."

We were halfway across the park. Sam slowed to give me more time to talk. I hadn't mentioned any of this to him before. The swings in the abandoned playground to our right started to sway in the increasing winds, their older chains squeaking slightly with each forward swing.

"They own a cute little two bedroom house. If she carries the baby to term, there won't be enough room, you know?" I kept my eyes focused on the path, not wanting to see his expression. "Because she hasn't yet passed her first term, they haven't notified my social worker."

I had no regret. I really did feel happy for Barb and Tim, and I'd moved around enough in foster care to know the drill. Plus, I counted down the days...months...until I turned eighteen, legally free from anyone's guardianship.

Sam remained silent beside me.

Leaving the park, we turned right on the sidewalk. The phone in my bag buzzed, and I quickly searched for it. The rain still held back, but the sky overhead rumbled ominously. I checked the message and smiled at Sam.

"Barb said she's very excited to meet you, and since you and I just ate, they'll have cake and coffee ready."

Sam nodded. A fat raindrop splattered on the sidewalk in front of us and without a word, we both started walking faster. When we turned the last suburban corner, I pointed out the Newton's house to him, not pausing the brisk pace we'd set.

Barb and Tim both waited for us on the front stoop. Tim had his arm wrapped around Barb's shoulders as he peeked around the awning to look up at the clouds. When Barb nudged him to point us out, he looked our way and waved.

They greeted Sam enthusiastically and invited him in. I could see Barb sizing him up and finding him acceptable. In a rare twist, Tim did most of the talking that night and asked Sam about himself. When Sam said he originally hailed from Canada and managed the family business investments, I figured he stuck as close to the truth as possible. They did ask him about my grandpa, and he wove a beautiful tale about them growing up together. Since I never talked about my grandfather, the Newtons didn't know any differently. The skill with which Sam lied made me a little uncomfortable. If he could lie that easily to them, how easily could he lie to me?

The rain stopped before he finished his second cup of coffee. Sam stood and smiled at Barb.

"The cake and coffee were wonderful. Thank you for letting me drop in like this." He extended a hand to Tim. "I won't overstay my welcome or the coffee."

Tim clasped Sam's hand with a warm smile as the adults all laughed.

"It was a pleasure to meet both of you."

"We appreciated you stopping in," Barb said, already collecting the cups to bring to the sink. "When Gabby said she ran into you, we were both very curious."

"I can imagine. Now that I found her, I don't want to lose track of her. If it's all right, I'd like to stop by now and again to check in on her."

"We insist you do." Tim patted Sam's back in a manly display of affection as they walked to the front door. I quickly helped Barb put the dishes in the sink so she could follow them. Barb was a little compulsive and couldn't walk away from a dirty kitchen.

"What about dinner next Wednesday?" Barb asked, raising her voice from the kitchen as she washed and dried her hands at the sink. She hurried to the front door where Sam bent to put on his shoes.

"That sounds like a good idea." Sam finished tying his shoes and turned to me. "Is that okay, Gabby?"

Leaning against the arch dividing the living room and the kitchen, I watched the adults interact. In a way, it reminded me of the animal channel. I struggled not to crack a smile at the thought since Sam really did have one foot in the animal world.

"After I finish volunteering at the hospital, it should work for me."

Satisfied they would see each other soon, the adults said their goodbyes and Sam left. Not bad for a first meeting.

Each time I met with Sam, I learned more about his world. Nothing that I could apply to myself, yet. I still had hope though.

SAM VISITED PERIODICALLY over the next two months, and life continued as normal for a while. Barb started to show, and the normally reserved Tim couldn't stop talking about it. My time with the Newtons ticked away like the seconds of a clock.

On one of our scheduled Wednesday nights, I opened the door for Sam as soon as he knocked. He didn't show any surprise when I swung the door open after just one knock, but then I didn't expect him to.

Despite meeting at my home where we couldn't speak freely, I'd managed to learn a little more about him and his kind. For example, he had exceptional hearing. He knew when I got nervous or upset by the change in my pulse. He could hear whispered conversations taking place in other rooms as long as the door remained partially open. He could even hear whispers through thin walls. In addition to keen hearing, he also had better eyesight. In the dark, his pupils expanded to a freakish dimension, allowing in as much light as possible and enabling him to see when a normal person couldn't. This explained the way his eyes reflected.

"Hi, Sam." I stopped him from taking off his shoes. "We're eating on the patio since it's nice out." He wiped his feet extra well on the rug before following me through the house to the back patio.

The solid concrete slab patio took up a fourth of their backyard space. The patio wasn't that big, the yard was just that small. But surrounded with a classic wooden privacy fence, it would make a perfect play area.

We walked onto the patio, and Tim looked up from the grill to our left and nodded a greeting. Smoke drifted lazily upward as he flipped a burger.

"Sam, thanks for coming."

Barb stopped setting the table and moved to greet Sam with a hug. Sam gave one back with a smile. She long ago stopped trying to hug me.

Tim brought the burgers from the grill, and we all sat to eat while Tim and Sam dominated the conversation with fishing stories.

When Sam asked if I'd ever been fishing, I nearly choked on my bite of burger. "No," I said definitively.

He put on a mock shocked face. "How can a girl your age never have been fishing?"

"Many have tried, and all have failed, Sam," I said slightly amused. "I'm not an outdoorsy type."

His next comment wiped the smile from Barb's face.

"You should come with me for the weekend. I'll take you to the cabin your grandpa and I went to before you were even born. It has indoor plumbing now, so I bet you could talk a friend into coming with."

I glanced at all the faces at the table. Sam still smiled, Barb focused on me with an alarmed expression, and Tim glanced between me, Barb, and Sam. I took another bite of burger to stall.

In private, Sam had asked about my plans for the future. Barb's baby bump was hard to miss now. He had mentioned he had a spare room at his place if I ever needed it. He'd also mentioned he would like to take me on a trip to meet others of his kind. I felt fairly certain that's what he meant now. Having him ask tonight without any warning took me off guard. I could have done some prep work, like dropping hints that I had an interest in spending more time with him or something. But it did make sense that he asked now. Why try to delay the inevitable? The doctors saw no reason Barb's pregnancy wouldn't go full term this time. School would let out soon, and I had no summer job.

Setting down my fork, I picked up my glass and took a long drink of water. They all waited. I decided to save the adults the long dance around a subject none of them wanted to face full on. I turned toward Barb and Tim.

"I've spent a lot of time getting to know Sam over the last two months and told him about the baby on the way." I looked at Barb, meeting her beautiful dark brown eyes. "We all know that I won't be able to stay once the baby's here." Barb started to tear up and speak but I stopped her with a raised hand. "I also know that you want me to stay. I don't doubt that for a minute. You've both been so great to me, and I thank you."

I turned to Sam. "You said that you live in a three bedroom house and that I was welcome to visit anytime. What about visiting until I graduate?" I didn't want to go back into foster care.

Sam continued to smile at me and nodded.

Barb started to sniffle, and Tim reached over the table to pat her hand.

CHAPTER TWO

Friday night, Barb and Tim dropped me off at Sam's. Though it was only for a weekend, they knew what it would mean if everything went well. So I willfully squashed my discomfort and endured Barb's hug. Tim, thankfully, settled on a nod and a wave as I climbed into Sam's truck.

I used the eight-hour drive to ask Sam direct questions about werewolf life, and tried to soak up everything he said. I stopped talking when we turned off the blacktopped road onto a deeply rutted dirt lane I doubted saw much use. For a mile, I braced myself against the rough ride. Finally, we emerged from the tree-lined path into a wide clearing.

A large two-story log cabin style structure dominated the space, its wings branching out to connect to outlying buildings. Sam parked on the combination of old gravel, stubborn grass, and plain dirt in front of the buildings.

The werewolf community reminded me of an old wilderness resort, one closed for a few years. If not for the lights pouring from several of the windows, I would have locked the truck door instead of getting out.

I shouldered my bag and trailed Sam onto the covered porch. Sam pulled the solid wood door open without knocking. Inside, an eclectic array of rugs along the perimeter of the large main entry accommodated numerous sets of shoes. Hooks on the walls held a bounty of coats, jackets, and overalls.

"We don't have to worry about stealing here," Sam said when he caught me looking at the mass of shoes. "And it keeps the rest of the place cleaner if we leave our outside things here." He started taking off his shoes, and I bent to remove mine.

"You would not believe how messy this place was thirty years ago," a voice called from the hall.

I looked up from untying my shoes. A tall woman with blonde hair and a gentle smile walked into the entry. I estimated her to be in her late twenties.

"Hello, Gabby," she said coming to stand next to me. "I'm Charlene. Sam's told me about you. I'm so thrilled to meet another person like me." She held out her hand in greeting as I stepped out of my shoes.

Excitement coursed through me. Finally! Sam had mentioned Charlene, another human among the werewolves, during one of our many talks. The possibility that I wasn't as alone as I thought obliterated any hesitation I might have had, and I reached out and clasped her hand.

Charlene's grip was firm and sure, but I barely noticed it. The darkness of my other sight had burst open and the brilliance of the sparks surprised me; their normal soft glow amplified so much that the blinding light obscured their gentle colors. I let go of her hand while maintaining my focus. The lights dimmed considerably so I could again discern their soft colors.

Sam's spark glowed blue with a green halo and hers, while still containing the yellow center like any human, had a red halo. I'd considered the possibility that my orange halo was because I couldn't see myself correctly using my other sight. But seeing Charlene's assured me our uniqueness was real.

Beyond our sparks, I noticed other blue-green lights. Not in the immediate area, but spread throughout my area of awareness. The coloring of those lights matched Sam's. Werewolves then were blue-green, I thought. Color by species made sense, but Charlene and I didn't match. Why?

"Like me?" Her words suddenly penetrated my study of the sparks. Could she see lights too?

"So far, we are the only two humans who seem to be compatible with werewolves," she said, still smiling in welcome.

My hope sank. So we were human and...wait, what?

"Compatible?" I looked at Sam in confusion. I knew that I smelled differently to werewolves, but he hadn't mentioned anything about compatibility. Charlene answered before he could.

"Yes, werewolves choose their Mate—husband or wife—instinctually. They have no history of ever before selecting from humans for their Mates, but here we are. Whatever it takes to become a Mate, we apparently have it, too."

My mouth popped open in shock as I understood. I turned on Sam.

"You brought me here to hook up with a werewolf?"

"No, Gabby. I apologize for upsetting you," Charlene said from behind me. I turned to look at her. "Yes, we're different in that a werewolf might choose us, but that doesn't mean that they must choose us or that we have to choose them. At your age, there will be no hooking up."

She looped her arm through mine and gave me a motherly pat. As soon as she touched me, all the sparks around us brightened again. I didn't even need to focus. The lights just flared and continued to glow brightly without effort. Weird.

She led me toward the hall from which she'd entered. After a few steps, she stumbled and pulled her arm from mine. With relief, the lights in my mind extinguished, and I concentrated on her words.

"I asked Sam to bring you so you and I can talk. As I said, there is no one else like us that we've found. I came here when I was younger than you—long story—and met Thomas, the pack's leader. It was a very hard adjustment with a huge learning curve on both our sides. I don't want you to have to face any of that on your own. We'll introduce you slowly to this new world you're now a part of. If you have any questions, don't be afraid to ask them."

She led us down a second hallway and stopped in front of a closed door. When she opened it, I saw it led into a very small apartment.

"This is still a work in progress. Let me know if you need anything," she said, looking at Sam. He nodded.

I took a moment to take in my surroundings as Charlene walked away. The small, main room had only a few mismatched pieces of furniture. The bedroom, which I suspected had once been a walk-in closet, barely held a twin-sized bed, nightstand, and lamp. Sam insisted I take that room as he set his bag on the foldout couch. I didn't complain. I figured sleeping in a half-sized bed ranked higher than Sam's sleeper sofa.

A tiny bathroom right off the main living area completed the suite. The apartment definitely qualified as rustic, but I didn't mind.

SAM WOKE me after a few hours of sleep.

Despite Charlene's assurances that my stay didn't include finding a boyfriend, I still felt leery over Sam not telling me about the compatibility thing. I'd thought I could trust him, and his omission stung a little.

I wanted to excuse it—maybe it'd slipped his mind—but it'd taken eight hours to get here. Granted, most of that time we'd talked about the progress the community had made and the customs, like pack hunts, that they no longer followed. Still, he could have mentioned that doozy. *By the way, Gabby, werewolves will want you as their Mate.* I paused then shook my head at the thought. Yeah, I would have reached for the door handle and tried to jump from the moving truck. Maybe, he'd made an okay call. Only time would tell.

I got out of bed and dressed. Sam already had his bed made when I opened my door.

We left the apartment and he led me to a large room, which he referred to as the commons, to get a bite to eat. The space served as a cafeteria and an entertainment area with sitting arrangements scattered around the room. It even had a pool table set in the back corner.

Charlene saw us and came over to our table. Two young men followed in her wake. She introduced them as Paul and Henry. She thought I might like the opportunity to talk to people my own age. She even suggested we go into the woods so they could show me more about the werewolf way of life. Sam heard my panicked heartbeat, and before I could refuse, he suggested we use the lounge in the commons to get to know each other, instead.

Paul and Henry didn't treat me the same as human boys did. As curious about me as I was them, they asked a myriad of questions.

"What's school like?" Paul, the boy with dark hair and a carefree smile, asked while sitting on a padded dish-chair close to me.

"You don't go to school?" I couldn't believe it.

"Nah," said Henry, a short stocky kid with bright blue eyes. "We're home schooled here. It's way quicker to graduate since we can study at an accelerated pace because we don't have to break for holidays or anything."

"That actually sounds pretty great...what school should be, minus the no breaks part." I cringed inwardly at the thought of school year round then answered his original question. "The majority of the teachers spend their time hating their jobs and finding ways to be as disagreeable as possible while the students look at it as a popularity contest and spend more time worrying about who's dating who than studying," I explained.

"Date?" Paul glanced at Henry, who wore an equally puzzled expression. "I heard Charlene talking about that once. Sounds weird."

"Really? You guys don't date?" I didn't ask what they did to get to know a girl instead of dating.

"No, we get invited to Introductions," Paul said as if reading my mind.

"What's that?" Sam hadn't mentioned anything like that to me, and I wondered if I should add it to his list of omissions.

"When a female comes of age, she's brought to the Introduction room where she can meet werewolves she has never met before. The Elders are there to make sure the girl is safe and to give the guys a few minutes to talk to her. You know, to really get her scent. When there's a connection, a guy just knows and Claims her. If not, the next group comes in for their chance."

I started to sweat as I sat there. First, what did he mean by Claim? Second, they kept a girl in a room while guys came in to look her over and smell her? I reached for my water that sat on the coffee table in the center of our sitting arrangement. My hands shook a little, and I tried really hard to calm down and not let my imagination run away.

"Hey, Gabby, you okay? Did Paul say something wrong? Charlene said we could ask any questions we wanted..."

They had no idea how foreign what they'd just said sounded to me.

"Hey, Gabby, you don't have to worry about Introductions if that's what's scaring you." Paul looked at me with concern. "For you and Charlene, the attraction works different. She explained it to us when she said that you were coming. You guys have a level of appeal, or chemistry, with just about all werewolves." He is not helping, I thought while he continued. "Because the level of attraction to you varies, it wouldn't be safe to put you in an Introduction room."

"Yeah," Henry agreed and, with a spark of excitement in his eyes, leaned forward in his chair. "That's when the mating duels happen. It's rare with a werewolf couple, but when Charlene was first brought here, I heard the guys went crazy because they didn't know what was happening. They fought over who had the strongest tie to her. But you don't have to worry about that with us. Paul and I think you're okay, and you smell good and everything, but we knew when we met you that you're not right for either of us. That's why Charlene left you alone with us."

My stomach churned. Werewolves were going to start fighting each other for me? No thanks. They both smiled at me encouragingly. They probably thought their explanations helpful, but the information they threw at me stunned me.

"What did you mean by 'Claim'?" My voice came out light and airy with anxiety, but I needed to know.

"It's when we bite our Mate. The bite draws blood but doesn't hurt," Paul explained reassuringly.

"What?" I nearly shouted. My freak-o-meter bypassed meltdown. My head spun dizzily, and no doubt, all the color had drained from my face.

"Oh, not for you, Gabby," Paul said, quickly leaning forward. He made shushing motions with his hands. "We can't Claim humans like that. When your Mate finds you, it's up to you to Claim him."

So, I would need to bite someone? Not going to happen. It was easier to calm down now that I knew I had control. I didn't want to be "the right one" for anyone at this point in my life. I hoped that the rest of the werewolves, like these two, would correctly use their keen sense of smell to determine my unsuitability.

I heard the main door swing open and saw Sam walk in with an older woman and another older man. Sam nodded to me and then moved with his group to another area of the room. They sat down and started talking. Paul and Henry shifted their attention to the new people, listening. I couldn't hear the conversation but had no doubt they could. Just as I knew Sam would hear if I asked either Paul or Henry to tell me what the group said. I decided to change the subject.

"What about sports? I noticed there are no TVs. Do you guys play or go watch any sports?"

"Nah, we don't get good reception out here, and the television tends to hurt our ears, but we do like to play football. There aren't enough of us for a team, though."

The door behind us opened again, and I watched two younger men, about our age, enter. They glanced our way but headed toward the group with Sam. I turned around and took another drink of water while thinking about this Mate business. According to these two, I needed to watch for a werewolf who acted as most human men would toward me, intense and weird.

Sam startled me out of my thoughts when he spoke next to me.

"Gabby, I'd like you to meet Eric and Derrick. They are the twin sons of a couple who lives here. They're home from college and have to leave again tomorrow."

I smiled and said hello. They both nodded to me but didn't speak. Awkward.

Uncomfortable, I looked back at Sam, who nodded at the two. They turned and left. If they represented the normal reaction to me, I needed to watch out for someone even more intense and weird. Maybe I just needed a plan to avoid them all.

Sam waited until they'd walked out of the room to explain.

"I want you to get to know the people who live here. In summer, we'll spend a lot of our weekends here." He looked at Paul and Henry. "You two keep an eye on her. I'm counting on you to help explain our ways."

Sam walked back to the group, and I looked from Paul to Henry with an arched eyebrow. Was it just me or did that feel weird? I wanted to ask but remained quiet. There were still too many ears to overhear. They seemed to understand my unspoken question and both shrugged in return.

Sam interrupted our conversation twice more, each time bringing someone to introduce to me. My mind caught on the word "introduce."

Paul and Henry's assurance that I would never face the Introduction room clicked everything into place. Sam had started slowly introducing me to the eligible male population of this little community right here, right now—in this room. After the third set left, I caught Sam's eye.

"Sam, would you mind showing me around outside for a bit?" I stood and made my way to the main door, not waiting to see if Sam followed. After three months, I'd felt sure enough of Sam that I'd risked a trip to an unknown destination with him, alone. I'd been willing to explain away the little doozy he didn't mention on the way here; but now, his actions and omissions devastated my confidence in him.

Already familiar with the layout of the Compound, I didn't hesitate to walk out the front door and stride purposefully toward the dirt lane. Sam didn't take long to catch up to me. If I told him I wanted to go back to the Newton's now, would he take me? If he did, then what? I couldn't stay there forever.

"Sam," I said when we walked side by side. "I don't want to be on the streets, but that's where I'll go if you think you can pull this crap if I move in with you." I didn't look at him; I was too angry. And scared. "I understand the condition of living at your place is that we come up here. But my condition is that you have to be completely honest about our purpose in coming up here. Each time," I stressed. "I don't know if I can trust you."

"I'm sorry, Gabby. You can trust me. I have your best interests in mind. This is another one of those things that is easier to believe when you experience it firsthand." He kept pace next to me as I led us further from the Compound.

"No, Sam. You need to lay it out for me straight."

He stayed quiet for a few minutes, and I wasn't sure he had anything to say until he actually spoke.

"Well, I heard what Paul and Henry told you. That part's right. We do Introductions for our females in a controlled environment to keep them safe until they find their Mate.

"We learned from Charlene's time here that you'd need to be handled differently. I told you that werewolves would find your scent interesting. Since we're branching out into more urban areas, it would only be a matter of time before you attracted attention. So, we wanted to control your Introduction. A formal Introduction without mass challenges was out of the question.

"This is the compromise; they come into the commons, say 'hello' to you, then talk to the Elders. Because the level of attraction varies, we interview them. They must formally request permission from me to come see you again if they think of you as more than just interesting. They are not allowed to approach you while you are on your own. If they were to approach me for a second meeting, I would speak with you first before approving or denying their request."

The light filtering through the canopy cast the road into dusky shadow. I stopped walking and turned to Sam.

"What you're saying is, eventually werewolves would find me; but, if I stay with you, you'd be my buffer?" He nodded. I studied him. "And I'd only have to say hi to these guys. It'd be up to me if I wanted to spend any additional time with them?" He nodded again.

I liked Paul and Henry. They oozed useful information and didn't react to me at all. The others I'd already met hadn't seemed too interested, either.

When Paul and Henry had mentioned mating duels, I imagined drowning in a writhing mass of hostile bodies, all in various stages of transformation. I still dreamt about Sam shifting. The dreams and my fueled imagination bothered me. But since arriving, everyone had remained in human form and nothing freaky had happened. The general population of werewolves couldn't be all bad. I just didn't like the way I had to meet them. Yet, now that the werewolves knew I existed, trying to live on my own didn't sound like a good idea. I'd be better off with Sam. He'd keep the others away.

"Fine, let's go back."

Paul and Henry were playing cards while they ate their way through a stack of sandwiches set out on the coffee table. They waved me over, and I gladly joined their game and grabbed a sandwich for myself.

Several more werewolves came in throughout the day. Sam led each one to me. Most left after a polite nod of hello. A few asked for a second meeting. Each time, Sam would look at me and, at the shake of my head, reject the request. It relieved me to see him keep his word and restored some of my shaken confidence in him.

We packed up and left Sunday morning. I mostly paid attention to the scenery since I'd missed the majority of it on the way there. While I watched the trees flash by, I thought about the weekend. None of the guys I'd met seemed too upset over any type of rejection. For as much emphasis as they'd put on my smelling good to just about all werewolves, their laid-back attitude didn't make much sense to me.

"Why did the guys seem okay with their second request being rejected?"

"Although you smelled good to them, they knew it wasn't just right. When it is, they won't give up, which is why staying with me is so important. We have laws that control certain aspects of the social side of the pack. One is that unMated human females, like you, cannot be approached without the approval of the nearest Elder."

"Then, why can't you just tell them all 'no' for me in advance, so we don't have to mess with this whole Introduction thing?"

"Because I have to give them the chance to see for themselves that it's not right. Was it that bad? Meeting people? No one treated you the way some human men have treated you."

I couldn't disagree. "How often is this going to happen?"

"Once a month."

I sat up straighter. "No way." I shook my head for emphasis. It was a cool enough place, but sixteen hours of driving in a single weekend every month would get boring. "Once every two months."

"Every five weeks, with flexibility to switch weeks if needed," he said.

"Seven weeks."

"Six," he said with a sideways glance at me.

"Fine, every six weeks," I compromised. Then I threw in another condition. "Until I graduate. Then, I'm going to college and won't be obligated to take time out of studying for dating—or whatever you want to call this—if I don't want to."

"Deal," he agreed.

I stared at him. He'd agreed too easily. Was that a hint of a smile on his mouth? Why did I feel like I just got the raw end of the deal? I'd have to play my cards carefully so I didn't find myself hitched in some weird backwoods werewolf custom.

CHAPTER THREE

SAM SAT AT THE WORN, OAK TABLE IN THE MIDDLE OF THE SUNLIT
kitchen. He scowled at its dull surface, and when I walked into the room, he
transferred the glum look to me. I shook my head at him and went to make his
morning coffee.

Sam and mornings didn't mesh well. I'd realized that as soon as I'd moved
in. How a werewolf, usually graceful and strong, could stumble and mumble
until he had his caffeine still confused me. With his werewolf metabolism, I
doubted it really did anything for him. Regardless, I still took pity on him and
tried to wake up first to start a pot—even though it wasn't my drink of
preference in the morning.

Today, however, his familiar morning scowl didn't solely relate to his need for
coffee. After two years of almost monthly visits to the Canadian werewolf
community, this weekend would be my last, and he didn't like it. Happily, I
hadn't met a single werewolf who had any type of pull on me.

The way I figured it, I'd fulfilled my end of our deal. Though school had
scheduled graduation for Sunday, I'd opted not to attend. I had no desire to put
this visit off for another week. The faculty could mail my diploma. After this
weekend, I planned to work as much as possible to save up what I could before
going off to college.

I measured out the coffee grounds and reflected back on my time with Sam.
I'd kept him company, and his mere presence had kept me safe while he'd

provided me with the information I needed about the werewolves and the pack community. Although Sam had shared so much of the werewolves' life and culture, I acknowledged I still didn't know everything. It didn't matter, though. I'd learned enough...and not just about werewolves.

Sam was a great role model for responsibility and planning. It's what he did for the pack. Because of him, I already worked as much as I could after school. But, it wasn't just his example that pushed me to become so dedicated to work and financial responsibility. Shortly after I moved in with Sam, I'd discovered that work commitments ensured he couldn't talk me into going to the Compound more than we'd bargained. He knew I'd need the means to get an education and support myself and never tried to talk me out of working. So, I worked and I tried to bank enough money to hold me over while I went to school.

As an Elder of the pack, Sam was extremely down to earth and wise. He carefully thought through all decisions with a deliberate calm that I admired. He didn't think of himself when making any decision, only of the pack. Their welfare ruled his life. Thankfully, even though he hadn't managed to tie me to anyone, he considered me part of the pack. That meant when I talked, he listened with his full attention, which I really did like.

Coffee brewing, I leaned against the counter and openly smirked at Sam.

"Come on, don't be pouty about this. We made a deal, and I stuck to it. I've met more man-dogs than I can remember. Some, even twice." My made-up term seemed to amuse him.

I pushed away from the counter and walked behind his chair. Resting my forearms on his shoulders, I rolled them outward and pressed down with my full weight. The tension slowly left his shoulders, and I rested my chin on his head. Yeah, I was that short compared to him.

"Tell me you're going to be okay without me here." I couldn't remember my real grandpa, but over the last two years, Sam had filled that role well, despite our rough start. I knew he had managed his own coffee in the morning for years before I'd moved in with him, but I still wondered what he'd do without me here to keep him company.

He sighed gustily and reached back to pat my cheek, the extent of affection I allowed with him. It had been a gradual progress to work up to it. He knew most physical contact made me uncomfortable. He understood it and never seemed offended by it. I'd held myself away from people for so long, I wasn't sure I'd ever be completely comfortable with casually touching anyone.

"You know I will," he said sounding tired. "I don't understand why you won't go to the community college here. Out of state is so expensive."

"No, it won't be," I said, pulling away from him. "I have scholarships and aid because of being a foster." I made my way to the coffee. A warm breeze brushed past the kitchen curtains to swirl around the room. As I poured him a cup, I continued defending my choice.

"Besides, you know very well why I'm going out of state." It was an old argument. My place in pack society, forever the bachelorette, bothered me. I wanted out. No other female went through such a long Introduction period. Over the last two years, I'd become the one all the guys wanted to meet and hoped to Claim by the end of the weekend. Though they treated me with kind hopefulness, my attitude toward finding a Mate hadn't changed. I didn't want one. Besides, two years of being the family disappointment was enough.

"I want my own life before someone else tries to take it over. Sam, I've always had to follow other people's rules. I want to live by my own rules for a while."

Sam harrumphed. "What rules have I ever enforced on you?"

I gave him a steady look as I handed him the steaming cup.

"Besides insisting on the Introductions..." He dropped his gaze to the proffered cup and accepted it with a lack of enthusiasm. Not meeting my eyes, he blew on the brew and turned the cup in a circle on the table before he began to sip it slowly.

Suspicious, I continued to study his face as I waited for him to look up again. He seemed unexpectedly guilty for such an innocent remark.

Though I chafed at his rules, they were simple enough. Go to the Introductions. Spend the weekends getting to know the pack and the pack laws. Never stay out past dark without a way to get home, which meant a ride from Sam since owning my own car made him uncomfortable. How could he not see he completely controlled my life with those rules?

Though I understood the reason for the restriction, it didn't make them more palatable. The very real draw men felt when near me had only grown stronger as I'd matured. It made time alone risky. Sam had insisted I take self-defense classes. Those had been great until the instructor suggested one on one training sessions a bit too loudly in class. Before I bailed on the course, I'd learned enough to keep men at bay...but not werewolves. Despite knowing I had no protection against them other than Sam, I still wanted to try it out on my own. Sam's rules were simple, however, they weren't mine.

"It won't be safe," Sam said, interrupting my thoughts. He looked up from his half-empty cup. "You know it won't be safe."

"Sam, I'll get a dog." I could see by his expression that he was gearing up for another round in an old debate. Why couldn't he understand that I'd rather get a dog than be Mated to a werewolf? I hurried around him for the bathroom down the hall.

"I better go shower. We don't want to keep the wolves waiting." I spun into the bathroom and shut the door with a snick to stop any further objections.

JUST BEFORE DINNERTIME, I pushed open the door of Sam's old pickup and, ignoring its groan of protest, climbed out. My feet crunched on the gravel parking area. Not much had changed. Though, still rundown and in need of repairs, to me the familiar buildings exuded welcome. With a twinge, I realized I'd probably miss these frequent visits. I pushed the door closed, reached around to the bed of the truck, and grabbed my canvas bag.

"There a pack meeting tonight?" I asked Sam, looking at the other vehicles.

I couldn't remember ever seeing so many cars before. Yet, for the number parked in the yard, the Compound was unusually quiet. Typically, before a meeting, groups of people stood outside to talk and renew acquaintances. I glanced at the buildings again. Though quiet outside, thin lines of light escaped from behind thick curtains in many of the windows on the main house. Definitely, a full house tonight. But why stay inside?

Sam just grunted in response to my question, shouldered his own bag, and headed toward the main building.

I studied Sam's back. He certainly seemed rushed. He'd even sped so we arrived in just over seven hours. We'd only stopped once for a five minute, gas-up, eat, and pee break. I hadn't questioned why, but it was unusual.

He'd stayed abnormally silent and pensive the entire trip, too. I didn't mind the quiet, but he generally updated me on current pack activity during the drive. Bored, I'd alternated between listening to my mp3 player and watching the country pass in silence.

I turned a slow circle, studying the area while I breathed deeply, and began to focus. In two years, the area of my sight had expanded so I could see much further in the vast darkness of my mind. It didn't exhaust me as quickly as it used to.

I closed my eyes and continued to turn a slow circle. At the Compound, focusing was harder. Typically, for humans, some sparks came in strong and glowed bright like a newly replaced light bulb while others were weak, more like a lightning bug's glow. I didn't know why; it just was. The lights of the werewolves were different. Their sparks tended to flash in and out of focus regardless of how bright or dim I perceived them. I considered the flashing a false perception. Instead, I believed I was watching the amazing speed at which they moved—there one second, gone the next, then back again. Since I hadn't yet shared my ability with Sam, I couldn't confirm my suspicion.

In the darkness behind my closed eyes, I saw the usual flashes of light, but they jumped around in a pattern that made me dizzy. I could see flashes in the Compound and many more in the surrounding woods and beyond.

I stopped turning before I made myself lightheaded. When I opened my eyes, I faced the woods to the right of the Compound just inside the gate. I felt watched. Not moving, I listened. Nothing but silence and my own breathing. I mentally shrugged and turned away from the trees to walk toward the main building. If any werewolves lingered out there, they would show themselves, or not, depending on their nature and if we'd already been introduced.

Several men exited through the main entrance as I stepped onto the porch. Two gave me kind, but dispassionate—perhaps even indifferent—nods of greeting. Mated. The other two watched me alertly and nodded politely. UnMated. I nodded a greeting in return and walked past them, safe with the Mated males nearby. Pack law: Protect unMated females from unMated males. Another pack law: Don't place yourself in a situation where you'll be alone with an unMated male or it could be seen as acceptance of his suit.

Inside, further down the long hall that branched from the main entry, more men headed my way. I kicked off my shoes, nodded, and walked past them. Again, a Mated male amidst the unMated.

"You're early."

I smiled at Charlene, who walked briskly toward me.

"He drove fast. Are Paul and Henry around?"

"I haven't seen them, but I'm sure they're around somewhere. I'll see you at breakfast." Charlene didn't slow. She had a pile of clothes in her arms.

She seemed more hurried than normal. As a Mate to the leader, she tended to be busy, but she usually always made time to talk to me.

With a tingle of apprehension, I hurried toward our assigned apartment. The same one we'd first stayed in, but with big improvements. The once sparsely furnished apartment now made a cozy weekend getaway. A plush rug protected the refinished hardwood floors. Pictures decorated the walls and various knickknacks adorned the room, just a few of Charlene's efforts to make it homier for those staying here. It also now had a small kitchen, which included a sink, dishes, and mini fridge. It still lacked appliances for cooking since we all took meals with the rest of the pack in the commons. The kitchenettes in the apartments were there for private convenience. Sam and I never used ours, but we weren't the only ones who stayed here. Though we had priority on the apartment, I knew visiting Mated werewolves used it on our off weekends.

Sam had already thrown his bag on the foldout couch in the living room when I walked through the apartment door. I walked past him, tossed my bag on my own bed, and returned to the living room to watch him and to try to puzzle out his mood. The last few informal Introductions had been less than typical with an unusually high number of unMated males coming to the Compound from greater distances. I figured this one would be no different. Maybe he was worried about the number attending.

"So, when do we get started?" I paced around the room to stretch my legs after the long drive.

"Soon as you're ready, I guess." Sam riffled through his bag, looking for something.

"How many this weekend?"

He didn't look at me. In fact, he seemed to be making an effort not to look at me and had been making that effort since breakfast. My stomach wanted to do a flip, but I firmly smashed down my emotions. I needed to figure out what was going on before I reacted in any way. Emotions around werewolves gave you away. They could smell some and hear others.

"I'm not sure. All of the Elders put a call out since it's your last one. Ready?" He straightened, with pencil and paper in his hand, and still did not meet my gaze. He kept himself busy by tucking the pencil into the spiral of the notebook as he moved toward the door.

"Yep." I fell into step behind him. "So, what does that mean?"

"That there are more ears than usual." He opened the door for me.

A werewolf fun fact to keep in mind at all times: They have excellent hearing. I didn't say anything more. Sam typically stayed very open with me, but something definitely felt different about tonight. I followed him down the hall. Our footfalls echoed softly on the hardwood floor.

Despite my effort not to react in any way to the oddities I kept noticing, a tension built inside of me. Not about the Introductions. I'd grown used to those. They could throw as many unMated at me as they wanted. I knew it wouldn't work.

In the past two years, not once had I felt any physical interest in any werewolf. There'd been some nice ones I'd enjoyed talking to, but nothing more. No spark that Sam had insisted I would feel. He'd stressed that whatever I felt, the male would feel infinitely stronger, a compulsion that they wouldn't be able to deny.

No, the tension wasn't about meeting more werewolves. It was Sam. The tension continued to grow as I puzzled over whatever Sam hid, whatever made him act so nervous and guilty at the same time.

When we didn't turn to go to the commons, but instead, went down the hall I knew housed the infamous Introduction room, his odd behavior suddenly made sense. They planned to go old school for my last Introduction. Since Sam had stressed a formal Introduction could be dangerous to me, his nervousness and guilt were understandable. But I didn't understand why they thought a formal Introduction necessary. Did they really think the results would be different?

"Sam...you should have told me first."

He said nothing as he stopped and opened the door at the end of the hall. He motioned me inside. Resigned, I entered.

The windowless room had the same comfortable log cabin design as the rest of the Compound. However, near the center of the room, ten worn X's taped to the floor formed a gentle arch. A few feet away, a solid line ran from one side of the room to the other, separating the front and back halves of the room. On my half of the room, folding chairs waited along the wall, a place for Elders to wait and observe. Having Elders present meant disputes were resolved quickly and without bloodshed. It also meant better protection for the female. Each side of the room had a door.

According to tradition, five men would enter from the opposite door, which led outside, and remain in the room for five minutes. The Elders present would watch my reaction to these men and their reactions to me. Five minutes gave enough time for me to introduce myself to each of them. It seemed pointless to me, though. Through their own admission, true Mates would know within a minute of meeting each other.

All ten marks came into play during Introductions for older, unMated were-females. Once Introductions started, unMated males traveled from distant states until the Elder network announced a Claim.

The males competed aggressively for a Mate since fewer females were available to men. Sam had told me, statistically, the birth rate was about three to one. Some thought it nature's way to keep the werewolf population low. Other's disagreed. They argued that it didn't make sense when human females appeared to be evolving to fill in the need.

I understood the seriousness of this Introduction and stood near the door I'd entered. If trouble broke out, I would step through the sturdy, thick door, lock it behind me, and run like hell. The locked door wouldn't slow a determined werewolf. Without an Elder standing between an oncoming werewolf and me, I wouldn't stand a chance. Still, locking it would make me feel better once I stood on the other side. Declared a safety zone, I was supposed to remain in the hall beyond to wait until the Elders calmed whatever disruption might occur.

Although the setting had changed, the rules hadn't. They couldn't force a Mate on me. It was up to Nature. One more weekend to play it cool, then...done.

The Elders began to enter behind me. During the informal Introductions in the commons, two or three Elders always remained nearby. If informal Introductions called for at least two Elders, I knew to expect more for a formal Introduction. Definitely three. Maybe four.

Sam already sat on a folding chair to my left. Gradually, four more filed in; four men, including Sam, and one woman. The number surprised me, but I didn't mind the extra eyes. I'd met Nana Wini two years ago while still learning about Introductions. A kind and patient teacher, she'd explained so much to me. Having her here comforted me, and I looked forward to talking to her afterward.

Once the last Elder sat, the outer door opened and ten men stalked in. Ten? I successfully kept my feelings from my face, but I knew they would smell my confusion. Ten explained the extra Elders. Werewolves in their fur were all powerful and vicious, Elders more so because of their position in the pack.

In addition to the increased number of Elders, the ages of the werewolves who stood on the X's ranged from young to old without restriction. Screw Nature. No way would I be even remotely interested in someone old enough to be my father. Especially when I had no clue who my father might be.

Wanting to get the Introduction over with, I stepped forward so the toes of my socks rested just behind my safety line and met the eyes of the first man. I nodded a greeting, turned with military precision, and paced to the next taped X to meet the second man's eyes. I slowly walked down the line and met the eyes of each man I passed. At the last man, I turned around to face all of them.

"Thank you for coming."

They all stepped back from the tape and turned to leave.

I stayed on my side of the tape and watched their retreating forms. The door on their side of the room opened so they could file out. It felt weird not learning their names as I usually did in an informal Introduction. But I knew this was typical of a formal Introduction. Any man interested in me would remain on his taped mark while allowing the others to step back to leave. This would give Sam a moment to note the interested party. Anyone on Sam's list would have an opportunity for a second Introduction where I would actually converse with him. The second round had more danger.

Movement in the recently vacated doorway broke my chain of thought. The doorway had barely cleared before the next set of ten entered. Was it always this rushed?

Breaking protocol, I glanced at Sam. He watched the men, still not looking at me. Without frowning at him like I really wanted to, I turned back to focus on the men who now stood on their marks. In this group, all of them were over forty. I repeated the same process from the first group, acknowledging each of them as I walked past. One appeared to have the start of a black eye.

I thanked them for meeting me and watched one remain on his mark while the rest marched out. The remaining man waited for Sam to make a note then nodded at me before he turned to leave.

Again, ten more filed in as soon as the room emptied. This felt wrong. Too rushed. They weren't even waiting the full five minutes once the men stood on their marks.

Instead of moving forward toward my line, I put my hands behind my back and kept my eyes on the ground. The rules said that the Elders would not interfere unless they perceived danger. They would not speak unless it was imperative to my wellbeing. It ensured no outside influence to any decision I might make regarding my choice of Mate. That rule made it impossible to ask Sam for an explanation and actually get an answer.

Why did they change to a formal Introduction now? Why on the last visit? What were they trying to accomplish? The unMated males entered ten at a time and faster than the normal five minutes.

I looked at the line on the floor. The crisp tape looked new even though I'd heard from Henry and Paul, still my best sources of information, that it hadn't been replaced in years. It looked new because it had never been walked on, never crossed. You leave by the door you enter. That's the rule.

I looked up. Rules are meant to be broken. Answers waited beyond the opposite door.

Stepping to the line, I met each of the unMated males' eyes. While doing so, I noted dried blood under one man's nose.

"It's nice to meet you," I said and waited, saying no more. They all stepped back to leave, and the door swung open.

"A moment, please." As one, they stopped before any of them reached the door, and turned to look back at me. I could feel the Elders watching me but didn't look at them.

I broke protocol, crossed the line, and walked toward the door. Since none of the men acknowledged any interest in me, I hoped I'd be safe enough.

"Gabby, wait," Sam called.

Hearing him stand and follow me caused my stomach to dip. My steps slowed for a heartbeat. Stepping through the door could compromise my wellbeing...but staying inside wouldn't get me answers. The door beckoned. I stepped through onto a packed dirt path and looked around.

The light that spilled from the door illuminated a small area. The trees that crowded the building left only a small gap of about twenty feet between the treeline and the roofline, which cast the area in an early dusk. In the cleared space near the back door, twenty men waited quietly. I frowned, puzzled. Something still felt off. I'd expected to see many more given the rushed Introductions.

Closing my eyes, I breathed deeply and focused. Tiny sparks flashed around me in the darkness. Sam, I saw, stood to my right. His spark glowed steadily, not blinking at all. The group of twenty was different.

Some of the werewolves' lights blinked like strobes. Some faster, some slower. Some so slow, I at first thought they might have left. As I studied them, it began to make sense. I wasn't seeing werewolves quickly running all over the place, rather an arrhythmic indication of a werewolf's location. I focused beyond the twenty. Lights too numerous to count stood out in the darkness. It would take hours to meet them all.

Had all the prior Introductions been a farce, a game to keep me from running until Sam could arrange the real thing? How strongly were the Elders determined to see me Mated? Would they let me leave unMated? Had my thoughts of college been a dream? I struggled with my growing frustration and panic. No. Not a dream. I wouldn't give up.

I opened my eyes already knowing that the group of twenty had doubled. I studied their faces and noted more bruising and blood. Some men dressed in jeans and shirts while others wore clothes too filthy from fighting to identify. Seeing the filth and blood, I understood why they wanted to rush the Introductions. Too many werewolves had arrived for this; and the Mating challenges the Elders feared, had begun.

I didn't say anything. I couldn't. Anger churned in my stomach at Sam for not telling me. I felt tricked and yet sad for the men waiting.

"Sam," I said, turning my gaze on him. There was nothing playful in my look. I wanted to tell him that I would never forgive him for this but knew the werewolves listening would take my words as a rejection. It would take away what little hope they had facing these numbers. Instead, I let my look convey everything I felt.

He lowered his gaze and broke eye contact, something he never did first. Good. He knew.

I turned away and studied the growing crowd. I'd lived among them enough to know not to show intimidation. They respected strength. With their hearing, I didn't need to raise my voice. Even those still hidden within the trees would hear me.

"No more fighting. There's no need to wait and fight for your place in tonight's Introduction. I will meet you all. Start a line here, and I'll walk it. If I am not right for you, there is no need for you to remain after I've passed you. You may leave and know that I am honored by your presence here tonight."

CHAPTER FOUR

MEN SILENTLY STEPPED FROM THE TREES AND MOVED TO CREATE A line as I'd asked. They continued to emerge from the woods even as the line extended around the corner. Because of that, new rows started behind the first line. The shuffling continued until roughly five hundred gathered. So many men focused on me, all at the same time, made my stomach churn. If they were human...I suppressed a shudder at the thought.

Ignoring the vast number, I moved toward the first man, nodded stoically, then turned to start the slow walk down the line. The Elders kept pace with me. I didn't bother pausing to meet anyone's eyes. Only my scent mattered.

As I'd asked, those without a strong interest stepped out of the line and walked back into the woods. It allowed those behind them to move forward and take their place. When I reached the end, I turned around to walk it again. I paced the line several times in silence so all would get their fair chance. As the number remaining decreased, my mood lightened. Sam made note of names as needed. Soon only a handful of men remained.

While my future loomed brighter, theirs dimmed. I nodded solemnly to those remaining and watched them melt back into the trees. I truly felt for them, but I'd experienced no attraction to any of them—no pull that Sam and the other Elders and werewolves had assured me I would feel when—not if—I met the one. A triumphant smile wanted to break free, but I contained it, not wanting to offend anyone. Finally, my duty was complete. I breathed deeply of freedom, ready to go back to my room.

Behind me, the Elders moved, reminding me of their presence. My mood shifted. The anger and betrayal from their lack of warning resurfaced. With a stiff back and tight mouth, I made my way toward the door and the waiting Elders. I didn't meet any of their eyes.

Sam had hours during the drive to say something but hadn't, and now all of his secrecy had been for nothing. I hadn't found a Mate. Did he realize the pointlessness of his gesture? I seriously doubted telling me in advance would have changed the outcome other than to make me nervous during the drive up. That, however, would mean I shouldn't be mad at him so I quickly disregarded the thought. Honesty was honesty. He should have told me.

Walking the dirt path, which I realized I'd tread over several times in my socks, I saw a peculiar shadow on the ground melding with the shadow of the still open door.

I looked up at the space behind the door and saw the flash of eyes just before a man stepped into view. I froze. My stomach dropped, and my heart did a strange little flip. Before I could take my next breath, a shiver ran up my spine and gooseflesh rose on my arms. My anger spiked, uncontrolled.

"You have got to be kidding," I whispered to myself without thinking. I'd been so close to escaping.

His filthy long, dark hair trailed in front of his eyes and shadowed his face into obscurity. An old, dull-green army jacket, just as filthy as his hair, hung from his frame while his bare feet shone pale against the black sweats he wore. I couldn't tell his age, the color of his hair, or the color of his eyes—because of the tangle of hair—but I could see the glint of them as he moved away from the door.

He stalked toward me. I remained frozen and tried to deny the significance of the encounter as my stomach continued to do crazy little flips. Just before he reached me, he turned away and walked around the corner of the building, heading not into the woods as the rest had, but to the front of the building.

I stared after him, momentarily confused. He'd recognized me. Just as I had him. Why had he turned away? Did it matter? Move! Escape before he changed his mind!

Finally, my feet obeyed, and I lurched toward the door.

"Sam, I've more than fulfilled any obligation I had to you or the pack. I'd like to leave tonight." The Elders stepped aside before I bowled them over.

I rushed past them, through the Introduction room and into the interior hall. There I paused to pull off my dirt-caked socks. Charlene would have me cleaning floors if I walked through the halls in my filthy socks.

Maneuvering through the fortuitously quiet and empty halls, I struggled to control my emotions. Over the years, I'd learned control, knowing those around me would be able to smell things like fear, anger, lust, or even sadness. But tonight all that control evaporated. Anger and fear swamped me. Anger at Sam for arranging the whole damn thing, and fear that the Elders knew what had just happened.

I'd been so close to freedom. Sam had set me up, stacking the odds against me with the sheer number of werewolves in attendance. Why would it have to be the very last one I saw that sent a bolt of lightning right into my stomach? Was it too much to ask for just one break in my life?

Self-pity began to flood me, but then a spark of hope surfaced. Could it be possible that no one noticed? Maybe they had attributed my reaction to the way he looked. I turned a corner, almost to our rooms. If I didn't acknowledge him in front of others, then it didn't count...right?

Once in the apartment, I headed straight to my room and grabbed my bag from the bed. Thankfully, I hadn't unpacked.

Moving quickly, I went to Sam's bed and zipped his bag closed just as he walked through the door. His slightly mussed, grey hair gave away his agitation. Good. He deserved a little bit of it to match my own.

He met my gaze. I resented that he did so now, after the Introduction was complete, and he'd gotten his way.

"Now, Gabby," he started in his soothing tone.

"Stop." I held up a hand to forestall anything else he had to say and to keep my temper in check. He might not know he'd gotten his way. Even if he did know, he didn't deserve the pithy remarks running through my head. He deserved my respect for all he'd done for me in the past and for everything from which he'd shielded me. Still, I wasn't going to listen to any more tonight. Amazingly, he didn't try to continue.

"Are you driving me or not?" I asked as I picked up his bag.

He held out his hand. I surrendered the bag and wondered what I'd do once we got home. I still had a whole summer ahead of me. A summer filled with two jobs and roommate interviews. Would Sam still let me leave like I'd planned?

I followed him out the door and closed it softly behind me. I knew I couldn't escape this place permanently because of my tie to these people, but I hoped not to see it again for a long while.

Sam's easy stride annoyed me within two steps. Was he stalling? I took matters in my own hands and strode past him to get to the entrance.

The longer we stayed, the more likely I'd run into that guy again. According to the information I'd gleaned over the years, he shouldn't have turned away in the first place. Maybe he hadn't been attracted to me.

In the entry, I stuck bare feet into my sneakers, which felt wrong, but I didn't want to waste time to stop and put on socks. A part of the heel folded under and wedged itself behind my foot. I was taking too long. Scalp prickling with tension, I struggled to pull the crimped back out. Why had I crammed my foot into the stupid thing? I took my shoe off, fixed it, and slipped it back on as my gaze darted around the room searching for any sign of *him*.

Sam had continued his leisurely pace and just stepped into the entry as I tugged on the door.

Nerves strung tight, I almost screamed at the sight of someone standing there illuminated by the yard light. Instead, I only stopped abruptly. Not someone. Many someone's crowded the porch. A whole group of werewolves. For that split second, when I'd opened the door, I thought that man had returned for me.

The men fortunately didn't notice my near heart attack or me. They were too busy watching something in the parking lot. Standing shoulder to shoulder, they blocked my view. I didn't really care what had them so engrossed; I wanted to go home.

I heard Sam behind me, muttered a quick "excuse me," and moved around the small group. It took me less than a second to spot the object of their attention. Once I did, I couldn't look away.

Sam's truck had exploded. Ok, maybe not literally, but that's what it looked like at first glance. The detached hood leaned against the right front fender. Dark shapes littered the ground directly in front of the truck. My mouth popped open when I realized I was looking at scattered pieces of the truck's guts. Little pieces, big pieces, some covered in sludge. Deep inside, I groaned a desperate denial. Not Sam's truck. I needed it.

A clanking sound drew my attention from the carnage to the form bent over the front grill. He did this, the last man I'd met. He studied the gaping hole that had once lovingly cradled an engine—one with enough life to drive me home.

"Gabby, honey," Sam said from behind me, causing me to jump. "I don't think he wants you to go just yet."

My heart sank. Not only did the man's actions scream loud and clear "she's mine" but Sam's calm statement confirmed my worst fear. The Elders had noticed. My stomach clenched with dread for a moment, and I wrestled with my emotions. No, it didn't matter who noticed. I wasn't giving up or giving in. I'd told Sam I'd come to the Introductions. I had never agreed to follow their customs.

"There's more than one vehicle here," I said.

"If we go inside to ask anyone else, we'll come back to more vehicular murder."

I turned to look at Sam. He watched the man and his truck. He was right. I couldn't ask anyone else to deal with this guy's obvious mental disorder. As soon as that thought entered my mind, I felt a little guilty. I usually didn't judge people. I preferred to avoid them altogether. But this guy made himself hard to ignore.

"Fine." I shouldered my bag, turned, and walked toward the main gate, pretending I didn't hear Sam's warning.

"You won't get far," he said softly behind me.

The yard light's glow didn't extend under the branches canopied over the Compound's dirt road. Crickets sang and night creatures distantly rustled in the undergrowth. With a hint of anxiety, I marched toward the distinct boundary between light and dark. The dark didn't concern me as much as the things hiding within it. But my fear of that grimy man overshadowed any concern I had about crossing over that boundary. Darkness blanketed me. I slowed while my eyes adjusted.

I used my other sight to watch for signs of pursuit. None of the sparks from the yard moved to follow me.

My fear kept me walking for miles. No werewolves ever entered within the perimeter of my sight though I thought I spotted a bear. Maybe a werewolf escort wouldn't have been so bad.

Hours later, tired beyond imagining and satisfied that Sam's dire predictions had turned out to be false, I spotted a motel ahead. The empty parking lot screamed vacancy better than the creepy, flickering red sign mounted in the office's window. My feet and legs hurt too much to ignore the opportunity to rest. Sighing, I pushed open the office door and rented a room for the night using the emergency cash I always carried. My plan remained simple enough. In the morning, I would find the nearest bus station and buy a ticket home or as close to home as possible.

Key in hand, I walked to my door and let myself in. A damp, musty smell engulfed me. I stretched out a hand and patted the wall until I found the switch. I grimaced at the room. It didn't inspire any thoughts of recently washed sheets. I kicked off my shoes and set them near the door. About an hour into the walk, I'd stopped to put on socks, and as I padded across the dirty carpet toward the bathroom, I was thankful for their protection.

The shower curtain looked brand new, but the tub and floor hadn't seen a scrub brush in a long time. I used the toilet but didn't look at it closely before or after. Sometimes ignorance was bliss.

The water dripping from the faucet had stained the porcelain brown. So I let it run while I dug through my bag. My stomach rumbled, and I regretted not grabbing some food before leaving. Ignoring my protesting stomach, I scrubbed my teeth. When the water ran clear, I spit and rinsed, smelling the water too late. Rotten eggs. Instead of wishing for food, I wished I'd just left the toothpaste in my mouth.

I wanted to go home where a clean bed waited, where inadvertently swallowing water from the bathroom sink wouldn't put me in the hospital, where I could pretend this weekend never happened.

Purposely not thinking of anything but the present, I left the bathroom light on and moved to the main room. I set my bag on a chair, turned off the light, collapsed fully dressed on the bed, and pleaded with the universe that nothing gross contaminated the coverlet.

The drama of my day had taken its toll. My eyelids refused to stay open. Grossed out and hungry, my last thoughts were of the creepy guy at the front desk and chaining the motel door.

I STRETCHED, only half awake, and fell off the bed. For a queen-size bed, I must have rolled around on it a lot to work myself so close to the edge. Laughing at myself in the darkness, I pulled myself back up on the mattress and winced at the soreness in my legs. I paused. Darkness? My stomach flipped in fear as I remembered the light I'd left on in the bathroom.

I blindly stretched out my arm. There should have been a wall near this side of the bed. The door to my room swung open. Light flooded in, blinding me.

A shadow moved to block the light, and I suffered a moment of disoriented panic. Was it the man from the front desk? By my third squinted blink, I saw Sam standing silhouetted by light. Behind him, I spotted his foldout bed.

"You okay?" he asked.

"What am I doing here?" I turned and looked at my familiar room at the Compound.

"Dunno," he mumbled. "He brought you back before dawn. Didn't say a word, just knocked on the door carrying you. I let him in. He set you on your bed then left." Sam's hair stuck up in places, and he absently scratched the hair on his chest, wobbling a bit as he stood in his flannel house pants. He needed his coffee.

I looked down at myself. Dirt stained my clothes as if he'd dragged me all the way back here from the motel...by my feet...through mud. I reached up to comb my fingers through my hair, and a leaf fluttered to the floor. I stared at it in disbelief and let my hands drop back to my sides. He'd left me looking like a wreck. What was going on with this guy?

"What happened after I left? Did he follow me?" I watched Sam closely. If he didn't respond with complete honesty, I wouldn't be responsible for what I said next.

"Not right away. When you started walking, he looked up from the truck and watched down the road for a while. Long after you passed from sight anyway. Then, he just took to the woods, leaving my truck in a heap."

Apparently, he wouldn't let me go easily. Not that walking half the night had been easy. It also meant he'd left after I'd walked far enough that I could no longer see his spark. He'd probably tracked me by scent, keeping his distance. Clever. But why?

I needed to talk to him and figure out what he wanted. There were probably new rules—his rules—that I needed to learn, too. My impotent frustration grew. Better to get it done now so I could figure out a way out of this mess.

"Where is he?"

"Gabby. Before you do anything else, I'd like two minutes of your time. You need to hear what I have to say."

My anger at Sam still lay in a dark, dormant pool inside me. I didn't want to listen to anything he had to say. Some of my anger and frustration collapsed in on itself as I acknowledged the truth. Sam's dishonesty bothered me, but my brush with freedom, to have it so close and then ripped away in the last few seconds, hurt more. Besides, if I didn't hear him out, I'd wonder what he had wanted to tell me. Defeated, I agreed.

"Fine, but please hurry."

Sam turned and walked back to his bed. I followed.

"His name is Clay," Sam said, sitting on the lumpy mattress. "Clayton Michael Lawe." He looked up at me as I moved closer and eyed me from head to toe.

In the brighter light of the living area, I really did look like I'd been dragged, or at least rolled, in mud. How had I slept through someone carrying me for miles?

"He's twenty-five and completely alone. His mother died when he was young. An accident. Shot by a hunter while she was in her fur. His dad took him to the woods."

That meant he'd been raised more wolf than boy. Sam had explained much of the recent pack history to me when we'd first started coming to the Compound. They'd only maintained enough of the original buildings to keep up appearances and used the 360 acres that came with it to live as wolves. Charlene's arrival had brought about huge changes, mostly in the social aspect of the pack. Afterward, most pack members started acclimating to their skin. Only a few of the old school werewolves still preferred their fur.

"His father died a few years back," Sam continued, pulling me from my own thoughts. "Clay's been on his own ever since, still choosing to live in his fur more than his skin. He's quiet and has never been trouble. He comes when an Elder calls for him but still claims no pack as his own. So, by pack law, he's considered Forlorn."

Forlorn. I closed my eyes tiredly and recalled my werewolf history.

Prior to Charlene, the decimated numbers had only supported one main pack in Canada and a few packs overseas. Over the last two decades, the Canadian pack had grown enough to consider splitting their numbers.

Because of the dangers of discovery, joining a pack ensured an individual's safety and continuity for the pack. Some, like Clay, stubbornly remained reclusive. The majority of those who stayed solitary did so because they disagreed with the changes Charlene had helped to establish. Many felt the superiority of the pack entitled them to an elitist isolation from humanity and the world.

By staying on his own, Clay had effectively stated his opinion on the pack's reentry into human society. However, Sam's comment about never being trouble meant Clay had not yet actually sided with the other opinionated Forlorn.

Yet Forlorn, not having a link to a pack, still had the link to the Elders. A link all werewolves shared. Elders acted as the lawmakers and enforcers for all werewolves while the pack leader enforced the rules for the pack, settling disputes. Elders and pack leaders worked hand in hand to keep the pack healthy and growing. Though a pack leader did not control any Forlorn, the base society rules laid down by the Elders still bound them.

According to Sam, a werewolf could not break their society laws. Once an Elder declared a law, it became an ingrained piece of the werewolf. Sam had compared it to a hypnotist. The werewolves heard the law, could contemplate it, have opinions about it, but followed the law regardless of their thoughts and feelings. Most laws made sense and werewolves didn't try to fight them, but even when a werewolf disagreed with a law, there was no choice other than to obey it.

At least, no one had proven otherwise. However, I'd overheard Sam speaking with another Elder about several instances where a Forlorn had ignored certain aspects of their laws, which made the relationship between the pack and Forlorn even more strained.

Sam sighed and rubbed a hand over his face.

"He was here last night to help keep the peace. He didn't come to be Introduced to you."

At least that explained his presence by the door and not in the line with the rest of them. My conspiracy theory that Sam had set me up shriveled.

"There are two things I can promise you. Though he is technically Forlorn, he's always followed pack rules. He has no issue with humans. With him, you are safe. His control over the change is unusually strong."

When over stimulated, the change could burst upon a werewolf with less than adequate control. Sam had drilled that into me when I first started hanging out with Paul and Henry unsupervised. He didn't want me to freak out if one of them went wolf on me for no reason. He'd stressed that whether in their fur or in their skin, they had the same intelligence and instinct. The change was just a defense mechanism because in their fur, they had teeth and claws to fight. So, what he meant was Clay had control, and he kept his emotions in check.

"And he won't give up," Sam added.

Clay hadn't been looking for a Mate like most werewolves did once they reached puberty. Did that give me any advantage? I doubted it. Sam had repeatedly stressed that instinct ruled this business. And fighting instinct proved extremely difficult for werewolves. So Sam's final warning was a given. Once they scented their Mate, they couldn't turn back. I sighed. Why couldn't werewolves get strategically-timed head colds like the rest of us?

"All right, where is he?"

"I think he's still tinkering with my truck. Try there."

Sam slid back under his covers, and I turned off the lights for him before walking out the door. My sock-covered feet, the only thing on me that didn't seem too dirty, muffled the sound of my passing. By the front door, I found my mud-caked shoes and put them on. They hadn't been that dirty when I'd taken them off at the motel. I couldn't believe he'd put them back on me before abducting me. Had I really been that tired? Maybe there'd been something wrong with that water. But why were my shoes caked with mud if he'd carried me?

CHAPTER FIVE

When I stepped out the door, the sun, already high in the cloudless sky, shone brightly. Moving off the porch, I closed my eyes for a moment and tilted my head back to soak in the warmth. The sound of a ratchet drew me back to my purpose.

I found Clay right where Sam had said, his torso bent over the grill of the pickup. He looked closely at the engine. Purposefully relaxing my shoulders, I started toward the truck. The yard was empty compared to yesterday. It left Clay more room to spread out the pieces he continued to remove.

Slowing my approach, I studied him a bit. The mid-day sun didn't make him look any better than he had in last night's shadows. He still wore that heavy jacket, despite the warm day, and some type of very dirty, baggy cargo pants. His bare feet looked surprisingly clean after walking miles last night, then carrying or dragging me back.

I looked at his feet again, then down at my shoes. No way! How were his feet cleaner than my shoes? He couldn't have worn my shoes; his feet were bigger than mine. Didn't Sam just tell me he had complete control over his change? Couldn't he have partially shifted his feet? Maybe. It still didn't explain how I slept through being carried.

He continued his examination of the truck. I knew he could hear me coming, but I waited to speak until I stood next to the detached hood.

"We weren't officially introduced last night. My name's Gabby. Gabrielle May

Winters." I tucked my hands in my back pockets and hoped I wouldn't have to shake his hand or anything.

He straightened, turned toward me, and gave me his undivided attention. I didn't think it possible, but he was even dirtier than I'd first believed. Long hair hung in clotted strands obscuring his eyes while his unkempt facial hair covered the rest of his face. I kept my thoughts about his hygiene to myself.

At no less than six feet to my five-five, he intimidated me, and I fought not to show it. His continued silence didn't help matters. It puzzled me until I remembered Sam's comments about his upbringing. Maybe he didn't even have the social skills to return a greeting.

There had to be a way out of this. Please let there be a way out of this.

"Sam said that your name is Clay." I waited for some type of acknowledgement, but didn't get one. He just continued to look at me. At least, I assumed I had his attention. I couldn't really see his eyes to know for sure.

"Listen, Clay, I know you think I'm the one for you..."

I decided to change my approach. Choosing my words carefully, I started again.

"I don't have a sense of smell to depend on, like you do. Although the Elders say to trust the instinct of werewolves, I don't trust blindly."

He didn't move. How was I supposed to know if he understood what I was saying? We stood maybe five feet apart with the front quarter panel of the truck separating us. I couldn't read his expression or anything in his body language to hint at what he might be thinking. I decided just to say what I wanted.

"I really want to go home. If I asked to borrow someone else's car, would it live?"

He turned away and continued with his examination of the truck, his body language, finally, easy to translate.

"Ok. I'll take that as a no," I mumbled more to myself than him.

He surprised me by turning back toward me again. I struggled to decipher his mood from his face. His ridiculously long and shaggy facial hair obliterated any trace of a smile or frown.

"Clay, I'm not trying to be rude here, but I'm struggling to figure us out. What's the plan?"

No visible response.

"Am I just supposed to stay here until you decide I'm not really your Mate?" I hated saying that word.

Again, nothing.

"Would it help speed things along if we spent a little time together?"

This time a shrug. One-way conversations rarely worked well when trying to get to know someone.

"Do you talk?"

And again, I lost his attention to the truck engine.

"Ok. No talking. Got it."

Did being raised in his fur mean he'd turned feral? The thought of spending time with a Tarzan mentality werewolf worried me. Who knew what he might do? Only Sam's assurance of my safety eased my fear before it could fully take hold. No, he couldn't be feral. He appeared to understand everything I said. For whatever reason, it seemed that Clay had no intention to speak to me.

I sighed, pulled my hands from my back pockets, and leaned against the truck. Chin in hands, I watched him check the different fluids.

"You seemed to like the idea of spending time to get to know each other," I said. He turned toward me again. "But what's the point in spending time together if you don't want to talk to me? Isn't the point to get to know one another?"

And he turned back to the truck. Good to know the windshield washer fluid was getting low.

Frustrated, I wanted to kick a truck tire but figured I'd just hurt my toe. Instead, I walked back to the main entrance. The one-sided conversation hadn't given me any useful information. Why keep me here if he didn't want to talk to me? And he obviously wanted me here. First, he'd killed Sam's truck. Then, he'd brought me back to the Compound in the middle of the night after letting me walk for hours. That reminded me...I needed a shower badly.

Inside, the hallways remained empty. I let myself into the quiet apartment. Sam no longer curled under his covers. His bed was made. He'd probably left in search of coffee.

I grabbed some clean clothes, headed to the bathroom, and cringed at the sight of myself in the mirror. He wouldn't speak and dragged me through mud and leaves. How exactly was that a good start to a relationship? I spent longer under the hot spray than I would have liked as I tried to work the leaf debris from my hair. Too late, I concluded brushing the leaves out first would have been better.

Someday, I'd have to get the full story about how I got so dirty. But how could I? He wouldn't speak to me. He seemed willing to listen though...until I said something he didn't like. When I talked about talking, he stopped listening.

Did that mean he wanted me to do all the conversing? It made sense that he wouldn't really want to reveal anything about himself given what Sam had mentioned about his childhood. I could empathize. There wasn't much I wanted to share with a stranger about my childhood either.

I tugged on the last of my clean clothes, a pair of cotton shorts (I'd been counting on a lounge day) and a tank top. Having planned a three-day weekend, I hadn't packed much. I balled up the dirty clothes, tossed them into a plastic bag, and set it by the bedroom door. Hopefully, Sam's washing machine could take the abuse.

I sat on the edge of my bed and, swinging my bare feet over the carpet, thought over my options. Stay and accept my fate or find a way back home to continue with the plans I'd made for my own future? Sure, I could stay and make an effort to understand and learn more about Clay. But I'd already made my plans. How fair was it to expect me to change them? If Clay truly lived in the wild, it wasn't as if he had any plans. Maybe he didn't even understand the concept of planning. Could I possibly talk Clay into letting me go? He didn't seem too fond of me.

Absently, I started to towel dry my hair. When I had hinted we might not be Mates, he hadn't turned away. Did that mean he had doubts too? If he did, maybe I had a chance.

Determined, I tossed the towel aside and stood. Due to the pull I had on human men, I'd honed my skills of reason and avoidance. If reasoning didn't work, I avoided them. This would be no different. Piece of cake.

I gave myself a pep talk as I hurried through the halls. A few of the men I passed gave me curious glances. I remained focused on finding Clay, while thinking of, and rejecting, the possible reasons for his doubt.

The main door swung open with a nudge. I hopped off the porch into the sun and winced when my bare feet met with the sharp gravel. Too absorbed in my purpose, I hadn't thought of shoes. Resolute, I tiptoed across the parking area as quickly as possible.

Clay still tinkered with the truck. However, when he heard me, he turned to watch my approach. Other than a few quick glances at him to ensure he didn't leave, I focused on placing my feet in the smoother areas where tire treads had cleared the stone and left sand behind. My ill-timed, stiff steps made a prancing dance. I hoped no one had a video camera.

As I neared, he took a shop rag from his pocket and set it on the ground near the truck. I paused mid-prance and looked down at the soiled rag. I'd just showered. What was with getting me dirty? Not a fair thought. My soles were probably already filthy. The insistent bite of the gravel decided it. I stepped onto the rag, wiping my feet on the grease and carbon stained surface to dislodge the piercing shards still stuck to them. The relief made it worthwhile.

"Thanks," I said looking up at him.

Since he'd set the rag directly in front of the truck, I stood closer to him than I would have liked. I could see brown eyes staring at me from behind the stringy hair. He studied me intently, and I felt that strange pull in my stomach again. It reminded me of my problem. We had an obvious connection; one I didn't want and one he might not want. Maybe, instead of trying to figure out why he might doubt our connection, I needed to explain why I didn't want it in terms he could relate too as a Forlorn werewolf.

Taking a breath, I plunged into a lie. I knew I played with fire. Living with Sam had taught me werewolves could sense a lie through increased heart rate, smell of fear, or anxiety. But, the simple beauty of the situation—the dash across the gravel, which had elevated my pulse—made the lie hard to detect.

"Sam just told me that you're to be confined to a room for the remainder of the day. With me. They want to see how we react to each other so they can determine if you really do have a Claim to me."

A low growl rumbled from him before I finished speaking.

"What? You don't want to spend time with me?"

He stopped his growling and looked down at my feet on the rag. I glanced at them too and noted what the gravel hadn't done, the rag had. They were filthy again. If Charlene found me walking though the hallways with feet this dirty, she'd give me an earful.

I looked back up at him. "You do want to spend time with me, don't you?"

He shrugged, still looking down. Not staring at my feet, then, but thinking. I continued to press my point before he caught on.

"So, it's not me. Don't you like being indoors?" He shrugged again, this time looking up at me. "Ok. If it's not me, and not being indoors, then what?" I let the question hang briefly before I said what I already knew. Ultimately, Forlorn didn't join packs because...

"You don't want to be told when or how to spend time with me. You don't want someone telling you what to do. Is that right?"

He didn't look away. Didn't move at all.

"Yeah, me either."

I watched him closely, waiting for some sign he understood I'd lied to him.

His motionlessness felt like a standoff and temporarily shriveled my hope. Maybe there was no reasoning with Clay. No, I just chose the wrong tract.

Ignoring the pain, I stepped off the rag and bent down to pick it up. I shook it out and handed it back to him.

"I'm sorry I lied to you, Clay. I thought maybe if you knew how it felt to have your choices taken from you, you'd understand why I want to leave. It's nothing personal."

He took the rag from me and turned back to the truck. Someone had brought him more tools, and he was in the process of taking something off what I assumed was the engine. He picked up a ratchet and started to loosen a bolt.

His inattention didn't deter me. I had to keep trying.

"Your instincts say I'm the one. I don't have those instincts. Instead, I just keep thinking how I don't even know you. And the little bit Sam's told me...that you spend most of your time in your fur, doesn't help me understand how there can be an us. I have no fur. I can't just run off into the woods with you." The clicking of the ratchet began to slow. He listened.

"I've enrolled in college—one I chose—despite Sam's opposition. Do you know why I picked it? Because it was far enough away that I knew it'd be harder for people to tell me what to do. Major decisions, up until this point, have been made by others based on what they thought would be best for me. Sure, they ask me what I think and try to consider it, but not always. How do you think Sam got me to Introductions for the past two years? It wasn't by asking me each time if I felt like going."

The ratcheting stopped, but he remained facing the engine.

"I don't mean to sound heartless. I've been through enough Introductions to know what they mean to your kind. I'm not trying to throw your traditions back in your face. I'm just asking for some compromise. Don't ask me to forget the one thing I've chosen on my own."

My pleading didn't appear to sway him any further so I switched tactics and offered him a little hope.

"If you're serious about me, then come to the city with me and learn while I learn. We can get to know each other. I need that in order to even consider there being an us." He still didn't move. Frustration crept into my words. "I know I'm asking a lot. You'd need to start talking, stop growling, and bathe. No offense meant, but you look like a crazy man the way you are."

He moved slightly as if I'd poked him in the ribs. So he did understand how bad he looked. Inside, I jumped up and down on the balls of my feet, clapping my hands excitedly. I leaned against the truck to take some weight off my bare feet and pressed my case further.

"I know it wouldn't be easy on you. You'll be surrounded by people. It'll probably be uncomfortable after you've been on your own for so long. But we'd be able to spend time together, to get to know each other—the normal, human way—and see how things go. We'd both be giving a little, then. Well, you'd be giving a little more, but...will you think about it?" I didn't wait for his reaction. I turned and walked back to the Compound. It had to work. Please let it work.

I spent about five minutes trying to wipe my feet clean on one of the entry rugs before I gave up and walked back to my room. My speech continued to run through my head. Either it would work or not. We both knew I couldn't live in the woods. He would need to rejoin society. He'd see I wasn't worth the effort.

With a mental sigh, I pushed it from my thoughts and focused on the present. I planned to lounge in the apartment and finish the novel I'd started over a month ago. My stomach rumbled loudly. And eat.

THE NEXT MORNING I woke early. I'd grown so bored reading the day before that I'd gone to bed by eight. So it was no surprise when I opened my eyes and saw my phone flashed five a.m. Sam would kill me if I woke him up. I only hesitated a moment before I threw back the covers and got out of bed. In the pitch-dark room, I managed to pull my zipper hoodie on over my tank top, tiptoe to my door, and open it without a sound.

I only managed three steps into the living room when the light near the sofa clicked on, blinding me for a moment.

"Doesn't anyone sleep around here?"

"Sorry. I should know better than to try not to wake you." His hearing made him a very light sleeper.

"What are you doing up already?" He sat up and ran his hands through his hair as if trying to wake himself up more.

I doubted it would work and didn't think he would appreciate an offer to make him coffee given the time. He'd rather just go back to bed.

"I was going to check on the truck. He had it mostly taken apart yesterday afternoon. I wanted to see if he'd started putting it back together."

"What did you say to him yesterday?" Sam surprised me by getting out of bed and stripping the sheets. We always changed the bedding just before we left so it was ready in case anyone else ever used the rooms. But it was five a.m....

"What do you mean?" I took a few steps backward to lean against my door and watched his progress. He almost tripped over his bag while pulling off the fitted sheet.

"Do you want me to start some coffee?" It wasn't normal for werewolves to be anything less than agile. Coffee couldn't be good for him.

"No, I'm fine," he said, answering my last question first. "I mean, he asked for the keys to the truck last night and brought them back earlier this morning. Truck's fixed. I checked myself. So, I'm wondering what you said to him."

My mouth popped open. I couldn't believe he'd actually listened to me. A silly smile tugged at my mouth. Did this really mean he'd let me go? My barely formed smile faded. Or would I just wake up back in this apartment tomorrow morning if I tried to leave?

Sam continued to remake the bed with the clean sheets from the hidden compartment in the matching sofa ottoman.

There had to be a catch. Sam had told me a tied pair didn't part until completing the Claim. When Clay had scented me, and I'd recognized him openly, the Elders saw us as a pair. They, in turn, announced it to everyone over their mental link. Every werewolf, whether in a pack or Forlorn, recognized our tie. If my words truly changed Clay's mind, great—but Sam's question caused me to begin to doubt that possibility, and I struggled to come up with what I'd overlooked.

"The truth," I said answering Sam's question. "Let's say he is my Mate. He's an uneducated man from the backwoods. How are we going to live? I can't turn on the fur like you guys can and live as a wolf like he's done for most of his life. Where does that leave us? I just pointed out that I had to go to school to get the education I needed to land a good job to support myself because he can't."

Sam had stopped remaking the bed and looked at me in disbelief.

"Well, I said it nicer than that."

He gave me a disappointed look.

"You don't know anything about him, Gabby. He may have lived most of his life in his fur, but it doesn't mean he isn't intelligent or that he's more wolf than man. You may have caused yourself more trouble than you intended."

I shifted against the door. "Hold on, I didn't say either of those things to him." Granted, I did tell him he needed to bathe. "And what do you mean 'more trouble'?"

"He said that you suggested he live with you so you could get to know each other better."

I froze in disbelief. That is not what I said.

"Wait. Did he actually talk to you?"

"Well, I had to put on my fur to understand him since he was in his, but yes."

Sam's kind communicated in several ways when in their fur—typically, through body language or howls. Claimed and Mated pairs shared a special bond using an intuitive, mental link. Once establishing a Claim, the pair could sense strong emotions as well as each other's location. Mated pairs had the same ability to communicate with each other as the Elders had with everyone in the pack.

I closed my eyes and thought back to my exact wording.

"I didn't say we should live together, but that he should come back with me to get an education." Fine, I hadn't worded it well, but how did he get "hey, we should live together" out of that?

"Like I said, you've got trouble." He gave me another disappointed look, folded the bed back into the sofa, then picked up his bag from the floor. He strode to the bathroom and closed the door on any further conversation.

Crap. I needed to talk to Clay again and find out what he intended. I'd been counting on his feral upbringing and his need for freedom to cause him to reject my suggestion—a suggestion that hadn't included him living with me. I'd meant he should find a place nearby so we could go through the motions of human dating, which was the extent of my willingness to compromise. I hadn't thought he'd take any of it seriously but that, instead, he would just let me go.

I left the apartment and stole through the deserted hallways. At the main door, I paused to put on shoes then stepped out into the pre-dawn darkness. The yard light cast shadows near the vehicles. I stood on the porch for a moment but heard nothing.

Cautiously walking across the empty expanse, I found the repaired truck, but no Clay. My stomach knotted as I studied the truck. Sam's words about Clay's intelligence haunted me. A man raised in the wild knew how to dismantle and reassemble an engine. I'd underestimated him. No matter which way I looked at it, it all pointed back to the fact I didn't know enough about Clay to try to guess what he'd do next.

Back in the apartment, Sam waited, ready to leave. I didn't bother with a shower but remade the bed and grabbed my own bag.

We made it back to the truck without any sign of Clay. Sensing my mood, Sam didn't say anything to me as I climbed in, and we started the long drive home.

It was several hours into the ride when I finally stopped looking behind us or stretching my second sight to search for werewolves. There'd been no sign of Clay following us, but there'd been no sign of Clay following me the night before last, either.

CHAPTER SIX

I WAS ON EDGE THE FIRST WEEK BACK, UNSURE IF, OR WHEN, CLAY would show up.

Desperate for distraction, I plunged into my two part-time jobs and worked as much as possible. I woke up early each morning, showered, ate breakfast, and packed a lunch, all long before Sam got out of bed. And because I still cared, I started his coffee before I walked out the door. In the evenings, a dark house greeted me when I returned home, worn out from the long day. Usually, Sam had something set aside for my dinner. I'd eat, go to bed, then start the cycle again the next morning.

I could have asked Sam if he knew what Clay planned, but he hadn't mentioned Clay since we'd left the Compound. I feared, if I brought it up, he would think I missed Clay or something. Since I didn't want Sam sending out a call that might cause Clay to show up when he otherwise wouldn't, I kept quiet. Worry ate at me; but, as time passed, and my hectic schedule successfully prevented thoughts of Clay, I started to feel safe again.

Three weeks before the start of school, I found the perfect roommate, Rachel. I'd been watching the papers near school when I came across her ad for a roommate. We hit it off the first time we spoke on the phone. She attended the same school in which I'd enrolled and was going into her third year in the nursing program. She rented a two-bedroom house. Her roommate from the prior year had moved out after graduation. Rachel had tried living on her own over the summer, but the bills grew too expensive and the house too quiet.

After our call, I did some research and found the house wasn't in the best part of town, but I couldn't find anything closer that I could still afford. Plus, the unoccupied bedroom she offered came furnished with a bed and a dresser; I didn't own the bed I slept on now and didn't feel right taking it with me when I left. So, I called Rachel back and let her know I wanted the room.

Sunday, a week before school started, I once again packed my possessions, an old familiar routine I'd forgotten while living with Sam. Sam pretended not to care I was leaving, but I knew he did. I'd only stepped out of my room for a minute to grab my shampoo and brush from the bathroom, and when I walked back into the room, I caught him slipping some money into the emergency cash I kept hidden in a half-full tampon box in my dresser. He pretended to check the dresser as if ensuring I hadn't forgotten anything. I went along with it.

Packing didn't take long. Everything I owned fit into several messenger bags and an old suitcase I'd gotten at a secondhand store. By lunch, we had what I needed loaded into the back of Sam's truck. A passerby wouldn't have noticed the small pile.

After one last look around the house to make sure I had everything, we climbed into the truck and started the journey. Sam looked slightly depressed as he drove. Excitement filled me, but I fought hard to keep it from showing. I didn't think my joy would give him any comfort.

"You'll call me if you have any trouble?" Sam asked, yet again.

"Yes, Sam. But I'm over four hours from you. I'll need to face things on my own."

"Not on your own. Elder Joshua has moved nearby. I'll be able to contact him if you have a need."

Sam had mentioned Elder Joshua to me a few days after I'd found Rachel. I knew Elder Joshua's recent move was for me but didn't make any complaint. As long as he stayed away until I needed something, we'd get along just fine.

When we arrived, Rachel sat waiting on the front step of the small ranch house. She'd described herself on the phone as just over average height with brown hair and eyes. She'd left out everything else. Her deep, brown hair hung silky-straight, and the beautifully bronzed tone of her skin had me wondering if she had any African-American heritage. Her perfectly arched brows didn't appear tweezed or penciled, and they highlighted her darkly lashed eyes.

At about five-foot ten inches, she surpassed average height. Long, lean legs extended from her cutoffs, and her V-neck top showed sufficient cleavage to know she didn't need to stuff her bra, either. Overall, she was gorgeous enough to make a straight girl wonder if she should switch teams, and that worried the hell out of me. Oh, not that I'd switch teams. As annoying and obsessive as men were, I still preferred them. No, her attitude the first time a man overlooked her and focused on me, worried me. Let's face it. Pretty girls can be very mean.

I drew my brief gaze from her as she stood to watch Sam do a Y-turn to back into the driveway. Using the side mirror of the truck, I studied the house.

A cracked and uneven sidewalk led to the front steps. Faded yellow aluminum siding and brown trim gave the small house a slightly run down look. Rachel had mentioned room dimensions to me to prepare me. After living at Sam's place, this house did appear small from the outside. Only two windows adorned the front of the house. There was a large picture window, which probably meant a living room, and, on the side of the house close to the driveway, a much smaller window. With the shade half-drawn, I assumed it belonged to a bedroom. How many houses had just two windows on their front? At least, they looked new, as did the roof.

As Sam backed into the driveway, I smiled and waved to Rachel. She walked toward the truck while Sam parked.

"Hi! Gabby, right?" Rachel said with an excited smile.

"Yes." I opened my door and stepped out of the truck. She caught me off guard by pulling me into an embrace. With my arms pinned to my sides, I fought the urge to pull back. "I hope you're Rachel." With that, she let me escape from her exuberant hug.

"I'm so glad to see you look so normal," she said looking even happier than she had a moment ago. "I was worried I'd end up with someone weird when I put that ad in the paper." Ah, that explained the happiness. Too bad, she had no idea how "weird" I was.

Sam came around from his side of the truck.

"Rachel, this is my grandpa, Sam."

"Hi, Sam!"

He quickly extended his hand for a friendly handshake, and I hid my smile. He'd noticed her boisterous hug.

Rachel clasped his hand. "Would you like to come in and see the place before we carry everything in?" She darted a puzzled look at the back of the truck.

I smiled. "We'll be able to carry it in and take a tour at the same time. I don't have much."

We grabbed my bags and walked around to the front of the house. The door opened to a tiny entry, with the vacant bedroom immediately to the right, a small hall closet straight ahead, and the living room to the left.

We all stepped into my room to set down my things. I'd been correct about the window being a bedroom window.

As Rachel had promised, my room came furnished with a full-sized bed. I had just enough space around it to walk. Accustomed to a twin, it seemed overly large. Thankfully, I had the correct bedding for it. A gift from Sam. The closet was a small rectangle, but more than enough space for what I owned. The only other piece of furniture—a small, battered wood dresser—leaned against the interior wall. Nothing decorated the walls, which Rachel said she'd done on purpose, so I could add my own flair to the room.

Rachel gave us the grand tour of the five-room house. The living room was long, but not very deep, and occupied the rest of the front of the house. Rachel had it tastefully decorated. Two sets of curtains hung in the picture window. The soft cream-colored ones faced the road, while the inside set matched the color of the worn, brown leather couch centered in front of the window. Square, wooden end tables held cream-colored lamps with matching shades and crowded each end of the couch.

A chair, set at a sharp angle against the interior wall, used the remaining space in the living room. The TV wall she'd painted a medium brown while the standard off-white covered the rest of the walls, which included my bedroom and the entry. A large, dark-brown rug, a shade close to the color of the couch and the curtains, covered all but a small swath of the living room's beige carpet. Overall, the room looked comfortable.

Through the living room's arched doorway, on the same wall as the TV, a small hallway connected the living room, her bedroom, a tiny linen closet, the kitchen, the bathroom, and the door to the basement.

Rachel turned left and briefly showed her room, the larger of the two bedrooms. Then she turned us and opened the door between the living room arch and the bathroom. She flicked on the basement light and told me we had our own washer and dryer and plenty of room for storage.

She gave the bathroom, opposite her room, a quick wave. "It's small, but it could be worse."

I noted that, although the bathroom measured half the size of the one at Sam's place, it didn't feel cramped. The pedestal sink, tub, and toilet abutted the wall shared with my bedroom. White tile covered the walls to about midway, except for the shower area where the tiles ran from tub to ceiling. Dark-blue paint coated the walls and offset the overabundance of white. She'd also defused the white of the plastic shower curtain by layering a dark-blue, cloth shower curtain over it and used a cute, white flower clip to swag it to the side. Everything looked neat and clean.

Finally, she led us to the kitchen. An addition there extended the room five feet into the backyard and brought it from worthless to functional. Just inside the kitchen arch, to the right, a table for four sat against the interior wall. Along the wall that faced the driveway, a wall-to-wall counter supported the sink and provided four cupboards. Two separate wall cupboards hung on either side of the sink, allowing light through the kitchen's only window. The refrigerator stood to the left of the arched kitchen entry, along with four more cupboards top and bottom. Standing free, the stove occupied the unclaimed space on the exterior wall. Just enough room separated the cabinetry from the stove to allow the bottom cabinet door to swing open. A garbage can hid between the stove and the door that led to the wooden deck and backyard.

Overall, the exterior condition of the house didn't match the inside. The exposed carpet in the living room looked worn but relatively stain-free. The walls and ceiling could use a fresh coat of paint, but with the string of switching roommates over the last five years, the landlord probably hadn't had a chance.

Rachel concluded the tour on the back deck.

"We'll take turns mowing the lawn and shoveling the snow, and since it's only a one-car garage, we'll switch parking, too. But we'll work that out when it starts snowing."

I nodded in agreement as I looked at our small backyard. A new looking barn-red wooden fence separated our yard from the neighbor's behind us while evergreen hedges barred the rest of the yard from the neighbor's on each side. With the deck and garage, there really wasn't a lot of grass to mow in back, but the front yard made up for it a bit. It reminded me of the Newton's place, and I suffered an uncomfortable moment of longing before I strangled the feeling.

During the tour, Sam had remained quiet as he followed us and scrutinized the house. Outside, he stood beside me, studying the backyard as well.

"Well, Gabby, looks like you'll be comfortable here. I'd better start heading back. You need anything, let me know." He patted my cheek and stepped off the deck, neither of us comfortable with drawn out goodbyes.

I watched him climb into his truck and waved when he looked back. Again, my emotions ran amuck for a few moments as he pulled away, nostalgia robbing me of my moment. I'd been so ready to leave and start out on my own I'd not inspected my feelings for Sam too closely. Now I knew. I'd miss him. A lot.

Rachel seemed to understand my mood as we went back into the house.

"You have a nice grandpa," she said, sitting on my bed as I unpacked.

I agreed and tried to shake the unhappiness that lingered. Less than five hours ago, I had looked forward to making my own rules. Here, in this house, I had the freedom I'd wanted. No more obligatory weekends in Canada. No meeting men I didn't want to meet. My internal pep talk began to work, and I started to unpack with more enthusiasm.

Rachel took a few of the wire hangers from the closet and helped hang the t-shirts I'd crammed into a bag.

"Please tell me there is more in these bags than t-shirts," she said. "I don't mind them—they're comfy—but where's the clothes for going out?"

"Um, I really don't own any." Watching her while I said it, I didn't miss the shocked expression that briefly flitted over her features. I looked over my small pile of clothes, most of them already on hangers thanks to her help. They lacked diversity. I'd never noticed before.

She changed the subject. "Got your bathing suit handy? With the backyard surrounded, the deck is perfect for working on a tan. Join me when you're done." Without waiting for my answer, she popped up from the bed and left the room.

Bathing suit? I didn't even own one. I finished unpacking and heard the back door a few minutes later.

Tucking my suitcase under the bed, I covered the mattress with the sheets from Sam. Instead of feeling sad, a new feeling bloomed. Resolve. I needed this, living here with Rachel, someone my own age. Well, close to it. And female. Normal things like lying out in the sun had escaped me over the years. She'd help me catch up. That she didn't seem adversely affected by me, gave me hope. Granted, she hadn't yet faced rejection from a man because of me. Maybe we could work on becoming friends first. Who knew, it could help prevent the ugly hostility I'd grown accustomed to. I liked the idea of having a real friend. Sure, I had Paul and Henry, but I wanted a friend of the same gender.

I changed into the shortest shorts I owned and a strapless top that Barb had given me for my eighteenth birthday. I'd kept in touch with my foster parents because of their insistence. Even though they had a beautiful little girl of their own, they still thought of me, especially on my birthday. Feeling light at heart, I headed out to the deck.

Rachel turned her sunglassed-gaze my way when I closed the screen door.

"Where's your suit?" she asked curiously.

"I don't own one," I admitted, lying on my stomach on the cartoon beach towel she'd laid out for me. "Didn't want to embarrass my grandpa. He's a little old school." Honestly, I kept my wardrobe modest because it was safe...and I hadn't wanted him to suggest I bring a swimsuit with me to Canada.

"Really? You don't own one?" She propped herself up on her elbows and glanced at me over the top of her sunglasses. A wide smile spread over her lips. "Wanna go shopping? I'll use any excuse to go."

I hesitated. If I declined, we'd be starting out on a poor note. If I said yes, we'd most likely have an issue with guys somewhere along the way. But if I didn't say yes, how could I hope to win her over as a friend? Any normal girl probably wouldn't even stop to think about this. I really wanted to try for normal.

"Sure, let me go change," I agreed.

"Yay!" She jumped up, grabbed both towels, and danced into the house behind me.

Since she had the car, she drove us to an outlet mall that she promised was the best and cheapest place to shop. Stunning in a tank top, short shorts, and cute little sandals with a heel, she outshined my drab, worn t-shirt, jeans, and sneakers. Still, I twisted my fingers in my lap and tried to quell my worry.

"While we're here, we should look for some clubbing clothes for you." She pulled into an open space and parked the car. "And don't be afraid to tell me if I'm being too pushy. I love shopping, but have too many clothes already. By shopping for someone else, I get my fix without adding to the mayhem in my closet."

"No, you're not being pushy. I could use a swimsuit and a few new tops. But, I have to be honest...I'm not really into the party scene. Guys act too weird around me, and it makes me uncomfortable."

"Weird how?" she asked as she reached for the door.

"Wait."

She paused, turning to look at me.

I'd rather tell her where no one else would overhear. I took a deep breath. Normal. I needed to sound normal.

"Every friendship I've ever had was ruined by competition over a guy. Only problem was, I was never competing. I wasn't interested in the guy my friend was. But the guy was interested in me."

Behind her sunglasses, her eyes searched my face. I struggled not to squirm or look away. Anxiety bloomed. I should have kept my mouth shut.

Her lips curved into an amused smile, and she laughed.

"You're a serious one. I can see that already. Don't worry, Gabby. If a guy doesn't trip over himself to get to me, I'm not interested. I don't want to waste my time chasing what doesn't want to be caught." She opened the door to the sunbaked parking lot, and I followed.

We'd just crossed the black expanse, stepping onto the sidewalk in front of the stores, when Rachel nudged me.

"Check out this hottie."

The man she'd spotted exited the same door we headed for. As I expected, he first looked at Rachel then at me. I looked down and kept my eyes on the sidewalk as we strolled past him.

Rachel obviously didn't know about the "wait for the door to close" rule because she started laughing before I'd even made it over the threshold.

"He kept his eyes on you the entire time. I can't wait to see what happens the first time we go out."

I wanted to groan.

The clerk at the register glanced at us just then because of Rachel's laughter. His double take at me caused her to start laughing even harder. I pulled her toward the back of the store before he decided he wanted to talk to us. Her carefree attitude about my effect on men did bring a smile to my face. Maybe things would work out.

After helping me pick out a swimsuit, a rather daring bikini that she insisted would not cause her the least bit of animosity no matter what attention it brought me, she talked me into a few more stores.

In three hours, I'd purchased two "clubbing" tops and a black mini skirt. I probably wouldn't wear any of it. Sexy was a dangerous look for me. Heck, mildly attractive was even dangerous. But I liked spending the time with her. My careful spending slowed the process down a bit, but she didn't seem to mind.

Back at the house, the pleasantly warm breeze and inviting deck beckoned us, and we decided to catch the dying rays before calling it a night. Really, I just wanted to try on my bikini.

I shook my head at the sound of the back door opening and closing five minutes after being home. How she managed to change so fast amazed me. My new clothes hung in my closet, except for the bikini. Since I was pale from spending most of my summer working, Rachel had insisted I purchase a bright pink number with vibrant yellow straps. She said it would give me a little more color. Normally, I'd be reluctant to wear anything that called attention to me, but Rachel had been adamant that people our age didn't wear one pieces with built in skirts, the style I'd deemed safer. The top with its strings and triangle coverage concerned me, but I'd given in because of the boy-shorts style bottom. When she'd held up a different option with even less material, I'd quickly judged the pink and yellow suit the better option.

I pulled the tags off the bikini and slipped it on. Then, I twisted and turned in front of the mirror in my bedroom, worrying. The string top covered me decently. The boy-shorts bottoms hugged my backside. However, a lot of skin reflected back at me. I did like the suit...I just needed to get used to it.

Grabbing the sunglasses I'd bought, I left my room. When I reached the kitchen, I heard Rachel's crooning voice outside. I stopped. Was someone here? Did I want to go out there in this?

I looked down at myself. Hiding myself because of the pull hadn't made me self-conscious...more like extremely cautious. Men reacted less if I kept to myself, which included staying modestly covered. What would happen in a bikini? Better to find out now, at home, if I could wear it in front of someone else than to go to a beach with it. I straightened my shoulders and walked out onto the deck.

"Gabby, look," Rachel squealed as I pushed open the screen door. "A dog!"

On the deck, Rachel reclined on her side, stretched out on a beach towel. Between her towel and the one she'd set out for me, lay a monster of a dog, relaxing in the sun. I stopped and stared. What was that thing? Although the size of a mastiff, it looked nothing like one. At least seven feet from nose to tail, the dog's shaggy brown coat gave it a wild look. Rachel didn't seem to mind, though. She continued to pet its head affectionately.

It turned its head, which moved it out of Rachel's reach. Its soft brown eyes met mine.

Rachel shifted to a sitting position to reach its head again.

"It just walked up the porch steps and lay right down. I nearly peed myself. Have you ever seen a dog this big before? What kind do you think it is?" She continued to pet it lovingly.

I remained glued in place, my stomach sinking. Any lingering homesickness died as my suspicion grew. What are the odds that an extremely large, random dog just appeared at my door scant hours after Sam dropped me off? Improbable odds. When I'd said I would get a dog, I'd meant it as a joke. I couldn't afford a dog.

"And you're not going to believe what its tag says," Rachel said, not seeming to care that I hadn't answered her questions. "'If found, please provide a good home.' Isn't that funny?" She ruffled his neck fur, which made his hidden tags jingle. The dog continued to watch me and ignore Rachel's ministrations.

"Yeah. Funny," I mumbled. The size of the dog would ensure men didn't bother me. But a dog half its size would do the same. Why get one so big? Its size compared to Sam in his fur. Did Sam think some of his kind might bother me? If so, I didn't see how a plain old dog would help. My eyes widened as my own idiocy dawned on me. Not a plain dog.

I needed to call Sam, find out what he'd been thinking, and then give him an earful for sending someone to the house to keep an eye on me. I was about to turn and go back into the house when Rachel said something that made my stomach drop to my toes.

"His tag also says his name is Clay. What do you think? Should we keep him?"

CHAPTER SEVEN

I turned to look at Rachel, eyes wide with shock.

"What?" I glanced down at *him*.

He continued to watch me, his eyes not wavering from mine. He'd left me alone the whole summer. I had thought he'd truly let me go, despite Sam's ominous warning, and had forgotten about him.

"Aw, you aren't allergic are you?" Rachel said with a small pout. "The lease says a single pet is allowed as long as it's licensed."

I doubted the lease had taken into consideration that Rachel would fall in love with a freakishly large monster bearing similarities to a dog.

"No, I'm not allergic," I said distractedly. He had all summer to make his move. Why now? And why when I wore a bikini for the first time ever? A bikini did not say "stay away." I considered grabbing the towel and wrapping myself in it, but discarded the idea after I thought about how it would look to Rachel. Instead, I continued to stare at the frustrating dog until he huffed out a breath, turned away from me, and laid his head on his paws.

Clay had finally shown up and, apparently, he still didn't want to talk.

"Good. He's so cute!" Rachel reached over to scratch his ears, and he closed his eyes.

"I'm going back in," I said as I turned toward the door. Clay sprang to his feet before I reached it and crowded behind me. I looked down at him then back at Rachel, who watched us with an enormous grin.

"Looks like another guy who can't take his eyes off you. Living with you is going to be a riot." She laughed and picked up the towels. "Let's all go in. The neighbor's tree is going to shade the deck soon anyway."

Having little choice, I opened the door for Clay. His fur brushed my bare thighs as he moved past me into the house. His head came to about my sternum. He really was huge...a huge problem.

Sam had warned me Clay had taken my speech as an invitation to live together. At least, Clay had shown up in his fur. However, any relief I might have felt went unnoticed as I contemplated how he'd found me in a completely different state. If Sam told him, I'd have to kill Sam. Since I didn't have the stomach for outright murder, I'd break his coffee maker.

I took a deep breath to clear my hectic thoughts and followed Clay and Rachel inside. She patted him again, and I knew I wouldn't be able to tell him to leave. Especially with Rachel around as a witness. It'd make me look like a complete psycho if I started to speak to the dog, not only as if I knew him, but also as if I was giving a breakup speech. I didn't really have much of a choice...for now.

"We can keep him. But he's going to shed everywhere," I predicted then walked away.

Wisely, Clay stayed in the kitchen with Rachel. She continued to talk to him. She told him how cute he was and asked him if he wanted anything to drink. I heard dishes clank as I closed my door.

Even knowing Clay could probably hear me, I grabbed my cell phone and called Sam. Sam answered before it rang on my end; he knew I wouldn't call so soon for just any reason.

"Gabby, what's wrong?"

"Clay is here. In fur," I said as quietly as possible.

After a brief pause, Sam chuckled. "What did you expect, Hun? He scented you as his Mate. He's probably been following you since. Only, when you were with me, he trusted me to protect you and kept his distance. Moving away...well, you might have forced his hand a bit. Then again, I think he had planned on joining you from the start."

"Right..." I heard a creak of leather and knew Sam had sat in his office chair to get comfortable for a long conversation.

"Listen, this isn't so bad. With him there, you won't need to worry as much about other men, right?"

"Yeah, but what about him?" I went to my dresser to look for clothes.

"I told you...he has control. You won't have to worry about him becoming aggressive with you."

Before I could say anything, Rachel's muted voice called from the kitchen.

"Hey, Gabby?"

"I gotta go. Just wanted to tell you he was here. I'll call if anything stranger pops up." I didn't wait for his goodbye. I closed the phone, tucked it into one of my messenger bags on my dresser, and hurried to change. After putting on lounge pants and a tank top, I headed toward the kitchen.

"What's up?"

"Do you think I can feed him leftover steak?" she said sounding a bit muffled.

Bent at the waist, Rachel riffled through the fridge. Clay sat off to the side with a perfect view of her string bikinied backside, only he wasn't looking. He faced the arched door, watching for me. Should I be happy that he'd ignored the perfect view or annoyed? Instead of thinking about it, I answered Rachel.

"I'm pretty sure people-food is bad for dogs." Yes, I knew it wasn't nice, but if he wanted to play the dog, I'd play along. "We can pick up some dog food for him in the morning. He'll be fine overnight."

I sat at the kitchen table, pulled my legs up, held my knees, and watched Rachel straighten from the fridge and let the door close. She turned to look at Clay with concern, but Clay ignored her and continued to watch me.

My stomach growled.

"But dinner does sound good," I said to Rachel, ignoring Clay. "I should have thought of groceries while we were shopping."

"No problem. I forgot to tell you during the grand tour that there's a cupboard over there that you can stock and call your own. The top shelf in the fridge is mine. But don't worry about it for tonight. I was lazy yesterday and ordered take-out pizza. There's still plenty if you don't mind leftovers."

"Leftovers are fine with me." My stomach rumbled in agreement.

"We've got cheap plastic plates in the cupboard to the left of the sink—inherited from a prior roommate. Grab two, will you?" she said as she re-opened the fridge.

I unfolded myself from the chair and grabbed the plates while Rachel pulled the pizza from the fridge. Clay lay down where he sat and put his massive head on his paws. I could see his eyes move to follow my progress.

Rachel chatted about our neighbors and the university while we warmed the pizza in the microwave. She was easy to be around and fun to listen to.

"What kind of movies do you like?" she asked changing topics abruptly once both plates held several steaming slices.

I had to think about it for a moment. "Action-comedy, I guess. I don't watch movies often."

She handed me a plate. "Let's eat this in the living room and watch a movie."

Clay stood and walked toward the living room before either of us moved. When he passed through the arch, he only had two inches of clearance on each side. I wondered if his fur made up his bulk. Not that it mattered. Our tiny house didn't suit a dog his size.

Rachel laughed as she watched him. "I think he's going to fit right in."

She had no idea how much he didn't fit in. I turned off the light in the kitchen and followed them into the living room. Clay settled on the floor and stretched out in front of the couch, which forced us to step over him. Rachel sat on one side of the couch, and I took the other.

The movie Rachel selected not only held my interest, but it seemed to hold Clay's as well. I ate two of the three pieces of pizza Rachel had put on my plate and set the remaining piece aside. During a quiet moment, Clay stood, stretched, and turned to study my pizza. Rachel noticed.

"Just one bite?" Rachel begged.

"If he's never eaten it before, he might throw up. Are you willing to clean it up? I'm not." I wasn't about to make living with us easy for him.

She pouted prettily, not really upset. Her easygoing personality allowed me to speak without having to censure my words too much. A few minutes later, I saw her break off small pieces and set them on the edge of her plate. Clay innocently turned around and snatched the pieces.

"Fine," I said when the movie ended. "Give him the steak."

Rachel cheered, hopped off the couch, and called to Clay as she went to the kitchen. He looked at me dolefully and followed her.

"Your choice, bud. Not mine," I whispered knowing he'd hear me over Rachel's puttering as she heated the steak for him.

I grabbed my plate and cup and made my way to the kitchen to quickly wash and dry them.

"Thanks for the shopping and movie, Rachel. And the leftovers. You've made this feel like home in less than a day." I quirked a half-smile at her. "But I'm beat and going to bed. See you in the morning."

Before I left the kitchen, I looked back to make sure Clay didn't follow. He sat near Rachel, watching me. Hastily looking away, I escaped to my room. The last thing I needed was for him to think that backward glance had been an invitation to join me.

Odd as it sounded, having Clay in the house made it easier for me to fall asleep. Although still a stranger to me, I knew his world and his rules. He'd keep me safe. Yet, regardless of Sam's assurance that I needn't worry about him, he remained a concern.

THE NEXT MORNING I woke feeling great. Sleeping on a full-size bed definitely beat sleeping on a twin. I didn't think I would ever be able to go back. The new comforter had done a better job keeping in the heat than my old one. My feet were nice and toasty.

I stretched my legs from their curled position and hit something warm and solid through the covers. No...he wouldn't. I sat up and glared at Clay, who was already awake and contentedly stretched out at the end of my bed. His eyes met mine.

"No," I whispered. "No dogs allowed on my bed."

He snorted out a sigh and laid his head down, closing his eyes.

"Seriously, Clay. Don't you think this is just a little inappropriate?"

He didn't move.

"Fine." I used my feet to try to push him off the bed, but he didn't budge. Leaning back, I braced my hands on the wall and pushed harder, straining to move his stubborn, irritating fur from my new comforter.

He still didn't move but did open one eye to look at me.

I gave up and glared back. "If you shed all over my comforter, I'm locking my door at night." I tossed back the covers and got out of bed. "With an eyehook," I added for good measure.

He wisely didn't follow me as I made my way to the bathroom. Rachel already moved around in the kitchen.

"Are you a coffee drinker?" she called to me.

With a mouthful of toothpaste, I had to spit before I could answer.

"No. More of a milk or orange juice person." I finished up in the bathroom, joined her in the kitchen, and noticed her scrubs.

"Going to work?" I asked as I sat on a kitchen chair and pulled my feet up from the cool floor.

"Yep. Sorry to leave you on your own so soon. I'll be back around five. If you need anything, just call my cell. If I don't answer, leave a message, and I'll get back to you." She filled a travel mug with the coffee she had made and rinsed out the pot. "Oh, when I went to bed, Clay whined at your door, so I let him in. Hope that was okay..."

"Yeah, that's fine." What else was I supposed to say without sounding weird or bitchy? Inspiration to pay him back for his sneaky method struck.

"Have you thought of taking him to a vet?"

Rachel paused mid-rinse. "I hadn't, but you're right. He should probably go if we're going to have him in the house with us. I'll call around and make an appointment. I need to check into licensing him, too. Ugh. Shots are probably going to cost a fortune." She looked at me pleadingly.

Darn idea to get back at him would cost me money. "Yeah, I'll go in halves." I got up and started back toward my room.

"Great. Talk to you tonight," she called as she went out the back door.

Clay still sprawled on my bed. He took up the full width with his back paws folded in toward his stomach so they wouldn't fall off. I stood in the doorway and studied him while he, in turn, watched me. We were finally alone, and I was determined to set some rules.

"First, I'd like to clarify that this does not qualify as getting to know each other. Second, you smell like wet dog. If you want to continue to sleep in my room, on my bed, you'll let Rachel give you a bath when she gets home." He snorted at that but didn't get off the bed. "Third, once I'm awake, you get out. I know what you are, and I am not changing in front of you."

He outright harrumphed at that one, and I swore I saw a canine smile. But, he did hop down from the bed. He left the room with quiet dignity.

I closed the door behind him, remade the bed—thankfully, he didn't appear to shed—and grabbed some clothes. I had two goals for the day. First, I needed to figure out how long it would take me to walk to the campus from here. Then, I needed to learn the bus schedule for the days I ran late or the weather prevented walking. If worst came to worst, I'd buy a beater car to drive.

Opening the door, I was startled to see Clay sitting there patiently waiting for me.

"What are you doing?" I asked when he didn't move. Of course, he didn't answer.

I eyed him warily and walked past him. In the kitchen, I grabbed the house key from the counter then moved to the back door. Clay's nails clicked on the floor as he followed me.

"I'm going for a walk, and you're staying here," I said when he made to follow me outside.

Clay growled slightly in response.

His deep growl gave me pause. He sounded scary.

"Please don't do that. Unless you really *are* trying to scare me."

His fur continued to bristle, but his growl stopped. Our relationship wouldn't go anywhere if he thought he could bully and maneuver me to his way of thinking.

"And don't crab at me. I'm not the unlicensed dog without a leash. Do you want me to talk Rachel into buying a pink collar for you?"

He coughed out a strangled bark then turned and walked back to the living room.

"See you later," I said, feeling a little smug.

The walk to campus took about forty minutes. I didn't mind the time, but the distance and the number of catcalls I'd received made walking impractical and unsafe. After checking the bus schedule and stops, I knew I'd need to buy a car. A necessity that would put a significant dent in my savings.

On the way home, I stopped at a small grocery store to pick up some essentials. Browsing, I found a new bar of soap, an extra toothbrush, dog food, and groceries for the week.

Loaded down with the bags, it seemed to take forever to reach the house. When I finally got there, my arms ached. I would need to remember to bring one of my messenger bags if I ever walked there again. It made carrying things so much easier. I made my way to the back of the house and saw Clay sunning on the deck.

"Nice to know you can let yourself out," I said as I walked past him. I nudged open the door and kicked it closed behind me. With a sigh, I put the bags on the table and began to unpack.

After a sharp bark from outside, I grudgingly turned to let Clay in.

"What? Can't let yourself back in?" He didn't respond, except to sit by the sink. I went back to the table and reached into one of the bags.

"Look what I got you." I pulled out a small bag of dog food.

Clay growled again, but it lacked any menace.

"You want to look like a normal dog don't you? Well... as normal as a dog your size can look, anyway." I set the bag on the floor next to the bowl of water Rachel had set out for him and continued to unpack, saving the soap and toothbrush for last.

MELISSA HAAG

"These are for you. You have two choices. You can use them when Rachel's gone, or you can wait until she's back, and I'm sure she'd be happy to help you."

He studied me for a moment then walked out of the kitchen, turning toward the bathroom. I followed a few steps behind.

A startled yelp escaped me when I rounded the corner and caught sight of a naked backside. Without much thought, I tossed the soap and toothbrush in and slammed the door shut.

"You could have waited until I put the stuff in there," I said through the door as my heart thundered in my ears. I took a steadying breath and heard the water turn on, the clink of his dog tag hitting the sink, then the shower curtain move.

Who would have thought he would even know how to use a shower? I hadn't. On the way home, I'd started to think of all the different things I would need to explain, like making sure to position the curtain inside the tub. Standing outside the door, still reeling from the view I'd gotten, I realized I might see the same thing again if I didn't get him a towel.

I'd packed two bath towels. Purchased from a discount store, they both sported gaudy floral designs. I grabbed one and waited outside the door again until I heard him splashing in the shower. Then, I knocked.

"I have a towel for you," I said through the door. "If you're still in the shower, I can open the door and toss it on the toilet seat. Okay?" I didn't hear anything. No surprise. "Okay, I'm coming in." I waited a moment for any indication that I shouldn't enter.

When the water continued to run, I cautiously opened the door. As soon as I saw a clear path to the toilet seat, I tossed the towel. Standing just inside the bathroom with my hand wrapped around the door handle for a quick exit, I paused. His new toothbrush rested on the sink.

"My toothpaste is the one marked with the pink nail polish on the cap. I'll let you use it as long as you promise not to squeeze the tube from the middle."

His answer took the form of an accurately aimed splash of water over the top of the shower curtain. I barely dodged it.

"You're cleaning that up."

I closed the door, grabbed a book, and went to the couch to wait. I hoped he would use the towel before he turned back into a dog. He'd make a mess if he shook out in there. After a minute, I actually opened the book and started to read.

Several minutes later, the water turned off. With my attention divided between listening and trying to associate an action to each sound I heard, I couldn't concentrate on my book. A moment of silence. Then running water. It sounded like the sink. Brushing his teeth? Then silence again. It remained quiet until I heard the doorknob turn. Quickly, I held the book higher to block my view, just in case he chose not to wear his fur...or the towel. A chuffing bark, apparently his dog version of a laugh, had me lowering my comically high book.

He strolled over by me and hopped up on the couch. Incredibly, his fur looked even fluffier.

"Don't get too comfortable, I don't know Rachel's rules about pets on the furniture." I curled my legs under me to give him more room.

Forgetting myself, I leaned over to smell him.

"Much better," I said straightening. At his intense look, I went back to reading my book and pretended I hadn't just leaned over and smelled a man. We stayed like that, side by side in companionable silence, until lunch when both our stomachs rumbled.

On the way to the kitchen, I noticed his wet towel on the bathroom floor.

"Next time, fold it over the edge of the tub," I said. The bathroom lacked any other available space to hang a towel, and I didn't want his towel hung in my room, either. That seemed a little too domestic.

I made us both dry ham sandwiches. Dry because I'd refused to pay four dollars for a miniature jar of mayo.

"I'm guessing your bowl of dog food will always be full," I said as I set his plated sandwich on the floor. Sitting at the table, I started to eat my own sandwich. He finished his in two bites.

"So, we have a week before my classes start up. What's your plan?"

He cocked his head at me.

"Did you want to try to enroll in any classes? Study anything?"

He lay down on the floor next to his empty plate, eyeing it sadly.

"Okay...well, if you change your mind, let me know."

I washed our dishes and went back to reading. Eventually, he joined me on the couch.

Later that night, Rachel breezed into the house and tossed her keys and purse on the table. She had a manly spiked collar in her hand along with a leash.

From my position on the couch, I watched her kneel down next to Clay, who stood near his bowl of water. I wasn't sure, but she appeared to have interrupted his contemplation of drinking from the bowl. The thought made me smile.

Trying to ignore the pair, I focused on my book. Shuffling movements sounded from the kitchen. Rachel mumbled something that was too quiet to hear. When the noises didn't stop, I went to investigate.

"This is a joke," she said. She knelt in front of Clay, face to muzzle, trying to get the collar on him.

I laughed from the doorway as I watched them struggle. She would wrap her arms around his neck to buckle the collar, and he would duck or shift to avoid her but he never got up and walked away. I caught a twinkle of amusement in his canine eyes.

I knew Rachel wouldn't give up getting a real collar on him. He needed proof of license. Yet, he appeared very determined to avoid the collar. It served him right. He was the one who chose to be a dog.

Rachel mumbled again, and I decided to take pity on her. I knew how to reason with him. If Clay ever wanted to leave the house with me, he had to have a collar. I just needed to point that out.

"Here." I held out my hand. "I'll try."

"Good luck," she said with a laugh as she got off her knees and handed me the collar. She took my position in the doorway.

"It was the biggest collar they had. I don't even know if it fits, he won't let me get close enough."

With a half-smile on my face, I knelt in front of Clay. I liked that he had a sense of humor when he interacted with Rachel. It made having him in the house tolerable...almost. I looked him in the eye.

"Clay, if you want to be able to go anywhere with us, you need a collar we can clip a leash on. Not just the twine you have holding your tag around your neck."

He didn't move so I leaned forward and reached for the string that held his current joke of a tag. He held still for me while I removed the twine and replaced it with the real collar.

"At least it's not pink," I said and patted him before I realized what I was doing. I'd forgotten myself again and treated him like a dog.

I quickly stood and avoided Clay's direct gaze.

Rachel laughed. "Hey, I wouldn't do that to him. No pink for our man. I don't know why he sat still for you and not me."

I'd forgotten about Rachel. She moved to pet and praise him for his good behavior. If I wanted a chance of having a friend as a roommate, I knew I needed to deal with Clay as a pet. But, I needed to watch myself. The direction of my thoughts—his assumed permanent residency in the house—troubled me.

Making him comfortable and buying him a license wouldn't help me get rid of him.

Rachel gave him a kiss, and he sighed. Maybe, he'd grow tired of her affection and run back to Canada. I held onto that happy thought.

"He's moody," I said, looking into his eyes. Moody and stubborn with a quirky sense of humor. Not a good combination.

CHAPTER EIGHT

As soon as Rachel sufficiently praised Clay for wearing the collar, she went to her room to change. From her room, she asked if I wanted to join her for a girl's night out. She explained she typically didn't stay in too much; when not busy working, her social life called. Still too unsure of our relationship—I didn't want to risk having someone Rachel might be interested in hitting on me—I declined. Thankfully, turning down her invitation didn't seem to bother her.

While Rachel exceeded my expectations as a roommate, adjusting to Clay's presence was something else entirely. When I woke Tuesday, Rachel was already gone. Clay still lingered at the foot of my bed.

"Get out," I said as soon as I opened my eyes. He left without complaint.

I took my time to dress, then went downstairs to check out the basement. Clay followed me. I tried to ignore him as I looked around. There wasn't much to see. The washer and the dryer were right by the steps, and there were a few utility shelves against the walls for storage.

With nothing else to do, I decided to take advantage of my idle time by sunbathing. I walked back upstairs and went to my room to change. After our talk the day before, Clay didn't attempt to follow me.

The second time wearing the suit was a little less nerve-racking. I didn't stare nervously in the mirror and eye all the pale skin glaring back at me. Instead, I appreciated the vivid coloring on the suit. Rachel had good taste.

Intent on finding the beach towels Rachel had used, I opened the door and stopped short at the sight of Clay. His huge dog head moved up, then down, as his eyes traveled the length of my body. I flushed, slammed the door, and changed back into shorts and a tank top. I opted to cut the grass, instead.

Clay sat on the porch and watched me push the mower back and forth. When I moved to the front, he followed. He was never in the way, just always there. After I went back inside to read, he did disappear for a bit. He had apparently taken my complaint about his hygiene seriously and had chosen to shower again. I hoped he would make it a daily routine.

Since he'd bathed and given me privacy as I'd asked, I had no reason to complain when I went to my room that night and saw him lying on the foot of the bed. However, when I woke Wednesday morning with him lying next to me, I did complain. Lividly.

"Now, just hold on," I whispered with a scowl. "You're a dog. Act like one. Fur stays at the foot of the bed."

He grudgingly moved to his place at the foot of the bed, watching me the whole time.

"Don't give me your doleful eyes. This is your choice, not mine." As soon as I said that, I recalled his talent for misinterpretation which had caused this co-ed housing in the first place. "Not that you'd get to sleep next to me in your skin either. So, don't even think about it. If you don't like the end of the bed, you can always sleep on the floor."

AFTER GETTING THE PAPER, I scoured the classifieds for a beater car and found two promising ads. Both required a long walk. I fetched my bag, tucked the folded newspaper inside, and grabbed the house keys.

Clay beat me to the door. I scowled down at him. He stared back at me. After a moment, he shook his neck, jangling his tags. Defeated, I clipped on his leash. He negotiated well without using a single word.

I used my cell to call the number for the first ad. The man sounded a bit brusque as if my planned visit inconvenienced him. Shrugging it off, I led Clay to the address. A rusty car parked on the front lawn with a "for sale" sign affirmed I had the right place. Clay and I walked toward the car.

A man called hello from the open garage and made his way toward us. As he neared, his demeanor changed, and I inwardly groaned. He introduced himself as Howard and looked me over with interest. Clay moved to stand between us, his stoic presence a good deterrent.

Howard talked about the car for a bit, going through the laundry list of its deficiencies. Then he popped the hood so I could look at the engine. In the middle of Howard's attempt to impress me with his vast mechanical knowledge, Clay sprang up between us. Howard yelped at Clay's sudden move and edged away as Clay placed his paws on the front of the car to get a good look at the engine, too. I fought not to smile at the man's stunned expression. At Clay's discreet nod, I bought the car, not bothering with the second ad.

No matter what errand I wanted to run during the week before classes started, Clay insisted on tagging along. On Friday, when I drove to the bookstore, Clay rode a very cramped shotgun and waited in the car while I made my purchases. Later, he sat in the hot car again while I bought some basic school supplies.

However, Monday, when I tried leaving for my first class, I put my foot down. He bristled and growled and tried to follow me.

"Your license only wins you so much freedom. Dogs aren't allowed on campus and definitely not in the classroom."

Thankfully, Rachel had left first and didn't hear me scold him.

I tried to leave again, but he stubbornly persisted. Finally, exasperated, I reminded him that he slept on my bed because of my good grace. He resentfully stepped away from the door.

AFTER THE FIRST week of classes, I didn't have time to mind Clay's constant attention. Maxing out at eighteen credits, desperate to get the general requirements out of the way so I could delve into clinicals sooner, I spent much of my day on campus in a classroom or in the library. When I actually found myself at home, I spent my time studying. I'd known when signing up for the courses that they would occupy all of my time and prevent me from having much of a life. Other than the fact I couldn't get a part-time job while taking the overload, I hadn't minded the commitment.

Even though I ignored him, Clay still stayed close to me. I realized how bored he'd grown when I came home and found one of my books on the couch, the bookmark on the wrong page. The next day, I took pity on him and brought back some books I thought might interest him. The one I thought particularly clever, about flora and fauna of North America, I included to remind him of home. He eyed the titles dispassionately. The day after, a bookmark nestled between the pages of two of the books.

I woke up one morning with a single-word note on my dresser. It simply said "mechanics." The first stack of books lay next to the note.

I turned to glare at Clay, who still lounged on the end of the bed.

"So you can write words to me, just not speak them?"

He blinked at me.

"Whatever. You're going to get caught creeping around the house at night."

Later that day, I returned the books on forestry and wildlife and checked out several books on mechanics. For fun, I threw in a do-it-yourself book for home repairs.

THE SECOND FRIDAY after school began, I sat on my bed with the door to my room closed. Clay lay in his usual spot beside me, his eyes devouring the words of his current book. He'd spent enough time reading next to me that I'd grown used to our system, a nudge when he needed a page turned. Trying to turn the page with his nose hadn't worked out well for him or the first book.

When he nudged me, I turned his page without looking up from my own book. When he did it again, I lifted my head. He read fast, but not that fast. He briefly met my eyes then turned toward the door. Just then, I heard the front door open, and I froze at the sound of Rachel's voice.

"...and this is where I live. Please have a seat, and I'll change quickly. My roommate and our dog should be around here somewhere."

"No rush," a man answered. "Our reservations aren't until six."

I turned wide eyes to Clay. Rachel had brought a man home? I didn't have time to think about it further because she knocked on my door. I wanted to ignore it, but instead, quickly closed the book in front of Clay.

"Come in."

Rachel walked in still wearing her scrubs. Her smile and flushed cheeks spoke volumes, as did the way she tactfully closed the door behind her.

"There you are. Come meet Peter." She walked close and leaned in so she could whisper more. "Don't kill me, but he has a friend without a date tonight, and I said I had a friend without a date tonight...please come with."

I groaned quietly. "Don't do this to me, Rachel. This won't end well, and you'll probably never forgive me."

"Come on...please?" she said, sitting on the bed next to me. "I really like this one."

"That's the problem. Remember what I said? It's always a guy that ruins a friendship. I don't want to go out tonight." I looked at Clay from the corner of my eye. He glared at Rachel. Not good. Too human. I nudged him with my foot while keeping my focus on Rachel.

"I like having a friend," I said.

She smiled at me. "If he hits on you, then it wasn't meant to be. Don't worry so much." She pulled me off the bed, and I reluctantly followed her out the door. Clay was close behind.

Peter, a pleasant looking man with light blonde hair and blue eyes, stood when we walked into the living room. He was an inch shorter than Rachel and, with his coloring, seemed her polar opposite. He immediately smiled at Rachel, and I could tell he had eyes only for her. I sagged with relief. His kind were rare.

"Peter, this is Gabby. Gabby, this is Peter. He's going to med school. I bumped into him at the library last week. Peter, why don't you tell her about Scott while I go get dressed?"

Rachel left the room in a rush, probably so I couldn't retreat. I smothered a grin as I watched Peter's gaze follow her. It took him a moment to collect himself.

"Nice to meet you, Gabby."

"You too. Want to sit?" I motioned him back to the couch and took the chair for myself. Clay settled on the floor between us. "This is Clay."

"He's huge," Peter said, appearing to notice Clay for the first time.

A huge pain in the butt, I thought without any malice.

"Yeah," I said instead. "So, who's Scott?"

"Oh, a friend of mine," he said looking up from Clay. "He's also in med school. We had plans to go to O'Donell's tonight for dinner and a drink or two. Then, I ran into Rachel and invited her to join us. We thought it'd be more fun if you could come, too."

Rachel waltzed back into the room at that moment. Amazingly, she had already changed into a skirt and complementing silky top. She'd heard Peter's last comment.

"Of course you will, won't you, Gabby?"

Two love-struck fools, who wouldn't even consider my presence if it weren't for Scott, had me cornered. Rachel really didn't know what she was asking of me. A public restaurant wouldn't be enjoyable. Yet, as she watched me hopefully, I knew my answer.

"Okay...but I need to be home early enough to let Clay out." A lame excuse, but I needed to prep the idea now so I would have an out later.

"I'm sure he'll be fine for that little while." Rachel waved her hand dismissively at Clay. Clay huffed, but she didn't notice. Instead, she shooed me toward my room.

"Go get dressed."

I stood to go to my room, but Clay leapt to his feet in front of me. I stepped to the right to go around him but he mirrored my move, blocking me.

Rachel laughed. "Come here, Clay. Come here and let Gabby get ready." She squatted down and patted her leg.

I'd seen her do this a few times before. Usually, Clay grudgingly responded. Not this time though. He kept his gaze focused on me and copied my feinted attempts to get around him.

"I've never seen him act like this," Rachel said to Peter.

I kept my narrowed gaze on Clay.

"I'm surprised you have such a wild looking dog. It seems too big compared to the house...and the two of you." Peter eyed Clay, too.

Giving up, I dropped to my knees and wrapped my arms around his thick neck, pretending to hug him so I could whisper in his ear.

"I'm not crazy about the idea either, but you have to let me go and stop acting weird." I pulled back. "Ready to be good, Clay?" I said as I stood and scratched him behind the ear just as a pet owner would do.

He turned and trotted into my room. Nope, not ready to be good.

Rachel laughed again. She knew I usually kicked him out when I wanted to change and had already teased me about it. I'd pointed out she wouldn't know how awkward it felt because he never tried to watch her change.

Resolutely, I followed Clay into my room and closed the door. I could just barely hear Peter and Rachel talking as they waited for me. Clay sat on my bed, watching me.

I folded my arms and kept my voice low. "I am not changing in front of you."

My words evoked an eerie canine smile from him, and he settled down onto my comforter and continued to watch me.

"Fine. I'll change in the bathroom."

I went to my closet and started looking at my clothes already knowing very few things in there compared to the style Rachel wore. The skirt I'd bought a few weeks ago would look nice but added to my pull, it would scream "hit on me." Biting my lip, I reached for the skirt. Clay began to growl fiercely.

"Zip it," I mumbled and grabbed one of the dressier tops I owned, a fitted cowl neck top with three-quarter sleeves.

Clay started barking, a deep menacing sound that raised the little hairs on the back of my neck. I spun toward him.

"What the hell, Clay? Cut it out." I knew he didn't like that because he got louder.

Rachel burst in without knocking, and Peter followed right behind her. Clay, who had been sitting at the end of my bed, sprang to his feet as soon as they entered.

"What's wrong?" Rachel looked at Clay, who continued to bark at me.

If possible, his volume increased, and I had to yell over him.

"Nothing. Just give me a few minutes to calm him down, okay?" I walked to Clay with the clothes still under one arm, and he growled at me. I faltered and eyed him with a hint of fear.

"Uh, I'm not so sure you should do that right now," Peter said.

Clay turned and started barking at Peter.

"Enough." My voice echoed in the small room. It apparently took Clay by surprise because the noise stopped. However, his attitude hadn't changed. Teeth still exposed in a fierce snarl, he glared at all of us. At least he'd finished barking and growling. For the moment. I turned toward Peter and Rachel.

"I'm fine. Thank you. Just give me a few minutes to change."

They shared a glance then left the room and shut the door behind them.

Closing my eyes, I took a deep breath. Without trying, I could "see" Clay in a painful burst of light. A first. My other vision usually required an amount of focus.

With a sigh, I opened my eyes and turned to him. He looked seriously pissed. My stomach churned. Sam had promised he could control himself.

"Will you bite me if I sit next to you, Clay?"

He snorted, and I watched the silent snarl ease from his muzzle. His hackles slowly laid flat. When he settled onto his haunches, I knew he'd calmed down and sat next to him.

"You know I don't understand dog, right? It'd be so much easier if you just told me what was wrong."

I turned my head to meet his gaze. Our faces were close together. Because of his height, he was looking down at me. He let out a gusty sigh and bent his head to nudge the clothes I still held.

"You don't like the clothes or that I'm going out?" I watched his face, trying to figure out what he was getting at. He actually bobbed his head yes.

"You don't like both?"

He lowered himself down onto the mattress and watched me with his sad puppy eyes, not trying to communicate further.

"You're really frustrating me, Clay." I moved to get up, and he growled again.

"Now, hold on..." I did get up, but spun with my hands on my hips to look him in the eye. Aware that only a door separated us from the suspiciously silent couple in the living room, I kept quiet despite my anger.

"I'm trying here, Clay, and you're not. So stop growling at me. Got it? And so what if I go out? Do you trust me so little? Have you not been paying attention? I'm not comfortable around guys. It's not as if I'm going to go out tonight and come back with a boyfriend or something. So, just chill out about your Claim, all right?"

He continued to growl at me and gave me a dog-eyed glare. In his mind, he and I shared a tie. I knew that. I also knew from a werewolf standpoint, in a strongly tied pair, the male often acted in an extremely possessive manner. If other unMated males came near before the Claim was completed, a fight typically broke out. Sometimes to the death.

"But we're not talking unMated males," I whispered to him, thinking aloud. "They're just men."

He chuffed out his canine laugh and hopped from the bed to walk toward me. I couldn't help it, after all that barking and growling, I stepped back from him. His sides heaved as he sighed and stopped advancing. I knew my fear disappointed him.

"Sorry," I mumbled automatically. Although, he'd done nothing but try to communicate why he didn't want me to go out tonight, I didn't appreciate his chosen methods of communication. They could use improvement.

"Let me think, Clay." I sat on the edge of the bed while he stood on the floor, and watched me. I still didn't understand what continued to bother him. The date wasn't with a werewolf. I had no interest in Scott. I only wanted to go as a favor to Rachel. And the clothes were the only going out clothes I had.

"Can we compromise? I don't want to spend the entire year sitting at home with a possessive dog who won't talk to me." Yeah, that sounded weird. "What if we went somewhere dog friendly? There's a bar with cute little bistro tables on the sidewalk. If you're on your leash, you could come."

He stood, turned around so he faced away from me, and sat again.

"Is that a yes?" I leaned to the side in an attempt to see his face. He didn't move.

"I'm taking that as a yes. If you turn around while I'm changing, I'm going to have you neutered."

He just laughed again, so I hurried into my skirt and switched my t-shirt for the fitted top. As my head cleared the neckline, I met his eyes in the mirror. Thank the stars I hadn't changed any underthings.

"Hope it was worth it," I said. "You're on the couch tonight."

Rachel and Peter sat talking on the couch when I walked out of my room.

"All set, but can we change our plans? I think Clay was freaking out because he knows we're leaving. He's been left alone so much this week..."

Predictably, Rachel made soothing noises and went to cuddle Clay. He tolerated it with as much dignity as a man in fur and a collar could muster.

"What if we went to that bar with the bistro tables that you were telling me about?" I said to Rachel.

Rachel leapt at the idea. "That'd be perfect. It's still nice enough out. Besides, I think this is the last week they do the outdoor dining. We should go before it's closed for the season."

Peter stalled. "Are you sure he will be okay? He looked pretty aggressive in there."

Rachel stopped petting Clay to look back at Peter. "He's never done that before. I think Gabby might be right. We've been leaving him alone a lot. I even forgot to let him out this morning before I left."

Peter looked adoringly at Rachel, and I knew we'd be going to the bistro bar.

"Let me grab my shoes. I'll follow you guys in my car just in case I need to leave early."

"I'll let Scott know about the change in plans." Peter pulled out his cell and started tapping the screen.

"I'll let Clay out." Rachel got up, walked to the back door, and called to Clay. Clay looked at me imploringly but, after what he'd just pulled, I had no pity.

"You know the drill. Go do dog business."

He left the room without a backward look. I went to the hall closet to search for my black flip-flops, the best footwear I had to offer the outfit, and grabbed a light jacket.

"You talk to him like he's a person," Peter said.

"I tease her for it all the time," Rachel said with a smile as she rejoined us. "You should hear her scolding him at night for taking up too much room on the bed."

Annoyingly, I started to blush. "Well, he's huge. Most of the time I have to sleep curled up. But, I'm sure I'll appreciate him more in winter." I slipped my feet into the plain flip-flops and made my way into the kitchen where I grabbed my keys.

I locked the back door while Rachel and Peter left via the front.

Clay already sat in the passenger seat when I turned toward the car. It meant he'd switched into his skin to open the door. I shook my head, got in, and started to buckle up.

"You're going to be seen doing stuff a dog shouldn't do. That or someone's going to call the cops because a naked man keeps popping up in my backyard." He didn't laugh this time. I turned to look at him while I started the car.

"You okay?"

Clay met my eyes, but I couldn't tell what bothered him now. I wished I could read him better.

"Fine. No growling, no biting, no barking. Pretty much no anything but acting like a passive, well-behaved dog," I said, laying down the rules as I backed out of the driveway.

I followed Peter's red compact through traffic with ease.

"I'm really nervous about this and don't want to worry about you, too." I sighed and started to doubt my decision. Although Clay had witnessed how the man who'd sold me the car had acted, he didn't know how guys acted around me in general. Maybe this wasn't a good idea. He would flip out when someone started to hit on me.

"Clay, you should know...men make me uncomfortable because of the way they act around me. They usually start flirting or ask me on a date. Most girls would be flattered, but if you really pay attention, there's something unnatural about it. It's like they can't help themselves. And sometimes, after I tell them no enough, they walk away with..."

I groped for the right word, but came up blank.

"I don't know...a look. Like they've been caught doing something they're ashamed of. I just want to try for normal tonight, okay? It'll be hard enough being in a public place. You'll see. I just need to know you're not going to make it any harder on me."

Out of the corner of my eye, I saw him turn to look out the window and reached over to ruffle his fur gently.

With increasing frequency, I caught myself touching him as if he were a dog. If I didn't think about him as a guy, petting him comforted me.

"Does it bother you when I pet you?" I asked, keeping my eyes on the road. I knew his answer when he contorted his large body to lay down with his head against my leg so I could reach him better. I laughed, feeling lighter than I had in a long while.

"Okay. If I start annoying you with it, just move away. I promise I won't pester you."

Peter considerately picked a parking spot with a free space next to it for me. Clay unwedged himself as I parked. I grabbed the leash and snapped it on. He watched me exit, hopped out after me, and stayed close to my side as we walked.

Rachel and Peter politely included me in their conversation. It helped distract me from my nervousness about meeting Peter's friend. I knew what to expect even if neither Rachel nor Clay fully understood. Peter's lack of reaction had pleasantly surprised me. But, his response wasn't the norm. I just hoped Clay would behave.

Scott waited for us at one of the outside tables. He stood and flashed a welcoming smile when he saw Peter. From a distance, I saw several female patrons at nearby tables cast speculative glances Scott's way. Fit and tall, with light brown hair and a carefree smile, no doubt his good looks warranted it. But, something about the way he held himself bothered me. It sent off an insincere vibe as if he'd practiced his pose.

His smile turned secretive and cunning as his pale blue eyes fixated on me. The subtle change probably escaped everyone else's notice, but not mine. Depressed, but hiding it well, I rested a hand on Clay's back. Whether in comfort or restraint, I couldn't be sure.

"Scott, this is Gabby," Peter said when we stood next to the table.

I smiled a tentative greeting but didn't offer my hand.

"A pretty name you don't hear often," Scott murmured, pulling out a chair for me.

Taking the chair he offered would put me across from Rachel and force me to sit between the two guys. Clay wouldn't like that. He didn't like the comment about my name either, but other than a twitch I'd felt with my hand on his back, he behaved.

"Would you mind if we switched spots, Scott? That way our dog won't be so close to people walking by. He's very friendly, but big. I don't want anyone to be intimidated by him."

"No problem." He gave me a reassuring smile and pulled out his own chair for me.

Loosely holding Clay's leash, I moved to the chair next to Rachel. Scott politely pushed the chair back in as I sat. Then he leaned close to move his drink. Clay quickly went to lie between my chair and Scott's. He nudged Scott's chair further away before Scott could sit. I pretended not to notice.

We made small talk while we perused the menus. I felt Scott's gaze continually return to me but refused to look up.

After we ordered, each of the more experienced students shared their knowledge of the university. Scott offered—twice—to take me on an official tour when I admitted I didn't know many of the campus locations they mentioned. As soon as I declined the second time, he looked less like the nice guy I'd met and more like a guy who would give me problems. I looked down at Clay. He still lay next to me, head on his paws. Only the twitch of his ears indicated his attention to the conversation.

"Why not have a drink with us, Gabby?" Scott asked, pointing at my water.

He hadn't worried about what I drank until I'd turned down his invitations for a tour.

"I'm a bit younger than the rest of you." I glanced at Rachel and saw her studying me. Crap! Was she noticing? Was she getting mad? I should have stayed home. Folding my hands in my lap, I tried to play it cool.

"Really? How old are you?"

"Eighteen. I'm not much of a soda drinker either, so water works." I tried to turn the conversation off myself. "How much longer until you graduate?"

"It depends on how far I want to go," Scott said, his intense smile relaxing a little. He nodded toward Peter. "Peter told me he declared his major freshman year and has never changed. I, on the other hand, have changed twice. I like what I'm learning now, so I hope I won't change it again, but you never know. What about you?"

"I'm going for massage therapy. So, I won't be here as long as the rest of you."

"Massage therapy? I hear they ask for volunteers to come in for those classes." He leaned closer with a fascinated smile on his face. "If you ever need someone to practice on, let me know. I'd be happy to come in." He reached over to pat my hand. The timely arrival of our food saved me from having to avoid his touch.

Clay nudged my leg with his surprisingly warm and dry nose, and I glanced down. He stared at me a moment then shifted his gaze to Scott, who was moving his drink for the waitress. Clay returned his glance to me and pulled his lips back in a silent snarl. Without the growl, it looked more like a scary, crazy wolf smile, but I got his meaning. Scott was getting on Clay's nerves, and Clay wouldn't put up with too much more.

Peter spoke up while Scott was distracted. "I think you'll both be in some of the anatomy classes next semester, Gabby. If you want a study group, you should let Rachel and I know. I've already been through them." He gazed admiringly at Rachel. "And since you're graduating in spring, I know you have, too."

"Thank you, Peter, but I really do study best on my—"

"That's a great idea," Scott said. "We should start now so the class won't be so hard later. What do you think about Tuesday nights?"

"It's a good idea to get a head start," I said ignoring Clay's insistent bump against my leg. "But I'm so swamped with classes and homework now that I don't even have time to take poor Clay for walks."

I reached over to pat Clay reassuringly, but stopped when I noticed Scott's gaze drop to my chest. The cowl neck had dipped away and revealed a little glimpse of the shadows within. Scott's eyes went from glassy fixation to glazed obsession. This was getting ridiculous.

Turning back to my dinner, I stuffed a few bites in my mouth to prevent me from needing to converse. Unfortunately, Scott took the opportunity to try to slide his chair a little closer. Thankfully, Clay didn't give an inch.

"What's your dog's name?" Scott asked, looking down at Clay.

"Clay," Rachel answered after seeing my mouth full.

Clay, I noticed, didn't look up at the sound of his name. Instead, he tensed and laid his ears back. Time to go.

"Nice name," Scott said, but I could tell he didn't care. "Let's bring him home after this and go out to a new club that opened downtown."

"Rachel?" I looked at her pleadingly, hoping she'd know that I wasn't begging to go out dancing. Her perceptive gaze locked on Scott.

"I see it," she said with a serious expression.

"See what?" Peter said. His gaze bounced between the three of us.

"Exhaustion. She's been studying like crazy." She waved over the waitress and asked for boxes and the check for the two of us.

"And she needs rest, not a night out. Although, I am really glad we came." She looked at Peter with a smile.

My weak smile didn't cover my gratitude at her diplomacy.

I reached for my purse which I'd hung on the back of the chair. Desperate, Scott moved to grab my hand. Clay stood abruptly. He successfully knocked Scott's hand out of the way but also bumped the table in the process. Peter reached out to steady his and Rachel's drinks, and I hurried to pull a twenty from my purse.

The waitress returned with the bill and the wrapped up leftovers. Since Rachel was still digging in her purse, I just handed the waitress the twenty after a quick glance at the bill. I was willing to pay for Rachel if it helped us leave faster.

"I better drive her home," Rachel said to Peter. "You have my number. Give me a call if you want to do something next weekend."

I stood, and Rachel shadowed me, ready to go. Clay bumped into me, knocking me off balance so I had to grab Rachel for support. I looked down at him and noticed Scott stand and hand the waitress his portion of the bill.

"Rachel, you can stay with Peter. I don't mind taking Gabby home," Scott said. Oily enthusiasm dripped with each word, and I didn't even need to look at Rachel for her to decline.

"No, Scott, I think we're done for tonight." She waved to Peter and grabbed my hand.

Poor Peter looked at us all, bewildered. His night out with Rachel had fallen apart fast, and I truly felt bad about it.

I went with Rachel, relieved to escape before Scott's recklessness grew. An "oof" sounded behind us, and I panicked, realizing I'd forgotten Clay. I spun around in time to see Scott hit the ground. He'd tripped over Clay in his hurry to catch me. I suspected Clay had done it purposely to slow Scott down.

Clay wasted no time. He ran to me and bumped his head against my back to get me moving before Scott could pick himself up again. There wasn't yet enough distance between the table and us to mute Peter's next words.

"What the hell is wrong with you, man? You come on too..." What he still had to say faded as we quickly walked away.

"I'm sorry," Rachel said. "You told me, but I didn't really get it. Even the men sitting around us were eyeing you."

I'd been too busy keeping an eye on Scott and Clay to notice. We continued to speed walk to the car.

"No big deal. You should see me in some of my classes. 'No' is the most common word in my vocabulary. Scott's reaction was worse than most because he already considered me his date. If you say 'no', consistently and to everyone, it doesn't get so bad." I handed Rachel the keys when we reached the car. "You really can drive."

She nodded, and we got in. Clay climbed into the back and stretched out so his head lay on the console between the two front seats. Rachel wasted no time backing out and leaving.

Halfway home, she pulled into a gas station. "Tonight's an ice cream night. Be right back." She jumped out and strode into the convenience station with the determination of a girl on a shopping spree.

Laying my head back, I sighed, and my hand found its way to Clay's soft fur. I pet his head and ears. He exhaled loudly, but stayed still so I figured he didn't mind. I was just glad he wasn't rubbing in that it'd been a disaster of a night out.

I looked out the window, watched traffic zip past, and allowed myself just a small amount of self-pity. I'd wanted normal so badly. No werewolves. No second sight. No weird pull on men. Yet, I *knew* I would never be normal. I would never have a normal date. I kept trying to mold myself into something I could never be. Why?

Clay lifted his head under my hand, and I reigned in my emotions, knowing he could sense my melancholy.

"I'm fine," I said as I met his gaze. "How are you doing?" He scooted forward to lay his head on my lap in response. Yeah, that was pretty much how I felt.

The door opened, startling us both.

"I got double fudge brownie for each of us," Rachel said as she slid in behind the wheel and handed me the bag. "Sorry, Clay. Chocolate's poison for dogs. None for you."

She made me smile.

When we got home, I went straight to my room to change. Clay stayed with Rachel as she praised his good behavior and good sense to trip Scott when he'd started to follow us. No doubt, he'd get the other half of her burger before I finished. Tossing the shirt into the closet, I vowed never to wear it again and pulled on the comfortable clothes I slept in.

Shaking off my mood, I walked into the kitchen.

"Where's my chocolate?"

Clay moved to my side, and I patted him again. I'd asked a lot of him tonight, and he deserved a real reward. He'd been surviving on sandwiches and leftovers from Rachel. Tomorrow, we'd go to the store, and I'd buy him a big steak.

Rachel handed me my pint with a spoon standing in it. She'd already dug into hers. After eating another spoonful with a blissful groan, she set her container of ice cream on the table.

"I'm going to go change. Want to watch a movie or something?" Rachel stripped out of her shirt on her way to her bedroom.

I looked at the wall clock and savored another spoonful of ice cream. It was only seven, but I was tired. I put the lid back on and tucked my container in the near empty freezer.

"What do you think?" I asked Clay, noting he watched me and not the striptease Rachel had unknowingly put on or the chocolate ice cream she'd left unguarded. "Stay up and watch a movie, or go to bed early? Lead the way." I waved him forward, and he trotted through the living room to my room.

"Rach, we're just going to go to bed early. 'K?" I leaned against the wall in the living room, waiting for her answer.

"It's okay. Go ahead," she said, appearing again. She wore short shorts and a tank top for bed. "I won't keep you up with a movie, will I?" She glided past me and flopped on the couch.

"I'm so tired I doubt anything will keep me from sleeping."

"'K. Night, Hun. Thanks for going with me even if it did suck," she said, giving me a smile.

"Don't worry about it. Night." I walked into my room and closed the door behind me as she turned on the TV.

Clay lay on the foot of the bed, his usual spot. His head rested on his paws. He still had his eyes open.

"Thanks, Clay." As I passed him, I stopped to kiss the top of his furry head. He made a funny grunt noise that made me smile. Probably his wolf version of "no problem." I crawled under the covers and wiggled my feet under his body to the spot he'd already warmed.

I felt Clay relax a moment before he let out a gusty breath. He started to breathe deeply, and I tried to unwind as well. Going on a double date hadn't turned out as badly as it could have.

CHAPTER NINE

IT WAS STILL DARK WHEN I WOKE. NOT ONLY DARK, BUT ALSO colder. The mild weather we'd enjoyed last night while eating outside had apparently fled with the sun. I nestled under the covers, trying to avoid the chill in the air. When I stretched my legs searching for Clay's weighted warmth, I felt nothing. His spot was cool.

"Clay?"

My bedroom door creaked open, and he jumped up on the mattress, causing it to bounce. He settled on my feet, and his heat immediately warmed me.

"Thanks."

Laying my head back down on the pillow, I burrowed deeper. The warm nights of summer, of sleeping with the window open, had retired for the year. Soon, going outside during the day would require a jacket. The thought was a little depressing. I didn't really care for the cold.

I wanted to sleep a little longer and tried to close my eyes again but they popped back open on their own. Clearly awake, I knew I should really get out of bed and do something. Yet, the thought made me cringe...until I remembered I owed Clay for last night. This early, there'd be no one around outside, especially with this first cold snap. We needed to take advantage of the still above freezing weather and do something together. He'd like that.

"Hey, Clay. Wanna go get breakfast with me?"

With a sigh, he jumped back down off the bed.

"You could have said no," I said with a soft laugh as I rolled out from under the covers.

Grabbing my clothes, I tiptoed to the bathroom. When I reemerged, Clay sat next to the back door, waiting patiently. I glanced at the car keys. Drive or walk? Walking would save money, and I enjoyed it.

"You up for a walk?" I kept my voice low since I didn't want to wake Rachel.

The idea of walking outside with Clay before dawn made me smile. He looked like a beast. Any sane man would keep his distance. It would be vastly different from the heckling first walk I had taken to campus.

When he didn't move away, I took that as affirmation and clipped on his leash, loosely looping it around his collar so I wouldn't need to hold it. He turned to me with a questioning look.

"What? I'm following the law...you're on a leash. Let's go."

I opened the door, and we soundlessly slipped outside. As expected, crisp air engulfed us, but the lack of wind made it tolerable. After pulling the hood up over my loose hair, I tucked my hands into the pockets of my hoodie and stepped off the porch, suspiciously testing the air to see if my breath clouded. Clay trudged next to me, still looking a little tired.

We walked in the direction of the campus, toward a small diner that was open all day, six days a week, closed Sundays. Well-known on campus, Ma's Kitchen served good, cheap food for the perpetually broke college kid. With ten dollars in my pocket, I figured we could stuff ourselves before walking back home.

The sidewalks remained empty. Streetlights buzzed overhead. The soft scrape of Clay's nails on the pavement comforted me, and I filled my lungs, relaxing. Very few cars passed us as we made our way from one pool of light to the next.

The walk to campus offered an eclectic array of buildings. Businesses jumbled in with residences. Some so close together their shadows merged, creating perfect places for hiding. But Clay's calm presence allowed me to enjoy the walk without using my sight.

We strolled in companionable silence for a few minutes before I spoke up.

"So what do you like for breakfast? Oatmeal?" He laughed, and I smiled back. "Yeah, I was thinking you're more a steak and eggs kinda guy."

"Who you talking to dar'lin?" a man called as he stepped out from the shadows across the narrow street. His sudden appearance made my heart race.

"My dog." Even though I considered this area safe, it paid to be smart. So I whispered to Clay, asking him to bark. He obliged with a deep "woof" that almost scared me. The sound bounced off the surrounding buildings. I hoped it wouldn't wake anyone.

"Damn," the man called back, keeping pace with us on the opposite sidewalk. "That thing on a leash?"

"Yep, but there's no holding him back. I'm safer letting him go or he'd just drag me along."

The man laughed. "I bet. Have a good morning," he called before turning at the next corner to walk around the block.

"You trust that?" I asked Clay, watching the man's retreating form. Clay harrumphed.

"Me neither. And thanks for warning me there was someone close by," I said. He made a noise I interpreted between a snort and a laugh.

"Brat." I smiled down at him.

Night sounds began to fade, and I heard the occasional bird call out, though dawn was still an hour away. Clay continued to pace alertly by my side until we reached the diner. Judging from the empty parking lot, they didn't get much business this early. Still, the air outside smelled like frying breakfast sausage. Delicious. Beside me, Clay's stomach rumbled.

"Since they don't allow dogs, I'll go in and get our food for carryout," I said, pulling open the door. He obediently sat just outside, the position enabling him to watch me through the glass.

When I entered, the waitress set down the basket of jellies she'd been using to refill the jelly holders on the tables and moved to the register.

"Good morning," she said with a chipper smile. "How are you this morning?"

Wow. A people-person and a morning-person. I weakly smiled back and ordered.

As soon as I had our breakfast, I brought it out to Clay. We sat together on one of the cement parking blocks in front of the building. The early-morning traffic crept along quietly, keeping the illusion of solitude.

I opened his container and started to cut up his steak. He laughed at me again, and I shushed him. He could laugh all he wanted. He usually ate so fast I worried he'd choke. I set his container on the ground for him when I finished. He dug in, making it hard to think of him as a man.

"I hope you're a slower eater when you're in your skin," I commented.

He stopped eating and looked at me. Too late, I realized how critical my comment had sounded. I tried to soften it.

"It's just that you eat faster than me. That's all." It sounded lame.

I felt worse when he made an effort to eat slower. He still finished first. In an attempt to make up for my thoughtless comment, I offered him the rest of my breakfast, too. When he finished, I threw our containers away in the parking lot trash can.

We began the long walk back, with each of us lost in our own thoughts. Well, I was lost in mine, anyway. I didn't know what to say to take away the sting from my words. Why didn't I think before I spoke to him? I sometimes forgot about the man beneath the fur and tended just to talk, letting anything flow from my mouth without much thought. Sure, I may have meant what I said, but I could have found a better, nicer, way to say it. Maybe.

Distracted and dwelling on my own thoughts, I paid no attention to my surroundings until Clay began to growl. My head snapped up in surprise at the soft, menacing sound. Clay stopped walking. His head turned so he watched the space between two houses on our left. Dawn still hadn't lightened the sky, so I saw nothing but shadows.

I closed my eyes and focused, depending on my other sight—something I'd mostly ignored since coming to school—to see what my eyes couldn't. The yellow-green sparks of the people in the houses around us glowed softly. To the left, closing in fast, a blue-grey light surged. Stunned, I blinked at it and glanced at Clay's spark. Blue-grey compared to his blue-green. Another color variation?

"What is it, Clay?" I whispered, taking a cautious step back. The colors I saw classified into werewolves, humans, and anomalies like Charlene and I. This new color moved too fast for a human.

Clay remained alert to the other werewolf's advance.

"What should I do, Clay?" I tried not to panic, but I could think of only one reason a werewolf would run at us like that. It wanted to challenge Clay.

If I walked away, it would think I was rejecting Clay's Claim. As much as I didn't want to Claim Clay, I didn't want a tie to anyone else.

Clay's growl increased in volume. I looked at the darkened houses around us. Perhaps I could use them to our advantage.

Clay tensed in front of me. I retreated a few more paces until I stepped into the road, no more than five feet from Clay. The faint, rapid thud of the werewolf's paws hitting the ground resonated from the darkness ahead. I tracked its spark. It sped forward. Suddenly, the rhythmic sound of its approach stopped even though its spark continued toward us.

Clay braced himself. In that moment, an enormous object soared at us from the darkness. I scrambled back. Its large body rivaled Clay for size. But, it was the newcomer's dark grey fur and bright blue eyes that forever burned into my memory.

The flying mass hit Clay hard. Clay let loose an aggressive snarl as he twisted, and worked to keep his back legs under him. His claws dug into the asphalt, scraping and scrabbling to slow the skid toward me. The two werewolves grappled, swiping claws and snapping jaws.

Eyes wide, I continued to maintain my view of the human sparks while watching the fight before me. Focused on each other, neither looked my way.

The challenger scuttled out of Clay's reach and regained his own footing. Clay lunged forward and snapped down on the other's muzzle. His sharp teeth ripped into tender flesh. I wanted to cheer when the other werewolf yelped in pain. They broke apart. Clay continued to growl. The low rumble made my heart beat even faster. The challenger responded with his own snarl but didn't attempt another attack. Instead, he sidestepped, looking for an opening.

I moved with them and maintained a small distance from both.

The noise escalated as they stalked each other. The challenger feinted toward Clay, lips drawn back and teeth parted. My heart beat harder with fear. Clay gave no ground, carefully keeping himself between the newcomer and me, while I tried to stay out of the way. The dogs in the neighborhood started to bark. The continued use of my sight began to strain me, but I saw a spark moving in a nearby house.

Time to take the offensive.

"Hey!" I yelled loudly.

Clay didn't jump, but the other werewolf did. His bright blue gaze flicked to me. A light turned on in the house.

"Whose dog is this? Someone help me get him off my dog!" Another light went on in the house.

Clay took advantage of his opponent's momentary distraction and went for its throat. The other wolf dodged the attack, but just barely. Bleeding freely from Clay's first strike, red began to color its muzzle.

With a deep-throated bark, it lunged again at Clay, refocusing its efforts. The lunge caught Clay in the shoulders and almost knocked him off balance. I forgot to breathe for a moment. Clay exposed his neck in an attempt to bite his opponent's front leg rather than to spin away and leave me unprotected.

The other wolf grunted in pain as Clay's teeth clamped down. Still, he went for the opening. His teeth clicked against the metal that studded Clay's collar.

The wolf growled, pulled back, and made to try again. Clay quickly released his hold on the wolf's leg and backed away, as did his limping adversary.

Clay's leash unraveled from its coiled pile under his collar and trailed in his wake. The other werewolf noticed it, moved forward, and attempted to step on it. Brown fur ruffled as Clay twisted sharply to flip the leash out of the way.

I looked around, trying to figure out how to stop this. In the houses closest to the fight, more lights burst on. In the house across the street, someone pushed back a curtain to peer out.

Behind me, I heard a shrill whistle. "Duke! Come here, Duke."

The neighborhood was waking.

This time, the sudden interruption didn't distract either of them. Both maintained focus on their opponent. This had to stop now before Clay got hurt.

"The noise has everyone waking up, whoever you are," I said. "You don't have enough time to finish this. It'd be better to leave now when Clay won't be able to chase you. Someone's going to call the police, and when they get here, they'll see a dog that's neither licensed nor leashed. You'll either have to change and expose yourself, or let them take you away thinking you're a dog."

The challenger continued his circling attack as if I hadn't spoken.

The front door of the house closest to us opened and a man shined a flashlight at the fighting dogs, then at me.

"Can you help me?" I called, my voice purposely coming out high-pitched and fearful. "Do you know whose dog this is? It came running at my dog from the direction of your backyard."

"It's not ours. Want me to call the police?" he yelled over the snarls and growls.

I didn't get a chance to answer. The grey werewolf broke away from the fight and bolted back into the darkness from where he'd come. Apparently, he had heard my warning.

Clay, panting heavily, stayed close to me and watched the other wolf retreat. The challenger conceded with his withdrawal. For now.

"Did you see what kind of dog it was?" the man called as he left the safety of his house to look at his side yard where the wolf had disappeared. He cautiously shined his flashlight to search for it.

I let out a shaky, thankful laugh, knelt beside Clay, and wrapped my arms around his neck. My hands shook, the strain and fear taking their toll, as I ran my hands over the area around his collar. I didn't find any injuries. Relieved, I leaned against him. He really was growing on me.

"Ma'am? You okay?"

The man pointed his flashlight at us but stayed near his house. Any closer and he'd feel the pull. I didn't need to deal with any more problems. Across the street, a door opened, distracting the man.

"They okay, Mike?"

I lifted my head from Clay. "You okay?" I whispered.

He turned his head and licked my cheek, reassuring me.

"Next time I'll just carry the leash," I promised. My eyes watered. It had been too close. It would have only been a matter of time before the other wolf would have pinned him because of it.

"We're okay," I said as I stood. I kept a hand on Clay's head. "The dog was as big as Clay here but had dark grey fur."

"Doesn't sound like any dog from this neighborhood, but I know there are some big dogs a few blocks away. Do you want me to call the cops?" The man started toward us.

I picked up Clay's loose leash and nudged him to get him moving.

"Nah. I think we're fine," I said taking a step back. Too late. The man had gotten close enough that the pull had him. I saw the interest in his eyes.

After a few moments reassuring him that neither of us had suffered injuries and that police involvement was no longer necessary, I grudgingly gave him my phone number just in case anyone had called the cops and they showed up. Clay remained quiet and unusually calm throughout the conversation.

Crisis averted, we hurried home. I didn't talk. Instead, I concentrated on scanning with my second sight. I pushed to see further than ever before, and it drained me. My legs grew heavier with each step. I tried not to let it show.

While I scanned, so did Clay. His eyes missed nothing, and he constantly scented the air.

The sun cleared the surrounding rooftops, and its bright rays lit the sidewalk. My hurried walk degraded to a plodding step somewhere along the way, and it took us much longer to get home. No further sign of that weird light reappeared during the rest of the walk.

Because I watched my shuffling feet as we retraced our steps to the back door, I didn't see Rachel standing on the porch.

"There you are!"

My hand flew to Clay's thick mane at the same time my heart skipped a beat. The scare distracted me from my second sight, and it snapped closed at my loss of focus. I struggled to reopen it but a sudden pain in my head stopped my attempt. I'd done too much.

"Nice morning for a walk," she said, moving toward us to pet Clay.

I unclenched my fingers from his fur, not wanting her to notice my death grip. She fingered one of his ears. He shook off her touch. She laughed and bent to kiss the top of his head. He endured the kiss but rolled his eyes at me. Some of my tension melted at their antics. He appeared more relaxed, too.

"I made a call this morning and can get him into the vet for his shots," she said as she tugged the leash from my loose grasp. "I figured after the way he acted last night, we should have him current...just in case."

It took a moment for what she said to click. My stunned gaze dropped to Clay. He calmly met my eyes, not giving any indication what he thought of her announcement. I looked back at Rachel. I didn't know what to say.

"You okay, Gabby?" She looked at me with concern.

No. Not okay. What had started as a nice thank you breakfast for Clay had turned into a dog fight. And now she wanted to take him to the vet? He didn't deserve that. Besides, after the attack, would he be willing to leave me? Wait. Could a vet figure out he wasn't really a dog? I tried to contain my panic.

"Uh, I didn't budget for it," I blurted, hoping at the very least to put the visit off until I talked to Sam about the risks.

"Don't worry." Rachel untangled his leash. "I can cover it for now, and you can pay me back."

"Let's all go." The words popped out of my mouth before I thought about it. What good would that do? Did I think I could block the vet from touching Clay? Rachel would definitely know something was up, then.

"No offense, Gabby, but you look like hell. I think you'd be better off with some quiet time. Don't worry; we'll be fine." She tried to pull Clay toward the garage again, but he didn't move with her.

Instead, he nudged me toward the back door, almost knocking me off balance. Rachel tugged on his leash and scolded him, but he ignored her and stayed focused on me.

"Would you mind giving him your standard pep talk? I don't know why he only listens to you. I'm the one that feeds him treats." She handed the leash over to me. I rubbed my forehead still unsure what he wanted me to do.

"Is it safe for you?" I breathed in his ear as I bent to give him a hug.

He snorted, which I took as a yes. Did he want me to stay here, then?

"I'm so sorry about this. I'll need to call Sam and let him know what happened."

I straightened, looked him in the eye, and smoothed the fur on his head. "It's your choice." I dropped the leash and stepped back.

He gave me a long look as Rachel moved to open the car door. He sighed then followed her.

"The control you have over him is weird but cool," Rachel said as he jumped into the back seat.

Control? I didn't have any control over him. He only listened when I threatened to kick him out of my room or leave him behind.

"Yeah. Just don't be gone too long. He'll get upset."

"The vet's just a few minutes from here. We should be back soon." She climbed behind the wheel, closed the door, and rolled down her window.

I couldn't believe we were actually doing this. What did a vet usually check for? Shots...Age...Neuter... Crap, crap, crap! The engine roared to life.

"Just don't have him neutered! Or anything that involves blood or blood work. It's expensive, and I promised him he'd keep his jewels." Oh how I wished those words back when Clay started to make an odd coughing noise. I could only assume it was his version of laughter. I really needed to start filtering what I said.

Rachel swiveled to check on Clay. "Maybe we should have the vet check his lungs."

"He's fine. Think cost," I said from the deck as she backed out of the driveway.

I went inside and immediately called Sam to let him know about the attack. He assured me of my safety, but I wasn't worried about that. Paul and Henry had long ago educated me in regard to challenge etiquette. A challenge questioned Clay's right to me. If present, I needed to stay near him to show my support of his right. Fleeing rejected him. Though rejecting him sounded tempting on the surface, doing so would put me back into the eligible pool. I didn't want that.

Sam said he would let Elder Joshua know about the attack, too. He also felt certain the challenger wouldn't try again anytime soon given the extent of his injuries.

A werewolf's tough hide deflected many things that could damage human skin. What it couldn't deflect, it reduced in severity. A knife could still cut a werewolf, for example, but not lethally like it could me. On top of the nearly impenetrable skin, nature also threw in a phenomenally fast healing process. A shallow cut would knit together in less than an hour, with no scar visible in less than a day. However, injuries from another werewolf tended to take twice as long to heal. Still faster than a human's, however.

Talking to Sam helped settle my nerves. Though the werewolf's odd light still bothered me, I couldn't bring it up. I'd never shared the details of my ability with Sam. However, I did almost bring up the vet visit. Only Clay's willingness to go had me keeping it to myself at the last minute. I felt guilty enough and didn't need to add a lecture to it.

Before I hung up, Sam reminded me that challenges weren't unheard of and that I had no reason to worry, yet. I agreed, and neither of us said what I already knew. Challenges occurred when more than one werewolf became interested in the same potential Mate and the potential in question didn't have a preference. So, the challenge was my fault.

AN HOUR AND A HALF LATER, I had showered, scrubbed the kitchen floor, and vacuumed every room in the house in an effort to keep myself awake.

At the sound of Rachel's car in the driveway, I ran through the house and out the back door. Rachel parked the car in front of the garage and smiled at me. I leaned over the porch railing in an effort to see into the back of the car. I spotted Clay lying on the back seat with his head down. He didn't look up at me.

Rachel opened her door.

"How'd it go?" I said, trying to sound indifferent.

"He took it like a champ." She opened the back car door for Clay. He lifted his head and stood with obvious effort. Then he hopped down with care and pathetically climbed the deck steps to my side. I stared at him for a moment.

"What'd they do to him?"

Rachel shook her head and closed the door.

"He wasn't acting like this when we left. I swear. I think he's hamming it up for you." She patted Clay's head with a laugh.

He accepted the pat with a defeated grunt, stopped hobbling, and started to walk with his usual gait. I heaved a relieved sigh. He looked up at me and winked. I quickly checked to see if Rachel had noticed, but she had already walked away from us and into the house. I shook my head at him before we followed Rachel in.

"So what shots did he get?" I poured some orange juice from the refrigerator and took a drink to keep myself busy. Clay's eyes never left me.

"Just rabies. The vet had a hard time determining his age by his teeth, but thought him to be in his prime."

I choked on my juice.

"That's great," I managed to gasp out as I glanced at Clay.

A small smug smile curled his lips. I needed to find a nice way to tell him his wolfie smile looked creepy.

"Hey, while I was waiting for him, Peter called. He said he had a good time last night and hoped Scott hadn't ruined his chance by coming on too strong. He's never seen Scott act in any way but smooth. He naturally thinks Scott's falling hard for you."

Both Clay and I gawked at her. I know my jaw had dropped a little and wondered if Clay's had done the same.

"I'm just repeating." She held up her hands with a laugh at my expression. "Anyway, Peter said Scott's already been bugging him about getting your number to set up another date. Given what you told me, I said no, that last night was just a friendly get together and that you were seeing someone else."

Clay's gusty sigh of relief competed with mine. We'd been through enough today. Okay, fine, he'd had to go through all of it while I just stood by. But still...the stress of it, along with the overuse of my sight, wore me out.

Looking down at him, I realized how much I didn't mind having him there. We'd at least become friends of sorts. But I worried I treated him unfairly by allowing him to hang around. Would that mislead him to think our relationship might grow to more than friendship? I hoped not. If he ever thought I asked too much, he could always walk away.

"You know, sometimes that dog creeps me out with how human he acts," Rachel said, shaking her head. "Anyway, I'm going to meet up with Peter for another try at a date. We're going to see a movie, and this time, I'm not asking you to come with." She had a huge smile on her face as she walked past us toward her room.

"Thank you!" I called to her retreating form.

CHAPTER TEN

THE REST OF THE WEEKEND PASSED IN A BLUR OF STUDYING. Whenever Rachel left to meet Peter, Clay and I would sprawl on the living room floor. I would read my books while he read his, and I turned his pages. We didn't talk much. He seemed content just to lie by me.

Because of Clay's sensitive hearing, we always moved back into my room before Rachel could get from the car to the door.

"I bet I'm looking for a new roommate before the next semester starts," I said to Clay when I heard Rachel come through the door late Sunday night. He didn't have much to say one way or the other.

On Wednesday, I realized I hadn't done my laundry in days. My meager wardrobe lay in a mashed pile in the corner of my closet. With a sigh, I plucked out a semi-clean shirt and the jeans from the day before. After I dressed, I grabbed what I could from the remaining heap and ran downstairs to cram it into the washer. Clay watched me from the top of the stairs. If I didn't leave now, I'd arrive late for class. I threw in the detergent, ran up the stairs, and nearly plowed Clay over on my way out the door.

When I pulled into the driveway that evening, there was a service truck parked in front of the house, and Rachel's car already sat in the garage. Baffled, I watched her hurry out the back door. She wore a wide grin.

"You are brilliant!" she said as soon as I opened my car door.

"What'd I do?" I took my bag loaded with library books out of the front seat and closed the door.

"There's a hot repairman working on the washer in the basement. Thank you for breaking it." She linked her arm through mine and walked me to the house.

"I didn't do anything but throw in a load of laundry before I left," I said quietly as I glanced at the open basement door.

Clay sat in the hallway, staring down the stairs. When he heard me, he turned his head to watch us.

"Hey," Rachel said. "I'm not blaming...I'm just thanking." She continued to grin.

"I thought you were into Peter," I whispered.

"I am. It doesn't mean I don't window-shop. Go down there and flirt with him and see if we can get twenty percent off our bill."

"I will not," I huffed with a laugh. I moved away from her and got myself a drink of water. "It'd be safer to send Clay down there to learn how to fix it than me trying to get us a price break."

"If our dog starts fixing things, we're hitting the road and making some money," said Rachel.

We both heard the heavy tread on the basement stairs at the same time. Rachel's face lit with anticipation while I eyed the door with dread. Was it too late to run past and hide in my room? With Clay so close to the door, I'd probably trip on him, and the repairman would find me lying at his feet.

Then, I saw the guy. Denim hugged his long, lean legs, and a snug shirt displayed his biceps and abs to perfection. I knew better than to stare; he would take my attention as a come-get-me signal for sure. But with a body like that, a girl had to look her fill. When my eyes finally met his, he smiled broadly and flexed.

Well, that just ruined the whole window-shopping experience. A conceited hottie. Their vocabularies didn't include the word no, which made it difficult to fight them off. The situation called for a retreat. I turned to Rachel.

"I have to go pick up my ring before Clay gets here. He'd be heartbroken if he found out I bent a prong on the setting already. Plus, my hand feels naked without it." While I spoke, I held out my left hand dramatically and gave it a wistful look. Maybe it was over doing it, but I wasn't sure he'd get the point otherwise.

"The dog?" the man asked with a puzzled look at Rachel.

A nervous laugh escaped before I could stop it. "We named the dog after my fiancé. He has a good sense of humor and likes the dog, too."

I bolted out the door and got back into my car. Clay hadn't been fast enough for a change, and I had to leave him behind.

Not knowing what else to do, I went grocery shopping and took my time to read the labels of the different orange juices the store offered. Even after the drawn-out shopping trip, I had to drive past the house three times before the truck finally disappeared.

When I staggered in through the back door laden with groceries, Clay sat waiting for me in the kitchen. I set down the bags and peeked around the corner to look for Rachel. When I didn't see or hear her, I spoke to Clay in a whisper.

"You better keep reading the books I bring home. You can be our repair guy. It gives me the willies that he knows where I live."

Clay nodded his head in agreement...which Rachel saw as she walked into the kitchen. She paused mid-stride, her eyes wide.

"Did he just nod?" she demanded.

I acted natural. "Yep. I've been working on it with him. He caught on really fast. The nodding isn't bad, but his smile can be a little scary."

Rachel stared at us for a moment then shook her head.

"You're weird, Gabby, but in a good way. Anyway, it was one hundred and twenty-five dollars to fix the washer. I covered your half. With the vet bill, you're up to one hundred, minus the burger and drink from disaster night."

Ouch. "Okay. I'll run to the bank after class tomorrow." I chewed my lip for a moment. My pathetic savings couldn't take these kinds of unexpected hits. Life was more expensive than I'd anticipated.

I turned to unpack the rest of my groceries and noticed Clay watching me closely. Not wanting to draw Rachel's attention to him again, I ignored his look and finished up so I could go study.

ON FRIDAY AFTERNOON, Rachel rushed in through the back door while calling my name in a panicked tone.

"In here!" I said as I jumped up from the bed.

We nearly collided as she flew through my bedroom door at the same time I tried to leave it. I caught her by the arms.

"What's going on?"

"Peter broke and told Scott he had plans to go to dinner with me tonight," she panted.

I stared at her. She ran through the house to tell me she had a date? I really didn't see how I qualified as the weird one sometimes.

"So...?"

"Peter's coming here to pick me up, and Scott's coming with. Gabby, I don't think he's going to take no for an answer tonight. Peter can't shake him." Her emphatic expression told me the degree of insistence Scott had used to accompany Peter.

I groaned, flopped back on my bed, and forgetting about Clay, landed on him. He didn't even twitch, but I still reached back to pat him.

"Sorry, Clay." I froze mid-pat then bolted upright. "I've got an idea! Rachel, if you have any clothes that would say I've been dating a guy for a while, can I borrow them?" I didn't want to spend any money unnecessarily.

"Sure, but who are you dating?"

Rachel moved out of the way as I rushed from my room. I heard Clay hop down from the bed to follow me. I grabbed shoes from the closet. My plan could work. I just needed to convince Clay. They both trailed behind me as I struggled to slip on some shoes while I walked to the kitchen. It wasn't easy. I almost tripped twice and covered most of the distance hopping instead of walking. I grabbed my car keys.

"I'll let you know when I bring him home. Come on, Clay," I called, holding the door open for him. With a baffled glint in his eyes, he followed me.

I rushed to the car and waved for him to hurry. I had the doors slammed closed and the engine rumbling seconds later. Clay studied me as I careened out the driveway and took off in the direction of the shopping district.

"You're here to keep me safe, right?" I took his grunt as a yes. "Then, I need you to be more than my dog." I risked a glance at him. He tilted his head at me clearly confused. "I need you to put on your skin. Be my date tonight. Please?"

I sounded desperate, but I didn't really care. The thought of Scott cornering me gave me shivers. His normal personality probably qualified as nice, but I'd seen how the obsession had worked on others. Scott's fascination with me had obviously advanced. Yet, if Clay were to run interference as my date, it could permanently dissolve.

"You took a shower today, right?" I expected the harrumph he let out. "Do you know what size you wear? Shirt, pants, shoes?" Unhelpful, he continued to stare at me.

Given what he'd worn when I first saw him, he probably didn't know. It made my work a little bit more difficult, but I would manage.

I found an open spot and careened into it, slamming on the brakes at the last second. Only Clay's good balance kept him from falling out of the seat.

"I'll be back in a few minutes," I said as I rushed out the door.

Inside the store, I tried to remember how he'd looked as a man. Hairy. Dirty. Tall. Well, taller than me. Had he seemed thin or chubby? I couldn't remember. His jacket had obscured most of his shape, and I'd been distracted by the whole "hey, I'm your Mate" thing.

Usually, when I shopped on my own, it didn't turn out well. However, my crazed sprints from rack to rack held most of the men I encountered at bay. So, I scoured the clearance racks and guessed at sizes while trying to stick with safe styles.

Panting for breath, I raced to a register. I bought Clay a linen pant and shirt set, the largest brown foam bottomed sandals I could find—I could always cut the foam down to size—and a few other essentials.

Then, I ran out of the store. Clay was standing on the seat. He just stared at me as I opened the car door and tossed the bags at him. They landed at his feet.

I started the engine and tried to think where I could take him to get dressed. Somewhere he could walk in as a dog and out as a man. I couldn't think of a single place that allowed dogs in changing areas. I'd just have to try to pull a fast one on Rachel. I put the car in gear and drove it as if I'd stolen it. I made it to the house in record time.

Rachel was already dressed and standing outside by the back door when we got home. She had a stack of clothes in her arms.

"Where's the date?" she said as her eyes searched the empty car. "They are going to be here in fifteen minutes."

I waved her back into the house. "He'll be here in a few minutes. I hope."

We followed her in, and I paused to toss the bag of new clothes in the bathroom for Clay. I really hoped he'd help me.

"Let's go in my room, and you can help me pick what to wear," I said to Rachel.

"Really?" she said with an excited smile. She'd already noticed I liked my privacy and usually left me alone. But, I expected the opportunity to dress me would distract her from noticing that Clay hadn't followed us from the kitchen or, later, his absence.

"I need something a little tropical, or hippie-ish," I said as I closed the door and started to undress.

Rachel set the clothes on the bed, her expression filled with suspicion.

"Who is this guy? Why do you need to dress like a hippie?"

"He's a good friend, and he didn't have much notice to go home to change. Because I'm cheap, I got him some clean clothes from the summer closeout racks." I spoke a little louder for Clay's benefit. I wanted him to know why I purchased what I had.

Rachel looked up at my sudden surge in volume. Clearly, my weirdness had just increased a level. I motioned to the pile of clothes to distract her. She began to riffle through them, searching for something to fit my requirements.

"He's got longish hair so I think he might look like a hippie in what I bought." At least, I thought he might still have longish hair. It'd been months since I last saw him. "He was just behind me. I told him he could use our bathroom to change."

"How good of a friend is he?" she asked.

I smiled. "Well, we've slept together."

She surprised me by not saying anything. Instead, she held up a few options. I picked a flowing, knee-length, cream skirt with a light yellow, scoop-necked top and hurried to get dressed.

"You do know that the best way to appear like you've been dating a long time would be to look like you don't care how you look, right?" she asked.

I rolled my eyes at her, gave the skirt one last tug to straighten it, and studied myself in the mirror. Dressing up was a gamble. It might send the wrong message to Scott even with Clay present. Maybe I should follow Rachel's advice and dress down. But then Clay would look out of place in his clothes.

"That looks great on you," Rachel complimented as she scooped up the rejects.

Worried Clay might need more time, I stalled by asking her how I should fix my hair. I didn't own any make-up to apply.

"So what's the guy's name?" Rachel watched me closely.

"Clay," I admitted reluctantly. Since I'd asked a huge favor of him, I couldn't lie about his name.

"Shut up," she said with a laugh of disbelief.

"Not lying," I said, holding up my hands in the mirror. "He talks as much as the dog, too. So don't bother trying to make conversation."

I figured I'd pushed our time limit and turned to let Rachel inspect me. She smiled her approval then dashed to her room to ditch the extra clothes. We crossed paths in the living room as she went to look out the picture window, and I went to find Clay.

The door to the bathroom remained firmly closed. I tapped on it.

"Do you need help?" I whispered.

Unfortunately, Rachel overheard and started sniggering behind me. Apparently, there was nothing to see out the window. I tried to shoo her away with a wave, but she shook her head and leaned against the hallway wall to watch.

"Please hurry, Clay," I begged.

The door opened. I took a step back to avoid the cloud of steam that rolled out. Clay stepped out with it. Stunned, I stared at him. I hadn't seen him since the beginning of the summer. Well, excluding that brief look at his backside. I'd been too shocked to notice the rest of him, then.

He still looked scruffy. Between the beard that concealed his cheeks and entire neck, and the full mouth-covering mustache, I still couldn't see much of him. His damp hair hung in limp, wavy strands in front of his eyes and covered the top portion of his face almost down to his nose. Yet, clean and dressed in the clothes I'd forced onto him, he looked amazing.

His shoulders filled the short-sleeved shirt, and although snug on his chest, it fell loosely to his waist. He put his hands in his pockets as he waited for my inspection to finish. Embarrassed, I tore my gaze away, but not before I noted he'd left himself barefoot.

"Brat," I muttered. Then, I cleared my throat and added, "You'll do."

I turned and caught Rachel's smirk. "Quiet from the peanut gallery."

Mercifully, the doorbell rang then so she just laughed and rushed to answer it. Their arrival spared me from having to look at Clay again. In a way, I'd forgotten the man under the fur.

I followed Rachel slowly, feeling curiously lost. Clay walked softly behind me.

"Come on in," Rachel said to Peter. Peter stepped in, and Scott followed inches behind. Peter gave me an apologetic look as he moved aside. Scott's eyes found mine, and he smiled widely. I flashed a politely cool smile in return.

I could see the moment Scott spotted Clay. His face first fell then firmed in tense appraisal.

"Hi, Peter," I said. "Nice to see you again, Scott." His face lit at my statement, and I felt badly that I needed to hurt him in order to end his fixation. "We were going to join you guys, but Clay just got off of work a little while ago and suggested he and I take advantage of the empty house tonight." My heart skipped a beat or two at my bold words, and I struggled to control the blush that wanted to paint my face. Thankfully, Clay stood behind me so I didn't need to witness his reaction to my words.

Scott's face was a different story. I watched it turn red.

"Isn't Clay your dog?" he asked suspiciously.

"We named the dog after my boyfriend. It's a bit of a joke. Clay, meet Peter and Scott, Rachel's friends." My disassociation of Scott broke him. His shoulders slumped, and the familiar look of shame stole over his face. Why did this happen? I hated it. Pity and remorse swamped me.

Clay lightly set his hand at the small of my back. A casual touch. His palm slowly warmed a large area. Even in man form, he could sense some of my anxiety.

Scott noted Clay's hand on my back, glanced between us, then turned to his friend.

"Peter, Rachel, I'm sorry to back out on you, too, but I think I'm going to head home. I've been fighting a cold all week." Without waiting for acknowledgment, he turned and left.

Peter, who'd looked apologetically anxious when he entered, watched his friend leave with a concerned frown. Rachel murmured something to him. He nodded and went to the closet to retrieve her jacket. Rachel looked back at me as Peter held out her jacket to assist her.

"Are you sure you want to stay in?"

Rachel accepted Peter's help with an ease that usually came after being together for years. I doubted they even realized how in tune they were with each other. That often happened when people found their perfect match. Their lives blended in a seamless perfection they simply called love. It was more than that, though. Their deep connection put them in tune with each other's needs and wants. It kept them open to suggestion and reason so they would always listen to each other. Yep, I'd need to look for a new roommate soon.

"We're sure," I said with a smile and waved them out the door. "Don't come home early."

When the door closed behind Peter and Rachel, I exhaled slowly, and turned to Clay, breaking our connection. I smiled at him.

"Home free. Thank you, Clay."

The subtle difference between living with Clay-the-dog and standing in a room alone with Clay-the-man tickled the nerves in my stomach. I refused to show it.

He simply watched me as he placed his now empty hand back into the front pocket of his pants. The air cooled the spot on my back that he'd warmed.

"Um..." I wasn't sure what to do. I hadn't thought past getting rid of Scott.

Clay's calm gaze made the nervous butterflies in my stomach worse. Silly, really, considering he watched me all the time as a dog. I took a breath and tried again.

"Did you want to do something since we're both dressed up?"

He shrugged.

"You can talk to me, Clay," I said with a little hope. I really began to wonder if he could speak. When he didn't respond, I spoke again. "Okay, do you want to go out or stay in?"

He moved to the couch and sat in the middle, his choice clear. Stay in tonight.

I hesitated. The chair, set at an odd angle to the TV, gave you a sore neck if you tried to watch a movie from there. That meant I'd need to sit next to him to watch a movie. But I felt so exposed in a skirt and sleeveless shirt. I wasn't sure if I could sit next to him for a full movie.

While I debated my options, he watched me closely.

"I'm going to go change," I stammered. "I'll be right back."

I turned and made it one step before the back of my shirt snagged on something. Surprised, I looked over my shoulder and found Clay standing right behind me. He held a fold of my shirt between his thumb and forefinger. I could see the glint of his brown eyes behind the still damp strands of his hair. He tilted his head back toward the couch and gave a slight tug on my shirt. My stomach dropped, and I couldn't tell if it was in a good way or a bad one.

When I hesitated, he gave another tug. I surrendered, turned back, and sat on the couch.

He padded over to the movies, made a selection I couldn't see, and crouched to start it. It amazed me that he knew how to do that. Then again, he watched everything Rachel and I did. I wondered if anything escaped his notice.

He pressed play, stood, and walked toward me with fluid strides. I felt graceless in comparison. He settled next to me and watched the previews. I tried to focus on them, too, but couldn't. Instead, I noticed our bare feet, the scratch on the wall next to the TV, his leg lightly pressed against mine, the sound of the water as it slowly dripped from the showerhead in the bathroom, his hands loosely resting on his lap. The long list of unimportant details would not let my mind settle.

It was midway through the movie when my mind calmed enough to notice we watched an action-comedy I'd wanted to see. I'd just mentioned it to Rachel this past week. She must have gotten it after that.

Slowly, I began to relax and enjoy the movie. I even laughed aloud at one point. Clay's echoing chuckle startled me, but in a good way. So, he *could* do more than growl as a dog. His deep laugh sounded pleasant.

When the movie ended, I stood and went to put it away. It was still early, just about six.

"Do you want to watch another one?" I asked as I knelt to look at the movie selection. "I can throw in a pizza for us."

When I heard nothing, which wasn't unusual, I turned and saw a pile of folded clothes on the couch. But no Clay.

"Clay?"

I went in search of him, but he wasn't in the house. In the living room, I glanced at the pile of clothes again. He had been so quiet I hadn't heard a thing.

It took me a moment to think about using my second sight. Because of school and Clay's presence at home, I'd fallen into patterns where I didn't use it often. I felt safe enough that I didn't *need* to use it. Still, I checked. He wasn't anywhere in the immediate area, but I wasn't too worried about it. He did occasionally leave my side, but he never stayed away for very long.

With a smile, I picked up his clothes and headed to my room. Good thing I took forever to pick a movie.

Since I had nothing else to do, I decided to watch the movie I had spotted just before Clay disappeared. I changed into some sweats and a tank top then scrounged around in the kitchen and found what I needed to make a big bowl of buttered popcorn.

Popcorn in hand, I headed for the TV. When I walked into the living room, Clay once again lay on the couch. I smiled at his familiar furry presence.

"There you are. Want some popcorn?"

I didn't wait for an answer but went to the kitchen to get him his own bowl and split the popcorn between the two. In the living room, I set his bowl on the floor within his reach. Then, I curled into my end of the couch and tucked my feet under him. With my bowl balanced at my side, I reached for the remote.

I'd barely started the movie when he sighed gustily, repositioned himself, and laid his head on my curled legs. The heat of him relaxed me, and I settled in comfortably, content not to move him. I ate a piece of popcorn as I watched the intro. His head shifted on my leg, following the piece of popcorn. I absently took another piece and offered it to him. He gently ate it from my fingers. I offered him a few more pieces, not fully paying attention when he licked the back of my hand.

The second movie was more an action-suspense than comedy. Halfway through the movie, I'd abandoned my bowl of popcorn to the floor. One of my hands burrowed in the thick fur at Clay's neck, and the other lightly worried his fuzzy ear. He didn't seem to mind my grip as I stared at the screen. At a particularly suspenseful part, the front door opened. It scared me so badly that a strangled scream tore through the air. My scream. My heart pounded as both Rachel and Clay stared at me.

"And that's why I don't watch suspense movies," I said to both of them once I could breathe again. Clay didn't stop laughing for two minutes. Rachel laughed just as hard and thankfully didn't notice Clay's reaction.

Clay licked my exposed midriff then, finally, settled down.

I gently tugged on his ear. "Cut it out," I scolded softly.

"So when did Clay leave? I thought he'd still be here after you said I shouldn't hurry home." Rachel kicked off her shoes and flopped sideways on the chair.

I turned off the movie to give her my full attention. "Nah, I turned my back, and he took off on me." I patted Clay on the head, and he snorted. "It's okay, though, I have my favorite guy here." And I realized it was true. I liked no man better than I liked Clay in his fur. Sam used to take first place, but I still felt disappointed in him for not warning me about the last Introduction and about the possibility of Clay showing up at the back door.

"He was a little scary looking if you ask me," Rachel said as she reached over to pet Clay. Turned away from her, he took the opportunity to arch a brow at me. I fought to keep my face straight.

"When I first met him, I told him he looked like a crazy man. I still think he's crazy, but he's also nice and dependable." Clay heaved a sigh. It seemed werewolves didn't like to be described as nice either.

"So does he ever act like Scott?"

"No way." It came out so fast I had to pause and rethink it. Nope, I definitely spoke the truth. "Most guys talk about themselves to try to impress me, or they just act scary obsessive. Clay's different. I don't think I affect him like I do other guys."

I looked away from both of them, thinking. At times, he showed his possessive streak—like when I'd gone on the double date—but he didn't act obsessive. According to my reliable sources of werewolf lore, Clay did feel a strong pull for me, but it was dissimilar to what human men felt. His pull, the werewolf version, should make him territorial and controlling, but he never seemed affected by any of that. Yet, for some reason, he stayed.

"I think he just likes being with me," I said. I noticed Clay looking up at me and met his gaze. Even when he wrecked the truck back at the Compound, he didn't creep on me like most guys had. "And I'm grateful that I get to be normal around him."

Rachel laughed at me. "You sound like you're really serious about him. Why didn't you talk about him before this? And why didn't you say the dog had the same name? We could have changed it."

I decided to ignore the part about being serious. "I wasn't sure if or when he'd make an appearance. And I like the name Clay. Besides, he doesn't mind." I wasn't sure if I was talking about Clay-the-dog or Clay-the-man anymore.

Rachel switched topics. "We should probably talk about overnight visitors. What rules do we want to set?"

"Um...no loud noises?"

"Come on!" Rachel laughed louder. "I meant, weekends only? Maybe guests till midnight on weekdays? Notice needed? You know, that kind of stuff."

She grinned at me, still lounged sideways on the chair. I really didn't want to have this conversation with Clay present. He lay quietly, head on my lap, considerately pretending to sleep.

"I don't know. I trust you and your judgment, and you can trust my lack of a social life. I really don't think I'll see Clay very often so you don't need to worry."

"Oh, he'll be back. I saw the way he watched you. Are you sure the only rule you can come up with is no loud noises?"

I thought of adding that she should warn me when we had a visitor, but I looked down at Clay and figured we had it covered.

"Yeah, I think we're fine."

"Great!" she said with a huge grin. Then she cupped her hands and yelled, "Peter!"

The front door immediately opened and a sheepish looking Peter entered.

"You were supposed to text me," he muttered uncomfortably.

I laughed. "Come on in, Peter. Clay and I were just going to bed." Clay jumped off the couch first, and I got up to follow him into my room. "Night, guys."

"Another early Friday night for us," I whispered to Clay after I closed the door.

I pulled back the covers and slid between the sheets. Clay settled in his usual spot and began to breathe deeply while I lay awake thinking about the conversation with Rachel.

As she'd pointed out, Clay wasn't like the other guys. At the Compound, when I'd felt the pull Sam had warned me about, I'd panicked. I'd thought Clay would be just like the rest and that I would spend the rest of my life trying to avoid him.

When he'd shown up at the door as a dog, and not as a man, he'd thrown me off guard. Now, I realized he'd been pretty smart about it. Somehow, he'd known I would be more likely to give him a chance as a dog than as a man. Again, I'd underestimated his intelligence.

Rachel was also right about Clay watching me. He followed me everywhere. I assumed his attentiveness was to observe and learn. What if it wasn't? His quiet presence had already lulled me into indifference over his company. I needed to be more careful.

CHAPTER ELEVEN

THE NEXT MORNING, I TIREDLY WENT TO THE KITCHEN AND OPENED the fridge. My deep thoughts had kept me awake longer than I'd intended, and I felt like Sam looked most mornings. Instead of coffee, I wanted my OJ.

I squinted against the harsh light and scanned the sparse contents of my designated shelf for the orange liquid of life. No orange juice. Shuffling the contents around didn't change the answer. Nope, not there. Straightening, I surveyed the kitchen and spotted its remains in the recycling.

The shower turned on in the bathroom, and I remembered Peter had stayed over. I looked down at Clay, who silently accompanied me, as usual.

"Great. Another non-coffee person," I complained to him.

Since I drank the last of the milk yesterday, I went for a glass of water instead. The faucet handle jiggled loosely in my hand, and only a trickle came out.

"Seriously?" I mumbled as Rachel glided into the kitchen.

"Looks like I'll have to call the hottie plumber back."

"No, thanks. And no big guy showing two inches of crack, either." I settled for a third of a glass of water and turned off the faucet.

Rachel might have thought the plumber hot, but he'd been bigheaded about it. I knew I wouldn't be able to get rid of him so easily a second time. Having narrowly avoided one potential stalker, there was no way I would invite another one in.

"I was going to go pick up Clay later, anyway," I lied. "I'll have him look at it." I smiled at Rachel as Clay's head whipped up at me. I'd beg him again if I had to.

"Really? No-talk, leave-early, Clay?"

"Yeah, that one. Not the dog."

"I believe you said you didn't think he'd be around much." She smirked at me while she measured the coffee. I stuck my tongue out at her, but she just laughed.

"Don't remind me. I'm probably going to need to beg."

"Does he know much about plumbing?" Rachel asked as she moved to the sink to fill the coffee pot.

"Don't know...we don't talk much." I laughed while she groaned.

WITH NOTHING TO DRINK, I dressed to go shopping. Clay waited for me just outside my door.

"Wanna come shopping with me or stay here?" I knew he'd want to go even if he did have to stay in the car. He moved to stand by the back door.

We drove to one of those discount supercenters. I left Clay in the car with the windows cracked—it was more for show than actual airflow. If he got hot, he'd just let himself out.

It worried me a bit that I needed to shop several days sooner than planned. In order to feed Clay and myself, I had already made compromises in my original budget. Yet, at this rate, I would surpass even my revised spending allowance for groceries. That meant I needed to change my shopping habits, not just to save money but to fill the pantry with more food. I didn't mind eating light, but looking back, since Clay didn't eat his dog food—not that I blamed him—he ate light, too. A little too light when I recalled how much Sam could consume.

The orange juice I liked cost more than a five-pound bag of potatoes. I put the potatoes in the cart and walked past the fresh juice. Maybe I could buy a decent concentrate. I went to the freezer section, found some cheap veggies, and ignored the speculative look from a man a few yards away.

Everyone found shopping a pain at some point. I found it a pain all the time.

In the next case, I studied the meat options. The flash-frozen chicken breasts were cheaper than the steaks per pound so I went with those. The man moved from the veggies to the meats as I eyed the cart and tried to envision our meals. Meat, potato, and veggie.

Before the man tried to start a conversation, I moved on to dry goods. A large tub of generic peanut butter and another of grape jelly joined the growing heap in the cart. I used my other vision to check for and skillfully avoid as many men as possible while I wove through the aisles. Not for the first time, I wished I could tell men and women apart.

Always on the lookout for deals, I spotted the day-old bakery rack and found two loaves of bread for a dollar. The cart held more than it usually did when I went shopping. Although, it lacked variety, it had quantity; and I'd managed to keep it under twenty dollars. My smug happiness lasted until I recalled I needed something to drink in the morning. Dang. And cereal. Oh, well. Under thirty still helped the budget.

When I thought back to what Clay had already done for me, like putting on clothes last night, I couldn't regret spending more to feed him. And there was still the faucet that awaited him. I frowned as I realized all he had to wear was the linen getup. Surely, I could spare enough to buy Clay a decent set of clothes.

I turned the cart around and hunted the store for the best bargains. The store had off-brand denims on sale. I guessed at his size and tossed a pair in the cart. Next, I stumbled upon a returned three pack of t-shirts that looked poorly repackaged. I saw nothing wrong with the shirts and figured the low price correlated with the packaging. Whatever dropped the price down by three dollars worked for me.

A flannel shirt, hidden within the mass of other shirts on the clearance rack, caught my eye. I looked it over closely. The shirt lacked most of the middle buttons. An easy enough fix. I put it in the cart. It would get chilly soon, and he'd need it. I paused. Would he stay that long? Probably. He showed no sign of wanting to leave. I went to find some warm socks then looked for shoes. I had to guess the size based on the feet that I'd seen last night.

Waiting in the checkout line proved painfully annoying. I couldn't avoid men while standing still. However, I did manage to find an open lane with a female cashier. Two men lined up behind me and persistently tried to start up a conversation with me before I unloaded the cart. The woman gave me a look. Whatever.

I left the store in a hurry. Usually, if I put enough distance between us, my admirers forgot about me.

The cart clattered over the blacktop as I made my way to the car. Clay watched for me from the back seat. His steady gaze tracked my progress. I looked forward to showing him what I'd managed to purchase and smiled at him.

Unfortunately, the man who'd just pulled into the space beyond my car thought I'd meant the smile for him. I mentally groaned as I kept pushing the cart toward my car. The man climbed down from his truck. Like Clay, he didn't stop watching me as he stepped out from between the vehicles to wait for me. Clay tensed inside the car.

"Hi, there. Need a hand?" the man said.

I stopped near the trunk.

"No, thanks. I got it."

He didn't leave.

"My name's Dale. I own Dale's Auto Body on South Mitchell. You should bring your car by. It looks like it might be due for an oil change."

Did I really look dumb enough to believe he could determine the car needed an oil change just by looking at the exterior? It certainly wasn't leaking oil as a giveaway.

"That's a nice offer, but my boyfriend does the oil changes." I unlocked the trunk and started to load groceries.

Dale didn't take the hint and go away.

"He's a handy guy, then?" He grabbed the potatoes and set them in the trunk for me. Unfortunately, it brought him closer.

"Yes, very." A brief conversation sometimes worked to get rid of a pest.

"I'm sorry, I didn't catch your name," he said.

I could see Clay through the back window. Crouched down, he watched the man though the small gap between the trunk lid and the trunk. I bent forward and set a bag in the trunk so Dale wouldn't see me as I rolled my eyes at Clay. Clay's gaze briefly flicked to me before returning to Dale with serious intent.

"Gabby," I said as I closed the trunk. "Thanks for helping me with the groceries, but I need to get going. My dog's been in the car for a while already."

Not waiting for his reply, I moved the cart to the empty spot next to my car.

"We have an opening at the shop. If your boyfriend's looking for work, send him by. We'll see how good he is," Dale said, opening the driver-side door for me.

Clay hopped from the back seat to the driver's seat. With bristling fur, he growled at Dale, who backed away a step.

I nodded to Dale and nudged Clay over so I could slide in behind the wheel.

Braving Clay's wrath, Dale closed the door for me. I started the car and pulled through the empty spot in front of me.

"Well, that was a challenge if I ever heard one." I reached over to pet Clay's head. "But no challenges until you fix the sink." He looked up at me, and I smiled.

When we got back to the house, both Rachel and Peter were gone. That seemed to make Clay happy. It definitely made me happy. I hadn't been sure how Clay would get dressed with Rachel around.

"You go shower while I unpack. Then you can look at the sink and see if we have to call that bigheaded plumber back."

He willingly trotted to the bathroom. After that first time, I'd learned to let him close the door on his own.

It didn't take long for me to put the groceries away. When I finished unpacking, I picked up the pile of things I'd bought for Clay and went to my room. The stuff from yesterday already hung neatly in my closet except for some underclothes which I'd hidden in my bottom drawer. I grabbed an item from his drawer—it made it less personal if I didn't over think it—then moved to the bathroom. I could hear the shower running and tapped on the door.

"I'm coming in, so please stay behind the curtain." I waited a moment then entered. Steam already filled the room. "I have some clothes for you. Better stuff for looking at a sink than what I bought yesterday." I realized then that I'd never actually asked him if he would help.

"Clay, I'm so sorry," I apologized sincerely. "I'm being rude and making assumptions. Will you look at the sink? Please?" I asked using my syrupy voice.

He splashed me over the top of the curtain...again.

"Ok, ok. I'll just leave the stuff here on the floor. If something doesn't fit or you don't like it, leave the tags on it, and we'll take it back. I guessed on the shoes. Some of the stuff isn't for now, but I figured you could try it on." I realized I was rambling at the same time I remembered the missing buttons on the shirt. I closed my mouth and quickly grabbed the flannel from the pile.

The water turned off just then, and I rushed from the bathroom.

In my room, I pulled out my travel sewing kit and got to work moving buttons around. The two spares on the inside seam remained intact. With those and a close match I found in the sewing kit, I solved the missing button problem.

While I stitched, I listened for Clay to leave the bathroom. By the time I finished, I still hadn't heard anything. I set the repaired shirt aside and went to look for him.

I found him in the kitchen. He already had his head bent over the faucet. The jeans hung loosely from his hips. The white shirt clung lightly to his back, outlining the curve of each muscle and his broad, firm shoulders. I blinked twice, swallowed hard, and caught myself a moment before I tried clearing my throat to swallow again. The clothes I'd picked out looked good. A little too good. And looking at him in them did funny things to my stomach.

Thankfully, he didn't look up and notice my gawking. I pulled myself together and moved to the refrigerator. Opening it, I studied the contents then grabbed what I needed to make him a big breakfast: eggs, bacon, potatoes, and yes, orange juice...from concentrate. I set everything on the table.

When first staying with Sam, he'd amazed me with the amount of food he'd consumed on a daily basis. He'd explained that the werewolf's metabolism ran a bit higher than the average person's did. So, I planned to make enough breakfast for three and only serve myself one portion, leaving the rest for Clay.

While he ran down to the basement, I washed the potatoes under the pathetic trickle of water. When he came back, I noticed he still had bare feet.

"The shoes didn't fit?" I moved to the table to peel the potatoes and stay out of his way.

He shrugged in response. I tried to guess what that might mean.

"So they fit, but you didn't want to wear them?"

No response. He continued to tinker with the sink. I started to cut the potatoes.

"Did you like them, or should we bring them back? I wasn't sure what style you liked. There were several different colors. They're cheap shoes, but I figured it was better than walking around barefoot in the snow. That's got to be cold even for you."

Halfway through my one-sided conversation, he'd turned to look at me. I knew I'd rambled a little...again. Then I realized I'd just referred to him still living here in winter. I had really grown used to having him around. Kind of. I hoped he wasn't looking at me because of that.

"I just don't want you to think you have to keep them if you don't like them. It won't hurt my feelings if we take them back. Just wear the flip flops for now, and you can come in with me next time and pick out what you like." The plain, grey and blue running shoes were muted enough that I'd thought they'd look okay with whatever he wore in the future. I hadn't given the style more thought than that.

I got up from the table and put some butter in the pan on the stove. When I turned to get the diced potatoes, he was sitting on a chair at the table. He already had his socks on and was bent forward to slide his feet into the shoes.

"No, no, no, Clay." I hurried over, reached out, and almost touched his back before I caught myself and pulled my hand away. "I wasn't saying you *had* to wear them." He continued to tie the shoes. "It's okay to bring them back if you don't like them."

When he finished tying, he stood and looked down at his feet. I could see him wiggle his toes through the canvas and mesh tops. The length seemed to fit well enough. The loose, untied lacing told me they ran a little snug in the width. He moved past me and walked to the sink then back to try out the shoes. What little I could see of his expression appeared relaxed, as did his stride.

"You like shoes but you don't wear them much, do you?"

He answered with his typical passive shrug as he moved back to the sink.

The sizzle of the potatoes called my attention, and I got another pan out to start the bacon. He used the tools he'd brought up from the basement to try to fix the sink while I cooked. The sound of water running at full pressure heralded breakfast.

"Good to have a handyman," I commented setting our plates on the table.

Clay cleaned up the tools and disappeared downstairs. I wondered if he would come back in his fur and eyed the plate I'd set on the table for him. We had eaten together before but always with him in his fur. Before I could stop it, an image of him trying to use a fork for the first time popped into my head. I quickly squashed the picture and sat down to wait for him in whatever form he chose. I would not underestimate him again. Nor would I thoughtlessly remark on his table manners no matter how poor they might be.

The soft tread on the stairs warned me that he remained a man. He sat across from me and dug in. He didn't eat like Clay-the-dog or use his hands. Instead, he had perfectly normal table manners. Though his beard shredded it, he even used his paper napkin in an effort to keep himself neat.

"What are the chances of trimming that beard?"

He used his napkin while he finished chewing and then flashed me a full view of his teeth. His canines remained completely elongated as if he still wore his fur. I froze briefly with my fork suspended midair. Then I gave myself a mental shake. The view scared me, but I reminded myself of Sam's words. I had nothing to fear.

"Do they stay like that all the time?"

He didn't answer but continued to eat, slowly clearing his plate. I waited patiently, hoping he'd give me some type of response. This was the second occasion we'd spent time together without his fur since he'd arrived. I knew so little about him and wondered if this was a sign he was ready to start talking to me.

When he finished, he moved to the sink and ran the water. I wasn't ready to give up. I followed him, leaned against the counter, and studied the little bit of his face I could see.

"Is this something you don't want to talk about?"

He shrugged. Okay, not a closed topic...and apparently he wasn't yet ready to speak.

"Is it something I need to guess or can you explain it to me?" I felt like I was playing twenty questions.

He turned to consider me for a moment then went back to washing his plate and fork. Taking the hint, I cleaned up my place while he moved to wipe the stove. I washed and dried my plate and tried to figure out what to ask next. Obviously only yes and no questions even though he hadn't answered when I asked whether his teeth stayed like that all the time. Perhaps asking about them embarrassed him.

When he returned to the sink, I briefly thought of letting the subject drop, but then he dropped the washcloth into the sink and turned to me. He crossed his arms, leaned against the counter, and watched me. Not just looking at me, but studying me...all of me...as if he weighed a decision. I couldn't help but return his stare.

We stood just a few inches apart. The close proximity brought the corded muscles under his snug t-shirt to my attention. I tried not to notice. He was downright drool worthy. I considered reaching out to touch him, just to see how he felt without fur. But his possible reaction stopped me. Would he take it as a sign of acceptance? Of interest? I'd meant what I'd said to Rachel. Clay didn't act like other guys. I didn't want to push my luck.

With a sigh, he uncrossed his arms and leaned forward. His movement shot a wave of panic straight through me, and I froze. Had he caught me eyeing him? Did he think that meant I wanted him to try to kiss me? I didn't know what to do.

His nostrils flared. He slowly shook his head and pulled back, and I knew he had smelled my fear. He didn't completely move away, just distanced himself enough so that I could breathe and think and not freak out. I caught the glint of his eyes behind his long hair. Calm. Patient. So this wasn't about a kiss. But then what was he trying to do?

"You're trying to explain the teeth, right?" I sounded pathetic, like a child who needed reassurance. I tried not to fidget on top of that.

He gave me the reassurance I needed in one of his rare nods.

Okay. No kissing. Just him moving closer. He slept at the foot of my bed every night. That was pretty close—right on my feet—and no big deal. But he had fur on when he did that. Now he looked...

I eyed him again. My stomach did a funny flip. Maybe my fear wasn't about his reaction, but mine. I was afraid I'd forget myself. I needed his control. I took a deep breath.

"It's okay then. Go ahead, explain. I'll behave," I promised quietly. I saw his mustache twitch with a quick smile. The canines explained some of the facial hair, but the full-bearded, crazy-man look seemed overkill.

After a slight hesitation, he leaned forward again while keeping his hands loose at his sides. I pushed back the fear and held still. He didn't stop his slow approach until his whiskers tickled the side of my neck and collarbone. There he paused and inhaled deeply.

As soon as he inhaled, I knew what he was doing, and although I didn't move, fear blossomed. Heart pounding, eyes wide, I waited for him to finish scenting me as a werewolf would a potential Mate, not a distant inhale, but an up-close sample of my scent, infinitely more potent. His warm exhale sent goose bumps skittering over my arms. I braced myself, anticipating some type of slip in his highly-praised control. He leisurely inhaled once more then lifted his head, exhaling as he went.

With his face only inches from mine, he opened his mouth to display his teeth again. The canines had grown even more pronounced, the surrounding gums swollen from their thickness.

I didn't know what to say. He had canines when in his human form because of me.

"So, when you're around me, they're worse? I guess that means they're like that all the time."

He shrugged and casually took a step back. I was unsure what the shrug meant.

We both heard a car pull into the driveway, and I knew questioning him further would have to wait. I remembered the new clothes still on the bathroom floor and moved away from him.

"I gotta move your clothes. I'll be right back."

When I returned, Rachel was kneeling, petting Clay-the-dog. She asked me why we had a man's clothes on the kitchen chair. Clay impassively met my gaze. Darn him. Why hadn't he just stayed Clay-the-man?

"Clay stopped by and fixed the sink. He figured he would leave a change of clothes because of last night," I lied. Thankfully, Rachel focused on the fixed plumbing rather than the fact I had a man leaving clothes behind at our house.

"The sink's working? And for free?"

I shrugged, feeling very Clayish, and grabbed the clothes. As I walked from the room to put them away, she continued to talk to Clay using her normal nonsense babble. He was such a good boy and so handsome. Did I treat him well while she was gone? Did he want a treat? I sniggered, put the clothes away, then sat on the couch and left Clay to his torture.

Done with her affectionate praise, she released him. He trotted from the kitchen and sat on the floor near me. She went to her room to change, leaving her door open so she could talk.

"I just heard the weather report, and we're going to get a cold snap this week. Frost. With past roommates, we always tried to make it to November first before turning on the heat."

"That's fine by me," I answered.

"Even though the landlord replaced the windows, air still somehow gets in. They're better than they were and seemed to help the AC run less. But if Clay knows anything about weatherproofing, maybe that'll help us save even more on the heating bill."

I looked at Clay. "Know how to weatherproof a house?" I whispered.

"What?" Rachel asked from her room.

"Nothing, just talking to Clay."

THE REST of the weekend passed like the one before, with studying and turning pages for Clay-the-dog. Although I still wanted to know about his pronounced teeth in man-form, I couldn't come up with any reason to ask him to shift again. When I tried asking him about his teeth while he wore his fur, he just walked away from me. I couldn't tell if he did that because he was moody or just bored with my conversation.

Monday night, I got home and Clay stood in the kitchen cooking dinner for two. I had to suppress the happy-dance I wanted to do and, instead, nonchalantly walked by him. A note on the table from Rachel explained she had gone out with Peter and would be back late. The note stressed alone.

Since Clay's last appearance, I'd thought of several questions to ask him—starting with his teeth—and hoped he wouldn't get annoyed and go fur on me again. I decided to ease him into my agenda.

"Wow, I didn't know you cooked. It smells great." I set my messenger bag on a chair and hovered behind him, watching him work.

He pulled baked potatoes from the oven. To the side, two plates waited with steaming chicken breasts. Seeing dinner almost ready, I grabbed flatware for us and sat down.

"So, other than cooking, how did you keep yourself busy today?"

He set a plate in front of me and sat down. He pointed to the last batch of books I'd brought home that he had piled neatly on the table between us.

"You read them all already?"

He nodded.

"That's a lot to read in just five days. Are you skipping chapters?" I teased.

He glanced up at me then back down at his food. Maybe I needed to work on my teasing. I supposed smiling would have helped.

"So, about the beard...are your teeth ready to play nice?" That got an actual laugh from him. A short one, but still very nice.

"Does that mean we can trim your beard?" I asked, excited by the prospect. The scissors would also make a beeline for his hair. How could I read his face when he kept it so hidden? Since he didn't actually speak, it hindered our communication even further.

He shook his head, and my face fell. I looked back down at my plate, feeling silly for the stab of disappointment because I wouldn't get to see more of his face tonight. Lost in my own thoughts, it took me a second to realize he'd stopped eating. He leaned back in his chair and studied me.

Pretending not to notice, I gave him a slight smile and, for a change, I kept my thoughts to myself.

"This tastes great. Thank you for cooking. Do you have a favorite food? I can put it on the next shopping list."

He watched me for another minute as I ate. I tucked away my

disappointment and annoyance, and tried not to let my face show anything I felt. I knew neither emotion did me any good, and both made it hard to enjoy the food. I pushed a few bites around on my plate before he finally uncrossed his arms and picked his fork back up to start eating again.

"Actually, let's keep a shopping list on my dresser. When you think of something, you can add to it so I know what to get without guessing." Maybe writing fell into the talking category, and I'd be out of luck there, too.

I ate the majority of the food on my plate then brought it to the sink. Not wanting to risk him going back to his fur just yet, I grabbed my messenger bag and sat at the table to work on homework while he finished his meal. I usually did homework the same day and left the bigger projects and in-depth studying for the weekend, if needed.

"If you want, when you're done, we can watch a movie," I said.

He shrugged and moved to clean up his plate. I hopped up to help, but he motioned me back to the table, pointing to the open book. I sat and read while listening to him move about the kitchen.

As soon as he washed the stove, I packed up my homework for the night. He wiped down the table, and I hovered with my bag over my shoulder. I did not want to put it away and give him the opportunity to change again. When he had everything clean and the dishrag rinsed, he walked into the living room. I followed him and sat on the couch.

He bent to the cabinet below the TV and picked the movie for the night. A suspense.

"If I scream again when Rachel comes home, no laughing," I said as I curled on the couch and waited for him to start the movie.

A strong wind blew outside, and the curtains moved slightly. Considering where I lived, it seemed pointless to dread the cold, but I did. Soon I would probably start to consider wearing snow pants just to walk to the car. I gave the fluttering curtain one last glare and turned my attention to the movie as Clay settled next to me.

This time, I didn't feel so nervous and actually concentrated on the movie. Clay never twitched, but I jumped twice within the first ten minutes.

The temperature in the room dropped to the point that I ran to get a hoodie during a suspenseful scene. Thankfully, Clay didn't pause the movie for me.

By the time the movie ended, the wind really howled outside. I sat on my fingers in an effort to warm them and knew it would be a long wait until the first of November.

"Hey, Clay. Do you like cookies?" I sprang from the couch and moved toward the kitchen. I could bake cookies to heat the house, and Rachel couldn't scold me for turning on the heat.

I rummaged through the cupboard, and I saw we didn't have any of the main ingredients. No sugar of any kind or flour.

"Shoot," I grumbled.

I had splurged and bought Clay clothes, something I considered a necessity. Along with many of the other unplanned expenses, it set me behind in my budget. Keeping the heat off longer would help make some of it up. But that meant no frivolous spending, not even for ingredients to bake cookies to warm the house.

I closed the doors and turned to tell Clay the disappointing news. Instead of staying in the living room as I'd thought, he stood right behind me. All that came out was a strangled "gah." He flashed a smile so wide that I saw teeth and couldn't help but smile back.

"Har-har. I told you no suspense movies. Life is scary enough without them. Oh, and false alarm on the cookies. We're missing some main ingredients."

He picked up my car keys and dangled them in front of me.

"It's tempting, but unless I want to get a part-time job, I can't afford to keep spending the money I've saved. I've got to stick to the budget so it lasts through till spring. If we can manage to keep the heat off until November, I should have cookie money for Christmas. That's when cookies are best, anyhow. I'll just need to start wearing more clothes inside."

I took the keys from him and put them back in the dish on the counter. When I turned, Clay wasn't looking at me, but off to the side. I tried to follow his gaze, but he didn't seem to be looking at anything. Shrugging, I left him to his own thoughts.

"I think I'm going to bed." I almost asked if he would come with, but didn't know how to word it so I would be asking Clay-the-dog not Clay-the-man. As a result, I went to my room alone.

Not long after, I heard him enter; and I wondered what I'd do if he tried to climb into bed with me as a man. I anxiously listened to the rustle of his clothes as he removed them. The quick pounce on the end of the bed told me Clay had once again become my personal foot warmer.

CHAPTER TWELVE

ON TUESDAYS, MY FIRST CLASS STARTED LATER. IT GAVE ME TIME TO catch up on things around the house. After falling behind on laundry once, I made a point to wash at least one load each Tuesday.

Clay padded softly behind me, following me down into the basement as I carried a basket of our combined clothes. I teased him that the discount detergent I'd purchased smelled like babies—not very manly. He chuffed out a laugh and watched me fill the machine. Nothing I did seemed very exciting to me, but he followed me as faithfully as a real dog would.

After I finished, he trailed behind me as I skipped back up the stairs. The closed basement door silenced the whir of the washer.

I moved to the bedroom and pulled the sheets from my bed to start making a pile for the next load. While I worked, I told Clay about what we'd covered in my classes so far. He sat off to the side, out of the way, but I could tell he listened by the tilt of his head. Glancing at the clock, I groaned at the time, called goodbye to Clay with a promise to see him at dinner, and ran out the door.

Not only did I like Tuesdays because of the delayed start, but also because Tuesday nights Rachel spent time with Peter. It gave me the house to myself. Well, and Clay, too, but she didn't know that. I looked forward to dinners with Clay since it meant spending time with him as a man.

I rushed to the car. The door protested loudly when I yanked it open. I tossed my bag in, closed the door, started the engine, and thought of Rachel as I backed out of the driveway.

Rachel and Peter's growing relationship made the increasingly frequent dinners with Clay possible. She hadn't come home last night and probably wouldn't come home tonight as well. It amazed me to see two people so meant for each other. When I focused on them, their lights, the essence of who they were, pulsed in harmony.

Although I'd never stopped wondering why I saw the lights, learning werewolves existed had tempered my need for answers. After all, if a completely different species could evolve unknown to the rest of the world, why couldn't one girl develop a uniquely strange ability? Oh, I still believed my ability to see the sparks served some purpose I hadn't yet identified, but I no longer actively searched for answers.

Before meeting Sam, I'd volunteered at the hospital, thinking I'd learn to use my ability to identify different illnesses. But no matter the patient or their illness, I always saw the same yellow-green color. However, because of my time at the hospital, I'd found what I wanted to do with my life. Massage therapy had benefited some of the elderly patients with whom I really liked working.

With a few minutes to spare, I pulled into the student parking lot, grabbed my things, and started the walk across campus. Students milled around outside a few of the buildings or purposefully strode the sidewalks, like me, to get to their next class.

Someone called my name. I stopped and saw Scott cutting across the dying grass. He jogged to meet me on the sidewalk.

"I think we should start drawing straws or something," he said when he reached me.

"What do you mean?" I shifted my messenger bag, eager to get to my class. Telling someone no only worked as long as I didn't send any cross-signals, and a long conversation definitely qualified as a cross-signal.

"Peter and Rachel. We should draw straws to see who has to put up with the lovebirds. I didn't get much sleep last night." He rolled his eyes, and I noted the dark circles under them.

"Ah. I didn't know you and Peter were roommates. I usually don't have a problem sleeping when he comes over, so if you want them to stay at our place, just tell Rachel. I certainly don't mind." He opened his mouth to say more but I cut him off. "Sorry, I have to get going. I'm going to be late for class."

He nodded, and I walked away without a goodbye. I hoped that counted as a short conversation. I knew Rachel had been staying at Peter's place because she felt guilty if he stayed at ours more than twice a week. I'd never stopped to consider Peter might have a roommate, too. Maybe I should say something to Rachel. They never kept me up when Peter stayed over. I wondered, belatedly, if they kept Clay up.

Realizing I'd slowed a little, I picked up the pace. I wanted to arrive early enough to talk to Nicole, the shy girl in my basic massage class. Today we would start doing more hands-on practice to try the few techniques already described to us along with muscle identification, and she'd agreed to work with me.

Last week, the instructor had warned us we would work in pairs and would be switching partners over the next few weeks. The announcement had given me a mild panic attack. Although the majority of the students were female, the few men had glanced my way. So, I'd carefully prearranged partners.

On the positive side, the instructor had also stressed we wouldn't need volunteers from outside the classroom this term. It was a relief to know I wouldn't need to fend off Scott as a volunteer.

AN UNUSUALLY QUIET house greeted me. The brisk wind rattled the kitchen window as I set my keys down and searched the house for Clay.

I didn't find him but did see evidence of his busy day. The neatly folded items from the laundry I'd put in, and the load I'd set aside before leaving, filled my dresser drawers. Clean shirts hung in my closet. Clay had even remade the bed with the fresh sheets. The baby powder smell of the detergent permeated the room. I grinned, thinking of him wearing his clean clothes.

A knock sounded at the front door. Still smiling to myself, I turned and answered it.

An older gentleman stood on the stoop. Dressed in a smart grey suit that complemented his dark grey hair, he reminded me of Sam, and I felt a moment of guilt. Sam had called several times to check on me, but I hadn't returned any of his calls.

A smile lined his face, reaching his warm hazel eyes. "Gabby? I'm Joshua."

My polite smile froze in place. This was Elder Joshua? I'd pictured a younger man. Doubt crept in, and I did a quick scan. His bright blue-grey spark glowed before me. That color...my stomach dipped in fear. Joshua had the same color light as the werewolf that had attacked Clay. Coincidence? I doubted it. So far, only Charlene and I had unique sparks. A knot formed in my throat.

In the distance, a child squealed in laughter. The sound snapped me out of my other world. I held myself still, clutching the edge of the door while I fought hard to push back the sudden burst of fear.

His nostrils flared slightly, and I knew my efforts were too late. I wanted to slam the door and run but knew it wouldn't work.

"I apologize for startling you, Gabby. Sam was concerned when he didn't hear back from you after the confrontation. He asked me to stop by and check on you."

"Confrontation?" My voice sounded dry and strained.

"Yes, we heard there'd been a failed challenge. Is everything okay here?"

I swallowed hard. "Yes, thank you."

Think, Gabby! Why would the werewolf launch itself at Clay from out of the darkness only to politely knock on my door? And why the front door? The neighbors could see him.

Staring at his puzzled face, his hazel eyes called my attention. The other wolf's eyes had been blue. What did it mean that he had the same color light as the werewolf that'd challenged Clay? I really wanted to believe it was just a coincidence. I had to call Sam and get a description of Elder Joshua to be sure the man before me was who he said.

"How are things going with Clay? Any other problems? Is he becoming too aggressive?"

"Everything is fine. He's very polite." But missing when I really need him, I thought. Convenient that Elder Joshua just happened to show up when Clay wasn't home.

"We were surprised to hear of a challenge. Usually, strong ties aren't challenged," he commented.

I didn't know how to respond so I remained quiet.

He reached into his pocket and withdrew a business card. "Well, if you need anything give me a call, or call Sam. We're here for you." He handed the card to me.

The card simply had his name and number printed on it, no title or business name. I nodded, hoping he would leave so I could give into the panic attack I barely held back. He smiled, bobbed his head in farewell, and turned to leave.

I closed the door and tucked the card into the front pocket of my jeans. This time I watched through the peephole as he got into the car he'd parked in front of the house. The door muffled the sound of the engine as he started it.

When he drove out of my line of sight, I closed my eyes and leaned my forehead on the cool wood of the door. First, a wolf with a uniquely colored spark challenged Clay. Then, Elder Joshua appeared with the same color. For more than two years...through every visit to the Compound...not once did I ever see a variance in the color of a werewolf spark. Just like humans, they remained consistent.

If not for the challenge, I wouldn't have worried about it. But I knew without a doubt, I'd never met Clay's challenger before. And if I'd never met him, why would he dispute Clay's tie with me? I needed to know who the challenger was and why Elder Joshua had an identically colored spark. Yet, no one knew about my ability to see the sparks. I could ask Sam outright if Joshua was different to their kind in some way. The best I could do was verify Elder Joshua's identity without raising too many unwanted questions. I needed to calm down and call Sam. If I called sounding freaked out, he would probably send Joshua right back over.

I pushed away from the door and turned to go into my room. Someone stood right behind me. I produced a full-throated someone's-sawing-off-my-arm scream before I realized it was Clay dressed in jeans, t-shirt, and running shoes. By his shocked expression, I'd just scared him as bad as he'd scared me.

Heart stuttering, I clapped a hand over my mouth. No way would I call Sam now. I wasn't even sure I could speak. The hand over my mouth shook from the adrenaline rush.

He tilted his head, studied me, then reached into my pocket to pull out the card. He glanced at it, shrugged, and shook his head, clearly puzzled. How did he even know it was in there? Had he been watching me?

I dropped my hand and did another round of deep breaths to try to calm down.

"Did you see who was here?" I asked. My voice wavered so I cleared it.

He shook his head.

"How did you know that was in my pocket?"

He briefly lifted the card to his nose. So, he could smell the other werewolf? That was good.

"Have you ever met Elder Joshua before?"

He shook his head.

"Have you ever smelled him before?"

Again, he shook his head.

I closed my eyes briefly and let out a relieved sigh that sounded a bit like a sob. Joshua wasn't the werewolf Clay had fought. Even though I remembered blue eyes, I'd still worried.

The new color variation bothered me, though, and I wished I had someone to talk to. Now that Clay had confirmed Joshua wasn't the same werewolf from the challenge, I didn't see much point in calling Sam other than to yell at him for sending Joshua over.

Lost in my own thoughts, I jumped when Clay lightly tapped my forehead with his index finger.

I gave him a weak smile. "You want to know what's going on in my head?" I guessed.

He nodded, and I finally recognized that my someone-to-talk-too stood right in front of me.

"I'd like to know what's going on in my head sometimes, too." If only I could figure out those lights. "Let's make dinner while I talk. Let me know if you hear Rachel or anyone else."

He nodded, kicked off his shoes, and put them in my room before joining me in the kitchen. He took the lead on dinner prep and gave me busy work so I could talk. I started to peel a potato while he clanked pans on the stove.

"That was Elder Joshua at the door. He stopped by because I haven't talked to Sam lately, and Sam asked him to check up on me. I guess he was worried after that challenge." I picked up a second potato. "Something was odd about him, Clay."

When I was quiet for too long, Clay nudged my chair on his way to the sink with the potatoes I'd peeled. His way of saying I should keep talking, but I struggled with how to tell him everything.

"I'm different," I said abruptly.

He turned from the sink, looked at me, and shrugged as if to say it didn't matter.

"No. Really different. It's kind of hard to explain. Sam told me I was different when he met me, but he doesn't know all of it. He said that I was rare because I was one of only a few humans compatible with werewolves, just me and Charlene."

I sighed and ran my hands through my hair. Based on my mom's reaction when I'd told her the truth, the idea of telling someone everything scared me.

He picked up two more potatoes and handed them to me. I started peeling again as he went to the stove. I spoke slow, essentially thinking aloud.

"Since as long as I can remember, I've seen lights. Not with my eyes, but in my mind. When I was younger, I had to close my eyes and concentrate to see a relatively small area around me. As I got older, I didn't need to concentrate as hard and could see a much larger area. Now, I can see these lights at will, briefly, with little effort, and over a longer distance. And I don't need to close my eyes.

"These lights are people, Clay. I can see the neighbors moving around in their houses right now. It's not an aura I'm seeing.

"To put it in perspective, I can see a square mile around us, but in my mind, the area looks like an inch. The lights within that area are small pinpricks, but I can see them so clearly, they could be the size of quarters three inches from my face. And all those dots are the same color. Every human around us has the same yellow light with a green halo."

Clay handed me a glass of water, breaking my train of thought. He rescued the potatoes I'd cubed into tiny pieces.

"Thanks." I took a drink and studied the glass for a moment before continuing. "You and I, in the middle of those dots, stand out. I have the same yellow light as everyone else, but my halo is orange. I'm different from the people around us. Even from you. Werewolves have a blue core with a green halo. At least, that's all I ever saw in the past two years, until the night you were challenged. That werewolf had a blue-grey light. Now, imagine my shock when I opened the door and saw a man, who introduced himself as Elder Joshua, with the same color light. Only the difference in the color of their eyes kept me breathing.

"I've been like this my entire life, and I have more questions than answers about this second sight. Why are all humans green and yellow except Charlene and me? We're human. Why does Charlene have a red halo? Or me an orange halo? The only similarities are the yellow cores. I've been thinking it means human, but don't know what the halos mean.

"And I'm sure that you've caught on to the whole guy situation. I call to them somehow, as if I'm a beacon or something. Do I really send out some kind of signal?" I looked up at him questioningly.

He held a plate in each hand. Both loaded with some kind of chicken skillet dinner. He handed me a plate and studied me for a moment before shrugging and shaking his head.

"So nothing as far as you can tell. There's got to be a reason, a connection to it all." I sighed and played with the food on my plate for a minute, thinking.

"I've never told anyone all of this. People figure out there's something different about me if they're around me long enough. But no one knows about the lights. I'm torn. Do I call Sam and tell him everything? Do I tell him the light of the guy who challenged you is the same light as Joshua? There's nothing concrete I can offer about the coloring or why I'm so worried about it.

"Why would a werewolf I've never met challenge you? And why does he share the same coloring as Joshua? So far, the lights have had a category: humans, werewolves, and compatible Mates. I don't think the challenger and Joshua can be compatible Mates because Charlene and I are uniquely colored from each other." I shook my head to try to clear away my frustration at my inability to solve the puzzle.

Taking my first bite, I struggled to swallow the cold food. I looked up at Clay in surprise and saw his empty plate.

"Bet you're wishing you hadn't asked."

He shook his head slowly still watching me. I started to doubt the wisdom of sharing so much with him. What if he started to treat me differently? I didn't want to lose his friendship. It devastated me to think I could lose the one person with which I might have had a chance to be myself. When he didn't say anything, I forced myself to eat.

He waited until I finished eating, took both our plates, and cleaned up the kitchen while I sat at the table and did my homework. The spatter of running water, the soft clicking of dishes, none of it distracted me as much as my own doubts. Uncertainty over what I'd just shared and his lack of response ate at me. Granted, he hadn't spoken to me at all *before* my announcement, but still.

When he finished, he left the room for a few minutes. His nails clicked on the kitchen floor as he padded back in. I didn't have time to wonder why he'd changed to fur. He nudged my arm with his head and looked toward the living room. The tightness in my chest, which I hadn't even noticed, loosened slightly. He watched me expectantly, and I ran my fingers through the fur at his neck, hoping he wouldn't ever act like a real dog and run away from home.

Deciding I'd done enough, I packed up my homework and followed him. We watched some sitcoms then called it a night.

When he curled up on his usual spot at the foot of my bed, I sighed and closed my eyes. He hadn't seemed to treat me any differently after I'd told him everything. I hoped it would stay that way.

140

Rachel came home after a very late evening shift at the hospital. I knew she was alone because Clay only shifted on the bed to acknowledge he'd heard something. The nights Peter stayed, Clay grumbled a bit. They probably did keep him awake. Poor Clay.

CHAPTER THIRTEEN

SEPTEMBER PASSED IN A BLUR, TAKING MOST OF OCTOBER WITH IT.

While on campus, I still struggled to fend off a few stragglers who hadn't yet grasped the concept of no. Thankfully, those stragglers didn't include Scott.

At home, Rachel and Peter were inseparable even though they made a big fuss about giving each other their own time. It just meant they only did overnights three times a week. It limited my quiet time with Clay, but we managed.

On Rachel nights, Clay-the-dog usually waited for me by the back door. Occasionally, I came home to an empty house. Those absences explained why he no longer consumed five books a week, but they did make me wonder how he spent his time when we weren't together. When I tried to ask where he went, he never answered.

I began to notice things, though, like he now owned more jeans—I'd only bought him one pair—and had a few new shirts. Despite the extra clothes, he still seemed to favor the ones I'd gotten him, especially the flannel shirt.

On nights we didn't expect Rachel home, Clay-the-man waited for me. He was never missing for those nights. Tuesdays, still one of the nights Rachel stayed over at Peter's, Clay did laundry for me if I forgot to do it before then and always had dinner ready when I came home.

He still didn't talk when he was in man-form, but I gradually learned more about him through many well-phrased questions. I guessed at his favorite color for over a minute. Pink...naturally. What guy wouldn't have a feminine stereotyped color as a favorite? I gave up trying to guess *why* it was his favorite after twenty minutes.

I also found out he liked to try new foods and made it a point to bring home one unique food item each week. Fruits like pineapple and kiwi disappeared quickly. Vegetables like okra and Brussels sprouts...well, I laughed long and hard when I watched him eat those.

Besides the new clothes that he'd mysteriously acquired, I also came across his wallet on my dresser. Since he'd been crouched right behind me when I spotted it, I'd peeked inside. He could have barked or something to tell me to stop, but he didn't.

The contents of his wallet had been informative. On his driver's license, he looked just as scruffy—except with a clearer view of his eyes. I'd stared at that photo until his laughing penetrated my fascination.

Behind the license, I found a folded copy of his GED transcript. With a few questions, I discovered that his dad, now deceased, had taught him how to read at an early age. The education he'd received essentially comprised of home schooling. When I asked him how he managed to get his GED and a driver's license without speaking, he stopped communicating with me for the night. Moody.

The glimpse at his eyes in the photo started me back on the "off with the beard" kick. His standard response was to bare his teeth. Darn canines. But, in a way, his consistent answer proved to me that telling him about my abilities had no noticeable effect on our relationship, other than to open a floodgate in me. I couldn't seem to stop myself from sharing all the weird or exciting things that happened to me on campus—the only time he couldn't shadow me.

When I talked, he sat and listened, always giving me his full attention. I'd grown so used to his attentiveness that he confused me one day when he abruptly walked away after I told him I'd been invited to a Halloween party.

I'd wanted to tell him more, like it was Nicole from my basic massage class who had asked me. Her reason for the invitation was pretty simple. A guy from our class, who she really liked, planned on attending, and she didn't want to go alone. Everything in me had cringed at the idea of a party so I'd told her I'd never been to one because of the way guys acted around me. She'd admitted to noticing, but that didn't change her insistence that I attend. Her acceptance of me felt good. Yet I had to point out the obvious. Having me along could back fire. The guy she liked could start bugging me again. He'd tried for the first two weeks of class before giving up. She didn't care. She wanted the support.

However, after Clay walked away from me, I didn't mention it again.

THE LAST SATURDAY IN OCTOBER, I found myself getting ready for a party instead of studying.

Clay grumbled, making it pretty clear what he thought of me going. I'd borrowed some of his clothes, the stuff that would fit without falling off, and slicked back my hair under a ball cap. Then, I used some funky hair gel from Rachel to comb a portion of my hair to look like pork chop sideburns. While that dried, I began the process of penciling in some thick, manly eyebrows. Clay stood on the bed behind me so he could watch my progress in the mirror.

"What do you think?" I asked, turning to Clay.

He grumped again then jumped off the bed to leave. Obviously not a fan.

"Rach?" I called to let her know I'd finished. She'd started as my costume consultant until she presented me with a skimpy dress from her closest and suggested that I go as a call girl. I'd kicked her out then. Clay had looked ready to rip apart the dress.

The door flew open, and only Clay's agile reflexes saved him from a concussion.

"What the hell did you do?" she said after she took one look at me. Her shocked expression was priceless.

"I'm going for dude. It's safe, right? What guy is going to want to hit on a guy even if he knows that underneath, it's a girl? Guys get weird about that stuff." I thought I looked pretty authentic. My layered clothes safely hid any curves I had.

"You know what's going to happen?" She sat in the middle of my bed. "All the guys are still going to be attracted to you. Only they're going to freak out because you're going to make them think they're gay, and you're going to get your ass kicked tonight."

Clay let out a yowl that sounded like "that's it" and ran from the room.

Rachel stared after him. "I love that dog, but he creeps me out sometimes."

"Yeah, I guess I shouldn't be trying to teach him to say 'No way'. I thought it'd be cool to train him to say it to guys, but I guess it's encouraging him to make other sounds, too." I hated lying, but Clay had just acted much too human.

"Oh, I didn't know you were doing that. Still...weird." She smiled and got up from the bed.

She'd told me earlier that she planned to stay in. I had a feeling Peter would arrive soon. Like magic, someone knocked on the back door.

"I got it," Rachel said as she bounded out of the room.

Shaking my head, I checked myself one last time. I didn't think I'd get my butt kicked...I hoped not anyway. I looked at the clock, expecting Nicole shortly. Nicole wasn't as close to me as Rachel but she still seemed to genuinely like me despite the attention I usually received.

We'd decided I would drive in case fate smiled upon her, and she managed to hook up with the guy she liked. To make it easier to keep an eye on her, I'd suggested she drive here. That way I could see when she came home like a nosey friend should do.

"It's for you, Gabby!" Rachel called from the kitchen. A hint of laughter laced her voice.

I moved toward the kitchen, wondering why Nicole had gone to the back door. When I saw who stood just outside, I stopped abruptly.

He stood motionless in the yellow glow of the porch light. The blue coveralls he wore had the name Clay sewn on the right pocket. Spattered patterns of grease stained the material, and one arm had a tear, making the getup look far from new. I'd never seen the coveralls before but didn't give it much thought as I stared at his face. I could actually see it. Well, sort of.

Our eyes met, and I couldn't look away. He'd pulled his hair back into a ponytail, fully exposing a broad forehead, nicely shaped eyebrows, and thickly lashed brown eyes, for the first time. His beard covered most of his cheekbones, but everything above his upper lip, he had trimmed shorter.

Stunned, I said nothing in greeting. I could feel Rachel's curious gaze flicking between the two of us. His eyes crinkled at the corners, and I knew he smiled at my reaction. It warmed my stomach and set my heart fluttering.

Thankfully, Nicole chose that moment to knock on the front door.

"I got it," Rachel said, breaking the spell Clay's sudden appearance had cast. She rushed from the room.

Breaking eye contact, I looked at his uniform. "You have some explaining to do, I think." My heart still fluttered as I turned away from him.

"I love your costume," Rachel gushed from the other room.

I turned the corner then smiled in awe of Nicole who was dressed as a mermaid in all its shimmering beauty. The modified silky green body-hugging evening gown included a tail-like train. I anticipated people would repeatedly step on the end of her dress the whole night. A heart-shaped neckline adorned the sleeveless top. She'd altered it to make it appear as if she wore a bikini top. When she turned to give Rachel the requested full view, I also saw a cute fin strategically placed on the back just above her butt. A tasteful dusting of glitter decorated her sleek, straight hair.

"You're gorgeous Nicole," I said. "Are you going to be warm enough?" Both she and Rachel laughed at me. "Hey, it's a valid question. It's the end of October for Pete's sake."

"I'll be fine." She looked at Clay and smiled warmly. "Hi, I'm Nicole."

Clay nodded and stuck out a hand. She clasped it.

"Uh, this is Clay," I said for him. "He doesn't talk much. And this is Rachel, my roommate. Are we ready?" I didn't want to give Nicole or Rachel a chance to comment on Clay's quiet presence.

"Sure. I parked on the street."

"Great. Let me grab my keys." I turned in time to see Clay already walking into the kitchen.

Because of his head start and longer stride, the storm door was just closing behind him when I reached the kitchen. The car keys I'd wanted to grab no longer rested on the counter. Outside, an engine started. I peeked out the window and saw him sitting behind the wheel of my idling car.

He stunned me with his sudden appearance, distracted me from a vital question—how did he have coveralls with his name on them?—with the first real look at his face, and now sat in my car ready to play chauffeur.

Slowly retracing my steps, I listened to Nicole explain how she'd made the costume herself.

"Nicole, if it's all right with you, I think Clay wants to come with. The way he's acting, I don't think he's ever been to a Halloween party and is curious."

"It's fine with me," she said with a smile as she moved to follow me to the kitchen. "Are you two dating?"

"Don't you dare say you are," Rachel said from behind her. "He's almost never here and when he is, he doesn't talk and he leaves early. That's not dating."

Since I hadn't told Rachel Clay appeared most Tuesday nights, I kept quiet.

Better to just leave her with the impression she had than to try to explain our odd relationship.

"So, he's available then?" Nicole said.

"If you're asking my permission to make a move, go for it. Just don't be disappointed. I don't think it will go far," I said as I walked out the door. Giving her permission to hit on Clay didn't sit well, yet how could I not give it when I wasn't interested in making a move...right?

We hurried to the car. I sat up front with Clay, and Nicole shimmied into the back seat alone. I turned in my seat to look at her as Clay put the car in reverse.

"I don't know where we're going. Just tell Clay where to turn and be sure to give plenty of warning. This is the only car I have for the winter." I was nervous about Clay's driving experience. He had never answered how he'd gotten his license.

Clay expertly backed out of the driveway. Listening to Nicole's directions, he got us to the party in less than fifteen minutes. We couldn't park within a block of the address, therefore Nicole shivered as we walked. Within two blocks, I spotted the obvious party house. Music blared, ghosts hung from every tree in the yard, and I thought I saw a keg on the porch. So this was a college party? It looked interesting. People crowded the front lawn in groups that overflowed into the neighbor's yard.

As we neared, predictably, men turned to stare. Their eyes drifted to me, their expressions turned to confusion, then they looked at Nicole.

I wasn't the only one to notice.

"I knew you would make this fun," Nicole said with a laugh. "Oh, I see him on the porch. Do you think I should say hi?" Her teeth chattered though she maintained a brilliant smile.

"Let's push our way through the crowd and get inside. We can warm up for a minute. It'll be more attractive if you're not stuttering with cold."

Clay didn't wait, but took my hand and guided me through the crowd. Nicole followed in our wake. People moved for Clay, and it didn't take us long to reach the door where a man stood selling cups for three dollars. We declined and went to find a place inside.

The bass of the music echoed in my ribcage. Good thing Clay wasn't a talker. I would never hear him, even though he could probably hear me. I wondered how his sensitive ears handled the volume.

He kept hold of my hand and pulled us through the crowded entry into an equally crowded living room. He forced his way between people to reach the small couch then paused in front of it to glare at the two male occupants. They uneasily stood and left, making room for us to sit. Nicole and I sat while Clay perched on the arm right next to me.

Nicole warmed as I looked around. From the decimated state of the snack table, the party had started a while ago. That also meant the majority of partygoers were drunk. One guy caught me looking around and made his way over.

The man stopped right in front of me and swayed slightly on his feet. I didn't look at him, but watched Nicole's face as her eyes darted to the man.

The music decreased in volume as a ballad came on.

"Hey...wash shore name?" he asked, his articulation long gone.

"Go away." I spoke clearly and rudely, knowing he wouldn't even remember in the morning. It didn't seem to faze him in the least.

"Wanna go up shtairs? They have a pool table," he said drawing out the L's in pool table just a tad too long.

Nicole coughed discreetly next to me to cover her giggle at the drunk's poor attempts at a pickup.

"No. Go away." This time, I added a glare to go with the words.

He looked beyond me with a startled expression, which quickly relaxed into a smile.

"Oh, god it man. Sheesh yours."

He ambled away, and Nicole and I turned to look at Clay.

"What did you do?" I said. Maybe some secret man-sign for "not interested." Whatever he'd done had worked well. I hoped I could learn it.

Clay flashed his teeth, showing elongated canines.

I heard Nicole's whispered "whoa" and glared at him. If he kept flashing his teeth, people would start panicking.

"If you keep those in all night, you're going to have sore gums tomorrow," I said thinking fast.

"Those are so real looking. You have to tell me where you got those." Nicole looked at him in fascination.

"He won't say," I said then changed the subject. "Warm enough? Are you going solo or do you want backup?"

She hesitated. She looked uncomfortable and nervous. Honestly, I felt nervous, too.

A group of guys across the room had started watching us once the drunk walked away. Their gazes pivoted between Nicole and me. Most of them just looked confused. One focused on me with a frown. Maybe, this was a bad idea after all. Rachel's prediction of a butt whooping appeared likely. Since Clay had already flashed his teeth once with minor provocation, I didn't want to think what he'd do if the frowny man approached me.

Nicole's bright gaze flitted around the room oblivious to the tension I created. Normally an introvert, she seemed to bask in the attention we received, and I understood why she wanted me to come with. Without me, she would have been a wallflower. With me, she shared some of the notice I pulled in. I didn't feel used but did feel a little sorry for her. I wished I could help her get the man she so obviously wanted.

Deciding to speed things up, I reached out to pat Nicole's shoulder. She needed confidence.

When my hand touched her shoulder, a shock ran from my hand to her skin, the sting of it strong enough that we both yelped. I saw an actual spark.

"I'm so sorry, Nicole. I was just going to tell you that we should say hi now, and I go and scare you, instead." That's what I got for getting all touchy-feely.

"No, I know what that was. It was a jump start." She smiled at me, and I noticed the group of guys across the room completely shift their focus to her. The face of the man who'd frowned at me cleared as he watched Nicole.

"I'm going to go out there, now. If I can't get his attention, we can go." She got up and made her way to the door.

The group started to follow her while others in the room viewed her appreciatively as she passed. Girls who had previously smiled a greeting now frowned or outright glared at Nicole.

Too busy observing, I let Nicole's lead grow. Something was wrong. This was what typically happened to me. Granted, dressed as a man, the attention I normally drew had flagged a bit when we'd arrived, but if I'd worn something like Nicole wore...they would be eyeing me as they were her. Their behavior was so odd for me to see as a bystander and not a participant.

Automatically, I got up to follow at a distance. A sudden, dizzy spell sapped the strength from my legs, and I wilted a bit.

Clay had his arm around me, instantly. I didn't look up at him, but instead tried to keep my eyes on Nicole as I waited for the spell to pass. Maybe I'd gotten up too fast or skipped lunch a few too many days this week. Whatever its cause, it passed, and I did my best to follow Nicole despite the crush of bodies.

Clay had to physically shove a few people out of the way since they were too busy staring after Nicole to pay attention to my attempts to squeeze past. When they did see me, they barely spared me a glance. They just moved out of the way while trying to crane their necks to see Nicole. I didn't like their reactions to Nicole. Not out of jealousy, but out of concern. If all these guys didn't snap out of it soon, Nicole would be in trouble. She was too introverted to deal with all of this attention.

I made it to the porch in time to see Nicole say hi. She shimmered beautifully in the light. Randy, the guy from our class who she spoke to, appeared captivated. He'd dressed as the man from the Old Spice commercial, with a towel wrapped around his waist and nothing else. I figured it a frat house thing because I'd spotted several others dressed similarly. As the only spice-guy willing to brave the temperature outside, I guessed keeping the keg company also kept him warm.

He laughed at something Nicole said and offered her a beer. His own. He didn't seem willing to look away from her long enough to fill a new cup. I couldn't believe this was the same Randy. Since school started, he hadn't noticed Nicole once. What was going on here?

As unobtrusively as possible, I moved so Clay and I stood close to a railing. Better line of sight from there. The crowd continued to shift around us as people moved from group to group to talk.

After ten minutes of watching, I didn't know how she could stand the cold. Shivers shook me so badly my head ached. Naturally, I leaned back against Clay and wrapped my arms around myself. The heat of him penetrated through the back of my borrowed flannel and warmed me fractionally, but not enough to stop the shaking.

Giving up on the attempt to warm myself, I reached back, grabbed both of his arms, and pulled them around me. He willingly wrapped me in his arms and tried to warm me. His chin rested on the top of my head. I could feel his heat, but the tremors continued.

"I don't feel good," I said with chattering teeth.

When he placed a hand briefly against my forehead a few minutes later, I knew he'd heard my complaint.

"Do I feel warm?" I turned my head to look at him.

He met my eyes and shook his head. I lost my train of thought for a moment. I'd forgotten he'd pulled his hair back so I could see more of his face, and I smiled absently. He had nice eyes. Expressive. My brain began to feel foggy, and I knew he could tell when his brows drew down in concern. I didn't like his frown. It detracted from his lovely brown eyes. Chocolate. That'd taste good.

I realized my mind had wondered and reined it in.

"I think I'm ready to go, but I don't want to leave Nicole here. What are my chances of getting her away from him, you think?"

He shifted his regard to the couple on the other side of the porch. I followed his gaze.

A few of Randy's towel-wearing friends had joined them, and their quiet talk had grown into an animated conversation. Nicole still smiled, but I could read a new tension in her stance. I'd been right. She wasn't ready for all the male attention she was receiving.

"I think now's a good time to s-see." The chatter at the end slipped out despite my Herculean effort to keep it in.

Clay loosened his hold on me and let me lead the way while he kept a hand on the small of my back. Whenever someone moved in my way, an arm snaked out from behind me and jostled them aside. There would be a few hung-over people tomorrow wondering how they bruised their shoulders. But I wasn't going to complain. It felt like a plague had struck me, and I really wanted to get to Nicole so we could leave.

The men in the group saw our approach and bristled. I tried on a rare smile but knew it lacked wattage because I felt like crap.

"Hi, guys. Sorry to interrupt, but we need to pull Nicole away for just a minute."

"I'll be back in just a bit," Nicole said to them. "Can someone get me a soda?"

She took me by the arm and turned me around so fast that Clay had to step aside for us. We didn't look back but walked right off the porch and cut across the yard in the general direction of my car. Her arm linked through mine propelled me along more than she realized.

"Thank you for that. It was really weird the way they were acting tonight. I guess mermaid sends off the wrong vibes. I hope he remembers talking to me, though. I liked it until his friends showed up."

Her astute observations brought a trembling smile to my lips.

"Yeah," I agreed, "He s-seemed okay. D-don't trust his friends."

"Are you okay?" Concern laced her voice.

Behind us, I could hear Clay's soft footfalls.

"I think I'm getting sick or s-s-something." I felt colder without Clay's borrowed warmth. "Clay felt my head, but s-said I didn't feel warm."

"Is Rachel going to be home tonight? You said she's going to school for nursing, right? She'll probably know if there's something going around on campus. The nursing students doing clinicals always seem to know." Nicole switched position so her arm wrapped around me, chafing me in an attempt to warm me. I thought it funny since I wore flannel and she had a strapless dress on.

"Good idea." The sounds of the party slowly faded to a normal decibel. I tried using my sight to make sure none of the men followed us and felt a sharp pain in my head, instead. I flinched and immediately stopped. Nothing had appeared in my brief peek. No lights at all. That had never happened before.

When I spotted the car down the block, I sighed in relief. All I could think about was getting home, taking a hot shower, and going to bed. Clay surprised me by jogging ahead to the car. I heard the engine start a moment before he was back on the sidewalk, opening the door for me. He looked worried as Nicole helped me into the front.

"Do I look as b-bad as I f-feel?" I tried to joke.

Nicole looked at Clay but he kept his eyes on me so she answered.

"Well, you do look like you're coming down with something. I'm so sorry I begged you to come out tonight."

"Don't w-worry about it. It w-was r-really interesting," I said, forcing the words through my tensed jaw.

Very interesting. The sudden interest of the men...the animosity of the woman...I was certain I'd somehow passed my pull onto Nicole. And broke my mental fish finder in the process, too.

Clay drove fast, dividing his attention between the road and me. I continued to shiver despite the heat pouring from the vents. Minutes later, Clay smoothly pulled into the driveway. The house was dark.

"I hope you feel better," Nicole said. "I'll see you on Tuesday."

I nodded, unable to speak. My clenched jaw ached from shivering so much.

Clay was out as soon as he parked by the porch. He stalked around the hood. His eyes never wavered from me as Nicole slid from the back seat and left. I blinked tiredly and wondered how I'd get into the house.

He opened the door, and his eyes traced my face a moment before he wrapped an arm around my shoulders to help me out. Between the shaking, the headache, and the stiffness I felt from shaking, I had all the symptoms of the common flu. And I wanted it to go away.

With his arm supporting me, we made it around the car and to the porch. My shivers increased to spasmodic and he still easily managed to unlock the door without dropping me. I figured unlocking the door as a dog made this kind of move child's play.

The quiet house told me Peter and Rachel must have gone out after all, and I was glad. I would rather not have an audience to whatever had decided to plague me. I slipped from Clay's helpful embrace and started to tug off the flannel on my way to the shower.

"Clay c-can you get my towel?" I asked, dropping the shirt on the carpet outside the bathroom.

Had I felt better, I might have worried about how that sounded. But, really, I just wanted to stop shivering.

He moved past me and strode to the bedroom. His coveralls caught my eye again. I had to remember to ask him about those later.

I closed the door, struggled out of my t-shirt, and lost my balance as it cleared my head. I bumped into the sink. The chilly porcelain along with the cool air prickled my skin and caused more gooseflesh. Curling the fingers of one hand on the sink for support, I lowered myself to sit on the toilet seat.

Tired and cold, I weakly kicked off my shoes then began to remove my socks. Without meaning too, I started whimpering like a little kid. I needed to warm up. Shivering sucked. The more clothes I took off, the worse it grew. It messed with my finger coordination.

I stood and tried to manipulate the button on my jeans but couldn't get it. I'd just begun to debate if a hot shower was worth the effort when Clay tapped on the door.

"J-just a s-sec," I said in a panic. "I'm not ready, y-yet." I desperately yanked at the button and it sprang free a moment before Clay opened the door.

"Hey!" I crossed my arms over my chest even though I still wore my bra. Sick and outraged, I glared at him for a moment. It cost too much energy to maintain.

He tossed the towel on the toilet lid and moved past me without a glance. Nudging the shower curtain back slightly, he turned on the water. I wanted to groan and smack my forehead. I hadn't thought to turn it on so it would warm up.

He turned from the shower, bent, and had my pants unzipped and around my feet before I could move. I stared down at him in complete shock.

"Clay, g-get out!" Had I not stuttered, it would have been an impressive shriek. Instead, it came across weak, and he ignored it. Embarrassment flooded me. "Really, I c-can do the rest."

He stayed crouched, kept his eyes averted, and indicated I should step out of the pants. Of course, he wouldn't listen to me when I sounded ready to have a seizure. I looked down at his turned head so close to my belly, and wanted to push him over. But my legs quivered, and I knew I'd just end up falling over, too. Obstinate man.

Sacrificing my pride and my coverage, I placed a hand on his shoulder to steady myself and stepped out of the pants.

"N-now out, Clay," I said, crossing my arms again.

He picked up my pants and stood. Then, still turned away, he shook his head.

"The h-hell you s-say!" Oh, if my grandma had heard that, I would have gotten an earful; and then she would have laughed because I'd learned it from her at a tender age.

Clay reached around me and set the pants on the towel. His sleeve brushed my waist, and his hair tickled my arm. When he straightened, he pulled back the curtain and held out a hand for me. Steam started to fill the air as I stared at him belligerently. Did he really think I'd undress all the way in front of him?

He continued to look at the wall, patiently waiting for me. The shivers grew worse, and I debated my stubbornness. With his hair pulled back, I could clearly see his eyes and knew he wasn't peeking. Yet, I didn't understand why he continued with his own pigheadedness and wouldn't just leave to let me do the rest.

As if he'd read my mind, he nodded his head toward the shower and tapped the tub with his booted foot.

I looked down at the high ledge. The shivers prevented any coordinated movement. If not for Clay's support, I would have fallen when stepping out of my pants. Suddenly, he made sense.

"You're s-staying until I'm in? So I don't fall?" I guessed.

He shrugged, and I knew I'd guessed right.

With a defeated sigh, I uncrossed my arms and clasped his hand. The showerhead angled toward the front of the tub so I could step in without getting my remaining clothes wet. He closed the curtain behind me, and I waited to hear the click of the door.

Once I knew left, I finished undressing. I tossed my things on the bathroom floor and stepped into the hot spray.

It felt so good that I stayed there, just standing under the spray for several long minutes. My only movement was a slight side-to-side rocking motion to keep all of me as warm as possible. The shivers lessened but didn't disappear. I began to worry they weren't really due to the cold. My energy continued to drain , and my headache progressed to a steady thump. When I heard the click of the door again, I knew I'd pushed it.

"Clay?"

I heard a grunt, but peeked around the curtain to be sure. He held out a towel with his eyes closed. I turned off the water and grabbed the towel.

It took a moment to wrap the towel securely around me. Covered, I peeked out again. Clay faced the door but had a hand extended to help me. Clasping it again, I stepped from the shower. I was warmer but more exhausted than when I'd gotten in.

I hustled as best I could to my room. Clay remained outside the door as I threw on the warmest pajamas I owned and did my best to blot the water that dripped from my hair. My arms quickly grew too tired, and all the heat I'd gained from the shower left me. Giving up, I tossed the towel to the floor, crawled between the covers, and curled into a ball. I couldn't even rub my feet together to try to generate more heat.

Clay walked in and turned off the lights. I listened to the familiar rustle of clothes. Instead of the usual bounce of him jumping up on the end of the bed, he peeled back the covers, and the bed dipped as he slid in next to me.

I didn't bother to pretend I wasn't interested in what he offered. Heat radiated from him, chasing the chill from the sheets.

"I really hope you're wearing shorts or something," I said with a slight slur. I stuck my cold feet right on his legs and shimmied over to his side to huddle against his warmth. Boy, was he warm. It didn't matter, though. The shaking didn't stop, but I was too exhausted to worry about it.

Sighing, I immediately fell asleep.

BRIGHT LIGHT FILLED the room when I peeled my eyes open, still barely conscious. I lay against Clay, basking in his warmth. My headache had faded from a steady thump to an annoying dull ache. I felt drained and very tired.

I tilted my head and met Clay's observant gaze. Worry glazed the chocolate brown depths. I tried to swallow, but the muscles didn't want to work.

"I'm thirsty," I rasped.

He gently moved me and got out of bed. I closed my eyes; I didn't want him to prove me wrong about the shorts. After a few seconds of silence, I forced my eyes back open. He stood next to the bed, holding out a full glass of water.

Shakily, I leveraged myself up on an elbow and grasped the glass. The cool water felt good going down. I drank it all and handed him the empty glass. He watched me curl up with my pillow.

I closed my eyes.

THE NEXT TIME I WOKE, I checked my alarm clock. The red digits showed two in the afternoon. Turning my head on the pillow, I happily noted the absence of weakness and pain. Whatever I'd done to cause my sudden illness, over sixteen hours of sleep appeared to have helped.

Gingerly, so as not to bring my symptoms back, I boosted myself into a sitting position. Clay no longer lay beside me. I glanced at my closed bedroom door. He must have gotten bored watching me sleep. I didn't blame him.

Although I could have slept longer, I pulled myself from bed. I grabbed my books then hopped back into my warm nest of blankets. Pillows stacked up behind me, I spread the work out. I'd lost a night and most of today because of the party. I couldn't afford to lose more time. I still had a few assignments from Friday to finish. In addition, I needed to review the prior week's materials to make sure I didn't miss anything.

After about fifteen minutes, I smelled bacon. My stomach growled loudly. The aroma tempted me to leave my warm bed. As I sat thinking about closing my book, the door opened fractionally, and Clay peered in. When he saw me sitting up, he nudged the door further to show a plate of food and a glass of juice. His appearance ended my internal debate and saved me from exposure to the cold.

"Thank you. I'm starving." I moved the book to the side, and he handed me the plate with a fork and set the orange juice on the dresser. I dug in right away, not realizing the extent of my hunger until the first bite touched my tongue. Eggs, bacon, potatoes, and toast vanished in minutes.

Without a word, Clay handed me the glass of juice.

I drank it slowly, starting to feel the pull of sleep. Resisting it would prove difficult. I patted the bed next to me.

"Want to read by me?" Maybe company would help keep me awake.

He flashed me a smile, collected the dishes, and left the room. I heard him move around in the kitchen. The sound of running water had me wrinkling my nose; I knew I'd need to risk the cool air once again for a quick visit to the bathroom.

When I dashed back into my room eager for the warm bed, I saw Clay already lounging on the covers. He was reading a book.

We spent the rest of the day together in my room. Clay read next to me while I paged through notes and completed assignments. Each of the few times he left my side, he returned with a drink for me.

Near dinner, Clay closed his book with a snap and left the room. I heard Rachel's car pull into the driveway a few moments later. Before I heard her car door close, he returned wearing his fur again. Somewhere in the house, Rachel would see a pile of clothes.

I grinned at him as he jumped up on the end of the bed. He settled with a sigh, and I stretched out to tuck my feet under his warm body.

CHAPTER FOURTEEN

MONDAY MORNING I FELT BETTER AND GOT READY FOR CLASS UNDER Clay's scrutiny. He didn't voice any complaint when I left, but I knew he worried that a full day so soon after recovering would overtax me. And he was right. By the last class of the day, I wanted to go to bed.

Dinner waited when I got home; two steaming bowls sat on the table. I dropped my bag next to the back door and flopped into the closest kitchen chair. Soup. Perfect. Clay picked up my bag and carried it into my room while I started to eat. After the first bite, I eyed the contents. I couldn't remember buying it and guessed he'd somehow managed to go grocery shopping.

He rejoined me and sat across the table. We ate in silence for a few minutes.

"Are you going to tell me about the coveralls or where you got the money for groceries?"

He shrugged in response.

Sighing, I pushed my bowl away. "I know I'm supposed to start asking you a bunch of questions, but I'm still too tired. Just don't be doing anything illegal, 'K? It would be hard to visit you in jail on top of school."

I used a battered plastic container to put the rest of my dinner in the refrigerator and quickly washed the dishes, despite his silent protests. He dried. Skipping homework, I changed and went straight to bed.

AFTER ANOTHER NIGHT'S SLEEP, I felt more energetic and noticed more than I had the day before. The people I encountered during the day treated me indifferently. The continuation of the phenomenon I'd experienced at the party surprised me.

I saw Scott crossing the campus again. He only waved when he saw me and continued on to his destination. A friendly wave from one acquaintance to another. Confused, I made an effort to interact more. I smiled at the people I passed. I'd grown so used to the pull I had on men that it felt odd when they didn't turn to look. Eventually, someone did stop me, another freshman, but he only wanted recommendations for a nice place to take a date. Why he stopped me out of all the other people drifting around on the campus grounds, I had no idea. However, it was the most normal, random conversation I'd had in my life, and I loved it.

Nicole caught up with me after our basic massage class and gave me the details of her weekend. Randy hadn't forgotten her and had called her on Saturday to ask her out on a date Sunday night. She'd excitedly accepted.

"He was nice and everything, just not the way he normally is in class. He seemed a little more intense on the date. I talked to him before class today, and he seemed more like his old self. We're going to go out again tonight."

Then she told me about her walk across campus that morning. She'd turned down no less than eleven date requests and two blunt one-night stands. She giggled as she related the details, but the humor didn't reach her eyes. I gave her a few pointers about keeping her physical distance if she didn't want someone to bother her and to say no bluntly. She nodded her thanks.

I wished her luck and hurried home to tell Clay my suspicions. I felt sure that something had happened to make Nicole the magnet for unwanted male attention instead of me. The shock we'd felt seemed to have been the turning point. I wondered how long the effect would last.

RUSHING through the back door with a smile on my face, I felt a stab of disappointment at the greeting I received from the dark and empty kitchen. I set my bag on the table and dug the leftover soup out of the fridge.

While I leaned against the counter waiting for it to warm, I wondered again about Clay's coveralls. I'd never gotten an answer about them. He probably worked somewhere, which would explain the wallet with the GED and the driver's license. But where? I could drive around and look for him, but I had no idea where to even start.

I sighed and settled at the table to eat and study. That he might have a job didn't bother me. That he bailed on what I considered our dinner night without a note or warning, did.

When he wasn't home by six, I decided to head to the library to work on my speech. I needed the reference materials for research.

Studying at the library without my pull thoroughly increased my efficiency. Thanks to the uninterrupted work, I finished my speech by eight and headed home.

The windows glowed with light, and I felt a spark of excitement. I really wanted to share my unusual experience at the library. However, when I pulled into the driveway, I saw Rachel's car already in the garage. It meant I couldn't talk to Clay freely, but maybe I could still manage to whisper to him when we went to bed.

Inside, Rachel sat on the couch alone. There was no sign of Clay. She said she'd just gotten home and asked if I wanted to watch a movie with her. She didn't mention Clay-the-dog so I told her I felt a little tired and went to bed early. I had no explanation for his disappearance and didn't want her to worry. I hoped that she thought he was already on my bed.

THE NEXT MORNING I woke snuggled up against Clay, who must have snuck in at some point during the night. Though Rachel had technically turned on the heat, she kept it low. It made Clay's extra warmth nice.

When the sleep cleared enough from my head, I realized he laid next to me on his back...in man-form. I held still, trying to decide how I felt about it. When I'd been sick, he'd done it to help me. There hadn't really been a choice. I wasn't sick now. But he wasn't being weird about it. So, should I really make a big deal out of it? I decided not to. Warm feet felt nice; a warm all of me felt better.

Considerately, he wore a shirt, and although I wasn't going to check, I felt sure he'd included shorts. I shifted my head from against his side to look up at him.

He lay with both arms behind his head. His hair again covered the majority of his face. I thought he'd gotten over that phase. Since the party, he had kept it pulled back whenever he was Clay-the-man.

"It's annoying not being able to see you," I said in place of a good morning. I flipped to my stomach and propped myself up with my elbows to get a better look at him.

"If you don't talk, and I can't see your face, how am I ever supposed to figure out what you're thinking?"

I reached out to move some hair out of the way, but he stopped me in a blurred move, catching my wrist gently in his hand. He didn't let me any closer. First, he ditched me on dinner night then he wouldn't let me touch him? The thought stopped me. I really hadn't touched him before either, at least not as a man. Maybe he was like me, a little standoffish. I could understand that.

"Seriously, Clay, what kind of bribe is it going to take for you to get rid of some of that hair?"

He flashed his elongated canines at me again in explanation.

"Can't we at least trim it back some?" Okay maybe a lot, but I knew to start with baby steps.

He tugged my hand to his chest, laying it flat. So much for my theory about not wanting to be touched. I patiently allowed it because with him, everything was guessing or pantomime. His chest warmed my palm.

Using his free hand, he tapped my mouth. I frowned, perplexed.

"What, you want me to be mute like you?" Was he hinting I talked too much?

He shook his head and reached out again. This time, he cupped my jaw and lightly ran his thumb over my bottom lip. The gentle touch caused the pull in my stomach to intensify. Though I couldn't see his eyes, I read his intent.

"Whoa!" I scrambled out of the bed as if it had caught fire.

He stayed where I left him and turned his head to study me as I stood trembling beside the bed. I nervously rubbed a sweaty palm, the one that had moments before rested on his chest, against my leg. His whiskers twitched down. I couldn't recall him frowning at me before.

I almost asked where that idea suddenly came from, but guessed it was long overdue. According to the Elders, when an unMated male finds his female, he begins a courtship of sorts. The end goal is to Claim his Mate.

But Clay hadn't courted me. He just lived here in his fur. And sometimes cooked for me. And sometimes helped me with chores...and when he wasn't around, I felt disappointed and missed him. My fearful expression slackened to one of stunned amazement. He *had* been courting me these last few months. Clever dog.

Not comfortable with simple contact to begin with, I naturally balked at his request. Then I paused, reconsidering my hesitancy. Yes, I'd held myself back from everyone. Contact meant an emotional connection, either for me or for the other person. But Clay didn't act like the rest. He wasn't compulsively drawn to me.

Maybe I needed to stop treating him like the rest. Hadn't I already started doing that? I'd sat next to him to watch movies, ate dinner with him, and, yes, technically snuggled with him at night. At least, my feet did regularly. And I had to admit, I liked looking at him—the parts I could see. Thinking of that caused a blush. I sent another panicked look his direction, but he remained motionless.

But he didn't ask for just a simple kiss. Our current relationship placed so many strings on it. Strings I'd never before had to deal with. It definitely took us one step closer to Claiming in his book. As I thought of it, I realized my stance on Claiming had subtlety shifted. I wouldn't mind having Clay around indefinitely. We meshed well together. But there still existed aspects of a werewolf relationship I wasn't ready for. Like biting his neck hard enough to break the skin and establish my Claim. My eyes drifted to his throat. That didn't sound like something nice to do to someone you cared about.

Clay waited patiently for me to consider his request. Would it really hurt to give in to just one little kiss? I wiped my hands on my pants again.

The male's drive to Claim his Mate increased with each passing day, building to a compulsive need. There'd never been a courtship that lasted more than six months. Paul and Henry shared that tidbit with me long ago.

I calculated back and cringed. We'd just passed six months. He hadn't pressed for anything from me in that entire time. I'd been so focused on school that I hadn't given any thought to the Claiming stuff I'd learned other than to be glad he wasn't pressing me.

I edged closer to the bed and touched my bottom lip, thinking. Was he struggling to hold back his aggressive side? Could that be why his canines were elongated more often than not? Had I put too much faith in his control? But the toughest question was if I trusted Clay. If I did give him what he asked for would it be enough to satisfy him or would he want more and then become unbearable to live with?

Glancing up at him, I considered my options while he continued to watch me in silence. I really wanted to see his eyes again.

"I have some questions before we talk about my bribe and your price." I crawled back upon the bed and sat on my heels once I reached his side. "Will you try to answer my questions?"

He continued to watch me without answering.

"Are you able to physically speak?"

After a brief hesitation, he nodded.

"Are you ever planning on talking to me?"

He smiled wide and nodded again.

I nervously noted his teeth were bigger than they'd been a minute ago. My stomach did a flip, and I could feel the fading blush rekindle and spread across my face.

"Clay, were you asking for a kiss?" I had to know for sure.

He nodded slowly and reached out to twine his free right hand with mine. His thumb soothed the outside of my hand while he waited for me to decide what to do.

"Clay, I can't even see your mouth to know where to kiss. I hope this bargain includes a shave."

His whiskers twitched, and I guessed he smiled. He appeared laidback, completely calm as if my answer didn't affect him at all. It bolstered my courage.

I let go of his hand and leaned forward, bracing myself on his shoulders. I could see the glint of his eyes as he watched my slow descent. My stomach churned with nerves and anticipation. Despite my teasing comment, I found his lips without any problem and lightly touched mine to them. His warm breath fanned my face, and I pressed closer. Something inside me melted a little.

Closing my eyes, I reached a hand up to gently brush against his face, exploring his brow, ear, and jaw. He changed the kiss by tilting his head slightly. His lips began to nibble at mine, slow and easy. My stomach dipped, and my heart started to flutter with desire.

When I realized how easy it would be to keep kissing him, desire changed to panic. I pulled away then gasped at the sight of the black eye I'd exposed.

"What happened?" I said, forgetting desire and panic. Then, thinking of Rachel I dropped my voice to a whisper. "I thought werewolves weren't supposed to get hurt like this."

Seeing his eyes again gave me a nice advantage. I easily read the frustration in them. Before he could try something else, I bounded off the bed again.

"A deal's a deal. Go shower and shave. After you're done, we can play charades until I have the story behind the black eye." The stubborn look in his eyes had me adding, "That or I call Sam."

I stayed well back while he ran his hand through his hair in agitation. Then he sighed and sat up. The flex of his abdomen under his snug shirt dreamily distracted me. When he swung his feet over the edge of the bed, he turned his back to me. Part of his shirt had ridden up exposing more bruises on his back.

Forgetting to stay away, I rushed around the bed. He heard me and stayed where he was. He didn't fight me when I started tugging his shirt over his head, either. Numerous bruises covered his torso.

"What happened?" I demanded again. I nudged his right arm away from his side, saw a huge, ugly purple mark, and lightly ran my fingers over it. He held perfectly still for me.

"This is really scaring me, Clay. I thought werewolves were supposed to be this tough, nearly indestructible, race."

I'd lost my mom to a car accident and my grandma to cancer. With no other family, I had endured as an orphan, truly alone in the world. Then, when I'd realized Sam's plan to pair me with one of his kind, a single thought had resonated with me: If I found a werewolf Mate, he would never die on me and leave me alone.

"Is this why you were gone last night when I came home?"

He didn't move at all.

"Fine." I turned to leave him, but he caught my wrist again and gently tugged me to his side. He brought my hand to his mouth, kissed the back of it, then my knuckles. I felt a tug in my stomach. That stupid, annoying, kinda-growing-on-me-a-lot pull which tied us together. My annoyance at him evaporated. Unable to help myself, I brushed my fingers through his hair. I liked the feel of it.

"I've lost everyone that's ever really mattered to me. I thought caring about a werewolf would be safer," I admitted softly.

He raised his head to look at me for a long moment then pulled me into his arms.

Normally, I wouldn't like someone hugging me like that. But with Clay, it felt safe. I hugged him back gently, not wanting to hurt him more, and hoped the safety I felt wasn't because I'd already lost too much of my heart to him. I'd never fully recovered from losing my mom or grandma. I doubted I could lose much more and remain the same person. Losing Clay, even now, might break me.

Eventually, I pulled away first. His stomach began to rumble and mine answered. I tiptoed out of my room and moved my car, knowing Rachel would need to leave soon. Then, while Clay waited in my room, I made him breakfast. I didn't want Rachel to see him when she woke. We ate together on my bed. Before we finished, I heard Rachel leave.

While I washed dishes, he slipped into the bathroom with scissors and a razor.

It would be an understatement to say I was a little curious about what he really looked like under all the fur, er, whiskers. The anticipation built while I put away the dishes.

I walked by the bathroom door but couldn't hear anything. Trying to keep busy, I went back to my room and sorted laundry before deciding what to wear. It didn't take me long to dress. I paced around the house listening to the shower run.

CHAPTER FIFTEEN

THE ANTICIPATION HAD ME SO DISTRACTED THAT I JUMPED WHEN someone knocked at the front door. Of course, the shower turned off at that moment. Bad timing. I scowled, took a breath, then walked to the front door. Smarter this time, I checked the peephole.

Sam stood on the doorstep, and he looked very serious. He must have left in the middle of the night in order to get here first thing in the morning. I frowned. The surprises just kept coming, and it wasn't even eight.

Fixing a welcoming smile on my face, I pulled open the door.

"Morning, Sam. This is a surprise." I wanted to see Clay freshly shaven without an audience, but I motioned Sam in anyway. If he took the time to drive here, I would take the time to listen to whatever he had to say. Maybe it would be a short visit.

He stepped inside.

"Um, don't get me wrong, I like seeing you, but is there a reason you're here?" I said, trying to hurry him along.

"We'll wait for Clay."

His cryptic answer caught me off guard. It'd been more than two months since we'd seen each other. Sure, we had talked, but it wasn't the same as seeing someone face to face. I'd expected him to look at least slightly happy to see me.

Just then, the bathroom door opened. I excitedly turned to look for Clay. Dressed in a t-shirt and jeans, he stepped into the living room. But I didn't waste my time ogling him. My eyes honed in on his face. Only Sam's observant presence kept me from wrinkling my nose.

Clay still sported his beard, but he had trimmed it back. The neat length continued to obscure his teeth while revealing a hint of his lips. At least now, I'd be able to see when he smiled. The whiskers that had covered his neck were gone, leaving the clean-shaven column of his throat exposed. My eyes lingered on that skin for a moment before moving on. He'd also run his fingers through his hair so it lay back out of his face. The deep purple of his black eye had already faded to an ugly green-yellow. Even with his bruising, he looked really good. Just not shaven all the way.

I smiled warmly at Clay, wishing we were alone so I could tell him what I thought.

"You know why I'm here, Clay," Sam said from behind me.

My smile fell as I turned to look at him. What was he talking about?

"I'm told you didn't take the news well."

I turned back to Clay in time to see him shrug and cross his arms.

"What's going on? What news?" I said glancing between the two.

Sam gave Clay a sharp look. "You didn't tell her?"

"He's not talking to me, yet," I said, wondering what bad news Sam had to share.

Sam shook his head at Clay. "You've dug your own hole then, son." He focused on me. "A group of Forlorn have asked Elder Joshua to approach you for an unofficial kind of Introduction. Joshua approved, but he made it clear they were to keep it brief and then leave, unless any of them had a further request of him."

The meaning of Sam's words sunk in deep like a vicious bite. It also explained his less than warm greeting. He stood in my living room as an Elder on pack business, not as family or a friend. I struggled to contain my anger.

"I thought I was done with that. We had a deal." I crossed my arms and coldly regarded Sam. "I know I said I was done."

The carefully, composed expression on Sam's face faltered a bit. "Honey, there are rules we must follow to keep peace in the pack. Clay had six months to convince you of his suit. That time has passed. That means unMated can once again approach you, with permission."

My mouth popped open. Six months. Permission from an Elder. That's why they'd stationed Joshua here. A backup plan because they knew I didn't want to

Claim Clay. They failed to understand I didn't want to Claim anyone. I'd never been free. I clenched my fists. My temper boiled.

"That's complete crap," I gritted out. "First of all, I didn't reject anyone. Second, no one ever told me about this stupid rule." My voice rose to a yell, and I took a deep breath and closed my eyes briefly to restrain myself. When I reopened them, I felt more in control and able to speak calmly. "You know what? I don't care what the pack rules are. I gave you my word and my time. Now, I expect you to keep yours. I worked hard to get here, Sam. I won't let anyone take this away from me." My hands shook. That Sam had cared for me in the past and given me a place to call home for two years, kept my tongue marginally civil.

"By not completing the Claim, you've become eligible again. Charlene was granted a special consideration because, at that time, we weren't even sure a Claiming would be possible between a human and a werewolf. Now that we know it is, you fall under the same rules," Sam explained calmly, his face again carefully devoid of emotion.

"No, I don't." I knew I could stand there and argue all day with Sam, and he wouldn't budge. It would always be whatever's best for the pack with him. "Is this why Clay was beat up?"

Clay made a noise—like a snort of disagreement—behind me.

"Feel free to jump in at any time," I said, turning to arch an eyebrow at him. He remained mute, but his eyes softened when he looked at me.

Sam spoke up from behind me, but I didn't turn to look at him.

"Gabby, it's the reason he's been fighting. He's not relinquishing his tie to you. Every time an unMated shows up here, he will challenge that man for his right for an Introduction. Did Clay get beat up? Only as a byproduct of handing out beatings."

Clay steadily met my gaze the entire time. It broke my heart a little to know he was fighting so hard to keep me, and all I'd given him in those six months was a kiss. Not even spontaneously given, but relinquished as part of a bribe. I hadn't rejected him. I just didn't want to be forced into a choice. If I chose to be with Clay, I wanted it to be on our terms.

"Why is two years of school too much to ask for?" I said to Sam, tearing my guilty gaze from Clay.

"And after that? Then you'll want time to establish your career. Let's face it. There will never be a perfect time for this in your life. You just need to make the best with what you have."

As in, suck it up? My temper boiled over. Screw respect. He just crossed a line. I walked right up to him and poked him in the shoulder.

"No, Sam, you do. I'm not your pawn in this game you play with women's lives. I went to your Introductions and fulfilled any obligation I felt I owed you for the roof over my head. You have no say in who I see..." Poke. "...or what I do, unless you intend to drag me back to the Compound and physically force me to bite someone."

Clay growled slightly behind me, obviously sharing my sentiment. I stepped back from Sam and moved closer to Clay.

"It's time for you to leave, Sam. Don't come back." Saying those words hurt just as much as knowing I only mattered to him because of what I meant to the pack, rather than what I meant to him.

"You were never an obligation to me, Gabby." When I looked away, he tried to persuade Clay. "You know it'd be safer for both of you if the Introductions continued at the Compound. If you keep going like this, there might be someone you won't beat. Are you willing to risk leaving her alone, then?"

What did he mean by that? Clay could get hurt even worse? I thought they were nearly invincible. Glancing at Clay, I looked at each bruise and saw the real answer. They were hard to beat but made to break, just like the rest of us.

I walked to the door and opened it for Sam, signaling the end of the conversation.

"All right, then." He walked to the door and turned toward me. "Gabby, call me anytime. I'm here to help you, no matter what you might think right now."

I nodded stiffly and closed the door behind him. His help would only extend as far as it could help the pack. He'd just proven I meant less to him than they did, but I'd always known that. Why, then, did I let it hurt me?

For a few seconds, I just stared at the door's surface and tried to let go of my anger. Sam made his choice. I needed to make my own.

I turned to look at Clay. He'd moved closer to me, probably waiting for my reaction to everything Sam had just said. I didn't want to deal with it, yet. Instead, I reached up and teased my fingers through the whiskers along his jaw.

"Much better, but I'm going to keep at you until it's all shaved off, and maybe a haircut, too."

He briefly bared his teeth, re-explaining the reason for the beard.

I spent a moment studying his face. I ran my fingers over his forehead and traced his black eye. He held still, patiently letting me look my fill. Would things have progressed differently if I'd known about a timeframe? I doubted I'd have even let him in the door if I'd known he only had six months to try to convince me.

With a sigh, I stepped away. "I need to get ready for class. Before I go, would you show me where you got the coveralls from?"

He nodded and his lips curled in a slight, secretive smile. I definitely liked seeing his lips.

MY HUNCH HAD BEEN RIGHT. He pulled into a small auto body shop on South Mitchell. The street name tickled a memory. I couldn't place it until the mechanic currently working looked up at our approach. Cleaning his hands on a rag, he smiled at us.

"Dale from the parking lot?" I whispered, looking at Clay questioningly. He just nodded. It explained his secret smile and his interest in books about auto mechanics.

Clay exited the car and moved to open my door. I'd thought I would get a drive by tour, not a walking one. Wide eyed, I stepped out.

Dale walked toward us. "Hi there, Gabby. Glad Clay finally brought you around." He held out his freshly wiped hand. I clasped it briefly. "I have to tell you that I was surprised when Clay showed up and was as good as you boasted." I didn't recall actually boasting. "Although, it doesn't look like he's been taking care of your car."

Clay said nothing in his defense—of course—leaving the talking to me.

"I'm always running back and forth to my classes. It's hard to give it up for any amount of time." I shrugged away his question. "Speaking of which..." I looked at Clay. "I really need to get going, or I'll be late." I turned back to Dale. "It was nice seeing you again, Dale. I hope stopping in was okay. I really wanted to see where Clay was working."

"Stop by anytime." He waved as we walked out and got back in our car.

"I'm sure there was some type of logic to picking that place," I said to Clay as he drove us home. "Someday you'll have to tell me about it."

BY FRIDAY, everything seemed back to normal with my pull. Men once again noticed me. Their eyes followed me around campus. Thankfully, they seemed to remember my repeated rejections from the beginning of the semester and didn't approach me anew.

I did wonder what exactly had happened, though. The suspicions that floated around in my head needed further examination, but I wanted to talk through them while Clay listened.

When I walked through the door just before five, an empty house greeted me. I really needed to find out his work schedule.

Rachel got home a little after five. As soon as she walked in the door, she announced she'd decided to go out to a dance club. She continued to her room without waiting for a response from me. I followed her, needing the company. Life had just been a little too weird for me over the past week.

"Don't suppose you'd like to come with?" she asked, looking at the options in her closet.

I sat in the middle of her bed safely out of the way of any clothing options she tossed behind her.

"You know how it is," I said as I plucked at a string in her quilt. "It's just worse if they're drinking."

"Which one do you like better?" Rachel asked, demanding my attention. She'd pulled two dresses from her closet. "This one?" She held up a red dress with a tuck that crossed the middle to accentuate the wearer's curves. "Or this one?" She indicated a standard black dress with a twist. The real hemline was shorter than the red's, but a secondary hemline comprised of strands of beads hung from the first hemline giving the illusion of another six inches.

"I think the black one would be more fun to dance in."

"I think you're right." She set both on the bed and rummaged in her jewelry box. "I have an idea. Peter can't go out tonight. I think we should make it a girl's night out." She turned with something in her hand and arched a brow at me. "Unless you have plans with Sir Talks-A-Lot?"

"No, but—"

She tossed what she held in my direction. By reflex, I caught it.

"Have you ever tried wearing a ring? Some friends of mine do it when they want to go out to have fun and not be bothered by anyone." She grabbed the black dress, handed it to me, then begged. "Let's just try. It's a club with extremely expensive drinks. The prices discourage an all-out drunk, and it has great music."

I hesitated, thinking of Clay. Did I really want to sit here, waiting? It wouldn't help him get home faster. The niggling concern that his delay related to another challenge reared its head. But, Sam had assured me that the challenger would want to heal between fights. If Clay dished out more than he got, the other guy wouldn't be ready yet, anyway.

She pounced on my hesitation. "You know I'll leave anytime you say you're ready to go. You never seem to let your hair down and just have fun. With that kind of constant tension, you're going to end up with heart disease or something."

Her comment about never having fun hit home. I did tend toward the more serious course. When was the last time I did something just for the fun of it? For myself? The double date with Scott had been for Rachel. The party last weekend had been for Nicole. The Introductions for the last two years had been for Sam.

Pathetically, I hadn't done anything just for fun since before I went to live with Sam. Even going to school and getting an education was more for my grandma than me. Before she died, I'd made her a promise to get an education and find something that made me happy.

But would going out dancing really be something I would find fun? I toyed with the fringe on the dress. Yes, dancing would be fun. The men who I'd rather avoid made it a less than fun idea. I looked at the ring in my palm. The large stone sparkled brightly. It was meant to be noticed, but not gaudy. Would it work?

"We'd leave at the first sign the ring doesn't work? Even if we never make it in the club?" I glanced up at her and caught her hopeful expression.

"I've got your back," she promised. "First sign and we're home, curled on the couch watching a chick flick."

"All right," I sighed and grabbed the black dress. "I've got nothing better to do."

"Gee, thanks," Rachel said with a laugh as I left to change.

RACHEL and I had to stand in a long line. It seemed the college crowd favored the downtown club despite the overpriced drinks. We shuffled forward every few seconds while listening to the muted music that thumped from within. Each time the bouncer opened the door it briefly grew louder. The door didn't open frequently enough.

I shivered as we inched forward and tried not to move too much so the cold beads wouldn't touch my legs. Eventually we grew close enough that I could watch the man at the door methodically check everyone's ID. I wasn't worried. I knew I wouldn't have a problem getting in.

"Finally," Rachel said with a smile as she stepped up to the man. She showed her ID.

The bouncer barely looked at her. He eyed me closely, not even glancing at the ID I held out. I withstood his scrutiny, wishing he'd hurry so we could warm up inside. I'd pulled my hair back into a messy knot and added a touch of eyeliner and mascara. It wasn't much of a change, but between the makeup and the dress, he looked at me as if I were a goddess. Maybe this wasn't such a good idea.

Then his eyes settled on the ring I wore.

"You come get me if anyone inside gives you any problems," he said. I nodded. He opened the door for us, and I stepped inside after Rachel.

The music's bass reverberated in the floor and my body. I wouldn't be able to hear anything else but didn't care. The club's warm air enveloped me.

Rachel pointed toward the bar. A long blackboard above the bar, filled with neon colored chalk, listed their specialty drinks and prices. As promised, the drinks were expensive. Good thing we wanted to dance, not drink.

Grabbing my hand, she pulled me to the edge of the swaying crowd and started to dance. I did a little twist in the dress and smiled to myself as the beaded hemline flared out. The dress was as fun to wear as I'd thought. Then the beads slapped my legs on the back swing. The sting of it made me rethink the fun factor. If anyone got out of line, maybe I could use it as a weapon.

The music freed me from worry about male attention, about Clay, and about Sam and his stupid rules. I danced with Rachel and truly had fun.

Eventually, reality invaded in the form of our own all male crowd, and our dancing became a game of evasion. Rachel arched a brow at me. I shook my head, not yet ready to call it quits. The deafening music made it impossible for them to talk to me, and its fast heavy beat didn't inspire a slow, close dance. As long as I evaded the bump and grind, I could still enjoy myself.

After a few songs, I signaled to Rachel because a persistent member of the group kept rubbing up against my backside. She grabbed my hand, and we both ignored the protests of the men around us as she led the way to the bar. A few of the men followed. One of them managed to pull out his wallet and order drinks for both of us before we could stop him. Rachel took hers, but I shook my head and shouted to the bartender that I just wanted water. The generous buyer sulked a bit, but I ignored him and his shouted attempts at conversation.

Sipping my water, I looked around feeling watched—by someone not in the immediate group of men who surrounded us.

I spotted two women further down the bar. They weren't exactly watching me. They were eyeing the crowd of men around us. Neither looked angry, but both looked a little envious. Dressed very similar to Rachel and me, they stood isolated at the bar. The way they kept glancing at me, they probably wondered what I had that they didn't. I couldn't blame them. I looked a bit frumpier than they did.

I motioned to Rachel, and we moved down the bar so our group would spread out to include the two women, as well. I shouted my name over the music and pointed to myself by way of introduction. The women smiled and seemed friendly. They tried to make conversation with a few of the men.

I didn't notice someone leaning close to me until his breath tickled my neck and his unfamiliar voice spoke smoothly in my ear.

"About time you left your guard dog at home." He was just loud enough so I could hear him over the music.

Curious, I turned. He stood several inches taller than I did. No surprise since just about everyone towered over me. He looked even taller than Clay, but not as wide shouldered. He had copper brown hair and hazel eyes. A humor-filled smile flashed at me as I studied him.

"Excuse me, do I know you?"

He leaned in and spoke in my ear. "No need to shout, love. You know I can hear you just fine." His lips touched the curve of my ear, and I shivered as he inhaled deeply. "Mm, you smell good."

I pulled back, leaned against the bar to make some space between us, and really looked at him. In the background, the bodies on the dance floor moved in rhythm to the steady beat of the music. I opened myself to my other sight and wasn't surprised to see his blue-green spark or several other matching sparks in the crowd behind him. Blue-green I could deal with. The other color I didn't want to face until I knew what it meant.

"What do you want?" I said.

With humans, the "safety in numbers" rule worked. Not necessarily so with werewolves. But they did have their own non-human set of rules they still needed to follow, unless they were Forlorn. I'd be okay, as long as I followed the rules Sam taught me.

He leaned in again. "Just to say hi, love. You're hard to catch by yourself. Did you know your dog follows you to school?"

"Hi, then," I said refusing to respond to his last question. If Clay followed me to school, how did he ever find the time to work? Again, I wished he'd just start talking to me.

The man beside me remained close. I didn't like that his breath continued to tickle my ear. Clay would smell him on me.

Rachel noticed us and sent me a questioning look. I gave her a half-smile to reassure her that I didn't mind—even though I really did.

"I was hoping we'd be able to go somewhere quieter to talk."

"Really? Just us? Or those other guys in the crowd, too?" I took a sip of my water and glanced at him.

His smile stretched wider. "And I thought we were blending in well."

None of their kind could ever blend into a human crowd. At least, not for me.

I decided to be blunt. "Do you have permission to be here?"

"We have permission to approach you and request a second meeting."

"Second?"

"This would count as the first," he clarified helpfully.

"Ah." So talking me into leaving with him would probably be the second meeting that he had permission to request. However, I bet he didn't have permission to have the second meeting without Elder supervision. Typical Forlorn rule breaking. His eyes never left my face, and the longer I remained silent the more his humor slipped. I didn't think he would accept no to his request. It might even result in my immediate forceful removal from this bar. Could nothing in my life ever go easy?

"I can't go with you tonight. I'm with a friend. But I plan to be at the Compound for an Introduction tomorrow night."

"Really? It's odd that no call's gone out for it." He tilted his head and studied me, probably trying to sense a lie. Didn't matter. He wouldn't sense one as I'd just made up my mind.

"That's because I haven't told my guardian yet. We had a fight, and I'm still pretty pissed at him." Pretty pissed at him, and pretty pissed at you. Why couldn't everyone just leave me alone? "I'm tired of being told what to do and want the Introductions on my terms. I didn't think about the call. Sorry."

He looked at me closely for several moments. "I can understand not wanting to be told what to do. That's why we left our packs."

Forlorn. My stomach dropped, and my hand tightened on my glass. Bad grew worse the moment he smelled my fear. His nostrils flared minutely, and his grin widened.

"Don't worry, little one. We're not going to cause you any trouble tonight. We will see you tomorrow night."

Yep, that sounded like a threat. If I didn't go to the Compound, they would be coming to get me either way.

He nodded to me, turned, and disappeared into the crowd. I used my sight and monitored his progress as he and his group left the club. Once they cleared the building, I grabbed Rachel's hand to distract her from her shouted conversation and motioned for the exit. A true friend, she immediately set her barely touched drink on the bar and moved to follow me.

One of the women noticed and snagged my arm.

"Please stay!" she shouted.

I smiled regretfully at her and her friend. Both pleaded with their eyes as did the men behind them. But the men begged for a different reason—they were only feeling the effects of the pull I had. I felt a moment of pity for the women. At some point in our lives, we all looked for that one being to connect with. These two just wanted a chance to find their special someone.

Though I understood, Rachel and I needed to leave in case the Forlorn changed their minds about waiting until tomorrow. I reached out to the women ready to apologize.

As soon as my fingers made contact with their arms, a large shock took the three of us by surprise. I knew immediately what I'd done. It hadn't stung as bad as it had when I'd zapped Nicole, but the drain of it was worse. Now Rachel and I had even more reason to leave quickly.

The women looked stunned. I just laughed it away and patted their arms.

"Sorry," I shouted over the music and waved goodbye.

This time when I moved to go, no one paid me any attention. One of the men behind the girls had already called the bartender over to order more drinks for the group. I hoped the women would stick together and be smart about the attention soon to be showered on them.

The first wave of dizziness washed over me as Rachel and I pushed our way through the crowd toward the door. The bouncer didn't even give me a second glance as we left. No man did. It confirmed what I had already guessed.

Our heels tapped out a rapid cadence on the sidewalk, but the clipped sound seemed like it came from under water. I wondered how long it would take my ears to recover from the loud music.

"We need to get home," I said as soon as we were far enough away from the club that I could hear.

"Why? Is someone following us?" She turned to look behind us.

I hadn't thought of that. I hoped the Forlorn would keep their word because I couldn't look for them with my sight. I didn't want to drain myself further.

"No, I'm just really not feeling well."

We reached Rachel's car, and I slid into my seat. By the time Rachel eased into the driveway, I shivered uncontrollably. She had cranked the heat in the car, but it hadn't helped. After all, the shivering wasn't because of a chill or a fever. I didn't argue when she parked and told me to stay sitting. She came to my side of the car to help me out.

"Why didn't you tell me sooner that you weren't feeling well?" Rachel said with one arm wrapped securely around my waist as she helped me into the house. The cold beads of the dress tickled the backs of my legs.

"I d-didn't know. It c-came on f-fast."

Rachel unlocked the door. We'd stayed at the club an hour at least, but the house remained quiet and dark.

"Clay?" I called from the kitchen. No answer. How long did Dale keep him on a Friday night? Rachel helped me to my room and frowned at the empty bed.

"I wonder where he is," she murmured.

Too late, I realized my mistake. When I'd called for Clay, I'd wanted the man, forgetting all about Clay-the-dog. Thankfully, I hadn't said anything more.

She unzipped the back of my dress because I shook too badly to reach it, then left my room to search the rest of the house for Clay. I let the dress fall to the floor and struggled to put on my warm pajamas. Rachel came back a few moments after I'd managed to pull up the pants. She looked even more worried.

"I can't find him anywhere."

"M-maybe he got out. I'm going to bed. I'm sure he'll s-show up tomorrow," I said, crawling under the covers.

Rachel got me a glass of water, set it on the dresser, then felt my forehead.

"Doesn't feel like a fever. Maybe it's low grade."

"I'll be fine. Don't worry about me. I've had this before and just need sleep." I burrowed deeper under the covers and tried to curl up to stop shaking. I wished for Clay again. I needed him. He warmed me, comforted me, and I needed to tell him about my promise to go to another Introduction. That wouldn't go over well.

Rachel continued to watch me—nurse Rachel, not friend Rachel. I needed to distract her before she insisted I go see someone.

"I forgot to tell you. I have plans to leave tomorrow to see Sam. If Clay's back, I want to take him with me."

"You sure you'll be up for it?"

"Yeah, it's not something I have a choice about."

"All right. Wake me up if you need anything." She left the room but kept the door ajar. It made my heart ache as I recalled how, first my mother, and then my grandmother, had done the same for me whenever I'd been ill.

CHAPTER SIXTEEN

I FELT CLAY HOP UP ON MY BED AND FORCED MY EYES OPEN. Tremors still shook me, and the mid-morning light sent shafts of pain into my aching head. The last time this had happened, it had taken close to twenty-four hours of sleep before I woke up without a headache. Unfortunately, I didn't have time to sleep this one off. If I didn't show up at the Compound on time, those Forlorn would come looking for me, and Clay would get hurt again.

My mind worked sluggishly as I stared at the time. The clock displayed nine. It would take a little over eight hours to get to the Compound. We'd arrive around dinner.

"C-clay, we need to get to the Compound. Can you drive?" I struggled to sit up. He cocked his fuzzy head at me. "A lot happened last night while you were gone. I'll tell you about it on the way."

I tried to stand, but a wave of dizziness knocked me back onto the bed. Blood rushed to my head and pulsed in my ears. I almost didn't hear Clay move while I sat there panting. I waited a moment, took a deep breath, then tried to stand again.

This time, Clay wrapped an arm around me to help. He'd shifted. I glanced at the door. It stood ajar. Was Rachel still home? He needed to be more careful. My wandering eyes caught our reflection in the mirror.

He stood beside me, looking down at me with concern. No wonder. I had my arm curled around his bare waist in a death grip, just to stay standing. My pale face enhanced the dark circles under my eyes. A frizzy mass of hair haloed my head. I looked like hell.

He, however, looked—I stopped gazing at his naked chest long enough to see his eyes narrow—pissed. He'd just figured out what I'd done again, and for the first time, I experienced a sense of appreciation that he didn't talk. Not wanting to meet his gaze, I decided to go back to enjoying the view. He wore jeans, unbuttoned and low on his hips. One arm wrapped around my shaking shoulders. He started to rub little circles on my skin with his thumb. He reached up with his other hand and lightly touched my forehead. Though he was upset with me, his concern was plain, as was...I squinted in an attempt to see clearly and then scowled.

He once again sported bruises and what looked like a bite mark. How many challengers were there out there? I'd thought just a couple. He came home with bruises too often for it to be the same few. And a bite? I frowned at the mark on his shoulder, but my fuzzy brain distracted itself again. I lost my scowl. Even with his bruises and bite mark, Clay looked incredible. I would have drooled at the view he gave if I weren't so sick.

"I need to use the bathroom then start packing."

He nodded and helped me through the door. My head throbbed with each step. I leaned against him, let my head hang a little, and trusted him to guide me. Because of my position, I saw Rachel's feet as she intercepted us.

"Hi, Clay. How'd you get here?"

I forced myself to look up. Still in her pajamas and sleep rumpled, she looked gorgeous. How she pulled that off, I had no idea. Concern filled her eyes when she took in the sight of me.

"I called him. Sorry, Rachel, I didn't want to bug you."

Her gaze drifted to Clay. "It's okay, I get it." She eyed Clay's bare chest and his face as he continued to support me.

I'd forgotten she hadn't seen him cleaned up like I had. Although bruised and bitten probably wasn't the best first impression, being shirtless kind of made up for it. She certainly wasn't looking at him in a clinically concerned way, and it made me smile. Rachel was a free spirit and loved life. She didn't mean anything when she looked, but I could sense it made Clay a little uncomfortable. I shivered again. Perfect timing.

"Are you sure you should be going?" she asked, managing to look away from Clay.

"Yeah, Clay's going to pack for me, and then we'll go. Oh, and he came by last night, saw the dog out, and took him home. We'll take him with, so don't worry."

I closed the bathroom door on both of them and focused on pulling myself together. I splashed some water on my face, leaned heavily on the sink, and ran my fingers through the snarls. It didn't help much, but I didn't think it would matter anyway with a long drive ahead of us. I took care of business and shuffled out of the bathroom to look for shoes, not concerned about changing.

Clay came in from the back door before I could make it to the hall closet. He took one look at my chattering teeth and scooped me up in his arms.

My squeal brought Rachel from her room before Clay could make it out the door.

"When you're feeling better, let's talk about rental rates," she called after us with a snicker. "And I'm not talking about the house!"

A blanket waited for me in the front seat of the warmed car. My bulging messenger bag, packed to the point of bursting, sat on the back seat. I twisted, grabbed the cell phone from it while Clay closed my door, then I buckled up. My fuzzy slippers were on the floor, but I curled my legs under me instead and pulled the blanket snuggly around me.

He slid in behind the wheel and took some time to better tuck the blanket around me. His hand smoothed over mine briefly before he pulled away and backed out of the driveway. I struggled to keep my eyes open. Sleep pulled at me.

"I don't want to keep going on like this," I said once we cleared town.

His hands noticeably tightened on the steering wheel, and I could have smacked my forehead if it wasn't already hurting so badly.

"I don't mean being with you. I like that. But I don't like seeing you bruised."

He loosened his tight hold on the wheel and glanced at me. A smile twitched his lips. I scowled at him.

"There's nothing amusing about it. I don't like worrying."

I lifted my cell, dialed Sam's number, and struggled to hold the phone to my ear. My arm trembled from the effort. Sam picked up during the first ring. I didn't wait for his greeting.

"I'm on my way. Put out a call for tonight only." I hung up before he could speak. I wasn't ready to talk to him. He'd hurt me too much with his last appearance.

I tossed the phone on the back seat and ignored it when it started to vibrate again. My gaze drifted to Clay. He looked outright pissed now. He knew who I'd called and what I intended. I hurried to explain.

"It's not what you think, Clay. I don't want to do another Introduction, but something happened last night. I went out with Rachel to a club downtown, not my best decision, but I think I've figured out what's going on with me." I shivered and pulled the blanket tighter around me. Sleep continued to tug at me.

"Remember the party with Nicole? When I touched her, I gave her a huge shock. That happened again last night. I think I can transfer my gift, that thing with guys, to other people. I didn't know how it happened the first time. But I think I've figured it out.

"Last night, these two women at the club had been on their own until Rachel and I—and the groupies I'd collected—joined them. When we made to leave, the women had been so disappointed. They knew the guys would walk away when we did. I felt so bad for them that I went to...I don't know...pat them, I guess. I'd just meant it as an 'I'm sorry' gesture, but then it happened again just like before. A huge shock." My words started to slur, and I had a hard time keeping my thoughts coherent.

"Both times I was thinking about how I wished I could help find the person they were meant to be with. And I think that's the key." I noticed the speedometer hovered ten miles over what I considered a safe speed, but I didn't comment on it. "I don't understand why I can see the lights, but I know it must be all tied together because when I try to use my sight, it hurts. Really bad." Clay's expression hadn't changed, and I realized I'd skipped the explanation of why I'd agreed to an Introduction.

"Oh, yeah. Before I shocked those two, a Forlorn came up behind me and started a conversation. My fish finder still worked then. There were more of them in the crowd, Clay. The one talking to me said he just wanted a chance to say hi. He was very persistent so I told him I would see them at the Compound for an official Introduction. They left right after but gave me the impression that if I didn't show up, they'd come looking for me. I got the feeling they'd been pushed too far." I watched his face. "Has it been the same werewolves trying to see me or is it always different?"

He didn't answer, but I didn't really expect him to. I sighed and snaked a hand out from under the blanket to touch his leg.

"It hurts to see you like this, Clay. If I have to put up with an Introduction to keep you safe, then that's what I'll do." My lids refused to cooperate any longer and drifted shut.

"I'm sorry, Clay," I mumbled sleepily. "I wish I could just get over my need for freedom and Claim you. We both know you're the one. I just don't want to lose myself." I fell asleep without looking at him to see his reaction.

I WAS SURROUNDED by darkness and in a bed. Clay had carried me around while I slept again.

"Clay?" I whispered, reaching out to feel the mattress beside me. Empty.

Sam's voice came from nearby. "You're safe, Gabby. At the Compound."

"Where's Clay?" I asked, trying to wake fully.

"In the unMated's wing. I was surprised he chose to stay there. After I kicked him out of here, I thought he'd go to the woods."

Sam's words annoyed me. How dare he kick Clay out. He had no right.

Still tired, I could have easily fallen back asleep. Instead, I struggled into a sitting position to keep myself awake.

"You don't know anything about him," I muttered, using Sam's own words. "Can you turn on a light please? I can't see."

The lamp next to the bed clicked on. Sam sat in a chair near the bed. He looked worn, but I didn't feel very sympathetic. I looked around. I wasn't in the same room I usually occupied, but I didn't bother asking why.

"What time is it?"

He glanced at his watch then met my eyes again.

"Just after seven. You look worse than sick. Charlene came in to look at you. You have us all worried. You going to tell me what's happened to you?"

Of course, they were worried. They'd promised their horde an Introduction.

"Nope, I won't. Did you put out the call? Did anyone respond?"

He didn't care for my answer, but let it go. "Yes, there's about fifty or so. There were more, but we explained that you were ill and wouldn't be able to—"

"Put the call out again." Why did he choose now to care about my wellbeing? "They have an hour to get here. Get Clay for me, please." I swung my legs out from the blankets and started to get up.

Sam moved in a blur of speed and pushed me back down, his hand on my collarbone. He didn't have to use much force. I flopped back into the pillow and glared at him. He kept his hand on me for a moment, probably waiting for me to try again. As if I could move a werewolf.

"I get it, Gabby. I disappointed you and lost your trust, but you're sick. This isn't what I asked for when I said you'd be better off doing Introductions at the Compound." His voice turned gruff. "Please, don't push yourself like this. You'll get worse."

His expression and pleading tone swayed me enough to take pity on him. I patted his cheek sadly and half-smiled.

"Not everything is about you, Sam. Yes, I'm still mad at you, but this is about Clay and me. I don't want to see him hurt because he's trying to fight other werewolves away from me. Now, help me up, and go get Clay." I held out my hands, and he reluctantly helped pull me to my feet.

Wobbling a bit, I made my way to my bag that lay at the foot of the bed. Sam shook his head as he watched my determined, but slow, progress. I sat on the mattress and pulled the bag toward me. With a sigh, he left to go get Clay while I rummaged through my messenger bag.

I still dug in the bag when Clay walked in without knocking. He didn't walk past the threshold, though. Concern filled his expression when I looked up. I lifted my hand from the bag and let the bikini I'd found dangle from one finger.

"Really, Clay? You're killing me. Where are my jeans?"

His lips twitched with a smile as he leaned against the frame, content to watch me dig through the bag some more.

Despite my playful greeting, I felt winded and dizzy again. Shocking both of those girls took more out of me than I'd anticipated. I'd expected to feel much better by now, like I had the last time. The shocks hadn't seemed as strong as Nicole's had, but perhaps, because it had split between the two of them, it drained me more.

At least my head didn't hurt. I took a break from my search to look up at the fading bruises on Clay's face. He still wore his hair back. I loved seeing his face.

He must have seen something in my gaze because he pushed away from the door and moved closer. He stopped in front of me, and without breaking eye contact, reached into my bag and pulled out a pair of jeans. He held them out to me and tapped his lips.

I smiled widely. "A kiss for the jeans?"

He nodded. I grabbed the jeans from his loose grasp and tossed them on the bed.

He watched me, curious, as I stood and placed my hands on his chest for balance.

"I don't need bribes to kiss you, Clay. Come here."

His lips covered mine in a move so fast, my head spun even more. I clutched his shirt in my fists, not sure if it was his kiss or my condition that caused the current wave of dizziness. His arms circled around me. I felt safe. And so desired. I pressed myself closer, and he increased the pressure on my lips. His warm breath fanned my face. One of his hands roamed up to curve around the back of my neck.

My heart skipped a beat, and my breathing became more erratic. I knew he'd hear but I didn't care. Standing on my tiptoes, I loosened my hold on his shirt and slid my hands up and around his neck. I didn't want him to let go just yet.

Tentatively, I opened my mouth and ran my tongue across his bottom lip. He growled, and his hold tightened fractionally. A thrill shot through me, heating my limbs and tickling my stomach. I used my tongue again. His mouth opened in response. He took control of the kiss and turned it from tender-sweet to passionately melting. Our tongues touched. I stopped breathing. My world tilted then steadied. He anchored me. How could I doubt this? Us?

My lungs burned for air, and he gently pulled away even though I whined in protest. He kissed my cheek, then my forehead.

It took a minute for the world to right itself again while I caught my breath. Clay placed his chin on my head and held me tight. My head rested on his chest over his thundering heart. The kiss had affected him as much as it had me. It made me smile because now I knew without a doubt; *I* attracted him, not my strange pull.

I heard the apartment door open and figured it was Sam. With regret, I pulled back, and Clay let me go. I looked up at Clay.

"Can you come with me for this, or will that cause more problems?"

"It would be best if he stayed away, Gabby," Sam answered from the doorway behind Clay.

I moved around Clay to look at Sam. "I didn't ask what was best. Best went out the window years ago, Sam, when 'making do' moved in. Is he allowed?"

Sam flinched when I repeated his words then ran his hand over his face. The move muffled his sigh.

"It's allowed. He's unMated, but he's considered rejected. He'll be challenged by everyone for his place in the Introduction order."

I made a non-committal noise and looked at Clay. "Do you want to be there?"

He nodded sharply.

"All right then. Sam, please head over and get things ready. Clay will walk me there. Clay, I just need to change then I'm ready."

Both men stared at me as if I'd grown horns. I knew I looked like hell. I was probably still pale and definitely had a worse tangled mass of hair than I had that morning. But, it didn't matter. Sam wanted an Introduction, and I wanted peace for Clay. I arched a brow at both of them.

Sam grumbled to himself as he left. Clay followed and closed the door softly behind him, leaving me to dress. I smoothed down my hair, not really caring, and changed into a shirt and jeans. My legs shook by the time I finished, and I had to sit on the bed for a minute.

I took a fortifying breath, stood, and made my way out to the living room. Clay waited for me by the kitchenette. He had a glass of orange juice ready for me. He knew me well. I smiled my thanks and gulped it down. It felt good and gave me a tiny energy boost.

"I need just a minute in the bathroom. Can you find my shoes for me?" I held the wall as I made my way there and leaned on the sink while I brushed my teeth. As I brushed, I dwelled on the fact that Sam had kicked Clay out of my room. If it weren't for the long drive, I'd insist we leave right after the Introduction. But I knew Clay needed sleep soon, too. I wondered what Sam would do when I insisted that Clay sleep next to me later. He was warm and comforting, and I needed both desperately.

Clay stood right outside the door when I opened it. My slippers waited on the floor by his feet.

"Where are my shoes?"

He shrugged and pointed to the slippers. Hey, he'd packed for me and remembered the jeans. He'd even packed underclothes and a toothbrush. If he forgot the shoes, I really had no complaint. I stepped into the slippers then squeaked when my world spun, and I suddenly found myself in his arms.

"I can walk, Clay."

He shook his head and carried me to the door. There, he repositioned me to one arm and opened the door while I clung tightly to his neck. I rather liked the feeling. With an arm wrapped around him, I leaned my head against his shoulder and ran my fingers through his hair.

The few people in the hallways stopped and stared as we passed. At the intersection of halls, which led to the Introduction room, I stopped Clay.

"No, go outside and around back. I won't go in that room ever again." As childish as it might be, I wanted something about the impending Introduction to be on my own terms.

He grunted in acknowledgment. But, instead of turning to go out the nearby back door, he backtracked to the main entrance. He set me on my feet, snagged a spare jacket from one of the hooks, and carefully buttoned me in. I studied his face as he concentrated on each snap. Always thinking of me. When he finished, he scooped me back into his arms. I didn't protest.

Bundled warmly in a thick coat, I didn't cringe when he carried me out into the cold. The sky was dark, and the yard light didn't reach very far. Clay carried me toward the back of the building. I couldn't hear the werewolves as we approached, but saw their sparks briefly before a sharp pain not so gently reminded me not to look. I guessed close to seventy-five waited out there. It meant some of them had returned.

"Put me down, Clay," I said before we rounded the corner of the building. "I'll walk now." I didn't want to give the waiting unMated any reason to believe this wasn't a fair Introduction, even though it really wasn't. I still felt the pull for Clay.

Clay hesitated. It'd be safer for both of us if I stayed in his arms. He wouldn't fight, and I wouldn't fall. Yet, despite my anger over another forced Introduction, I truly felt sorry for the men who waited. The Introduction was just a false hope. One I couldn't take away from them.

"It'll be okay Clay. There are a lot of fast people here. I won't fall on my face." I spoke normally so everyone could hear. I really didn't want to fall on my face.

As soon as he set me on my feet, I walked around the corner with my shoulders back and head held high, determined to look strong. The slippers probably ruined the image, but I pretended otherwise.

The Elders stood by the back door. Only three of them this time.

"I'm Gabby. There will be no Introduction order. I won't have anyone left out, or leaving without a fair chance. So, instead of the stuffy cabin, let's just do this out here." The warmth of the jacket when not supplemented by Clay wasn't adequate, and I started to shiver slightly. "I believe the Elders mentioned I was ill, so if I start to stammer, bear with me."

The men began to line up. So many looking for a Mate, and this was just a fraction of what was really out there. Some were too far away to answer such a short notice call. I wondered how many of their kind I still hadn't met.

I met the eyes of several as I walked slowly down the not yet fully formed, long line. As I'd anticipated, the shivers grew more noticeable. This time the tremors were due to the cold, not my fatigue, and I fought not to duck further into my jacket. They needed to smell me. I kept walking and listened to Clay keep pace with me, just a few steps behind. Several of those I passed glanced at Clay, but no one actually commented on his presence.

Walking helped warm me a little. While the shivering didn't go away, it at least didn't increase.

A few exceptionally young Weres stood mixed in the line. I smiled kindly at each of them. For the most part, I paced in front of the line as if I performed a quiet military inspection. The males scented me as discreetly as possible, so hopeful for some type of connection. Many walked away after I passed.

About halfway down the line, I noticed a man step back and retreat into the woods. No unMated male walked away from an Introduction before being Introduced. It just wasn't done. The possibility of meeting a Mate was too important to them. Suspicious, I used my other sight despite the knowledge it would hurt. I pushed myself to look as far as I was able and gasped. A jolt of pain pierced my temple and forced me to close my other sight. My hand flew to my head, cradling it.

Clay moved so quickly, my hair lifted in his breeze. He stood close enough that I felt his heat at my back. I forced myself to straighten. The werewolf I faced looked confused. His eyes moved to the Elders standing several steps behind us.

"Gabby," Sam began, but I held up a hand.

"A moment, please," I managed to say.

Although it'd been a brief glimpse, I had seen a blue-grey spark moving away from our group. In the distance, three other blue-grey sparks waited. I couldn't say anything to Clay since I held everyone's attention, but I glanced at him. He studied the worry on my face for a moment then looked around. I felt safer because of it but still wished I could reach out to take his hand.

Instead, I turned to the men in front of me.

"I'm sorry. Like I said, I'm not feeling well. The pain in my head just took me by surprise." I took a steadying breath and continued my slow progress. The werewolves I passed watched me with concern. I probably looked even worse than I had just a moment ago.

More than halfway down the line, I came across a face I knew. He studied me, his playful smile from our last meeting absent. I used him as an excuse to stop and rest for a minute. I'd started shaking again, not from the cold.

"A f-face I know. I'm here as p-promised."

His eyes turned slightly remorseful at my words.

"I see that, little one. Although, it looks like you should be in bed instead."

"I would b-be if people would j-just leave me alone." I felt bad for saying it as soon as it left my mouth. How many times had these men stood in line hoping to meet some faceless girl? "B-but it's not meant t-to be. So, you know my name, but I d-don't know yours." I made conversation to make up for my harsh comment.

"Luke Taylor, love." He offered his hand, politely. A human custom, not a werewolf one. With my pull gone, could I safely touch him without causing some type of obsession? I hesitated and studied his face. He'd been desperate at the club, but now he looked resigned. He knew I wasn't the one for him.

Feeling sorry for him, I accepted his hand. A mild shock went through me to him.

Time stopped as my vision tunneled. The world around me disappeared, swallowed by darkness until only a pinprick of light remained. Then the darkness exploded into a spark-filled view of the world in its entirety. The tiny lights dazzled me. The yellow-green of humanity almost consumed the world. However, diversity persisted, though small.

Slowly, the sparks of each human, werewolf, and the yet unexplained blue-grey winked out of existence until a single, faint spark tinted with a violet halo remained on the east coast. My focus changed, honing in on that light. Like reading a map, I saw its exact location. My eyes swam in the yellow-violet light for a moment. Then, with a snap like an elastic band breaking, I returned to myself.

My lungs sucked in a breath with a loud whoosh, and my heart hammered in my chest. I ached all over and felt like vomiting. Only Luke's steady, warm hand, desperately clutched in my own, anchored me and kept me from falling apart.

Clay paced directly behind me. I vaguely imagined he wouldn't like me holding another man's hand for so long. I met Luke's gaze and swallowed down my bile before attempting to speak. He eyed me warily.

"I need to talk to you. Don't leave until I do."

His brow rose in surprise at my heavily slurred words.

"Clay," I whispered. My head lolled to the side as I tried to catch his eye. "Catch me." I let go of Luke's hand, and the world disappeared.

MY POUNDING HEAD WOKE ME. I couldn't tell if I lay in a dark room or just had my eyes closed. It didn't really matter. My skull would certainly shatter if I had to deal with light, too. I tried to whisper for water but only managed a faint croak. When I attempted to clear my throat, the pain in my head brought tears to my eyes. I was dying. I had to be to feel this way.

An arm gently slid under my neck and lifted my head a bit. A cool glass pressed to my lips, and I slowly sipped the contents. I stopped when the darkness began to pull me down again.

I WOKE SEVERAL MORE TIMES, only drinking a bit of water before passing out again. Each time the pain in my head decreased a little until, finally, I woke with more clarity.

"Water," I whispered into the darkness.

Again, an arm snaked under me and lifted me for a cool drink. I drained the cup. The arm lowered me, and I settled back onto the pillow. My ears rang in the silence.

"How long have I been sleeping?" I asked just to hear something.

Instead of an answer, I got a tight hug.

"I really hope you're Clay," I whispered breathlessly.

His gruff laugh wrapped around me, just as comforting as his hug.

"Can we turn on a light?"

He moved away from me, and I took the opportunity to sit up a bit and lean against the headboard. My legs still felt shaky.

The bedside lamp clicked on. I squinted against the light and regretted my request. My head ached slightly. I rubbed a hand over my face as my eyes watered. A tangle of my hair got in my way. I brushed it aside and felt the knots in it.

Blinking several times, I finally focused on Clay. He was dressed in the same clothes he'd worn outside. Maybe I hadn't been out that long after all. He stood near the bed and watched me with a tender, relieved expression.

"Clay, I think I know what's going on. Can you help me up? I really need a shower." And a toothbrush.

He shook his head.

"Clay, now's not the time to put your foot down. This is really important." I tried to sit all the way up, but couldn't. My head started to throb again. "Okay. Maybe you're right," I mumbled as I rubbed my forehead. "Can you get me something for my head, please? It feels like it going to explode all over the walls."

Clay leaned over me, smoothed back my hair, kissed my forehead, then left the room. The guest apartments didn't have any type of medicine in them because the werewolves typically didn't need it.

I waited until I heard the outside door close, then I struggled up again. My comment about my head was absolutely true. Therefore, I stayed in a sitting position for a minute before attempting to swing my legs off the bed. But headache or not, I needed to speak to Luke.

Reaching for my bag, I smiled again at Clay's packing. Flannel pants and a t-shirt were perfect, after all.

CHAPTER SEVENTEEN

I USED THE PANELED WALL FOR SUPPORT AS I MADE MY WAY TO THE bathroom. Sweat beaded my forehead when I finally stepped onto the cold, tiled floor. I flicked on the light and fan then set my clothes on the toilet tank.

Knowing I had limited time, I immediately turned the shower on to let the water warm. I moved to the sink, caught my reflection in the mirror, and cringed. Sunken eyes, hollow cheeks, and hair that stuck out at varying angles, reflected back at me. Without a doubt, Clay really did care about me. I shook my head then brushed my teeth, giving the water an extra minute to heat.

When I finished, I struggled out of my clothes and further depleted my waning energy. I eyed the high edge of the tub and thought back to when Clay had insisted on helping me. If I fell, I'd never hear the end of it. Bracing myself, I successfully stepped over the edge and tugged the curtain closed.

The hot spray felt great, but I didn't pause to warm up. If I stayed too long, I'd lose what little energy I had or Clay would discover me. I grabbed the all-in-one hair wash and lathered my natty head. My arms grew heavy as I rinsed, and with relief, I turned off the water. Navigating the high edge proved more difficult the second time, and I clutched at the wall after a near fall.

The fan worked to suck the built up heat and steam from the room as I hurried to dry off. My unsteady legs forced me to sit down to finish dressing. The cold helped hurry the process.

I used my towel to bundle my dirty clothes then moved to the door. Though it felt like the process took forever, I knew only a few minutes had passed since Clay left. If I could get to my room and dry my hair, I'd be home free. I pulled open the door and yelped. The steady thump in my head increased its tempo.

Clay stood just outside the door, leaning against the wall. He held a glass of water in one hand and two pills in the other. I tried to read his face, but he kept it perfectly blank. I hoped that meant he wasn't angry with me. Desperate to relieve the pain in my head, I released my death grip on the door and gulped down the pills.

When I tried handing him the empty glass, he shook his head and picked me up again. My feet had been getting cold, anyway. Holding the empty glass, I sighed and rested my head against his chest.

He went toward my room, and I almost complained until I saw what he'd done. He'd changed the sheets and remade the bed. Socks, slippers, and my hairbrush lay on the quilt, waiting. He'd known I would go for the shower and had given me privacy even though he hadn't wanted me to get out of bed. Not only that, but he'd gotten everything ready for when I finished.

I looked at him. He studied me, his arms still securely around me. I leaned in, kissed his cheek tenderly, and hesitated there. He smelled so good. I just wanted to curl back up with him. But I couldn't. I pulled back and looked at him again.

"You are so sweet, and I truly appreciate this, but I'm not going back to bed, Clay. I need to see Luke."

The muscles in his jaw clenched as he stepped into the room and carefully set me on the bed. He left without a backward glance.

I stared at the empty doorway puzzled until the outer door slammed hard enough that I heard the wood crack. I flinched.

"I shouldn't have said I needed to see Luke."

I hurried to put on my socks and slippers while hoping Clay wouldn't go too far. The movement made my head feel like it would fall off at any moment. The pills needed to kick in soon. I rubbed my brow again, but it didn't relieve the pain at all. This wasn't a normal headache. I just needed to deal with it. With a sigh, I stood.

I'd only made it to the living room when the door burst open again. I stared at Clay as he dragged Luke in by the cuff of one pant leg. Luke didn't appear to mind. Instead, he was laughing. His hands clutched the waistband of his pants to keep Clay from pulling them off entirely. After they cleared the threshold, I saw a crowd watching from the hallway. Not good. News of this would get back to the Elders. No doubt Sam would want to talk to me as soon as he found out I was awake. I moved from the couch to the door and slammed it closed. The poor door would need some repair work.

Clay reached the middle of the room, dropped Luke's leg, and without pause, turned back to the door. I didn't move away from the exit. He reached for the knob without meeting my gaze, but I stopped him with a hand held up.

"Clay, I need you to stay and listen. Please."

He still didn't look at me, and I knew asking to speak with Luke had hurt him. Why wouldn't it? Had I really ever given him much hope we had a future together? Sam showed up at our door just days ago saying I'd rejected Clay and needed to do the Introductions again. Instead of putting my foot down, we went back. Granted I'd told Clay I didn't like to see him hurt and admitted we both knew he was the one for me, but we hadn't talked about what we'd do about it.

"Please," I said again, when he hadn't moved. "Give me a chance." I touched his face and forced him to meet my gaze. "I've asked so much of you already and know it's not fair to ask again, but I am." I chose my words carefully aware of our audience inside the apartment and in the hall.

He sighed, reached up to cup my face, and gently smoothed his thumb over my cheek. A tender look crept into his eyes before he abruptly dropped his hands, turned, and headed toward the still laughing Luke. Clay dragged his feet as he stepped over Luke. Luke grunted when a foot connected with his ribs, and his laughter started to quiet.

As Clay settled on the chair against the wall, Luke sat up.

"Most people wouldn't laugh while being dragged through the Compound like that." I stayed by the door because I didn't want either of them leaving. I knew I couldn't stop them physically even on my best day, but I'd cry if I had to.

Luke stood and turned toward Clay with a grin, ignoring me to taunt Clay.

"I've never seen anyone hold a transformation like that. He was man, but the fangs, ears, fur...it was amazing, and hilarious, mate," he said as he settled himself on the couch.

"Um, isn't that a sign that he's in an extreme emotional state?" I asked Luke. He didn't appear to hear me.

I walked behind Luke and smacked him hard on the back of the head. It really hurt my hand, but it got his attention.

"Meaning, you should stop trying to annoy him."

Since Clay sat across from Luke, I moved to Clay and gingerly perched on one of his knees. He held still for a moment then his hands gripped my hips. He pulled back so I fully sat on his lap and turned me so we could both see Luke. Much better than sitting in my own chair. Warmer, too.

Having successfully gained both their attentions, I decided to get to the point.

"Luke, what happened when I touched you? What did you feel?"

"One hell of a shock. Listen, did you bring me here for a reason, or was it just to rub your relationship with him in my face?" Luke nodded at Clay, and though Luke's usual smile still curved his lips, his words conveyed the agitation he tried to hide.

"It's for a reason." I tried to lean forward, but Clay wrapped his arms loosely around my waist. He didn't give an inch, and I didn't fight it. I'd pushed him enough for the night...or day. I still didn't know how long I'd been out.

"How long have I been sleeping?"

"Two days, love. Everyone's been pretty worried, and the Elders are waiting to talk to you."

"I bet." My eyes drifted to the door. I focused and immediately cradled my throbbing head. My eyes watered as I tried to breathe through the pain. "Crap."

Behind me, Clay grunted in annoyance.

Luke's smile slipped. "Listen, I think you should still be in bed, little one. No disrespect intended, but you don't look well."

My hair hung wet and uncombed around me. I could imagine what I looked like. I pressed my cool fingertips to one temple and wished I hadn't been so stupid. Clay started to rub my back soothingly, working his way up to my neck and then lightly stroking my hair. It helped.

"I know you're right, but I can't go back to sleep yet. I need you to tell me what happened."

Nicole told me that she'd really connected with Randy. Even after my pull wore off, they had continued to date. I couldn't go back to the two women at the club to find out what they'd experienced. I needed to get more information from Luke.

"I don't know what happened, love. You shocked me, told me not to leave, then fainted. After that, Clay picked you up and ran inside with you. He hasn't let anyone near you for two days. We only knew you were still alive because he didn't take off into the woods."

Clay's tight hug when I woke made more sense. He'd been worried about me, taking care of me and keeping the Elders away.

I forced myself to stay focused on Luke.

"And after Clay left, what about you? What did you do?"

Luke began to look uncomfortable. "Uh, I went out for a bit then came back here."

"The constant attention probably went to your head," I muttered. Luke was too sure of himself for any woman to have a chance.

His startled expression told me I was right.

"Did you meet anyone special while I was out?" I asked glancing at the door again and wishing we didn't have an audience.

I looked back in time to catch Luke shaking his head. Still unMated. I'd thought as much but had to be sure. Normal humans wouldn't tempt him, and there were too few unMated females at the Compound. I had an idea but needed sleep and time to think through everything.

"Luke, there is so much I don't understand, and I really need your help." I nodded toward the door and hoped he'd know I meant with the Elders who probably waited outside. "I need some time to myself to understand what I'm feeling." This is why Clay had to be in the room with me. Anyone standing in the hall would probably think I felt torn between Clay and Luke.

Luke looked from me to Clay then back again. He started to ask a question, hesitated, then gazed at the door once more. Finally, he stood.

"I'll be around," he said.

I hoped he'd understood I wanted his help to get us out of here. The door had barely closed behind him when a knock sounded.

Still sitting on Clay's lap, I turned to him. He met my gaze. I shook my head and wrapped my arms around his neck. His arms cradled me as he stood and carried me to the bedroom. He set me on the bed, covered me, then closed the door. I listened to him answer the apartment door.

I heard Sam's voice but didn't bother trying to hear what Sam had to say. The Elders would come to get me soon enough. My exhaustion didn't wait for them. I fell asleep again.

MY STOMACH GROWLED SO LOUDLY it woke me. I listened for a minute before opening my eyes. Clay had left the lamp on so I could see. I turned my head. He lay next to me, on top the covers. Given the steady cadence of his breathing, he still slept. I let my mind drift, content to think and let him get the rest he needed.

Whatever I had in me, I could temporarily pass to people via a shock, but the effect only lasted until I recovered. I could also zap more than one person at a time, and I felt certain now that my emotions, in addition to my touch, triggered the transfer. The drain I experienced afterward varied. It felt like the flu the first time, but when I passed it to the two women, the symptoms intensified.

Shocking Luke had been different. I couldn't say if the drain had been worse since I'd started out drained. However, focusing on a specific person's spark was new.

Based on the yellow-violet coloring, I guessed it belonged to another compatible, like me. Could it mean my ability was to find Mates for the people I touched? But then, why hadn't I zoomed in on a single person when touching the others? Maybe a werewolf amplified my ability, and the view appeared whether I wanted it or not. Or maybe one spark had stood out when I'd touched the rest, but I hadn't focused on my spark-sight to check.

But what about my pull? Where did that play into this? There were still too many possibilities. I needed a test group. Immediately, I thought of Rachel and Peter. When I sensed them without touching Rachel, I knew they were a perfect match. If I tried to pass my pull to Rachel and saw Peter's spark, I'd have my answer. If it didn't work on them, I wouldn't rule out my theory completely. The difference between human and werewolf might be the key to the results. I could experiment on Clay. He knew I was his match.

In addition to figuring out why I had the ability to pass on my gift, I needed to understand why I saw different werewolf colors. The one who'd left the line and the others waiting for him worried me.

Regardless of my anger at Sam, if trouble stalked the pack, he needed to know. But I needed to talk to Clay about it before I could talk to anyone else. He would help me figure out how it all tied together. However, I couldn't talk to Clay here. There were too many ears, and I was still uncertain if I could trust Sam with everything.

I needed to leave before the Elders started pushing me for answers I didn't have. What reason could I give Sam for my sudden faint during the Introduction? He'd know any lie before I told it. And if I gave him the truth, would he then share it with all the Elders? After seeing those werewolves leave the Introduction, I couldn't blindly trust Elder Joshua. Too many werewolves of that same color acted unusually.

Feeling a light caress on my hair, I turned to look at Clay, who watched me again.

"Do I say good morning or is it close to goodnight again?"

He smiled at me, reached down to twine his fingers through mine, and brought my hand to his mouth. Instead of kissing it, he whipped his head toward the door. A silent snarl pulled back his lips. The bedroom door opened, and Luke poked his head in.

"Better hurry. You carry her, and I'll grab her things," he said, speaking directly to Clay.

I let out a relieved breath. Luke had understood and come through. I opened my mouth to thank him, but Clay leapt off the bed and quickly scooped me into his arms, covers and all. With the blankets twisted around me and partially covering my face, I felt a moment of disoriented panic as he lifted me.

I shook my head to dislodge the blanket and sent Clay a quick scowl. His lips twitched.

Over his shoulder, I saw Luke cramming my things into my ragged messenger bag. My bag wouldn't last through another werewolf packing.

Clay left the room. Just in case anyone else roamed the halls, I laid my head on Clay's shoulder. He held me closely and walked quickly. We quietly made it out the main entrance with Luke following us.

The black sky twinkled with stars, and crickets conversed with their night song as the two werewolves stealthily moved over the graveled parking area. It had to be Monday night. I regretted missing a day's worth of classes, but there'd been no way to help it.

The car faced the gate. Luke must have moved it. The door's loud creaking groan made us all cringe. Clay quickly settled me inside, reached across me to secure the seat belt, then silently jogged around the hood to get in behind the wheel.

Luke handed me my bag then moved to close the door. I motioned for him to wait and dug in a side pocket of my bag for a pencil stub and paper. In those few moments after I shocked him and before I passed out, I'd gleaned some information about the person I saw. Whoever she was, Luke needed to find her and help me understand if some of my suspicions were right. Was she like me? Was she his Mate?

I jotted him a hasty note and handed it to him with a wave. He quickly closed the door. I hoped giving him the information was the right thing to do. I barely knew him. Would he even try to find her or just hand the information over to an Elder? Worried, I looked at him through the window. He didn't see me. His eyes scanned my note. He crumpled it in his hand and spun toward a waiting motorcycle.

Clay pulled away from the Compound, spitting gravel with the tires. The motorcycle roared to life and quickly zipped past us. Luke saluted me with a wicked grin then disappeared from sight. I peeked in the side mirror and caught the reason for their loud exit. Sam stood on the porch, his gaze locked on us. He grew smaller as we sped away. I wished I knew whom to trust.

I laid my head back and closed my eyes. What a crappy Introduction weekend. The worst yet. I hoped there were no more in my future.

The drone of the engine and the soothing vibrations of the tires put me right to sleep. I dozed the whole way home, waking when Clay lifted me from the car. With blankets still twisted around me, he carried me to my room and gently set me on the bed.

A few minutes later, he settled next to me. It didn't matter anymore if he wore his fur or stayed as a man. He remained with me. It was enough.

CLAY TRIED to keep me home Tuesday. First, he planted himself, in his fur, in front of my door so I couldn't get out of the bedroom. Then, when I pleaded to use the bathroom, he allowed me out and took the opportunity to hide my keys.

My suspicion rose when he calmly watched me get ready. I discovered the missing keys and resorted to further pleading. I explained my need to talk to Nicole in hopes of piecing together the puzzle of my abilities. The one-sided conversation reminded me of the first time I'd reasoned with him.

Of course, Rachel caught part of my serious chat with our dog and did a double take on her way to the bathroom. I laughed and waved her away, then gave Clay a look. Grudgingly, Clay led me to my keys, and I made it to campus on time.

I parked and took a minute to lean my forehead against the steering wheel, still recovering from sharing my ability with three people in one weekend. Clay had obviously sensed it. If Tuesday hadn't been the only day I saw Nicole, I would have stayed in bed. Steeling myself, I got out of the car and trudged across campus.

For the first time ever, I didn't pay much attention to the instructor. Instead, I sat by Nicole and whispered questions freely, but failed to uncover anything more than what she'd already shared. Men had hit on her quite a bit after the

Halloween party. She attributed the attention to the costume, which she planned to reuse. Since it wasn't a bad costume, I didn't dissuade her of the idea. Better to think it was the costume than a freak friend passing some kind of power to her.

I smiled and waved goodbye to her at the end of the class. People pushed past me to leave. I watched them go and dreaded the long walk back to the car. With my pull gone, thanks to Luke and two strangers, I could safely ask someone for a piggyback ride. I'd seen it happen before. Yet, I couldn't picture explaining to Clay why I smelled like another guy.

RACHEL AND CLAY-THE-MAN stood in the kitchen together making an early dinner. Surprised, I hesitated in the doorway. Rachel typically spent her free time with Peter or at work. And Clay tended to stay in his fur when she was home.

Rachel paused her one-sided conversation to wink at me. I glanced at Clay, stepped further into the room, and slowly closed the door behind me. Clay remained focused on the food he stirred in the pan. Rachel walked past me on her way to get silverware.

"You didn't tell me he could *cook*," Rachel stage whispered.

Giving her a crooked smile, I made my way to a kitchen chair. I was exhausted.

"He cooks, he cleans, he warms up my feet at night, and he keeps the toilet seat down...so hands off. He's mine."

Rachel laughed, and Clay turned to give me an undecipherable look. I had a feeling he liked the "mine" part.

"How you feeling?" Rachel said, coming over to touch my forehead. "I asked Clay, but he didn't say." Rachel gave Clay a pointed look. Clay shrugged and went back to cooking at the stove.

"Not the best, but it's getting better. I think it's mental exhaustion, nothing contagious."

"Mm," she said in a noncommittal way as she eyed me speculatively. "I still think you should go to the doctor. Could it be something you didn't think of yet?" She casually leaned close to me. "Pregnant?" she whispered.

Clay dropped the spoon. It hit the stove and bounced back at him. He caught it tight after a close fumble. Both Rachel and I stared at his back, but with dignity, he stayed facing the stove and kept cooking.

I turned back to Rachel with a wide smile. "No. Now, behave."

We ate dinner companionably. After we finished, they shoved me out of the kitchen with orders to rest while they cleaned up. I went to my room and changed into my lounge clothes while listening to Rachel tell Clay about a cute pair of shoes she'd found. It made me smile. She would never break him. He'd never talk.

Dinner, though delicious and entertaining, had drained my reserves. I lay on top the comforter thinking I'd rest for a bit before I tackled that day's homework. I still needed to talk to Clay about what I'd seen in the woods at the Introduction.

SUNLIGHT PENETRATED the darkness behind my eyelids. I no longer sprawled sideways on the bed on top the comforter but underneath it, snugly tucked in. Clay sat up in the space next to me, pillows stacked behind him as he read a book. His posture didn't fool me. He really sat there to watch over me while I slept. I knew with an unexplainable certainty that he would never leave me again.

"Good morning," I said, pulling the covers up to my chin. Thanks to Rachel-the-heat-miser, the room felt cool, but I enjoyed lower rent.

Clay closed his book as soon as I woke and turned to examine me.

"I want to talk to you but keep falling asleep. If I do it again, wake me up." I smiled at him when he pulled me close to snuggle against him. It was much warmer that way.

"During the Introduction when I said my head hurt, I saw a man step away from the line. I know how your kind view Introductions. It didn't seem right so I peeked at his spark. It hurt like hell, but I saw he had the same color light as Elder Joshua and the wolf that'd attacked us. I thought maybe it could be the same guy, that he needed to leave because you'd recognize his scent. Then I saw three more, further away. Something's going on, but I can't figure out what.

"I know you didn't stay with the pack full-time, but did you ever notice any of them acting different?"

He shook his head, actually giving me a direct answer. It should have made me happy. Instead, I sighed. I still didn't have a clue.

He gently stroked my hair as I thought it through. "If only I could trust Sam.

If I could ask him questions about Elder Joshua without him repeating them, I might be able to figure this thing out."

My head started to hurt again. Maybe if I stopped thinking about it so much, the answer would just come to me.

SAM CALLED my cell the following weekend. I'd expected to hear from him much sooner. He surprised me by asking if I'd come back to the Compound over the long holiday weekend. I hedged. Did he want me to return so he could arrange another Introduction?

When I didn't give a definitive answer, he launched into a long speech about how he knew he'd disappointed me and how he really did worry about me, not just the pack. I tried to be understanding but didn't bend much.

Finally, he came right out and asked what had happened to me during the last visit. I answered vaguely, claiming ignorance. Werewolves couldn't recognize lies as well over the phone. A long moment of silence passed. When he spoke, he didn't comment on my answer but again asked that I consider coming home over holiday break. I knew he meant the Compound and told him I'd think about it.

After that, he continued to call me daily just to talk. Most of our brief conversations touched on weather, school, or investments. Anything pack related stayed off limits. I could tell he was concerned, but trust, once lost, took longer to earn back. I wouldn't tell him any of my suspicions until I could confirm some of them.

FOR THE NEXT FEW WEEKS, the challenges stopped, and I pushed the pack, strange colored sparks, and my pull from my head. Instead, I focused on my studies.

Clay worked at Dale's while I stayed on campus. I hadn't given up trying to figure out why he'd picked Dale to be his employer. However, whenever I asked, he responded with a shrug. I never asked him if he followed me to school as Luke had suggested. Some things I preferred to remain a mystery.

I thought Clay's expectations would change after our kiss, but he never pushed for more. He continued to stay in his fur most of the time, except for

Tuesday nights when he had dinner waiting for me. I looked forward to our nights together and not just because he cooked exceptionally well.

Rachel knew I was spending more time with him, and on one of our quiet nights together, she asked about Clay-the-man while Clay-the-dog lay curled on the floor next to me.

"You are so weird about him. What is it about the guy that keeps you coming back?" She sat on the couch, folding her summer clothes and packing them into a tote.

Smiling slightly, I turned the page of the book in my lap before I answered.

"You don't know him like I do."

"How can you know him at all when you two don't talk?"

"You don't need to talk to get to know someone. You just need to listen," I said absently, trying to concentrate on my reading. My words rattled in my head for a moment before what I said clicked into place. I froze and looked at Clay. His brown eyes met mine steadily.

Damn the patient, clever dog. A smile twitched my lips. I never had a chance...and I didn't mind.

"But that's what I'm saying. He doesn't talk. What are you listening to?"

I laughed at her and myself. "Actions speak louder than words," I quoted, finally looking up at Rachel. "He's there when I need him, he's kind and caring, he keeps me safe, and as you've seen, he cooks and cleans. What's not to like, Rachel?"

She grumbled under her breath but didn't have anything else to add.

Clay walked over to her and lay on some of her dresses, ending her mutterings that I should get out and meet other people. She laughed at him then tried to move him. He laid his head on his paws and winked at me. He wasn't mad but enjoyed giving Rachel some grief.

Shaking my head, I went to the fridge and left Rachel to tug her dresses out from under his bulk on her own. In the fridge, I saw a new carton of orange juice along with a double-chocolate cake. Two layers of chocolate frosted goodness. My mouth watered. I usually ignored the food Rachel bought, but that one begged my attention.

"Can I have a piece of your cake?"

"I thought it was yours. It was here when I got home," she called back.

I stood staring at the cake a long time. How could I be so blind? He'd shrugged when I'd asked why he'd gotten his job, but the answer, wrapped in layers of sinful chocolate mousse frosting, sat before my eyes.

Thinking back, I identified several of the little things I'd previously overlooked. Things I'd assumed Rachel had purchased, like movies I'd mentioned I wanted to see. He'd gotten his job for *me* because of my speech the day after we'd met. My heart melted a little as I thought of all the effort he'd put into trying to be what I needed, and I knew I fought a losing battle.

THE AIR GREW COLDER and snow started to fall the week before Thanksgiving. The wind howled outside, still finding a way past the new windows. Despite the low-set thermostat, the heat kicked in often, and I worried about the bill. Even with Clay warming my feet, I'd added another quilt to the bed.

Broke and out of quilts, I lay under the covers, shivering. I wore two pairs of lounge pants, a t-shirt, and a sweatshirt. If I could just fall asleep, I knew I'd warm eventually. During the night, I usually stripped to one layer. But warming the bed took forever...on my own.

"Screw this," I said, sitting up. I started pulling off my sweatshirt. The streetlight filtered through the curtains, so I could make out the shapes in my room. I tossed the sweatshirt toward the closet.

Clay lifted his head, tilting it just so.

I ignored him for the moment and shimmied out of my second layer of pants while trying to stay under the covers. The pants soared through the air and landed next to the shirt.

"Clay, will you keep me warm tonight?" I'd barely whispered the words when he jumped off the bed.

A moment later, he pulled back the covers and joined me. He wrapped his arms around me and pulled me to his chest. Bare chest. I sighed, pressed my face against his skin, warming my cold nose, and wrapped my free arm around his waist. Then, I tucked my feet under his calves. He grunted slightly but didn't loosen his hold.

"No more fur at night. Deal?"

The blankets and his chest muffled my voice, but I knew he heard me. He kissed the top of my head, the only part exposed. I smiled, figuring it meant yes.

The next morning my cell phone rang, waking me. Still wrapped in Clay's warmth, I didn't move right away. He reached over me, plucked it from the bedpost, and handed it to me. Only Sam and Rachel had my number.

I could hear movement in the house and looked at the display, expecting Sam's number. Instead, it was one I didn't recognize.

I answered with a questioning, "Hello?"

"Gabby, I found her, but..."

"Luke?" I hadn't heard from him since we'd left the Compound.

"Yes. I understand you think she's important, but she's not even eighteen. How am I supposed to get her to come with me?"

I sat up excitedly and knocked back the covers in the process, exposing both Clay and me to the cool air. Clay grunted a complaint.

"I can't believe you actually found her! I need to talk to her. If she's like me, which I think she is, you had better bring her to the Compound. I hate to admit it, but the Elders need to know."

"Fine. You better be there when we get there," he said with an edge. The line went dead.

I pulled the phone from my ear to look at it, puzzled. Luke never had an edge. Slowly, I grinned. Had I been right? Was he now dealing with his potential Mate? Smiling hugely, I hoped she gave Mr. Confident a little hell.

CHAPTER EIGHTEEN

WITH THE FREEZE CAME THE NIGHT RACHEL THAWED TOWARD Clay-the-man.

A heavy snow started to fall just as Clay and I went to bed. His arm curled around my waist, and my head rested on his shoulder. Asking him to sleep beside me was the best decision I ever made, and it made me finally understand that *I* determined the pace of our relationship. He had waited patiently for me to invite him in and would wait patiently for the next step, whatever I decided that would be.

My phone rang and pulled me from my warm cocoon. I recognized the number and answered.

"Hey. I'm coming home," Rachel said. "It's snowing too badly to go to Peter's." She'd caught on that Clay spent the night often.

"Thanks for the heads up," I said with a laugh. "We'll see you soon."

Clay got out of bed as I ended the call. Puzzled, I watched him dress in warm clothes. He left the room. The back door opened and closed. A minute later, I heard the rasp of a shovel on the driveway. I smiled, moved to his warm spot, and burrowed in.

The sound of the plow scraping past disrupted the silent world and kept me awake. Clay stayed outside, keeping the entrance to the driveway clear until Rachel came home. I heard her thanking Clay as they came in together. He didn't say anything in return, but I imagined he gave her one of his rare nods.

When he returned, I flipped the covers back for him and moved out of his place.

"I was just keeping it warm for you," I lied.

He laughed and pulled me close. Even after being outside so long, he still warmed me.

My lids grew heavy, and he kissed the top of my head.

WITH THE LONG holiday around the corner, I needed to cross a few things off my mental checklist. First, I needed to pin down my next victim for a power swap. After that, I needed to talk to Sam and hope for answers.

I'd planned to test my ability on Rachel before I went back to the Compound, but Clay watched me closely. Since he knew something happened when I touched other people, he subtly kept everyone out of reach. I pretended not to notice so he wouldn't become even more protective.

Luck turned in my favor when Rachel texted and asked me to meet her and Peter for lunch. Having just left my morning class, the timing couldn't have worked better. She suggested a small ma and pa diner close to the campus; the same one Clay and I had walked to so long ago for our sunrise breakfast. I quickly agreed, told her what to order for me, and rushed over the scraped sidewalks to my car.

I cautiously drove the few blocks to the diner. The salt on the roads made everything slushy, and my worn tires liked to slide when I least expected. I eased into the crowded parking lot and snagged a spot near the door.

Through the windows, I spied Rachel and Peter already snuggled in a booth. The waitress had just delivered our food, and they didn't notice me park or get out of the car. They stared at each other. I saw their lips moving in quiet conversation. Rachel kept stopping to grin at Peter.

I opened the door, briefly blasting the patrons with the frigid air. It caught Rachel and Peter's attention. They wore secret smiles as they watched me approach. I slid in across from them, the vinyl seat squeaking, and peeled off my hat and gloves. The warmth of the room heated my cheeks and turned them red in seconds.

"Hi, guys. This is a nice surprise. What's the occasion?" As soon as I said it, I noticed the glint on Rachel's ring finger. "Oh, wow..." It came out sounding as stunned as I felt. The rational side of me said it was too soon, but the part of me that saw them together and saw their synchronized pulses, knew it was perfect.

"Peter proposed last night, and I said yes." Rachel's happiness bubbled from her.

I stood and reached across the table to hug her. She bounced up from her seat and excitedly hugged me back. I grabbed hold of the opportunity. Focusing, I repeated what I'd thought and felt the other times I'd shocked someone. Was she doing the right thing? Was Peter the right one for her? What if I was wrong? I dredged up all my concerns and hope for her, held it tight within me and then let it flow through to her.

The shock jolted us apart immediately. The intensity of it burned my fingertips. Rachel settled next to Peter with a surprised laugh. I sat too, smiled, and opened my sight wide, forcing the full view of the world as I'd seen when I'd shocked Luke. It strained me a bit, but I didn't let go. This time I really looked. The tiny sparks of all living beings covered the world. I focused the view so I could see the occupants of the diner in detail.

Peter and Rachel pulsed in time as usual. I expected Peter to be different, somehow, to signify his match with Rachel, but I couldn't see anything unusual. They did appear a bit dimmer, like their light had faded. I remembered that happening when I'd touched Luke and quickly pulled back from such a close up view.

While I looked at Rachel's tiny spark, something caught my eye. Faint pulses rippled out from her. Much like the ripples made by a pebble thrown into a pond, they spread outward, passing through all other sparks. One approached Charlene's spark. Instead of passing through, it bounced off and came speeding back.

Startled, I scanned the sparks, zooming in and out as needed until I identified five uniquely colored sparks like me. The ripples didn't pass through them. Instead, they bounced off and came flying back. Right at me, not Rachel.

The return wave of the spark midway between Charlene and me hit. I absorbed it, and a wave of dizziness rushed through me. That was the first indication of the drain I'd felt previously. I watched Charlene's wave approach and knew that when it hit, I'd get worse. It made sense now, how I grew weak and sick shortly after transferring my ability. Each hit of return energy knocked me further on my butt. If I'd paid more attention to it before, I would have noticed it when I shocked Nicole and the other girls. But why had it acted differently when I'd touched Luke? Why had just one of the five become focused? I still had so much to figure out. For now, the clock ticked, counting down the time until I would turn into a shaking mess.

I'd noted all of this in the few short seconds it'd taken for Rachel's surprised expression to clear.

"I'm so happy for both of you," I said before she could say anything about my momentary pause.

I smiled while I braced myself for Charlene's energy wave, just minutes away.

"Gabby, after Peter proposed, we both decided we'd tortured you and Scott enough and should get our own place. So as soon as we find something, I plan on moving out. I wanted to give you as much time as possible to find a roommate before I actually left."

I nodded and smiled at her as if I understood. Would another roommate really put up with Clay-the-moody-dog, or Clay-the-mute-man? I couldn't blame them for wanting to find their own place. I knew she missed Peter when they were apart.

She picked up her fork and started eating her salad. Peter took another bite of his BLT sandwich. My burger and fries sat before me, still untouched.

Her announcement and the continued strain of staying focused on the vast scale of lights for so long took their toll. My head started to pound. I saw the second wave rush toward me and couldn't help the slight wince when the pounding in my head increased to full force. I clenched my teeth to keep them from chattering.

Thankfully, Rachel still wore her love-goggles and didn't notice.

"Don't worry about me. Clay will be there enough that I'll make him pay the other half of the rent. So, did you set a date?"

The conversation turned to wedding plans until Peter glanced at his watch and reminded Rachel of their next class. She pouted playfully. I smiled, barely holding back a shiver, and assured her we'd make time to talk wedding stuff soon. The third wave hit, stunning me. Two to go, and they weren't far off.

"You feeling all right?" Peter asked as they stood. "You look very pale."

"I'm fine. I skipped breakfast, and I think my blood sugar is getting revenge. It will pass." I picked up a fry and ate it. My stomach rebelled.

"You should have that tested," Peter warned, helping Rachel into her jacket.

I nodded and reached for the ketchup while they walked out the door. Squirting a big pile on my plate, I looked up in time to wave to Rachel as they backed out of their spot. I pretended to nibble on a fry as I watched their car.

Once they left, I dug out my cell with shaking hands and dialed Dale's Auto Body. It looked like I would need to miss a few more classes.

Dale answered after the third ring.

"Hi, Dale, it's Gabby...Clay's girlfriend." It felt weird giving myself that title, but I pushed it aside. Bigger issues to deal with. "If he's there, can I talk to him?"

Dale chuckled. "Sure, but I don't imagine it'd be much of a conversation."

I heard him call out to Clay. A moment later, a husky voice said, "Hello?"

After not talking to me for so long, hearing his voice startled and annoyed me slightly. He would talk to a perfect stranger, but not me? I opened my mouth to say something about it, but the pain in my head insistently prodded me to get on with the important news.

"Clay, I did it again. I'm at the diner where we had breakfast. I need you to come get me before it gets worse."

He didn't say anything for so long that I looked at the phone to see if I still had a signal. The screen said disconnected. Would it have killed him to say "Okay" or maybe even "Bye" before hanging up? His hello had been too shocking to recall the sound of his voice.

I sighed and put my cell away. With Sam's frequent calls and Rachel's occasional texts, my remaining minutes dipped into the double digits. I needed to adjust my budget to buy more airtime. Did life really need to throw me this many curveballs? And all at once?

I forced myself to eat more of my mostly untouched meal so the waitress wouldn't bother me as I waited.

The last of the waves hit me. Only determination and a hand over my mouth kept me from whimpering. After about ten minutes, I settled the bill and watched out the window for Clay, barely checking the need to curl into a ball and lie down on the padded bench. The waitress kept a close eye on me, probably thinking she would need to clean up barf soon. She might.

Dale's huge tow truck pulled into the parking lot. Clay opened his door and leapt out while it still rolled to a stop. Through the window, he spotted me. His eyes never left me as he strode in and Dale pulled away.

Clay still wore his greasy coveralls, and with his hair pulled back, he looked like an angel—a grimy one—coming to save me. Again.

"Hi," I whispered, tilting my head to meet his gaze.

His eyes softened as he looked me over.

My legs trembled just sitting there but with so many students from campus,

I wouldn't leave by any means other than my own two feet. I handed him the keys to my car, slid out of the booth, and reached for him. Standing, I wrapped my arms around his waist. I hoped it looked like I wanted to snuggle instead of holding myself up. He maneuvered us out the door and to my car with no trouble.

Minutes later, he carried me through the back door. He knew the drill and gave me a drink before he tucked me into bed.

CLOSE TO DAWN, I woke feeling much better. The shivers had faded while I slept, and the lingering headache was manageable. The full bladder wasn't.

I snuck to the bathroom, hoping not to wake Clay. But when I got back, the light was on and he lay awake waiting for me. With his hair still back, I easily read his expression. I hated when he looked at me like that. All disappointed and hurt.

I stalled saying anything until I slid back under the covers. Warmer, I met his gaze.

"I'm sorry. I didn't plan it..." Technically. "...but I think I've figured out what I am, Clay. I'm like a GPS for werewolves. I can find people. Not just people, but compatible Mates like me." My feet refused to warm so I tucked them under his legs. He didn't even flinch. Probably because I did it all the time.

"When I touched Rachel yesterday, I really paid attention. I saw the energy I release when I shock a person. It goes into them and pulses outward, passing through almost everyone else. And everyone this energy passes through fades in my mind, almost dimming to the point of non-existence. Five people didn't fade, Clay. In the whole world, there are only five. Six if you include me. And when the energy I release touches them, it bounces off to come crashing back on me. That's what's been knocking me on my butt."

Unsure if I should bring up the rest, I played with the quilt for a second. He nudged me, and I smiled at him. I should know better. Even when he didn't like what I had to say, he listened. He always listened.

"It was different when I touched Luke. With him, I zoomed in on one specific spark, a yellow-violet one on the east coast. The paper I gave Luke? That was directions to find her. I think she belongs with him. I think I found his Mate just by touching him." I grinned when I recalled the phone call from Luke. "I don't think he appreciates my help, though."

Through my entire monolog, Clay lay on his side, up on an elbow, and watched me intently. His serious expression conveyed his concentration.

When I finished, instead of shrugging as I expected, his head snapped toward my bedroom window. He snarled softly as he threw off the covers and crouched on the bed, head moving to track something I couldn't see.

I scrambled to my knees, staring at him. Fangs exploded from his mouth, and his ears changed. Now I knew why Luke had laughed at Clay's partial transformation but didn't find it a bit funny as I watched.

Clay remained frozen in a crouch, listening. I held my breath and strained to hear what he heard. The beating of my own heart filled my ears.

Both our heads turned toward a chuffing laugh near the window. A taunt to draw Clay out.

I opened my mouth to point it out but never made a sound. Clay's hand darted out and nudged me backward. I lost my balance. As I tumbled over the edge of the mattress, he leapt toward the bedroom door. He cleared it and switched off the light before I landed on the floor.

The front door slammed against the wall. The explosive sound echoed through the house as did the chilly breeze that gusted along the floor. I shivered, hidden in the semi-darkness beside the bed. The door closed itself on the backswing, cutting off the cold.

I righted myself as I caught my breath. Luckily, I'd landed on a pillow which I'd knocked off with me. Any recovery I'd experienced while I slept had vanished as soon as I hit the floor. My head pounded with renewed vigor, but I thought clearly enough to wonder if Rachel had spent the night here or with Peter. The sudden noise outside distracted me from my thoughts.

Loud snarls and low growls filled the air.

Despite Clay's obvious wish that I stay down, I risked a look over the mattress as my eyes adjusted to the gloom. The window gave a soft glow from the streetlights. The sound of my frightened breathing echoed in the room. I quieted it, pulled myself up, and crawled over the bed toward the window. Cautiously, I inched the curtain aside to peek out.

Clay and another man fought in the snow on the front yard. I cringed at the sight of Clay's bare feet and chest. The challenger at least had shoes and a shirt.

Clay swiped at the man, ripping a good portion of his shirt away. Good. Clay wouldn't be the only cold one.

They skirted the direct glow of the streetlight, but didn't stick to the shadows closest to the house. The neighbors would not only be able to hear them but see them as well. Hadn't the idiot challenging Clay thought of that before he approached our house from the front? Pack law forbade public shifting.

The snow crunched under the challenger's feet as he rushed Clay. Clay spun and avoided the charge. He used the man's momentum to trip him and knock him into the snow. As the man fell, he shifted noticeably.

Clay shifted further as well. His mouth extended to enable the use of his fangs. I cringed at the thought of the neighbors spotting him. There would be no way to explain away the disconcerting appearance of his ears and fangs.

The other man rolled and rose to his feet. His head had almost completely contorted to wolf form. My eyes rounded. He snapped at Clay, narrowly missing Clay's chest. His attempt distracted Clay from blocking a well-placed punch to his gut. I cringed, then silently cheered when Clay gave back as good as he got.

The sky began to lighten, and down the road, a few of the streetlights blinked off. They needed to end this soon, but the fight didn't seem to be winding down.

Their movements increased in speed until they mostly blurred. I heard each time one of them connected—the solid thunk of it reverberated through the house—but didn't see anything. I hoped Clay gave more than he received.

Twice the other wolf feinted away from the house, but Clay refused to follow, forcing the challenger to come back to him. Clay would not distance himself any further from the house and leave me unprotected. The other wolf's attempt had me wondering.

Knowing I'd regret it, I stretched my sight. I saw another blue-grey light nearby and began to doubt this fight was just another Mating challenge. As quickly as I opened my spark-filled view of the world, I closed it. It hurt, and I couldn't afford to distract Clay with my pain.

I studied the man fighting Clay. He didn't look like the same werewolf who'd attacked us on our way back from breakfast. The sprinkling of fur starting to cover his skin appeared lighter than the original challenger's dark grey fur.

Despite their noise, I heard the back door open. So did Clay.

In a fierce move, he hit the other werewolf in the head with a sickening crack. The man dropped to the ground. Clay didn't wait to see him land. He turned and ran for the house before I could even think to scramble under the bed and hide.

The front door slammed again. I thought of the damage and winced. The temperature in the room dropped further.

Clay and the new werewolf met in the living room with a thud. I didn't think, just sprang from my crouched position near the window to scramble over the bed. It might have been safer to stay hidden, but I worried more when I couldn't see what was happening.

I eased off the end of the mattress and edged closer to the door, trying to make them out in the dim light of the living room. I stared at the fight raging in front of me.

Two shapes struggled in the center of the brown rug. I identified Clay by his long hair. His back was to me. The other man had his arms wrapped around Clay, attempting to squeeze him. Clay fisted his hands together and hammered them down on his attacker's face. They broke apart, the attacker almost bumping into the TV.

Cold air wrapped around my legs. I glanced at the front door, which stood ajar, but didn't move to close it.

When I looked back at the men, I had a clear view of the attacker. I stopped breathing and stared at the man, stunned.

I'd grown accustomed to the stomach acrobatics I suffered every time I looked at Clay. Feeling them when I looked at this new wolf devastated me. I gasped in a ragged breath, hurt by fate's cruelty. The sound distracted the newcomer, who met my eyes with recognition then calculation. Clay took advantage and brought the man down like he had the one outside. The sickening thud made me cringe.

Without thought, I moved out into the living room and stared down at the unconscious man. His short, sandy blonde hair contrasted with the brown of the rug. It moved in the breeze that swept the floor. I didn't feel the cold as I studied his tall, lean frame. He had no facial hair. Except for the tall part, he looked like Clay's opposite.

How could I feel that pull for two men? Sam assured me that I would know when I met the right one because there would be a pull, a burning curiosity like no other. This didn't make any sense.

The man's hand lay on the carpet close to me. Some of his fingernails had shifted to glossy black claws before Clay had knocked him out. Looking closer, I saw his ears had shifted, too.

"What do we do, Clay?"

I looked up at him and found him watching me closely. I shivered and didn't look back at the man on the floor. Having all the doors open made the heat kick in, but it did little to warm me.

"He's part changed. With all the noise, I think the police will be here soon. Can we leave him here like this?"

Clay nodded and motioned me back into the bedroom. His knuckles bled, and he had the start of another black eye. I wanted to walk to him and hug him, but felt too confused. Instead, I turned away to hide my watering eyes.

In the distance, I heard sirens.

Clay put me back into bed then left, closing the door behind him. Moments later, I heard the back door close and then nothing as the sirens got closer.

Fate or not, I belonged with Clay. I wasn't sure anymore if I was his prize or punishment, though. Regardless, he'd earned my loyalty. Reacting to someone other than Clay felt like cheating, and it bothered me a lot. I didn't know what to do about it or how to stop it. It wasn't something I could talk to Clay about. I had hurt him enough already. If I could trust Sam, I could maybe ask him.

The sirens quieted with a chirp before they reached the house. Muted red and blue lights danced on my bedroom wall by my head. I wondered what Clay planned to tell the police. No matter what I'd just felt for the man passed out on the living room floor, I trusted Clay completely. He had a plan, and I just needed to wait.

But Clay didn't come back in. Instead, I heard a knock on the front door and the murmur of several voices. Exhaustion and pain, from pushing myself too soon, shivered through my body.

CHAPTER NINETEEN

An hour later, the full light of a new day—Wednesday morning, the beginning of Thanksgiving break—lit my room.

Clay, still bloody from the fight, stood with the officers to show them out. They had his written statement and my phone number, since I didn't plan to stay in the house for a few nights. I'd decided we'd go to the Compound a day early. I'd waited long enough. I had too many questions to answer on my own, and a certain Elder waited for me there. I needed to talk to him.

The police believed we'd experienced a simple break in. Their deduction suited me fine. I could just imagine the line of questioning I would have endured if I'd mentioned the men had broken in to kidnap me. After seeing the second man, I had no doubt that had been their intent.

The front door closed, and I listened to Clay walk through the house and close himself in the bathroom. He needed to wash the dried blood from his face. It had served its purpose and hidden his noticeably advanced healing from the police.

Flipping back the covers, I got out of bed and started to dress. The dizziness and headache that had returned when I fell off the bed had faded while they questioned me.

I finished dressing, grabbed my messenger bag, and began to cram clothes in it. My mind wasn't on packing so I didn't treat it anymore gently than Clay or Luke had when they had packed it. How had I felt anything for that man on the floor? It shouldn't have been possible. Agitation burrowed deep. When I turned toward the door and saw Clay watching me, I dropped my gaze to the floor unable to meet his calm regard. He sighed, stepped aside, and motioned for me to lead.

In the kitchen, Clay had my jacket and shoes waiting. I slipped them on, remembering at the last minute to call Rachel to let her know what had happened. Thankfully, she hadn't been home. She promised only to come back home with Peter, just to be safe.

Clay didn't say anything as we got into the car, which was normal, but I sensed his extreme tension. My stomach churned with guilt. However, I didn't know what to say, so I closed my eyes and tried to nap. Still needing to regain my strength, sleep wasn't too hard to come by.

Several times, I woke to the sound of him tapping his grey nails against the steering wheel. When I opened my eyes to look at him, I could see his elongated canines. At those times, I wanted to reach over and pat his leg, but I held myself back.

When I woke to see his ears pointed too, I quietly studied him for a few minutes. I knew I was the cause of his agitation. He'd sensed my withdrawal. I hadn't wanted him to see my confusion. I wanted to talk to Sam first, before saying anything to Clay. But my approach obviously wasn't the right one. Clay had stuck by me through everything. I needed to trust that he wouldn't turn away from me after I revealed what had happened.

"Clay..."

He paused his tapping.

"Could you pull over for a minute?"

He glanced at me, lifted a concerned brow, but did as I asked. The tires crunched on the snowy shoulder. He stopped the car then turned toward me.

A sad smile lifted my lips. I hated to see him like this. I tapped my lips. I needed affirmation that we still had our connection, and he needed assurance I was fine.

His tight grip on the steering wheel loosened, and he shook his head in amusement. I held my breath as he leaned toward me.

Clay cradled my face in his hands and kissed me tenderly. I clutched his shirt, dragging him closer. When he opened his mouth to nip my bottom lip, I groaned and willingly let him in. We steamed the windows. My lungs burned for air. Finally, I had to pull away to catch my breath. He wrapped his arms around me and placed small gentle kisses on the top of my head.

His neck hovered in my line of sight. I could give him what he wanted. A quick bite and I wouldn't need to worry about other potential Mates. I could Claim him as my own. But I didn't want to hurt him anymore. Physically or emotionally. I pulled back from our make-out session.

Clay gave me one last kiss on the lips then put the car in drive. The smooth, tan skin of his very human ears called my attention, as did his clean, pink nails. He looked content, no longer tapping his fingers while he stared ahead at the snow-covered roads.

I turned away and pretended to sleep, condemning myself for my lie. My hesitation to Claim Clay didn't stem from a concern that I would hurt him. No, just like Sam said, I selfishly didn't want to give up my plans.

Deep down, I was unwilling to bend and try to make it work.

WE ARRIVED at the Compound just as the sun's last rays sank below the tree-topped horizon. Vehicles crowded the parking area. I didn't worry though. Holidays always drew a crowd.

Clay grabbed my bag then walked around to open my door for me. Staying close, we walked inside the Compound. Jackets and shoes filled the entry. It meant cramped quarters for the holiday, but I'd done it before.

We went to the apartment I usually stayed in with Sam, but another family with small cubs had commandeered it. After several minutes of knocking on doors, we gave up trying to find an apartment in the main Compound. We turned down a hall I typically didn't travel—the unMated wing—and found the majority of the dorm quarters also occupied. Several men passed us as we searched. They gave us curious looks as they scented the air. I stayed close to Clay.

Clay and I grabbed the first open dorm room and put our stuff on the twin bed. We would figure out our sleeping arrangements later.

"I need to talk to Sam," I said once we were back in the hall. Clay nodded and led the way to the main hall.

Charlene and her crew had done a wonderful job decorating the large room. Cornucopias with harvest produce sat on each of the long tables. Several turkeys with feathers made of construction paper hands hung on the walls. The cubs had obviously partaken in crafts while visiting. It amused me that Charlene insisted on celebrating the US holiday while living in Canada. Her extended adopted family didn't seem to mind. I could hear women laughing in the attached kitchen. Fresh pumpkin pie perfumed the air.

In the midst of all the decorations, I spotted Sam. He sat with his back to me, conversing with several other men at one of the many sitting areas in the main hall. I noticed the weary slope of his shoulders. Part of me—the part that lived with him for so long and thought of him as "grandpa"—wanted to run over and hug him. I ignored that part.

Before he noticed me, I strode over and interrupted their conversation.

"It's time we talked," I said, tersely.

He turned toward me with a hesitant smile then quickly nodded to the others, who got up to move to another group.

"Gabby, I didn't think you'd be up until tomorrow."

Clay and I shared a glance. The main hall didn't afford privacy since all the werewolves present would hear me. Then again, very few places in the Compound qualified as private to that degree. Normally, I wouldn't care who heard me, but I had the mystery of the blue-grey werewolves to solve. I did a quick scan of the room and managed to hold back a wince of pain.

Clay gave an annoyed grunt but gently rubbed my back. He'd become adept at knowing when I used my gift.

In the brief glimpse, I'd noted the sparks all appeared normal. Well, for a werewolf anyway. But it only assured me to a degree. Although I didn't think Sam responsible for what had happened, I still wondered if he might know something about it.

"We came early because two werewolves tried breaking into my house." I watched Sam closely as I said it.

"What?" Sam said, giving Clay a sharp look. Sam appeared genuinely upset and concerned.

"He's still not talking," I said. I slumped into the chair across from Sam. "I believe their intentions were to kidnap me."

Clay lowered himself into the chair next to me. He always stayed close, and I couldn't imagine it any other way. If it hadn't been for Clay, the men probably would have taken me. What would have happened then? I thought about the blonde man who'd been lying on the floor, and my stomach clenched with worry. My troubled gaze swung to Clay.

Clay met my look with calm, brown eyes. Staring into their depths, a tense breath eased out of me. Sure, I had questions, but I wouldn't let the answers to any of them affect the tie Clay and I had.

I gave Clay a small worried smile then turned my attention back to Sam. Different colored lights...a pull to another man when it should only happen once...I could come up with the only possible explanation.

"Is there more than one kind of werewolf?" I asked bluntly. Maybe I'd stir up trouble with my public questioning, but I was tired of waiting.

Sam frowned and leaned forward. "Not sure what you mean, exactly."

Sam watched me closely. I nibbled on my lip and thought back to the original challenger. Physically, he'd looked like any other werewolf. So if Sam didn't already know about another kind of werewolf, I didn't think there would be a way for him to differentiate. Then I thought of the last one I saw on the floor.

"When you go fur, what color variations are possible? Different shades of fur, eyes...what about nose, or nails?"

The door to the commons opened, and a few more werewolves drifted in, slowly walking toward other groups. While they progressed across the room, they kept their heads tilted, listening as if already aware of the important conversation occurring in our small group.

"What does this have to do with—"

I held up a hand. "Bear with me, Sam. I need answers to give answers."

Sam turned his attention to Clay.

"I already told you, he still isn't talking. Look, is there another Elder I can talk to? One willing to answer my questions?"

I wanted to take my harsh words back when Sam's face fell.

The expression cleared after a moment, and he slowly answered. "Fur is like hair and varies just like a human's. Same with the eyes. We are more like dogs when it comes to our noses. Mostly dark, but we sometimes have unusual markings. Did you see an identifying mark, Gabby?"

I ignored his question. "What about the nails?"

He shrugged. "Shades of grey. Mostly a dark grey."

"Black?"

"Well, like I said, a dark grey is possible."

"No. I mean black. A very glossy black you could see your reflection in."

Sam remained introspectively quiet for a full minute. The intense silence claimed my attention. Looking around, I caught the eyes of a few others in the room before they quickly looked away.

"I don't think I've ever paid that much attention to our claws before. But, no, I don't believe so."

I slumped back in my chair, thinking. Everyone in the room watched me, waiting for what I'd say next.

Could there really be another species of werewolf? The sparks I saw indicated the possibility. But if I followed that line of reasoning, did that then mean I was another species of human? Maybe these werewolves just had different abilities. I chewed on my lip for a minute. What about the nail color? Could that small difference carry enough significance to classify two separate species? I was grasping. I needed to grasp. If there were two kinds, it could explain why I had two potential Mates.

Frustrated and still tired from my stunt with Rachel, I scowled and got to the heart of my angst. Sure, I wanted to know what the color differences meant, but I needed to know why I felt what I did when I saw that man unconscious on the floor.

Sam cleared his throat, and I ignored him. Someone spoke softly further back in the room. Others moved restlessly.

So what if I felt the same pull for another guy? It just meant I had a choice. Wasn't that what I'd wanted all along? Yet, now that I had options, I couldn't see myself walking away from Clay...not for school, not for a career, and not for some creep who snuck into my house.

I peeked at Clay, unable to hide my turmoil. He reached out, offering his hand. His hair hid his eyes again, making it hard to read him. I looked down at his hand, calloused and so real.

Realization dawned. Clay and I held the answers. I kept my eyes trained on his hand to hide my thoughts. When I'd focused on Luke, I saw the yellow-violet spark. When I'd focused on Rachel, I'd expected to see Peter, but I hadn't. Human vs. werewolf testing. If I was right about different species and tried the same test with Clay, I foresaw two possibilities. I would see myself as Clay's Mate or I would see two potential Mates for myself, thus supporting my theory of another werewolf species.

Doubt crept in. What if I didn't see myself? What if it didn't work that way, and I saw the werewolf that Clay had knocked out?

I needed to know.

Lacing my fingers through his, I closed my eyes and focused. I held onto my need to find the perfect Mate for Clay and my hope I'd see myself.

The shock jumped from my hand to his, and my vision of the real world narrowed. I held my breath, terrified of the answer. My second sight exploded into existence. Not the great void filled with billions of sparks, but with the vibrant intensity and color of the sun. The white yellow core pulsed, its energy radiating outward, cooling to a molten orange. Hope flooded me as I realized my own spark filled my vision.

The vision closed, and my eyes once again focused on the real world. My hand still rested within Clay's, but I caught the change in his expression. Clay glared at me. He knew what I'd done, but I couldn't feel bad about it. Joy filled me. I'd been right. It didn't answer my question about the variances in sparks, but I didn't care. It had given me the answer I needed.

I smiled sweetly and leaned over to kiss him lightly on the lips. When our lips touched, something tangible changed. The joy I felt remained, but something else crept in. I pulled back, eyes wide. My heart hammered and my stomach clenched as I stared at him, unable to look away. Mesmerized.

In shock, I realized what I'd done. I'd transferred my pull to him. Only he wasn't pulling in men. He pulled me in, and the force of it consumed me. He represented a hot fudge sundae to a diet-starved girl. Even knowing that what I felt was a result of my power, I couldn't ignore it. He was so handsome, so perfect, and so clueless as he continued to scowl at me.

His fingers still twined through mine, but I needed more from him. I needed an affirmation of us as a pair. I wanted to touch his face and smell his skin. I wanted to hold him tight and never let go.

With speed I never imagined I possessed, I moved from my seat to his, straddled his lap, and leaned my forehead against his. He grunted in surprise, but otherwise didn't move.

Breathing in deeply, I smelled the soap he'd used and closed my eyes. His hair tickled my nose. I pressed my lips to the tip of his nose. My heart twisted painfully. His hand came up, lightly resting on my side. It heated my ribs. The contact of each finger branded me. Better, but not enough. My mind kept chanting "more." I opened my eyes and smiled.

Forgetting our audience, I ran my hands through his hair and pulled back to kiss his exposed forehead. His cautious brown eyes met mine. I lost myself in their depths for several moments as I recalled the first time I saw them. On his driver's license. I needed more from him. No more hiding from each other.

I tilted my head and kissed his cheek. The whiskers abraded my lips, but I didn't mind. I moved lower, finding his lips. He didn't resist me, but didn't join in as he had in the car. I frowned slightly. A stab of doubt pierced my heart. This didn't feel right, yet. He still hid from me.

Nudging his jaw with my nose, I made room to nuzzle his neck. My lips skimmed his smooth skin. His pulse jumped under my mouth. Finally, he reacted. Both his hands came up, holding my sides, kneading me, encouraging. My breath quickened, and my heart hammered. Yes! This was right.

Something took possession of me. With one hand, I gripped his hair and tugged it. He tilted his head to the side and exposed his neck, giving in willingly. My eyes traced his neck where his pulse skipped erratically. The beat matched my own. I couldn't look away from that clean-shaven spot. I recalled when he had started shaving it. He'd known I would need to see it. For this. I kissed it lightly and felt him shudder. Before the shudder ended, I bit him hard on the same spot. Hard enough to draw blood.

The taste of his blood on my tongue broke the hold he had on me and created a new one somewhere deep inside. I pulled back slightly to look at the small marks I'd left. They had already begun to heal.

The pull he had on me and the euphoria of the moment faded as the horror of what I'd just done washed over me.

Clay stared at me in stunned silence...versus his everyday silence. Behind me, someone moved and called attention to the fact that we still had an audience. A Claiming typically occurred in private.

A deep blush seized my cheeks, and embarrassed tears began to gather. I wiped the blood from my mouth with a shaky hand. I didn't regret Claiming him, but wished we could have talked first. I needed reassurance. Would this mean I'd have to quit school? Would he want me to live in the woods with him? If he did, I owed it to him to try after everything he'd done for me.

Then, a really ugly question floated to the surface. Had I just forced him?

Panic bloomed in my chest. Before I could scramble off his lap, he reached up and gently stroked my hair. I froze, hands braced on his chest for stability, ready to flee.

"I've been waiting for that since the moment I saw you," he said in a deep and husky voice. He sounded like a midnight radio DJ.

Hearing his perfect voice ignited my temper. *Now*, he could talk? I scowled at him. The man had the audacity to laugh then scoop me up in his arms.

The room around us erupted in cheers, and I hid my blazing face in his chest, my thoughts a confused jumble. I felt him walk, but didn't have the courage to look up to meet the faces of the people who'd witnessed our Claiming. The sounds of cheering faded as he moved out of the commons. My tears of embarrassment dried before they spilled over.

Part of me couldn't wait to get him alone and yell at him for not talking to me for so long. Another part of me wanted to skip talking altogether and get back to the kissing part. And yet another part of me wanted to ask his thoughts about my gifts and the lights I saw.

When he carried me into our little room and set me on my feet after closing the door, I did none of those things. I stood mere inches from him still too stunned, and very unsure, to do anything but stare. Where would we live? How would we support ourselves? What about my education? His job? Was he upset I bit him under the influence? Should I tell him about the other wolf? Did he have ideas about the weird colored lights?

I trembled. He no longer smiled, but his eyes still twinkled.

"Why?" My high, strained voice made me sound like a child. I cleared my throat and tried again. "Why wait until now to talk?" Apparently, my curiosity had won.

He quietly studied me for a moment then opened his arms. I didn't hesitate, but stepped right into them. I needed his comfort. He tucked me against his chest and gave me his explanation in a simple, heart-melting way.

"If I'd spoken, even just one word, I would have never been able to hold back what I feel for you. You would have run."

I remembered the day he'd plopped down on the towel next to Rachel. Had he arrived any other way, I would have tried to kick him out. If that wouldn't have worked, I would have...run. Even then, he'd known me. I hadn't been ready for any monumental life changes then and wasn't sure if I was now.

I pulled back and met his gaze.

"Can I finally get answers from you now? You'll keep talking?"

He smiled at me and nodded. Well, he'd never be a chatterbox.

"Do you think I'm right about the—"

With sudden seriousness, he interrupted me. "Now's not the time. We'll talk later."

"No way, we're talking now. If not about that, then something else. I've waited over six months to hear your voice."

He didn't look too motivated to talk, yet.

"You owe me. I bit you." It sounded a little backwards, but he smiled for a moment before the look turned puzzled.

"How are you feeling?"

His question gave me pause. Where were the waves of backlash? Shouldn't I feel sick or something by now?

"Good, actually." I'd felt great since I bit him.

Curious, I stretched my awareness. Two of the waves had already hit me, but I hadn't felt a thing.

"It's weird, but I don't feel sick." No backlash. Did that mean I would no longer have a pull on men? The idea excited me. I tried pushing my sight further, and it worked.

In Clay's arms, I focused easily, seeing things I'd missed before. The humans dominated the majority of the space while the werewolves claimed an insignificant portion. Far to the east, a large gathering of blue-grey werewolves hid among the humans. I stayed focused on their group, concerned. If they congregated together, they understood their difference.

"I think we need a safe place to talk." Although werewolves tried to respect each other's privacy, I didn't want to chance anyone overhearing what we needed to discuss.

Clay nodded, but glanced at the door without moving. I followed his gaze and my shoulders slumped as I looked at the wood panel. I had a good idea who hovered outside. He'd given me my answers and now wanted his own.

I slipped from Clay's arms and yanked the door open. As I expected Sam leaned against the wall opposite the door. Waiting. Probably listening, too.

"Sam, since we don't have any privacy, we'd like to use the conference room. There are a few things we need to discuss."

"I couldn't agree more," Sam said, motioning for me to lead.

"Clay and I, Sam," I clarified as I stepped from the room. "I don't have any answers for you."

"Gabby—"

"No. Now it's your turn to be bossed around and told what to do. I did what you wanted and Claimed one of you. Lay off." My stomach churned, and a little fear crept in. Talking to Sam like that was like poking a bear with a stick. Though he'd never given me reason to fear him, he could rip my head off in a blink. I never forgot that.

Sam didn't say anything behind me, but continued to follow me. I didn't turn around to look but knew Clay followed Sam. I needed to stop baiting Sam and smelling like fear. It didn't help any of us.

I opened the door to the soundproofed conference room and turned to face Sam. He'd schooled his features to appear perfectly calm and blank, but his spark glowed like a fanned ember.

"Sam, I'm trying to do what's best for me, Clay, and the pack. There's a lot I haven't told you, things I haven't told Clay. Give me some time to sort everything out. I need to make sure your goals mesh with mine before I can fully confide in you." He looked hurt by my words, but I didn't regret them. I was trying to be honest and give him what information I could to help explain my behavior.

He studied my face for a long moment then stood back and let Clay join me in the room. "I'll be here."

I nodded and gently closed the door. I'd figured he would wait.

When I turned to Clay, I found him watching me. He looked puzzled. Probably trying to figure out what I hadn't told him. He knew so much already. But what would he think about my reaction to the man who'd broken into our house?

I rubbed my hand through my hair. "I'm not sure where to start."

He pulled me into his arms. "Anywhere. I'll listen."

He always did. I smiled and started with the easiest thing. "I can see everything, Clay. Without pain." I pulled out of his arms and continued to look. "Even without touching you, there's no pain. I can see so much more than before. Why?"

"It's our link."

"Wait. I thought the link happened when..." I didn't really want to bring that up. We'd moved a little fast with the Claiming, and I didn't want to seem overly eager about the Mating. No mixed signals.

He read my hesitation and quirked a smile. "The full link happens after the Mating is completed. With the Claiming we have a more limited version of that connection." His smile faded, and he looked at me sincerely. "It can still be broken. If there's another potential Mate out there...by biting him, you can break our bond and create one with him."

My jaw dropped. I couldn't believe he'd said all those words. I hoped he didn't say that potential Mate part because he thought I still doubted us.

"Don't use up your word quota for the day." He grinned, and I stuck out my tongue before getting serious again.

"Clay, I won't be biting anyone else. Ever. But I do have something to tell you. When those wolves attacked...the second one..." I trailed off, trying to find the right words. I didn't want to hurt him. This should qualify as the best day for us. Would telling him turn it into the worst? He nudged me as he often did when in his fur. It made me smile sadly as I admitted the truth.

"I felt the same pull with him as I do with you. I don't understand why that would happen. Sam said just one. Experiencing that with someone else confused me and made me feel horrible, like I cheated on you."

He sighed and shook his head, smiling softly at me. "I saw what happened. It worried me, but the kiss in the car helped me understand how you feel. Don't worry about it."

He'd known all along? His impatient finger tapping made more sense now.

I met his eyes and smiled back. His easy acceptance of everything that'd happened finished melting my heart.

"I love you." My admission took me by surprise.

I didn't see him move. He embraced me again, crushing me in a spinning hug. The room twirled around us at a dizzying speed, and I didn't attempt to focus on it. Instead, I looked down at Clay's face. He wore a huge smile. I grinned back and noted his canines were normal for the first time ever.

"Oh!" I squirmed to get down, excited at the size of his teeth. He grudgingly released me. "Please can we get rid of the beard?" Yes, I hopped from foot to foot like a kid begging for cotton candy. I wanted to see him just once without facial hair. If he wanted to grow it back, I wouldn't mind. I'd fallen in love with him as he was, after all.

He nodded, laughing at me.

"And I still want to get my degree. Can we stay where we are until then?"

Before he could say anything, his eyes shifted to the door. My joy-filled smile faded. I still needed to figure out what made Elder Joshua different from other werewolves. No doubt, it related to me in some way. Why else would I be able to see the colors? For a moment, I thought about my mom and all the questions I would ask her if she still lived.

I stepped closer to Clay and laid my head against his chest, wrapping my arms around his waist. "Everyone I've ever loved this way I've lost," I said, recalling my earliest memories of my mom and grandma. I hugged him close. "Don't let me down."

"I won't. You're stuck with me forever," he whispered as he held me close.

I pulled back enough to meet his eyes and knew without a doubt I'd found the perfect man. He *would* stand by me. Always.

I kissed his lips, wishing we had time to be just Gabby and Clay, the newly engaged couple. Then, I smiled. We would have time. Eventually. Like he said, he wasn't going anywhere, and neither was I.

Something chirped behind me. It took a second chirp for me to recognize the sound of my own phone. I groaned at the interruption, but pulled back from

Clay's warm embrace, not quite leaving it, to pluck the phone from my back pocket. Luke's number flashed on the screen.

As soon as I hit "talk," Luke spoke in a rush without waiting for my greeting.

"Gabby, I have a problem," he shouted over the roar of an engine. Something popped loudly in the background. Luke swore. The phone went dead.

The three-second conversation left me speechless. I pulled the phone away from my ear to look at it. What the hell was going on? Safe in Clay's arms, I stretched my senses and searched for Luke. I found a yellow-violet spark and a lone blue-green spark—Luke...and the other spark like me—swarmed by blue-grey sparks.

"Clay, I don't think I have a choice anymore. Something's happening to Luke. The other werewolves are all around him. We need to get Sam." I turned to look at the door. "I don't know who to trust."

Clay nodded and leaned his forehead against mine. "I'll stand with you, always."

NOTE TO THE READER

What is going on with Luke? *crowd starts chanting, "We want Luke!"* I know, I know. I'm dying to share what sexy pants is up to. But, before I can, I have to introduce Michelle. Trust me. She's important like Gabby. And her story also ties into Luke's story. Keep reading! You won't be disappointed.

MISFORTUNE

JUDGEMENT

OF THE SIX

BOOK 2

MELISSA HAAG

CHAPTER ONE

CLOTTED POTATOES STUCK IN MY THROAT WHEN I TRIED TO swallow. I tried again, and they slowly slid down. My overladen plate of food mocked me. I didn't want to eat. I wanted to go hide in my room, away from our dinner guests. I almost blanched just thinking the word guest. It didn't at all describe the men sitting at the table with us.

Blake asked my stepfather, Richard, a question about their latest stock investment, and I dutifully looked up. Just as quickly, I looked back down at my plate like the meek little mouse Blake wanted me to be. I didn't mind playing a meek part when sitting with these men. Blake didn't give me any trouble, but the other ten men with him often did. Dinners went smoother if I kept my eyes on my plate.

Blake sat at one end of the table, and my stepfather sat at the opposite end. I, unfortunately, always took the middle seat on the side with five chairs. It gave me more room than if I sat on the other side. If given a real choice, I would have rather sat next to Richard.

The six men across from me stared at me through the entire meal. At every dinner, different men stared at me. How many business associates did Blake really have? These dinners had been happening since my mother died four years ago. Once a month, every month. I hated them. I felt like a freak on display. *Hey, come on in! Have dinner with the freaky girl who predicts the market and makes us all rich. Don't worry, she doesn't bite. She'll do exactly as I say.*

I thought of my brothers, who slept in their beds, and forked another bite of potatoes into my mouth. Yep, I would do as Blake said. He'd made it painfully clear who he would punish if I didn't.

One of the men across from me nudged my foot under the table. I didn't look up. It would just play into whatever he planned. Probably some lewd gesture. For business associates, as Blake usually introduced them, they dressed more like mill workers, wearing torn, stained jeans and ragged shirts. They were sometimes unwashed, too. I didn't judge them by their appearances, though. Their actions told me what I needed to know about them.

The man kicked me again, harder. I tucked my feet under my chair in an effort to avoid his long reach as Blake asked me a direct question.

"Michelle, my dear, are you trying to withhold your latest premonition?" He sipped his wine and watched me. Blake's medium build and salt and pepper hair gave him a distinguished look that hid a very mean personality.

"You know I haven't," I said in a quiet, biddable voice as I met his gaze. If I tried keeping a premonition to myself, I got sick. First, it was just a niggling headache. However, the longer I held the information inside, the worse the ache grew until, finally, I broke down and started babbling the information with pain-filled tears.

"Sorry, Blake," Richard said from down the table. "Michelle gave me the information yesterday. When I went in today, I just invested what we discussed last night. I didn't think you wanted me to bother you with it."

I lowered my gaze to my plate again. A puppet, that's all I was. Just then, the man across the table kicked me again. The hard toe of his boot bruised my shin. I looked up, eyes blazing with hate, and whispered two words—they rhymed with "pluck you"—that sealed my fate.

In a blur, Blake shot from his chair, sailing toward me over the table. His hand curled around my throat and the momentum of his move carried me backward, lifting me up. My long skirt tore when it caught briefly on my tipping chair. Before I could blink, Blake slammed me against the wall. My feet no longer touched the ground.

My stunned mind couldn't comprehend what had just happened. *No one should be able to move that fast.*

Barely breathing, I panicked and fought to pry away his hand, forgetting to be meek. He laughed and squeezed my neck a little harder. My eyes darted around the room looking for help. Behind him, Richard stood, but said nothing. No help. There never was for me.

I focused on Blake. The calculated look in Blake's eyes reminded me of his expectation. Swearing at his "associate" hadn't been a bright move. Still trying to wheeze in air, I stopped clawing at his hand and instead wrapped my hands around his forearm for support. His hold loosened, and I gasped. The air burned, but I didn't stop pulling it in greedily.

All the men at the dinner table watched us, and the one who had kicked me, smirked.

"The time for niceties is at an end. We've amassed our fortune. It's time for the next step. You will choose one of us and evolve your abilities as you were born to do."

I barely heard his words. His teeth claimed my attention. As he spoke, they grew. Elongating. Already panicked because of the hand at my throat, my racing heart kicked into overdrive at the sight of his canines. His face changed slightly, his jaw expanding to accommodate his teeth.

He can't be human. What is he?

He tightened his grip with his next words.

"You will allow each male here, and every male I bring from this night forward, to scent you. If we decide you are his Mate, you *will* bite him and establish your Claim."

His hold loosened. Still gasping for air, I didn't immediately register that my feet again touched the ground. *Bite one of them?* He dropped his hand and moved away from me, but his piercing gaze continued to hold me in place.

"Frank, since she offended you, you can go first."

Frank quickly leapt over the table, his teeth also abnormally long and pointy. Swaggering toward me, he leaned in close and licked my neck. A shiver of revulsion ran through me.

"You're mine," he whispered before he moved to allow the next man close to me.

I turned my face from them and pressed myself against the wall. Despairing, I closed my eyes. Tears fell from their scrunched corners. I couldn't escape.

After the last man leaned in close to my neck and inhaled deeply, Blake commanded me to leave. I fled to my room and locked the door behind me.

WHEN I WOKE, I found a manila envelope shoved under my bedroom door. A Post-it decorated the front of it. I easily read Richard's scrawl.

Run as fast as you can. Everything is in your name.

I gazed at those words with a growing feeling of dread. Somewhere in the house, a phone rang. I quickly stashed the envelope in my pillowcase without looking at the contents and started to make my bed. Before I finished, a key rattled and the door swung open.

David eyed me as I stood next to the bed, tugging the quilt into place. I still wore my pajamas.

Since Blake needed Richard in the office and didn't trust me home alone, he'd brought in David as my keeper. Well paid, David did as Blake said. I wondered if David knew about Blake's teeth.

"You're not supposed to be in here until I knock," I said, repeating Blake's rule.

"Today's an exception. Blake's on the phone." David held out a cell phone.

I stared at him a moment before I approached to take it. What game did they play now?

"Yes?" I said, putting the phone up to my ear.

"Richard's dead. This changes nothing. We'll be back tonight." The line went dead. Richard's scrawled message ran through my head.

David walked further into my room, a suspicious look on his face. He moved past me and pulled back the quilt.

I looked at my shelf where my softball participation trophy from middle school sat. When he lifted my pillow, I quietly lifted the trophy.

I could hear my brothers' muffled voices on the other side of the wall, still locked in their own room, waiting.

David never heard the envelope crinkle.

IN JUST OVER FORTY-EIGHT HOURS, the spark of hope, ignited by the escape from my bleak life, grew dim. I had no idea what I was doing or where I was going as I pulled into the almost empty parking lot of a small town diner.

Parking, I glanced at the mirror and cringed at my reflection. Naturally olive-skinned—thanks to my mom—I would never look pale, but I did appear ashen. My light blue and brown-flecked eyes looked bloodshot and glassy from lack of sleep. My long, warm brown hair that I'd pulled back into a ponytail, needed to be washed and brushed.

I shifted my attention to the passengers I also saw in the mirror.

Liam and Aden stared at me from the backseat of my mom's car. The means of our escape. I was thankful Richard had held onto it after she passed away, letting it sleep peacefully under a dust cover in the third spot in the garage.

My brothers' solemn faces hadn't changed since we'd left. They were taking their cues from me. Barely holding myself together, I leaned my head against the steering wheel.

David's knees buckled, and he tipped forward as he crumpled. My broken trophy fell from my hand. The top half of David's body landed heavily on my mattress. With my heart seizing in my chest, I grabbed the envelope from the pillowcase and quickly broke the seal to look inside. Keys, cash, and a few important documents fell to my bed when I shook out the contents. Nothing else from Richard to explain what I needed to do to escape.

The keys I recognized from my mom's car. But how did I drive it? Since I hit fifteen, I'd been locked in Richard's house. A secured house. I didn't know how to disarm the alarm. As soon as I opened the door to the garage, it would go off.

Run as fast as you can...

I inhaled a shaky breath. We'd done it. We'd run. But where were we going? I lifted my head and smiled tremulously at my brothers. Neither smiled back.

Liam looked a lot like Richard, with sandy blonde hair, light blue eyes, and a stubborn chin. At five, he could negotiate a deal like a pro when David wasn't in the immediate area to intimidate him. Most of his deals involved a later bedtime or more dessert. Aden, at four, had my mom's coloring and looked more like me with medium brown hair, deep blue eyes, and a dimple. When given the chance, they both had a smile that could light a room. I wondered if they would ever smile again after the scare I'd given them.

Initially, my driving had almost killed us. I didn't know how I'd managed not being pulled over. Since squealing out of the garage in a cloud of blue smoke, I'd tried keeping a low profile, sticking to the back roads, and stopping only when absolutely necessary.

I twisted in my seat. Empty snack bags littered the seat between the two. "Are you guys hungry for some real food?"

Liam looked out the window at the red and white paint-faded diner across the blacktop expanse. Large windows dominated the front of the squat building, allowing the diners to look out.

"Is it safe?" Liam asked.

"I hope so, buddy. I need a break. My eyes keep closing on me."

He nodded and reached over to unbuckle his brother. I let him help Aden while I fumbled with my own seatbelt. I would never again take a good night's sleep for granted. My head felt fuzzy, and my ears rang. I got out of the car and stood for a moment, waiting for a wave of dizziness to pass.

When I opened the back door, they spilled out of the car in a rush. They ran around chasing each other in the open parking spot next to ours. I let them. I'd parked us in one of the furthest places from the door. Two parking spots away, a motorcycle sat parked in the otherwise empty part of the lot.

I leaned against the closed driver side door and watched them have their fun while I let the fresh summer air clear my head. After a few minutes, I pushed away from the door and had to pause until another wave of vertigo passed. I eyed our destination. It suddenly seemed like a long walk. With a sigh, I herded them toward the diner.

As we neared, I noticed a man. He sat in one of the booths against the large, front windows. Dressed in faded denims and a t-shirt, something about him caught my eye.

He had cropped his dark hair so short I could see his scalp on the side of his head. A five o'clock shadow covered his strong jaw and upper lip, making him look a little scruffy despite the haircut. He had nice ears—why did I notice that? —and my stomach did a tiny flip just staring at his profile. I rolled my eyes at myself.

How could I stand in a parking lot window-shopping a cute guy while on the run from some fanged monster who had kept me locked up for four years? I needed to get a grip on life. Sleep deprivation had robbed me of common sense. Yet, I didn't look away.

The man sat slightly bent over his plate, eating a hearty breakfast. It was just after three in the afternoon. His long legs folded under the table with just barely enough room, and his t-shirt hugged his biceps as he reached for his drink. A black leather jacket lay on the seat next to him and matched the sturdy black work boots he wore. Then I saw the helmet set on the table near his coffee. The owner of the motorcycle.

When we were within a few feet of his window, he glanced up and froze when our gazes locked. The fork he held remained suspended in the air part way to his mouth. My stomach started going crazy doing little flips, and my heart stuttered out an odd pattern before returning to normal.

It was a moment more before he moved again and brought the fork the rest of the way to his mouth. He finished chewing and lifted the coffee to his lips, not once looking away. I forgot to breathe as he studied me with an unnerving intensity. It vaguely reminded me of how Frank watched me at dinner, minus the creepiness...and the kicking. The man held me spellbound. I couldn't look away.

If not for the boys holding my hands, I would have stopped to stare some more. As it was, they continued to pull me forward past the window. When our eye contact was broken, so was this man's hold on me.

What had just happened? The way he looked at me, the way my stomach flipped, and my hands started to sweat...these weird reactions confused me. Did I subconsciously recognize him? Could he be one of the many men Blake had brought over to the house? The thought scared me, and I tried to remember all their faces. I couldn't recall his face, but there'd been so many. Yet, I didn't even consider turning around and going back to the car. I would kill us for sure if I didn't take a break. Besides, there was a very real possibility that my exhausted mind had devolved to a state of cluelessness that meant...I couldn't even think what it meant.

The bell above the door rang as we walked in, and I glanced toward the man. He didn't turn to look. My fears eased a bit. If he knew me, he'd have turned to look, right? I gazed out the windows and scanned the parking lot again. Nothing out there.

I looked down at the boys. Both watched me. I gave their warm little hands a gentle squeeze of reassurance then viewed the diner.

The inside of the place appeared clean and smelled wonderful, like grilled meat. Booths lined the front of the building by the windows as well as the right exterior wall. Scattered tables took up the rest of the open room. Two kitchen doors occupied the left wall, which divided the dining area from the kitchen. A large opening in the section of wall between the two doors gave the cooks a counter to pass the completed orders to the waitress.

The waitress passed us on her way to refill some of the patrons' coffee and told us we could sit anywhere.

Tugging the boys forward, I passed the man in the booth and chose a spot near the bathrooms at the back. A strategically sound location. I could see everyone inside as well as the door. I let the boys slide in first. It probably looked weird with all of us sitting on one side, but it felt safer. Anyone walking up to the table would need to go through me to get to them. However, I doubted I'd put up much of a fight in my current state.

"Mimi," Liam said, calling me by the pet name they'd made up for me. If he and Aden had their way, they'd call me mom, having never known our mother.

He had to tap my arm to break into my thoughts. I'd been staring at the placemat, not paying attention, and hadn't noticed the waitress standing next to us.

I looked up at her. "I'm sorry. What did you say?" I attempted to return her smile.

She gave me an overly patient look. "Can I get you anything to drink?"

"Yes, apple juice for all of us if you have it. And can I get the special and an order of french fries?" I didn't want to wait to order. We needed to eat then keep running.

She asked if we wanted anything else, and I tiredly shook my head. She offered the boys some crayons before she left. Liam thanked her politely and turned over their placemats. They took turns drawing shapes while we waited.

I didn't know what to do next. The need to keep running had kept me awake so far, but I would soon need real sleep or I would risk running us off the road. Where could we go that we would be safe? The image of Blake's teeth popped into my head, and I doubted anywhere would be safe enough.

Propping my chin in my hands, I aimlessly looked around. My eyes found their way to the man in the booth. He had finished his meal and sat sipping his coffee, not looking at anything particular. The waitress grabbed his empty plate on her way past.

My attention started to drift, and before I could prevent it, my eyes closed. It took three attempts to open them again, and when they did, I struggled to focus. Safe from Blake or not, we might not be able to leave the parking lot when we finished eating. I blinked to clear my vision and saw the man glance my way. I sat straighter and rubbed my eyes.

When I glanced back at the man, he again looked out the window while he sipped his coffee. His bill lay on his table, and I hoped he'd leave soon. Even though I felt certain I'd never seen him before, something about him made me very aware of him. Maybe just the fact that he'd caught me dozing. I really didn't want any witnesses when I face-planted my meatloaf.

The waitress brought our drinks, and I took a big gulp for something to do. I leaned back in the booth and saw the man watching again so I arched a brow at him. If he wasn't after me, what was his deal? Didn't his mother teach him it wasn't nice to stare?

He had the nerve to grin at me. My stomach did a weird flip again. I frowned and looked away then started asking the boys about what they'd drawn.

The man's smile hadn't been a leer or even a smile-because-she-looks-crazy type of smile. It had been a kind, hi-how-are-you smile...with a dimple. So, what was up with the stomach flip? Sure, he looked attractive. But hadn't I learned not to react to how someone looked?

After a few minutes, the waitress came back with our meal and extra plates. I divided the special between the three of us and placed the french fries so they could share. Hot mashed potatoes were a nice change from chips, but reminded me of the last dinner with Blake and his men. I shuddered and took a bite of the meatloaf instead.

The boys dug into their food, and I felt a pang of guilt. I'd been caring for them for four years. Crying babies, diapers, throw-up, you name it. In the beginning, Richard had helped, but Blake made the rules and didn't want Richard near me. In reality, Blake had wanted me to bond with the boys so he had power over me. Yet, he never allowed me to care for them without supervision. David watched everything and controlled our time together.

I brushed Aden's hair back tenderly. I loved them so much...even at their most annoying. I just wanted them to be safe.

We'd made it over forty-eight hours without any Blake sightings. That had to mean something.

The few other customers who'd been sitting when we entered slowly trickled out as we ate. Eventually, only the man remained. The boys finished their meals and nibbled on the fries while they continued to draw.

I forced myself to keep eating, diligently working my way through the small piles of food on my plate. I needed the nourishment as much as I needed sleep. Eating while I drove hadn't worked well for me. Split concentration had almost landed us in the ditch. I just hoped after this break I wouldn't confuse the pedals again as I had in the beginning.

My continued to struggle to keep my eyes open—they felt hot and gritty—eventually made me set my fork aside. I stood and let the boys out to use the ladies' room behind us. My legs felt weak and achy so I leaned against the back of the bench seat.

The waitress spotted me beside the booth and came over with the bill. I handed her the cash and told her to keep the change. She smiled her thanks and walked away. Before I could move, the room started to tilt. I held onto the back of the booth, waited for it to pass, then went to check on the boys.

When we walked out of the bathroom, the man's booth sat empty. I felt slightly relieved...and maybe a little disappointed, too.

We stepped into the afternoon sun, and I noted that the parking lot had cleared since we'd arrived. Not paying attention, I staggered a little when we stepped down from the curbed sidewalk that surrounded the diner. I looked around to see if anyone had noticed.

The man stood near his bike, searching in the panniers. His lingering presence should have made me nervous, but I was too tired to care. If he left before we reached the car, I'd take it as a sign I should nap in the parking lot.

Between walking, wishing for sleep, and the motorcycle man, I didn't notice the vehicle parked on the far side of my own. When I recognized David's vehicle, I faltered and my stomach sank. Beside me, Aden whimpered, and I gave both their hands a reassuring squeeze. We all knew what David's presence meant.

My tired, strained eyes darted around the parking area, trying to locate David. He didn't let me look too long. With a mocking smile, he stepped from behind his SUV. Dressed in his usual khaki pants and dark V-neck sweater, he looked fresh and ready to drag me kicking and screaming back to my prison. He looked me over, unconcerned that I'd stopped walking and stood several feet away.

Suddenly, I didn't feel so tired.

"Michelle, you look terrible," David said in a patronizing tone. "In fact, I'd have to say you look like hell. Not surprising since you've only been sitting still a few minutes at a time." His smug look evaporated, leaving impatience. "I've followed you long enough. It's time to come home."

Followed? I stared at him blankly. I'd been checking my mirrors and staying to the back roads. I never planned where I was going to turn until I turned. I would have seen him.

David laughed at my expression. "Good thing Blake knew Richard arranged for you to have this," he patted the car. "You might have disappeared without a trace otherwise."

I stared at the car for a moment before I understood. Angry, I swallowed hard and met his eyes again.

"How's your head?" I asked, refusing to acknowledge the fact that our escape had been a lie. "You went down pretty hard."

He narrowed his eyes at me, but I didn't cower. That part of my life was behind me. We were in a moderately populated area. If I screamed, someone would notice. If I sent Liam running back into the diner to call the police, David would be in trouble. He had no hold over my brothers or me, and thanks to Richard, I had our birth certificates to prove it. I only needed to keep him away from the boys until help arrived. If he got one of them, he'd have the advantage he needed to force my compliance.

"Walk away, David."

He stuffed his hands in his pockets and looked down at his shoes briefly before meeting my eyes again.

"You know I can't."

His look held no apology, only determination and, perhaps, a bit of fear.

So he did know about Blake. Then, we both knew he couldn't walk away.

He took a step forward, and I nudged the boys behind me. David looked deceptively calm as I stood my ground. He took another step toward me, and I could see the promise in his eyes.

I opened my mouth to tell Liam to run for help, but David paused. His attention shifted as he looked past me.

"This man have any legal rights to these kids?" a smooth baritone said from somewhere behind me.

I didn't turn to look at the speaker. I knew who it was because I hadn't heard the motorcycle leave yet. I hadn't expected his help, though.

"None," I said, keeping my eyes on David. "Their father recently passed away. This man is no relation to me or my stepfather." I listened to the faint scrape of the man's boots on the blacktop as he came closer.

The man's calm voice held no a trace of anger or threat when he spoke.

"Then you and your partner should walk away like she said."

The word partner made my stomach sink, and I risked looking away from David. Another man had been making his way around the other side of the car, obviously trying to circle behind us. I felt a surge of relief that it wasn't Blake, himself.

David didn't look very concerned that someone wanted to help me. In fact, he smiled, and I understood why. Both David and his partner had bulk—not the fluffy kind—compared to the motorcycle man's lean, muscled build.

"Two to one. Better for your health to move along," David said using a tone that usually meant punishment. Lockdown for me. And for my brothers, a cuff upside the head and then a lockdown.

The man behind me gave a low chuckle. "I'm not too worried about it."

I was. The boys each clutched one of my legs and peeked around me. I reached back with both hands and hid their faces in my shirt as David pulled a gun from behind him. A small sound of terror escaped me as the barrel swung toward the man. Then David's partner moved toward us, walking right into David's line of fire.

From the corner of my eye, I saw motorcycle man dive for David's partner. He hit the guy hard and brought him to the ground. David grunted and swung the gun in motorcycle man's direction. I shuffled back a step. David caught my movement and glanced at me as motorcycle man's elbow drew back then shot forward, lightning fast. A sickening crunch sounded.

Motorcycle man ducked around the front of the vehicle, leaving me alone to face David. I couldn't blame him for running.

Flushed with anger, David glanced at me then cautiously backed up a step. He glanced around the side of his SUV, and I understood he thought the man wasn't gone. After a moment, David quietly rounded the back of his vehicle. The loud thud I heard made me jump. Then, there was silence. I started backing up again, too afraid to hope.

A scuff of noise drew my attention. The man with the smooth voice and friendly smile emerged from behind the SUV. He looked completely unharmed. His eyes swept over us, and he gave me the faintest smile.

My throat tightened with the need to cry as I stood there shaking with relief. My stomach started doing those crazy dips and flips again, but I didn't care. I loosened the death grip I had on the boys' heads.

"Thank you," I managed to whisper, not taking my eyes from him. His face held my attention. He felt so familiar. I wished I knew why.

He studied me closely with a slightly troubled expression. I could guess at what he saw.

"You're tired. Can you drive for a few miles?"

Could I? I didn't have a choice. We needed to keep running. So I nodded.

"I'll follow you to make sure these two don't."

Gratitude swamped me.

"Need help getting your kids in?" he said as he looked down at Aden and Liam.

My kids? I didn't correct him. Physically, I looked older than my nineteen years. The last several years had matured me.

"No, but thanks."

He stayed close as I opened the back door for the boys. I made Liam crawl through first with an order not to look out the window. They both listened immediately, wide-eyed and quiet.

Once the boys were in, the man held my door for me. He leaned on the frame, watching me as I buckled. Worry lined his face.

"Just drive south," he said. "I'll be right behind you."

I nodded, and his eyes glided over my face in another close study before he closed the door. He'd most likely been trying to figure out how long I would be able to drive. I honestly wasn't sure.

CHAPTER TWO

HIS MOTORCYCLE ROARED TO LIFE, A SIGNAL THAT I NEEDED TO PUT
my key in the ignition. I didn't look to the right as I backed out of our spot, but I
knew I'd cleared all prone forms when I didn't hit any speed bumps. The
persistent roar of the motorcycle reassured me as I pulled out of the parking lot
and headed south just as he'd said. After a few minutes, we passed the town's
sign thanking us for visiting.

The adrenaline from the confrontation stayed with me for a few more miles
then I started to slump.

The motorcycle suddenly grew louder, and I checked my mirrors, only
swerving a little at the distraction. He pulled out from behind me as if to pass
but, instead, stayed next to me. I spared a quick glance at him. He rode with his
visor up so I could see his troubled eyes.

He pointed to a spot in front of us—a small combination used car lot,
junkyard, and farm implement supplier—and motioned for me to pull over. I
nodded, fumbled for the blinker, and braked firmly. Thankfully, I'd pressed the
correct pedal. I turned onto the gravel driveway still going a bit too fast, and my
tires slid over the gravel for a few feet, making my backend swerve. I barely
managed to pull to the side and park.

Heart racing from the wild turn, I put my head back against the headrest,
closed my eyes, and willed myself to stop shaking. The boys remained mute
behind me. I knew I needed to reassure them, not just about my driving but also

about our future. I didn't know what I could say that wouldn't end up as a lie. Would everything be okay? David had found us, they could follow our vehicle, and I appeared to be listening to a complete stranger. No, I had nothing.

A knock on my window made me jump. The man stood next to my door, his motorcycle already parked behind him. He eyed me with concern. I hadn't even noticed the roar of his engine die. This close I could distinguish the deep blue of his eyes from his pupils. I cautiously rolled down the window a few inches.

"You were starting to swerve," he said quietly, stuffing his hands in his pockets. "How long since you last slept?"

I didn't want to admit that the swerving was just the way I drove. I considered his question. About thirty-three hours if I counted the very short nap I'd taken while stopped at a stop sign until someone had honked at me. I knew people could survive a heck of a lot longer than that without sleeping. I wasn't sure I could go much longer, though.

"It's been a while." My voice came out scratchy.

"That man, David, hinted this was how he followed you," he said gesturing to the car.

It took me a moment to catch up with his thinking, and I understood why he'd wanted me to pull over here specifically. I needed a different car.

I looked at the single small building on the property. A man stood just outside the door, watching us. When the man noticed my attention, he started walking toward us. My stomach flipped and not in a good way. I had no idea what I was doing.

"Come on, guys. Let's unbuckle and get out. Stay close," I said unnecessarily. The man backed up so I could open my door. He glanced at the salesman then turned his attention back to us...me.

I really needed to ask his name, but the salesman wasted no time closing the distance between us.

"Howdy, folks. What can I do for you?"

"I need a different car," I said while Aden climbed out and moved close to me. Liam already stood at my side. I gently ran my fingers through their hair, trying to give them what comfort I could without being obvious about it.

"A trade?" the salesman said. I nodded, and he looked thoughtful. "To be honest, your car is probably worth two of any of the cars I have."

I glanced at my mother's car. The bright red paint sparkled in the afternoon sun. I didn't know a thing about cars, but even four years old, it still looked new. Part of me wanted to cry at the thought of leaving it behind. I had nothing else of hers. When we'd run, we'd run fast, just as Richard had said. I hadn't even grabbed any clothes.

"It's okay," I lied. "The insurance on this thing is too much for me. I need something worth a little less to bring down the premiums." Not bad for someone using the few cells still awake in her brain. Even locked away as long as I'd been, I wasn't completely clueless. Blake often rewarded good premonitions with simple things like magazines and books.

We trailed behind the dealer as he moved through the collection of vehicles on his tiny lot. He showed us a dark blue truck flecked with bits of rust. It had dual gas tanks, but I would probably only get half the mileage I'd been getting. Not that it mattered. I still had a good chunk of Richard's cash.

"I'll take it," I said firmly. The motorcycle man looked a little surprised that I'd agreed right away. I didn't care about fair deals. I just wanted to keep moving.

"Come inside, and we'll sign the papers. Do you have the title with you?"

It took me a moment to process his request. Title. Paperwork from Richard. Glove box.

"Yes, I think so. Let me go get it."

"I'll get it for you and move your things," the man said from behind me, making me glad he hadn't left yet. My thoughts didn't flow as quickly as they should.

The boys and I walked to the office building with the salesman. The motorcycle man joined us a few minutes later with the papers from the glove box. It didn't take us very long.

We walked out of the office fifteen minutes later with the truck's unfamiliar keys biting into my palm. I questioningly glanced at the motorcycle man as he walked next to us. Why hadn't he taken off yet? It wasn't that I minded him being there. It was just unexpected, as was his motorcycle already sitting in the bed of the truck.

"I hope you'll accept my help for a little longer. You need to move from here, but you don't look like you'll be able to stay awake for very long." He glanced from me to the boys, who craned their necks to look up at him.

Since my driving sucked even when I was well rested, I needed to think of the boys. If I got behind the wheel, I'd be just as dangerous as David. But could I consider the man in front of us any less dangerous? He'd just beaten two men with apparent ease, and I still didn't know his name.

"Who are you?" I asked.

"Emmitt, for now. When you're more awake, I'll give you whatever details you want."

I nodded, too tired to think of another option. Accepting a stranger's help was better than falling asleep somewhere and risking recapture. If that happened, it wouldn't be me who Blake would punish. I gently squeezed Aden's and Liam's hands.

Emmitt walked with us to the passenger door and held it open while we piled in. The truck only had a single bench seat; we would be driving illegally for a while. I put Liam in first and kissed the top of his head. After putting Aden next to him, I buckled them in together. Out the back window, I noticed the car seats in the bed with the motorcycle.

I settled myself into my own tight space aware that Emmitt was waiting until I buckled up to close the door. As he walked around the hood of the truck, his eyes scanned the road, the direction from which we'd come, and it made me glad he was still with us. Plus, I liked looking at him. My stomach agreed.

He slid into his own seat, asked Liam if he had enough room, then started the truck. He pulled out and nodded to the salesman as we passed.

"Which direction should I head?" he said after a few minutes of silence.

The sound of his voice startled my eyes open. I couldn't remember closing them.

"Doesn't matter," I said as I drifted again.

Aden pressed against my side. I felt him reach over and run his fingers through my hair, his security blanket.

For the next few hours, I lightly dozed. Each time I surfaced, I heard Emmitt talking to the boys. Mostly he played I-spy with them or talked about things like favorite foods. Despite his efforts, the boys remained quiet. The sound of his calm voice and Aden's hand in my hair reassured me enough so I could sink into a light doze again.

When we stopped moving, my still gritty eyes popped open. We sat in the parking lot of a motel. The sun hung low on the horizon, casting long shadows everywhere.

"Michelle, the kids could use a break, and I think you'd benefit from some real sleep," he said.

I liked his smooth voice but didn't care for his suggestion. Stopping at a motel with a strange man? Bad idea.

"How about I get the three of you a room while I stay with the truck?"

Oh. Well, that didn't sound so bad. But I still cast a worried glance at the keys. If he took off while we slept, we would be screwed. I didn't have enough cash to buy a new car. When I looked back at him, he was studying me.

"You can hang onto the truck keys, of course," he said.

The idea of a bed called to me. Just three or four hours. Then we could move again. I grudgingly nodded my acceptance.

He told the boys to keep an eye on me as he opened his door and stepped out. Before he closed it, he pressed the lock down. I reached over to lock mine, but it already was. I didn't remember doing it.

I glanced at the boys who gazed after Emmitt, tracking his purposeful stride across the blacktop to the office. They looked a little curious.

"How did it go while I was sleeping?" I asked them.

"He's nice," Liam said quietly. "He played games with us like you do. He stopped because Aden has to go."

I looked over at Aden who nodded. We'd driven a long time, again, especially since they'd each had a large apple juice at the last stop.

"Sorry, buddy. You could have woken me."

"Emmitt said you were tired. He said we could wake you up if we were scared but should try not to," Liam said.

I thoughtfully studied the motel, a single story structure with russet wood siding. It looked like something from the seventies but seemed well maintained on the outside. Emmitt really seemed to be trying to help us. He was doing way more than what just some guy who'd been in the right place at the right time would do. But why?

He came out with a room key just then. He held it up and smiled at the boys. His gaze met mine briefly, and my heart fluttered. Troubled, I looked away. I needed sleep. My emotions were all over the place. He was just being nice and didn't need some silly teen constantly staring at him because she didn't have her head on straight.

Climbing back into the cab, he apologized to Aden for taking so long then moved the truck to park it directly in front of the room's window. With a small smile, he handed me the room key and the truck key then quickly got out to open the door for me.

I didn't know who he was beyond his first name, or why he wanted to help, but I wasn't ready to question him. I wearily climbed out of the truck and helped lift the boys down.

He waited by the truck as I tried to unlock the door. When I failed the second attempt, he came over and held out his hand. I willingly surrendered the key and backed up a step to give him room. He slid the key into the lock, and the door immediately clicked open.

"If you need anything, I'll be right here. Yell, and I promise I'll hear you." He moved aside to let us into the room.

Before I could walk past him, he caught my hand. I turned in surprise. He lifted my hand, placed the key in my palm, and wrapped my fingers around it. I realized I would have walked into the room without asking for the key back.

Trying not to dwell on his warm touch, I nodded, stepped into the room, and closed the door. I watched through the peephole as he went back to the truck and got comfortable. He didn't lock the doors for himself as he had for us. He closed his eyes and appeared to sleep right away.

I clicked the bolt into place and tiredly turned around. Aden and Liam stood beside me, watching.

"Both of you use the bathroom," I said, bending to kiss their foreheads.

Aden made a beeline for the toilet, and I shook my head. Poor guy.

I looked around the room. It appeared clean enough with a queen-sized bed, television, and small table for eating. Honestly, it could have been a cave with a pile of straw in a corner, and I would have found it inviting.

Pulling back the bed covers, I kicked off my shoes and listened to the boys giggle as they washed. The bed tempted me, but as soon as my head hit the pillow, I knew I'd be out. I waited until they finished in the bathroom.

"I like Emmitt," Liam said softly after taking off his shoes. Aden did the same and nodded.

"I'm glad you like him. I think he might be willing to help us for a while. At least until I get some real sleep."

They climbed up on the bed. I knew they weren't tired but would stay close to me while I slept. Thankfully, the room had cable with a cartoon channel. I showed Liam how to turn on the television then went to use the bathroom. As I washed my hands, I saw a plastic-wrapped cup on the bathroom counter. I opened it, filled it with water, and brought it back to the bed with me. Liam watched me set it on the nightstand.

"Use this on my face if you need to wake me up fast," I said. He looked at me in surprise. "It's okay, buddy. Use it if you think you need to. I won't be upset."

I gave them both tight hugs and planted a kiss on top of each of their heads. *No one but me to keep them safe now.* I studied them as they watched cartoons. Neither smiled nor laughed. We were such a broken family. Tears gathered in my eyes for them, and I wiped them away quickly. I just needed some sleep.

DISTANTLY, I became aware of a wet hand gently tapping my face. Peeling my eyes open, I saw Liam peering down at me. I blinked and focused on his concerned expression. He stood beside the bed, holding the cup of water.

It took several heartbeats for everything to click back into place.

"I'm up," I said quickly to avoid a soaking. "What's wrong?" I looked over and saw Aden sitting up in bed, quietly drawing on a piece of motel stationery. They must have been awake awhile.

"Emmitt is knocking on the door. I looked out the window and saw it was him."

I nodded and pulled back the covers, forcing myself to stand though I still felt tired.

I checked the peephole. Emmitt stood in the dark, illuminated by the outdoor light. My stomach did its strange flutter again. Apparently, my sleep-deprived brain hadn't imagined how good he looked. He watched the door. It felt like he was looking right at me, but I knew that wasn't possible.

He had left his jacket off and wore a plain, white tee with his jeans. I blinked slowly and looked at his hands. He held a plastic bag in one hand and a paper bag balanced on top a drink-carrier in the other. Food. I opened the door and stepped back so he could enter. He nodded at me as he stepped in. When he walked past, he seemed to slow, and I couldn't help but notice he smelled good, too.

The boys perked up and inched toward Emmitt when they saw him enter. He smiled reassuringly and waved them over to the table where he set the paper bag and drinks.

"There's a fast food place nearby. Since everything's been quiet, I made a quick run," he said as I closed and locked the door. When I turned around, he offered me the plastic shopping bag. "I noticed you didn't have much, so I also picked up a few things."

I took the bag, opened it, and blinked at the contents: toothbrushes, toothpaste, new socks, and t-shirts for all three of us.

"Thank you," I murmured, not looking up. Gratitude warred with suspicion. He'd bought us *things*. He didn't even know us but saw our need and shopped for us. Instead of trying to resolve my feelings over his kind gesture, I nudged the boys toward the bathroom.

While the three of us crowded around the sink and brushed our teeth, Emmitt set the food out on the table.

The boys brushed longer than usual to make up for the missed brushings—Liam's idea. I smiled at them. When they finished, we closed the door so they could change into their new clothes. The best part was the clean socks. Aden's little feet got so sweaty when he had to wear shoes for an extended period.

Emmitt leaned against the wall near the motel door, looking relaxed with a hand in his pocket as he drank his coffee. Two fast food wrappers already sat in the garbage.

The boys settled at the table and tentatively reached for some food. I went straight for the coffee then sat on the edge of the bed. I finally glanced at the bedside clock. I'd slept for five hours. Good enough for now, but it would catch up with me fast. At least I could think better.

Suspicions I should have already considered continued to creep in. Why would a complete stranger want to help me to the extent he had? Was it just chance he'd hung around so long at the diner? Feeling watched, I glanced at Emmitt and met his gaze. Did something lay hidden there? I couldn't tell anything beyond the intensity with which he watched me.

"Sorry for waking you up so soon. I could hear the boys saying they were hungry," he said quietly, shifting his gaze to look at my brothers.

Having his attention diverted brought relief. Perhaps I was just being paranoid, but it felt like he constantly watched me. Maybe he just wanted to figure out what he'd gotten himself into. Or maybe he already knew. The suspicion that he'd been planted at the diner rose in my mind, but I quickly killed it. David had been *following* me. I'd picked directions at random, never knowing where I wanted to go until I turned. He'd been halfway through his meal when we'd arrived. There was no way he could have been there for me.

I followed his gaze and smiled at the boys. They took huge bites, plowing through their burgers.

"Slow down, you two, or you're going to choke," I warned them. I glanced back at Emmitt. "We haven't been eating right, so it's good that you woke me. They needed this."

"And you need more sleep."

The soft concern in his voice made my stomach do a very large, very crazy spiral, and I decided to change the subject.

"I'm rested enough for you to tell me who you are and why you're helping me."

He nodded. "Name's Emmitt Cole. I was recently discharged from the military. Now, I'm just taking my time seeing the country as I make my way home to Montana. And I'm helping you because, back at the restaurant, you looked like you could use someone on your side." He paused a long moment. "As long as it wasn't anything illegal, I had no reason not to help."

I sipped the coffee in quiet thought, very aware the boys listened as they ate.

"I appreciate what you did. I wasn't doing anything illegal." *In the parking lot, anyway.* "They had no right to take us back with them."

He studied me and nodded. "I figured as much from what David was saying. I'm guessing you're running. Going anywhere particular?" His gaze flicked to the boys briefly. "I'd be happy to tag along to make sure you safely get to where you need to be."

His question brought a pang of guilt, and I waged another silent war with myself. The boys were counting on me. Could I really keep them safe on my own? Blake had changed before my eyes. He wasn't normal. Didn't appear human. My hand holding the coffee shook slightly. I wrapped my other hand around the cup, too, trying to steady it and my thoughts. How could I hide from what I didn't know, from what I didn't understand? I needed help. But, could I trust a stranger? Even if I did, was it fair to put him in danger, too?

"Emmitt, we could use help, but I don't think it'd be right to accept it." I looked at the boys. "There's a lot going on that I can't explain."

He didn't say anything as he studied me.

I took another sip of coffee then answered his original question. "I didn't have a place in mind when I left."

"Can I make a suggestion?"

I nodded. Never hurt to listen.

"Keep moving. As long as you're awake, get further from the last place they found you. He knows you're exhausted. He's going to count on you needing to stop. If I were him, judging from how rundown you looked, I'd bet you would crash hard, too. He's going to start checking likely places where you might have stopped, calling and asking for you by name."

I realized then that Emmitt had booked and paid for our room. I'd been too tired before to notice. He'd known what he was doing.

"If he can't find you still sleeping, he'll at least look for a trail to follow. Switching vehicles was a good start, but they'll have found the dealer by now and gotten a description of the new one. It's only a matter of time," he said slowly, meeting my eyes. "Unless you can disappear."

My heart stuttered in fear at his words, and I looked down at my coffee to hide my frown. I'd disappeared four years ago and didn't want to disappear like that again. I just needed a place to hide. A place where I'd be in control.

"What exactly do you mean?"

"I live on a big spread. No neighbors close by. Plenty of room for you to lay low without feeling like you're being locked away."

His words, echoing what I had just thought, continued to pluck a familiar chord of fear. I looked up, met his eyes, and searched for a hint of an ulterior motive.

"What's in it for you?"

He shook his head slowly and frowned slightly. "Haven't you ever had anyone help you just to help?"

I sighed. If someone had, it happened in a past I barely remembered. Should I trust again? And a stranger?

"May I see your wallet?" I asked cautiously.

I doubted he had anything to do with Blake, but I still needed to assure myself that he was whom he said and wasn't trying to hide something.

He didn't hesitate. A complete stranger reached into his front pocket to hand me his slim bi-fold wallet.

Liam, no longer pretending to eat, watched me closely. Fear had crept into his eyes. I gave him a weak smile, and feeling slightly embarrassed, I opened the wallet.

The name he had given me showed in print on his license, military ID, and library card. I looked at the library card for a long moment. I didn't own one. I studied the driver's license. Emmitt Alexander Cole, twenty-six years old and, surprisingly, not an organ donor. He would help a random stranger by fighting off two guys at a diner, but wouldn't donate? I stared at it for a second before looking at the rest. I pulled out a credit card and eyed the same name. Everything matched.

I found three pictures tucked into the main pocket, along with several large bills. The first picture showed a very attractive woman with blonde hair and eyes that matched his. When I looked at her, I had a vague sense of recognition, but couldn't place it. The other two photos were of men who bore an obvious resemblance to Emmitt.

"Family?" I asked, indicating the pictures.

"My mom, brother, and dad." He pushed away from the door and moved closer to look at the pictures with me.

The picture of his mom couldn't be recent. She looked amazing. I would have guessed sister because of the resemblance. I looked through the rest of his wallet and found a piece of paper with phone numbers, but no names.

"What are these?" I held up the piece of paper, and tilted my head to meet his eyes. The focus I found there made my stomach dip and heat suddenly. I looked back down at the paper.

"The first one is compliments of my mom," he said in an affectionate tone that made me miss my own mother. "It's the number for a friend of the family close to where I was stationed, in case I ran into trouble. The next one is my brother's number. I left just after he and I moved down here from Canada. I wasn't sure I'd remember the number."

"How can you be from Canada but in the U.S. military?"

"My mom's from the U.S. and insisted both Jim and I be born here. It drove my dad crazy because she didn't want to leave home until the last minute. He swore it was her sheer determination that kept us from being born on the 'wrong' side of the border." A genuine smile split his face, and I could see his family meant a lot to him.

I looked away and noted we also had Aden's undivided attention. I smiled at Liam and nodded toward the bathroom. It was a nod Liam knew. He had seen it many times before. Liam seemed more relaxed as he grabbed his brother's hand. Emmitt's answers must have passed muster with him, too, so far.

They moved into the bathroom to clean up, and I turned back to Emmitt.

"The last number?"

"My parents. I figured if something ever happened to me, those three numbers would be good emergency information."

It seemed like a normal wallet. I looked at the floor, debating. I hated driving. If we went with him, we were far more likely to arrive at our destination safely just because of that. But I didn't know him. I thought of Richard and scowled. Did you *ever* really know someone?

"Is it so hard to trust?" His quiet and curious question penetrated my thoughts.

"You have no idea," I whispered more to myself than to him. "Tell me more about this big spread."

He smiled wide. "It's been awhile since I've been there. It's an old three story with wrap-around porches. Before I left, my brother and I talked about dividing it into six apartments. From what he's told me, he's done the dividing and now just needs to complete the finishing work in three more apartments. It also has a huge backyard that's a pain to mow, according to him," he said with a slight laugh.

"Just you and your brother, then?"

"No, a friend of our parents, Winifred Lewis, who we call Nana Wini, moved in as soon as he completed the second apartment."

I really wanted the picture he painted. A quiet secluded home where we could roam outside all day and, finally, in the sun. I wanted that badly. But I needed to think clearly, beyond what I wanted. What were my options? I could cut ties with this man, and the boys and I could try it on our own. With the truck, I might have a chance...if it was just me. I listened to the boys whispering in the bathroom. I couldn't keep running as I was with them along. They needed a safe place, and if I wanted to give them that, I needed help. Accepting Emmitt's help sounded nice, but what would be the repercussion?

Why couldn't my premonitions just tell me what to do? I dropped my head into both hands, frustrated and afraid of making the wrong choice. Sometimes when things sounded too good to be true, it was because they were. His offer might be sincere. The place he described might even be real. But, he had no idea what he was getting himself into.

"You should know they won't stop looking for me. Ever." I had to give him the chance to turn us away, and part of me cried at the thought of never finding a safe place to stay.

"Doesn't matter to me. You'll be welcome as long as you like," he assured me.

I looked up as the boys walked out of the bathroom hand in hand. Both watched me closely, the little eavesdroppers. Their carefully blank expressions decided me. They tried to hide what they felt, just as we'd been taught, but I knew what hid behind their masks. We all were scared and needed somewhere to finally feel safe.

"We'll go with you and take one day at a time," I said, turning to meet Emmitt's eyes. A wide smile split his face. It stole my breath again, and I hoped I was making the right decision.

EMMITT DROVE the rest of the night. The boys fell asleep almost immediately. I tried staying awake but gave up after twenty minutes. Several times, I woke and looked over at Emmitt's face, illuminated by the dash lights. Each time my eyes fell on him, my stomach flipped and my heart fluttered. Without fail, he would sense my attention, meet my gaze, and gently say I needed more rest. My eyes always agreed and drifted closed again.

We continued driving the next day, stopping only for short breaks. Emmitt entertained the boys again with games, jokes, and stories while he casually watched the road behind us. I did the same. Whenever Emmitt caught me checking a mirror—he caught me every time—he assured me everything was okay. As the day progressed and there was no sign of David, my fears eased.

Before dinner, Emmitt posed a question.

"Do you want to stop for dinner or drive on to your new home?" He didn't look away from the road as he said it, and I was glad. The way he said home had filled me with so much longing that I flushed. I glanced at the boys, but they didn't voice an opinion.

"How much longer?"

"About thirty minutes," he said.

"Let's keep going." Then I started to imagine every possible scenario that we might find when we arrived, from nudist commune to axe murderer in waiting.

My nervousness grew, and I paid closer attention as we drove. We passed a bar, which Emmitt said had good food. Across the street from it, a small convenience store's window displayed a blinking neon sign for beer. After that building, there was nothing but trees and a few rutted driveways whose frequency decreased the further we drove. My stomach churned with worry. Please don't be a weirdo.

CHAPTER THREE

THE TRUCK BEGAN TO SLOW, AND I SPOTTED A RUTTED, GRAVEL path marked with a battered, metal mailbox. Emmitt eased onto the tree lined drive. I nervously clasped my hands in my lap and listened to branches scrape the truck as he followed the bumpy trail. After a distance, the trees gave way to an impressive view of a huge and slightly rundown house. Wider than it was tall, the building had a wrap-around balcony on each of its three levels just as Emmitt had described.

Emmitt followed the driveway to the rear of the house and parked near the back porch steps. Turning the key to cut the engine, he smiled down at the boys.

"Welcome home."

Home. My stomach lurched in a worried way while my heart excitedly fluttered.

He looked up at me, his smile fading slightly as if sensing my turmoil.

"Everything will be fine. I promise you're safe here."

Hope surged until Blake's crazed and determined face resurfaced in my mind. The building hope fell. I needed to remember my own words to Emmitt. They wouldn't stop looking for me. Emmitt had mentioned other people living here. Would my presence jeopardize them? Yes, it definitely would.

I nodded to show that I'd heard him; and despite knowing I was being selfish, I opened my door, hopped down from the truck, and turned to help

Aden. There was nowhere else for us to go, and this man was willing to help. But, telling myself that did little to ease my guilt.

Aden and I looked around as I set him on the ground. Trees boxed in the spacious yard on three sides. A garage, set back from the house, listed to the side within the overgrown grass.

Everything smelled so fresh. I breathed in deeply and eyed the green expanse of lawn. It had to take hours to mow. I itched to sit down and run my fingers over the blades. It had been over a year since I'd felt grass tickle the bottoms of my feet. Richard had let me walk outside in the moonlight as a reward after an exceptionally profitable premonition. The reward had lasted less than a minute, long enough for David to call Blake. I shut out the memory and took another deep, slow breath.

Liam slid across the seat and joined us in our rapt study. Like me, they had rarely been allowed outside. If the boys liked this view as much as I did, we'd never spend time inside.

A man dressed in jeans and a dark fitted t-shirt opened the back door, disrupting our awe. The boys moved closer to me, and I gave them a reassuring squeeze. I easily recognized the man as Emmitt's brother from the picture in Emmitt's wallet. He stood about six feet tall with enough muscle to nicely fill in the height. He wore his light brown hair a tad shaggy, which looked good on him. An impressive tan covered his arms and face, and I guessed he spent a lot of time outside. His wide, welcoming smile reached his grey-blue eyes as he stared at Emmitt.

"Emmitt! About time they let you go," he said as he sprang down from the porch. The brothers greeted each other with an enthusiastic hug. Emmitt pulled back and grinned widely at him. Then, they both turned to look at my brothers and me at the same time.

Emmitt's eyes locked with mine. "Jim, this is Michelle and her two brothers, Liam and Aden. Michelle, this is my brother, Jim."

Before either Jim or I could respond, an older woman stepped out onto the porch. Her long white hair, twisted into a thick bun, lay pinned to the back of her head. Dressed in tan slacks, white blouse, and pink cardigan, she looked the picture of someone's loving grandmother. I felt a pang of envy. We'd never had a grandmotherly figure.

She marched straight to Emmitt and pulled him into a tight hug. "It's so good to see you," she said. Then she turned to us.

Her warm smile grew as she looked at the boys. "I'm Winifred, but everyone calls me Nana Wini."

"This is Michelle," Emmitt said, introducing me. I held out my hand, and she clasped it affectionately. She emanated strength.

"I'm so glad he brought someone home with him." She turned her attention to the boys and bent to pull them both into a tight hug. Surprised by the brief embrace, they didn't even have time to think about fighting it before she straightened again. She looked back at me with a twinkle in her eyes. "I have to say, I always thought it would be Jim who brought someone home first."

Emmitt looked slightly embarrassed. "Nana—"

"But, I'm very happy. How long have you two been together?"

I looked at Emmitt helplessly while my face flushed scarlet.

"Two blissful days, Nana," Emmitt said dryly. "Michelle and her brothers need a place to lay low."

Nana looked over her shoulder at Emmitt, her expression unreadable.

Emmitt's expression turned quietly serious. "She needs us," he said.

"Of course she does," Nana said turning back to me. She smiled mischievously and winked. "Since you're not with Emmitt, would you be interested in going out with my nephew Cameron?"

"Nana!" Emmitt said in an exasperated tone.

She laughed. "It's good to have you home, Emmitt. Jim's been good company, but these young men are going to be a welcome distraction from the monotony around here." She held out a hand for each boy. "Let's go in and have dinner. After that, I'll see if I can find any of Jim and Emmitt's old toys. Believe it or not, they used to be smaller, like you two, and liked playing. Still do. So you better keep an eye on the things I give you. They're likely to try to convince you to let them play, too."

The boys looked back at me. I could read the hesitation in their faces as Nana waited patiently with hands outstretched.

"We'll follow you in," I said with a tentative smile, instead of encouraging them to take the hand of a stranger. I hoped she didn't think me rude, but I couldn't ask them to do what she wanted, which was to openly trust. Their exposure to the outside world had been limited to television. Their exposure to people had been limited to me, Richard, David, and Blake. They didn't have a good base for building trust.

Nana led the way to the house. Emmitt and Jim trailed behind us as we stepped inside. The oversized back door opened to a grand entrance, and our footsteps echoed on the newly refinished wood floor. The entryway was completely barren except for a sweeping staircase that led up to the second and third floors. At the base of the stairs were two doors, one on each side of the steps. Further along the walls, I could see more signs of the remodeling Emmitt had mentioned. Someone had patched two large, door-shaped places with plaster.

Nana moved toward the open door on the right and walked into a cozy living room decorated in rose and cream colors. Knick-knacks adorned the bookcase, and pictures of nature scenes hung on the walls.

She waved for us to follow her into the kitchen. Lemon yellow accent towels matched the color of the walls perfectly. The aroma of warm chocolate chip cookies enveloped us as soon as we entered. The boys eagerly looked around.

Nana laughed at their expressions and handed Aden forks.

"If you help set the table, I'll give you the big cookie I made for Jim," Nana said to Aden. Then, she handed Liam the plates with a promise that he'd receive the *other* big cookie she'd made for Jim.

Liam and Aden looked to me for approval before doing as she asked. I gave a slight nod.

Jim pretended to pout as he and Emmitt sat at the worn, light oak table. The two men playfully "helped" set the table by moving things around when the boys weren't looking. Neither boy knew quite how to react. Liam tentatively reached out to straighten the fork he'd already placed.

"Can I help with anything?" I said, turning back toward Nana.

She shook her head. "You just sit."

After all the driving, I wouldn't have minded standing but didn't argue.

Emmitt paused his antics and nudged out the chair beside him. His warm, inviting smile tugged at my stomach, and I felt a flush creep into my cheeks. I tried ignoring it, hoping he would too. He didn't look away until I sat beside him.

It felt weird to sit while someone else did all the work. Nana removed a pan of baked chicken from the oven along with a side of rice and buttered corn.

"If you're lucky, they'll leave some for you," she said with a laugh when I gave the enormous amount of food a questioning look.

Jim mumbled something that sounded like "maybe" as he winked at Aden.

"Liam, Aden, you had better pass your plates down. I'll fill them before Jim fills his," Emmitt said.

It turned out most of the food did go to Emmitt and Jim. Aden, who sat between Jim and me, kept a suspicious eye on Jim after his first piece of chicken went missing. To Jim's credit, he kept a straight face while he finished his meal. When both Emmitt and Jim leaned back in their chairs, not a crumb remained.

I couldn't remember a meal that had been so pleasant. Breakfast and lunch under David's scrutiny had been tolerable at best. The dinners...I shook off the thought, not wanting to ruin the pleasant feeling this meal brought.

After we helped clean up, Jim offered to give us a tour of Emmitt's apartment. I'd thought it odd that Jim would provide the tour until Emmitt confessed he hadn't seen the apartment yet. The boys ran up the two flights of stairs with ease then solemnly turned to watch us. At home, David would have yelled at them for running and closed them in their room for the night. Neither Jim nor Emmitt said anything about running as we followed them up.

Jim opened the apartment door with a flourish. I stepped back to let Emmitt through first, but he shook his head.

"You and your brothers can stay here," he explained. "I'll stay downstairs with Jim. So go ahead and have a look around."

The boys stayed beside me, waiting for permission. I stood there, stunned. Our *own* place? I'd said we would take things one day at a time, not intending to impose on them for too long. But the more I saw, the longer I wanted to stay. We'd just found a secluded place to hide with an awesome yard, two good-looking neighbors—I wasn't blind—and the grandmotherly figure I'd always wanted. And now he threw in our own apartment. I couldn't say no. I gave a slight nod, trying to mask my hopeful excitement, and stepped through the door.

The main door led to a living room similar to Nana Wini's. Unlike Nana's place, no wall divided the kitchen and the living room. While I looked around, Jim mentioned he'd been the one to decorate.

In the living room, a battered sofa helped fill some of the space. A single lamp was on the floor beside the sofa. I couldn't picture how it'd even be useful from there. A tube television sat on an old breakfast cart with wheels.

The kitchen lacked a table but did have a breakfast bar with two mismatched stools. I could eat standing up while the boys sat. A new queen-sized bed occupied the smaller bedroom, and I felt guilty that Emmitt wouldn't even be the first one to sleep on it.

I overheard Jim tell Emmitt he'd made the master bedroom into a weight room and office. The huge grin on Jim's face puzzled me until I saw free weights on the floor and an office chair in the corner. Nothing else.

Emmitt smirked at his brother and shook his head. They obviously shared the same sense of humor; Emmitt was just a little more reserved about it.

"We'll get better furniture soon," Emmitt said when he caught me watching.

"No, everything's perfect." And I meant it. I'd lived in a home furnished with the best money could buy and had been miserable. So what if the sofa had a few lumps, or I stood while we ate a meal. Because of Emmitt, the boys and I were together and free. I just hoped it would stay that way.

"I'll run down and get your things," Emmitt said pushing Jim out the door. Jim waved goodnight to the boys, who stood staring after the pair. They didn't close the door behind them so we all heard Emmitt chase Jim down the stairs. My brothers looked up at me. They were unused to that kind of play. I shrugged. I wasn't used to it either.

AT SOME POINT during the night, I woke with a start. I lay sandwiched between Liam and Aden. Breathing quietly, I listened for what might have woken me. The apartment remained quiet.

After several minutes of silence, I tried going back to sleep, but my imagination wouldn't let me. Every time my eyes closed, I saw Blake's face peering through the window, his canines extended like vicious, ivory blades.

I knew I wouldn't sleep again until I checked the apartment. Heart hammering, I untangled Aden's fingers from my hair and crept from the bed. I was still dressed from the day before. It made me feel safe. Ready. Despite my overwhelming desire to stay, I knew I needed to limit our time here to protect these people.

My wild imagination drew me toward the window. There, I stood torn. I had to know, yet I feared what I would see. Heart thumping painfully, I slowly pushed the shade to the side. Blackness filled the window frame. I panted with relief and let the shade fall back into place.

I left the bedroom and went to check the apartment door. There was no peephole so I pressed my ear against the panel. I didn't hear anything but that didn't stop my imagination as I gripped the knob. Would I open it and find Blake there? Maybe David again?

A light tap on the other side of the door almost made me pee myself. A startled squeak escaped me.

"Michelle?"

I recognized Emmitt's voice and opened the door with shaking hands. Emmitt stood barefoot, dressed in jeans and a t-shirt.

His dark eyes roamed my face, and a worried frown creased his brow.

"I didn't mean to scare you. I heard someone moving around up here and wanted to make sure everything was okay."

My stomach did its flip routine, which I ignored. "The walls are that thin?"

He shrugged. "I have good hearing and couldn't sleep either."

I didn't know what to say to that, so I stared at him while the silence and my discomfort grew. His eyes never left mine.

"Do you want to come down for pancakes tomorrow morning?"

I nodded. I hadn't thought about what we would eat while we were here.

He smiled, just a slight tilt on one side of his mouth. "Okay, then. I'll see you in the morning." He turned and quietly went back down the stairs, his steps somewhat reluctant.

I closed the door and went back to bed, oddly reassured that Emmitt listened below. Smiling slightly, I realized that for the first time in four years someone had made me feel safe. In spite of that happy feeling, my mind wandered to thoughts of the things we needed like food and clothes, to the envelope on the floor next to the bed, and to everything that tied me to the life from which I ran.

CHAPTER FOUR

Little tugs at my hair woke me. Aden lay next to me, eyes wide open as he stroked my hair. Sunlight peeked around the drawn shade.

"Morning, buddy. Did you go to the bathroom yet?"

He shook his head.

"Come on."

I sat up and helped Aden from bed. Liam, who was also awake, followed us. While they used the bathroom and brushed their teeth, I went to the kitchen to check the time on the microwave. On a typical day, David let us out of our rooms by seven. I'd slept past nine. They had to be starving.

After they allowed me a little time in the bathroom, we went downstairs. Both Nana and Jim's doors stood open. From Jim's apartment, I heard a shower running and someone singing boisterously. Aden giggled, and I looked down at him in surprise. He caught my look and grew serious again. I felt horrible that my glance had killed his amusement. I gave him an encouraging smile and his hand a light squeeze, but the moment was gone.

The sudden sizzle of frying food came from Nana's apartment and interrupted the singing. I led the way into Nana's while calling out a tentative hello.

"Good morning, sleepyheads," she called from the kitchen. "Come in and eat."

Only three settings waited on the table.

Nana caught my puzzled look. "As soon as they smelled the food, they started snitching. I told them they might as well eat," she explained. She then smiled at the boys. "I saved some for you."

Emmitt came in while we ate, followed closely by a still damp Jim.

"Ready to head into town and do some shopping?" Emmitt said.

Mouth full of pancake, it took me a second to answer. The thought of clean clothes appealed to me, but the likelihood of Blake finding us remained lower if we stayed hidden in Emmitt's home and tree-enclosed yard.

"Not today," I answered. Maybe not ever. I could live in these clothes forever if it meant Blake never found us.

Emmitt tilted his head and studied me for a moment. "If you're worried about money, I—"

"On Saturday's, I usually comb through the paper," Nana said, interrupting him. "This morning I found a few family rummages. Would you like to come with me?"

I set down my fork, feeling a little interrogated. "Thank you, but I think we'll stay here and play if that's okay."

From the corner of my eye, I saw Emmitt frown.

Nana smiled reassuringly. "It's not everyone's cup of tea. Would you mind if I looked for things for the boys?"

I eyed my brothers and knew I couldn't say no. I wanted to stay here for a few days, at least, before moving on. It would help to have some spare clothes.

"I don't mind."

She and I talked sizes while Liam and Aden finished eating. Jim and Emmitt stayed in the kitchen, listening. I felt Emmitt watching me and resisted the urge to meet his gaze.

Jim sat next to Aden and mischievously eyed Aden's plate. Aden pulled his plate away and shifted his body to give Jim his back. Jim grinned but left Aden's food alone.

After cleaning up our places, the three of us followed the rest outside. Nana wasted no time pulling her small car out of the driveway, and I wondered if I should have given her my sizes, too.

Emmitt ambled to the garage where a riding lawnmower sat with its deck removed. Old, dried grass clumps littered the area around it. Jim joined Emmitt, and they started talking lawnmower care. Emmitt pointed out the need to do general maintenance, and Jim congratulated Emmitt on his new job.

Liam, Aden, and I lingered on the porch and stared at the yard. Our eyes saw freedom, but our minds didn't quite believe it. Clasping hands, we walked down the steps together. At the last minute, I sat and pulled off my shoes. Liam and Aden did the same.

Grass tickled the bottoms of my feet as I stood. I smiled at the feeling and took a slow deep breath. The grass felt just as I remembered, and I wanted to do cartwheels and somersaults on it. A feral desire to hold onto this place claimed me, and thoughts began tumbling in my head. Maybe Blake wouldn't find us here. Maybe we could just stay. The boys held my hands, walking circles in the grass with me.

Eventually, I realized Jim and Emmitt's playful banter had stopped. When I looked up, I found both men watching us.

I self-consciously cleared my throat and turned to the boys. "What do you want to play?"

"There's no swing," Liam said as he looked around the yard with a very serious expression.

Without Jim and Emmitt's gazes, I would have shown my brothers the things I wanted to do. Instead, I bent and plucked a blade of grass from the overgrown lawn.

"We don't need one to play. Here." I handed each boy a blade of grass and proceeded to teach them how to make a whistle using the grass, their thumbs, and cupped hands.

I entertained them with simple things I remembered from a long time ago, until Aden's stomach growled.

"I'm hungry," Jim called out, right on cue. "Anyone else?"

Aden immediately answered with a quiet "Me."

As I stared at Aden in surprise, forgetting that I needed to encourage him rather than stare, a premonition hit. Like a song played too often on the radio, it crawled into my head and stuck there on repeat. I didn't visibly react but did start to worry. When I'd run, I hadn't given any thought to what I would do with them.

When it came to my premonitions, my brain acted as a broken ticker. A string of letters and numbers, the market code followed by the gain, repeated until I passed the information on to someone else.

I'd once tried withholding the information from Richard, but that hadn't worked out very well for me. I discovered that the longer the letters and numbers repeated, the more uncomfortable I became. My head began to ache annoyingly, and I grew irritable. The pain gradually expanded until it reached an agony so piercing that it brought me to my knees, sobbing and clutching at my head. I ended up screaming the market code to Richard. I never willingly withheld the information after that. But I did learn something very significant from the attempt; as soon as the information left me, the pain ended.

I bit my lip as I followed everyone toward the house. I couldn't just give the information to Liam and Aden; I'd tried that once, and it hadn't worked. My need to stay hidden limited my options to the other three adults in the building. If I gave it to one of them, they wouldn't think anything of it the first time. But what about the fifth or sixth? Offloading a tip always earned me a week's reprieve until the next premonition struck. Always seven days apart. To the minute. They'd notice and would start asking questions I couldn't answer. Maybe I *should* have gone with Nana. I could have given it to some random person, then.

Both Liam and Emmitt stopped on the porch to watch me when I lagged behind. I suppressed a sigh and followed them up the steps. I would easily make it through the rest of the day. Tomorrow, though, I'd suffer if I didn't come up with a plan before then.

Emmitt stood aside while Liam and I entered Jim's apartment. The back of my neck tingled, and I knew he studied me. I couldn't consider him as an option. He saw too much.

Jim stood in front of the refrigerator, listing out possibilities for lunch. His large frame put emphasis on the tiny boy standing next to him. Aden barely passed Jim's knee. Jim seemed to understand Aden's timid nature and only asked yes and no questions in a teasing manner. By process of elimination, Jim helped Aden choose cold cut sandwiches.

I sat quietly and watched Jim explain to the boys how he made his triple-decker sandwich. The meat-stacked sandwich towered on his plate, and I wondered how he'd even bite it. I studied Jim and realized he might be a perfect answer to my current problem. He seemed like the type of person who teased and smiled a lot, not taking anything too seriously. The kind of person who wouldn't take a stock tip seriously. I tried to think of a way to pass the information to him without being obvious, but with Emmitt's gaze still on me, nothing inspiring came to mind. So, I kept quiet.

We were still eating when Nana walked in, carrying three paper bags. Emmitt quickly rose to help her.

"I think you'll be happy with what I found," Nana said, setting two bags on Jim's couch. "Emmitt, can you get the other bags for me? They are on the porch." He nodded and stepped out.

Nana reached into one of the bags and pulled out a ball cap. "I have one for both of you. It's good to wear outside so you don't burn," she said to the boys. She set the caps on the couch then turned for the next item in the bag.

I glanced at the boys to see what they thought but, instead, witnessed Jim reach over and take a huge bite of Emmitt's sandwich. He grinned at me while he did it. My lips twitched, surprising myself. Both the boys smiled when they saw my reaction but ducked their heads down to keep eating.

Emmitt walked back through the door with three more bags. He set them on the couch and went back to his sandwich, and I turned my attention back to Nana. From the corner of my eye, I saw him give Jim an annoyed glance before eating the rest of his sandwich in two bites.

From the bags, Nana pulled out a stack of shorts for each boy, several pairs of long pants, shirts, shoes, sandals, and swim trunks. She had provided both with a full wardrobe, including brand new underwear and socks. Two of the six bags remained untouched.

"Michelle, I hope you don't mind, but I found a few things that I couldn't resist getting for you." She indicated the bags. "Would you like to see?" She gave me a hopeful look, so I nodded. Who was I kidding? I felt giddy that she'd thought of me.

Like the boys, I now owned several pairs of shorts, two additional pairs of jeans, and several printed tees.

"I'll let you look through the rest on your own," she said, stopping halfway through the second bag. "If something doesn't fit, just let me know."

Jim piped up behind me. "What? No suit for her? Come on Nana, tomorrow's the fourth. We could go to the lake."

Nana shot Jim a dirty look. "Of course, I bought her one. She can look for herself."

Jim grunted loudly, and I turned to look at him. Emmitt stood close beside him. Neither met my gaze. Both Aden and Liam smiled down at their plates. Suspicious, I looked down at my plate. Empty. The last two bites had vanished. My lips twitched again, and I shook my head and looked at Jim. Jim widened his eyes and pointed discreetly at Emmitt. Aden burst out in giggles.

I turned away from the foursome. Jim's antics would bring the boys out of their shells. But what trouble would they learn from him?

Nana apparently had the same thought as she repacked the bags.

"Jim, if you can't behave, you can go mow the lawn. Boys, put your plates in the sink if you're finished. Emmitt, can you help me bring these up to their apartment?" She indicated the bags as she picked up two herself.

The way she said "their apartment" warmed me, and I smiled at her as she passed. I liked how she brought everything to order easily.

Jim put his plate in the sink, winked at Aden, and sauntered out the door as Emmitt grabbed several bags from the couch. Aden quickly put his plate in the sink and followed Jim, saunter and all. I caught Emmitt do a double take. His lips tilted at the corners before he left, too. Having Aden out of my sight for even such a short time worried me, and I was glad Liam remained by me. Together, we quickly cleaned up lunch then went outside. I easily spotted Aden.

Jim squatted next to the mower, Aden at his side mirroring his pose. I could hear Jim explaining the names of the tools Emmitt still had laid out beside the now attached deck.

"What do you think, should we take her for a test drive?" he asked Aden. I eyed the mower with concern.

Jim looked up at me. "What do you think, Michelle? If I hold him, can we go for a ride around the yard?"

Nana's voice rang from inside the house, saving me from answering. "Jim, I think the boys would be better served if you went to the basement to look for some of your old things. I recall seeing gloves and a ball somewhere in that mess."

Both Aden's and Jim's faces fell, but I was relieved that she'd discouraged the idea and saved me from saying no.

"Aden, you and Liam can wait on the porch with me," she said as she walked out holding two plates, each with a cookie. "It won't take Jim long."

The boys walked toward the porch.

Jim scowled playfully. "Where's my cookie?"

"You had more than your share of food at lunch. If you want dessert, learn to eat what's on your own plate," Nana said mildly and patted each boy's head as she handed over the cookies.

Jim walked past me and mumbled, "Notice Emmitt doesn't get a cookie either."

I smiled and rolled my shoulders. The ticker continued its repetition, and the symptoms crept in, a tightness in my shoulders and back of my neck.

"Michelle, I can keep an eye on them if you want to go look at the clothes quickly. You might find something you can change into. I can send the boys up as soon as they finish."

I hesitated to leave them. Everyone here was nice, but we'd only been here a day. Both boys, still full from lunch, nibbled slowly at their cookies. Liam watched me closely.

"Is that okay, Liam?" I asked hesitantly.

He turned to look at Nana, and she patiently let him judge her. Finally, he nodded.

"I'll be right back if you don't come up first," I assured them.

I took the stairs two at a time and arrived at the door out of breath just as Emmitt stepped into the hall. He gave a small smile as he passed me. I hesitated in the doorway until he reached the second landing. I didn't want an audience when I looked through the clothes.

The bags lined the couch. I knelt and started digging through them, hurrying to sort everything into piles. At the bottom of my bag, I found new underwear, a swimsuit, and a sports bra. Gratitude swamped me. Clean clothes!

Tromping footsteps announced Liam and Aden's impending arrival. I helped them change into shorts then begged them to watch some fuzzy cartoons on the TV while I showered and changed.

Excited, I closed myself into the bathroom, and then realized I had a problem. The towel rack sat empty. No shampoo lined the shower ledge.

Nana had graciously provided the clothes, but we still needed a few other basic items. I went to the bedroom and counted out the remaining cash. Thanks to the magazines I'd read, I could guess the cost of new shoes, tops, or designer jeans. But what did second-hand clothes cost? And what about basics like flour, milk, shampoo, and deodorant? Uncertain, I plucked two of the one hundred dollar bills from the pile. She'd brought back six bags of clothes...it had to be close. I assured the boys I would be right back and ran downstairs.

The lawnmower droned outside. Both Nana's and Jim's doors stood open, but I didn't see anyone.

Before I could decide if I should knock or just start shouting out names, Nana called from the porch. Both she and Jim sat on the steps, watching Emmitt mow.

Jim leaned back in the sun, barefoot, shirt off, and wearing jean cutoffs while he grinned at his brother. Emmitt glanced our way when I walked out the door. Jim definitely looked good, but he didn't give my stomach fits of churning delight like Emmitt did. Thankfully. One distracting me was enough.

"I wanted to thank you for the clothes, Nana," I said ignoring both men. I handed her the money, which she accepted. "And I was wondering if I could borrow a towel and shampoo for a shower."

She looked at the bills. "This is more than what I spent on the clothes."

At least it wasn't less. "It's okay. I really appreciate what you did for us. It saved me from having to—" I caught myself. "It would have been boring for Liam and Aden, and I didn't want to leave them alone."

She nodded in understanding. "How about we send Jim to the store to buy some picnic food? Then, we can go to the lake tomorrow like he suggested. It's a public lake but remote enough that not many people go there," she said before I could decline.

My mind raced through several possibilities. One being that if we stayed on this property, hidden, Blake might not ever find us. Sure, I knew he wouldn't give up, but how would he know to look here? I liked it here. I liked Emmitt, his brother, and their neighbor and knew that Liam and Aden did, too. But, I knew that by tomorrow my pain would be worse.

Staying here meant I needed to find a way to deal with the premonitions. A random conversation with Jim about stocks, a topic just about everyone my age would naturally avoid, wasn't the best idea. If we went to the lake, I could put something on someone's car window. Or draw it in the sand where someone would see. The lake provided more opportunities.

I nodded, and she handed Jim one of the bills. He laughed mischievously.

"I'll be right back." He went into the house and came back out a minute later wearing sturdy boots and a sleeveless shirt. Small keys dangled from his little finger.

"Jim..." The warning in Nana's voice was clear as he jumped from the porch.

Emmitt looked up from his mowing as Jim swung a leg over Emmitt's motorcycle and inserted the key. The drone of the mower died as the bike's engine roared to life. Jim laughed loudly and revved the bike over Emmitt's shouted words. Saluting us, Jim took off.

"Nana!" Emmitt called in frustration. It reminded me of Liam when Aden wouldn't share a toy. "You couldn't stop him?"

Just then, we heard Jim rev the engine again and squeal a tire on the blacktop road. The sound faded much too quickly.

Nana glanced at me with a small smile. "Jim was lonely without Emmitt."

"I can tell," I said absently, turning to watch Emmitt run a hand through his hair. His lips moved rapidly, and I guessed if I stood closer, I would hear swearing. "Did Emmitt miss Jim, though?"

She laughed. "Let's get you that towel."

EMMITT FINISHED MOWING the backyard and moved to the front before Jim returned. Pieces of grass stuck to our feet when Liam, Aden, and I ventured out onto the newly cut expanse. I loved the smell of it.

Nana called to us from the porch and presented the boys with the gloves and ball that Jim had unearthed in the basement.

I helped them fit their small hands into the large gloves as she went to the garage to fetch a rake. Without a glove to play, too, I grew restless watching the boys toss the ball to each other.

Living in confinement hadn't been bad if I followed the rules, but it had been boring. Given our options at that time, boring had been better than David's harassing presence or Blake's furious attention when I did something outside of the boundaries he set. But being bored while the ticker ran in my head just brought my increasing tension into focus and reminded me that the ache would only get worse.

I went to the garage, found a second rake, and helped Nana, stopping occasionally to roll my shoulders. I caught Liam watching me with a knowing look and was glad Emmitt wasn't within sight.

The motorcycle roared into the yard while the mower still rumbled in the front. The boys stopped their play to watch Jim park. He put his feet down to stop and grinned widely at the boys.

"I've got some cool stuff for tomorrow!"

Liam looked at me for permission, but Aden inched his way toward Jim before I even nodded. Jim stood and swung a leg over the bike, handing a bag to each boy as they crowded close.

I set the rake on the grass and joined them. Through the plastic bags, I saw boxes for sparklers, smoke bombs, spark fountains, and more. I didn't see one food item. I glanced nervously at Nana. Jim had blatantly disobeyed.

The mower in the front quieted. Jim grinned wider, looking down at the boys' rapt expressions. I doubted they even knew what they looked at. Nana set her rake down and strode toward Jim to peer into the bags.

"James Grayson Cole. That wasn't your money." The growled intensity in Nana's voice surprised me. Even the boys looked up at her.

Though Jim's grin remained on his face, it started to look a little forced.

"I got what we needed, Nana." He met her eyes steadily.

I watched the scene play out, feeling uncomfortable. There was an obvious silent message there, but I didn't know what. Would they start arguing?

Emmitt walked around the side of the house just then. My heart skipped a beat at the sight of his damp shirt and glistening skin. His eyes met mine as he closed the distance, and he gave me a wink. My stomach did an extra special twirl. On top of my nervousness, it didn't feel too good.

He set a hand on Nana's shoulder. "Let's save this conversation for another time."

Nana's eyes didn't leave Jim's, but she did nod in agreement.

Emmitt bent to look in the bag that Liam still held with uncertainty. "Do you think we should light some of these tonight?"

Liam's eyes darted to me, then between Jim and Nana. I didn't blame him. It felt like the wrong answer could set off a landmine. Even Aden looked at the group in confusion, his bag hanging loosely from his chubby fingers.

"I think we should go inside," I said softly, holding my hands out. Liam dropped his bag, and Aden immediately did the same. They ran to me, wrapping their little hands in mine.

The three other adults didn't move as I led the boys away. I felt Emmitt's eyes on me and risked a backward glance. Our eyes met, his concerned and sad gaze followed my progress. I quickly looked away.

Both boys remained quiet as we walked to the house, as did the group behind us. I wondered what lecture waited for Jim.

We spent the rest of the evening in Emmitt's apartment. I discovered paper in one of the kitchen drawers and played tic-tac-toe with them. When we grew bored with that, I found a movie we could all watch while lounging on the lumpy couch. We remained quiet just like we used to do when David grew angry. If we were quiet, he eventually calmed down; and we avoided being locked back in our rooms.

Dinnertime approached, and the annoying ache officially upgraded to a headache. Since coming inside, I hadn't heard anything from below. Back home, a quiet house after Richard returned home from work meant trouble. Neither boy mentioned anything about dinner so I ignored it, too.

Eventually Aden started to yawn, and I suggested we all get ready for bed. Thanks to Nana, we changed into pajamas and snuggled in for the night.

Despite the pain in my head, I slept hard.

CHAPTER FIVE

"BUT I'M HUNGRY..."

The faint whisper penetrated my foggy mind. Pain throbbed in my skull, steady and insistent. I wanted to drift to sleep again, but I heard Liam's solemn answer.

"Mimi's head hurts."

At five, Liam knew the power of my pain. In the past, Blake had used it to gain my obedience. It worked just as effectively as threatening the boys.

"It's okay, buddy," I mumbled lifting my head. I pretended it didn't feel like it would fall off. "I'm hungry, too." I blinked, and it took a moment to focus.

They stood beside the bed already dressed in swim trunks. I wondered if we would still go to the lake after yesterday's discord.

I pulled back the covers and stumbled from the bed. Aden backed up, giving me space, and held up my swimsuit. I smiled shakily and took it from him, unable to disappoint him.

"I'll change after we eat, okay?" He nodded and led the way to the kitchen. When he turned the corner, I tossed the suit over my shoulder, not caring where it landed as long as he didn't notice.

In the kitchen, I opened cupboards only to stare at their empty cavities. The refrigerator equally disappointed me. I looked at the boys. We would need to beg from our neighbors again. I hoped that Nana and Jim had worked out their differences yesterday and there wouldn't be any lingering tension.

Forgetting about personal hygiene, I shuffled to the door. The boys followed. I heard Aden's stomach growl.

"We'll see if Emmitt has some food. 'K?" He had been the coolheaded one of the bunch yesterday.

The stairs challenged me, and I needed to grip the railing to keep my balance. I rolled my shoulders, subconsciously trying to ease the pain. Liam moved beside me and held my other hand. I tried smiling again and gave his hand a light squeeze.

Before the end of the day, I would be babbling and crying. I needed to get rid of the information.

Emmitt stood at the bottom of the steps, waiting for us. He tilted his head slightly as he monitored our slow progress. The concern from yesterday crept back into his eyes.

When we reached the bottom, he stepped forward and gently touched my forehead. He pulled his hand back before I could lean into the comfort of it. His light touch, though brief, lingered on my skin.

"What's wrong?"

"Nothing. Just a headache," I said clutching the railing.

Liam stayed beside me, but Aden stepped forward, craning his neck to meet Emmitt's eyes.

"I'm hungry," he said with quiet uncertainty.

Emmitt smiled down at him. "Of course you are. You skipped your supper. Would you like some pancakes?"

Aden nodded enthusiastically and reached up to hold Emmitt's hand. I looked at their joined hands, and my heart ached for Aden. He obviously wanted a man in his life who could care about him. I empathized.

"Would you like some aspirin or something?" Emmitt asked as Aden tugged him toward Jim's apartment.

I shook my head—very gently—and followed them, still holding Liam's hand. Jim stood at the stove, cooking. When he glanced back at us, he caught my eye and winked. Had my head not hurt, I would have smiled. Whatever happened after we left yesterday hadn't changed Jim's mood.

The smell of the grilling pancakes turned my stomach, but I sat with the boys at Jim's kitchen island. Emmitt nudged Jim to the side while talking to the boys.

"If you add a big scoop of batter in the middle," he turned slightly to show Liam, "and add two smaller scoops to the top on each side, do you see what we can make?" Liam shook his head, and Emmitt's lips twitched in a smile. "No? Well, we'll see if you can guess it when we're done."

We all watched Emmitt reach into the refrigerator and pull out the can of whipped cream. He set it on the counter in front of Liam then turned to flip the pancake. He let it in the pan for another minute before he put it on a plate.

"Ready, Liam?"

Liam nodded, and Emmitt uncapped the can. Within seconds of applying the cream, Liam began giggling.

"Know what this is, yet?" Emmitt asked tilting his head to look at his creation.

Aden laughed with Liam. For a split second, it'd looked like a famous mouse, but then the heat of the pancake had melted the cream so it looked more like a bear with a grimace.

"Well, that didn't work so well," Emmitt said, sliding the plate toward Liam. "Try a bite and let me know if it tastes better than it looks. I'll start another one for your brother and sister."

I struggled to swallow down the bile that rose at the thought of eating. Sliding back, I nudged Aden off my lap and onto the stool then quietly excused myself.

I escaped outside into the fresh air. On the porch, I leaned against the column near the stairs and looked out at the yard. A warm, early morning breeze swept away the smell of cooking food, easing my stomach but not my head. My eyes watered with the increasing pain.

Inside, a phone rang. The sound chipped at my skull. Thankfully, Nana answered on the second ring.

Emmitt came out to stand next to me. "Liam said your head really hurts. Are you sure I can't get you something?"

Liam didn't understand the cause, only the level of pain I endured.

"No, I'm fine." I didn't move.

I could hear Nana's conversation. *"Sam, I don't know any better than you do. I thought all you did was research the trends, read financial reports, and watch for promising growth opportunities. When I read the paper, I look at the funnies. Now that I can help you with..."*

My ears perked up.

Emmitt moved down to the step in front of me, bringing him closer to eye level as he faced me. "If not aspirin maybe Nana has something that could help."

I shushed him and turned slightly to look at Nana's window, fully listening. He tilted his head, watching me.

Nana rattled off four characters, paused, and said four more. "Just pick?" she questioned the person at the other end.

"Pick the first one," I said over the pain. Emmitt's eyes widened slightly at my volume. I could barely hear myself over the thumping in my head. The information spilled from my mouth. "Ride for a one point six increase then drop it."

The pain abruptly disappeared, and I sighed before I could catch myself. Emmitt still watched me, his expression carefully blank. His striking, dark blue eyes saw too much. My pulse picked up as I noticed details my headache had obscured. His damp hair. How close he stood. The concern still in his eyes.

In the background, I heard Nana repeat my recommendation and wanted to cringe. Instead, I forced my face to relax, keeping it blank. How could I have been so stupid? So obvious?

Emmitt's calm gaze gave nothing away. "We were still thinking of going to the lake after breakfast. Nana went for groceries this morning. Will you come with?"

I nodded slowly, waiting for what would come next. Questions I couldn't...wouldn't...answer. But he didn't say anything about my headache or spontaneous yelling.

Instead, he nodded at my clothes. "You might want to change."

I looked down at myself and winced. I still wore lounge pants and a baggy t-shirt. Fuzz coated my teeth. A blush crept into my cheeks as I looked up at him again. Amusement twinkled in his eyes.

DRIVING to the lake posed a bit of a problem. My truck, technically, fit three; Nana's cute car fit four; Jim apparently didn't own a vehicle; and Emmitt had his bike. Clearly, I didn't want to drive, which meant tagging along with someone else. Jim suggested we leave the truck because it drank gas and go with the motorcycle and car. Everyone looked at me, and I didn't immediately understand why.

Nana spoke up. "It would be safest if the kids rode in the car. That leaves the front seat open for someone while the other two follow on the motorcycle."

Oh. I looked at Emmitt and Jim. Well, I couldn't see them riding together.

Jim had a smirk on his face as he watched me have my epiphany. It would serve him right if I insisted on driving with the kids. I shifted my attention to Emmitt's ever-watchful gaze. He hadn't questioned me when I acted weird before. I owed him. The thought of being so close set my stomach twisting and jumping.

"Do I need to go change, again?" I wore shorts over my swim bottoms and a t-shirt over the top. Sandals covered my feet.

"No," he assured me. "You'll be completely safe."

I didn't contradict him but knew differently. Not about the bike but about the stupidity of going to the lake or anywhere public now that my headache was gone. However, after agreeing to it and my weird behavior this morning, I didn't think there was a way to back out quietly.

Mentally sighing, I smiled slightly at my brothers who excitedly spoke to Jim. If our freedom was limited, I couldn't rob them of today's adventure. The problem of Blake would still be there after the lake.

I helped the boys buckle in and told them I would follow them. They didn't seem to care as they began to pepper Nana and Jim, who had already claimed his spot in the front seat, with questions about sand castles, swimming, and picnics. This whole experience would be new to them.

Emmitt waited for me by the bike. He sat first and held it steady while he pointed out where I should place my foot to swing my leg over. He didn't say anything about where to put my hands once I was on, though, and my palms started to sweat. I mounted quickly without touching him and landed with a thump that bounced the bike slightly. I mumbled an apology and reached behind me to hold on to the bar back there, not completely comfortable with wrapping my arms around him. My stomach dipped in disappointment. Stupid thing wouldn't settle down around Emmitt. Just another reason not to get too close to him. I wasn't sure how I'd really react.

Nana's car pulled out, but Emmitt didn't start the bike. Instead, he turned to look at me. "Are you sure you can hold on like that?"

I nodded, blushing, not meeting his gaze.

He hesitated, opened his mouth as if he would say something more, then turned around. He slid sunglasses on and handed me a pair. I would have rather had a helmet. I loosened my hold briefly to put on the sunglasses. The engine purred awake, and he eased the bike forward.

Nana waited at the end of the driveway. When we approached, she turned right, and Emmitt smoothly did the same.

I discovered a love for motorcycles. The wind whipped my hair in my face with stinging lashes, and bugs occasionally hit my shins with brief piercing bites. But, I learned to crouch a little and tuck myself closer to Emmitt, who shielded me from the wind and bugs. By doing so, I could revel in the freedom of the open ride.

At the first stop sign, I asked Emmitt to wait and struggled to braid my hair quickly. Knots and tangles slowed my progress. When I finished, I tucked it into the back of my shirt and told him to go. The car had already disappeared.

He pulled away smoothly and sped up, quickly catching up to them. Jim held something out the window—a camera—and Emmitt nodded. He twisted the throttle slightly and pulled around the car. I looked over in time to see two grinning boys in the back, cheering, and a bright flash from the front seat.

Emmitt pulled ahead, taking the lead.

A few minutes later, we turned onto another gravel lane, much nicer than their driveway, and followed its length to a sun-speckled body of water. A sandy beach lined the shore beyond the empty parking area. Seeing the vacant lot, I felt relieved that I'd offloaded my ticker information before arriving.

Emmitt pulled to a stop. I quickly hopped off and stood on shaky legs as I waited for the boys.

"Did you like it?" Emmitt asked, studying me.

I nodded. Far too much.

AFTER TESTING THE CHILLY, clear water, I chose to sit on the blanket Nana had spread on the sand. It was the perfect spot to keep an eye on the boys. Jim and Emmitt didn't hesitate to join my brothers in the water. I overheard Emmitt explaining the game of chicken to Liam. He had Aden's attention, too.

The sunglasses hid my wandering eyes as I watched water run down Emmitt's chest. I rationalized away my guilt over my pathetic eye groping. After all, Blake could catch me at any moment and shove me back into my prison. Was it so bad to create a few happy memories before that happened? My tiny, rational voice insisted it was, and that I shouldn't be wasting mental resources gazing at Emmitt's beautifully sculpted and glistening chest; I should be trying to think of a way to be free of Blake permanently. I shushed that voice.

Nana reclined next to me, reading and occasionally flicking a glance at the water antics. When she offered me a magazine, I took it to further disguise my growing fascination with Emmitt's water-coated torso.

Despite the sunglasses and magazine, Emmitt always seemed to look up when I drifted from idle ogling to fully immersed fantasy. My telling blush would cause him to flash a small, knowing smile which tweaked his dimple and set off a firecracker in my stomach.

Before the sun started to set, we packed up. When Emmitt mounted the motorcycle, he offered his hand to help me, but I ignored it. I didn't do it to be rude. I'd spent a good portion of the day mentally drooling and didn't think physical contact would be in my best interest. Still, I enjoyed the ride back as much as I had the ride to the lake. Maybe more...

Nana went into the apartment to make dinner while I brought the boys upstairs to change. Emmitt and Jim promised to have the fireworks ready by the time we returned. I slipped into a pair of cotton shorts and a tank top and had the boys do the same.

The boys raced ahead of me down the stairs. When I reached the door, they already stood in the darkened expanse of grass with Jim. Each held sparklers and drew designs in the air. Nana sat on the porch steps, watching their pretty patterns.

Emmitt waited by the bottom step. The two sparklers he held illuminated his face. A hint of a smile tickled his lips as our eyes met, and he drew me in with his dark-eyed focus. When I stepped down, he handed me a sparkler. Our hands brushed. With that contact, I left the real world behind.

A very young girl dressed in lounge pants and a loose top, sat cross-legged in a spot of sunlight on a living room floor. At first glance, she appeared twelve, but as I watched her move, I guessed she was closer to her late teens than her early teens.

So many open books littered the brown area rug under her that they surrounded her in an almost complete circle. She removed one from her lap and set it on top of another open book. Turning slightly, she pulled a new one into her lap and leafed through the pages. She kept her ash blonde head bent over the text, intently studying it as she took notes in a spiral notebook also resting in her lap.

I looked out the window to try to see where we were. Oddly, despite the sunlight, the other side of the street lay shrouded in mist. I could only see as far as the curb bordering her front yard. Turning back, I tried to look for anything else that might help me figure out who she was.

Next to her lay a huge dog. Its massive head rested on its paws. As I watched, I noticed its gaze on the book set directly in front of it. I looked closer in amazement. Its eyes moved as if it read the words on the page.

Whoever this girl was, she owned an unusual pet. I tried to move closer to get a better look at her partially hidden face, but it felt as if I were wading through mud. I gave up and watched some more. The dog turned to look at the girl who'd been mumbling to herself. It showed its long sharp teeth, not in a menacing way but more of a weird doggy smile. The girl reached over, absently petting him, and he laid his head back down. Whoever she was, she looked peaceful and happy. And so did the dog.

The vision disappeared abruptly.

"Michelle?" Emmitt said, trying to get my attention. His hand still touched mine.

"Sorry," I whispered in disbelief. "Daydreaming."

He gave me a funny look but didn't say anything further.

After years of wishing to have a premonition of something other than the stupid stock market, it had finally happened. And when I had touched Emmitt. Holding the sparkler, I pulled my hand away and moved into the darkness. I wanted to think where his watchful gaze couldn't observe my every reaction.

The premonition didn't make much sense. I hadn't recognized the girl, the room, or the dog. I waited for the premonition to repeat, but it didn't.

I snuck a peek at Emmitt as he helped Aden light a new sparkler. He remained focused on the task and an abrupt pink glow lit their faces. My heart skipped a beat, and my stomach flipped. Maybe Emmitt was the key. I reacted to him physically every time I saw him.

My sparkler sputtered out, and I wandered back over to the porch to sit next to Nana.

The boys burned through the sparklers then sat on the porch to watch Jim's small fireworks show. They loved it. Their first Fourth of July ever. And it really meant something. Three days without a sighting. Real freedom.

I watched Emmitt and wondered if I'd found where I was meant to be. But, was it actually safe to stay?

CHAPTER SIX

A soft knock on our door woke me early Monday. I slid from between my sleeping brothers and quietly answered it.

"Morning," Emmitt said. I liked the way he smiled at me.

"Could I borrow your truck?"

"Sure," I whispered. I left him at the door and went to get the keys. "You can drive it any time you want," I said handing them over. "But why the change from the motorcycle?"

He frowned a little. "Jim took it to work."

I smiled at his disgruntled expression. "Tell Jim to take the truck tomorrow."

After Emmitt left, I showered and got ready for the day. When the boys woke, we went downstairs, still not having any food in our apartment.

Nana called out to us when we reached the first floor. She had breakfast waiting and told the boys that Jim would be at work most of the day. Aden was noticeably disappointed. Three mornings of eating downstairs left me feeling like a mooch, but Nana didn't seem to mind. When we finished, I insisted on doing the dishes.

Nana and the boys played a board game in the other room until I finished. Then we went outside. I sat on the step by Nana and watched the boys toss a ball back and forth.

The vision I'd had the day before of the girl and her dog still hadn't repeated itself, and I suffered no ill effects from it. The sudden variation in my ability worried me because I didn't know the rules. What did I need to do with the information? How long did I have to act on it? What consequences were there if I didn't act on it?

I had no answers. I nibbled at my thumbnail, slowly removing the excess with my agitation. It didn't help that I had nothing to do to distract myself from my thoughts. So, I fidgeted when I ran out of nail.

The crunch of gravel heralded Emmitt's return several hours later. The boys dropped their ball and ran to watch him pull up to the porch. Lumber, a grill, and a bright yellow slide stuffed the back of the truck. As soon as Liam spotted the slide, he started to cheer. Aden, still clueless, joined in weakly.

Stunned, I sat on the porch and stared at the supplies for a swing set. I hadn't even committed to how long we would stay. Sure, I *wanted* to stay, but I still hadn't figured out what to do about Blake. He would track us down eventually. Leaving here permanently might keep these people safe from him, but it wouldn't help us. I wasn't sure what would. I needed to know more about what he planned, but the only way to learn more was to ask him. The thought of facing Blake sent slivers of ice through me, and I pushed all thoughts of him away.

The supplies in the back weren't all Emmitt had purchased. A mountain of grocery bags clogged the front seat. When Emmitt opened the door to step out, I stood and asked if we could help carry in his things.

"Actually, they're your groceries."

He'd purchased a ridiculous amount of food, but I didn't comment. I handed a bag to each of the boys, and they took off into the house. Fewer trips to the store were better, less exposure. Plus, cooking would give me something to do. But the swing set just seemed too much for temporary guests.

"Why the worry?" he asked, studying me as he handed me a bag.

I didn't pretend I wasn't worrying. "The swing set is great, but I don't know how long we can stay here." It hurt to admit it aloud.

"I told you, you can stay as long as you want."

He didn't understand, and I couldn't explain. Instead, I just nodded in agreement as a feeling of hopelessness and longing consumed me.

"I'm not sure my freezer will be able to hold all of the meat," I said, grabbing another loaded bag.

"Don't worry. We'll put the extra in Jim's freezer."

Given Jim's appetite, I seriously doubted the meat would be there when we needed it.

I continued carrying up groceries while the boys helped Emmitt unload the swing set.

On the way back down to grab more from the truck, I met Nana on the steps. She carried three paper bags. I smiled my thanks. I didn't know how she managed without dropping something. It had to be a practice thing. I strained to carry two up the stairs.

She helped me put all the groceries away; and together, we marinated steaks and made a salad. With the windows open, I could hear the boys animatedly talking to Emmitt. His responses were much quieter and harder to hear than theirs were, but I could tell from his tone that they amused him. He even laughed aloud a few times. It was a toe curling sound.

Jim came home before dinner, took one look at what they worked on, and pitched in. Thankfully, they were all starving and easy to pull away from their task once they smelled the cooking steaks.

The next day followed the same routine with the exception of Jim stealing the motorcycle. Before Jim came home, Emmitt announced the swing set, with its plastic climbing wall, slide, and fort, was complete. The boys cheered and began scrambling all over the thing.

I sat on the step, slightly bored again. Watching Emmitt assemble the swing set had been a nice distraction. I sighed, and he moved to sit by me.

"I bought a movie when I went to the store," he said, looking out over the yard.

I turned to study his profile. He had a strong jaw, straight nose with a slight bump on the bridge, and firm lips. My stomach dove for my toes for half a heartbeat before it sprang back with a twist. I caught Nana watching me from the chair she'd brought out to the porch and blushed.

"Would you like to watch it with me?" he asked softly.

The way he said it, a soft rumble of invitation, made my heart jump with excitement. I looked away, focusing on my brothers as they played in the yard. I struggled with what I *should* say versus what I *wanted* to say.

Nana interrupted my thoughts before they fully formed. "I can watch the boys out here if you two want to go in."

That decided me. He and I needed to talk. I stood and told the boys that I would be right inside if they needed me. Emmitt let me lead the way to Jim's apartment.

The movie waited right next to the TV. Emmitt went to it and lifted it with a dimple-showing smile. I stood behind him and arranged my features into a serious expression while my insides went crazy.

"Emmitt," I said with quiet reluctance. "I really appreciate you letting us stay here, but I need to say something." He turned toward me. His smile faded, and I swallowed hard. "I don't know how long we'll be here and can't afford any emotional distractions."

He was quiet for so long I thought he wasn't going to say anything, and I started to worry.

"What are we talking about, exactly?" His voice, low and steady, sounded a bit upset.

"The way you look at me..." I whispered with a blush.

Though my mind would willingly paint us in a white-picket-fence dream, the reality was that any emotional connection with these people would just be another way for Blake to hurt me if—no, when—he caught up with us. Plus, I couldn't afford any entanglements that would prevent me from leaving when the time came.

"I see." He didn't sound mad, just thoughtful. "Michelle, when I saw you in the diner, and again when you faced David, I knew you needed a friend."

Friend? As if someone had thrown a boulder down my throat, something heavy hit the bottom of my stomach and embarrassment began to flood me. Had my attraction to Emmitt twisted what I thought I saw into what I'd wanted to see? I wanted to disappear. Instead, I tried to salvage the humiliating situation with a stab at ignorance.

"Friendship might be more than I can manage."

He slowly nodded and looked down at the movie in his hands, making it hard to read his thoughts. After a moment, he looked up with a relaxed, easygoing smile and slightly lifted the movie. "So, is that a no to a movie?"

Cherry red and wanting to run, I still couldn't say no. I was too curious about my reaction to him. Too tempted. At least, we both knew where we stood, and I could breathe again. Well, not really. Not with him so close, but he didn't know that.

For the next two hours, we sat side by side, not quite touching. We watched a movie but instead of focusing on the story, my mind kept wandering to the premonition and the talk we'd just had. Was it just coincidence I'd had a vision when I touched Emmitt?

Jim got home as the movie ended and plopped down on the couch next to me. He slipped an arm around my shoulders. He felt hot and sweaty, and it made me wonder what he did for a living.

"Where do you work?" I asked, turning to him.

Emmitt got up to turn off the television. Jim's eyes followed him, and a knowing grin split his face. I didn't understand it and turned to look at Emmitt. Knees bent, he squatted in front of the DVD player, his back mostly to us.

"Roadside construction. Thanks for letting me use your truck," he said and leaned toward me, planting a quick kiss on my cheek before standing. The kiss surprised me.

"You need to shower," Emmitt said in an oddly flat voice, not turning around.

Jim laughed and sauntered back to the bathroom.

I stood, too. "Thanks for the movie, Emmitt."

He nodded, not looking at me, and I left to check on Liam and Aden.

The swing set hadn't yet lost its appeal, and I watched them climb around on it for a few minutes before I called them in for dinner and baths. They groaned, but listened. Beside me, Nana chuckled at their reaction, and I thanked her for watching them. She assured me they were a joy.

Once they slept, I paced the apartment. Though I had freedom, I stayed close to the boys and had nothing to do. I recalled Nana's packed bookcase and left the door open as I skipped down the stairs. Her door stood open, as usual. Before I could call out to her, Emmitt opened Jim's door.

"Do you know where Nana is?" I asked pointing at her open door.

"She stepped out for a walk," he said in a hushed voice as he closed the door behind him. I heard Jim's chuckle through the door and understood why Emmitt had closed it. "Did you need something?"

"I wanted to ask if I could borrow a book."

He smiled and motioned for me to follow him into Nana's apartment. "She would insist you take your pick." He waved his hand indicating the large bookcase. "She used to be a teacher, you know. She loves curious minds and reading."

His last comment assured me that she wouldn't mind, and I stepped up to look at the titles. I plucked two from the many rows and asked Emmitt to let her know what I took.

I felt his eyes follow me as I jogged back up the stairs. Carrying one of my selections to bed, I read until I passed out.

THE NEXT MORNING, I listened to the boys plan what they wanted to do that day. Play on the swing set, of course. After they finished their oatmeal, I put on my suit with a tank top over it as the boys quickly dressed. With my book and a blanket from Emmitt's closet tucked under my arm, I followed them downstairs for another sunny summer day.

Both apartment doors on the first floor stood open, again. It made me smile. We went from a house with bars and alarms to a house without doors, and I loved it.

We left the cool, quiet indoors and stepped out into the singeing heat. Birds chirped in the trees, and crickets spoke to each other in the tall grass next to the house where the mower couldn't reach.

A metallic clink echoed within the dim recess of the garage, explaining where Emmitt hid.

The boys contented themselves with playing pirates on the swing set while I spread my blanket near the porch in the first sunny patch of the morning. I lay down on my belly and began to read my science fiction novel.

Eventually, I heard Aden's excited exclamation and looked up. They no longer played in their area. They had wandered to the back corner of the garage where they hunkered down on their heels, heads bent, and pointed at something on the ground. I set my book down and rose to investigate. *Please don't let it be a snake.*

When they saw me coming, they ran toward me and excitedly told me about a large animal track. Aden tugged on my hand to lead me to the corner and pointed to a huge, muddy paw print the size of my hand.

"Um, new rule," I said staring at the monstrous mark. "No petting strange dogs. Ever."

"You don't have to worry about that here," Emmitt said, startling me.

I turned as he came closer. He wore cutoff jean shorts and a light blue t-shirt that bore a few grease smears. Friends, I reminded myself as my stomach did its happy dance.

"I've seen the animal before," he continued. "Met it. It's completely friendly to kids," he assured me.

I nodded but still cautioned the boys to stay where I could see them. They continued to gawk at the print while I fled to my blanket and book.

Eventually, the sun rose too high, and I knew I needed to find shade or burn.

I retreated to the house to change into shorts then spent the rest of the day on the porch, reading and inspecting whatever new object the pair discovered.

Thursday morning proved to be as uneventful as the prior day. I didn't really mind. Uneventful was better than discovery. However, moments of consuming anxiety began to occur. I'd find myself relaxing then wonder how close Blake was to finding us. The urge to move, to run again, would flood me. Thankfully, no one was close enough to see my agitation when one of those moments claimed me since Emmitt and Nana had stayed inside to work on the unfinished apartment on the third floor.

By midmorning, the day seemed to drag. I loved my brothers, but never having spent so much concentrated time with them before, I began to feel a little short-tempered when dealing with them. Aden seemed especially whiny in the sun so I moved him to the shade. There he threw a fit because I didn't make Liam join us. After I called Liam over to appease Aden's sense of fairness, they just fought.

Taking a calming breath, I suggested they come in to help with lunch. It turned into an argument over who should pick what we'd eat. I settled it by making slightly smashed peanut butter and jelly sandwiches. They both looked down at the mangled food on their plates and said nothing. Their internal sensors had finally warned them to save themselves by remaining mute.

I opened the windows throughout the apartment and the French doors in the kitchen to allow a breeze while they ate quietly. Before they finished, I decided I needed more quiet time and plugged in a movie. However, paint fumes from the apartment next door gradually permeated our living room, and the boys started begging to go outside. I agreed and trudged after them.

By the time Jim pulled into the driveway, I wanted to rip the keys from his hand and drive to the mountains.

"Rough day?" he called from the truck with a smile.

I nodded, not trusting what I'd say if I opened my mouth.

"Me, too. Want to go out for a drink?" he asked as he dropped next to me on the porch step.

I turned and gave him an are-you-stupid stare. I wasn't opposed to alcohol, but leaving the boys completely alone while I consumed it—no matter how annoying they were—was not going to happen.

He grinned and stood just as I heard footsteps rapidly descending the stairs inside.

"Let me know if you change your mind," he said.

He walked in as Emmitt stepped out. Emmitt gave Jim a dark look as they passed each other, but his expression cleared when his eyes fell on me. He sat next to me, and my stomach danced while my heart stuttered. A solid smear of brown paint decorated the side of one of his hands. Tiny speckles of white paint coated his hair.

"Want to watch another movie with me?"

I agreed without hesitation.

Inside, I heard a shower turn on. Seconds later, Jim began to sing. Emmitt's expression changed, appearing more guarded.

"Let's watch it upstairs," he suggested.

I SAT on the lumpy couch with a relieved sigh. The door to the apartment remained open. I could faintly hear Jim's baritone and Aden's answering giggle as the group made cookies in Nana's kitchen. It was enough noise to know where they were but not enough to bring on a twitch.

Emmitt popped in a movie he'd borrowed from Nana and, still colorfully adorned with paint, joined me on the couch. This time, I focused on the movie and relaxed...or tried to. My insides continued to go funny around Emmitt, and it proved as distracting as my worry about Blake.

An hour and a half later, I frowned at the rolling credits and wished for another thirty minutes. "I made grape drink at lunch," I said, standing. "Want some?" I just wanted to stall going back downstairs. I still felt out of control emotionally and wasn't ready to take on my brothers again.

He nodded, lips twitching, and I moved to the kitchen to pour a glass.

"Were they that bad today?" he asked from behind me.

I wrinkled my nose. Either Jim had told him, or he'd witnessed my reactions to them at some point throughout the day. At least he hadn't noticed my other freak-outs.

"No. I'm just not used to being around them so much."

"How much time are you used to spending with them?"

I shrugged, determined not to say more, and turned to hand him his glass of purple, flavored water.

He didn't take the glass. Instead, he reached out and tenderly tucked a strand of hair behind my ear.

A girl stood in a busy, mall food court. She wore heavy makeup. The girls with her talked and laughed. She smiled but didn't stop scanning the crowd. Dark shadows circled her eyes. I guessed she was younger than she appeared. Probably sixteen or seventeen. It seemed as if she wanted to hide her youth behind the makeup and clothes.

Her skittish gaze began to make me nervous. I looked around, trying to figure out what she searched for. I saw in the food court clearly, but the shops further away faded into a haze. I wondered what it meant that I could only see the immediate area in these visions.

Looking closely at the area visible to me, I spotted a man watching her from across the food court. He appeared several years older than she did. She hadn't noticed him, yet.

He pulled a phone out of his pocket and dialed a number. I could hear his end of the conversation clearly even over the distance that separated us. It would have been impossible in the real world, but perhaps in my vision world I could hear anything I could see.

"Gabby, I found her, but—" He stopped and listened, never taking his eyes from the girl. "Yes. I understand you think she's important, but she's not even eighteen. How am I supposed to get her to come with me?" He paused again. "Fine. You better be there when we get there." He hung up the phone and slipped it back into his pocket.

I became aware of the present and Emmitt's thumb softly trailing across my cheek. My heart skipped a beat, and I struggled to breathe. He stood so close. Friends, I reminded myself.

"What are you thinking about?" Emmitt asked.

I took a slow breath. "Nothing."

He dropped his hand, and his eyes searched mine. "We all have our secrets, Michelle."

I wanted to snort in disbelief. What secret did Emmitt have that could possibly rival the laundry basket of secrets I carried?

He continued to watch me then frowned slightly.

"I want to show you something," he said slowly as if just making up his mind. "My secret." He moved half a step back and held out his arm. "But I don't want it to freak you out. I just want you to see you can share your secrets with me. I want you to be happy here."

I doubted knowing any secret of his would encourage me to reveal mine, but I dutifully looked down anyway. He had nice hands. Strong hands. A light dusting of hair covered his corded forearm. How could looking at someone's arm make my stomach go crazy? I struggled to focus. At first, I thought I needed to find a tiny hidden tattoo or something. As my eyes searched, I noticed his arm hair change. It grew longer and thicker. Startled, my gaze flew to his.

"You can make your hair grow?" My gaze flitted to the hair on his head. It didn't look any longer than it had a moment ago.

"Sort of," he said lowering his arm. "There's more." He pulled back his lips in a parody of a huge smile.

I stared at Emmitt's elongated teeth in horror. Panic bloomed. Clutching the glass in my hand, a growling scream erupted from my throat, and I drew back my arm to throw the glass at him. At the same time, I lifted a knee and clipped his groin. He dropped like a stone before I launched the glass.

Eyes wide, I looked down at his prone form. He had closed his eyes, and his gritted teeth still exposed his canines. I couldn't look away from them. Panting, I tried to make myself move. Run. Run! RUN. The word echoed in the cavern of my mind until I broke free of my paralysis. I dropped the glass and sprinted for the door, clearing it as the glass shattered and Emmitt grunted.

How many of these things existed? *Protect the boys.* Was this all just a game? *Protect the boys.*

I sprinted down the stairs, taking three at a time in my panic and almost fell. Jim met me a few steps from the bottom. He held both hands out in front of him, palms toward me.

"Michelle, it's okay. We can explain."

No, not him. Of course him. They were brothers.

"God," I whispered, skirting around him. My eyes darted to Nana's door, which stood slightly ajar.

He let me pass, but his eyes flicked up the stairs. I didn't turn to look.

Reaching the bottom, I pushed the door the rest of the way open. Both the boys sat on the couch. They remained focused on the movie still playing, unaware of the danger. My sudden appearance didn't disturb them. Nana however, stood waiting for me just inside the door. Her stance partially shielded them from my view.

"Michelle, let's talk in the hallway," she said calmly.

My heart hammered in my chest. They would not take the boys from me. I braced myself, ready to fight, but didn't get a chance. Fingers curled around my biceps and pulled backward. Nana stepped forward and nudged the door shut, closing her in with my brothers as I bumped against a hard chest. I struggled until I heard Emmitt's voice.

"Please," he whispered, holding me firmly. "Let me explain." His breath tickled my ear.

Eyes wide, I panted in fear and wondered what he'd do in retaliation for the kneeing. A tear leaked from the corner of my eye. I stared at Nana's door and tried to think. There had to be a way to get them out safely.

"Shh," he soothed, running a hand down one arm. "You're still safe. I promise."

I used his distraction and loose hold as an opportunity to elbow him in the ribs. It hurt my elbow.

He grunted again but didn't let go. Instead, he leaned in closer, his nose touching the tender place just below my ear.

"Please," he whispered. His lips brushed the lower part of my neck.

A tremor ran through me in response. I froze, holding my breath at my reaction. It didn't fall in line with my let's-not-be-friends-because-I'd-rather-unman-you attitude I'd had upstairs. I struggled to think past the mind-numbing panic.

His exhale tickled my skin as he pulled back slightly and trailed the tip of his nose around the shell of my ear. All thought stopped.

"I'll take every knee, elbow, or fist you throw at me because it means you're still here, and I still have a chance to explain."

I couldn't make myself move. I didn't know how to fight like this. What was he, and why did I react to him? It was too unnatural. A sob escaped, and I shook in his arms.

"No," he whispered fiercely as he turned me to face him.

I braced my hands against his chest, trying to put space between us. He didn't seem to notice. He cradled my face and touched his forehead against mine.

"Please," he whispered. "Give me a chance. Give me time. I'm different, but nothing to fear." Desperation laced his words.

Nothing to fear? He was everything I feared. How soon before they called Blake? When would he show up to gloat over my stupidity?

"I want my brothers," I said in a broken whisper.

"Of course. Nana only wanted to protect them. She didn't want them to see you like this and worry."

The disbelief I felt showed on my face, but his earnest expression didn't change. I experimentally pulled away, and he reluctantly dropped his hands. Warily, I watched him as I put distance between us. He straightened and met my gaze steadily. Clotted blood adorned his forehead. Remembering his forehead pressed against mine, I reached up and wiped my face free of tears and potential blood. Emmitt was right; I didn't want the boys to see me like this, but I wouldn't leave them in there, either.

I darted a glance to the side and saw Jim sitting on the steps. For the first time ever, he neither teased nor smiled. His sad and concerned gaze tracked my moves.

Angling myself so I could see them both, I reached out to rap my knuckles on the door. It immediately swung open. Nana had a hand on each boy's shoulder. Gently, she pushed them toward me. Aden and Liam stepped out and curiously looked at the adults around them. I extended my hands and only felt moderate relief when their fingers curled around mine.

Now what? Emmitt watched me. I could still feel his lips on my neck and shivered. I doubted he would let me walk out the front door, but I debated trying. If I would get just one chance, I needed to plan. I was good at waiting...as long as Liam and Aden were safe.

I nudged Aden toward the steps, steering him to the side to give Jim wide berth. Liam trailed behind. I didn't take a decent breath until we reached Emmitt's apartment.

The boys remained unusually quiet as I cleaned up the glass, fed them dinner, then got them ready for bed. I considered trying to sneak out with them that night, but Jim still had the truck keys. We wouldn't get far without a vehicle. So, instead of running, we crawled into bed together, and I took comfort in their little bodies pressed against me. Aden tangled his hands in my hair, again.

I waited until they both slept soundly before I let my tears of frustration fall.

CHAPTER SEVEN

When I woke, my head ached from too much crying the night before. I hadn't planned to fall asleep.

Both boys still snuggled beside me, oblivious. Weak light peeked around the window shade. Rain tapped on the roof in a steady rhythm.

Sneaking from bed, I checked the clock in the kitchen. Not that time really mattered. I listlessly sat on one of the stools and dropped my head into my hands. At least in this prison, they allowed us to go outside, I thought.

A soft knock startled me, and I spun around on the stool. I stared at the door, wondering if they'd already called Blake. The bubble of safety I'd once felt no longer existed.

The knock sounded again, making me flinch and forcing me off the stool. I drifted to the door. Fear weighted my stomach as I set my hand on the knob. I wanted to cry again. Instead, I pulled the door open.

Emmitt stood in the hall. Freshly showered, he still didn't look like he'd slept or shaved. He took in my puffy, red eyes with a quick glance and stepped into the apartment without invitation.

"Michelle," he breathed. "I'm sorry." He wrapped me in his unwanted embrace.

I didn't have a chance to fight his touch as I slipped into another premonition.

I stood in an empty bedroom. A king-sized bed with a white, down comforter monopolized the space. Two towels sat on the bed. Folded into the shape of swans, they faced each other to form a heart with their heads and necks. A black, white, and brown abstract painting hung on the wall above the bed. To the left, long black and brown patterned curtains dominated the wall.

Emmitt strode through the door on my right. In his arms, he cradled a woman dressed only in a robe. They were completely lip-locked. Emotions warred in me, mostly my physical attraction to him against my good common sense.

Then, I realized he carried me and gasped. My fingers tangled in his hair, fisting it to hold him in place. The groaning noise the other me made caused me to blush in embarrassment.

When Emmitt gently laid me on the bed, I tried to look away, but my gaze drifted back. Because of my discomfort, I missed what I said, but heard Emmitt's reply.

"It hurts to wait."

I watched in shock as I bit Emmitt hard on the neck.

My heart raced wildly as the vision left me. I'd looked very much in love and happy. He'd been completely ecstatic when I'd bitten him. Definitely not how I'd look if someone bit me.

Emmitt still held me in his arms. I struggled to breathe. Not because he held me tight. No, his gentle hold didn't hurt in the least. A monster held me. One I would bite. Were these visions really the future, or were they a warning?

"Give me three weeks," he said, oblivious to what I'd just witnessed. "Stay. Give me a chance. Get to know me. If you can't accept me after three weeks, I will help you go wherever you want to keep you safe from whatever you're running from."

I pulled away at his words, and he let me go. Taking a step back, I put space between us. Did he really not know? He watched me calmly, his expression not revealing his thoughts. I looked down at the floor, my mind working quickly.

Blake's teeth elongated. So did Emmitt's. Emmitt had shown me more, though. Could they be different? No. I didn't believe in that much of a coincidence. How could two people do the same thing and not be the same?

If I didn't believe in coincidence, then meeting Emmitt at the diner had been a setup. But how could it? I'd driven randomly. Granted, they'd tracked my car, but how could they know where I'd stop. And, Emmitt had been halfway through his meal.

I remembered the way he'd looked at me. He'd frozen in surprise as much as I had. I started thinking of the things he'd done since we'd met. He'd helped us run, found us a place to sleep, offered us a place to stay, bought us toothbrushes, watched movies with me, played with the boys, built a swing set, and made me feel safe. None of that matched with what I knew of Blake and his men. They wouldn't have done anything remotely nice like Emmitt had. I'd told Frank to stuff himself and ended up pinned to a wall. I'd kicked and elbowed Emmitt, and his only response had been to hold me gently while he begged me to listen.

I peeked up at Emmitt's solemn face. Perhaps, if there were a lot of them out there, he really didn't know Blake. Though part of me worried that there might be an untold number of them in existence, I also realized that abundance might work to my advantage. Emmitt could truly be the help I needed. Could I learn something useful from him? Learn what I was up against?

Before I grew too hopeful, the memory of the last premonition swamped me, and my insides twitched as if I'd consumed too much caffeine. If I stayed, would that be my fate? To be with Emmitt?

"What are you?" I asked, afraid of the answer.

He smiled slightly, maybe nervously. "The most common name would be werewolf, but we're not the ones from legend. Not really."

Werewolf. I recalled those men as they sat at the dinner table, ate, and eyed me hungrily. The details of my past four years scared me.

Emmitt continued a quiet litany of his characteristics unaware of my train of thought.

"We change when we want to, mostly as a defense, not because of the moon. We eat like everyone else. Pancakes rank as my favorite food in case you haven't noticed. We're the same as humans, but enhanced. I hear better, see better, can move faster, am stronger, and heal rapidly. And I'm not an organ donor for obvious reasons."

I blinked as I remembered I'd noted that fact when I'd looked at his driver's license. Did he see everything? He watched me closely, now.

I hated not knowing what to do. A premonition about his alliance, or lack thereof, to Blake would have been better than the soap opera I'd witnessed.

Behind me, I heard Aden softly call my name.

"It's supposed to rain today," Emmitt said quietly. "I pulled a few more games from the basement if you want me to bring them up."

I shook my head. I wanted nothing from any of them, not now, maybe not ever. He gave me one last look then left, closing the door softly.

Rubbing my puffy eyes, I contemplated the closed door. Did the premonition change my determination to leave? No. Maybe. The way he acted confused me. I sighed and turned to look at Aden who hovered in the hallway.

"I'm hungry. Can we go by Jim's?" he asked hopefully.

"Not today, buddy. Let's eat breakfast up here." *So I can plan a way out for all of us.*

Liam stumbled into the kitchen as I poured cereal into two bowls. While they crunched, I dressed and cautiously slipped through the French doors onto the porch.

Rain fell lightly on the roof. Dry under its protection, I leaned over the railing to look for my truck. It sat next to Nana's car. So tempting, yet not. Emmitt's secret terrified me, but *he* didn't. Why did he have to be one of them? I was either living in the safest place or the second most dangerous. If they truly didn't know about Blake, who better to help me? Emmitt's litany of strengths rang in my ears. And if they did know about Blake, or were working with him, this was still better than Richard's house.

Still looking at the truck, I frowned. Jim should have taken it to work already.

"I wouldn't have told you," Jim said softly, walking around the corner of the house.

Startled, I whirled to face him. He wore a sad smile. Seeing him didn't send a shock of fear through me as it should have. It was hard to fear someone who always teased or laughed.

"I would have waited for the fear in your eyes to leave. I would have given you a chance to know me better." He leaned on the rail beside me looking out at the yard. "But not telling you felt like a lie to him. And he couldn't stand lying to you."

I looked at Jim then glanced at both ends of the porch, wondering who else hid just around the corners.

"It's just me," he assured me. He nodded toward the garage below. "He's in there."

The door gaped open, but I couldn't see anything within the shadowed interior. It didn't matter, though. I knew whom he meant.

"So, are you going to stay?" he asked bluntly.

I thought about asking for the keys. "Why should I?" I said instead.

"Because whoever you're running from is still out there. Here, you're safe, whether you believe it now or not. Because we care about you...*he* cares about you."

A part of me did a tiny little cheer hearing that. Still, I worried what it meant.

Jim straightened to his full height and looked me in the eye with a stern and serious expression. "Can I have some cereal, too?"

Through the doors, Aden shouted his approval. I slowly nodded, coming to terms with several facts.

First, Blake *did* still lurk out there somewhere.

Second, the actions of an individual or even a handful of individuals within a race...er, species...shouldn't be used to pass judgement on the entire species. That didn't mean I was willing to risk the safety of my brothers by trusting Emmitt, Jim, and Nana. Yet, I couldn't ignore the fact that they'd given me no reason not to trust them other than showing me they grow fur, too. Blake, on the other hand, had given me so many reasons not to trust him. And, that was before he had even shown me his fur.

If Blake and the people here were the same, would it be wise to pass up the opportunity to learn about their kind while we were still relatively safe? Between the opportunity to learn more, the potential protection they could offer, and the way we'd been treated so far, the reasons to stay outweighed the reasons to leave. But, not by much.

Lastly, maybe I wanted to stay because I was curious about Emmitt and the vision.

I joined the boys inside and watched them laugh when Jim fished out a mixing bowl as his cereal bowl.

He stayed with us for the rest of the morning, acting as an indoor jungle gym. The boys climbed all over him, used him as a horse, had him hold blankets while they built a fort, fed him, of course, then settled down to watch fuzzy cartoons with him. The rain continued to fall. Without Jim, I would have gone crazy with their energy.

I watched how he interacted and reacted to the boys' antics. In his eyes, I saw the typical amusement but also concern when Liam accidently rolled into Aden, causing Aden to cry. He acted nothing like Blake. Heck, he acted nothing like David who was *human*. It helped further ease my concern about my lost determination to leave.

Before lunch, Jim apologized and said he needed to go back downstairs. With sad eyes, we all watched him go. Werewolf or not, I was glad he'd spoken to me, and I was glad he'd stayed.

The afternoon progressed slowly with Aden and Liam requiring all of my time and attention. My annoyance with them bubbled to the surface again, as it had the day before.

They fought, whined, and pouted their way to just before dinnertime when it finally stopped raining. Not caring about wet grass or mud, I nodded when Aden asked to go outside then sat in the middle of the retired warzone. Lunch shrapnel still stuck to the counters. Overturned stools blocked the hallway to the bedrooms. Cushions from the sofa littered the floor.

Jim found me in the same spot fifteen minutes later.

"Rough afternoon?" he asked grinning.

"I think I'm ready to start drinking," I tiredly joked as I threw a cushion closer to its home.

"I'll make you a deal. You cook me something, and I'll watch the kids for you."

"Deal." I didn't care if I just made a deal with the devil. I'd lock Aden in a room myself if I had to spend another ten minutes with him. As soon as I had that thought, I felt horrible.

Jim ducked back into the hall and bellowed downstairs that I would make dinner. Then, he disappeared, leaving me with my guilty thoughts. Outside, I heard faint, childish cheering. I drifted to the porch and watched Jim run out the door and chase Aden and Liam around the swing set. Jim's low laugh reached me on the third story. It didn't feel fake. He enjoyed spending time with them. These people seemed so *real*. Please let them be just as they seem. Please don't let them turn out to be like Blake. I turned away from their play, an act of trust that filled me with apprehension.

After straightening the apartment back to its original state, I went to the refrigerator to examine the ingredients. Whatever I made, I needed a lot of it. I wondered if Jim's and Emmitt's appetites had to do with what they were.

For dinners with Blake, he'd always provided me with a strict menu along with the required quantities, expecting me to cook it all. The largess made more sense now as did his pickiness. I'd learned to hone my cooking skills after he'd criticized my first few attempts. He'd smelled the hint of scorch on a batch of biscuits even though I'd thrown away the burnt ones.

I opened the freezer and pulled out the five-pound package of ground beef to start it defrosting.

"Can I help?" Emmitt asked from the door.

My stomach flipped with joy at the sound of his voice. I glanced at him. He casually leaned against the wall just inside the door, watching me with a wary, yet hopeful, gaze.

My heart hammered, and I frowned. It was easier dealing with Jim because I had no particular reaction to him. Emmitt divided me. He pulled me in too close without even trying and that scared me as much as it thrilled me. Avoiding him would be safer. At least, until I sorted out my reactions to him and gave the vision of us more thought. It hadn't exactly enforced his claim that he just wanted to be friends.

As I took a breath to politely decline, he held up a bottle that he'd held half-hidden behind his leg.

"I also brought up wine. Jim said you needed it."

"One glass," Nana called loudly up the stairs.

Emmitt grinned at me and winked. His boyish smile and dimple disarmed me, and I found myself nodding. He didn't hesitate. He left the door open and joined me in the kitchen. Darn it! Why had I nodded?

He found the biggest glass in the cupboard and filled it to the top with wine.

"You don't have to drink any," he said when he caught my look.

I picked up the glass and took a large swallow. It wasn't my first glass of wine. Blake had insisted on wine at the table and me drinking it. I didn't mind the taste or the mellow feeling that followed after a few sips. But I knew better than to drink the whole thing. I couldn't afford the resulting dull senses.

The microwave beeped. I turned the meat, removed the thawed pieces, and put them into a large bowl. Then, I washed my hands and tossed Emmitt an onion with a request to chop it.

We worked together to assemble meatloaf. Eggs, oats, spices, ketchup, onion, and brown sugar crowded in the bowl along with a growing pile of meat. Emmitt mixed while I dug out a pan.

Each time I came back to the counter, I took another sip. The wine did its job, and I began to relax. I realized just how much when I opened my mouth to ask for pepper and said something else entirely.

"He locked them in their room when he got tired of them." I froze and stared at my hands. I couldn't believe what I'd just said. Obviously, I still felt guilty about my own thoughts in regard to locking Aden in a room.

The water ran behind me briefly. Then he touched my shoulder, turning me toward him. Standing a foot apart, I tilted my head a bit to meet his eyes. He didn't look at me with pity or any other emotion I could name. But something in his face, understanding maybe, caused a dam to break.

"My mom died just after Aden was born. My stepfather, their dad, died two days before I saw you at that diner. I'm all my brothers have. I won't let them be locked in a room again."

He didn't touch me, just stood close, listening.

"David will never get the chance," he promised. Determination laced his voice, and his eyes took on a steely glint.

Huh? David? As I frowned at him, I realized I'd never spoken about Blake, and a spark of hope that he really had nothing to do with Blake surfaced again. I studied him and tried to read the truth from his face. I couldn't see truth or lie, but I saw a flash of something else as his eyes met mine. Tenderness.

"I'm not afraid of David." I turned away, poured the rest of my wine into the sink, then put the meatloaf in the oven.

Emmitt said nothing.

I dug out a bag of potatoes and started peeling. He stayed by my side and worked through the pile with me. It hurt to be so close to him. My stomach wouldn't settle down. But I didn't move away.

I WASHED dishes in the silence of the apartment and exhaled a sigh. Outside, the boys cried encouragement to Jim and Emmitt.

With a hot dishrag, I began to wash the counter after I lifted the wine bottle out of the way. Downstairs, Aden erupted in a fit of giggles. Playing with a werewolf. No, werewolves. My brothers were playing with *werewolves*. I grimaced at the thought and continued to wash the counter, wiping away the remains of a dinner that had gone well. Jim had brought the boys upstairs, and they'd served themselves as Nana joined us. Everyone had been nice. It felt like a family. The thought turned my stomach to ice because I knew what I was doing. I was deciding to stay—to live—with three werewolves. What exactly did that mean?

I threw the dishrag into the sink and shook my head in frustration. I needed to settle this in my head, settle what it meant for us. I needed to start asking questions. I needed to talk to Emmitt. But the thought of seeing Emmitt change again made my insides turn to Jell-O.

My eyes fell on the wine bottle he'd forgotten. More than half remained, enough to give me courage to ask hard questions and to stay and listen to scary answers. I pulled the cork back out with a pop and slugged down the remains. Lowering the bottle, I wiped my mouth with the back of my hand then washed the stove.

After a few minutes, I grew warm and the tension eased from my shoulders. Not all of it, but enough. I wished I had more wine but headed to the stairs, anyway. I wasn't trying to use alcohol to hide from the answers, just to make the answers less terrifying.

At the top of the stairs, I hesitated. Part of me—the part that was still listing off reasons alcohol use, when discovering the existence of werewolves, was completely reasonable—wanted to march right back into the apartment and go to sleep. The other part of me agreed. I turned to go back into the apartment and stopped myself. No. I needed answers. Better now, not later. I made a face, turned back to the staircase, and marched toward the unknown knowledge I really didn't want to face, yet.

Emmitt was on his hands and knees being kicked in the sides by Liam with an order to *giddy-up* because Jim and Aden were in the lead. They raced around the porch. I didn't envy Jim's or Emmitt's knees, but they didn't seem to mind. The boys didn't look the least bit tired.

I slipped on the sandals I kept by the front door and joined the fun on the porch. Nana sat in her chair, acting as a judge to keep the race fair.

"Ready for them to come up to bed?" Nana asked.

Aden protested loudly before he and Jim disappeared around the corner.

"Not yet." My stomach dropped a little knowing what I needed to do. "Could you watch them a little longer? I was hoping Emmitt and I could go for a ride."

She turned and considered me. "You smell like wine. Are you sure that's a good idea?"

"It's the only one I have," I whispered miserably.

She gave me a sympathetic look. "Of course, I'll watch them. I'll put them to bed for you, too."

I nodded and waited for the racers to approach again. Before I could say anything, Emmitt stopped in front of Nana, and with great disappointment, Liam dismounted. Emmitt ruffled Liam's hair.

"This doesn't mean they won. We'll just need to race them again tomorrow. K, bud?"

Liam perked up at Emmitt's promise to race again and nodded in agreement.

Emmitt turned toward me and extended his hand. Swallowing the fear the wine hadn't killed, I touched my fingers to his.

"Nana will watch you, Liam," I said as Emmitt wrapped his hand around mine. Liam nodded again, and Emmitt gave me a gentle, playful tug.

My heart thumped heavily as we walked to the garage. This time, I used him as a brace to mount because I was just a little unsteady. I settled on the seat, placed my feet, and reached for the bar behind me.

"No holding the bar this time," he said, starting the bike. "Hands around me so I know you're still with me."

I nodded and tentatively wrapped my arms around his waist. After hesitating for a moment, I laid my hands flat on his shirt over his stomach. I could feel the hard muscle beneath, and the heat of him warmed me more than the wine had. My stomach went into freak-out mode, twisting and tumbling in a thrilling way.

He slowly pulled out of the garage, and I waved to our audience on the porch while I tried to calm my racing heart. It was hard to do when his muscles twitched under my fingers with each slight movement.

He turned left and drove for a bit. I began to relax, loving the ride.

When the bar we'd passed on the way to his house that first day came into view, I tapped his stomach and motioned for him to pull in. One more drink, and I could do this. I could ask him to show me what he meant by "werewolf" and see what Blake really was so I could start asking questions.

He pulled over to the graveled parking lot. The rather small building's dark wood siding blended a little too well with the trees pressed up against the back of it. With a faded sign above the entrance and a flickering neon light in a window, it didn't look like much from the outside.

"I can't take you in there."

"Yes, you can." I knew I looked old enough. If they carded, we'd leave. But I really didn't think they'd card in the sticks. I climbed off the bike.

"Nana will kill me."

"I think you can take her," I said sarcastically.

"You have no idea," he muttered as he got off the bike.

He led me into the bar. Dressed in cutoffs and a tank top, I blended in well with the few patrons inside. Emmitt walked up to the bar and ordered himself a beer and two shots for me. My eyebrows rose.

"Isn't that what you wanted? Alcohol?" He looked slightly annoyed with me as he handed me the first one.

I was dealing with the surreal weirdness of my life as best I could and didn't much care for his attitude. Narrowing my eyes at him, I drank the tiny drink. It burned a trail down to my stomach.

"That was awful," I said making a face. I definitely preferred wine.

The annoyance left his gaze, and his lips twitched. He nodded in agreement and handed me the second one.

"Isn't there something better than that?"

"There is, but that will do the trick."

I swallowed the second one quickly and waved the bartender back over to ask for a glass of water. We sat there as he nursed his beer and the fire spread through my veins.

"I think I'm ready," I said unsteadily.

"For what, exactly?" he asked, taking a sip while he watched me.

"To get to know you."

His eyebrows rose comically, and I realized how what I said sounded. A giggle escaped me, and my IQ dropped. The downside of liquid courage.

"Not that," I assured him. "Like you asked."

A fleeting sadness filled his eyes, but then he shook his head and stood, offering me a hand. I needed it.

Night had fallen when he led me back outside to his motorcycle. The ride home was dangerous and exciting. He went slow, and I held on tight. Maybe my hands wandered over his chest a bit. I wasn't quite sure how much, though, because I couldn't feel my fingers.

When we parked, I asked my first question. "What was in that little cup?" Darn mouth wasn't saying what I wanted it to. Shot; I knew it was a shot.

"Tequila."

"It didn't taste good," I said as I struggled to get off the bike.

He twisted and lifted me off as he stood. It was so effortless that I blinked at him in awe as he got off the bike and stood before me.

"What now?" he asked.

No lights glowed in the windows of the house. The yard light's weak illumination just reached the garage. Enough to see, anyway.

"Show me?" I asked. My world tilted a little, and I reached out a hand to steady myself. When the world righted, I absently petted the bicep under my fingers. Lovely muscle.

"What exactly?" Emmitt's voice rumbled quietly in front of me.

"You said you're a werewolf. Show me what that means exactly." I slowly blinked at him, watching the shadows the yard light cast on his face.

He studied me for a moment then reached up and gently ran his fingers down my cheek. "If I show you, will you answer some questions for me?"

I nodded gamely.

"Turn around for a second."

I spun on my heel and almost tipped over. Giggling, I pin-wheeled my arms for a few seconds and struggled to regain my balance. When I found it, I spread my arms wide like a tightrope walker. My fingers touched fur, and I gasped and looked at my hand.

Beside me stood a huge dog. The light from the house barely glinted off the beast's dark eyes as it watched me.

"Hi, there!" I petted its head. Then, wondering where the dog had come from, I peered around the garage looking for Emmitt.

"Did you see where he went?"

At the dog's feet, I noticed a neat pile of clothes. Wait, weren't those Emmitt's clothes? I imagined a naked Emmitt running around and grinned.

I bent, picked up Emmitt's neatly folded shirt, and held it to my face. It was still warm. I inhaled deeply and closed my eyes. He smelled so good. The dog nudged me, and I realized I'd almost drifted off to sleep.

"Good boy," I said, patting its head again.

It harrumphed and used its teeth to try to pluck the shirt from my grasp.

"Bad!" I scolded, tapping the dog on the nose. Its head came to my chest so it wasn't a hard reach.

Suddenly, the dog began to change, comically distorting in lurching phases. Fur disappeared, showing smooth skin. A naked expanse of man-chest.

"Oh!" I said, finally understanding. I spun on my heel, still clutching the t-shirt. The ground lurched under my feet then held steady.

The rasp of his zipper had me closing my eyes in humiliation.

"Is it too late to ask for another shot?" I whispered in mortification.

"Yep," he confirmed from behind me, a second before he scooped me into his arms.

The world spun in slow motion, and I leaned my head against his chest. Being carried was kind of nice.

"Now, you promised to answer a few questions," he said in soft amusement.

CHAPTER EIGHT

STEADY POUNDING WOKE ME. I GROANED AND PULLED THE PILLOW over my head. It didn't block out the noise.

"Mimi," Liam said, shaking my shoulder. "Someone's at the door. I think it's Uncle Jim."

Uncle Jim? What? I tossed aside the pillow, struggled to lift my head from the mattress, and tried to focus on Liam's face.

Last night came back in a rush, and I groaned aloud, letting my head fall back down.

"Should I get the door?" Liam said quietly, shaking my shoulder.

Worst. Sister. Ever. I pulled my hung-over butt from bed and looked at Aden. He still slept on my other side. Thankfully, only Liam witnessed my current state. I stumbled into the kitchen and checked the clock. Six a.m. I was going to kill Jim.

I yanked open the door with a scowl and glared not at Jim but at Emmitt. In one hand, he offered two coated pills. In the other hand, he had a glass of water. He elevator-eyed me, and a slight quirk lifted his lips. I took the pain relievers without comment and swallowed them.

"I heard Liam moving around and wanted to know if he'd like to come down and eat with me." His warm, soft voice melted my middle and brought back the memory of last night's question and answer session that had followed Emmitt's big reveal. I cringed.

Emmitt: *"If you're not worried about David, who are you worried about?"*

Me: *"Can I sleep in your shirt tonight?"*

Emmitt: *"Why did David keep you locked away?"*

Me: *"Blake told him to. I really liked when you kissed my neck even though I tried not to."*

Notable pause in questioning.

Emmitt: *"Who's Blake?"*

Me: *"I like you without a shirt. A lot."* *Long pause.* *"I think I'm going to be sick."*

It could have been worse.

"I'm never drinking again," I whispered.

Emmitt grinned. "I like your pajamas."

I looked down at myself. I wore his t-shirt. Damn.

"We're not on speaking terms today," I said, meeting his eyes again.

He laughed and greeted Liam who joined us, dressed for the day.

"Send Aden down when he's up."

I MANAGED another hour of sleep before Aden woke. Enough time to lose the headache. I sent Aden downstairs, jumped in the shower, and contemplated the night before.

After failing to answer Emmitt seriously, he'd carried me upstairs. I flinched as I recalled how I'd clung to him. So much for my little talk about being less than friends.

He'd opened the door and set me on my feet, then waited in the living room while I shuffled into the bathroom with his shirt. I'd sniffed it and grinned like an idiot for a moment before changing. When I'd stumbled back into the hallway, I'd hesitated. Despite the tequila, I'd realized the danger in getting too close to him again. From a good ten steps away, I'd wished him a good night. He'd grinned at me, wished me sweet dreams, and closed the door. I'd crawled into bed between the boys.

I took my time drying my hair and getting dressed. Moving slower seemed wise. When I left the apartment, the smell of cooking food hit me, and I almost gagged. I concentrated on the steps to distract myself, and my stomach settled.

At the bottom of the stairs, both apartment doors stood open. Aden's voice came from Jim's place so I stepped through that door.

Nana sat at the island, supervising Aden's attempt at cutting a sausage until I walked in then her watchful gaze fell on me. She looked me over from head to toe, turned to Emmitt, and glared at him. He wouldn't meet her eyes. Pretending not to notice, I planted a kiss atop each boy's head.

"What do you guys want to do today?" I asked quietly. Though the headache was gone, my head still felt tender.

Jim piped up. "It's going to be hot and humid. Can we go back to the lake?"

I nodded, not really caring. Napping on the beach didn't seem like it had a downside.

"Michelle and I will get the groceries this time," Emmitt said, pouring syrup over a stack of pancakes. He handed the plate to me.

I wrinkled my nose but reached for it.

"No," Nana said. "I think you should take Jim to teach him how to shop."

Emmitt turned back to the pan, but I caught his slight frown. I managed a forkful of pancake before my roiling stomach let me know it wouldn't tolerate more. I discreetly slid my plate toward Jim. He took it with a wink and ate the rest in a few large bites.

Emmitt and Jim left with the truck, and while the boys changed into their suits, I helped Nana Wini pack the car.

"So are you staying?" she asked with her head in the trunk.

"It's not like I have a choice." It slipped out before I could stop it.

She straightened and gave me a curious look. "What do you mean?"

Handing her the towels, I shrugged. "There's nowhere else for me to go."

"And if there were?"

"Then, I wouldn't have come here in the first place." I would have headed straight to that mystery place of safety and never met Emmitt in the diner.

She nodded and put the towels in the trunk next to the blanket. "Fate has a funny way of working things. I'd like to say it does things for the best, but how can I when there is so much death and tragedy in the world. No, the best we can do is think there must be some kind of purpose to this mess."

Words of wisdom. There had to be a reason I met Emmitt and came here. I liked thinking like that. Better than dwelling on the possibility that he was in league with Blake.

NANA and I drove the boys to the beach. They ran to the edge of the water while we carried our things to the shore. I set my armful down, and Nana spread out the blanket. Since they were content to play in the sand, I eased down onto the blanket, ready to soak up the warm sun. From her beach bag, Nana pulled out a floppy sun hat and wordlessly handed it to me. I didn't realize how much the sun hurt my eyes, thus my head, until plopping it on.

Sighing, I laid back and closed my eyes. With the heat relaxing me, I slipped into a light doze.

A drop of something cold splashed on my stomach, startling me awake, and I sat up with a squeal. Emmitt stood over me. I squinted up at him. The sight of him glistening in the sun, without a shirt, made it hard to swallow. In his hand, he held a sweating bottle of water, the source of the drip.

He apologized with a grin, not looking very repentant. Before I could say anything, he sat behind me and handed me the water.

"Your head will start hurting again. Drink up."

As usual, my stomach went crazy with him so close. Unable to lie back down, I accepted the bottle and eyed the water level. It didn't reach the top. He shrugged and grinned when I arched a brow at him.

I took a few large swallows and handed him the bottle, expecting him to leave. Instead, he settled back on his elbows and looked out at the water.

Nana mumbled something I didn't catch, stood, and joined the boys at the water's edge.

"About last night," Emmitt started.

"Don't want to talk about it." I moved over to Nana's spot and lay back. My head hit abs, not sand. I sat up again and did a double take.

"How did you move..." I didn't finish my question. I didn't want to know.

"I thought after showing you what I am, you'd have more questions for me. Other than if you could wear my shirt."

My face flushed. I tilted the hat to block his view of me and wrapped my arms around my knees. "Nope."

"You sure?"

"Yep." I didn't really have questions, just a whole ton of worry and what-ifs. Nothing I could talk about without getting into the deeper subject of *me*.

"Green."

The random word caught me off guard, and I turned to look at him without thinking. "What?"

"It's my favorite color. What's yours?"

"If I tell you, will you let me lay down again?"

He flashed me a wide grin but didn't answer.

"I don't know that I have one," I said honestly. It wasn't anything I'd given thought to. "I like looking at the sky, though, so maybe blue."

He moved over on the blanket. His attention stayed on the water. I drank some more, and after a few minutes of quiet, I cautiously lay back down. With the hat blocking the sun and a light breeze to keep me from getting too hot, I gradually relaxed. My breathing slowed.

Lying in the sun's restful rays, I floated on the cusp of sleep.

"What kind of music do you like?" Emmitt asked quietly.

"I don't remember," I mumbled.

"Why not?" His soft voice neither lulled nor intruded on my peace.

"Blake hated the noise," I said on an exhale and drifted away to that leg-twitching place between awake and asleep.

A gentle tug on my hair anchored me to the beach.

"Who's Blake?"

A good question, and I wished I knew the answer. The memory of Blake's contorting face bobbed to the surface in an ocean of memories. This time his long teeth didn't draw my attention. Behind him, the men at the table changed in small ways, too. Hairier arms, miss-happened ears. Nothing I noticed that last night but saw easily, now. Richard's ashen face, shaking hands, but otherwise calm presence as he sat at the table. *Run as fast as you can.* He'd known. *Richard's dead. This changes nothing.* And Blake had killed him. Why? He had a plan. *Scent you...bite him...establish a Claim.*

Another memory bubbled to the surface. Emmitt leaning close as he held me still. His breath tickling my neck on an exhale. His nose gliding along my hairline, near my temple on an inhale.

I SAT UP ABRUPTLY. Twisting, I saw Nana reclining in the spot Emmitt had occupied when I fell asleep. Water splashed. Giggles erupted. Squinting against the glare of the reflecting sun, I spotted the other four in the water.

Nana glanced up at me.

"How long was I out?" I asked.

"About an hour. Almost time for lunch."

I waited for my stomach to rebel at the thought of food, but it remained steady. A good sign. Digging my toes into the hot sand at the edge of the blanket, a sigh escaped. I rested my chin on my knees and watched their water play. Emmitt showed the boys how to cascade a wave of water at Jim, using his fisted hands. As he spun, the muscles on his back rippled.

"Can I ask you a question?" I asked quietly, recalling the way Emmitt had held me when he'd begged me to stay. Nana set her book down, an indication of her willingness to answer. "Do I have a scent?"

"Everyone does, dear. As unique as a fingerprint."

I liked that she didn't ask me what I meant. I needed to face the truth. Get the facts. Start learning. I watched Emmitt in the water.

"Why would a werewolf want to scent me?"

Emmitt's head swiveled my direction. Instead of blocking Jim's spray, he unflinchingly caught it on his left side. I bet he had an ear full of water. He didn't move as he stayed intensely focused on me.

"I'd be happy to answer that question, but I need to explain more than that for you to understand. If you're willing..."

I nodded. Liam tugged on Emmitt's arm, encouraging him to get revenge on Jim. Emmitt turned away to rejoin the fun.

"Emmitt shared with me that he showed you who we are. People use the term werewolf, but we are more than a shape-shifting creature of the night."

I briefly gazed down at the sand the first time she used we, having a hard time picturing her with teeth like Blake.

"We are the opposite of a person with multiple personalities. We are one personality with two bodies. Who we are doesn't change, no matter the form we choose. However, there are benefits to each form we wear. We are faster on four legs than two, but not by much. When in our fur, we have better protection because of our teeth and claws. However, some things don't change. Our sense of smell, hearing, and sight.

"Our sense of smell is more vital to us than our sight. We can smell an object long after it has disappeared. A scent can tell us more than we could ever see. Emotions like fear and desire can flavor a person's usual fragrance. Through our senses, we read the world and react to it.

"Scenting is when we use our sense of smell to identify potential Mates. Their scent calls to us. It's more than just liking the fragrance. It's the rightness of it." She paused for a moment and smiled kindly at me. "I've never had to explain this to someone who didn't have our noses. So let me know if I'm not making sense.

"I like the smell of strawberries, but I wouldn't want my clothes to smell like them. It's a good smell, but not right for clothes. So, although my scent may be pleasant to several, it might not be just right for any of them. Because of the nuance between an alluring scent and the rightness of that scent, nature threw in a backup plan. It's something we feel deep inside ourselves, like a tug in our stomach, reeling us toward the one we're meant to be with. The scent calls us, possibly from a greater distance than we can see, but the pull cinches the deal."

My eyes locked on Emmitt, and my stomach somersaulted as usual. Panic flared. What was Nana telling me? Emmitt continued to play with the boys, but I could tell by the cant of his head that he listened. Was he waiting for me to try to run?

Nana reached over and patted my hand.

"It's a lot to take in, but nothing to worry about. With humans, we werewolves typically don't feel or scent anything that would indicate we're compatible with you. Oh, a few have tried to have relationships, but they were shallow connections that never lasted long."

Emmitt cast a quick scowl at Nana over his shoulder before returning to the game he played with my brothers.

Nana picked up a water bottle lying in the shade of her bag and handed it to me. "Would you like me to tell you more about our kind?"

Until she mentioned the last bit about humans and werewolves not working, I'd been tying my mental running shoes, thinking my vision an inevitable outcome. Could I take more? *Think of your brothers*, I told myself. If I wanted to avoid the fate Blake had planned for me, I had to understand what his words had meant and why he'd forced those monthly dinners.

I nodded, took a sip of water, and tried to relax.

"Werewolves live in packs. Historically, at least as far back as we can remember, packs were small with an alpha pair leading maybe three other Mated pairs and their young. Since Charlene came to us, Emmitt and Jim's mother, there have been several changes, which include all of the smaller packs merging into a large one. Charlene put the backbone back in our pack and brought us together by sheer determination. It's because of her plans for pack growth that I am here with Emmitt and Jim. We are trying to establish another pack location because the main one in Canada is growing too large for the space.

"Our society is like any other in that we each have a place in it. Elders are the keepers of knowledge and peace. Pack leaders keep the peace within their own pack, but Elders keep the peace between packs. Almost all werewolves belong to a pack. However, some werewolves choose to live on their own. Those we call

Forlorn. They can still hear the Elders and have the same compulsion to obey, but they follow no pack leader."

"So Emmitt's mom is the pack leader?" I asked trying to wrap my head around everything she'd shared.

Nana laughed softly. "Technically, no. Emmitt's father is the leader. But Charlene influences the pack in her own right."

I mulled over the information. General information about werewolves was helpful and none of it sounded too bad, but I didn't see how it connected to what Blake had said the night he pinned me to the wall.

"Where in there does biting become involved?" The question slid out of my mouth before I could consider how it sounded.

Nana gave a little cough, Jim roared with laughter, and Emmitt gazed at me, looking troubled. I dropped my eyes to the sand, feeling a flush creep into my face. Apparently, biting wasn't a polite topic of conversation for werewolves, either.

"Can I ask where these questions are coming from?" she asked after a moment.

"Just curious," I mumbled. "Maybe we should eat lunch," I suggested diverting the direction of our conversation.

I didn't ask any further questions for the rest of the day even though Nana offered to continue her explanation of their race. Instead, I moved away from the water to sit in the shade of the trees that lined the beach. Humidity weighed the air, making it difficult to breathe as the day progressed.

Before the sun set, we packed up and headed back home. I insisted on dinner in our own apartment. No one liked my answer. My gaze locked briefly with Emmitt's before I turned to go upstairs.

If werewolves and humans weren't a thing, why had Blake's men scented me? More to the point, why had Emmitt? I had no doubt that was what he'd done when he held me just outside of Nana's door. Were they all just looking for a "shallow connection" with me because of my premonitions? That answer would make sense if Emmitt *knew* about my premonitions.

MY STOCK MARKET premonition struck before the boys finished breakfast. It marked the end of our second week away from Blake. So much had happened in that time yet, other than moving locations, nothing fundamental had changed.

Blake still trapped me. He held me through my fear of discovery. That, and the fact that werewolves were still present in my life, kept me wary. I'd been used for my predictions for too long to trust easily.

Liam and Aden raced downstairs to bug Emmitt and Jim, and I absently followed. How could I smoothly pass along the information without being obvious?

The humidity from the day before still lingered. Sweat beaded on my forehead as I sat in the shade of the porch. Jim eyed our glistening faces and ran into town, returning with a sprinkler. The boys squealed with excitement once he explained its purpose. Another first for them.

I watched them from the porch, not feeling up to joining in the fun. Emmitt stayed close, watching me. I struggled to hide any visible sign of the worry I felt as the ticker continued to run.

Nana stepped onto the porch, making her first appearance of the day. She held her cordless phone to her ear.

"Michelle, I have my friend on the phone from last week. He wanted to thank you for your recommendation, which looks really good so far, and he wanted me to ask if you had any other advice."

I stared at her for a moment, thinking. This was perfect, but I couldn't just spew out the information again with Emmitt watching so closely.

"Uh, I haven't looked at the paper, yet. If we have one, I can take a look at it. Maybe you could give your friend a call back later this afternoon?"

I hoped it would look like I had researched the information and had just been very lucky. I would have to figure out something else for the next one, though. Three in a row wouldn't go unnoticed.

Nana nodded and disappeared inside as she conveyed the message. She came back a moment later with the paper.

THE NEXT MORNING, the boys excitedly ran downstairs. I had no reason not to let them terrorize the neighbors. Aden came back up a minute later crying because Jim had already left for work.

To console him, I suggested we cook for Jim. Aden perked up at the prospect. We decided on some cookies. While we measured out the flour, Nana knocked on the door.

"Good morning, Michelle. Liam mentioned he didn't know the ABC song.

Would you mind if they spent some time with me a few times a week so I can work on their alphabet with them?"

I stared at her as a horrible, sinking guilt made me shrink inside. My brothers had been denied so much. As soon as they could speak, they hadn't left the house, and their care had fully fallen to me. Defiance on my part had meant a lockdown for all of us. When locked in our separate rooms, they went without food or contact, except for each other. David hadn't liked kids and only tolerated them outside of their room when they kept quiet. I'd taught them basic things that applied to our caged life at the time but hadn't thought of teaching them more.

Something must have shown on my face because Nana stepped further into the apartment, looking concerned.

"There's nothing wrong with them not knowing the ABC's, yet. Four and five is just the right age to start learning. I have so many of my old materials left, and, frankly, I miss working with children. I thought I would offer."

Emmitt's comment came back to me. Who better to teach them than a teacher? I reluctantly nodded and promised to send Aden down as soon as we finished the cookies. He felt strongly that he needed to help make them for Jim.

When he tromped downstairs a while later, I sighed. As much as they drove me nuts, they also kept me company. With nothing else to do, I lounged on the couch and read the book I'd borrowed. Their enthusiastic singing echoed down the halls as the oven warmed the apartment to unbearable. Baking cookies in summer was not a good idea.

Sweating, I tossed the book aside and changed into my swimsuit. I opened all the windows and doors to let out the heat. When I opened the French doors to the porch, a nice breeze shifted past me, and I stepped outside. Protected by the overhanging roof, shade cooled the wooden deck. I stood there for a moment letting the wind tease my skin and realized I'd found the perfect place to read.

I went back inside, took the last batch of cookies from the oven, then grabbed my book and blanket. The porch didn't just give me a cool place to read. It also muffled the boys' boisterous singing. I relaxed on the blanket and enjoyed the breeze.

An hour later, Emmitt stepped onto the porch from the door of the adjoining apartment. I glanced up from the book. When he saw me, he paused. He was laden with paint cans, rollers, and plastic and looked like he could use a hand.

"Let me help," I said, jumping up. I took two of the cans from his hands and smiled up at him.

His face flushed. He swallowed hard and glanced down at what I wore.

I pretended not to notice his reaction and lifted a can. "What are you doing with all of this?"

He met my eyes again, and his voice was rough when he spoke.

"The outside needs painting, too. I thought I'd start on it while the paint dried in there."

He gave me one last look, turned, and walked to the far corner of the porch where he set down the painting supplies.

"Is the apartment almost done?" I asked as I trailed behind him. I set the two cans next to his pile.

"I still need to work on some plumbing, but its close. Want to see it?" he said, looking at me once more. The flush had faded, but he was careful to maintain eye contact. The steady look made it hard to pretend I didn't feel underdressed.

"That's okay."

"I could actually use your input on the colors in the bathroom. Nana bought a variety of cans on clearance, and I'm down to a yellow and a grey."

The idea of talking about paint colors shouldn't have caused my stomach to dip or a pink flush to spread across my skin. Yet, it did. I pushed down the jitters, resisted the urge to tug at the edges of the bikini top, and nodded.

He smiled at me. His dimple made my heart stop. He extended a hand to indicate I should lead. I turned and walked to the apartment's porch entrance. The door led into a large, open-concept living room and kitchen. Thick, clear plastic covered the beige carpet immediately inside the door, protecting it from paint spills. White speckles already decorated it from painting the ceiling. He had painted the wall dividing the living room and kitchen from the rest of the apartment a dark brown. A warm, light brown coated the remaining walls. The main door to the apartment was located just inside the kitchen area where the beige carpet transitioned into large earth-toned tiles.

"Wow. This looks great."

"I'm glad you like it," he said quietly. "Let me show you the bathroom."

He led me to the hallway where an orphaned toilet waited for installation. He stopped just outside the bathroom door.

"We can't go in. The grout is still wet, but you can see the colors in the tile from here."

He moved aside so I could lean against the wall and peek into the room.

In the process of leaning forward to look, I knocked over a loose piece of molding. It tipped inward toward the newly grouted floor. I didn't even have time to wince before Emmitt snapped it out of the air, impossibly fast. The move reminded me of our differences, and a tiny bit of fear grew in the pit of my stomach as I recalled how quickly Frank had leapt over the table to claim his right to scent me first.

A shudder ran through me.

"Don't," Emmitt whispered hoarsely.

I turned to him, confused.

"You are the one person who will never have to fear me."

Fear him, why would he say that? Usually, I just felt confused. Like now. The only time I felt fear around him, I'd ended up kicking him in the...

"I'm sorry I kneed you."

He reached out and gently touched my cheek, feathering his fingertips over it from temple to jaw. My heart started to beat faster.

"I'm sorry I scared you," he murmured as he moved closer.

I glanced down at his lips. My breath hitched. I looked up, and I couldn't think. His deep blue eyes held me in place, waiting, anticipating. His head lowered. My lips parted.

"And I'm sorry I missed it," Jim said from the living room, startling me.

Emmitt's hand dropped back to his side, and his eyes flicked down the hall in annoyance.

Free of the spell, I put some space between us, tried to calm my thundering heart, and peeked at the bathroom one more time.

"The yellow won't work, but the grey might. Too bad you didn't have a blue-grey to match the flecking in the tile."

I kept my eyes locked on the bathroom, not wanting to explore what might be in Emmitt's gaze. He apparently hadn't understood my friendship speech as well as I'd hoped. He needed to be the strong one and stay away from me, because I had very little willpower when it came to him.

"Thank you," Emmitt said.

I nodded and led the way down the hallway, thankful for Jim's intervention.

"Why are you here, Jim?" Emmitt said before we reached the end.

"Aden mentioned something about cookies..." Jim's words trailed off as I stepped into view. Then, he wolf-whistled.

"I regret my decision to think of you as a sister," he said with a grin. "Nana can sure pick a suit. I think you should really wear a t-shirt over that, though."

"Shut up, Jim," Emmitt said flatly behind me.

I blushed and kept walking toward the porch door. Emmitt and Jim stayed behind in the apartment. I could hear their low, murmured voices as I picked up my blanket and book.

In that moment before Jim interrupted us, Emmitt had wrapped me in his spell. I'd wanted nothing more than his kiss. Nana's comment about shallow connections rang in my ears. While the boys played school with Nana, I vowed I'd use that time to learn, too. Time to start Werewolf 101. Tomorrow.

AFTER NANA COLLECTED the boys for their morning lessons, I grabbed a cookie and went to search out Emmitt. He wasn't hard to find. I followed the sound of a quick, metallic rasp outside on the porch. Paint flakes decorated the decking by our doors. Free of loose paint, the third floor of the back of the house awaited its turn at rejuvenation.

Turning the far corner, I almost ran into Emmitt and smashed the cookie between us. His quick reflexes caught me and robbed me of the cookie. Grinning, he took a bite before he offered it back.

"I actually brought it for you," I said.

His face lost a little of its playfulness. He tilted his head, studying me with a silent question.

"Will you tell me about your family?" I reached for the nearby broom. "Please."

"What do you want to know?"

"Anything. Everything." I shrugged. My stomach was in knots. I wanted to know, but I didn't.

"My dad's side is from Canada. My mom, from the states. They met when she was pretty young. The way my dad tells it, it was love at first sight. My mom just rolls her eyes." He grinned at me between brisk scrapes. He made quick progress, stripping the boards of paint. I struggled to keep up with him as I trailed behind with the broom.

"My dad's brother lives in Canada with them at the Compound."

I stopped sweeping and looked at him.

"It's a collection of old buildings; the community I grew up in. It has been struggling for decades to support itself while keeping away from the corrupt influences of the outside world," he said with a hint of humor.

"Corrupt?"

He quickly swiped around the window. "Some believed that humans would lead the world to devastation through their wars, pollution, and overpopulation. They thought, by withdrawing from it, they could save themselves.

"The day my mom showed up, about thirty years ago, changed the direction they'd been headed. She made them see they were hurting themselves by hiding from the truth. They'd created their own distrust by not learning about the changes they were scorning and made it harder for future generations to rejoin the world. That's part of the reason they sent me back here to live with Nana Wini.

"The more of us who leave to learn about the world, the better it is for others when we go back and share what we learned. The money we earn doesn't hurt, either. Part of the reason I know what I'm doing here is because I grew up helping with this kind of work back home."

We rounded the corner, and he began scraping the front of the house. Behind us, I left neat little piles of paint chips.

"My mom started making improvements as soon as there was money, and she hasn't stopped. People actually have beds to sleep in now." He looked at me after he said the last piece as if he wanted to take it back.

How horrible to be so poor that there wasn't even beds to sleep in. After Blake appeared in my life, I'd found the opulence of Richard's house distasteful as it represented a way of life I wanted nothing to do with. Clothes, food, an exercise room. Everything had been high-end and bought at the price of my freedom. I'd run from it, willingly risking a potential future without beds, warmth, or food, to save us all from a worse fate. And poverty would have happened, if not for Emmitt.

I reined in my thoughts. "So the remodeling inside, the painting outside, you learned all this from your mom?"

He nodded, looking adorable with paint flakes dusting his hair. "Can I ask you a question now?"

Reluctantly, I nodded. I didn't promise to answer it, though.

"Will you tell me about your stepfather?"

I sighed and stopped sweeping again, remembering how it'd been in the beginning. "It was just me and my mom until after my thirteenth birthday. She met Richard through a friend of a friend."

"Richard?" he asked, looking puzzled.

I nodded and realized I'd never mentioned Richard by name before. "He was nice. He treated my mom well, and I think he really loved her. Then, things changed." Things I wasn't ready to share with Emmitt.

My premonitions had struck. I hadn't understood what I'd been seeing and wrote it down on paper to show my mom. By that time, they had married and were expecting their first child. Richard had found the paper and known what it was. He'd been amused by what I'd written, but after seeing the accuracy of my predictions, he'd started to use them. He hadn't demanded anything from me, just said I could give them to him when I thought of any more.

Everything had been fine for a while. We'd moved into a better house, the one in the gated community. We'd been happy. Liam was born, time passed, I went to school, had friends, went on my first parent-supervised date, and my mom got pregnant again.

I wasn't sure how Richard got involved with Blake, but he had; and Blake had started coming to dinner. My mom had disliked him immediately. Seeing past events clearly for the first time, I understood how much Blake had truly controlled our lives. It had started with my mom's death. An accidental death that I could now see wasn't so accidental. Blake had killed her just as he had Richard. After she died, Richard had become Blake's lackey.

"How did they change?" Emmitt asked quietly, watching me closely.

I'd daydreamed through half the front of the house. I shook myself and finished sweeping quickly.

"My mom died just after Aden was born," I said softly, remembering how alone I'd felt. "Richard shut us away from the world for four years."

Emmitt had stopped scraping and studied me closely.

"Richard. Then, who's Blake?"

With Blake's identity firmly glued to my secret, at least in my head, I couldn't talk about him without everything spilling out. I didn't want to tempt Emmitt with the power he could gain by possessing my premonitions. I didn't want him to turn out like Blake.

"I have to check on the boys," I said in a rush. I leaned the broom against the wall and fled.

I sequestered myself with my brothers for the rest of the day. The other occupants of the house let me be.

CHAPTER NINE

EMMITT KNOCKED ON MY DOOR THE AFTERNOON FOLLOWING OUR talk. The boys were outside playing, and I was alone. I quietly backed away from the door. It seemed every time we spent time alone, I let too much slip. We needed distance. I needed distance. So, I snuck to the bathroom and avoided him with the skill of a master thief.

After his footsteps faded in the hallway, I risked a quick look out the bathroom door. The sunlit pattern of the French doors on the kitchen floor caught my eye. The island blocked a good portion of it, but not the top half. The shadow of a man drifted through the bright patch. I spent the afternoon reading on the toilet.

It proved more difficult to avoid Emmitt the following day. He stood outside the apartment door when the boys ran out in the morning. Stunned by his unexpected appearance, I gaped at him for a moment before my brain kicked in.

"I have to take a shower," I said in a rush then slammed the door in his face.

I stayed under the hot spray until my fingers pruned, then I crept around the apartment, stealthily checking the windows and doors. When time passed without spotting Emmitt, I changed into my swimsuit and grabbed a book. No more toilet reading. My legs had gone numb the day before. I eased open the French doors and tiptoed onto the porch.

The warm summer air surrounded me, and I took a slow, deep breath and shook out my blanket.

"Michelle?"

The sound of his voice directly behind me almost made me scream. Heart hammering, I clutched the blanket to my chest and spun to face him. My master thief skills were more like apprentice level. I caught a glimpse of his hurt expression before he smoothed his features into a carefree mask of indifference.

"I need to go into town for more paint soon. I was wondering if you wanted to come with me and help pick out the color." His eyes held mine as he spoke. He stood a few feet from me, wearing paint splattered cargo shorts and an equally colorful printed shirt. A brush hung from a loop on his shorts.

I didn't answer immediately, and he tucked his hands in his pockets, waiting. My stomach did its weird flutter. After talking to Nana, it felt more like a tug. It made me nervous all over again. Why did I react like that to him? It had to be the reason I couldn't seem to keep my mouth shut.

"I'll pass. I'm more comfortable here," I mumbled. Riding to town to get paint meant taking the car since Jim had the truck. Thinking of any amount of time in the confines of Nana's little putt-putt, alone with Emmitt, did funny things to my insides.

"Okay," he said with a small nod. Then he turned and walked away. My shoulders sagged in relief.

He left me alone for an hour. Laying in the shade of the third floor porch, I heard his footsteps approaching, but didn't scramble to my feet fast enough. He caught me on my knees.

"Thirsty?" he asked holding out a sweating glass of water. *Who is Blake?* The last time he'd offered me something to drink, I'd said too much.

Fine. The drink had nothing to do with it. Not really. Emmitt was the problem.

"No." I popped up as if pulled by a string connected to the top of my head. "I have to pee." I dashed through the French doors and closed myself in the bathroom. Again.

After a few minutes, I ducked into the bedroom, threw on a shirt, and rushed downstairs to ask Nana and the boys if I could join them. The boys eagerly welcomed me while Nana gave me a curious look. She didn't stop her lesson, though.

Since she kept her door open, I saw Emmitt pass by several times before lunch. Each time my stomach trembled, and I wished the stupid thing would stop causing me so much trouble.

When Nana announced her lessons complete for the day, I left the apartment with trepidation and led the boys upstairs for lunch. Our door stood open. I made Liam go in first while I hid around the corner.

"Emmitt! Are you cooking lunch today?"

Liam's excited greeting caused me to throw a spontaneous quiet tantrum in the privacy of the hallway. There was a lot of silent foot stomping and some pantomimed fainting involved. Thankfully, Aden walked in right after Liam and missed my awesome display.

Straightening my shoulders, I stepped through the door. For the first time ever, Emmitt didn't look up at me. Not even briefly. He focused on the boys and their sandwiches.

"Yep. I thought maybe I'd eat with you guys. How about we carry these sandwiches downstairs and eat on the grass?" He handed each boy a sandwich and, carrying one for himself, left with the boys.

Owl-eyed and confused, I stared at the empty door as the lone sandwich he'd left on the counter mocked me. I'd hurt his feelings with my avoidance. Drifting to a stool, guilt ate at me. Dejectedly, I took a bite of the sandwich. Turkey. With bacon. Frowning at the delicious taste, I set the sandwich aside. Didn't he know I had no choice? Couldn't he stop asking me questions for five seconds? Cradling my head in my hands, I grimaced remembering his questions today. Simple, harmless questions.

I sighed and admitted an ugly truth. The problem wasn't Emmitt. It was me. I *wanted* to tell him everything. How stupid could I be? Not even a week had passed since he'd revealed his secret. Though I'd decided to learn what I could from him, I'd yet to resolve a few things in my mind. Primarily, the trust issue. It was too soon for that.

Hardening myself against the guilt, I decided to keep avoiding him.

A BRIEF RAIN shower Friday morning, followed by a hazy, breezeless sky, spiked the humidity. Instead of lessons inside, Nana encouraged the boys to play in the sprinkler while they recited the things they'd learned during the last few days. The sweltering heat of the apartment drove me outdoors, too. I brought the blanket and book with me.

Emmitt painted upstairs until the heat drove him out. He stepped outside without a word to me. Calling to the boys to save him some water for later, he disappeared into the shadows of the garage and returned carrying a weed eater.

After a few sharp pulls, it started with a loud drone, and he moved to the tree line, turning his back to the porch.

Part of my frustration with myself was my inability to stop looking at him. My eyes drifted to his back repeatedly, watching the play of muscles as he held the machine inches off the ground. I tried lifting my book higher to block the line of sight, but the book always drifted back down on its own. If only I could get over my fascination, maybe my stomach would stop freaking out and I would lose the urge to spill my guts.

He took off his shirt and tucked it into the waistband of his shorts. I lost the battle and outright stared, book forgotten.

Finished with the first section of trees, Emmitt killed the motor and moved to the next, glancing up as the boys shouted to him. I was in his line of sight. Caught staring, I blushed and lifted my book again.

When the motor started, I quickly offered to make lunch and sprinted upstairs. I could feel my resolve weakening. I needed help.

After lunch, Emmitt left with Nana's car to get the paint he needed. He hadn't repeated his invitation.

Nana asked if we wanted to walk in the woods where it would be cooler. Liam heartily agreed. Aden, pruned from so much time in the water, nodded. I insisted they go without me if Nana could manage. She laughed, assuring me they would be no trouble.

I ran upstairs, changed into cutoffs and a tank top, then waited on the porch. It didn't take long for Jim to pull into the driveway.

"Jim!" I called popping up from my spot on the porch and moving to the truck before he parked. "Will you teach me how to drive?"

His eyebrows rose lifting his sweat soaked hair. "You don't know how?"

"I'm self-taught and need practice. Everyone else is gone." I crowded up to the driver's side door and gave him a pleading look. Inside my head, a clock ticked. We still had hours before dinner, and Emmitt would soon return with the paint.

"Sure," he cut the engine. "Can I shower quick?"

"I guess." I didn't bother to keep the disappointment from my face. I really wanted to leave before Emmitt got back.

He eyed me for a moment then grinned. "I'll be back in less than five minutes."

I stepped back as he opened the door. With a blur and a breeze, he vanished.

Blinking, I looked around. What game did he play now? We didn't have time.

Striding to the house, I heard him singing inside and stopped. A shower ran. I smiled. He moved fast.

I returned to the truck and settled into the driver's seat. The keys dangled from the ignition. I touched them lightly. I could leave. So easy. Of course, my brothers held me—I wouldn't leave without them—but I could take the keys and wait. Tell Jim I changed my mind. No. At some point, I had come to terms with the fact that we lived with werewolves. Did I like it? Not really. Did it bother me? Only when I thought about it, which I needed to do more often. The urge to leave primarily stemmed from my growing fascination with Emmitt. I needed to figure out a way to deal with that so I could become serious about getting answers about Blake.

The passenger door opened and closed with a gust of wind. Jim sat beside me. He was freshly showered and wearing clean shorts, sandals, and a wife beater.

"Start her up. What do you need to know?"

I cranked the starter and took a moment to remember our quick escape. "I figured out the gas and the brake. Sometimes I still mix them up," I admitted. He gave me a worried look. "But it's mostly the rules I need to know. Like who goes first at a stop sign, when to use your blinkers, what the 'N' stands for here." I pointed to the shifter display.

Putting the truck in reverse, I didn't wait for his reply. The gas pedal was touchier than I expected, and we flew backward. Had the garage door been closed, I would have bumped it. Just a little. I mumbled a quick apology, shifted into gear, then pulled forward smoothly.

Gravel crunched under the tires as I brought us to the road. I didn't quite stop. Rather, I rolled forward slowly until I could see both ways were clear then pulled out onto the road.

"Okay. Two things," Jim said. "If you're turning onto a road, use your blinker. It might not be a law, but it's polite. And always stop to look both ways. A complete stop."

I nodded and kept driving. He explained the gauges inside the truck while I kept my eyes on the road. Mostly. He suggested I take my foot off the gas when going into a curve instead of trying to keep the speed limit through it. His advice relieved me as the last curve had felt like one side of the truck had lifted off the road.

When we came to the bar Emmitt and I had stopped at, Jim begged me to pull in. This early on a Friday, cars hadn't yet crowded the parking lot so I didn't need to worry about avoiding anything as I jerked the wheel to make the quick turn.

I parked with a jarring stop and uncurled my fingers from the wheel. Jim was already out of the truck and headed toward the door before I could turn to ask what we were doing there. I unbuckled, plucked the keys from the ignition, and rushed to catch up. I caught the door on the backswing and followed Jim inside. Two window air conditioners hummed in the otherwise quiet bar. It felt nice inside. Not a bad place to cool off.

Jim called to the bartender for a double shot of whiskey. I shuddered, remembering the tequila, and sat on the stool next to him. The bartender gave him the glass with amber liquid. Jim drank it down and asked for another before the man could move away. He repeated the process four times then sighed and asked for two beers.

"Can you get drunk?" I asked Jim once the man moved away.

"Yep, but I have to work harder at it, and it doesn't last as long." He pushed a glass of beer toward me.

"But I'm driving."

"Nope, not anymore," he said as he reached over and plucked the keys from my hand. Considering what he'd just consumed, I thought the key confiscation a bit backward.

"Come on, Jim. I wasn't that bad, was I?"

Instead of answering, he asked the bartender to line up another four doubles of whiskey. He handed me his wallet and told me to stop him when he ran out. The bartender and I exchanged a look.

"Jim, if I'm not driving and you're drunk, how are we getting home?" I'd left my brothers with Nana Wini. What would happen when they got back to the house and I wasn't there? I began to worry. How could I be so stupid? When I'd asked Jim to teach me, I'd just wanted to put some distance between Emmitt and me for a while, not drive away.

He winked at me and drank his whiskeys, this time spacing them out by a few minutes. I took a sip of my beer and dug through his wallet to lay out a few bills. Jim laughed and pulled out a few more.

"So are you going to tell me why you really wanted to kill me today?" he asked when I glanced at the clock on the wall.

"Jim, we should really go back. Nana has the boys and won't know where I disappeared to."

Jim arched a brow at me, and I pouted a little before answering his original question. I didn't really want to talk about it.

"I'm avoiding Emmitt."

"I've noticed. Just can't figure out why."

I shrugged and took another sip of beer. Wine tasted better, but beer won over tequila. "It's hard to explain."

"Not really. You just need the proper motivation." He nodded toward the dartboard. "I win, you tell me. You win, I leave it alone."

I shook my head before he finished his offer. "No way. I have no idea how good you are." If he could run faster than I could see, how could he miss a dartboard?

"Dice then. A game of chance. I might be ready to go afterward."

Dice, I could play. I nodded, and he taught me a quick drinking game, only instead of taking a shot, the loser told a secret. In my case, why I wanted to avoid Emmitt. In Jim's case, who'd taught him to sing in the shower.

Jim whomped me. I took the last drink from my beer. Jim motioned for another.

"Because I'm stupid around him," I said in exasperation.

"Explain."

"I lose focus on what's important and start talking about things I shouldn't," I said then asked the bartender for a sweeter beer. He gave me a funny look but moved his hand from one tap to another.

"Why can't you talk about things?"

If only Jim had asked *what* I couldn't talk about; I would have clammed up.

"Because people take advantage of information. They use it to gain power, control."

The door behind us opened, and a few more Friday patrons trickled in. I replenished the money on the bar as Jim called for more whiskey. He grinned at me with a twinkle in his eye.

"So you're avoiding Emmitt because you're afraid you'll say something he'll use to control you?"

I began to nod then stopped myself. Had I said that? Damn. I eyed my beer.

"Don't blame you," Jim said interrupting my thought. "He's a bit of a control freak. O.C.D. Look at how driven he is to finish that apartment for you."

What?

"I mean, you haven't even decided if you will stay, yet. I tried telling him he needed to chill, but no. Be prepared. That's how he thinks."

"He's finishing that apartment for us?" I couldn't get past that tidbit.

Jim nodded and nudged my glass. I dutifully took a drink.

"Yep. Doesn't think his apartment is a good home for you and the boys. Apparently, my decorating doesn't meet his standards." He rolled his eyes.

I hid my grin with another sip.

"If he's not working on that, then he's always listening for you. Or Liam. Or Aden. He leaves the apartment door open 'just in case'. In case what? I say let it go already."

I thought he just opened the door in the morning to welcome the boys. But to have it open all the time? My heart melted a little.

The door opened, and a larger crowd of men came in. A few called hello to Jim. Jim nodded and smiled but didn't invite them to join us.

"You know what really puts me over the top?" he asked, looking at me with frustration. "He won't let me make the pancakes!"

Several people turned to look at Jim. I studied Jim in surprise, not sure how to respond to his outburst. Then, I caught a twinkle in his eyes.

"You brat!" I smacked him on the arm, and he laughed.

He'd picked on my concerns but had also revealed some interesting information about Emmitt. Things I didn't know. Did I have to worry about Emmitt using the information against me? I didn't know because I didn't really know Emmitt.

"Fine. You win. I'll stop avoiding him." My stomach flipped in anticipation, and I let out a shaky breath. *Friends only*, I reminded myself. That would be risky enough. I'd probably say more than I wanted.

"Good girl," Jim said, smiling approval. "Drink up. The music's about to start. It'll get too loud in here to talk."

I looked around the crowded room and wondered where everyone had come from. The glass in front of me was cold and full. Hadn't I been drinking out of it already? I thought I'd almost drained it.

"We can go now if you want," I offered.

"Please, no!" he said, holding his hands up in surrender. "I just need a few more minutes." After all the alcohol he'd consumed, he didn't seem the least bit affected.

Three more beer and two hours later, I needed to use the restroom. A crowded dance floor occupied the space between my goal and me. I leaned close to Jim to hear myself over the music.

"Be right back," I half-shouted and hopped off the stool.

He nodded at me with a grin and lifted his glass to sip the beer I suspected he'd been nursing for the past hour. If he didn't want me driving, maybe he was sobering up? Wait, was he ever really drunk? I felt a bit light-headed and unsure of the real answer.

Without tripping or embarrassing myself, I made it to the restroom. The small room did little to muffle the blaring music but did offer my ears a slight respite. The time away from Jim and his distracting conversation helped me remember my responsibilities. Liam and Aden.

After drying my hands, I stepped out of the restroom and carefully started to skirt around the group of bodies writhing to the music. I craned my neck, trying to spot Jim. We needed to leave.

Instead of seeing Jim, I met a startling pair of dark eyes for a moment before a random dancer moved in the way. I froze, doubting what I thought I'd seen. When the dancer moved, no one familiar stood there. Dark blue eyes or otherwise. I shook my head, blamed the beer, and continued to inch forward. Definitely time to insist we go home. Jim had to be sober by now. I wanted to get back to my brothers and needed to apologize to Nana.

The mass of dancers drifted, blocking my route along their edge. Taking a deep breath, I changed tactics and started to snake my way through the dancers. I mumbled apologies as I went. Shoulder to shoulder, bodies bumped and brushed each other as they swayed to the music. I struggled to make any progress. An arm encircled my waist, stopping me completely. I tried to spot Jim at the bar, but the crowd was too thick. The music too loud to yell. Defeated, I turned to face my captor.

Dark blue eyes, close cropped dark hair, and a perfect mouth swam before my eyes. Emmitt. My heart skipped a beat. He wore jeans and a faded blue t-shirt. His eyes unwaveringly met mine. He studied me with an intensity I didn't understand.

He leaned in to smell my hair. Tingles skittered along my neck and arms.

"Hi," I whispered, tipsy and unsure of his mood.

Folding me in his arms with a sigh, we swayed to the fast music. "You had me worried," he whispered in my ear. He rested his forehead against mine.

"My driving's not that bad," I protested, pulling back slightly. He let me have my space as his lips quirked and he shook his head.

"When you stopped talking to me, I thought you wanted to leave. Then, you did. With Jim."

"Oh." I didn't know what to say for a moment. His eyes burned into mine, capturing me even through the beer haze. My hands came to life at my side, reaching up to clutch the fabric of his shirt near his stomach. My knuckles brushed his hard muscles. I melted a little.

He exhaled and closed the distance between us. As he lowered his head, excitement burst like a bubble within me, randomly splattering my insides with a cold fire. The room tilted. My blood rushed, and my eyes fluttered closed. I held my breath, lifted my face, and forgot my vow to confine our relationship to the boundaries of friendship.

"Please stop," he begged.

My eyes popped back open. "What?" I asked confused.

His mouth hovered inches from mine. The song changed. A slow beat to match our sway. I lifted myself up on tiptoes and let go of his shirt to wrap my arms around his neck. I felt his breath on my lips. So close...

He moved quickly, nudging my head to the side with his jaw, giving him access to bury his face in the curve of my neck. His lips rested against my skin but didn't move. He inhaled deeply and groaned.

"Driving me crazy," he murmured, answering my question.

It took me a moment to understand him. I drove him crazy? The look in his eyes, the way he held me, and what he'd just said added up to one conclusion. Despite his previous assurance that he only wanted friendship, I thought he wanted to kiss me. Had I misread the situation? I tightened my arms around his shoulders, and he pulled me closer. Nope. I didn't misread a thing.

"I don't understand."

"If you'll let me, I'll explain in the morning. When you're more lucid."

The song ended, and he led me from the floor. I stumbled a bit, the floorboards doing their best imitation of a rollercoaster.

"You found her." Jim grinned at me. "Good." He handed Emmitt the truck keys and held out his hand, waiting for Emmitt to surrender the motorcycle key. "You two have fun." He sat back on his stool and began to speak to the woman on his right.

Emmitt shook his head and tugged me toward the exit. Tripping on the threshold, I fell through the door. He spun and caught me before my eyes even locked on the gravel rising up to meet my face. Without a word, he swung me up into his arms. I snuggled into his warm chest and smiled, touching his shirt.

CHAPTER TEN

I WOKE ALL AT ONCE. SILENCE SURROUNDED ME. TURNING MY HEAD, left then right, I looked for the boys. Their spots were empty, and I frowned and sat up. The taste in my mouth distracted me; I needed a toothbrush.

I swung my legs out of bed and stepped on a piece of paper on the floor. A childishly penciled arrow pointed to the hallway. I picked up the paper and walked out of the room, curious. I saw another paper in the living room but detoured to quickly brush my teeth and use the bathroom.

The arrow in the living room pointed to the door. In the hall, another paper pointed to the apartment across from ours. The fragrant aroma of browning bacon tickled my nose. I moved to the door but stopped when I heard a childish giggle below.

Before I could peek over the railing, the door swung inward revealing Emmitt. He held a spatula in one hand while he looked me over with a slow smile. Behind him, bacon sizzled on the stove. My stomach growled. Unlike the morning after tequila, I felt fine.

"Nice shirt," he commented.

I looked down at the blue cotton t-shirt that almost covered the bottoms of my hello kitty cotton sleep shorts and fought to hide my smile. "Thanks. It's really comfy."

"I know," he said shaking his head. "Want some breakfast before we face the music for last night?"

I nodded, and he stepped aside.

"How's your back?" I asked sitting on a new stool at the island.

Without furnishings, excluding the stools and cooking utensils, the sound of my voice rebounded off the walls.

"Fine." He grinned as he moved to turn the bacon. "Is the floor behaving this morning?"

I laughed. Last night, after he had carried me to the truck, the spinning had continued. So much that I begged a piggyback ride upstairs when we returned home. Not waiting for an answer, I'd leapt on him, bringing us both to the floor. The ruckus brought Nana to her door. She had looked at Emmitt with disapproval but only said that she would speak with us both in the morning. Before she closed her door, she assured me that both boys were sleeping upstairs and hadn't been any trouble. Guilt had pierced me, then, and still did. Sharp little jabs.

He set two plates next to the pan and split the bacon. There had to be a whole pound between the two plates. Leaving the grease in the pan, he fried up five eggs, sliding two on one plate and three on the other. He added two pieces of buttered toast to each and set the smaller portioned plate in front of me. I stared at the food, and my stomach gave a queasy twist.

"Too heavy after last night?" he asked, watching me.

I nodded.

He reached over, picked up a single piece of toast, handed it to me, then set the plate next to his. "Better?"

"Much." I nibbled at the toast and watched him put away the grease-soaked food. "I was thinking maybe we could spend today together."

"We could all go to the lake again," he offered.

I made a face. "Maybe somewhere less public. I'd like to learn more about you, like why a strong fast...person such as yourself could get knocked over by a nineteen-year-old light weight. I'd prefer my brothers not see anything."

"Nineteen?" His fork clattered to his plate as he whipped his head around to stare at me. He looked horrified when I hesitantly nodded. "She's going to kill me," he mumbled pushing away his plate.

"What's wrong?" I set the half-eaten toast aside as I watched various emotions flit across his face. Shock, concern, calculation, back to concern.

"We all assumed you were a bit older than that." He quickly gathered the dishes and stacked them near the sink. "Come on. Let's get this over with." He offered his hand.

With a frown, I accepted it and followed behind him.

"Are you telling me I look *old?*"

"Ancient," he threw over his shoulder with a wink.

As usual, both apartment doors stood open. So did the main entrance door. Outside, the boys were playing on the swing set. Emmitt led us straight into Nana's kitchen where Jim already sat contritely at the table. Nana leaned against the counter, her eyes boring holes into Jim's soul. Well, that's what it looked like anyway.

"Sit," Nana said.

Emmitt held out a chair for me before seating himself. I felt small and very guilty. Taking a steadying breath, I opened my mouth to apologize for leaving her like I did, but she spoke first.

Nana's gaze again drilled into Jim. "Your irresponsibility knows no bounds. What were you thinking taking her to a bar! Our job is to keep her safe, not keep her stocked with booze."

Keep me safe? I blinked at the two repentant looking men, feeling as if I'd walked into a conversation near the end. So this was about me being at the bar with Jim, not me leaving?

"And you," she said to Emmitt, "are supposed to have her best interests at heart."

Why was she putting so much of this on them? It was my stupid decision. I took a breath to say just that, but Emmitt beat me.

"That's why I tracked her down and brought her back," Emmitt quickly defended. Jim grimaced. That explained Emmitt's earlier look of calculation. He'd just thrown Jim under the bus.

She turned her steel gaze on me, and I felt myself shrink a little. "At nineteen, you have no right to be going out drinking."

Whoa. My mouth popped open, and my temper ignited at the absurdity of her misdirected concern. Had she called me irresponsible for leaving my brothers, I would have meekly nodded. But telling me I was too young to drink of all things!

"That is so—" I stopped myself from saying something stupid, knowing it would make me sound younger in their eyes. "My age doesn't matter. It never has," I said instead, thinking of Blake's use of me.

"You have a responsibility to your brothers," she said too late.

I flattened my hands on the table, trying to keep my temper under control. "No one knows that better than I do. Their wellbeing, their existence, depended on my obedience. Complete and absolute. Don't speak. Look up when addressed. Return to your room when your presence isn't required.

"I messed up last night. I get it." In essence, I'd left my brothers with strangers. I still didn't know enough about who they were to trust them with my secret, but I'd left my brothers with them? What if Blake had shown up? What would Nana Wini, a fellow werewolf, have done? Just hand them over? My fingers twitched on the surface of the table. Now I was getting angry with myself. I'd been so stupid.

"They could have been found, and I wasn't here," I said.

Nana made a slight noise as if she would continue.

"I don't need your lecture. I will not be ruled by another..." I clamped my mouth shut and closed my eyes with a flinch.

When I opened them again, three faces studied me with too much intensity. I had such a big mouth.

"I'm sorry."

I stood and left my stunned audience sitting around the table in Nana's cheery yellow kitchen. I took the stairs two at a time. As soon as I reached my door, I heaved a sigh of regret. I shouldn't have yelled at her. She had everything right. I shouldn't have left my brothers. Especially not to sit at a bar. Granted, that hadn't been the plan, but I could have insisted Jim drive us back. I could have walked.

With Blake, I hadn't spent much time with my brothers because I wasn't allowed. Now, I had all the time I wanted and didn't value it enough. Instead of being a self-absorbed brat who dwelled on her feelings concerning Emmitt, I needed to stay focused, learn about werewolves, and use the knowledge to protect us from Blake. And, I needed to find a way to test Emmitt's werewolf abilities without Liam or Aden seeing or hearing anything.

I quickly dressed in a tank top and cutoffs and grabbed the white shirt I'd originally borrowed from Emmitt then trotted downstairs. Both doors still stood open. I spotted Emmitt with the boys in the yard.

When I tapped on Nana's door, she called me in. Jim still sat at the table. Though I hadn't heard any yelling, from the look on Jim's face, Nana had continued after I left.

"Jim, I'm sorry I used you yesterday. I should have faced the issue instead of running from it." I glanced at Nana's set face. "Can I talk to you alone for a minute?"

Nana neither agreed nor disagreed. Regardless, Jim flew out of his chair as if it had spontaneously started on fire. There weren't even retreating steps to mark his passing. He simply vanished. Outside, the boys cheered.

"I shouldn't have said what I did. You're right. I'm not being responsible. My past, whether good or bad, doesn't earn me any hall passes. I'm sorry I left like I did yesterday."

Nana sighed and deflated a little. The angry light left her eyes. "You are an adult. You're correct that you don't need me to lecture you. We are here to help you, Michelle, if you would just let us. We don't know who you're hiding from or why. Is leaving here dangerous? Is there a chance the people you're hiding from could track you here?"

Hearing her echo my recent thoughts increased my worry. "I don't know." I ran my fingers through my still wet hair. "I'm so afraid, Nana," I admitted. "I'm afraid they'll find us and afraid if I trust..." I looked away for a moment, took a breath, and said as much truth as I could. "I'm afraid you'll be just like them."

She tilted her head and gave me a compassionate look. "Never, Michelle," she promised. "We are an entirely different species. Loyalty runs deep with us."

My stomach dropped and bile rose. She couldn't have said anything worse. They didn't know about Blake, yet. When they found out he was one of their own, would they just hand me over? Her words further cemented my decision to learn more about them and to learn it fast.

"You're right. You're different, and I haven't taken the time to learn about you like Emmitt asked. I'm sorry to ask again, but can you and Jim keep an eye on the boys? I won't ever again disappear like I did yesterday. I just want to take Emmitt to the front yard where the boys won't see or hear anything. Then, I'll ask Emmitt the questions I should have asked from the start."

"Of course we will. You don't have to ask Emmitt, you know. You can ask me anything as well."

I nodded hesitantly, and she smiled at the preference she saw in my eyes. I didn't want to face her in any other form than the grandmotherly one she wore. I thanked her and left.

Instead of going outside, I took a quick detour then headed back upstairs.

In the apartment, with the door closed, I tested his hearing. "Emmitt, can you come up here, please?"

I waited several minutes, but he didn't appear. Opening the apartment door, I tried again. Immediately, I heard his tread on the steps.

He wore an unsure smile. "Jim told me to pass on his pledge of servitude."

I smiled slightly in return. "He'll pay it back today. He and Nana are going to watch the boys so I can spend some time with you and learn what makes a werewolf tick."

"What do you have in mind?"

"According to your boast, you're faster, stronger, have better sight, hearing, and sense of smell. I'd like to know just how good you are at each."

He agreed, and we walked downstairs. I stopped just outside Jim's door.

"I went inside and hid something. Can you find it?"

He quirked a smile at me and walked purposefully into the apartment. I trailed behind him to watch.

When hiding the shirt I'd borrowed, I'd touched everything, leaving false trails. I even went so far as to change the hiding place twice.

He walked unerringly through the apartment to the spare room, lifted his pillow, and pulled out the shirt. Lifting it to his nose, he closed his eyes and inhaled.

"It will never smell like me again."

"Sorry."

"I like it better this way."

I blushed and looked away. "How did you know where it was?"

"Your scent is impossible to mask."

"But I touched everything along the way. I even hid it in two different places before picking here." Had he heard me moving around the apartment from outside?

He nodded. "I know. Under the couch cushions and in the silverware drawer."

"But, how..." He'd walked straight to the bedroom, not even hesitating.

"The fragrance of you led me. The lighter trails, I ignored. I went to the place where it was most saturated."

"How long will they last? My trails."

"The places you touched? Less than a week because of the contaminations here."

"Contaminations?"

"Your brothers, me, Jim. We are the contaminations. We touch the same things in here and eventually wipe away the traces of your scent. On the road, other vehicles do the same to the scent of your truck. Think of scent trails as delicate strings. If too many other strings cross them, they break and fall apart. We might be able to find fragments of the trail after a week, but the longer it sits, the harder it would be to try to follow."

So the longer we stayed the safer we were? I felt a small measure of relief. Maybe last night hadn't been such a glaring lack of responsibility on my part, after all. Yet, leaving my brothers alone with two werewolves when I suspected Blake of being the same thing...well, I didn't want to think about it too much.

I considered Emmitt's explanation for a moment. "Is it just my scent that's hard to mask or any person's?" The question appeared to make him uncomfortable. "Am I asking something I shouldn't?"

"No, you can ask anything. I just don't want to upset you with the answer."

"If I'm asking, please just answer honestly. I need the truth, not the dance around it."

"Everyone's scent is as difficult to mask, but their scent wouldn't be as compelling to follow."

"What do you mean?"

He stepped close to me, crowding into my space. I didn't move. Leaning forward, he inhaled deeply. "Your scent calls to our kind. Remember Nana mentioning a certain scent calls to a Mate. Yours teases all of us. Calls us closer to test it, to see if you really might be a match for us."

His cheek brushed against mine. This close, my stomach reacted. It clenched, and a flush crept into my cheeks. I fought to keep my breathing even and myself from leaning toward him.

"And when you do that, it just about brings me to my knees," he said softly against my ear.

His words brought a wave of embarrassment; I had an idea what I might have just done. Pulling away to make some space between us, I didn't meet his gaze. Instead, I retreated to the kitchen and thought over what he'd shared. His news that all werewolves would find my scent appealing disturbed me.

"If my scent is hard to mask, and you can smell my trails crisscrossing the apartment, why would one of your kind need to lean in close to scent me?" Blake's dictate to allow his men to scent me confused me. What game had he been playing at? The feel of Frank's tongue stroking my neck resurfaced. Revulsion skittered down my throat, and my stomach churned.

"I'm sorry for upsetting you," he said softly behind me. "I didn't think you—"

"Oh, no, not you," I said. "I just meant—" What did I mean? I meant the other werewolves you don't know about yet. I wanted to smack my forehead.

"I don't want to talk about it," I said quickly. He nodded reluctantly. "I'm sorry, Emmitt. I'm just not ready to divulge all my secrets, yet."

"I understand."

"Will you show me again how you shift?"

When he agreed, I led him outside. The warm air felt heavy with moisture already. Sweat beaded on my upper lip. I waved to the boys where they played baseball with Nana and Jim on the lawn. They barely noticed us as we followed the porch around to the front, staying in the shade.

The branches of the trees surrounding the smaller front yard extended over the lawn by several feet, shrinking the view of the sky above. Stepping off the porch, I walked to the center of the lawn and looked up, focusing on the white wispy clouds streaking the light blue sky while the leaves on the branches danced in the fringe of my view. The branches meant plenty of shade.

Emmitt interrupted my idle inspection. "Nana said no full shifting. She doesn't want me upsetting you."

"Um, okay." That put a damper on learning things. "Nana mentioned that the benefits of both forms differ. What are the attacking benefits of each form?" He canted his head slightly and studied me. "I want to know the strengths and weaknesses of each form. Like speed, for example. How fast can you move?"

One moment he stood near me, the next he watched me from near the tree line. Only a slight breeze had marked his movement. As much as it impressed me, I didn't like it. Blake could hide around a corner, grab me, and be gone in less than two seconds. Worse, he could grab Liam or Aden.

"Can you move as fast carrying someone?"

A strong heavy breeze lifted my hair from my neck as he abruptly scooped me up into his arms without warning and ran the perimeter of the front yard. Green flashed by in my peripheral vision. The wind stole my breath, and I buried my face in his neck.

The heat of his skin and the moisture in the air would have created an uncomfortable stickiness if not for the breeze he created. Even with me in his arms, he showed no decrease in speed or shortness of breath.

I felt his pulse against my cheek. Steady and slow. After a few seconds, I noticed how he smelled and leaned in a little closer, unintentionally touching my lips to his skin. He smelled like the woods after a storm.

Unexpectedly, the heat of Emmitt left me, along with the breeze, and I found myself sitting alone on the grass. The singing birds, who'd moments ago chirped out their happiness, quieted in the nearby branches.

Unhurt and confused, I set my hands on the cool grass and twisted around to look for Emmitt. I found him just a few feet away. He sat back on his heels, knees spread apart and fingertips touching the ground. His eyes were closed, and his jaw clenched. Fur rippled along the bare skin of his arms.

I had a clear view of his change. The bone structure in his face started to shift. As disturbing as I found the view of his body changing, another concern took precedence. Hadn't Emmitt mentioned werewolves changed as a defense mechanism? My head swiveled around looking for a threat.

"What is it Emmitt?" I scrambled close to him, clinging to a furry arm as I scanned the trees and hoped Nana Wini and Jim had the boys close. "Did you hear something?"

He tried to speak but, with his mouth already too far out of human shape, the sounds weren't intelligible. He took a slow breath. His face stopped contorting and began to move back into place. The fur slowly faded from his skin. Unclenching his jaw, he opened his eyes and looked at me with a hint of discomfort, but no alarm.

"What? What just happened?" If we weren't in danger, then why had he started to shift?

"I had to set you down."

"Yeah, the fur gave that away." I waited patiently for a better answer.

"I was taken by surprise, that's all." He stood and offered a hand to help me up. I took it but didn't let go once I stood.

"By what?"

"You were just a little close, and I wasn't expecting it."

I stared at him dumbly for a moment. "You picked me up, remember?"

He took another deep breath and looked down at our joined hands. "Michelle, Claiming is pretty serious stuff, equivalent to getting engaged in your world. If a guy would give you a small, velvet box, your first thought would probably be 'it's a ring'. Turns out, it's tickets to a ball game. Guys know girls associate those little boxes with rings, so it's cruel to use them for anything else, right? Claiming is a quick hard bite to the neck. We grow up knowing a werewolf's neck is a special area that you don't go near lightly. It's the small, velvet jewelry box. Do you understand?"

Claiming...bite...neck. Several pieces of Blake's speech fell into place. But why would Blake want me to become engaged to one of his men? I couldn't picture biting any of them.

The vision I had where I bit Emmitt resurfaced, and I blinked at him. Engaged? My stomach did a wild flip, and my heart stuttered in panic. My nearness to his neck had caused the change to burst upon him. He'd had to put me down or drop me.

"But you said you thought of me as a friend."

"If that's all you can give me, then I'll respect that."

Our gazes held for several long moments as what he said settled inside me. I knew he waited for me to say something.

"Stay away from werewolf necks. Got it. Sorry."

"No," he said a bit forcefully then grinned ruefully. "You can get as close as you want to mine. Just avoid anyone else's."

His intense gaze pulled another blush from me before I looked away. Clearing my throat, I suggested the next test.

"How strong are you?"

"Strong enough that any display would catch the attention of Liam and Aden."

Bummer. No proof of that one. Although, proof wasn't really necessary. I trusted what he said. So far, he hadn't given me any hope. Nothing I could use to put to rest my fears of Blake.

"So, how do you fight a werewolf?" I wondered absently.

Emmitt chuckled. "With another werewolf."

I turned away before he could see my despair.

CHAPTER ELEVEN

AFTER SAYING THAT I NEEDED A BREAK FROM WEREWOLF information, Emmitt and I joined the others in the front yard just in time for sprinkler races. I let the rest run while I sat in the shade, thinking. My mental list of questions wasn't any shorter than when we'd started. What could I do to stop Blake? Would he pick up traces of my scent and have enough of a broken trail to follow me here? Why did Blake want me to Claim one of his men? And if humans and werewolves didn't have relationships, why did I feel a pull in my stomach when I looked at Emmitt?

After Emmitt's explanation of my scent appealing to all werewolves, I really needed Nana Wini to clarify a few things for me. She'd said scent was how werewolves found their Mates but then hinted werewolves and humans didn't work. So what did that mean for me? And why was biting even necessary?

Since it was too early for lunch, I struggled to come up with an excuse to invite Nana upstairs. But, I needed the distance and closed door to ensure we wouldn't be overheard. I didn't want to embarrass myself with my line of questioning.

Perhaps my repeated looks her direction gave me away because she came to sit by me without any manipulation on my part.

"Everything okay?" she asked after a moment. For having run through the sprinkler several times, she didn't drip any water. In fact, her shirt only sported a few wet marks.

"Could we talk?" I said it quietly, but Emmitt glanced up at me anyway. "In private?" Might as well send up the red flag for everyone.

"Of course. Let's go inside. I saw you did a load of laundry. I'll help you fold."

I nodded, relieved. I hated folding laundry.

With a basket of freshly washed shirts and shorts between us, we sat on the couch in my closed apartment. The humidity and heat hadn't yet seeped in, but it wouldn't take long before it drove us back downstairs. Knowing I didn't have much time, I took a calming breath and prepared myself for the possibility of the werewolf version of "the talk".

"You and Emmitt mentioned a few things that I don't really understand. I have an idea, but...what does Claiming really mean?" Her brows rose slightly as I spoke. "Please keep it cliff-noted," I said desperately.

She laughed and patted my hand. "No details, I promise. I heard Emmitt explain that Claiming for our kind is a bite on the neck."

My heart thumped heavily in panic and the image from the vision I had starring Emmitt and me resurfaced.

"That bite has a purpose. It establishes a connection between the pair similar to what I have with each individual—"

I opened my mouth to ask for clarification, but she held up a finger in the universal just-a-minute sign.

"—but at a reduced level. A Mated pair will know what each other is feeling if the emotions are strong enough. It can also be a way to sense each other's location. This is especially important to the pair as separation can cause anxiety."

So it *was* more than a simple human engagement. It was a mental tie, an instant tracking device. A shiver of fear traced its way through my middle.

"Mating is the next stage."

Whoa! That got my attention. I turned crimson and thought about covering my ears. She laughed at my expression and held up her hands.

"As promised, no details. But I do want you to know that the connection the pair has because of the Claiming evolves when Mated. They will be able to send thoughts to each other. Complete silent communication regardless of distance."

I felt as if she'd slapped me then caught the other cheek on the back swing. "Telepathy?"

"Yes. A Mated pair's communication is much closer to what I, as an Elder, have with all werewolves."

"All of them?" Fear clogged my throat. I could feel Blake's hands around my neck again, and I gasped for air. I'd only wanted to know what scenting had to do with Claiming and how it applied to Blake. I didn't want to know she communicated with him.

She nodded as she eyed me curiously. Someone knocked on the door just then, and I jumped slightly. Nana continued to watch me. Glancing over my shoulder, I called out in a strangled voice. Emmitt walked in, saw me, and flashed an annoyed look at Nana.

"She's fine, Emmitt. We're asking her to take in a lot of information at a frequency that I would imagine makes it hard to assimilate everything." Nana set her stack of folded clothes back into the basket and rose.

She didn't understand the reason for my panic. I tried to calm myself.

Just because she had the *ability* to communicate with all of them, didn't mean she actually did. Or perhaps she didn't do so frequently. Maybe the last time she'd communicated with Blake, he hadn't yet found me. It could explain why they didn't know about my premonitions. But if he had been hiding me, amassing his fortune, where was his wolfie loyalty Nana mentioned? Shouldn't he have shared the money with the rest of his kind? Maybe his loyalty only applied to himself. I wanted to believe that hopeful thought but couldn't ignore the other possibilities.

My hands grew cold and sweaty at the thought of Nana inadvertently communicating my location to every werewolf in existence.

Emmitt stood beside me until she left then sank down on his heels, eye level with me.

"I can smell your fear."

I didn't look up. While staring at bare feet that glistened with water droplets, I tried to breathe through the dread that held me tight.

"I don't know what to do." The comment popped out without warning. Something about him just made me want to spill everything, to trust that he would keep me safe.

A gentle touch under my chin had me lifting my head and meeting his concerned gaze.

"About what?"

His fingers moved from my chin to feather along my jawline. Sighing, I closed my eyes and words spilled from my mouth again before I decided what I wanted to say.

"I want to tell you. I start thinking I should. Then I learn more, and I can't."

"I don't know what else to do to prove you can trust me. I'll wait forever if you need me to. There's nowhere else for me to be, but by you."

My eyes popped open. "That's part of what I don't understand. You talk about my scent. Nana talks about a pull. I see—"

I stopped myself just in time. Divulging that I saw the two of us together would lead to the fact that I had premonitions. I couldn't say anything about that until I had a better understanding of how Blake played into their lives.

"Well, never mind about what I see. But Nana said that humans and werewolves don't work, so why are you talking like I'm...that you and I..." I stopped, not sure how far I wanted to spell out my confusion. I already sounded like an idiot.

He tilted his head. Not like he usually did when I puzzled him, but as if he could hear something I couldn't.

"Do you want Nana to come talk to you some more?" he asked softly after a moment.

Why would she need to come and talk to me again? Realization dawned. *A shallow connection.* Was that what this really was about? My legs started to shake with my embarrassment. I was wanted too much by one werewolf for the wrong reason and not enough by the other for the right reason.

I looked away, displacing his touch on my face. "No, that's not necessary. I'm sorry I misunderstood. Like Nana said, it's a lot to take in."

He growled low, the sound reverberating deep in his chest. The noise reminded me of Blake, and my gaze flew back to him. He shook his head slowly, and his growl quieted.

"You're getting me in trouble. Nana is scolding me for growling."

She should. It had scared me. But how did she know? My eyes flicked to the closed apartment door. Was she just outside, listening?

"And I'm frustrated that we keep misunderstanding each other. May I please explain myself clearly?"

Heart still thumping from his growl, I nodded hesitantly. It couldn't hurt to listen to more. Everything else I'd learned churned in my thoughts until they turned into mud. What was one more glop of sludge?

His hand slid into my hair, and he closed the distance between us. "I saw you in the diner and felt an instant recognition. When you walked in, you flooded my senses until only one word beat through my mind." He leaned in until his lips brushed my ear. "Mine." A slight growl roughened his voice when he said it, and I shivered.

"So, when I say I'll wait forever to earn your trust, I will. My heart is yours. My loyalty, yours."

He inhaled deeply near the curve of my neck. My insides heated, and I barely stopped myself from wrapping my arms around him.

"If all you can give is friendship, I'll take it. For you, I'll take anything. Do you understand?"

I nodded, but the mud in my head remained.

"Liar," he whispered pulling me up off the couch. He looked into my eyes. "What don't you understand?"

"Nana said humans and werewolves..."

Emmitt distracted me. Freeing his hand of my hair, he trailed his fingers down the curve of my neck then traced my collarbone to the base of my throat. Tiny shivers followed their paths.

"You're different. Special. That rule doesn't apply to you." Like a bucket of ice water, his words penetrated the fog his fingers had made.

"Different?" I feared I'd found out their lie, that they already knew.

He continued to trace his fingertips along the collarbone to the other shoulder, and I struggled to stay focused.

"There's nothing wrong with being different. My mom's different. Human like you."

Hope flared. Could she really be like me?

"I'll make you a deal. You tell me a little bit about your past, whatever you *can* trust me with, and I'll tell you about my mom."

I considered his offer. He politely kept his fingers still so I could think, which told me he knew exactly what he did to me.

"I think my mom was killed. My stepdad, too. If they catch us, they'll hurt one of my brothers. Bad. To teach me a lesson. Their safety kept me there, a willing prisoner, until I realized the boys were only useful young. Their lives would end like my mother's and their father's as soon as they were no longer useful."

He pulled me into a tight embrace. Comfort radiated from him, and I gave into the urge and wrapped my arms around his waist, burying my face in his chest. I felt safe and protected. I wanted that feeling to last forever. To trust it.

"I have two big secrets." It came out muffled, but he didn't let me go. "One will test the sincerity of what you just said, and the other will give you power over me."

"Then tell me the first one. Test me to see if I'm worthy of the second one," he said, his breath warming my hair.

"I want to, but what if you're wrong. You'll hand me back over—"

"Never," he growled. His arms trembled against my back.

I looked up in time to catch the bones in his face shifting under the surface of his skin. Eyes closed, he struggled to control it.

"Mine," he reiterated, tightening his hold.

I couldn't keep living here, wanting to trust yet unsure where I stood with him, with Nana, with the werewolves in general.

"Blake killed them. My mom, Richard." I took a breath and whispered the words that I knew would seal my fate.

"He's one of you."

The words had barely left my mouth when Emmitt's body gave a huge lurch. Bones didn't just move, his shape exploded into his other form. His sudden shift bumped me backwards. He fell to all fours, facing me. He tipped his head back and started yowling. Eyes wide, I listened for barely a moment before the door swung open.

Nana and Jim rushed in. Nana, looking stern and concerned, planted herself in front of Emmitt. Jim picked me up from the couch and dashed down the stairs.

"Control is..."

I only caught those two words. The rest faded as we reached the second floor landing.

"We left the boys outside," Jim said. "They can probably hear Emmitt."

He set me on my feet before we reached the door. I wobbled a bit, and he had to steady me. We stood in the shadowed entry. The boys still played on the swing set, though I saw Liam glancing up toward our apartment.

"What happened?" I asked, looking up at Jim.

He chuckled a little. "We've talked about your secret and tried to guess what it might be. You'd mentioned Blake a few times. Emmitt thought he was your stepfather until you corrected him. Then he was sure Blake was a controlling boyfriend from your past. Human. Easy to deal with. Finding out one of our own mistreated you, someone we consider rare and special, well, it put him over the edge. He's still swearing."

"Swearing?" I couldn't believe that noise had been swearing. It'd been more like a one-sided dog fight. "Then why did you guys rush up there?"

Jim's face lost its humor. "After your admission, Nana thought his sudden shift might turn your fear to include us. She wanted to put some distance between the two of you until he calmed down." His gaze flicked to the steps behind me. I caught his lips twitching before he turned away. "Let's go check on the boys and give Emmitt a minute to get dressed. Our clothes don't shift with us."

I followed him, not wanting to check the stairs behind me. I wasn't ready for any more of an eyeful.

Once we stepped out in the sunlight, I started perspiring and wished we could sit on the porch. The boys didn't seem to mind the heat. Probably because they were still wet from the sprinkler.

"You really didn't know?" I asked as we walked toward the swing set. I waved at Liam to let him know everything was okay.

"Nope. That's a bit of a shocker. It will take Nana some time to figure out who Blake is."

"No!" I spun back toward the house, but Jim caught me before I could take a step.

"No one will do anything without talking to you. I promise."

I glanced nervously at the house then back at the boys. They stood tense, watching me because of my outburst. I relaxed so Jim would let me go.

"Emmitt's talking to Nana now. I can hear some of what they are saying. We understand what's at risk."

Both boys held themselves back from greeting Jim as we neared. I knew Aden just followed Liam's lead. Liam, ever cautious, eyed Jim. I hated lying to them but didn't want them to revert into their distrustful selves.

"Don't use the TV upstairs," I said to the boys. "The volume's broken. We'll have to get a new one." I turned to Jim. "Sorry for scaring you."

He nodded, understanding my lie.

Aden asked Jim to push him on the swing. My explanation for the noise and Jim and Nana's disappearance were good enough for him. I moved to Liam, who still watched Jim closely.

"He runs fast," Liam stated quietly, meeting my eyes. Too smart for five.

I nodded in agreement. "Just remember that if he and Aden challenge you and Emmitt to a race."

"I'll ask Nana to be my partner," he said seriously. "She runs faster."

It didn't take long for Emmitt and Nana to reappear. Emmitt stayed on the porch while Nana walked toward me.

"We need to know more to understand how best to protect you." She spoke in a low tone so that only I could hear. Well, probably Jim and Emmitt too, but at least the boys remained oblivious. "Would you mind talking to Emmitt on the porch?"

I agreed and shuffled toward Emmitt, unsure how he'd react to me. He met me on the bottom step, captured my fingers, and tugged me down to sit next to him. My stomach somersaulted at the contact, and I eased my hand away, wanting to concentrate. The churning didn't completely leave, though, because our shoulders still touched, and I couldn't bring myself to move further away.

"I apologize for losing control. It will never happen again." He rested his arms loosely on his knees and turned his head to study me.

His spontaneous shifting had surprised me, maybe even freaked me out a little at the time, but it didn't bother me now. "Did my secret change anything?"

"Not the way I feel. But it does change how we need to deal with Blake. Will you tell me more? How did he find you?"

"Remember when I told you Richard and my mom married and then things changed? Blake changed everything. I don't know how Richard got involved with him, but one day, Richard brought Blake home. He spoke smoothly. Salesman-nice is what my mom called it. She didn't like Blake.

"Looking back, I think that's why she died after Aden was born. I think Blake knew she would be a problem. She would have tried to stop what he had planned. So, he killed her. With her gone and two little boys to worry about, Blake had Richard on strings, dancing to his commands. Suddenly, I wasn't allowed to leave the house anymore. Disobedience wasn't tolerated." I watched my brothers play. "I tried to run once. When they caught me, Blake slapped Liam. Hard. His handprint turned into a bruise that covered Liam's little face from temple to jaw."

Emmitt growled low in his throat, startling me. When I glanced at him, he had his eyes closed and jaw clenched. The skin on his forearm rippled slightly. I glanced at Nana and Jim unsure what to do. The boys didn't need to witness Emmitt shifting, and I didn't want to get knocked off the porch steps.

Nana didn't acknowledge us, but she did move to block Liam's view. How did she know?

"I promised not to lose control, and I won't. However, I can't help reacting," he said after a moment. An underlying growl roughened his voice. He lifted his head and met my eyes. I could see his anger. "We don't hit children."

I nodded slowly. He might not, but Blake sure did.

"So I stayed and obeyed, and Blake had me by the same strings he had

Richard. Every month he brought men to the house. He called it a business meeting but the men never talked business. They never said anything. They just stared at me.

"Then, at the beginning of the summer, Blake became *driven*." I paused, looking off at the trees as I remembered my last night there. "The dinner before I ran, Blake went crazy. He grabbed me by the throat, and his face started to change. Not all the way like you did. Only a little. His fangs scared me. While he held me, he told me I would allow all of the men to 'scent' me. He said I would bite and Claim one of them."

I felt Emmitt shudder beside me and touched his trembling hand in comfort. When he stilled, I continued.

"I held myself still as they approached me one by one, afraid they would change like Blake had. After the first one, I closed my eyes. When they finished, Blake told me to go to my room.

"The next morning Blake called. He told me that Richard was dead. I don't doubt Blake killed him, and I think Richard expected it because that morning there'd been an envelope shoved under my door. Important documents, cash, and a number for a lawyer were in it. Richard had written a note telling me to run. I hit David over the head and ran fast. I took my mom's car, not knowing how to drive. I almost backed into the mailbox." I looked up at Emmitt. "He won't give up."

Something in his eyes gave me real hope. I wanted to believe I wasn't alone and unprotected in a world filled with strange beings. I shook just thinking about it.

Emmitt wrapped an arm around me and hugged me close, resting his chin on top my head. "You don't have to worry about him anymore. By exposing our kind to you and using humans like he did, he broke our laws. He'll pay for what he did."

"I don't understand. How is what he did different from what you did? Not that you've used us. I mean, you showed me what you are."

He lifted his head, tilted it as if listening, then sighed. "I'll let Nana answer the questions about the rules and laws tomorrow. We've had enough excitement for one day."

My gaze flicked to Nana. With her back to us, she pushed Liam on the swing. "Was she just talking to you?"

Emmitt didn't ask whom I meant. "Yes. She's worried about you. Jim gives you too much to drink last night. She scolds us this morning. I prove what werewolves are capable of. She reveals more about Claiming and Mating than you're comfortable with. Then we find out everything we've asked you to understand about us is on top of an exposure to our kind that's left you distrustful and fearful. And I burst into my fur in front of you." He paused, a small, self-depreciating smile playing about his lips. "It's a lot to take in before lunch."

I nodded in agreement. Yet, now that I'd told them about Blake, it didn't feel so bad.

After the silence between us stretched, Emmitt joined the boys in their sprinkler races, leaving me to my thoughts. One secret down. How would they deal with my ability, though? Staying in the shade, I contentedly sat on the porch and watched their antics while I dwelled on my premonitions.

Nana went inside after a while. I didn't know how she could stand the heat.

I knew I needed to plan for tomorrow's premonition, but instead, I watched the ripple of Emmitt's muscles while he twisted, turned, and jumped through the water. His chest was wet again from the sprinkler, and he was almost as tan as Jim from his time outside. I struggled not to drool. His words echoed in my head. I was his. Did that then mean he was mine? I liked the idea of that. My stomach tightened.

He turned, caught me watching, and winked. Given my thoughts, my face flamed. He frowned, stopped playing, and strode toward me. I felt my face heat further and looked away, trying to calm down. My averted gaze didn't last long. I couldn't *not* look at him.

As he approached, his nostrils flared. His lips curved in a knowing smile. My stomach went crazy, and my breathing spiked. With a gleam in his eyes, he leapt onto the porch, bypassing the steps, and stalked me.

"Do you have a phone with a data plan, or a computer with internet?" I asked randomly.

My question brought him up short. He tilted his head and studied me with a curious look before shaking his head.

Nana stepped out just then with a tray of sandwiches.

"Emmitt, go get the boys. Michelle, will you fetch a hand towel?"

Glad for the reprieve, I ran inside. Nana had the boys wipe their hands so their sandwiches didn't disintegrate when they touched them.

We all ate on the porch, and after Emmitt finished eating, he quietly excused himself. I watched him walk inside. When he stepped out again, dressed in a shirt and jeans, he said he'd be back later and strode to his bike. The roar of the engine and a cloud of dust marked his passage and left me wondering where he'd gone.

TIRED FROM AN AFTERNOON OF PLAYING, the boys fell asleep quickly, leaving me with nothing to do. I jogged back downstairs, returned the books I'd finished, and borrowed another one from Nana. Back in our apartment, I pulled the office chair onto the dark porch then settled down to read. Reading wasn't easy. I had to angle the book to catch the light from the kitchen. Still, I relaxed and listened to the night sounds.

Several chapters in, I heard the distant rumble of a familiar engine. I smiled to myself and stayed sitting in the dim circle of light, waiting. It didn't take long for Emmitt to pull into the driveway. I could taste the dust in the air; we needed rain again. He slowly pulled into the garage and cut the engine.

His eyes glinted when he stepped from the garage and looked up at me. I gave a small wave, knowing he would see me. A few minutes later, I heard his footsteps in the kitchen behind me.

"Nice chair," he said with a hint of laughter.

I glanced back at him. "It's my new office."

"Then you might need this." He lifted a dark object he'd been holding.

Spinning the chair around, I reached for it. The small sleek tablet caught the light, and I glanced up at Emmitt with a frown. He'd left to buy me a tablet?

"The guy at the store said you should be able to surf the internet, even out here."

I accepted the outrageous gift quietly. The sensibility of having it for tomorrow outweighed the need to protest at the expense.

"Thank you, Emmitt. I'll try to pay you back." But I doubted the stack of bills left in the envelope was enough to pay for it. When pulling a bill out here and there to give to Jim or Nana so they could buy us groceries, I never stopped to count what remained. The thinning pile told me enough.

"Don't worry about it. It's a gift."

He stepped onto the porch and moved to lean against the wall. In silence, we watched the stars twinkling over the trees.

"Pretty crazy day," he commented after a few minutes.

"Makes sitting in my office at night just that much better." I didn't really want to talk about the day. If I did, it would really hit home how messed up my life was. I preferred to bumble along in denial for as long as I could.

He pushed away from the wall. "If you need to talk about anything, I'll be here." Then, he left quietly.

I stared off at the stars until a distant howl reminded me I had work to do.

CHAPTER TWELVE

When the boys stumbled into the kitchen and saw me blurry-eyed, leaning over a piece of paper covered with scribbled notes, they froze. The tablet had taken some getting used to. Despite the learning curve, I felt I had enough research on the paper to warrant a plausible explanation of my impending prediction.

Pushing away from the island, I stood with a wilted smile and asked what they wanted for breakfast. A tap at the door delayed their response.

Emmitt swept open the door without waiting for an answer. Jim stepped in just enough for my brothers to see him.

"Come on, boys," Jim waved them to the door. "Eggs, bacon, potato pancakes and orange juice are waiting." Still in their pajamas, the boys ran out the door with Jim close on their heels. The three of them created a thumping racket on the steps.

Emmitt stood by the door, studying me. "You didn't sleep." Disapproval laced his words. His eyes drifted to the tablet and then the piece of paper.

I blinked at him stupidly, my brain replaced with fuzz. What had he expected when he handed me a cool new toy two hours before midnight? Of course, I stayed up to play with it. My eyes followed his to the paper. And I did some darn good work, too.

His movement interrupted my drifting thoughts. Two strides brought him across the room. A twist and lift had me up in his arms before I could squeal. He marched me to the bedroom, set me gently on the bed, and pulled a sheet up to cover me.

I didn't fight it much. Having the bed to myself felt lovely. I forced a weak protest for appearance's sake. "But I have stock information for Nana's friend."

"It can wait until you've slept a bit." He hung a blanket over the blinds to keep out all light.

"But..."

"Sleep, Michelle. I'll be listening." He closed the door.

My lips twitched in the dark. Plan perfectly executed.

THE TICKER TAPE WOKE ME. I didn't know how much time had passed, but I threw back the sheet and got out of bed. The still, warm air in the room left me feeling hot and sticky. Grumbling about stocks and lack of rain, I grabbed a change of clothes and stumbled to the bathroom.

As I showered on autopilot, I focused on the information playing in my mind and struggled to recall the closing rate from my research. Nothing came to mind. A seed of doubt sprouted. I rinsed, shut off the shower, and pulled on clothes while still partially wet. Why couldn't I remember?

Hair dripping onto my shirt, I yanked open the bathroom door and flew to the island. My eyes devoured the notes. I pulled the paper closer, my brain denying what my eyes saw.

"No, no, no, no, no!" I whispered fiercely. I'd stayed up all night. And for what? Some unknown entity to pop into my head. What did I need to do to catch a freak'n break?

I crumpled up the paper and threw the ball out the open French doors, watching it sail over the railing. Grabbing a new sheet, I set to work again, my fingers dancing over the tablet's smooth glass as I tried to figure out how to prove this new premonition viable. The scratch of my pencil against the paper kept the ticker in my head company.

Deep in thought, reading an article about the business in question, I noticed the sudden silence in my head. The ticker had just stopped. Turned off. I looked at the paper next to me where I'd started my notes about the business. In the top corner, I'd written out the premonition like a recommendation. I knew writing it down wouldn't turn it off. It never had before. But I had no other explanation. Setting down the pencil, I moved to pick up the paper.

"What are you doing?"

Emmitt's voice ripped a startled yell from me. Swiveling on the stool, I held a hand to my heart and gave him a wide-eyed look.

"Obviously, four hours of sleep isn't enough." He stood just behind me, reading the paper over my shoulder. "Why are you doing this?" he asked nodding to the paper. "And why did this one fly?" He held up the wrinkled sheet I'd tossed out the window.

"I know investments. Stocks. Richard invested. It's the only way I can pay you back." He arched a brow at the crumpled paper, obviously wondering about it. "Another thought woke me. That one wasn't right," I said, motioning to the wadded paper he held.

"Back to bed." He tilted his head indicating I should get moving.

"I'm not five. I don't need to be told to go to bed."

"Of course you're not five. A five-year-old would listen."

His words hurt a little. The scowl fell from my face, and I eyed him, wondering about his attitude. He didn't appear angry.

He saw something in my expression or scented something related to my emotions because he stepped forward and wrapped his arms around me, setting his chin on the top of my head. He didn't seem to mind my wet hair. My cheek rested against his chest.

"I'm worried," he admitted. "Last night you seemed fine with everything that happened yesterday, but then you didn't sleep." He paused for so long I thought he'd finished talking, but then he asked softly, "Are you planning on leaving?"

Leaving? Despite everything I'd learned, I still felt safest here. "No, Emmitt. I'm not leaving." He hugged me close, causing my stomach and heart to go crazy. I forced myself to keep still.

He cleared his throat and stepped back.

"Since you don't want more sleep, do you want to come outside? Jim and I were talking about going into town for a few things."

"Sure. Hold on," I hopped off the stool and went to the room to get some money. Two more twenties from the diminishing pile. We needed milk and fresh produce.

He accepted the money with reluctance when I told him what I wanted him to pick up. Before he left, he promised he and Jim would be back soon. I went outside to play with Liam and Aden. At least, I didn't have to worry about the premonition anymore.

THEY RETURNED WELL AFTER LUNCH, pulling a trailer loaded with furniture. Jim waved to the boys from the passenger window while Emmitt pulled up next to the garage to back the trailer closer to the house. Nana stepped onto the porch and helped direct Emmitt.

Liam and Aden climbed the tower attached to the swing set and watched. I shaded my eyes and squinted at everything stacked on the trailer and in the bed of the truck. There was so much. A sense of anticipation filled me when I thought of living in the new apartment. It would be our real home. The permanence of that thought didn't scare me as it once had.

Emmitt backed up until the gate hung over the steps then parked the truck. He and Jim hopped out and got to work unloading everything. No matter what it was, they made it look effortless. Leather sofa, love seat, recliner, queen bed, bunk beds, dressers. They never appeared winded nor did they need a break. I stayed with the boys until all the big pieces were inside. Then, we followed.

I hadn't been in the apartment since I'd given Emmitt my opinion on the bathroom color. This time when I stepped into the kitchen from the hallway door, I looked at it with new eyes.

The living room was no longer a big, empty cavern. The sofa and loveseat helped fill the space, making it look homey. Someone had positioned both so they faced a widescreen television. I wondered where the money had come from for all the new furniture. The boys raced to the back of the apartment. I watched Nana set the end tables near the sofa.

Feeling pensive, I moved to the boys' bedroom where I heard Jim and Emmitt talking. A bedframe, the first of a pair that would stack for bunk beds, lay half-assembled on the floor. The boys squatted nearby, eagerly asking to help. Jim handed them the screws and bolts to hold, and I smiled at their enthusiasm before glancing at the two matching dressers that sentineled one of the room's windows. A toy chest sat under the other window, leaving room for the bunk bed to abut the interior wall.

I watched from the doorway for a moment, wondering if my brothers thought of their room back home. Large and open with a few toys to entertain their lonely hours locked inside, it had originally been the master suite. After my mother died, Richard had contractors come to the house to make several changes. In my grief, I noticed nothing until it was too late. Bare, white institutional walls had replaced the beautiful decorations and colors my mom had contributed, and discreet locks had adorned the doors.

The room before me looked like a real room for two little boys. Bittersweet thoughts of how my mom would react to Emmitt's efforts filled me.

Leaving them to their work, I turned to check out the other room and froze in the doorway. A queen-sized bed, assembled and made, sat between the two windows that faced the backyard. A dresser sat against the wall to the right of the bed with a reading chair next to it. The light from the nearby window made it a perfect spot to curl up with a book. Beside the bed, the guys had set an end table with a lamp.

Decorated in shades of light brown and blues with green accents, the room reminded me of a day at the lake. Specifically, the day Emmitt had asked me my favorite color. My heart swelled a little though I tried to stop it. I gently touched the light blue quilt patterned with beige stitching. Why were my feelings toward Emmitt so chaotic?

Gorgeous, kind, and completely focused on me, I found him intense at times. Knowing he considered me his and witnessing the vision about us left me floundering, wondering where we stood exactly. If we were normal humans, I'd say we were just in the flirty stage of an almost relationship. After his "mine" talk, I highly doubted he'd agree.

I heard the brush of a foot on the carpet behind me and turned. Emmitt stood there.

"You worry too much," he said softly.

Yeah, I did. I smiled. "Thank you for this."

He nodded and seemed to want to say more, but Liam called him from the other room. With an amused tilt to his lips, he answered his helper's call and left me wondering what he hadn't said.

Eager to give Emmitt his apartment back and to settle in our own, I started moving our few possessions. With dressers for everyone, I enjoyed putting away our clothes.

"Michelle?" Nana called from the kitchen.

I closed Aden's dresser drawer and left the boys with instructions to make their beds. When I walked into the kitchen, I was surprised to see Nana there holding a large box.

"When I went rummaging, I was hoping you'd stay. So, I picked up more than clothes." She set the box on the island, opened it, and showed me a set of pots and pans. "There's more in the garage. Do you want me to bring it all up?"

I smiled and nodded.

After the boys finished their beds, they went to find Emmitt and Jim. All four left the apartment, suspiciously quiet. I walked through the rooms, looking for what trouble they might have gotten into. Through the windows in my room drifted the sound of Aden laughing. I peeked through the pretty gauze curtains and spotted him playing with Jim outside.

Smiling, I went back to help Nana. We had a mountain of flatware, glassware, pots, and pans to labor through. While we worked, she asked about my research the night before and told me more about her friend, Sam, who was her age, mild-mannered, and sounded like a nice grandfatherly sort. She admitted that she humored him when he called for her input on the market, having no interest in it herself.

I didn't notice how long we'd worked until Emmitt returned with two tired boys. The sun hung low in the sky. I glanced at the clock and saw it was almost eight. I hadn't even thought of feeding them. Emmitt saw my frown and assured me they had already eaten dinner.

"Thank you," I said to Emmitt. "Nana, I better get these two to bed. I can finish the rest on my own." She smiled and left with Emmitt. My stomach chose then to growl, but looking at my brothers' tired faces, I put off my own dinner to help them get ready for bed.

Liam and Aden excitedly tromped to their bedroom to get their pajamas on and then to the bathroom to brush their teeth. I thought they might fight going to sleep, especially in a separate room from me, but they didn't spare that a thought. Instead, they both tried to claim the top bunk. I stepped in to settle it before it got heated. As the oldest, Liam had the top bunk. Aden pouted until I pointed out the bottom bunk made a better fort by adding a few extra blankets.

I kissed them goodnight, turned off the light, and left the door open. Even after they lay in bed, they giggled and talked until I reminded them if they didn't close their eyes soon, they'd end up sleeping in and missing precious outside playtime. They quickly grew quiet.

I wandered back to the kitchen. Opening the refrigerator, I looked for something to eat. The vast empty belly mocked me. I'd moved our things but not the food.

Closing the refrigerator door, I crept to check on the boys before sneaking across the hall to snag some food.

Emmitt met me at the door. "Thought I might see you yet tonight." He held a fork. On the end, he'd skewered a bite of grilled chicken. I grinned and popped it in my mouth. The temperature caught me off guard, very warm, straight from the grill. He'd probably timed it.

"I didn't think you could hear through closed doors."

"I can if I'm close enough. Just across the hall from a closed door, I can hear some things. Like footsteps." He winked at me and stood aside so I could enter. Two plates waited on the island. "Will you eat with me?"

As if I could say no. My stomach somersaulted in the now familiar way it did when near Emmitt. I nodded. He smiled.

FOR THE REST of the week, Nana and I took turns making dinner. When I cooked, I insisted the boys help me. I'd realized how little I did with them when we were together. So I made an effort to change that. They still went down to Nana's apartment each morning to practice their ABC's and do projects. Our refrigerator already sported two colorfully glittered works of glue and construction paper. In the afternoons, I practiced baseball with them.

Friday Emmitt cornered me with a request. "We'd like to give you a surprise tomorrow but need you to leave with Nana for at least three hours."

I stared at him for a moment, knowing he meant without my brothers, and delayed answering. I'd been irresponsible with their wellbeing when I'd left them before. And I'd meant it when I said I wouldn't do it again.

A FLOOD of sunlight woke me. I lounged in bed for a moment enjoying the novelty of my room. The quiet apartment told me the boys still slept. Sighing, I stretched and got out of bed. For fun, I walked to the closet and stared at my clothes. Sure, there weren't many, but they hung neatly displayed, ready for selection. I picked a printed tee and cotton shorts and hurried to take a quick shower before the boys woke up.

When I finished, they still slept quietly snuggled in their new beds, so I decided to go talk to Emmitt. He hadn't pushed for an answer yesterday after I'd made it obvious I didn't want to talk about it. I owed him an explanation. I knew he just wanted to do something nice for me.

He opened his door before I could knock, startling me. He was dressed in jeans and a shirt as usual but this shirt ran a little smaller than the rest. The material outlined every ridge and dip on his chest. I stood there awkwardly for a second, trying not to eye him. The hallway flooded with the aroma of sausage and pancakes as he looked me over from head to toe. A shiver ran through me as his slow appraisal caused a deep blush.

"How did you sleep?" I asked, not knowing what to say about his look.

"Fine. The bed still smells like you."

I didn't know what so say about that, either. He'd clarified things nicely before, and I knew he was interested in me, but where did that leave us? I wondered what he'd do if I asked him to spell out where exactly we stood in the relationship game.

He didn't move to let me in, which I thought odd. So I stayed in the hallway, hesitating. His eyes twinkled. Was he laughing at me?

I heard a noise behind me and turned to see Liam standing in the doorway already dressed.

"Want some breakfast, buddy?" Emmitt asked from behind me.

"Yep," Liam said with a nod. He turned to look behind him. "Hurry up, Aden." Aden ran down the hallway from their bedroom as he pulled a shirt over his head.

"What are you up to, Liam?" I asked with mock suspicion.

"Nana Wini said if it was okay with you, we could spend the day with Jim and Emmitt so you could go do girl stuff with her." He looked up at me pleadingly. "Can we?"

I'd been setup by three werewolves and a kindergartner. They wanted me to leave my brothers in their care for three hours for a surprise. Could I trust them to keep Liam and Aden safe if something happened? I knew they would try. After all, they knew whom, or rather what, they faced now. But they didn't *know* Blake's determination.

"Emmitt..." I hated that I was about to say no.

"They will be safe," he promised stepping close. Liam's hopeful face bounced between us. "Everything's been quiet, and you've left them before."

"I know," I said emphatically. "But that wasn't right."

He sighed and looked me in the eyes in a way that curled my toes. "Do you trust us?"

I did. I just didn't trust Blake. "Just three hours?"

Emmitt nodded and stepped back from me, allowing Liam and Aden space to run into his apartment so they could start their fun-filled day. Emmitt laughed at my disgruntled expression and encouraged me to get shoes on to go down by Nana's.

Nana waited for me at the bottom step. She wore a pretty sundress and had a purse already slung on her shoulder. When I saw her purse, I hesitated. I hadn't thought of bringing any money.

"Where are we going? I didn't bring anything with me."

"You're fine as you are. We thought you needed a day out, free of responsibility just for a little while. Our treat."

A *day* out?

"Just three hours though, right?" She smiled and nodded. I reluctantly followed her out the door and got into her car.

After a few minutes watching the trees zip by, I relaxed enough to take a deep breath.

"Where are we going?" I asked again, curious.

"Emmitt wanted to treat you to shopping, and Jim thought you'd like a mani and pedi." I swung my stunned gaze away from the trees to her smiling face. "A little bit of worry-free freedom and fun. That's what Emmitt wanted for you."

I blushed, and my stomach warmed at Emmitt's consideration.

We drove to town, making small talk along the way. She asked about my plans for enrolling Liam in school, and I felt a moment of panic. I hadn't given it any thought. Blake would probably be watching for Liam to enroll in school. My blood chilled at the thought.

Nana Wini must have seen something in my eyes because she quickly changed the subject and asked me when I'd last had a manicure or pedicure.

Her question completely diverted me from my concern. I admitted I'd never had either. I looked down at my feet and wondered why Jim would suggest it.

As we drove into a large city, the other drivers casually glanced at us as we sped past. So many people seeing me. What if Blake or his men came here and started looking? What if they were already here?

"Michelle, I can smell your worry. Breathe through it. Talk about what's concerning you. Don't keep it inside."

"There are so many people. People who look our way and see me. Any one of them might remember me. What if Blake or his men come here looking for me?"

"Do you think he'll just stop random people and start asking about you? Maybe show your picture? No, honey." She reached over to pat my leg. "It would call too much attention to himself. He needs to be discreet. He probably still thinks you're out on your own. If he's one of us, I've given him no reason to think you've been found. Other than telling the other Elders, we've kept your association with us quiet." Her words reassured me.

She pulled into a space in front of a day spa and killed the engine. "Ready?"

I glanced at the screened windows of the small building before us. I couldn't see more than the reception desk. The only person visible, a young woman, sat behind the desk, looking down at her computer screen. I nodded, got out, and followed Nana's lead.

The inside smelled lightly perfumed, and quiet pop music played overhead. The woman behind the desk looked up with a smile and welcomed us.

Minutes later, we sat in massaging chairs while our feet soaked. Nana conversed with the person rubbing lotion into her calves. I half-listened to their conversation while I watched the woman on the stool in front of me. She sorted through her metal instruments, selecting two and lifted my foot out of the water.

"...mauled by some kind of dog."

The words caught my attention, and I glanced at the woman at Nana's feet. I didn't see how talking about a mauling counted as a relaxing day.

"Happened almost a month ago. I just read more about it this morning. I guess the guy's family went missing right after that. There's all kinds of speculation."

"Not that I don't feel sorry for the man, but why would that go viral?" Nana asked.

I tried not to smile at Nana's very modern terminology.

"The dog is crazy big. It stood chest high. They're trying to identify the breed but can't."

Great. Enormous, mad dogs on the loose. This planet needed a reality check.

The woman at my feet offered me two color wheels so I could pick a polish. I let the rest of the conversation drift over me while I studied a vibrant pink-orange.

NAILS POLISHED, purchases in the back seat, we headed home hours later. I thanked Nana for the day. I'd tried to be fun and gracious, but Nana probably noticed my lack of enthusiasm.

She waved off my thanks. "The nails were Jim's treat. All I sprang for was the phone plan, which we needed. Adding you to it was no hardship."

I toyed with the cell phone in my hands. It had a data plan. Probably Emmitt's idea. The phone could come in handy. I liked knowing I could call and check up on my brothers if I did have to leave them for some reason—like today.

Sitting back in my seat, I watched the country fly past. For an older person, Nana Wini liked to speed. Thankfully, she drove well.

When we pulled into the driveway, Jim and the boys waved from the backyard. They had the sprinkler on full blast. I'd known my brothers would be fine on a certain level, but actually seeing them melted the tension that had prevented me from truly enjoying the day.

I opened the back door to pull out my purchases while Nana Wini went to ask the boys if they'd had fun. Not only had Nana insisted on me getting a phone, but she'd also insisted I buy a dress and shoes, saying that every woman needed something pretty in her closest for any occasion. I didn't see myself ever going anywhere, so why bother with a dress? But, she'd persisted until I'd distractedly found a solid black dress. Without trying it on, we'd purchased it. I'd assured Nana I knew my size. I really had no idea if the dress would fit but had wanted to get back to my brothers.

Carrying my dress, covered by a white plastic bag so it wouldn't get dirty, I stepped onto the porch.

"Hold on," Jim called, leaving the boys to their sprinkler. "You can't sneak in without showing me." He looked at me expectantly, and I wiggled my toes for him, again glad I'd worn sandals. "Very nice. Now the dress."

"How did you—"

"Emmitt told me his contribution to your day."

Emmitt had wanted me to buy a dress?

"It's why I thought you'd want your nails done. Better hurry, I hear him coming."

I gaped at him. "I don't know if anyone will get to see me in this dress."

"Day's not done yet," he grinned back at me. I shook my head and thanked him for the special consideration. Then I gave him a quick, spontaneous hug.

"You keep that up, and he'll be treating you to spa days with Nana Wini every week." Emmitt's voice rang in the entry.

I turned and saw him coming down the steps. My eyes devoured him, and I realized I'd missed him, too.

"Thank you for the dress," I said sincerely.

Jim moved away from us, heading toward the boys who still regaled Nana about what they'd done.

"You're welcome. Just don't let Jim see it before I do."

"I think it might stay in the bag for a while."

"I hope not. I was wondering if you'd consider going to dinner with me. Next Saturday," he assured me when he saw my panicked look.

My panic had nothing to do with leaving Liam and Aden this time. "A date?" I asked before I could stop myself.

"If you're not too busy." He wore a teasing smile.

I shrugged, pretending indifference. "I'll see what I can do." First, I'd need to try on the dress.

He moved aside so I could carry my things up. "You coming back outside or going to research again?"

Without knowing it, he'd reminded me what I needed to do before playing dress up. "Both. I'll bring the tablet out here."

After tossing my things neatly in the closet, I grabbed my paper, pencil, and tablet before jogging back downstairs. Nana already sat on the steps, sipping a glass of tea, her toes sparkling in the sun. She'd selected a cool, silver polish. I settled next to her and started my research.

With the heat and the hard step, I struggled to stay focused. After only an hour, I set the tablet aside and ran in to get an iced tea, taking up Nana on her offer to help myself. When I came back, Emmitt sat in my spot and looked up at me hopefully. Nana held the tablet, staring at it intently.

"Can I have a drink?" he asked, looking at my glass. Since I'd already had a few sips and had gotten it more out of boredom than actual thirst, I handed it over with a smile. His gaze flicked to mine as he drank half the glass in a few long pulls. His request to take me to dinner echoed in my ears, and I flushed. Uncomfortable, I looked away and caught sight of the video Nana watched on the tablet.

Any blood rushing to my face immediately fled as I watched a huge, shaggy dog attack a man just outside of an office building. The grainy quality of the image and the distance between the camera and the attack made it hard to see clearly, but I couldn't mistake Richard's identity.

The person holding the camera swore, and the image on the screen dipped to show blacktop as the attack became savage. People screamed in the background. Some yelled for help. The person taking the video refocused on Richard's prone form as the attack ended. He had been savaged, covered in red gore.

People ran toward him. The dog turned to look around, its eyes catching the light and glinting for the camera before it leapt over a fence, clearing more than ten feet before sprinting away.

A strange popping sound filled my ears, then all noise ceased. The sun began to set suddenly and the sky grew dark. Nothing made sense. In the dim light, Emmitt's eyes appeared before me, filled with worry.

Thankfully, the lights went out. I was glad I didn't have to see any more.

SEVERAL SOMEONE'S called my name. I opened my eyes, disoriented. I heard Jim speaking.

"She's okay. She just fainted. Emmitt caught her. She's not hurt."

Fainted? The image of Richard came back to me in a rush, and I closed my eyes. Oh, Richard. Blake said he'd died, but he hadn't said how. I'd assumed something like poison or a setup mugging. Why would they do something so obvious?

"I don't know," Nana said. I hadn't realized I'd spoken my question aloud.

A hand smoothed back my hair. I opened my eyes again and saw Emmitt. His deep blue eyes caressed my face. His arms cradled me as I half-sat in his lap.

"Nice catch," I whispered. Some of the worry melted from his face, and his lips tilted up at the corners slightly.

"For you, always."

I sat up, and he kept an arm around me. Blood rushed to my head, making me dizzy. I smiled at the boys. Their expressions were just as worried as Emmitt's.

"I'm okay. Just got too warm. I think I need to go through the sprinkler," I suggested.

Liam watched me a moment longer than Aden. He knew I lied. Smart boy. Jim encouraged them to go back to playing with him.

"I'm assuming that was Richard based on your reaction and question," Nana said. I nodded. "This has gone too far. We need to find those responsible. They are killing, and that endangers us all. What we saw...that is not who we are," she said sadly.

She rose and walked into the house. A moment later, I heard her speaking. Emmitt stayed close, comforting me. My eyes traveled the trees, scanning. Nothing had really changed, nothing to think that Blake and his men were any closer to finding me, but it didn't matter. Fear ruled me, again.

CHAPTER THIRTEEN

AT FIRST, I COULDN'T BRING MYSELF TO LET THE BOYS OUT OF MY sight. Nana, Jim, and Emmitt all took turns talking to me, saying what I already understood. Nothing had changed except that we now knew how Richard had died. Though I knew they were right, it didn't ease my fears. Liam and Aden, clueless about what I'd witnessed, didn't understand my sudden smothering presence and started to rebel.

Reluctantly, I gave Liam and Aden a bit of much needed distance, but my concession didn't change my nights. The slightest noise would bring me out of a doze, and panic would set in much like our first night there. So the week passed slowly, and within a few days, my head ached from poor sleep and constant worry.

Each day the concern in Emmitt's watchful gaze grew. Thursday night after dinner, he pulled me aside.

"I'll sleep on the couch after the boys go to bed."

He didn't ask, and I didn't try to tell him no. I hoped having him there would help me sleep through the night.

When an ominous rumbling of thunder woke me Friday morning, I had mixed feelings. Liam and Aden would need to stay inside, but I'd forced too much inside time already this week. Today, they would mutiny for sure.

I heard a creak in the hall outside my door then the rapid patter of feet. Worried, I flew from bed, making it to my door just in time to look down the hall and see the boys disappear out of the apartment. Calling their names, I raced after them.

As I reached the end of the hall, Emmitt stepped into my path. He caught me in his arms and spun us, absorbing my momentum. It didn't prevent my nose from connecting with his sternum with enough force that my eyes watered.

"Ow!" I squinted up at him.

"I'm sorry." A tender look crept into his gaze as he studied me.

My breath caught as he slowly lowered his head. Was he really going to kiss me? I hadn't even brushed my teeth! I closed my eyes. My heart started to beat erratically, and I couldn't control my breathing. Then, his lips touched the tip of my nose. My eyes flew open.

"I wouldn't have stepped in front of you if I'd known you'd get hurt." He reached up and gently pushed back a strand of my hair that had fallen forward during our collision.

"Uh. It's okay." My thoughts jumbled together. "Just a minute." Instead of continuing my chase, I pivoted on my heel and fled to the bathroom.

I rejoined him a minute later, minty fresh and with untangled hair. He stood at the stove, watching the pan on the burner until he heard me approach.

"How are you feeling?"

I tried not to stare at his chest as he spoke. Smacking myself against it, though painful to my nose, had been wonderful for the rest of me.

"Fine," I said. "No permanent damage."

He gave me an odd look but said nothing. Instead, he handed me a plate with a single egg and toast. After a few home-cooked breakfasts, he'd caught onto my portion size.

With the second bite in my mouth, I realized he hadn't been asking about my nose but about how I felt in general. My fears revolving around Blake had abated with some decent sleep, but thanks to the platonic kiss on the nose, I was confused again. I took a drink of the juice he'd set before me, calmed myself with a slow breath, then asked the big question.

"What are we?"

He paused mid-chew to look at me, just like he had in the diner. It made me smile. He swallowed and tilted his head.

"I'm not sure I understand the question."

Of course not. I needed a morning blush to start the day off right.

Frustrated, I stood.

"I get this." I leaned forward and planted a light kiss on his nose, surprising him.

"And I get this." I moved close to his neck, inhaled his scent, and trailed my nose against his skin as he'd done several times to me.

"And I'm told..." His skin suddenly rippled beneath my touch, and I pulled back.

His eyes glittered as he struggled for control.

"I'm sorry," I said, stepping away.

He followed me, moving fluidly from his stool. His calm, midnight eyes tracked every move I made.

"Don't be. I'm fine. Finish your question." His voice was rough and intense, and it made my heart drop into my stomach.

Holding my ground, I let him crowd me. Better to leave room to turn and run than to be backed against a wall. Not that I thought I'd need to run from Emmitt, but it never hurt to leave options open.

He didn't stop moving until he was a hand's width away from me. I struggled to maintain eye contact. I knew what I'd done to him, and I really wanted to touch him again. But I couldn't. Not until I understood how he saw us.

"I, uh, was just going to say that...um." I cleared my throat. "You said I'm yours and that biting equals an engagement. But I don't understand where that leaves us now. What are we?"

"As you asked, we are friends," he said.

I felt a brief stab of disappointment. Then, he leaned in again. He didn't inhale or use his nose this time. He dropped his mouth to my neck. It wasn't a kiss exactly, just a brush of his lips that blazed a path on my sensitive skin. I couldn't help myself; I lightly rested my hands against his chest and leaned into the feeling as I struggled to focus.

"But, I hope we are friends who are working their way to dating."

It took a moment for his words to register. Ah. That's right. His dinner invitation.

"I'm not good at being friends," he said softly, breaking contact but not pulling back. My hammering heart appreciated the move, but my tingling skin felt bereft. "I struggle with the boundaries of friendship."

It was good to know I wasn't the only one struggling. I swallowed and dropped my hands.

"What boundaries?" As soon as I said it, I knew the answer because something in his gaze told me he wanted my hands back where they were.

"Friends don't get this close. They don't touch each other like I just touched you. And I really want to be that close."

I wanted that, too. Especially when he whispered it near my ear.

"What else?" I couldn't believe I'd asked.

"You'll have to let me know," he said, reluctantly retreating. "You set the boundaries."

He turned away from me and walked to the island. I wanted him back, crowding me. Stupid friendship talk. If I had more courage, I would tell him I wanted to be more than friends. But what did more than friends mean in the wolf-world? If I was the one setting the boundaries that defined our relationship, I needed to know the answer. Because I didn't, I said nothing.

Emmitt stood there a moment until the shaking stopped then he sat down. I joined him and slowly started to eat my food.

He'd answered my question about our relationship. But sometimes, knowing an answer was worse than dwelling on the question.

THE KIDS STAYED DOWNSTAIRS with Nana all morning. After we cleaned up breakfast, Emmitt stepped out. I used the time to research stocks.

The Sunday before, after witnessing the video, I hadn't cared enough to explain the tip I'd handed to Nana. She hadn't asked, either. This week I planned to be prepared, again. The boring work drove me to distraction. I knew some people loved it. Richard had. But, it wasn't my thing.

Rain continuously pattered against the roof, keeping me company. When Nana knocked on my open door near lunch, I willingly pushed aside my work.

"Do you have a moment?" she asked politely.

"Lots of them. What's up?"

She stepped in and took a seat next to me at the kitchen island.

"Emmitt's watching the boys while they color. I wanted to come up and let you know that I put out a call stating the person responsible for Richard's death should step forward immediately. No one has, yet."

My heart skipped a beat, and I felt a stab of fear. "How long will it take?"

"That's the problem. A response should have been immediate."

I shrugged slightly, not understanding.

"Our society has rules and laws like any other. They differ from human laws, not just in the message but in our people's inability to break them. When an

Elder like me speaks a law, it's implanted in our kind as a restriction. Because of that, our laws are few and well thought out. At least, we believe them to be. The rules are easy to break, but the repercussions are impossible to ignore.

"For example, one of our *laws* forbids the forced Claiming of a human. A *rule* states not to kill humans. We made the first one a law—unbreakable—because we could see no circumstance in which we could ever conceive applicable exception to warrant the act. However, self-preservation must be considered before passing a law forbidding the death of another. We made it a *law* that anyone responsible for breaking the *rule*, or a witness to the breaking of the rule, must admit the deed to an Elder.

"The same applies to shifting in public. Our rules state it shouldn't be done, while our law states that any who break the rule, or know of the rule being broken, must step forward."

"Someone should have come to you a month ago," I said, understanding.

She nodded.

We sat in silence for a bit, lost in our own thoughts. Had Blake done the killing himself or one of his men? Did it really matter? Either way, Blake had to have known. He should have stepped forward.

"Can you tell me where Blake kept you? We need to find him to figure out how he's avoided us."

I shook my head before she finished. Richard's address wasn't yet posted in any article I'd read online. Blake would piece it together if werewolves suddenly showed up at our old home. I wouldn't compromise the safety of Liam and Aden so Nana could find some errant werewolves.

She patted my hand. "I understand your reason for saying no. Just think about it." She stood and left.

The day had started out so well. With a sigh, I went back to my research.

A little while later, I heard a tap on the door leading to the porch. Emmitt motioned to me through the glass.

I stood with a wince because of sitting too long, unlocked the door, and stepped out onto the porch with him. The overhanging roof protected us from the rain while lulling us with the soothing patter. Behind Emmitt, a small patio table with two chairs sat near his kitchen door. Two plates and two glasses waited.

"Hungry?" he asked as I took in what he'd done for me. I nodded, and he went to hold out a chair for me. "I heard what Nana said."

"I have premonitions." The randomness of my confession made me cringe.

I'd decided that I needed to trust someone, that I couldn't keep going on so alone, but I hadn't decided how to tell him.

"Did you see what happens if you give us your old address?" he asked without pausing.

I blinked at his easy acceptance of my secret.

"No, I don't have those kinds of premonitions. The stock market." His brows rose. "I know, not very interesting. But think of what you could gain by controlling someone with my ability. The money. Power."

"I don't want money or power. Just you."

His words made my heart flutter, and brought back the memory of his lips on my neck. I blushed and pushed the memory aside.

"Blake's tasted that power. If your laws can't control him, what makes you think finding him will help? All it does is expose us. He will go straight for Liam and Aden. Through them, he can control me again."

He remained quiet for a moment. "Nana won't ask again," he said seriously. Then, in a Jim-like way, he grinned and said, "Want to spike your tea?"

I heard Nana yell his name two stories below and shook my head, breathing a sigh of relief. I'd shared my secret, and he didn't appear to care about it one way or the other. I was halfway through my turkey sandwich when he asked his next question.

"Why did you tell Sam which stock to invest in? Why not just keep it to yourself?"

My appetite fled. By sharing my last secret, I'd officially crossed the all-or-nothing line. I needed to spill the rest. I placed my half-eaten sandwich on his plate before I answered.

"I don't have a choice. The information comes to me every seven days. It plays in my head like a market ticker but with just one stock on repeat. If I don't share the information, it makes me twitchy. The longer I hold it, the more painful it becomes until I'm a mess. Blake figured that out. It became another way for him to control me. I *have* to share the information with someone. As soon as I do, the countdown to the next premonition resets."

"And that's why you didn't want to tell me." He schooled his features and nudged my glass. "Drink."

I did without questioning it. The cool tea soothed my worry-tightened throat.

"There's more," I said.

He continued eating but kept his focus on me.

"I told you a little about what Blake said the night before I ran. That he wanted me to bite one of his men. Before that, he talked about evolving my abilities. When you asked if I saw what would happen, I meant it. I don't have those kinds of visions. But since coming here, something has changed. I've gotten glimpses of people. Girls like me, mostly. I don't know why. Those visions don't work like the stock ones. They don't repeat."

"We'll figure this out." He reached across the table and wrapped his warm fingers around my cold hand. "Please, let some of the worry go. Trust us to keep you and your brothers safe."

I gave a small nod.

SATURDAY, the rain continued. Once again, the boys snuck out early. Emmitt surprised me in the kitchen, not with a cooked meal, but a simple bowl of cereal. Lucky Charms. It made me laugh.

He left me alone for a few hours, and I used the opportunity to page through the items Richard had stuffed into the envelope. Since Nana asked about our old address, I'd been wondering what had become of the house. So I dug for the lawyer's number, and I looked it up online. There was actually a legitimate sounding business associated with it. The site listed a physical address, fax, and an email address.

Tapping my fingers on the dark counter, I debated what to send. Richard hadn't explained the number or why I should contact the lawyer. Perhaps he'd wanted me to press charges against Blake. But on what grounds? Richard owned the house with all the locks and security installed. Maybe Richard had provided the number for custody rights to the boys. But who else would they live with if not me? We didn't come from a big family.

After creating an email address with no personal information, I decided on a short message. I provided my name, Richard's name, and Richard's request that I contact the firm. I sent the message then turned off the tablet. No point in sitting and staring at it on a Saturday.

Tromping downstairs, I found everyone playing board games in Nana's living room. We spent the rest of the morning, and most of the afternoon, cheating and having fun.

Jim's stomach growled in the middle of a card game with Aden, and he asked if I would get him a snack from across the hall. Emmitt and I took a break from our own game to go look.

When we stood in his kitchen with me rummaging in the fridge, Emmitt surprised me with a serious mood. He pulled me back from the open door, turned me, and framed my face with his hands.

"Do you know you've been here a month?"

I hadn't really thought about it. But apparently, he had; and it meant something to him.

"Let me take you to dinner tonight. Please."

His midnight gaze pleaded with me, and I found myself nodding. Dinner with Emmitt. My heart fluttered with excitement as his thumb feathered ever so slightly over my skin.

"Wear the dress," he said freeing me.

He opened a cupboard and pulled out a bag of chips.

Absently, I followed him out of the apartment. The dress? I panicked, not even remembering what it looked like. Black. It'd been black and knee length, maybe, on the hanger. Why hadn't I tried it on? Then I remembered. Nerves about leaving the boys for so long then the video about Richard.

A few steps behind Emmitt, I heard Nana Wini offer to watch the boys. Darn her excellent hearing. The boys turned their puppy eyes toward me, already pleading without words. My gaze flicked between Nana and Jim. Was it safe? I trusted them with the boys, but what about...no. Nothing had changed. Emmitt was right. It had been a month since I left. If they were going to find us, they would have already. Again, I nodded. Trapped.

"Could we leave in an hour?" Emmitt asked me while handing Jim his chips. Jim grinned at my stunned expression and passed the bag to Aden. He'd ruin Aden's dinner.

"Sure," I mumbled, taking a step back toward the hallway. An hour to try on the dress and, if it didn't fit, find something else to wear. The dress had better fit.

I didn't waste any time but bolted up the stairs as soon as I cleared the door.

In the apartment, I pulled my hair from its ponytail and ran a brush through it. It fell straight and smooth after a few minutes of brushing. I stalked to the bedroom, reached into the closet, and tossed the garment bag on the bed. Then, I bent to search for the shoes that weren't there. I straightened slowly, thinking back. After shopping, I'd carried them up to my room and put them in the bottom of my closet. I was sure of it.

I looked under the bed. Nothing. Hands on my hips, I stood in my room, scanning and thinking. They didn't just walk away on their own. Tracing my way through the apartment, I looked under everything, behind the doors, and in the broom closet. I was ready to go ask Nana if she'd seen them but walked to the boys' room just to double-check.

The shoes lay under the bunk bed while the box stood on its side with the lid propped at an angle to create a temporary shelter for Aden's army men.

"Seriously?" I mumbled, snagging the shoes and leaving the box.

Dropping the shoes in the hall, I closed myself into my room and unzipped the bag. The clock on the dresser motivated me. I'd wasted too much time looking for the shoes and only had thirty minutes left.

The black material slid from the bag. There appeared to be less of it than I remembered. Black burnished clasps adorned each shoulder, gathering the material to show more skin. The silky fabric fell softly to the waist panel where shining, black thread glinted in ornate patterns. The plain skirt ended abruptly not far below that.

I picked this? I turned the dress around. No zipper. Shaking my head, I stripped from my shorts and tee then stepped into the dress, tugging and twisting it into place. It felt okay. Not too tight or loose.

I left my bedroom and closed myself into the bathroom to get a better look. I couldn't see all of me at once, but what I did see had my stomach pitching wildly.

The dress was gorgeous but a bit more revealing than a simple date called for. The material draped loosely from the shoulders and gapped in the middle, showing the center of my bra. I turned around. Same with the back. The skirt ended mid-thigh, much longer than the cutoffs I wore, but short for a dress. Well, for *my* dress. A bit of anxiety crept in.

What else did I have? T-shirts and sweatshirts hung in the closet. No other options. I looked back at the mirror as I unclasped my bra and wiggled out of it. I tried tugging the material to hide the valley showing. Nope. Not going to happen. I'd just need to change quickly and run across the hall to see if we could go somewhere that wouldn't require a dress.

I opened the bathroom door and froze. Emmitt and Jim both stood in the hallway. Emmitt's gaze raked me, and Jim gave a wolf whistle.

"What are you doing here?" My voice sounded too high but I couldn't help it. What if I'd stepped out in a towel? Well, maybe that would have been safer. The big towels Nana gave us would have covered more.

"You sounded upset," Emmitt said absently as his eyes continued to travel my length. On the way back up, he closed his eyes briefly, swallowed hard, then returned to his slow appraisal. He didn't bother to look at Jim when he spoke.

"Okay, you saw. Now go away."

With a laugh, Jim left.

"Saw what?" I asked, looking Emmitt over as well. He wore dark grey slacks and a sport coat with a lighter grey V-neck sweater.

"He wanted to see how you looked in the dress. Nana Wini told him about it," he said absently, still studying me.

Nana remembered the dress, and I hadn't?

"Could we maybe go somewhere casual enough for jean shorts?" I fought the urge to cross my arms, knowing it would just make it worse. Then, I realized I still had my bra in my hand. Please don't let him notice, I thought.

"I can smell your nervousness. You look lovely. Please wear it," he said quietly, meeting my eyes again. "Do you need a jacket?"

A trench coat would work. Instead of speaking, I shook my head.

He bent to pick up my shoes, and I quickly tossed my bra behind me and turned off the bathroom lights. He motioned for me to lead the way to the door. There he bent and helped me with the shoes.

He didn't say anything as he slipped the black heel onto my foot. His light touch at my ankle made my legs Jell-O. Once the shoe was on, his hand lingered on my calf before he moved to the other shoe. The longer he stayed quiet, the more nervous I became.

When he stood, he smiled slightly and leaned forward. He carefully swept my hair back over my shoulder, moving it out of the way. The warmth of his palms heated my upper arms as he held me steady. His breath tickled the skin at the base of my neck as he breathed a path up to my ear. I forgot all about the dress.

"Thank you for saying yes," he said softly then pulled back.

Yes to what?

He clasped my hand in his and led us out into the hallway. My brain came back online when he closed the door with a soft snick. He wrapped my hand around his arm as we walked downstairs. I could feel his eyes returning to me but didn't look his way. Navigating stairs with heels required my full attention.

When we reached the bottom, I gave in and met his gaze. His intense regard sent shivers through me. He leaned in once again, his breath tickling my neck near my ear. I focused on the sensation of his lips brushing my skin. Please just kiss me already, I thought. The anticipation of it was driving me crazy.

"You smell wonderful."

I turned my head slightly and pressed my cheek against his. He groaned.

When he finally straightened and motioned me through Nana's open door, I walked in on autopilot, my neck still tingling from overexposure to Emmitt.

The boys already played a board game at the table with Jim and Nana. I could see Aden was in hero-worship mode when it came to Jim. Neither boy seemed to care too much that we were leaving for the night.

As I stood there saying goodbye, my head cleared enough that I started doubting the dress, again. I tried to think of an excuse to go back upstairs and change, but couldn't. At least, not a diplomatic one. So, I allowed Emmitt to escort me out the door. The rain had stopped, but the ground still glistened with water. My heels sank a little when I stepped off the porch.

"Where are we going?" I asked while he held the door open for me.

"A steak and seafood place just outside of town," he said as I carefully got in.

He hesitated then closed my door and walked around the front of the truck. The moment reminded me of the day I'd bought the truck, and my heart fluttered as he slid in behind the wheel. I wouldn't have guessed then that the attraction I'd felt would have led to the revelation it had.

Emmitt was a werewolf, and he was mine.

He reached over and brushed back a strand of my hair. I took a calming breath and hoped he thought my racing heart was due to leaving my brothers and not him. He started the truck and pulled out of the driveway.

I settled in and watched the scenery. After a few moments of silence, I glanced over at Emmitt and caught his gaze.

"You've never mentioned any family other than your mom and Richard."

I sighed and turned to glance out the window. "No family as far as I know on either side. It's just us, now."

He was quiet the last few miles to the restaurant. When he turned into a wide, paved drive, I saw the restaurant and was surprised. White Christmas lights wound along the fence and cast a soft glow over the parking lot. The place definitely looked more high-end than I would have expected being out in the middle of nowhere, though I could see the glow of city lights on the horizon.

Emmitt got out and opened the door for me. I watched his gaze stray from my eyes as he helped me down. A blush heated my face, and he gave me a small smile as he held my hand and led me inside. I couldn't decide if I wanted to cover up or bask in his attention. So, I focused on walking.

A maître d' stood at a podium, ready to greet us. Behind him, the polished wood floors of the bar area glowed in the soft light.

Emmitt gave his name and led me to an open place at the bar. He held out a barstool for me. I didn't miss the brush of his fingers on my exposed back as I sat. He settled beside me and ordered us each a glass of red wine.

I didn't say anything about the alcohol though I knew Nana would smell it on me. I wondered if I'd get another scolding. The bartender smiled a bit too warmly at me as he set my glass down, and Emmitt scowled in response. I took a sip. Nana would certainly understand.

I'd finished half a glass by the time the maître d' came to seat us at our table. I studied the menu and immediately spotted what I wanted. The last time I had chicken parmesan, my mom had been alive.

Glancing up to ask Emmitt what he planned to order, I found him studying me instead of the menu. I rolled my eyes and reached across the table to pick up his menu and wave it in his face. He laughed, took it, and finally opened it.

Our server wore a crisp, white shirt under a black vest and matching black tie. He was politely formal when he came to ask if we wanted a fresh drink before ordering. Emmitt ordered another one, but I asked for water, instead.

It was no surprise when Emmitt picked the biggest steak on the menu...and appetizers.

RELAXED BY THE glass of wine, dinner had progressed pleasantly, but nervousness had crept back in toward the end. Our ride home remained quiet, and I didn't mind. I doubted I could maintain any form of intelligent conversation. My focus was on what would happen at the end of our date. Would he finally kiss me?

The crunch of gravel under the tires announced our return. He parked the truck near the porch and got out to open my door. Although it wasn't far to the ground, he offered his hand to help me down.

"Did you enjoy yourself?" he asked as he closed the door behind me.

Had it not been for the very exposed feeling I'd had throughout dinner, I would have been able to answer with an honest yes. Instead, I tried for vague.

"I think it will take a while before I'm comfortable leaving my brothers."

We walked inside the quiet house. It wasn't yet past nine, and I thought the quiet odd, but Emmitt didn't appear concerned.

Nervous anticipation filled me as we walked upstairs. He opened my door for me, and I didn't know what to expect next. Would he come in with me? Would he try kissing me? My heart did a crazy stuttering beat at the thought. I wasn't sure what I wanted. I turned to face him.

"Thank you for tonight. Let me know if you want to go shopping with Nana again. You have amazing taste." His gaze slid my length again, but he remained in the hallway.

"I think I'll be fine for a while. Besides, I prefer shorts and t-shirts. Your t-shirts are the best." Usually, because they hung to mid-thigh and covered me well. It didn't hurt that they smelled like him too.

He handed me his jacket, and I watched as he pulled his sweater and t-shirt off over his head. The jacket almost fell from my hand. Emmitt, shirtless in the sun, was breathtaking. But this...I swallowed hard. If I appealed to him half as much as he did to me, I understood why he'd kept looking at me all night.

Seeing him in just dress pants made my knees melt. He handed me the white cotton shirt still warm from his body and reclaimed his suit jacket.

He stepped close. "I'll give you my shirt whenever you ask."

Clutching the shirt to my chest, I stopped breathing for a moment.

He grinned slightly. "So there's no misunderstanding, we're officially in the dating phase of our relationship."

I nodded dumbly, glad we were officially ignoring my friendship talk now.

He hesitated there, standing toe to toe with me, consuming my space and air as I gazed up at him, held in his spell. Then he shook his head, leaned in to brush his lips against the side of my neck, and left me with a racing heart.

His clarification of our relationship hadn't helped. When he announced we were dating, I'd expected—assumed—a kiss would follow. On the mouth. Instead, I stood staring at his closed apartment door in confusion and more than a little disappointment.

I spent the remainder of the evening dressed in his shirt and sitting in the kitchen as I researched for the next day's premonition. I wasn't sure if Emmitt had told Nana my secret or not.

CHAPTER FOURTEEN

An overcast, but dry, Sunday marked the end of our fifth week of freedom. My energetic brothers raced outside just after breakfast. As usual, they left the door open behind them. I didn't follow this time. Instead, I finished some last minute research while waiting for the actual premonition.

When I heard Emmitt's door open across the hall, I perked up but didn't look away from the tablet. So I wasn't surprised when he spoke from my doorway.

"Good morning."

I swiveled on the stool and smiled at him. "Morning."

He leaned against the doorframe. His wet hair lay in disarray as he slowly blinked at me.

"Didn't you sleep well?"

He shrugged. "Coming down for breakfast?"

I looked at him in surprise. Usually he already knew if we'd eaten. I figured his sense of smell helped with that. Granted, we'd eaten cereal this morning, which I didn't consider very aromatic, but the bowls still sat next to the sink.

He caught my glance at the dishes and smiled self-depreciatively. "Sorry. I'll see you downstairs."

Watching the empty doorway an extra moment after he left, I wondered if he wasn't feeling well. I glanced at the clock. Twenty more minutes to kill.

While surfing the web to fill the time, I came across the video of Richard's death and more speculation regarding the dog. I avoided the video but read the articles. In one, the author noted the disappearance of Richard's beneficiary. It gave me pause. Was that the point of the lawyer?

I checked my email and saw a reply not nearly as brief as my query. Sawyer Nolan introduced himself as Richard's attorney and, after offering his condolences, asked me to come to his office to discuss the will. He mentioned needing to coordinate with Mr. Blake Torrin regarding the date and time. That meeting was *not* going to happen.

I closed the email and worried at my thumbnail with my teeth. The latest stock tip popped into my head before I decided what to do about the email.

Notes in hand, I ambled downstairs and peeked out at the boys and Jim who played in the backyard. Barefoot, they splashed in the puddles from the day before. All three waved at me. Tonight my brothers would need baths. I waved back then went to find Nana Wini in her kitchen. She was making Emmitt breakfast.

"Did your friend, Sam, call already?" I asked, putting the papers on the table and sitting next to Emmitt. His eyes followed my moves. I couldn't put my finger on what felt different about his gaze, but it made me edgy.

Nana turned away from the pan and gave me a kind look. "Yes, we discussed your gift, though, and feel that it shouldn't be used. He thanked you for your help so far but will research on his own from now on."

With the ticker still stuck on repeat in my head, panic surged. "But, you can't—"

She shook her head. "We can. We won't use you. But, I did hear what you said about the pain. You can still give the information to me," she said indicating the papers on the table with the spatula in her hand. "I will read it so you won't suffer, then I'll destroy it."

I couldn't believe they would do that. Give up the information and power. I felt lighter, freer, and relieved.

"By the way, there are a few people coming today who'd like to meet you," Nana said turning back to the stove, missing my shattered expression at her words. "They should be here in about an hour."

She plated a heap of food and passed it to Emmitt. Though Nana didn't catch my initial expression, Emmitt had. He watched me closely.

"What people?" Please don't let it be men.

"They are from the Compound in Canada. Friends of Jim and Emmitt's parents. They are coming down with their sons to meet you and your brothers," she said.

Sons.

"Why are they coming?"

Nana shared a look with Emmitt. I caught the barest shake of his head before he focused on his plate and started to eat. Nana sighed at him.

"We thought it would be good to start exposing you to more of our kind whom you can trust."

"And who decides who's trustworthy?" I could feel my temper starting to simmer.

Nana tilted her head, studying me. Her nostrils flared slightly. Wisely, she remained quiet.

Was I overreacting? I just didn't know. I revealed everything to them, and suddenly friends of Emmitt's parents were bringing their sons to meet us.

"I'm sorry, Nana, but I don't feel like good company today."

Leaving them at the table, I went outside to the boys.

"Jim, may I have the truck keys?" I didn't wait for his answer but looked at the boys. "Want to go into town and see a movie in a movie theater?"

Their eyes lit at the prospect of it.

USING THE TABLET, I memorized the directions to the theater while the boys washed up. No one tried to stop us from leaving, but all three stood on the porch, watching me back out.

Not having driven since Jim's lesson, I didn't execute the Y turn to back away from the porch as smoothly as I would have liked. Almost quitting then, I scolded myself for being a stubborn control freak and inched my way down the driveway.

Aden and Liam talked excitedly as they sat buckled into their booster seats. What was I thinking? This wasn't safe. I drove like crap, hated big crowds, and had very little money left to live off. Would it kill me to stay and say hi to whoever Nana had coming over? No, but if I didn't put my foot down and keep it down, I feared becoming a pawn again.

The drive took longer than I expected. Liam and Aden were antsy to leave the truck and see the theater by the time I parked.

They stood beside me, holding my hands, while I studied the movies listed. The first movie didn't start for over forty minutes. I wished I'd been smart enough to check the show times online before we'd left.

I looked around, wondering what to do. The crowd shuffling by us on the sidewalk made me twitchy. I didn't want to spend forty minutes just standing in the open.

Across the street, I spotted an ice cream shop just opening.

FOUR SCOOPS and three cones later, we happily stood in line for the movie. Despite the ice cream we'd consumed at the shop, we were laden with the prerequisite popcorn and slushies. Aden bounced on the tips of his toes in anticipation.

When I glanced down to smile at him, a reflection in the glass panel of the ticketing booth caught my attention. A man stood outlined in the door behind us, the pane of glass separating us. His complete motionless in the shifting foot traffic stood out. I turned fully to see him, not just his reflection. When I did, he looked up at the marquee above his head for a moment then moved on. Perhaps he'd just been looking at the movie listings.

Aden tugged me forward as our theater's doors opened.

The laughter in a theater full of children melted some of my worry. It wasn't until I was struggling with Aden's buckle in the truck almost two hours later that I noticed the man, again. He leaned against the side of a beat up old car and had an elbow casually resting on the roof as he watched me.

When I looked directly at him, he winked at me. Something about him just hit me as off. Giving up on the buckle, I started the truck and pulled out, hands shaking. It didn't help my driving.

He stayed leaning against the car, watching. I watched his shrinking form in the mirrors. He never moved.

I kept an eye on the mirrors as I drove. The man had intentionally brought himself to my notice. Why? I hadn't recognized him and nothing about him said werewolf. So, I didn't think I needed to worry about that possibility. He'd just been creepy. Still, I looked back every few minutes.

The mirror stayed clear all the way home. I was relieved to pull into the driveway and find Emmitt waiting for us on the porch steps.

However, with my concern over the movie man, I'd forgotten about the company that had sent me running in the first place. An extra vehicle was in the truck's usual spot. I parked next to the garage and helped the boys out. They immediately ran for the house, saying they wanted to tell Jim about the huge

TV, not understanding the difference between a television and the movie theater.

When I closed the passenger door and turned, Emmitt stood behind me, waiting. His eyes studied every inch of my face.

"What's wrong?" I asked, worried.

Behind him, Nana and two adults stepped onto the porch. I tried to keep the distain from my face when I glanced at them. I wasn't ready to play nice, yet.

"Mary and Gregory were planning on staying the night," he said with little emotion. "Can I sleep on your couch?"

If I said no, would they go back to Canada? Maybe. But Emmitt on the couch didn't sound like such a bad idea after some creepy guy had winked at me. I nodded.

He held out his hand. I clasped it loosely, and he led me to the group on the porch.

The woman had neat brown hair a shade lighter than my own. She watched our progress with expressive brown eyes. The man, who stood beside her, towered over her diminutive frame. I couldn't decide if the woman was unusually short or if werewolves' heights were as diverse as humans. So far, they'd all been tall, but other than Nana, they'd all been men. The man's hazel eyes flicked to Emmitt's hand holding mine and then up to my face. I felt judged with that glance.

As we walked up the steps, Emmitt introduced them. "Michelle, this is Mary and her husband Gregory."

Husband, not Mate? Were they human?

"Nice to meet you," I said flatly, using the same tone I had hundreds of times before for the standard greeting at Blake's dinners.

"I doubt it," Mary said with a grin, "but I don't blame you. We're the long distance version of nosy neighbors. Our sons, Paul and Henry, are inside with Jim. Your brothers are adorable."

The adorable duo ran out the door just then, making a beeline for the swing set and calling for Jim as they went.

"Energetic," she added with a laugh.

With ice cream, slushies, and popcorn in their systems, they probably needed real food to counteract their obvious sugar jag.

"I better go and make them some lunch," I said to excuse myself.

Emmitt didn't relinquish my hand.

"I'll come with," he said.

Jim walked out the door. Two boys close to my age trailed behind him. They grinned at me, said hi, and followed Jim to the swing set, standing back to watch him interact with my brothers. I hadn't expected the sons to be so young. None of Blake's associates had been my age. Still not sure what I dealt with, human vs. werewolf, I hesitated to leave my brothers outside.

Emmitt seemed to read my concern.

"Jim, can you send them up in a few minutes to eat?"

Jim waved acknowledgement, and I let Emmitt lead me inside.

Our company stayed downstairs when Jim came up several minutes later. He took a huge bite from Aden's proffered sandwich, and I shook my head, guessing at the reason for his personal escort.

I tried to talk the boys into games upstairs, but they wouldn't hear of it and tore back downstairs as soon as they finished. Food gone, Jim followed them. Emmitt helped with the cleanup.

"My parents sent Gregory and Mary down," he said as he wiped down the counter.

I paused putting away the lunchmeat, giving him my full attention.

"They can't leave the Compound themselves and were curious about the girl who has captured their son's attention."

"Why couldn't you tell me that before?" I asked in mild exasperation.

He didn't answer right away, so I tossed the jar in the fridge and turned to him with my arms crossed.

"I didn't want you to worry about meeting them."

"When Nana said people were coming, bringing their sons, I thought it was going to be like Blake's all over again." I swallowed hard and looked away from him.

"No," he growled. "How many times do I have to tell you?" He backed me against the counter.

"You. Are. Mine."

His knuckles brushed my neck as he moved my hair aside, and he leaned forward, lips running along my jaw.

At first contact, my heart thundered painfully and heat burst in my chest, radiating outward. I reached up, fisting my hands in his short hair. It was just long enough to grip.

I wanted to pull him closer, to move beyond this limbo stage. Instead, I tugged him back by his hair. He didn't move at first.

"Emmitt, stop. I can't think like this."

He pulled back. The pupils of his eyes swallowed the midnight blue of his irises. The tips of two sharp teeth poked out from under his upper lip, drawing my attention to his mouth. I'd stared at his chest plenty, but never really his lips. I blinked slowly. What would it feel like to have them pressed against mine? I wanted...

"Do it," he whispered.

"What?" I breathed out the word, my gaze flying to his. Blood rushed to my face, and I nudged him back. He sighed and gave me room. Not much, but I could think again.

"Nothing." He gently brushed his fingertips along my collarbone. "I'm going to check on the boys."

I nodded and watched him leave, wondering how long Gregory and Mary would be staying and what kind of report they would take back to Emmitt's parents.

I spent the rest of the afternoon hiding in my apartment, too chicken to find out the answer to either of those questions.

Emmitt came back hours later and convinced me to join everyone for a picnic dinner. Liam and Aden sat near Paul and Henry, a new sheen of hero worship in their eyes. We lingered at the table after they ran off to play.

Mary asked me how I liked living at the house. The innocent enough question felt like a graded essay. Did his parents disapprove of me living in the same house? Should I say it made me uncomfortable? No. They would sense the lie. I weighed my choices and finally settled on admitting the truth; I felt safe there. She smiled kindly and asked if I'd given any thought to the future. I looked at Emmitt helplessly.

"We should probably go up and get everything ready for tonight," he said, standing and rescuing me. I followed his lead and started gathering plates to help clean up. "Paul and Henry can crash at Jim's," he continued. "You're welcome to use my place."

Mary nodded her thanks as I made my escape inside.

Emmitt and I worked together, quietly putting condiments away in Jim's fridge, then headed upstairs.

Sensing my mood, Emmitt put in a movie and steered me to the couch with a stern order to relax. He came in once during the middle of the movie with a pillow and a light blanket, which he set on the couch in anticipation of his overnight stay.

I WOKE in the middle of the night, heart hammering from my vivid dream. The man from town had tracked us, and I'd watched as he had scaled the outside of the house to reach the third floor. He'd had vicious, sharp teeth. Not just his canines, but all of them. As he'd walked around the porch, he had dragged his nails along the siding, making a terrible screeching noise.

Throwing off the covers, I got up to close the window. The cool night air felt nice, but a mere screen separating me from the outside world didn't feel very safe. I tiptoed to the boys' room and closed their windows, too. It was cool enough in the house, anyway, because of the recent rain.

When I reached the living room, I paused. I'd forgotten about Emmitt. His dark form sprawled on the couch. In the dim light, I caught the glint of his eyes and knew he was awake and watching me.

"Bad dream," I said quietly.

He sat up and opened his arms in invitation.

Still shivering from the image of the man scaling the porches, I quickly went to him. I sat on the couch and leaned into his side, resting my head on his shoulder as he wrapped his arms around me.

"Go to sleep."

I liked that he didn't ask me to share the dream. Talking about it would make it too real and harder to sleep again. His warmth eventually relaxed me, and I curled into him, getting more comfortable.

Werewolves made comfy beds, I thought sleepily. He kissed the top of my head, and I slept.

CHAPTER FIFTEEN

THE BOYS STOOD ON THE PORCH, SADLY WAVING GOODBYE TO THEIR new friends. Since Jim had already left for work, they were stuck with just Emmitt, Nana, and me. We were obviously nowhere near as exciting as Paul and Henry. Mary gave me a final wave as they pulled away from the house.

Emmitt stood beside me. I was relieved he hadn't said anything about my dream the night before or the way we'd woken up. A blush rose at the memory of waking practically on top of him. When I'd lifted my head to see if he still slept, I had found him studying me. My mad scramble to get off of him had seemed to cause a moment of pain, but I hadn't stopped to apologize. I'd flown to my bedroom and closed myself in until he'd left.

"Now what are we going to do?" Aden said softly to Liam.

Emmitt laughed. "How about a baseball game?"

The boys perked up and started planning teams. They called Nana out to join in. Since I didn't run as fast as the other two adults, the boys decided I should pitch. Liam wisely chose Nana for his partner.

When Jim got home from work, he found us still playing outside. Everyone agreed it was time to eat, and we had another picnic dinner on the porch.

Afterwards, the boys talked Jim into a movie at Nana's place and raced off to pick what they would watch and get ready for bed. Nana followed, leaving me alone with Emmitt for the first time since that morning.

Emmitt didn't give my nerves a chance to build. Instead, he took me by the hand and led me to the truck. He wrapped his hands around my waist and, with little effort, sat me on the open tailgate. He hopped up next to me. Shoulder to shoulder, we watched the sun set.

"I'm sorry about last night," I said, finally working up the courage.

"Why? It's the best night sleep I had in a while."

I rolled my eyes at him, doubting the truth of his statement.

His lips twitched at my expression. "The longer I'm with you, the more I want to be near you. When you first came here, being apart at night didn't bother me. You were only two floors away, and I'd started working on the apartment so I knew we would be closer soon. Then, sleeping in a bed that smelled like you helped, but it's been getting difficult again." He smiled ruefully. "If you asked, I'd sleep on your couch every night."

After the dream I had the night before, the offer tempted me; but I had to think of Liam and Aden, too.

"I'm not sure how Liam and Aden would take that. They'd probably worry that we aren't safe again, no matter what explanation we gave them for your overnight stays. I don't want to scare them."

"We could always share your bed?" he half-asked, half-stated in a serious tone.

I floundered for something to say. Share a bed? Were we that far?

"No hidden agenda. Just sleeping," he said, amused.

I opened my mouth to thank him for the offer and to decline but never got the words out.

Emmitt's head whipped up. His gaze locked on the woods at the back of the yard. Without looking away, he leapt off the tailgate, lifted me, and set me on the ground toward the house.

"Get onto the porch."

His low voice worried me. He took a step backward, trying to herd me in the direction he wanted while positioning himself to shield me. What was out there? Peeking over Emmitt's shoulder was no easy feat, but I managed.

At first, the yard appeared empty. Then, the deep shadows near the trees at the back of the yard moved. I frowned, trying to focus on the area.

Two men emerged, but I couldn't see them clearly. I wanted to ask Emmitt who they were, but he reached for my arm and nudged me toward the porch as he'd ordered.

I took a step back, hoping to see more, however, he shadowed my move. His skin rippled and started to sprout fur. The first thread of fear started to creep in.

I glanced over my shoulder and backed up onto the porch steps. With the additional height, I could see past Emmitt.

The two men continued to advance. Their bent, partially transformed bodies moved with a slinking stealth I found disquieting.

A cloud drifted away from the moon, briefly lighting the yard. Moonlight caught pale skin, highlighting the odd elongated arch of a thigh before another cloud snuffed it out. It'd been enough to recognize one of them. Frank. Fear bloomed.

Another cloud shifted. Frank smiled at me before shadows obscured him again.

Emmitt growled low in warning. Dread filled me. We'd managed to stay hidden for a little over a month. Why had they found us now? Thinking of my brothers sent another wave of fear crashing through me. We couldn't go back to the life we'd had.

The thought gave me courage to speak up.

"Where's Blake?" I said in a voice that definitely didn't sound fearless.

Both of the werewolves stopped their approach.

I took a breath and tried to sound more confident.

"Give him a message for me. He won't get what he wants. I've seen it."

I really didn't know what I had seen but hoped it would give Blake a reason to doubt his plan. Maybe even a reason to abandon it.

"You know nothing, little girl," Frank said from the darkness. "You just played dress up and sat at Blake's dinners like the puppet you are. If not for the curse that causes you to be born to humans, we would have wiped out humanity long ago." As he spoke, he began to shift further. "You are nothing more than a tool."

I wished I knew what he meant.

Behind me, the door creaked open. A light footfall gave away Nana Wini's presence, saving me from having to respond. She moved just behind me, and I fought the urge to turn around and look for the boys.

The men in the dark shadows didn't react well to her appearance. Their faces extended forward, canine muzzles just starting to form. Fingers contracted and nails grew longer, glistening ebony in the yard light. The men remained on two legs, but those legs shrank as their torsos stretched.

"Leave now," Nana said in a low and commanding voice.

Had she not been behind me, blocking my way, I would have been tempted to go inside. It wasn't a voice easily ignored.

"Quiet old woman," the other werewolf growled. The moonlight shifted enough that I recognized him, too. The man from the movie theater. I cringed. I'd jeopardized us all.

Nana's furious snarl startled me. I whipped my head around to look at her. Bits of fabric flew at me as she burst from her lacy cardigan and tweed pants. An enormous, snowy white wolf stood where she'd been.

She gathered herself and leaped over Emmitt and me, clearing the space between the porch roof and our heads with precision. She landed lightly on her paws several yards in front of Emmitt. Crouched and ready to spring, she gave a low warning growl that sent chills down my spine. Neither werewolf budged.

Nana and Frank stared at each other. For several minutes, they remained locked in a silent standoff. Though she continued to growl occasionally, Frank did nothing.

"What's going on?" I whispered to Emmitt, who still stood in front of me as a shield.

"She's trying to talk to them through her link," he said calmly. His skin had stopped rippling once Nana had arrived.

Nana let out another furious snarl, and Frank laughed in response, a guttural taunting sound. Her muscles bunched a second before she launched herself at them. The half-changed werewolves burst into their own fur, meeting her onslaught.

The three collided with an audible thud. I flinched and gripped Emmitt's shoulder.

"Help her, Emmitt," I said.

"Michelle, she's an Elder. She has more strength than Jim and I do combined, more than enough to take care of those two and several more. You need me more than she does."

My gaze never wavered from the swirling mass of fur and legs. Frank and his friend, similarly colored, made it hard to distinguish who was who. Thankfully, Wini stood out with her white.

I leaned into Emmitt. My limbs trembled as I watched her evade bite after bite. The two wolves were cunning and fought as a team. Her speed and skill kept her just out of reach. Then one of the wolves made a mistake and exposed his neck. She almost had him by the throat when the other lunged forward and tried to take a bite out of her back leg.

Nana spun and tore into the one trying to sneak a bite. He emitted a high-pitched continuous yelp of pain. I hoped it was Frank.

The unharmed wolf used that distraction to go for Nana's throat. I made a small sound of denial and clutched Emmitt. Nana coiled, and I knew she saw.

Using her hold on the yowling one, she tossed her head back, swinging the captured wolf into the other, effectively blocking the attack. My jaw dropped at the show of strength. Those wolves were as big as she was. The hit wolf grunted at impact and flew back a few feet. The wolf in her maw fell silent and looked a bit dazed.

She loosened her bloody hold, and he fell to the ground. She backed up a step, crouched, and waited.

The bloody one scrambled to his feet and joined his friend, who was up and ready. However, they didn't make another attempt at her. They turned and ran.

Nana Wini took off after them, almost catching them at the edge of the yard. There she stopped and paced.

Emmitt turned toward me.

"Let's go inside. The kids heard some of the noise and are scared."

I whirled and ran to my brothers. Already dressed in their pajamas, they both huddled on Jim's lap. He continued softly speaking to them when I entered.

"Sometimes wild dogs come into the yard and fight over a bone. It doesn't mean they are bad, just that they are misbehaving. Nana will set them straight. You'll see." He looked up and met my eyes with relief.

The boys got up and ran to me.

"I'm here," I said dropping to my knees to hug them. My shaking remained. Emmitt stayed by the door.

Jim stood and picked something out of my hair. When I looked at him questioningly over the boys' heads, he showed me a piece of cardigan. My mouth popped open in a quiet "oh" as he strode to Nana's bathroom. He came out carrying a robe and went to the hallway.

I hadn't thought about Nana Wini's clothes. It was a good thing he had.

"Are they gone?" Liam asked, his face still buried in my hair.

"Yeah, buddy. Nana chased them away."

A few moments later, Nana strode in, unharmed. I assumed she'd chased them off, but her next words worried me.

"Chasing away those dogs gave me an idea," she said looking at the boys with a calm smile. "You haven't yet met Jim and Emmitt's parents. They live with several other families in a house bigger than this one. Paul and Henry live there, as do some much nicer dogs. So, I think we should take a vacation and visit them. In fact, we should make it an adventure and go tonight. Should we let Jim come with us?"

They both nodded, but didn't let go of me.

"Should we have Jim and Emmitt race to see who can pack first?"

This time Aden pulled away a little, slightly interested. I wondered what he thought of Nana's sudden appearance in a robe.

"To make this fair, we'll have Emmitt pack for your sister and Liam. Jim, you go pack for Aden and grab all personal affects."

Aden cheered in approval and began telling Jim where his things were so he could win.

Nana met Jim and Emmitt's gaze for a moment then they both walked out of the apartment, leaving the door open. Silent communication. My anxiety grew. We were running. Again. A wave of panic almost pulled me down.

"Michelle, let's take the boys into the bathroom and wash them up before we leave. It's a long trip."

She closed the three of us in the bathroom, saying she'd pack for herself while we waited.

I went through the normal motions but didn't open the door when we finished. Instead, I sat on the toilet lid and asked Aden and Liam about their time with Paul and Henry. Liam, for a change, didn't say much and let Aden do most of the talking.

Emmitt opened the door a few minutes later.

"It was a tie," he said to the boys. "Ready to go?"

We all nodded. Emmitt met my gaze over the boys' heads and sent them out to Jim and Nana.

He held out a hand. "You're not alone this time," he said.

A bit of the tension eased. He understood. I wrapped my fingers around his, and he pulled me into a quick tight hug before we joined the others.

In the living room, Jim already had Aden up in his arms. Emmitt scooped Liam up in a way that flipped him in the air, eliciting a shocked squeal and bringing a smile to his small, and otherwise serious, face.

Jim and Emmitt carried my brothers out on the pretense that they didn't have shoes on. They buckled the boys into the back seat of Nana's car while Nana stood near me.

After closing the back doors, Emmitt took my hand and led me to the truck. He held the door for me, waiting until I buckled. I heard Liam quietly tell Nana

Wini she had something in her hair. I didn't look up to see what it was, but I hoped it wasn't blood. Emmitt closed the door on her response.

I kept my eyes on the trees lining the driveway while Emmitt drove out. What once seemed so quiet and peaceful now menaced. I imagined Frank and his friend watching us from the shadows. How long before Blake joined them?

Leaving the driveway, Emmitt turned north. Jim, driving Nana's car, followed. I knew we were heading to Canada and the mysterious Compound of Emmitt's childhood. The thought of going to a place with even more werewolves churned my stomach. What would we find there?

"You're killing me," Emmitt said, pulling my attention from the trees.

"Excuse me?"

"Your fear. I can smell it. Even when you were facing down David in the parking lot of that diner, it wasn't this bad." He reached across the seat and wrapped his hand around mine. "It will be okay. I promise. There is no need for this fear."

"No need?" I said in soft disbelief. "Werewolves are real. One of them kept me locked away for four years and wants me back. The infallible laws, which your people *can't* ignore, no longer seem to work. After all, Richard's murderer hasn't stepped forward.

"I'm heading to an unknown place filled with an unknown number of werewolves who will think I smell delicious and may or may not treat me like Blake has. If I don't want to go, my only other option is to run again, zigzagging scent trails across the North American Continent, waiting to be stumbled upon. How exactly am I supposed to get rid of my fear?"

Emmitt lifted the hand he held and brought it to his mouth, tenderly kissing the knuckles. My heart flipped. I wasn't upset with him. I was angry with myself for believing there could be an easy answer. Emmitt kept my hand in his and remained quiet.

Nothing had been easy since Blake had entered my life. I needed him out of the picture for good. The premonition of me biting Emmitt should have assured me everything would turn out all right, but Frank's reaction worried me. Why had he laughed when I'd told him?

And how was I a tool for Blake? The way Frank spoke, it had to be more than just stock market information. Frank's comment about wiping out humanity scared me. How many werewolves looked at humans like that? It had to be a select group because I didn't get that vibe from the three werewolves I lived with.

I stilled, recalling his exact words.

"If not for the curse that causes you to be born to humans," I whispered.

I looked at Emmitt with chills skating over my skin.

"They knew I would be born? How had Blake known I'd be born?"

He squeezed my hand reassuringly, but I caught his quick frown.

"Nana's hoping to find answers at the Compound," he said. "Another Elder is there waiting for us."

I had serious doubts she would find anything useful. Blake held the answers I—we—needed. How could I get them, though, without going back? If not for Nana, Jim, and Emmitt, Blake's men would have me, and I might know the answers. But I didn't want to go back like that. And, now that Blake knew who I had protecting me, I doubted he would risk exposing himself again.

We lapsed into silence for so long I started to drift to sleep, still trying to think of a way to get answers. Next to me, I felt Emmitt move in his seat. A moment later, his jacket, which he'd brought with him, settled over the front of me. I curled my legs under me, snuggling under the jacket. It smelled like him, and it was all I needed to drift off to sleep.

I VAGUELY REGISTERED the sound of a car door opening. Even the sudden chill as the jacket left me couldn't completely wake me. I turned toward the seat's warmth, trying to get comfortable, already sinking back into sleep.

The feel of a thick arm sliding behind my back and another under my knees tickled my awareness. Emmitt's smell surrounded me, and I shifted to snuggle against him. Then, he lifted me. The air born, weightless feeling yanked me from my sleep. I let out a yelp and wrapped my arms around him, prying open my unwilling eyes.

He smiled down at me while turning so he could nudge the door closed behind us. The sound echoed in the surrounding silence.

I looked around for the boys, noting the sky had started to lighten. Jim carried Aden, and Nana Wini held Liam. Both the boys slept soundly. The adults were already making their way toward the vague outline of a building.

"Emmitt, put me down." I didn't want anyone's first impression of me to be that of a helpless girl.

He set me on my feet. "I was trying to let you sleep."

"I know. Thank you." I clasped his warm hand.

The rest had helped relieve some of my anger and frustration. I felt bad about venting at him but didn't want to say anything out in the open. The ears here would hear far too much.

I turned to look back at the road we'd come from but saw only a rutted trail leading into more trees. The surrounding woods reminded me of our home in Montana. I could see why Emmitt and Jim had settled there. It must have reminded them of this place.

Hearing a door close, I turned to see the boys gone.

"Is this where you grew up?" I asked Emmitt quietly.

"Yeah." He gently tugged my hand, encouraging me to start walking.

A long, two-story log cabin, winged by several outbuildings, encompassed the area we'd parked in, which was more dirt than gravel. Constructed before the 19th century, the buildings had seen better days. Pieces of chinking were missing here and there from between the grey, aged roughhewn logs. Near the ground of the first story, most of the chinking was new, showing that repairs were in progress. A few of the old, single-paned windows rattled slightly in the breeze. I wondered how they could possibly stay warm in winter. The outbuildings were all in equally poor repair. Emmitt hadn't been exaggerating about their need for money.

Despite the building's run down appearance, the area around the buildings showed signs of upkeep. Flowers bloomed in pots near the main door and in the window boxes under a few of the first floor windows, improving an otherwise unfriendly exterior. Branches from surrounding trees showed signs of recent pruning, and the weeds near their bases, trimmed back.

The oversized front door was one of the few things that looked new. I eyed the unevenly spaced deck boards that raised a step above the ground. In a few places, the wood looked newer. Even with the replacements, it still looked questionable. At least, I didn't have far to fall if one of the boards snapped under me. I stepped up on the planks and was surprised they felt sturdy.

Emmitt reached around me to open the door. I walked into a huge entry and paused, relieved to see the inside in much better repair. Rugs stacked with shoes lay around the outskirts of the room while a variety of outerwear hung on the hooks screwed into the walls. I felt like I had just walked into a huge coat closet. Emmitt's hand on my lower back prompted me to step further into the room.

"Nana Wini sent a call out for a pack meeting in a few hours."

That sounded intimidating.

"Pack meeting? Why?"

"It's time you are introduced to the pack. It lets everyone know you are under the protection of the Elders."

What protection? Their laws didn't work. Physically, Nana fought off two rebel werewolves, but I knew there were so many more out there. I didn't voice my doubts.

"What about the boys?" I was less afraid for myself than I was for them.

"They've already been put to bed."

He led me down a long hallway.

"I mean their safety."

His expression filled with soft understanding. "It will be discussed in the meeting as well. We will keep them safe." He walked beside me in silence for a moment.

I could tell he was struggling with something. He didn't leave me guessing for long.

"I know you're probably tired, but my parents would like to meet you." He glanced at me. "If you're up for it."

My stomach did a tiny flip, and not in a good way. The leaders of the pack and parents to the man I now dated wanted to meet me. I'd just dozed in a truck for several hours and probably had crazy hair and looked rumpled. Great first impression. No, I really didn't want to meet them, but I nodded anyway.

Emmitt's face lit with a relieved smile. "They're waiting for us in the apartment we'll be using."

Emmitt and I followed several hallways before finally climbing a set of stairs. He led me to a door that opened to a newly remodeled, modest apartment.

A small area in the back left corner of the main room was set aside as a kitchenette, complete with a mini fridge, coffee pot, and small breakfast bar. There was no kitchen sink. Getting water from the bathroom had to be more cost efficient, especially if the apartment was only used occasionally. I could see where this kind of updating moved slowly. It had to cost a fortune.

The rest of the room was setup as a living room, complete with occupied sofa and chairs.

Six sets of eyes turned toward us as we walked in, interrupting a quiet conversation. I recognized Mary and Gregory, and of course Jim and Nana.

Everyone stood, and Emmitt led me toward the two I didn't know.

"Mother, Father, this is Michelle."

Emmitt's father, a tall formidable man with a bulk of bulging muscles and a serious expression, stood beside Emmitt's mother. I'd caught how he watched her intently while she'd spoken with Mary. The slight softening of his expression when his gaze settled on her assured me he had a soft spot.

His mother was tall and lean but not thin. She wore her hair pulled back into a ponytail. Dressed in worn jeans and a t-shirt that sported a rock band from the seventies, she fit into her surroundings. She looked beautiful and much younger than in her forties. Apparently, women aged well, here. In fact, I hadn't noticed any old and wrinkly werewolves. Nana Wini's hair might be white, and she might be old in years, but she didn't have any other signs of aging.

"Call me Charlene," Emmitt's mother said. She gave me a warm smile that reached her dark blue eyes—Emmitt's eyes—and offered her hand.

I returned her smile and reached for her hand. When we touched, my world tilted precariously. I *really* didn't want to faint in front of Emmitt's parents.

The room and all the people faded from my sight. I stood in a black void and knew something wasn't right. Shouldn't I have fallen? I reached out a hand and slowly turned in a circle. I couldn't see, hear, or feel anything except myself. There was no floor beneath me. I appeared to be floating. I looked around, feeling panicked. Where was I?

I spotted a pinprick of brilliant, white light in the distance. It looked like a tiny star. Yet, even its brilliance didn't explain how I could see myself in the inky abyss surrounding me.

As I watched, the pinprick of light began to expand. It rapidly grew to the size of a baseball but didn't stop there. It bloated to the size of a volleyball within seconds. Its radiance hurt my eyes, but I didn't turn away. Instead, I squinted, trying to see it clearly.

The light wasn't growing but swiftly flying toward me—or me toward it. I tried to move. The result was a moment of helpless flailing since there was no floor to use to propel myself. My heart started to race painfully in my chest. Death couldn't come this way. I wanted to see my brothers. Emmitt.

I threw my arms in front of my face and braced myself. Light flashed brightly through my scrunched eyelids. I cringed, waiting for the impact of whatever it was. When nothing happened, I tentatively lifted my head and peeked through my arms.

Everything around me had changed although I still couldn't move, suspended in nothing. The area directly below my feet was a brightly lit white space. Around me, millions of images overlapped each other like frozen stills on a monitor. I wondered what waited behind them and blinked in shock when the one I'd been looking at jumped out of the way to expose another image behind it.

Turning my head, I focused on other images, willing them to move, and they did. They flew to the side to make room for the ones below. Most of the images were clear and crisp, but some were fuzzy or dark. All had people in them.

Before I had a chance to focus on any one image, I flew backward. The images behind me moved to create an opening in the weird, white emptiness. The whiteness clung to me, briefly stretching into the black void before letting me go, leaving me in darkness again. I watched the light shrink in size as I zoomed away from it, or maybe as it zoomed away from me. It was hard to tell.

Just as suddenly as I'd appeared in the void, I snapped back to the present. My hand stretched before me, holding empty air. Charlene had let go.

"You okay?" Emmitt asked.

I mentally shook myself and dropped my hand to my side. I wasn't sure what had just happened.

I'd thought I'd glanced images, some violent, containing several of the people in this room. At first, the images had appeared infinite. When they moved to allow me to leave, I'd seen they weren't. They had been stacked on top of one another, several layers deep.

Had I just seen the source of my new premonitions? Could that really be where they came from? I desperately wanted to go back and study them.

I looked at Charlene. She watched me with concern, but I noticed dark circles under her eyes that hadn't been there a moment ago. Perhaps now wasn't the best time to ask to shake her hand again. Whatever had happened to me, something must have happened to her, too.

All the werewolves around me were watching expectantly, waiting for me to offer an explanation for my weird behavior. If only I had one.

"Sorry, I'm a little tired." I gave Charlene a weak smile then glanced at Emmitt's father. He met my eyes directly and though I could see he didn't believe me, he didn't appear upset about it. Instead, he nodded in greeting. I could see where Emmitt got his height and coloring from.

"This is Thomas," Charlene said, continuing with the introductions. I was glad Emmitt's father didn't hold out his hand. "And you already met our friends, Mary and Gregory."

I smiled and said a quiet hello to the others.

"Nana told us some of what you've been through. I wanted to let you know that we will do everything we can to protect you and your brothers so you can feel safe here." Her earnest expression lent credence to her sincerity. "We'll let you get some sleep and see you at breakfast." She turned her warm gaze on Emmitt and gave him a quick hug before leaving. Mary and Gregory followed the pair out.

"I'll see you after breakfast," Nana said, leaving as well.

Jim remained with us, closing the door behind Nana. "If it's okay with you, I'll stay on the couch tonight."

He glanced at Emmitt when he said it, but I answered. "That's fine. The boys will probably wake you up in about two hours, though." I liked knowing he would be between us and the door while we slept.

"I can handle it." He stretched out on the couch and closed his eyes.

Emmitt said nothing. He pulled me toward the back of the apartment, down a short hallway, and nudged open the door on the right. I peeked in.

Dim, pre-dawn light illuminated two small bumps under the covers of the full-sized bed. I stepped forward and pulled back the light quilt so I could see them clearly. They both lay on their sides, facing each other.

I bent to give them kisses and gently touched their cheeks before covering them up again. The fear that sat heavily in my stomach since seeing Frank and his friend fight Nana Wini wasn't for me. It was for them. I hated feeling so helpless.

Crossing the room, I pulled the curtains on the window closed. It would give Jim a few more minutes of sleep.

Emmitt stepped into the room. I waited by the door while he smoothed back the hair from each boy's head. When he finished checking on them, he motioned me into the hallway and pulled the door partially closed behind him as he left. He had werewolf hearing, but I didn't and appreciated the consideration. With their door cracked open, I'd hear them when they woke.

We walked across the hall to another bedroom, which mirrored the boys' room. Emmitt flipped on the switch so I could see clearly. The full-sized bed and matching dark dresser complemented the forest green walls. Sheets and a light quilt covered the bed. An extra quilt lay folded on a trunk at the foot of the bed. Our bags rested on top of the spare quilt.

Staring at the bags, I felt a blush creep into my cheeks. Did he plan to sleep with me? When he'd suggested sharing a bed last night, I thought he'd been kidding.

I could feel him standing behind me, waiting for my reaction. Too much was coming at me too fast. Thinking of him...us...right now made my head hurt.

"I don't know what to say."

"How about don't hog the covers or I'll push your furry butt to the floor," Jim called from the living room.

Emmitt snorted behind me, and I turned to look at him.

"I just want sleep. I won't get it out there with Jim or if I'm further away from you than the next room."

I recalled what he'd said about having a hard time sleeping away from me and sighed as I nodded my acceptance of the situation.

Quirking a smile, I quoted Jim. "Hog the covers and I'll push your furry butt to the floor."

He grinned in return.

"Now, go away so I can change." He obliged, and I quickly changed into the pajamas he'd packed for me then slid under the covers. "Okay. I'm decent."

I rolled onto my side, facing away from the door so he could change if he wanted to. Listening, I heard him enter, the rasp of the zipper, and the rustle of clothes. I closed my eyes while wondering if he felt as self-conscious as I did.

He stepped to my side, surprising me enough that I opened my eyes. I saw his loose shorts as he reached up and closed the curtains, and I mentally breathed a sigh of relief. He moved to his side and slid into bed beside me but didn't reach for me.

We lay quietly, side-by-side, and I wondered if he could still smell my fear or if all my other emotions where flooding it out.

"I'm sorry about in the truck before. You're right. I don't need to be afraid right now. I need to be strong and face whatever happens. I just don't want to drag anyone else down into my problems. I wish there was a way I could face Blake and still keep my brothers safe."

Emmitt rolled to his side so he faced me. "We will find a way."

He moved his hand, lightly resting it on my side. I didn't mind. The warmth of his palm soothed me to sleep.

CHAPTER SIXTEEN

A FEW HOURS LATER, THE BOYS BURST INTO THE BEDROOM, AND I heard them pause when they saw two lumps under the covers. Either Emmitt had been sleeping deeply or Jim had set us up. I lifted myself up on my elbow, trying to play it cool.

"Good morning, you two. Is Jim awake?" They both nodded. "Good, tell him we'll be up in just a little bit." They didn't move.

"Who is that?" Liam asked pointing to the lump that was Emmitt.

I glanced down at Emmitt. He was watching me, letting me deal with the situation however I saw fit.

"It's Emmitt. Jim had the couch. You two had the other bed. So, I let him sleep here after he promised not to steal the covers."

Liam quietly gazed at the floor before he took a deep breath and lifted his head.

"If you married Emmitt, we could live with Nana and Jim forever."

My eyes widened in surprise as I scrambled for something to say, but Liam saved me from a serious answer.

"If you don't want to marry Emmitt, we would be okay with Jim, too."

My face flushed, and the bed started shaking due to Emmitt's silent laughter.

"We'll talk about who I'll marry some other time, but I'll keep what you said in mind. Now, go get dressed and wait with Jim."

Both boys scampered out of the room, and I got out of the bed without looking at Emmitt. I'd never given marriage a thought. Had Emmitt? He might have because he'd called me his repeatedly. I wasn't sure how I felt about a permanent relationship, though, and couldn't afford to dwell on it. There were bigger issues in my life.

I grabbed some clean clothes and left the room, pretending I didn't notice Emmitt's scrutiny. Shutting myself in the bathroom, I started to get ready. I didn't take too long. The boys were probably hungry and trying to talk Jim into leaving without us. I pulled back my wet hair and opened the door.

Emmitt leaned against the wall, waiting. His sleepy smile and slow appraisal had my stomach doing acrobatics. He winked, and I realized he knew what he did to me. With an embarrassed smile, I indicated the bathroom was all his and fled to the bedroom where I ditched my dirty laundry.

I went to join Liam and Aden in the living room where I could hear Jim entertaining them with stories from Emmitt's youth.

"Morning," I said, walking into the room. "Did you two sleep well?"

"Yep, until Aden woke me up," Liam complained.

"I'm hungry," Aden said to explain his purpose for waking his older brother.

Jim reached forward and plucked Aden from the floor. "Me, too. Let's hope Emmitt hurries or we'll have to leave without him." He used his big hand to cover Aden's stomach and flexed his fingers. Aden squealed and giggled, the childish laugh making me smile.

Freshly showered and dressed, Emmitt strode into the room. He spared me a quick wink then focused on Aden.

"I'm starving, too. Let's go eat. If I get there first, I'm eating all the food."

Aden flipped off Jim's lap and made a dash for the door, but Emmitt reached it first. Jim and Liam shared a brief look. Jim smiled mischievously, and Liam took off running after Aden and Emmitt.

Jim laughed. "Come on, little sister, or you'll be left crumbs."

As we finished eating, Paul and Henry came and asked to take Liam and Aden on a tour. Jim immediately offered to go with. I watched my brothers leave the common room, both excitedly following the younger pair of werewolves, then helped Emmitt carry our plates to the adjoining kitchen.

He deposited the dishes into a large tub of soapy water and turned toward me.

"Are you ready?"

I looked at him blankly.

"The pack meeting." His gaze flicked to the doorway behind us.

I looked over my shoulder. In those few moments since leaving the room, a growing number of people had entered it. I wrinkled my nose and shook my head. He smiled, gave me a tender look, and took my hand to lead me back. As I suspected, ready or not, I would be attending the meeting.

People gathered along the outskirts of the room. Those that didn't have a place to sit stood near the picnic tables or the open patio doors. They looked like normal people, but I knew better. This was the pack.

As we headed toward Charlene, Thomas, Mary, and Gregory at the front of the room, I scanned the faces in the crowd. Thankfully, I didn't see anyone I recognized. Most just looked curious about me. However, the intense stares of a few made me nervous. I tightened my hold on Emmitt's hand.

The hush that fell as we delved deeper into the crowd drew Mary's attention. She smiled reassuringly, and I tentatively smiled back.

Emmitt stopped next to his parents, and we turned to face the pack. My anxiety reached new heights as I stared into the sea of bodies that watched us. Thomas stepped forward, drawing their attention.

"There was a challenge last night, which Elder Winifred declined. Michelle has acknowledged Emmitt in front of Elder Winifred."

Challenge? I'd acknowledged Emmitt? What were they talking about?

The collective eye of the pack focused on me. Emmitt's hand lightly squeezed mine as I struggled not to squirm under the sudden attention.

"All challenges will end now," Thomas said. "Not only is this a command from me—"

"It's from me as well," Nana Wini said from the back of the room.

There was a minute shuffling in the crowd then everything stilled.

"Just as we count Charlene as one of our own, we now count Michelle." Thomas glanced at me and gave me a warm smile. "Michelle has brought two cubs with her."

Cubs?

"They are under pack protection, but I am looking for a Mated pair to protect them as their own, to put the safety of the cubs above the safety of the pack." There was a slight murmur at this.

"I'll keep them as my own," Mary said from beside me.

"We will," Gregory agreed.

Thomas nodded to Gregory. As if it were a sign, people started to leave. Many of them looked back to study me before they quit the room, and I wondered what they were thinking. I wasn't even sure what I was thinking. The six of us stayed where we were.

"I'm sorry about that, Michelle," Charlene said. "We needed to lay down the law right away so you wouldn't run into any trouble."

"And my brothers?"

"That's what Mary and Gregory are for. While you're here, they will be an extra layer of protection. Mary and Gregory will always be close by, and if you need to leave your brothers for any reason, they will step in while you are gone, protecting Liam and Aden even more ferociously than you could. They were guardians for Jim and Emmitt while they were growing up."

It touched me that they already knew Liam and Aden's names. But I wasn't sure I could trust complete strangers to watch over my brothers, even knowing they were friends of Emmitt's for a very long time.

Charlene must have sensed my hesitancy. "Nana Wini also spoke a command to the room. No one will harm them."

I wasn't about to mention Nana Wini's word didn't seem to work too well if Nana hadn't already mentioned it.

"Now that that's settled, we are hoping you will discuss your past with us. We want to help you," Charlene said.

I gave a slow nod, not knowing what more I could share other than Richard's address. I didn't think the address would do much good. I highly doubted Blake would be sitting at the house with all the news coverage I saw online.

Charlene motioned for Thomas to lead the way. Emmitt's thumb smoothed over the side of my hand as we followed. His touch momentarily distracted me from my thoughts.

Thomas opened the door to a small, windowless room. Its sole furnishing was a battered rectangle dining table, surrounded by mismatched chairs. Nana Wini and another man I'd never met already sat at the table. Everyone moved to join them.

"Michelle, this is Elder Sam," Emmitt said as he held out a chair for me.

I recognized the name of Nana's stock market friend and said a quiet hello as I sat. Sam nodded in greeting but remained silent. He looked just as I imagined him; aged, but not stooped, with neat, grey hair and kind brown eyes.

Emmitt took a seat beside me. "This room has been soundproofed, so we won't be overheard."

Charlene nodded. "Nana Wini told us the Forlorn ignored her command to leave. That is cause for concern. But I'm more concerned about the things you said on the way here."

I gave Emmitt a sidelong glance.

"You shouldn't need to live in fear," Charlene said. "I've seen these people do amazing things. Let's face this together. But in order to do that, we need to know everything you know about those men. Do you have any idea why they could ignore an Elder?"

I wanted to laugh. "How could I possibly know anything like that? I've known about werewolves less than a month."

"Emmitt mentioned you thought Blake was one of us. You were near him for more than four years. Tell us about him," she said.

Did I know something I hadn't yet realized? I thought back to the beginning, scrutinizing everything I could remember. Sure, it had been Blake who was responsible for my prison, but he hadn't been there most of the time, just at the dinners and infrequent visits to confer with David or Richard. There wasn't much else.

They remained silent, patiently waiting.

"I don't know what you're looking for," I said finally. "I thought Blake was just like everyone else. Human. But, he was mean. He'd come over and ask me about my premonitions. He sometimes asked if I saw anything other than market tips. I always wished I did see something more. But it wasn't until..."

It wasn't until I met Emmitt that they'd changed. With that thought, I realized Blake had known that my premonitions would evolve. It explained why he kept asking; he'd been waiting for my answer to change.

I looked down at the table in shock. Was that why he'd brought his men over?

His men. The thought stuck in my head and pieces fell into place.

"No. You're wrong," I said looking up at Nana Wini, yet still lost in my own thoughts.

"About what, dear?"

"Pack leaders control the pack. Elders keep the peace between the packs through the pack leaders," I said slowly, reasoning it out. "Yet, there are some of your kind you have trouble communicating with." My thoughts felt right, but the implications scared me. "Before the night he shifted, I thought Blake's control over the men he brought with him was just a businessman's hold over his lackeys. But that night, it was more. I think he's their leader. A pack leader. Those were *his* men. I think Blake is different. You can't communicate with him, and because of that, his men. They are their own pack. A large pack.

"Many of his men commented on my smell. No, not smell. Scent. I never understood what they meant." I looked at Emmitt. "I believe Blake brought those men over because he knew my premonitions would change when I met the right werewolf. They changed after I met you."

Emmitt's lips twitched, and the look in his eyes grew warm. Before I blushed, I turned my focus on the other members of our group.

"Now, I've seen actual people in my premonitions, not just stock tips. I think Blake meant to unlock that new piece of my gift. He knows more than we think, not only about my gift, but about why Elders can't communicate with everyone like they should."

The room remained quiet.

"I think you're right," Thomas said finally. "He does sound like he knows more." He looked at Sam and Nana Wini. "But, is it worth the risk to find out what he knows when we have no way of controlling him?"

Sam and Nana Wini shared a glance.

"These gifted women are rare," Sam said.

Huh? What gifted women? I glanced at Emmitt, confused, but Sam kept speaking.

"And we have yet to determine why these gifted women are compatible with us. Are they gifted because they are compatible or are they compatible because they are gifted? Are there other human women out there who are compatible but not gifted? There's so much we don't know. Charlene, your gift has never been clear to you; and with Gabby less than a month away from leaving for college, I think we need to find out what Blake knows."

"Gifted?" I said to Charlene then swiveled toward Sam. "Who's Gabby?"

Sam reached into his pocket and removed his wallet as Charlene answered my first question.

"So far, the humans who are compatible with werewolves are gifted." When I looked at her speculatively, she said, "Yeah, I can manipulate people's minds, plant thoughts in there, and make them do what I want."

The idea of that scared me, but no one else in the room seemed too bothered by it.

"I learned at an early age what I could do wasn't a good thing and started to fear people would come take me away because of it. So I ran and ended up here."

Though her gift concerned me, it also gave me comfort because now I knew I wasn't alone. Maybe she knew why my gift had suddenly changed.

"Did anything happen to your ability when you met Thomas?" I asked, absently accepting the picture Sam had plucked from his wallet.

If my suspicions were right, her ability would have changed when she met her Mate. But, without knowing exactly what these strange abilities were for or where they stemmed from, it was hard to say if my theory was right or not.

"No," she said, disappointing me. "But when I Claimed him, he changed." She looked at Thomas, and he nodded as if encouraging her to continue. "A pack leader can only hold together a pack size equal to his mental strength. His command needs to encompass the entire group. When it can't, the members see weakness and leave. So by nature, the pack size remains equal to the power of the alpha. Once I Claimed Thomas, his capacity to control more members grew. Even now, we could welcome more members if they wanted to join us."

So Charlene's gift hadn't changed, but Thomas had. Why after the Claiming? Could it be that her ability had changed before that, but she hadn't noticed? Did this mean when...if...I Claimed Emmitt, my gift could change again?

Stumped, I finally looked down at the picture in my hand. I felt the same sense of recognition as I had when I first saw Charlene's picture, but this time I had an explanation for it.

"This is the girl from my first vision. She was studying. College texts, I think. One of you was lying beside her. A huge dog with a long, shaggy brown coat. I saw her petting him." I looked up and saw Sam's surprised expression. "Did I say something wrong?"

"No, no. It's just...she tolerates coming here but doesn't really have a fondness for any of us."

I wasn't wrong in what I'd seen. "I guess we just have to see what comes to pass. Maybe it was just a picture of a possibility." I passed the photo back to him.

Sam stared down at the picture in his hand, a slight smile on his lips. The girl in the picture might not have a fondness for them, but Sam definitely had affection for her.

"Do you know of a way to reach Blake?" Thomas asked.

I started to shake my head no but then paused. "There's a lawyer who seems to be in contact with him."

"A lawyer?" Thomas said.

"Before I ran, my stepfather left me an envelope filled with documents and stuff, including a number for a lawyer. I looked the lawyer up online and sent him an email. He replied right away, asking for a meeting to read Richard's will. But he mentioned Blake too, so I never responded."

"Perhaps we could work through the lawyer," Charlene said, hope buoying her words.

"If the Elders can't communicate with him, the only chance we have to get the answers we want is face to face," Thomas said. "Not through a lawyer."

Sam nodded in agreement but looked troubled.

They were right. I doubted Blake would respond willingly to a phone call, email, or third party. If we wanted answers, Blake would need to be confronted face to face like Thomas said. And, I realized, I would have to do it. He had no reason to acknowledge anyone else in the room.

Ice formed in my limbs.

"I need to go back."

Charlene and Nana Wini shared a worried look.

"No, honey," Charlene said. "We'll think of something else. Now that you're here, and Nana put out a call about your protection, there's a possibility he'll come to you."

Fear swamped me.

"No. I don't want Blake here."

I didn't want Blake anywhere near my brothers. Yet, that's exactly what would happen now that he'd found us again. He was probably already tracking us or trying to. If I left the boys here, surrounded by werewolves not controlled by Blake, and went back to Wisconsin to lead Blake away, my brothers would be safe. Well, safer. Still, I wasn't willing to throw myself at Blake for the sake of a few unanswered questions—no matter how much I wanted the answers.

"Michelle, it would be better for you to stay here," Charlene said.

"For me, but not for Liam and Aden. They are how he controlled me before." I didn't want to go back, but I would to keep them safe.

Compassion flooded Nana's expression. I wished I had her strength. That was it, I thought with realization. Maybe there was a way for all of us to stay safe.

"Emmitt said Elders are stronger, more powerful than any other pack member. Maybe one could come with me, and one could stay here," I said, hopefully.

The group remained quiet for several moments before Thomas spoke up. "Neither you nor your brothers will be put at risk if we lure Blake here."

"I understand that you don't believe so, but you don't know Blake." And neither did I, not really. But the memory of his hand tightening around my throat made me desperate to keep my brothers safe. He was coming for me. I didn't doubt that. If I left without my brothers and he caught me again, at least I wouldn't have their wellbeing holding me back from trying to escape.

Sam cleared his throat. "Let's think on this for a while."

"Not too long," I said, wondering if Blake already knew of our location.

"We'll meet again tonight," Charlene said firmly.

I had little hope they would come up with a plan that didn't involve me facing Blake. But, my worst fear wasn't that Blake would recapture me. I feared never seeing my brothers again and never knowing if they were as protected and loved as I wanted them to be. Another thought pierced my heart. Would they grow up without any memories of their parents or me? Because of their ages, it was a possibility. Yet, what other choice did I have but to leave them here? My selfish need to stay with them wouldn't protect them.

Knowing what I needed to do, I nodded at Charlene. That's all they were waiting for. The others stood and started filing out completely unaware of the probable future tearing me apart.

Emmitt's hand settled on my shoulder. A comforting touch. A reminder that it wasn't the future yet and that I still had today to make unforgettable memories with my brothers.

I rose, took Emmitt's hand, and headed out the door.

GREGORY AND MARY found us while we were on our way to dinner. I sent the boys ahead to eat with Jim, Paul, and Henry while Emmitt and I headed to the soundproofed room.

When we entered, Charlene was in a whispered conversation with Thomas. Whatever they discussed, she looked very adamant.

Sam and Nana spoke with two newcomers, imposing men who stood just inside the door. The older of the two closed the door behind us. He was leaner and older than the other, but in no way less impressive. The younger, larger man rivaled Jim's size. With long, thick legs, he towered over his partner and stood with his massive arms crossed as he silently listened to Sam. I much preferred Emmitt's leaner build but didn't mistake their size differences to directly relate to their abilities. I knew better; I'd watched Emmitt and Jim "rough house" at the lake and Nana take on two larger men.

Emmitt led me to an open chair, and as usual, he held it out for me. The papers on the table caught my eye—four airline tickets. Two had names I didn't recognize. Another had Emmitt's name. The last ticket had my name on it.

My heart skipped a beat. I'd known I would have to go back, but I couldn't settle on how I felt about it.

"We spoke at length," Thomas said, noting the direction of my gaze. "We think an information-gathering trip to your old home, with the protection of an Elder, is a good idea. Those tickets are only if you agree to our plans."

Charlene moved toward the table, and Thomas considerately pulled out her chair even though she scowled at him. They'd obviously disagreed about something.

"Jim and Nana Wini will stay with the boys at all times as will Mary and Gregory," Thomas said. "Paul and Henry will be with them, as well, but no other werewolves will be permitted near them as a precaution."

I sensed Nana Wini's influence in the decision to limit their contact. Gratitude swamped me. It had to be tough to find out the complete control she'd thought she had was just an illusion.

Thomas continued. "While keeping Liam and Aden safe, we will not let them feel isolated. We'll keep them busy, just like today. In the event something does happen, Mary and Gregory will be their first line of defense followed by Jim and Nana Wini."

My hands grew cold at his words.

"At that point, Nana Wini would put a call out. I promise you, the entire pack will answer."

I could only nod in agreement due to the lump in my throat. It gave me chills hearing Thomas talk like that, but I was glad they'd thought it through. My brothers would be well guarded.

Under the table, Emmitt reached over to give my hand a gentle squeeze.

"Good," Thomas said. "Next, let me introduce you to the men who will be protecting you. This is Carlos and Grey."

The two names on the tickets. Carlos, the muscled man with a beautiful tan, black hair, and incredibly dark eyes, nodded at me when Thomas said his name. Grey, less bulky with a head of thick, curly grey hair and merry blue eyes, winked at me.

"Both Nana Wini and Sam have examined their intentions," Thomas said. "In addition to that, I personally vouch for them. Grey is my older brother. He has been with me through many challenges and has never let me down. Carlos has been with the pack since the day he was born. Even as a youth, he displayed tremendous courage and loyalty at the risk of personal harm.

"We don't want to take any unnecessary risks. Either Grey or Emmitt will be with you at all times, and you will not be going to your old home, yourself. The closest we agree you should go is to the city. From there, Carlos will act on your behalf."

Everyone's eyes rested on me. Though in their eyes three werewolves might seem like good protection, I would rather have an Elder. Someone who could trump Blake.

"Will Sam be coming with us?" I asked hesitantly.

Sam smiled slightly. "Grey is an Elder and can communicate with us as needed."

"Oh. I thought there were just two Elders," I said, meaning him and Nana.

"No," Nana said frowning slightly. "Though, our numbers do concern me."

Sam heaved a sigh but didn't speak.

"I think we need to give it consideration," she said looking at Sam then Grey.

"Give what consideration?" I asked, not understanding.

"There is a candidate waiting to become an Elder," she said with reservation.

"Waiting?" I said.

"We can't communicate with him like we should and hesitate to allow him to take the oath," Grey said, speaking for the first time.

"He might be the key," Sam said. "What Winifred experienced when those two came to challenge has been noticed before." He sighed. "But, never to the degree she experienced. We don't give commands very often. We believe in free will, so we've never tested the completeness of our communication with each individual. We just send out information when it's needed."

He looked at Nana Wini. "What you discovered is a bigger issue. We need to think of the possibilities. The new candidate, with this communication limitation, might be able to communicate with the others like him."

I didn't understand their concern. If they had someone who could communicate with the others, why not use him. Nana seemed to read my mind.

"An Elder has vast power and a huge responsibility to that power," she said. "When a candidate approaches us, we inspect their mind thoroughly. If we allowed a candidate to take the oath without making sure their intentions were honest and true, they could die." I frowned, confused. "When we take our oath, we are bound to serve the pack's best interest. Always. Our decisions may not be right all of the time, but they must be made with the right intentions. If we ever did anything knowing it would cause the pack harm, or wasn't in the pack's best interest, we would die instantly. It's the tie to all of our kind that controls us as much as we control them."

I stared at her, stunned for a moment. The connection she shared with all pack members could backlash and kill her? What a scary risk. Then again, putting so much control into one person was a risk, too. If there weren't some kind of check and balance, they could grow into a power-hungry Blake.

"So, because you can't inspect his mind, you don't know his intentions?"

"He's been waiting for three years. He has studied with each of us. We've tested him in many ways; but we haven't been able to inspect his mind. We can touch areas of it, just like I was able to with the two that appeared last night, but not all of it. And just like the two that appeared, he can choose to ignore a direct command."

"So, if he's an Elder, he might be able to control them?" I wondered.

"He might. Or, he may die taking the oath," Sam said.

Werewolves were getting more complex. Everything I knew about them whirled in my mind.

The Forlorn were on their own, controlled only by Elders, but in some cases even Elders weren't able to communicate with them. The pack leaders controlled pack members. Through the pack leaders, the members were then fully open to the Elders. Due to the oath Elders took, pack members indirectly controlled them.

One important question swirled in the center of my mental hurricane. Where did that leave special people like me?

According to Nana, all werewolves wanted us, most protected us, but we answered to none of them. We were part of their lives but not held to their rules. Even the Claiming was different for us. They couldn't choose us. We had to choose them. There had to be a reason for these differences.

Charlene brought us back on track.

"We can decide this later. Right now, we need to finalize the trip. I still think it's too dangerous for Michelle, even with an Elder along. No offense intended, Grey."

Grey winked at Charlene but remained quiet.

Dropping my gaze to the table, I considered their condition that I didn't go near the house and the impracticality of it. I still thought Blake would only speak to me; but, even with the stipulation, the plan achieved my goal. I would be closer to Blake and further from my well-protected brothers. Going to Wisconsin put me in a better position to learn more about Blake's real plans and would hopefully keep Blake away from Liam and Aden.

"I think it's worth the risk," I said quietly.

"All right," Thomas said, standing. "The flight leaves at 10 a.m. We'll see you at breakfast."

So soon? I felt a little tug in my chest as everyone else stood. While Grey and Carlos left with Nana and Sam, talking about someone named Joshua, I wondered how I'd actually bring myself to leave Liam and Aden.

Charlene must have read something in my expression because she stood when I did and moved to hug me. I accepted the gesture of comfort without thinking.

As soon as she touched me, the room faded. This time when I flew through the darkness toward the growing white glow, I prepared myself to focus. I was determined to look for two things: the outcome of the confrontation with Blake and the safety of my brothers during that confrontation. If anything looked off, I'd back out of the trip immediately.

The white room closed around me, and I quickly looked about. Each image flew out of the way as soon as I decided I didn't want to view it, and a new one crowded forward. It was like flipping through a book. Most images I barely gave a cursory glance.

I didn't find any starring Blake but did see the one of Emmitt and me. As I focused on it, it started to play again and distracted me from my purpose. I had complete control of it, rewinding or forwarding through the scene. Before I bit him, however, the room blinked out of existence.

My consciousness returned just in time to see Charlene crumple toward the floor. Thomas's quick reflexes saved her from a complete fall. He gently laid her down. I attempted to kneel beside her, but Emmitt caught me by my arms.

"No," Emmitt said, pulling me back from my semi-crouched position.

Thomas already knelt beside Charlene, tapping her cheek and calling her name.

"What happened?" I asked Emmitt.

"One minute she was hugging you, the next she started breathing funny and fainted. Did you have another vision? You had that same look."

"Yes. No." I stared worriedly at Charlene's prone form. "It was different. I think my ability is changing again, but I don't know how or why. I think I did that to her," I said to Emmitt in quiet fear.

On the floor, Charlene started coming to.

"No, it's just part of my gift," she assured me calmly as Thomas helped her up. "I'll tell you about it some other time. You need to go spend time with your brothers. I'm fine."

She didn't look fine. She looked pale and shaky as she moved to sit on a chair.

Emmitt gave my hand a quiet squeeze of assurance. I squeezed back. Had I almost killed his mom?

"She's stronger than she looks," Thomas said to both of us.

"She's still here and listening," Charlene said with a roll of her eyes, and I felt a little relieved.

Emmitt moved as if to leave, but Thomas stopped us.

"Michelle, could I have a moment with you? Privately?"

Emmitt scowled at his father but left, closing the door softly behind him. Charlene remained, and I stayed by the door, waiting.

Thomas rested a hand on the back of Charlene's chair, opened his mouth several times, but didn't say anything. This was the first time I'd seen him look anything but confident and calm.

Charlene gave a snort at his prolonged silence. It seemed to motivate him. He gave her a look and ran his hand through his hair—a gesture I'd seen his son do numerous times.

"I wasn't sure what to do about sleeping accommodations. Jim mentioned Emmitt stayed with you last night, and I was wondering if you wanted one room or connecting rooms."

Heat flooded my face, and I wished I could disappear.

"I wouldn't mind if we shared a room," I said truthfully, hoping they wouldn't think poorly of me. "I'd feel safer."

Thomas nodded and moved to leave, but Charlene stopped him with a slight clearing of her throat.

"Two beds, then?" she asked politely.

I nodded, relieved she didn't assume the worst. Sleeping next to Emmitt after I had the bad dream, and again at the Compound, had been nerve-racking, yet completely wonderful, experiences; but I didn't want to get into the habit of sharing a bed. I had Liam and Aden to think of.

She winked at me. "I know how male minds work. If you don't clarify, they'll

weasel their way under the covers and have you believing it was your idea."
Thomas snorted but didn't deny the accusation. "We raised Emmitt to be a good
boy. Set your boundaries, and he'll respect them. But like any werewolf, he'll
look for loopholes," she said with a laugh.

"Are you done?" Thomas said to his wife with an arched brow. She smiled at
him sweetly and stood to plant a light kiss on his lips. He huffed a sigh and
shook his head at her.

She turned back toward me. "You'll learn," she added with another wink and
led Thomas to the door.

I let them step out first. I needed that extra moment to cool my blush.

Emmitt waited for me in the hall. After a small wave goodbye to Charlene
and Thomas, he and I walked slowly back to our apartment. We didn't talk about
anything since we were out of the secured meeting room. Instead, he just
reached over to hold my hand. I willingly surrendered it.

That night, to Emmitt's disappointment, I slept snuggled between my
brothers. In Aden's sleep, he tangled his fingers through my hair. Somehow, he
knew something bad was coming.

CHAPTER SEVENTEEN

THE NEXT MORNING I HAD THE DAUNTING TASK OF BREAKING THE news to the boys. Worried they'd cry or beg me to stay, I wasn't prepared for the cheering or the rush to help me pack.

"Aren't you going to miss me even a little?" I asked them in a half-teasing tone.

"Mimi," Liam said rationally. "You said four days. That's not a long time. We get to have sleepovers with Paul and Henry."

I laughed and hugged him. Obviously, there was no competing with Paul and Henry.

We went to breakfast, and the boys excitedly greeted Paul and Henry, telling them about all the things they were going to do together.

Mary grinned when she saw my face and gave my arm a quick, reassuring squeeze.

"They'll want to miss you, but we're going to keep them so busy they'll forget to. It will be easier for them that way."

I knew she was right.

We finished our breakfast then left Liam and Aden with Mary after another round of hugging. Emmitt stayed close beside me as we walked the quiet halls. When we were in the apartment, he spun me around to face him. Understanding filled his gaze. My eyes watered, seeing it. He tucked me tight against his chest, held me for barely a second, then stepped back.

"You don't have to go." It was the first objection he'd voiced regarding this trip.

"I do. I want to be free. I want to protect the boys. This is the only way to do it. Why are you saying this now?"

"I see how hard this is, leaving your brothers. I can go alone. There's no need to come with us."

"You know better. I'm the bait." It was the first time during this whole plan that I'd admitted it, and he scowled hearing it. "You'll keep me safe," I said seriously. "I don't doubt that."

A CAR WAITED for us just outside the main entrance. Emmitt put our bags in the trunk. The sound of it closing struck me with cold finality. Would I ever see my brothers again?

I'd done the math. Four years with one dinner a month; ten guests each time with few, if any, repeats—I hadn't paid close attention. Blake led more than five hundred men. The number made the likelihood of my return to the Compound a scary improbability. So why go? One way or another, Blake would come for me. I'd rather it be on my terms with my brothers safe.

Emmitt reached for my hand again and gave it a gentle squeeze. We both slid into the backseat, and I said a quiet hello to Grey and Carlos.

Carlos drove, heading straight to the airport. Grey kept up a stream of conversation, ribbing Carlos about everything from his hairstyle to his driving, both of which were impeccable and precise. Carlos remained stoically quiet. I could see his silence amused Grey. Under different circumstances, I might have found his playful banter diverting.

As it was, my stomach churned with anxiety. I doubted my decision and wondered what would happen to my brothers if I couldn't return. I leaned into Emmitt. He would care for them...if he made it back.

I casually reached into my pocket, found my phone, and sent a quick text to Nana Wini to ask for her promise that my brothers would go somewhere permanent and safe if I didn't return. Seconds later, Emmitt sighed and pulled me even closer.

Grey turned in his seat. "Wini said to stop worrying. You're bruising my ego with your doubt. We will keep you safe."

Darn werewolf telepathy.

"We'll be at the airport soon," Grey said, passing back our tickets.

I straightened away from Emmitt and grabbed my ticket before Emmitt could. It would be my first time flying. My reasons for nauseous anxiety continued to grow. I took a deep breath and let it out, feeling Emmitt's eyes on me. I needed to remember my purpose: Keep my brothers safe by whatever means necessary...and try really hard to come back home.

I THOUGHT I would be terrified to be back in the same town as Blake but didn't feel anything but squished as I sat between Carlos and Emmitt in the cab we took to the hotel. Mercifully, it wasn't a long ride.

Carlos and Grey checked us in while Emmitt grabbed our things from the trunk. He shouldered both bags and held out his hand. I wrapped my cool fingers around his warm ones. My stomach twisted happily at his touch as we walked toward the entrance.

Two glass utility doors opened to a small, chlorine-scented lobby. Carlos and Grey waited just inside and handed Emmitt a room key. We all silently walked the hallway to the left. Their room was two doors down from ours.

I blushed when Emmitt opened our door and I spotted two queen beds. I wondered if his father had mentioned the sleeping arrangements to him. The room, tastefully decorated in brown and gold tones, had a sitting area opposite the door.

"If it's all right with you," Grey said from behind us, "we'd like to get started right away."

I nodded, and Carlos and Grey came in with us. Emmitt set our bags on one of the beds while I cleared the hotel advertisements and guidebook off the coffee table. Carlos and Grey sat on the wooden chairs from the table while Emmitt and I sat on the small brown sofa. Grey spread out a map of the area that he'd grabbed from the airport, and I pointed to the area where I used to live.

"I don't know if David's still there. I'm guessing probably not since David was employed by Blake and had no ties to Richard or the house. But Blake might have someone watching the place. If it's possible, could you sneak in and grab a few things? You'll need to be careful. The house has a security system. I set it off when I left."

I explained where to find photos of my mom and a few other things that I wanted for my brothers. "Then, you could go back tomorrow and see if you stirred up any trouble."

Grey smiled wide. "I like the way you think. We'll call when we get there to let you know the state of things. If anyone's there, we'll watch for a while."

They both stood to leave. My worry and fear had evaporated while we talked, and now impatience grabbed me. It would take them at least forty minutes to get to my house. I didn't want to wait that long to find out...well, anything. I knew whatever would happen, would happen, but I just wanted to get it over with. I'd given Blake enough of my life.

Emmitt closed the door behind them and turned to study me.

"Let's go next door and get something to eat."

We left the room and walked to the restaurant next door. The smell of grilling burgers hit me when we left the hotel. Crossing the parking lot, my stomach growled. Emmitt grinned at me.

Inside the restaurant, we decided on burgers and ordered takeout to bring back to the room. The wait seemed to take forever. I kept glancing at the clock, worried we'd miss Grey's call.

When we returned with our food, we ate quickly. Emmitt's phone chirped just as I finished. He'd been done within minutes, of course.

Emmitt listened for a while, adding affirmations occasionally. Finally, he said, "I agree. I'll let her know. Call back if there's a change in plans."

He hung up the phone and gave me a slight smile. "They're watching the house but say it looks abandoned. The grass is overgrown, and the papers are piled up. There's even a notice on the door. Grey's content to sit and watch it for the rest of the day to see if they're mistaken. Tonight, they'll go in for the things you mentioned. We can send them back to watch tomorrow."

I nodded, surprised, but not concerned. I had a plan B.

"So it looks like, in order to find Blake, I'll need to call the lawyer."

"It can't hurt," he said.

I picked up the hotel phone and dialed the number I'd memorized. A receptionist answered. I gave my name and asked to speak to Mr. Nolan. She said that he was in a meeting and asked for a return number. But when I said I'd just try back later, she quickly asked me to hold.

The line clicked, then a man came on.

"Ms. Daniels. Thank you for contacting us." He went through the usual offer of condolences then explained why he'd been looking for me. He wanted to read the will and discuss the details of Richard's estate with me.

Estate? Will? I'd never given any of that any thought. I glanced at Emmitt. He had his head tilted, watching me. I was sure he could hear both ends of the conversation.

"How soon can we meet?" I asked.

"Mr. Torrin said he would be available whenever you were. My schedule is open on Thursday. Is there a time that day that works for you?"

"Let me check." I put my hand over the receiver, needing a minute to think it through. Why would Blake not watch the house? Why would Richard give me the number of a lawyer with whom Blake also had contact? The answers lay in the meeting with the lawyer. I moved my hand.

"How does ten sound?" I asked.

"Perfect. I'll see you Thursday at ten."

After I hung up, I sat on the bed, thinking. Although I wanted to meet with Blake to find out what he knew about my gift, I didn't want to walk into a trap. I needed to get more information about the will and Blake's involvement.

Emmitt sat back and watched me as I grabbed the phone book.

THREE HOURS LATER, when I hung up the phone, my head spun from all of the information I'd won. The will, which was straightforward, had gone to probate. Richard's estate included properties I hadn't known he owned. Everything went to me as the sole beneficiary.

I didn't understand why he'd left everything to me, his stepdaughter, when he had two sons of his own. Then, I realized by not naming them in the will, Richard had protected them. Blake had no reason to pursue my brothers, unless he still wanted to use them to control me. It also meant that Richard had put a lot of faith in me to take my brothers with me when I ran. And, he had trusted me to keep them safe.

Since Richard hadn't specified an executor, one had been appointed. There'd been no surprise when I'd been told Blake was trying to contest it. By being an executor, he'd have control of everything in my absence. After speaking with the court appointed executor, I could see no reason there even needed to be a meeting other than to get us in the open so Blake could do whatever it was he had planned.

"I don't think we should go," I said to Emmitt.

He frowned thoughtfully. "If we don't, Blake is still out there and this trip will have been for nothing."

He moved to sit near me on the bed and wrapped an arm around my shoulders. "The lawyer's in the phone book. I checked, so we know he's real. Even if he's being paid off, he'd have to be careful with what he's involved in."

"But what if Blake brings people with him, like Frank and that other guy?"

"We'll bring more powerful people."

I liked Grey and Carlos well enough but didn't think they could take on Blake's entire following. "Three, no matter how strong or fast they are, against an unknown number, doesn't seem like a good idea."

He grinned at me. "Not just us. One thing Blake won't want is people knowing what's going on. I heard you talking and heard how much Richard's properties are worth. Call the news. Bring them with. Say you want to donate half of your inheritance to a charity. With a camera on you, he can't touch you."

I remembered the video of Richard's mauling and doubted his plan would be as safe as he thought. Blake hadn't seemed too concerned about public exposure, then.

We debated what to do until just past dark and our stomachs growled. With no better options, I called the local news.

Emmitt was right. As soon as I mentioned an eight-figure inheritance, I had the media's attention. The person I spoke with took down the information for the lawyer and agreed to have someone there.

I managed to say goodbye before Emmitt plucked the phone from my hands.

"Enough for tonight," he said gently.

I nodded in agreement. I was emotionally drained and ready for bed, but Emmitt insisted we eat. I grinned, knowing he was the hungry one this time. He ordered room service while I took a shower.

My thoughts kept running over what I knew about Blake. Why fight to get control of Richard's assets? Yes, the number was large, but what about Blake's take? He should have made at least that amount. I'd always given the tips to Blake via phone or in person. Except that last time.

Briefly towel drying my hair, I wished again that I would have better premonitions. Something useful like what Blake had planned. Sighing in frustration, I pulled on my pajamas and joined Emmitt in the room. There was no point in dwelling on what I couldn't control, and my premonitions fell into that category.

My hair had mostly air dried by the time the food arrived. Emmitt tipped the room service person and groaned in appreciation of the aroma coming from the trays as he set them on the table. I teased him by reaching for the half-pound burger, and he playfully growled before offering to share a bite. Shaking my head, I reached for the smaller burger and carried it over to one of the beds.

"I'll take this bed," I said sitting down on the end of it.

He stopped mid-chew and looked up. He studied me for a moment then resumed chewing the bite in his mouth.

I watched him swallow and take a drink from his soda, wondering at his reaction.

"No," he said. Then, he took another bite still watching me. His look, so intense and focused, made me a little uneasy and very confused.

"Okay. I didn't know you had a preference." I got up and moved to the other bed. This time I didn't look at him but reached for the remote and turned on the television.

He moodily dropped his burger on his plate. "I don't want to sleep apart from you."

I almost laughed aloud. So that's what this was about? Remembering his mother's words, I primly set down my own burger and walked over to him. Leaning in, I pressed a quick kiss to the tip of his nose as he'd once done to me.

"Too bad."

Before he had time to react, I walked back to my plate. "Eat your burger, Emmitt."

It was hard, but I finished my burger while watching television. He remained quiet, eating his own meal. I could feel his steady scrutiny the entire time.

When he finished the burger, he ate both of our fries and the side order of onion rings. I didn't know how he had the room. He hesitated when he finished, looking slightly frustrated, but then walked over by me and politely asked if I had finished, too. I handed him my plate, and he stacked it on the tray before placing everything outside the door.

I felt like I'd started a fight when he quietly closed himself in the bathroom.

I brushed my teeth then crawled into my acquired bed. The room was a comfortable temperature and the pillow soft. I didn't think I'd stay awake long enough to hear back from Grey and Carlos.

Mentally exhausted, I fell asleep before Emmitt came out of the bathroom.

THE NEXT MORNING, I knew I wasn't in bed alone. His breath tickled the top of my head, and his arm lay casually draped over my waist. Slowly, I opened my eyes. Curled on my side, I lay facing him. He slept, his eyes closed and face relaxed. He'd made a gesture toward compromise and laid on top the covers. Since I'd said no to sharing a bed, I wasn't sure it was much of a compromise.

Shifting slightly to get comfortable, I paused when I felt the edge of the mattress under me. How was that possible? I lifted my head to look. He'd moved the other bed, pushing it up against mine. Technically, he wasn't sleeping in the same bed as me.

I studied him again, amazed. His dark lashes fanned his cheeks, making him completely irresistible. Irresistible and mine, I thought with a smile. Mine. His clarification of how he felt about me rang in my head. He'd known I was the one for him when he first saw me well over a month ago. His complete certainty awed me. As did his patience. I frowned suddenly. He'd waited a month for a first date, a date with no first kiss. Why hadn't he kissed me yet? A kiss to the tip of my nose didn't count.

Looking at his peaceful face, I wondered what it'd be like to really kiss Emmitt. My stomach did a quick flip, and a flush consumed my face. I decided it was time to get out of bed before I woke him up.

I snuck to the bathroom and quietly closed the door. I couldn't stop thinking about what he'd done after I'd fallen asleep. He'd moved not only the bed but also the small end table, which had been between the beds, and a lamp. He'd relocated everything, neatly arranging it all on the side of the room near the window. So much effort just to be next to me.

What was wrong with me? I feared starting the relationship I really wanted with Emmitt because of the looming danger of Blake. With Emmitt, I was happy and peaceful. Why was I letting Blake stand between us?

I crept from the bathroom and quickly brushed my teeth, trying not to wake him. In the mirror, I saw the covers on the opposite bed lay in disarray with the sheet trailing onto the floor. The pillows lay in a pile near the head of the bed. A few had signs of being squashed. He'd tried to do as I'd asked.

Though I tried to deny it, I wanted to be near him, too. Always.

I quietly rinsed then crawled back into bed, easing onto my side to face him. I lightly ran my fingers over his hair. It already needed a trim. He looked a bit like a porcupine. I focused my attention on the stubble on his face. He shaved each morning, but by evening, it grew out again.

While I was tracing his jaw with my fingers, he opened his eyes.

429

"Good morning," I whispered, removing my hand.

He caught it and brought it to his mouth, placing a kiss on my palm. A surge of heat spread through me. His pupils dilated and his irises grew slightly, a sign of a partial shift.

With thoughts of kissing still drifting in my mind, my gaze shifted to his lips. Why did Emmitt need to be the one to kiss me?

He kissed my palm again then released my hand, running his fingers through my hair.

I hesitantly touched his chest. Could I lead? His heart thumped under my fingertips. I leaned in slowly.

The fingers in my hair twitched when I stopped just inches from his face. He didn't move, but his eyes begged me to close the gap. Gathering my courage, I lightly brushed my lips against his.

Tiny explosions started in my stomach, sending out waves of warmth through the rest of me. He groaned. I pressed closer, absorbing the feel of his firm lips. My insides began melting with the heat the kiss created. It distracted me so much that I, at first, didn't notice the bed shaking. This time, it wasn't due to laughter on his part.

Reluctantly, I pulled back and looked into his eyes. What I found there humbled me. The dark blue irises were almost lost to his pupils. Very little white remained.

"Thank you for trying last night," I said softly.

He reached up, gently touching my jaw. My skin tingled. I really wanted to kiss him again, but I could see his effort to control the slight tremors running through him. I didn't think kissing would help. He disagreed.

He skimmed his hand around to the back of my neck and pulled me close for another kiss. Our lips brushed lightly, and I couldn't help my smile. I nudged him so he lay on his back and moved closer to him. Not fast enough to suit him, however. He lifted me, moving me so I half-lay on his chest, an arm on each side of him. My heart stuttered and another explosion of heat went off inside me.

A low rumble echoed in his chest. Not a growl really, it was more a satisfied purr. I studied him for a moment to make sure he was okay with the situation before slowly leaning forward again. He lifted his head slightly, his smooth lips meeting mine. Possessed, I lightly nipped his bottom lip.

The tremors grew worse. The bed was going to shake apart. I reluctantly pulled back. His teeth had elongated, reshaping his lips. Any hint of white in his eyes had disappeared beyond his expanded irises.

"Maybe, I had better stop," I said more to myself than him. I really didn't want to, but...

In a flash, I lay on my back while he leaned over me, his arms caging me in.

"No."

At least, I thought the growl had a hint of no in it. He tried clearing his throat and speaking again, but it was still more growl than human. Giving up on communication, he lowered his head, his intent clear.

"If you change into your fur, we're done," I said a moment before he claimed my lips.

His kiss was hot and thorough, sweeping me from the hotel room to a magical place in my mind where only the two of us existed. I had no concept of time, but when he pulled away, I was gasping for air, stunned by the intensity of emotions running through me.

He held still, watching me as he shook violently. I wanted to pull him back down despite his obvious struggle for control. It took several long moments before my breathing slowed from ragged gasps.

I could now comprehend how I'd be able to bite him. From that single kiss, I already had a slight urge to nip at his neck. A good make-out session and it'd be done. I needed to be careful when I kissed him. And there was no doubt; I would be kissing him again. Soon.

His pupils dilated further as he leaned in to nuzzle my neck. I shivered as he inhaled deeply. I wished we were staying in this hotel for fun instead of Blake. It'd be easy to let go then. When he inhaled again, lapping my neck, my insides started to liquefy, and I forced myself to push lightly against his chest.

"We need to stop." It came out sounding breathless. When he didn't stop, I took a deep, calming breath and tried again. "Emmitt, please stop."

Grudgingly, he pulled away; and, instead of facing me, he rolled to sit on the edge of the bed, quickly averting his face. Wondering if he was angry, I reached for his arm, catching him before he left the bed. He stilled when I touched him, but he didn't face me. Tremors continued to wrack his body.

"Are you mad?"

He shook his head in response but remained silent.

"This thing between you and me, it's definitely right. I don't doubt it. I just don't want to get so involved that we forget why we're here. Once I deal with my past, I can focus on our future."

He turned to me, a wild light burning in his eyes. "As long as it takes, I'll wait. I'm not going anywhere."

His voice was guttural, devolved due to the partial change. A light fur covered his arms, and the tips of his ears were no longer rounded. Even with fur, he made my stomach churn in a good way.

I hugged him hard. I was lucky to have him. He didn't show fear. He showed me how to be strong, how to have fun. He was exactly who I needed. As soon as I thought that, I slipped into my vision world. Not the white master room, but the single feature version.

I stood near the bar in a dimly lit, crowded club. Had I really been there, the press of bodies would have crushed me. Music dominated the air, thumping out a loud, aggressive beat. Colored lights shifted back and forth over the writhing mass on the dance floor, making it hard to see any one person for more than a second.

The flashing exit sign above the entrance caught my eye just in time to see a woman walk in. She was tall and trim with curly, bright red hair, pale skin, and a smattering of dark freckles. Her green eyes shimmered in the multi-colored light. She was stunning, and she was pissed.

She stalked into the club, roughly pushing her way through the bodies to get to the bar. As she passed the other patrons, they stopped moving and turned to stare at her. I initially thought she was going to get her ass kicked for pushing her way through the crowd. Instead of looking angry, the people she'd shoved out of the way looked serene. Their serenity seemed to make the woman even angrier.

"Another vision?" Emmitt asked pulling away from me and stopping the scene. He looked and sounded calmer.

"Yeah. There's an angry redhead out there somewhere who I wouldn't want to run into. I just wish I knew what I was supposed to do with this information."

"We'll figure it out." His stomach grumbled loudly.

"Go shower," I said, "and then let's get something to eat."

I smiled at his disgruntled expression and knew he'd rather stay in bed. But kissing Emmitt was intense, and I wasn't ready for another round. I had been serious about losing focus. We couldn't afford that.

He reluctantly agreed, and I enjoyed the solitude as I dressed and thought about my visions.

So far, the visions were all about women. The first one had a werewolf in it and a girl Elder Sam had identified as Gabby. The second girl had to be related to werewolves as well since the man on the phone had been talking to someone named Gabby. I didn't think it a coincidence. And, though this last vision didn't have any sign of werewolves, without a doubt, the girl had powers. The people she'd passed seemed as if she'd put them in a trance.

Three visions of different women. In each vision, I'd felt a sense of recognition as if I should somehow know the woman. Charlene had a gift like me. And the third girl appeared gifted. Could the recognition be because we all shared that tie? If so, how many of us were out there?

Based on the vast majority of images in the white room, I wasn't done having premonitions. I just wished I knew how to control them so I could get some better answers.

Emmitt strolled out of the bathroom damp and looking good in his jeans. My stomach somersaulted, its version of a happy clap. His bare chest glistened in the vanity light. Muscles rippled as he walked. The need for food had me averting my eyes. I didn't want him to catch me enjoying the view and start something again.

"Did you hear from Grey?" I asked as he pulled a shirt on.

"They got back late with the things you wanted. Everything's in their room. They left early again to watch the house. We'll hear from them later."

We walked to the restaurant from the night before and had an enjoyable breakfast. We took our time, talking about ourselves and our plans for the future.

I pointed out both of us were jobless and asked if we wanted to stay that way.

"My father sent Jim and me to Montana to establish another branch of the pack," he explained.

I watched in amusement as he forked in a large bite of syrup-covered pancakes and waited for him to continue.

"When the apartments are all finished, I'll need to find something to do. But something from home." He met my eyes. "I don't want to go far."

His answer warmed me. Then, he asked what I wanted to do.

"I want to work on my GED. Thanks to Blake, I missed out on graduating. After that, I'm not sure. I can't think of getting a job and leaving my brothers, yet. And the thought of sending them off to school in the fall terrifies me."

"We should consider inviting other families to come live with us. Nana Wini could homeschool."

"Would Nana really want to do that?"

"I think so. We all want to keep those boys safe. Cubs are usually homeschooled because of their unpredictable shifting. Even though yours don't shift, they should still be treated in the same careful manner. It would mean they'd need to be told, though. Unless you want them surprised the first time a friend pops into fur."

"Just another thing for me to think about," I said with a sigh.

"We'll figure this out together." He reached across the table and squeezed my hand.

When we finished, we walked back to our room. I felt a little restless with the waiting, and we still had more than twenty-four hours to go before the meeting. I wouldn't have minded being trapped in a room with Emmitt after this morning's kiss, if I'd intended to continue. As it was, I needed a distraction. I recalled Emmitt had thrown my swimsuit in my bag.

"Did you pack a suit, too?"

"I have something that'll work."

Ten minutes later, I stood at the edge of the hotel's indoor pool, hesitantly testing the water's temperature with a toe. Emmitt took a two-step running start to jump in and hooked an arm around me as he passed. Grinning widely, he twisted in the air so he landed first and kept my head above water. I sputtered and laughed.

FEELING SHRIVELED AND WATER LOGGED, we made our way back to our room before lunch. Emmitt called for room service as I rinsed and changed.

Tired from all of the swimming, I suggested watching a movie while we waited. We flipped through the channels, but the movie we wanted to watch didn't start for another hour. We settled for a cooking show while we waited. It just made Emmitt hungrier.

I wasn't surprised when he got up and opened the door before the poor room service boy could even knock. Emmitt pretty much ripped the food from his hands, tossed him the tip, and closed the door in his face.

"Remind me not to forget to feed you. You turn a bit feral."

He just grunted at me as he tore into his burger.

We ended up watching two movies back-to-back, reclining on our stacks of pillows. Of course, we were on the same bed. Emmitt wouldn't have it any other way. He took every opportunity to touch me, random touches as if to assure himself I lay next to him.

By the time the second movie's credits were rolling, Emmitt's stomach growled again.

"Why don't you call in an order at the restaurant next door then run and get it? We can watch this next movie, then. If you're fast, you won't miss much," I said.

He called in the order and groaned when they said it'd be ready in thirty minutes. We settled next to each other on our bellies to watch TV, but his stomach kept getting louder.

"You need to think about something else so we can hear the movie," I said with a laugh.

"I can't. I'm hungry, and someone down the hall had pizza delivered."

I leaned over and nipped his earlobe. He let out a defeated sigh and turned toward me.

"I thought I wasn't supposed to think about that, either."

I grinned at him then turned back to the movie. His stomach was quieter, but he kept moving around on the bed, uncomfortable on his abdomen. When he got up to leave, I crooked my finger at him. He obligingly bent down, and I sweetly kissed him.

"Hurry back or you'll miss the rest of the movie."

"I'd rather stay here and skip the movie and the food."

"Ha! You're only saying that because you're distracted from how hungry you are. Go. I'll be here when you get back."

CHAPTER EIGHTEEN

LESS THAN A MINUTE AFTER EMMITT LEFT, A SOFT TAP SOUNDED AT the door. I smiled to myself and sprang off the bed. Emmitt must have·used his super speed, I thought as I pulled open the door.

My smile fled when I saw Frank's cocky grin. Shirtless, barefoot, and sweaty, he looked as mean and ugly as I remembered. I tried to slam the door in his face, but he moved too fast. He thrust his arm in the opening and shoved. I stumbled back, catching myself before I fell. His angry, bloodshot eyes narrowed on me as he advanced a step into the room.

The last time I'd seen him, the dim lighting of the backyard had spared me a detailed view. This time, the florescent light of the vanity cast him into harsh focus. The ragged cutoffs he wore were a superficial token at being clothed. They had more holes than actual material. From the amount of dirt and other unknown stains, he'd most likely pulled them out of the trash somewhere after shifting from his fur.

I glanced around the room, looking for something I could use to defend myself before my brain kicked in. There was no use fighting him. The best I could do was hope for Emmitt's arrival. I started to scream Emmitt's name, but Frank clapped his hand over my mouth before I could form the second syllable.

"Time to go," he growled as he grabbed me. His fingers bit into my arms as he tossed me over his shoulder. I landed forcefully on my stomach and grunted in pain. I quickly braced my arms on his lower back to alleviate the throbbing ache, then I filled my lungs for a second yell.

Frank suddenly turned and took off at high speed out the door. The abrupt turn sent me swinging to the side, and my head connected with the doorjamb so hard my vision tunneled. I hung limply for a few stunned moments and struggled to think coherently. Another hit to the head would knock me out. I feebly wrapped my arms around his waist and pulled myself in closely. I couldn't let go and hit my head a second time. Being unconscious was not an option. I closed my eyes against the growing nausea, forgetting to call for help.

He turned several times, then I felt cool, fresh air as he began to run faster. My hair flew out behind us, and I held on tight.

With my head so close to him, I couldn't help but notice his smell. My stomach continued to churn unbearably. He smelled like leftover soup, the kind that was slowly shoved to the back of the refrigerator and found three weeks later.

Bile rose, or rather, fell. If he didn't put me down soon, I would throw up all over his back. I couldn't decide if it would help the smell or not.

He stopped abruptly and turned sharply again so my head flew out, despite my hold, and connected with something solid again. I slowly registered the sound of an idling engine as he gave a mocking laugh. Dark spots further clouded my vision as he lifted me from his shoulder.

We stood by the back door of a car. I could see blood on the back quarter panel. My blood. He opened the door and shoved me forward. I reached out to brace myself as everything went black and my legs crumpled under me.

WHEN I CAME TO, my cheek was stuck to the vinyl of the back seat. Before I could lift my head, the car stopped unexpectedly, and I flew from my semi-sprawled position to the floor. I felt too sick to move. My head pounded steadily, matching the rhythm of my heart.

A door opened and closed. A moment later, the door by my feet opened. I hadn't even tried opening my eyes yet, but the feel of his rough hands clamping around my ankles motivated me. He violently pulled me out before I had time to reach for anything.

My chin thumped on the tan carpet of the middle floor divider, and I bit my tongue. Once my waist cleared the door, he stopped pulling, picked me up, and tossed me over his shoulder again. I groaned but was grateful he hadn't yanked me all the way out of the car. Landing face first on the asphalt would have been much worse than having a shoulder planted into an already bruised stomach.

My fear raised a notch when he turned and started walking again. I wanted to fight but my arms felt like noodles when I attempted to brace them on his back once more. He opened a door and dropped me onto a wooden chair.

I tried to scramble from the chair but was slow and clumsy. He used one hand to pin me in place and the other to zip tie one of my ankles to a chair leg. When I realized he intended to bind me, I fought harder. I connected a fist to the side of his head. It bruised my hand, but he didn't even notice the blow.

Desperate, I bit his arm and gave a disgusted cry when he groaned in pleasure. It guaranteed there'd be no more biting on my part. I tried kicking with my free leg, but he just caught it and zip tied it to the other chair leg.

He slowly backed away. Hurting and out of breath, I stared at him as he stalked to the window. He moved the curtain aside with his finger to create a minute gap and checked outside. Satisfied with whatever he saw, he moved away from the window.

"I'll leave your hands free and your mouth ungagged if you behave," he said as he sat on the bed.

"You need a shower," I slurred, angry at him and at the taste of rotten soup now in my mouth. My vision swam dangerously as I panted in pain.

"Your coy invitations won't work on me. You smell like him, you know."

I stared at him for a moment, shocked. Who would have guessed he'd know how to use the word coy?

Then, I turned away from him, not wanting to hear how I smelled like Emmitt. How long had I been out? Was there even the slightest chance Emmitt had heard me scream?

I carefully looked around the old hotel room. The blue curtains and worn carpet matched the faded paisley comforter on the bowed bed. Streaks of yellow from the prior occupants' smoking habits ran down the once white walls of the room. Mustiness, sweat, and stale smoke permeated the air.

When I turned too far, trying to look behind me, I winced at the pain in my stomach and head.

I turned to look at Frank again. He'd been studying me while I examined the room.

"How soon until Blake gets here?" I asked.

He grinned nastily. "It'll be awhile. He's out of town trying to tie up two loose ends."

I knew he was talking about my brothers so I smiled back sickly-sweet, not letting a hint of fear or concern show. "He'll be back soon, then. There's no way he's going to get them now, not without exposing himself to a whole lot of angry werewolves."

Frank narrowed his eyes at me again. "You're choosing the wrong side in this, Michelle. You side with those mongrels, and you'll get hurt."

"Hate to break it to you, but you're the same mongrel." And I was already hurt.

He grunted his disbelief. "We may have started out the same many millennia ago, but we are nothing alike now. When this is over, it will be the Urbat who rule the earth, not you humans or the werewolves."

He got up and walked over to me. Grabbing my arms, he forced me to overlap my hands so he could zip tie them together. So much for leaving my hands free, I thought as the small strip of plastic bit into my tender flesh. It was just one more pain to add to the list. The worst, by far, was my head. When I turned, I could feel a slight tug on the back of my neck where dried blood had glued my hair to my skin.

He stepped back, putting distance between us. "I think you're right; I do need a shower. I need to wash your deluded filth from me."

Despite his appearances, I was beginning to see he was no idiot, just crazy.

"I'm not the deluded one here, Frank. You are if you think you're going to rule the world. You may be strong, but there are more humans than you can deal with. And you know it, or you wouldn't be hiding the fact you're a werewolf."

"You know nothing. You're just a tiny, insignificant piece in a global puzzle."

"There is no puzzle, just a greedy, crazy werewolf leading other crazy, greedy werewolves. And if I'm so insignificant, then why take me? Let me go."

"The only crazy thing about Blake was his decision to let Richard keep you for four years. Your time's up. We've waited long enough for you to come to the right decision on your own. Now, we will decide for you. We'll start with you, and then we'll help the rest of your sisters. We will stop this cycle, and a judgment will be made."

He slowly approached me with a wild light in his eyes. He didn't look upset anymore, and that worried me. He slowly knelt in front of me, spreading my knees so his hips were against the chair. His stench was overwhelming.

"You can end this now." He tilted his neck so I could see the dirt rings there.

"Claim me. I will raise your brothers to be strong, not the little weaklings Richard made them."

They were *not* weaklings. The courage they'd displayed when I'd run with them and when David had found us again, was undeniable. Weaklings were men like Frank and Blake who bullied and hurt people. Torn on how to respond, I simply chose to turn away from him. Spitting in his eye like I wanted to do would probably just result in more bleeding on my part.

He growled furiously and shoved himself to his feet. I watched him from the corner of my eye. At first, I thought he would hit me and inwardly cringed. After a moment, he seemed to calm himself and swung away to move toward the bathroom. He left the door open, no doubt so he could hear me. I averted my eyes and thought back to what he'd said.

He was right. I didn't know anything. What sisters was he talking about? I was an only child from my father and had two brothers from my mom. No sisters. And what was an Urbat? He made it sound different from a werewolf.

Perhaps I didn't need Blake. It seemed Frank had some answers, too. I just needed to figure out how to get them. The thought of being nice to him made my stomach roll. Maybe it wouldn't be so bad once he was clean.

The water turned on, and the shower curtain rustled. I risked a quick glance at the bathroom where I, thankfully, couldn't see him, then turned to look for something that might help me get out of the ties. Even the slightest tug hurt so I didn't try too hard. What was the point if I bruised myself so badly I couldn't run? I knew they wanted me alive. I was too valuable to them, which was probably why I hadn't been hurt worse.

The sudden silence from the bathroom brought me back from my thoughts. There was no way his shower had been long enough to get rid of the smell. I quickly turned away, afraid he'd come marching out in the nude. I grew nervous when he didn't make any noise for several minutes.

"Afraid you'll see something you like?" His voice, inches from my ear, startled me.

I squeezed my eyes shut and answered with more bravado than I felt. "Hardly. I just don't think my stomach can take much more—"

He smacked me upside the back of the head, stopping the rest of my comment. I winced and swallowed hard against the pain. It could have been worse.

Risking another smack, I kept talking, hoping he'd give away some useful information. "You know, it's that kind of treatment that had me running in the first place. If you wanted me to stay, you could have tried some kindness."

"Richard and your brothers were your kindness. You were allowed to stay with your brothers, yet you still resented the monthly Introductions. You were provided for and kept safe. What more do you think you needed?"

Think? My estimation of his intelligence dipped.

"My freedom," I said, risking a look.

He wore the same dirty cutoffs and stood near the bed. Most of the grime that had coated his skin was gone. I wasn't about to trust the smell had disappeared, too.

"And what would you have done with your freedom?" He tilted his head as if really interested in my answer.

"If I would have had it from the beginning, simple things, like shop for my own clothes or take the boys to the park."

He considered me for a moment. "What if it would've been given to you later?"

There was no point answering because his smug expression said it all. We both knew I would have run. What did he really expect? How long could you treat a person like a prisoner before they started dreaming of escape?

His pocket buzzed softly. Given his state of dress, I would have never guessed he owned a cell phone. He dug it out and answered it abruptly. He listened for a moment then started to pace. As he moved, he kept eye contact with me. It was like watching a lion at the zoo. I wished I had werewolf hearing. Whatever the caller said, Frank didn't like it. His face flushed and a low growl erupted from him.

"Get rid of him. I don't want to hear from you again until he's dead." He slid the phone closed, ending the conversation as abruptly as he'd begun.

Hope flooded me. He could only be talking about Emmitt. I frowned, and hope turned to worry. Someone was helping Frank and had seen Emmitt. I wondered if Grey and Carlos were with him. I needed to distract Frank from planning anything further.

"What is an Urbat, Frank? And what decision were you waiting for me to make?"

"If Blake wants you to know, he'll tell you." He continued to pace, his steps agitated. He occasionally stopped by the window to look out the gap in the curtain.

I thought quickly. "It has to do with Claiming one of you...the men he brought to dinner, doesn't it?" I asked. "Why does Blake want me to Claim one of you? Why not Emmitt?"

"The puppet has a brain. Impressive."

I wasn't getting enough of his attention. "How could I have ever thought of any of you in that way? I was fifteen when all that started." Frank ignored me so I tried again.

"What's so important about Claiming one of you? He already had me under his control."

"Hardly. Mated to one of us, you'd never be able to run and hide like you did. We'd sense exactly where you were and come for you. That is control. But that's not the real reason."

He started walking toward me but paused before he made it halfway. He tilted his head as if he heard something. I'd seen that same look on Emmitt; Frank listened to something I couldn't hear.

I glanced toward the door. A crackling noise filled the air as the wood bulged. A moment later, the door flew inward and hit the wall with a loud thud.

Emmitt stood in the opening, outlined by the fading light of the sun. His grey t-shirt sported several tears and bloody patches. The rips exposed skin that was blemish free so I knew the blood wasn't his. He did, however, have a bruise shadowing his jaw under his emerging whiskers.

His gaze skimmed over me before it locked on Frank. Anger boiled beneath Emmitt's features. He flexed his hands. His usual pink, blunt cut nails extended into long, lethal grey claws.

Frank crouched and rolled his shoulders. Spotty patches of fur erupted from his skin and the tips of his now pointy ears. One leg started to transform, the thigh shortening while the foot elongated.

Tendons stood out on Emmitt's neck as his canines burst forth from his mouth. His face started to shift, elongating slightly, making room for his teeth. I could barely understand him when he spoke.

"Your mistake was her blood," he growled just before he lunged for Frank.

They met, snarling in the center of the room. Emmitt grabbed Frank by the shoulders and pulled him in for a head-butt before Frank could swipe at him. I cringed at the sound of the solid thunk, but Emmitt didn't seem fazed. Frank, however, staggered—partially due to his foot. Emmitt lashed out toward Frank's chest in a move so fast I almost didn't catch it. Frank leapt out of the way.

There wasn't much room for them to maneuver as they circled each other looking for openings. Emmitt seemed to be waiting for Frank to do something.

When Frank's back was to the door, Frank lashed out with his right fist just after feinting with his left.

Emmitt dodged Frank's swing, ducked under it, and raked his claws over Frank's exposed side. Four bloody furrows erupted. Frank swore. His control slipped, and his feet fully sprouted claws and fur. Frank started panting with the effort.

Emmitt gave him no opportunity to recover. Instead, he pushed Frank harder, striking repeatedly with his claws, once even biting. Frank didn't moan in pleasure, then. His howl of rage ricocheted off the walls.

Through the damaged hotel door, I saw the parking lot lights click on and watched three men run from the main office.

"People are coming," I said to both Frank and Emmitt. They couldn't be caught fighting in their current state.

Emmitt nodded slightly and blocked Frank's swing with his left forearm. He drove his right fist into Frank's face. There was a sickening crack as Frank's head whipped back. I glanced at the door again as he staggered.

The men were halfway across the parking lot. One of them spotted me tied to the chair and pointed.

An odd raspy exhale drew my attention back to Frank just in time to watch him fall hard. His eyes rolled back into his head. His face bled from several scratches. His nose bled, too. It was badly broken. I had a feeling Emmitt had been toying with Frank up until that final blow.

The air in the room stirred as Emmitt used his supernatural speed to turn and slam the door shut. He bolted it before the men could reach it. Just as quickly, he moved to me.

The men reached the door and started pounding on it.

Emmitt softly swore when he saw my hands. He knelt and carefully used his teeth to bite through the plastic.

Frank groaned on the floor.

"Hurry, Emmitt. I think he's waking up."

The pounding on the door stopped, and I could hear sirens in the distance. The plastic band on my wrists popped free, and Emmitt moved to the ones around my ankles. There, he used his claws to rip through the plastic quickly. I was sure the sharp tug would leave a mark.

Emmitt stood and yanked the curtains back from the window directly behind me.

I struggled to my feet, cringing at the pain in my head and stomach. The room tilted dangerously as I hobbled toward the window.

The motel was set on a slight slope. From here, the room afforded a view of a swamp. Emmitt slid the window open. We were only four feet off the ground. He popped out the screen as the sirens grew to their loudest then stopped altogether. The sudden silence was eerie.

I turned and shuffled toward Frank. The movement made me nauseous, and I had to fight the urge to vomit. I reached into his pocket, and wrapped my fingers around his phone. I hoped it contained Blake's number.

Frank twitched on the floor, opening one eye to look at me. Panic flared until I noticed Frank's wolf parts shift back to normal man parts. I breathed a sigh of relief. Frank wouldn't do anything; he didn't appear to have the strength even if he wanted to. He looked like hell, and part of me actually felt sorry for him.

"Don't try this again," I said. "I choose who I Claim. Not you." With effort, I straightened away from him. My stomach cramped from his rough treatment.

"You're not the only one," Frank said, sounding nasal. He closed his eyes again.

I moved away from him as I tucked the phone into my pocket. Emmitt waited patiently by the window. When I got close, he scooped me into his arms; and I suppressed a flinch.

Knowing his intent, I looped my arms around his neck and buried my face against his chest. I felt him jump out the window and then the rush of wind in my hair.

Risking a peek over his shoulder, I watched the motel fall behind.

HE RAN FOR A LONG TIME. First, through the marsh behind the motel, then through the trees that bordered people's backyards. When we eventually came to a business area, night had fallen; and he ran on the sidewalk or through parking lots. He moved with stealthy speed, keeping to the shadows. No one noticed us.

I had no idea how much time passed, but he finally slowed from a run to a walk. Lifting my head, I saw we were in a bad area near another sleazy looking motel. Emmitt held me with one arm as he opened the door for us. He didn't seem inclined to let me down, and I was glad. I had no shoes, and the floor looked like it hadn't been cleaned. Ever.

The man behind the desk eyed Emmitt and then me.

"We need a room for an hour," Emmitt said quietly, his voice back to normal. "I need soap and a towel. A clean one." He set money on the counter, and the man nodded. He reached under the counter, handing Emmitt soap and a towel along with a key.

I reached out and grabbed everything. The man cleared his throat uncomfortably, looking at me.

"You okay, lady?"

"I am now," I said as Emmitt turned away. I rested my head on his chest as he climbed a dimly lit set of stairs.

He opened the door for us, and I eyed the room, dismayed to see it in worse condition than the one Frank had used. The air conditioner rattled ominously, obviously not circulating the dank, musty air that saturated the room. The bed, though made, looked rumpled.

Emmitt carried me straight to the bathroom. When Emmitt elbowed the light switch, only one of the three vanity lights flickered on. Stains decorated the laminate counter around the once white sink. He didn't seem to notice.

He sat me on the counter, and I tried not to flinch as places that I'd thought fine started to ache.

He wet the towel and rubbed the soap against it. Carefully, he cleaned the blood from my face and hair, avoiding the gash on the back of my head. He worked quickly, but gently. I didn't say anything. Instead, I focused on his face as he concentrated on me. I loved watching him. He'd never been this serious around me before. When he was close to finished, I realized he hadn't met my gaze yet.

Ignoring what he was doing, I leaned forward and pressed my lips to his. He grunted in surprise but didn't disappoint me. He kissed me tenderly. His fingers ever so lightly touched my jawline. Soon every ache and scrape I had faded to the background. All I could feel and taste was Emmitt. I sighed contentedly. He pulled back from my kiss.

I opened my eyes to find him watching me.

"That's more like it," I said with a slight smile. "If you tell me we don't have to sleep here, we can kiss all night long."

My comment seemed to upset him. His brows drew down slightly, his expression, unreadable. "How can you even want to look at me?"

It was my turn to make a face. "What do you mean?"

"I promised you, you would be safe."

He started to turn away, but I grabbed his arm, stopping him. It hurt my wrist. "You're beating yourself up because I was dumb enough to open the door for Frank?"

He turned toward me again, frustration plain on his face.

I shook my head at him. I wasn't mad. How could I be? Emmitt had found me before anything really bad had happened.

"To me, safe doesn't mean I'll never get hurt. It means you'll be there to help pick me back up when I do. Now, do we really have to stay here?" I remained on the counter, not wanting to step on the bathroom floor without shoes.

A slight smile lifted his lips. "This was just to get you cleaned up. I couldn't take you anywhere nicer, looking like you did, without someone calling the police."

He grabbed the towel and started to rinse it. Vivid pink water ran down the drain. I wondered how I'd looked to the guy downstairs. I hoped he wasn't calling the police. Regardless, we had to keep moving.

"Frank got a call while I was with him. Were you followed?"

"Not for very long. I met up with Carlos and Grey on my way back with our food. As soon as we entered the lobby, I smelled your blood." He rang out the towel and folded it neatly beside the sink. "We tracked you. A few of Frank's friends were waiting. Grey and Carlos stayed back to deal with them."

"So, now what? Are they meeting up with us somewhere? Do you think the guy downstairs is going to call the cops?"

"Now, we go to another hotel. You'll be harder to follow by scent without the fresh blood. I'll call my father to make arrangements when we find a payphone. He'll coordinate with Grey."

Just then, the phone in my pocket started to buzz. Pulling it out, I looked at the screen. I didn't recognize the number but didn't expect to, considering the phone belonged to Frank.

I met Emmitt's gaze as I answered it.

"Michelle," Blake's voice boomed through the receiver. "Good to hear you sounding so well. I was afraid Frank might have been a bit rough." His voice conveyed no concern.

"He was as gentle as a lamb," I said it without inflection, but Emmitt's face grew red again. "Why are you calling, Blake?"

"Isn't this why you took Frank's phone? To talk to me?"

So, Frank had managed to get out and call Blake. I'd hoped he sat in a jail cell somewhere by now.

"I guess it is. I have a lot of questions and, according to Frank, you're the only one who will answer them. What's an Urbat? What decision was I supposed to make, and who are my sisters?"

There was a long pause before he answered. "Ah. I see. I'll explain everything if you meet with me." He sounded confident and reassuring.

"I'm already meeting with you. Tomorrow morning. Didn't the lawyer call you?"

"Yes, of course." A hard edge crept into his voice. "I was hoping for something a bit more private."

"I don't think that'd be in my best interest. At least, not until I Claim my Mate."

Emmitt's anger vanished as I spoke. Instead, he appeared slightly sad. I wished I knew what he was thinking.

Blake's frustrated growl distracted me, and I smiled. "Come on, Blake. You don't think I'm going to sit around and wait for you to try this again, do you?"

"Then, we part ways for now. You'll hear from me again, though."

Before he could hang up, I added, "Oh, and I spoke with the court appointed executor. Looks like you'll have to spend your own money and leave mine alone."

He wasn't quick enough to disconnect the call. I heard him swear before the line went dead.

I tossed the phone in the garbage and smiled at Emmitt. He shook his head at me in disbelief and plucked me from the counter.

CHAPTER NINETEEN

IN LESS THAN OUR ALLOTTED HOUR, WE LEFT THE SEEDY HOTEL.
Emmitt once more cradled me in his arms as he ran carefully, sticking to the
shadows and putting distance between the hotel and us.

Even with his smooth pace, my head throbbed with each step. Nausea
continued to roll in my tender stomach. I didn't acknowledge any of it because I
knew he was worried; I felt him look down at me several times.

"I'm okay," I said running my fingers through the hair at the base of his
skull.

He lightly kissed the top of my head.

A few minutes later, we found a payphone. I held the receiver to Emmitt's
ear and dialed since he wouldn't put me down. I didn't mind. The position
allowed me to lean close and listen to the conversation.

Emmitt's father let out a relieved breath when he heard Emmitt's hello.

"Grey called," Thomas said. "He and Carlos dealt with your would-be
followers. Are you two safe?"

"Are my brothers safe?" I asked before Emmitt could answer.

"They are. We had two incidents earlier, but everything is quiet now. Mary
and Gregory are with the boys, and several of our pack are patrolling."

I sagged with relief.

"Michelle's been hurt," Emmitt said, his voice deceptively calm. He shushed
me when I tried to insist I felt fine. "She needs to rest."

448

I heard Thomas cover the phone with his hand. A murmur of voices continued for several seconds before Thomas came back on and asked us to wait while Charlene booked us another room. I could hear Charlene speaking rapidly in the background but couldn't make out the words. After a few minutes, Thomas gave Emmitt directions to a new hotel.

"Emmitt, be careful." There was a lot of love in those three words.

"We will," Emmitt said.

I hung up the phone, and Emmitt took me by surprise with a long kiss. He poured his relief into it, tenderly holding me close. In the distance, someone shouted encouragement. It cooled the moment. Emmitt pulled away and rested his forehead against mine, breathing deeply.

"I won't be able to let you go for a while."

I kissed his cheek in response. He walked away from the phone, carrying me snugly. Once he reached the shadows of a side street, he sprinted away from our audience.

A SMILING attendant greeted us outside the new hotel and moved to open the door for Emmitt as we approached. I felt silly being carried but didn't try to get Emmitt to put me down, yet.

The red and gold patterned carpet in the expansive reception area muffled Emmitt's steps, and every piece of highly polished metal we passed gleamed in the lights.

The person behind the desk welcomed us with a smile. "Mr. Cole. Good to see you. Your mother's description was very accurate." The man held out a room card, which I accepted on Emmitt's behalf. "Room service will be up with your meal. Please let me know if you need anything else. I hope you enjoy your stay."

Neither Emmitt nor I said anything for a moment. I wondered what Emmitt's mom had done or said to have completely registered us before our arrival. The man should have at least made us sign something.

As long as he was being accommodating, I decided to see if he could help a little more. "Do you think someone could get me some socks and shoes? I lost mine."

The man smiled serenely and nodded as if it were an everyday occurrence to have a guest request shoes. "I'll have something delivered as soon as possible."

I thanked the man, then Emmitt turned away, heading toward the bank of elevators. I pressed the button for Emmitt, and he stepped in as soon as the doors slid open. After checking the number on the room card's envelope, I selected the top floor. The doors slid shut, and the elevator started moving.

"Could you set me down? I don't want to attract any more attention than we already have."

He grudgingly obliged, but as soon as he set me on my feet, he wrapped my hand in his and rubbed his thumb in slow circles against the pulse in my wrist. I stood carefully, trying not to wince at the aches I felt.

When the elevator chimed and the doors whispered open, Emmitt breathed deeply before we both stepped out into a deserted hallway.

"Are we okay here?" I asked softly. I didn't think he'd scented anything but after being taken once, I was feeling cautious.

He pointed to a camera mounted just outside the elevator. "Better security."

He led me left from the elevator. Our movements were strangely hushed, making me feel like we were in a library rather than a hotel. Several feet down the hallway, just before the first numbered door, I noticed another camera. This hotel definitely had more security. And more space. The doors were so far apart, I wondered what kind of room Charlene had gotten for us.

Our room card opened the second door on the right side of the hall. Decorated in neutral colors with black accents, the suite not only looked clean but smelled clean, too. The door closed behind us with a click. After one last swipe of his thumb, Emmitt released my hand.

The light cream walls of the kitchenette flowed into the main room where a fireplace danced with electric flames. The leather sofa and oversized chair beckoned, but I hesitated to step from the dark laminate floor that ran from the entry door to the light carpet. I didn't want to leave dirty footprints.

I noticed a bathroom through an open door to the right. It was immaculately clean, and I stared in grateful appreciation. Three times larger than the one at home, it had a glass corner shower with dual shower heads, a whirlpool tub big enough for two, and a heated towel rack.

"I call dibs on the tub," I whispered, half-reverently.

Emmitt laughed but didn't follow me as I drifted into the bathroom, flicking on the lights. I moved to the tub and turned on the water. Fluffy, white towels sat on the tub's ledge along with a pair of white robes.

When I saw the robe, I paused. It struck a familiar chord, but I couldn't place why. Given the other crappy hotels, I was sure it hadn't been because of them. I continued staring at it. Seeing it didn't alarm me; it made me feel like I'd forgotten something important.

Absently, I wandered from the bathroom, forgetting to worry about my feet as I looked around again. Nothing in the kitchen or living area looked familiar, and I started to doubt the odd feeling I'd gotten.

Emmitt, who sat on the sofa, lifted his head from his hands and watched me with a sad light in his gaze. I crossed the carpet, sat beside him, and rested my head on his shoulder.

"Don't dwell on the past. It doesn't do any good."

He kissed my forehead. "Go take your bath."

Reaching around him, I gave him a quick hug then got up to inspect the bedroom.

"What are you doing?" he asked with curiosity in his voice.

"Just checking things out. Something seemed familiar, and I can't figure out why."

I moved to the doorway and froze. The king-sized bed with a white down comforter dominated the room. Two towels folded into swans faced each other at the end of the bed. Their heads and necks formed a heart. On the wall above the bed, a black, white, and brown abstract painting hung. To the left, long black and brown patterned curtains dominated the wall.

This was the room from the vision where I bit Emmitt. My stomach dropped, and a blush consumed my face. My stomach continued twisting nervously, and my heart gave a quick unsteady beat.

"Are you okay?" Emmitt asked quietly from behind me.

Startled, I jumped and turned. "Yep. Fine. I'm going to rinse in the shower then take a nice long soak. Let me know when the food's here, okay?" My gaze drifted to his throat briefly before I forced it back to his eyes.

He tilted his head, probably trying to figure out what I wasn't saying. I just smiled nervously and moved to step around him. He mirrored my move, blocking me.

"Michelle, tell me. What is it? Should we leave? Find another room?" Concern etched his face.

Despite my discomfort, I couldn't let him worry. I wrapped my arms around his waist and laid my head on his chest. His heart beat strong and steady. Mine still raced.

"No. The room is fine. I just connected it with a vision I had."

"What was the vision about?"

I made a face against his chest, not wanting to say anything, but knowing he'd think the worst, if I didn't.

"You and me." I pulled away, feeling nervous. Then, the filter between my brain and my mouth broke. Every thought that crossed my mind spilled from me unedited.

"I don't want to bite you. I don't care if it looked like you liked it or not. It's going to hurt you, and I just don't think I can do it. Not yet."

He quickly masked his shocked expression and didn't try to stop me when I fled toward the bathroom. I wasn't nervous about being "engaged" to Emmitt. The biting part scared me. I'd bit Frank because I was angry and desperate. I'd meant it to hurt him. Granted it hadn't, and all I had to show for it was the lingering taste of rotten soup in my mouth, but still...

I glanced back at Emmitt just before I stepped into the bathroom. He watched me with concern. I'd put him through enough lately, and as I turned away, I wished I could take back my mental spill.

I left the door ajar for comfort; I needed to be able to hear him moving around out there. Though I wasn't about to let myself dwell on the mistake I'd made when I'd opened the door for Frank, I wouldn't soon forget the fear.

The tub was at least halfway full, so I shut it off and moved to the shower. I was about to peel off my clothes when I realized they were the only ones I had. The hotel probably had a laundry service but what would they think of the blood that smattered my shirt? I stepped out of my shorts, but kept the rest on as I ducked in under the spray. First, I peeled off the shirt, cleaning it with shampoo until the bloodstains were gone. Then I rinsed my under things. I wrung everything out and hung the clothes over the glass shower door.

The water ran pink again when I washed my hair. Would I really be Claiming Emmitt tonight with a head injury? What kind of crazed person was I? The word "tonight" echoed in my head. I needed to think about something else. I needed a toothbrush.

I ran my fingers along my scalp to assess the damage. Wincing at the sting of the shampoo, I determined the blood was from a scrape rather than a cut. Relieved there wouldn't be a need for stitches, I hurried to rinse. Then I washed my mouth out with soap.

Free of the blood and Frank's lingering smell, I quickly moved to the tub and eased into the hot water. When I started the jets, the water churned so much, the level rose to the rim. I leaned back and sank down so it lapped at my chin. Slowly, I began to relax.

My mind drifted to everything Frank had said and the call with Blake. Talking to Blake hadn't been as helpful as I'd hoped. Could I trust that he'd really given up on me for now? I thought so. At least, Frank's comment about me not being the only one made it a possibility. Yet, I wondered what "sisters" I had that Blake meant to find. It disturbed me to think of another woman having to deal with Blake like I had, as much as it frustrated me that I hadn't gotten the answers I wanted. I had a lot to share with the group when we got back, though. Maybe some of them would have more insight.

The water hadn't even had time to cool when I heard a knock on the outer door. I fumbled with the jets, turning them off, and listened. Emmitt walked by the bathroom door. I sunk low in the water, but he only pulled the door shut as he passed.

I left the water as quietly as possible, grabbed a towel, and quickly dried off. All the while, I strained to hear anything. Was it too quiet out there? I tossed on the robe, crept toward the door, and pressed my ear against its surface.

"Food's here."

I jumped at the sound of Emmitt's voice directly on the other side of the door and yanked it open in time to catch his slight smirk.

"Not funny." I pulled the belt tightly around my waist and flinched when my bruised stomach immediately protested.

His expression grew serious, and he looked me over as I loosened the belt. When his eyes lingered on the side of my head, I turned slightly to show him the scrape.

"It's not as bad as I thought," I said turning to look at him again. He wasn't eyeing my head anymore, but the robe. Too late, I realized what I'd done. The vision had shown me in a robe.

Before I could become more nervous, he indicated the food he'd set out on the kitchenette's island. His mother had ordered steaks topped with blue cheese, sides of mushrooms, and baked potatoes with the works. There were three full meals. My tender stomach rebelled at the thought of eating so much, but I knew it wasn't all for me. Emmitt needed more food due to the miles he'd covered.

I settled on one of the stools, heard a clink, and looked down to see one of the meals already set in front of me. I opened my mouth to argue, but Emmitt gave me a warning look. Was I two-years-old, now? Yet, I kept quiet about why I didn't want to eat.

The scrape on my head and marks on my wrists and ankles were enough for him to worry over. I wasn't about to give him a full inventory of my aches so he could dwell on each one. He was already upset Frank had gotten me. If he knew the extent of it, he'd just feel worse.

We ate in silence. I picked at the meal, eating a few bites from everything before pushing it away. Emmitt reached for my plate, scraped it together with what was left of his second meal, then put the leftovers in the refrigerator.

Hunger satisfied, I leaned against the counter, propped my head up with my hand, and fought to keep my eyes open. Funny that I'd started out the day thinking it'd be boring when it'd been anything but boring. Banged around, kidnapped, rescued, carried for miles, I needed sleep. I yawned hugely and tried to smother it with my hand. I wasn't ready to go to the bedroom, yet. No matter how tired I was, I couldn't forget my vision.

Emmitt noticed my yawn. He had me up in his arms before I could blink.

"I'm not tired," I protested. We both knew that was a lie.

He looked down at me for a moment. I gazed back, my fingers nervously plucking at the fabric of his shirt. It had a small bloodstain on it, too.

"Frank didn't hurt you, did he?" I asked, feeling horrible for not asking sooner.

He gave a pained laugh then leaned in to kiss me. A light kiss. He pulled back and searched my face, his expression bittersweet and sad.

I didn't want him to be sad. We'd made it safely away from Frank, and we were together. I pressed my hand against his shirt over the steady beat of his heart. Together was what mattered.

I slid a hand to the back of his neck and pulled him down for another kiss. His lips feathered over mine, and I sighed, reassured. It was too sweet to pull away even though my heart started to hammer and my face flushed.

His lips moved over mine, hesitantly at first then more aggressively, as he held me in his arms. He stole my breath with his passion, and his desperation caught fire in me. I feathered my fingers through his short hair, while I explored the curve of his shoulder and ridges of his arm with my other hand.

I barely noticed when he lay me down on the mattress. I hadn't even been aware we'd moved. He continued kissing me, forearms braced on either side of me, careful not to hurt me further. With my hands free, I tugged his shirt up to smooth my fingers over his stomach.

I'd lost control over the situation. Not that it mattered. He was doing a wonderful job of taking me to that magical place where just the two of us existed.

He smoothed a gentle hand over my hair then trailed his fingers down to toy with the sensitive skin of my neck. Chills danced along my skin. I broke away from his kiss to pant for a quick breath. Before I could recapture his lips, he proceeded to kiss my brow, then my temple.

The move brought the column of his throat close to my mouth. I strained forward slightly and kissed him just below his jaw. He froze above me, and fine tremors shook the bed.

Something about him, about this, called to me. I tentatively ran the tip of my tongue over his skin.

"I don't want to hurt you," I whispered, nipping his neck gently.

He groaned in frustration.

"It hurts to wait."

Everything in my vision was happening just as I'd seen. I didn't hurry. I continued to kiss and nip, slowly becoming the aggressor. He groaned every time my teeth scraped his skin. He kissed my collarbone and shoulder, giving me plenty of room. Bursts of hot need filled me and pushed me closer to what he wanted, to what I wanted. I finally understood biting him was about me making a choice. And I chose him.

I bit down firmly, just enough to break the skin. The bite healed almost instantly. I tenderly kissed where I'd bit him. Mine. He claimed my mouth in a searing kiss then pulled back.

I studied his face, expecting to feel different. My stomach flipped wildly as it always did when I looked at him, but as far as I could tell nothing fundamental had changed. He looked relaxed and very pleased with himself. A feeling of complete contentment washed over me.

"Go to sleep, now," he whispered, shifting me so I lay curled against his side.

Exhaustion caught up with me, and my eyes closed against my will. I frowned sleepily. I wanted more kissing.

He leaned over to place another kiss on my forehead.

"I love you," he murmured in my ear.

I didn't have the energy to respond.

CHAPTER TWENTY

I SLOWLY BECAME AWARE OF EMMITT'S ARM ON MY STOMACH. Although it wasn't extremely heavy, it did rest right on top of the bruised area. I kept my eyes closed, wanting to go back to sleep. If I could just move out from under him and then roll over, I'd probably sleep another hour.

Carefully, I tried rolling away, hoping he'd feel it in his sleep and remove his arm. My stomach cramped. I cringed and gingerly settled onto my back again.

"Might as well open them."

My eyes popped open at the sound of Emmitt's voice. Reclined on his side with his head propped in his right hand, he studied me. He lifted his offending arm and ran his fingers over the skin of my stomach. The skin of my stomach? I let out a squeak. I was supposed to be wearing a robe.

I lifted my head to look, but doing so caused more pain in my already tender stomach. I flopped back down, frowning at the ceiling. Damn, that hurt.

He'd used a bath towel over the robe to cover the important bits, exposing the rest of me. I wanted to be offended, but I knew he'd only been checking me over for injuries.

It wasn't how I'd expected to wake up, but I didn't mind. I remembered what he'd said before I fell asleep. He loved me.

Turning on my pillow, I gave him a shy, sleepy smile. I'd been so busy making sure I was covered, I hadn't noticed his serious expression. Was he still upset about my injuries? I thought he'd gotten over it last night, after I bit him. I blushed thinking of it. My heart stuttered a beat. Had I really Claimed Emmitt?

"You lied to me. You're not fine." His fingers stroked my stomach again, just over the most tender part. "How much pain are you in?"

Ah, so that was it. I looked down again, surprised to see an actual surface bruise. I'd thought it more of a muscle pull. I looked at my wrists. They were tender but not as bad. Given what I'd been through, I thought I was lucky. When Frank had strapped me to the chair, I'd expected far worse.

"Emmitt, I'll live. Don't make a big deal out of this."

He said nothing as I modestly gathered the robe around myself, tied it, then tugged the towel out of the way. Though I wanted to sit up, I knew better than to try. Instead, I rolled to my side, facing him so he could see me, held my stomach with one arm, and used the other to boost myself up. It wasn't a pain free effort. My stomach protested, and boosting hurt my wrist; but I withheld every twinge from my expression.

Emmitt watched me closely from his reclined position, his expression growing more guarded by the moment.

Maneuvering carefully, I turned away from him and eased my legs off the bed. As I sat there, taking a small break, I noticed the time on the alarm clock beside the bed.

"We need to get to the lawyer's office. How long will it take from here?" I paused, looking around the room, remembering the long run. "I don't even know where we are."

"About thirty minutes," he said getting up from the bed and moving to stand near me. His continued guarded expression puzzled me.

"Really, Emmitt, I'm fine," I said to reassure him. He didn't look convinced so I leaned forward, ready to stand and prove it to him.

He quickly offered his hand. I clasped it and was glad for his help. I hadn't been aware of the number of stomach muscles used when standing. If my stomach had felt tender lying there, it now felt like it'd been punched...repeatedly.

He wrapped his arms around me and held me close as I waited for the pain to fade. To distract him, I nipped his neck again. He twitched then pulled back, shaking his head with a small, amused curl to his lips.

With a tender look, he helped me to the bathroom. He left me at the threshold without a word. I closed the door and turned toward the mirror to assess what the reporter would see. The girl in the mirror actually looked better than I felt.

The light bruises on my wrists were easy to overlook, but the scattered bruising on my stomach wasn't. A shirt would cover it, though. Even the injury on my head would be invisible thanks to my hair. I ran my fingers through the tangles on the uninjured side but just smoothed the strands down on the injured side. It was good enough for now.

I brushed my teeth with the new toothbrush that waited for me on the counter then dressed in my freshly laundered clothes. Emmitt must have been awake for a while to have everything ready for me.

My stomach rumbled, and as I opened the door, I wondered if we'd have time to eat the leftovers. It wasn't meant to be. The empty containers filled the small trashcan in the kitchenette, and Emmitt stood waiting for me.

I studied Emmitt. The blood on his shirt was gone too, but he still sported the rips I had noticed last night. Going out in public like that would cause stares.

"We're going to need to get our things," he said, noting the direction of my glance.

I wrinkled my nose but knew he was right. Our plane tickets were still there.

"They dropped these off this morning," he said, showing me a pair of black, slipper flats. He didn't let me take them, but went to a knee to help put them on so I wouldn't need to bend. The flats fit me well enough.

He stood again. "Ready?"

"Just a second."

I walked back into the bedroom to make sure we weren't forgetting anything. Not much to forget since we'd arrived with just the clothes on our backs, but I still felt the need to check. Maybe I simply needed to look at the room one more time.

It was hard not to stare at the bed for a moment as the reality of what I'd done settled over me. Engaged. I didn't really feel engaged. Of all the different ways I'd imagined last night playing out after the bite, it had been completely different than I'd expected.

I wondered when I'd feel something from Emmitt like Nana Wini had mentioned. All I felt at the moment was my complete contentment. I paused. Was I really content? A little. But I felt nervous about meeting the lawyer, tired, and sore, too. I missed my brothers and wanted to get back home.

Emmitt stood in the doorway behind me, watching, and gave me a questioning look. Understanding dawned, and I smiled at him in wonder. It wasn't my contentment I was feeling, but his.

I moved to twine my fingers through his. "I'm ready."

He kissed the back of my hand, and we left the room.

The person at the front desk called a cab for us, and within minutes, we were making our way back to the old hotel. I still worried Blake had lied on the phone and would be waiting either at the hotel or at the lawyer's office. I didn't trust him after everything he'd done to me.

The cab pulled up to the hotel's drop off, and I eyed the building. Everything looked normal from the outside, but I really didn't want to go back in there. Emmitt seemed to sense my concern and told me to wait in the cab while he ran in. It was a nerve-racking wait. I scanned the parking lot around us the whole time. I caught the cabbie looking at me several times and figured I wasn't being as casual about it as I'd hoped. If I'd seen anything, I would have been yelling at the cabby to "go, go, go!" like in the movies.

Thankfully, Emmitt returned before I had to do anything so drastic. Grey and Carlos trailed behind him with their bags. I couldn't believe they had stayed in their old room. What if Blake had come back? I couldn't say anything as they piled in. The cabbie already looked ready to tell me to get out.

Emmitt gave the driver the lawyer's address as he handed me my slack bag. He caught my look at the bag and shrugged.

"There was nothing else worth taking."

I wondered what they'd done to our things and dejectedly faced forward. I wanted to go back home. I wanted Blake to leave me alone for good. I wanted to see my brothers. Above all, I wanted some time with Emmitt where we could just be normal. Well, as normal as an engaged werewolf and human could be.

With Emmitt beside me, I calmed slightly, and we rode in silence to our next stop.

The news crew waited outside the lawyer's office. Carlos and Grey hung back, looking like personal bodyguards. In a way, I guessed that they were.

After the reporter introduced herself, we started talking about my sudden fortune and the cause of it. I had to look appropriately upset since Richard had passed away scarcely a month ago. Thankfully, that topic was short-lived. They recorded most of our conversation, but I knew they'd edit the heck out of it to make it news worthy.

I answered as many questions as I could; and by the time we needed to go in, I'd committed to a charity and an amount. Though I invited the reporter to come inside with us, she declined. She already had the information she needed from the copy of the will she'd acquired and our talk.

Trepidation filled me as I watched her walk away. If the news crew left, were we still safe? Emmitt gently put a hand at the small of my back, a touch of reassurance. So, I smiled and waved as they departed.

When we walked inside, the posh reception area reminded me of Richard's home office. The woman behind a glossy counter looked up at us with a friendly expression.

"Can I help you?"

"I'm here to see Mr. Nolan."

"Michelle?"

"Yes."

She glanced at the four of us as if not sure what to do with such a large group. "Please have a seat."

She picked up the phone and dialed. As she spoke softly, Grey winked at her, a slow lowering of an eyelid accompanied by a slight teasing smile. She paused mid-sentence, obviously having lost her train of thought. I hid a smile behind my hand as she struggled to maintain her end of the conversation.

A moment later, she moved to lead us into Mr. Nolan's office. Grey and Carlos stayed behind in the sitting area. I shot Grey a quick look, hoping he would behave.

When Emmitt and I walked in, Mr. Nolan stood and greeted each of us with a firm handshake. The decor in his office was more down to earth than the reception area. Pictures of his family, including grandkids, perched all over the shelves and desk.

I didn't see Blake and glanced at Emmitt. He seemed completely relaxed. Could Blake have been telling the truth? Was I getting a reprieve? At what cost, though? His comment about parting ways for now, and Frank's comment about getting my sisters worried me. If they were shifting their focus from me to some other poor unsuspecting girls, I'd rather they just stayed chasing me. After all, I had Emmitt. Who knows what the other girls would have for protection.

"Thank you for coming, Ms. Daniels. I'm not sure if you're aware of this, but the reading is just an unnecessary formality. Everything is already in order." He indicated we should have a seat and moved to take his own seat. "I have to admit the only reason I asked to meet was because Mr. Torrin wanted this meeting. I've worked with him in the past in conjunction with some of Mr.

Daniels' interests and know Mr. Torrin can be a bit insistent. So I'm surprised he's not here."

"He's not coming?" I asked.

"No, he called yesterday afternoon to say he wouldn't be able to make it. He wanted to reschedule, but I said we were already committed to this time."

The lawyer didn't read the will but did go over some of the details and some additional information Richard had shared with him before his death. He took his time explaining everything to me and provided some referrals to investors I might want to try. I smiled politely and accepted the information though I had no plans to use it. I wasn't concerned about investing because of my premonitions.

As it stood, my net value was ridiculous. He helped me set up two trusts, one for the werewolves and one for my brothers. If anything happened to me, the money wouldn't be easy for someone else to obtain.

Several hours later, he walked us to the lobby and shook our hands again.

"If you have any questions, big or small, call me. I'll be happy to help."

"Thank you, Mr. Nolan."

He nodded and went back to his office as the receptionist called us another cab.

While we waited outside, my tender stomach grumbled.

"Hungry?" Emmitt asked.

"More homesick than hungry. Can we just go straight to the airport and see if we can get an earlier flight?"

"Of course."

The cab pulled up, and he opened the door for me. I carefully slid in, trying not to strain my bruised stomach.

Emmitt waited until I was settled before climbing in next to me. Both he and Carlos tried not to crowd me.

The complete contentment I'd felt this morning was still there, but something else was creeping in. It wasn't quite worry but close. That, on top of Emmitt's continued reserved behavior, worried me.

"What's wrong?" I asked as we drove toward the airport.

For the most part, the cab driver ignored us. Grey, however, swiveled in his seat to look back at us, a mischievous glint in his eyes. I ignored him and focused on Emmitt, pretending we were alone.

Emmitt glanced at me and shrugged.

I slipped my hand into his and leaned against him. "Is this something I have to figure out for myself? Because, if it is, I have to say it will be awhile. I'm fried. I just want to get home and be with you, my brothers, and...well, my family."

I felt him smile as he leaned down to kiss the top of my head.

"Nothing's wrong."

I looked up at him. "Are you feeling neglected? Like it was a bite and run?"

Grey howled with laughter in the front seat. Carlos calmly told him to turn around or else. It was the most I'd heard Carlos say the whole trip. Carlos acted more like I thought an Elder should act than Grey.

Meanwhile, Emmitt rolled his eyes and gave a slightly pained grin.

"No." He ran his thumb over the back of my hand. "I'm just worried about you."

I gave him a reassuring smile. "I'm here. I'm fine."

I pulled his head down and gave him a long kiss to show him. When I pulled back, I noticed his teeth were starting to extend.

"Enough of that, I think," I said.

He nodded reluctantly, flicking a glance at the driver and the quietly grinning Grey.

THE AIRPORT HADN'T YET FULLY COME to life. Inquiring at the desk, we found a flight leaving in an hour that had four open seats. We booked the flight and checked in so we could look for somewhere to eat within the terminal.

We found a restaurant by following our noses. Both Emmitt and Grey were practically drooling as we crowded into a booth. Grey slid in first and patted the seat next to him while looking at Carlos.

"Come here, honey," he said with a laugh.

Carlos sighed tolerantly and sat down.

I wondered about their story. Though Grey teased about being a couple, I didn't think they were. It seemed like he enjoyed tormenting Carlos, and Carlos put up with it.

I sat across from Grey and shook my head as he and Emmitt both reached for a menu. This was probably the longest I'd seen Emmitt go without eating.

Looking over the menu, I debated what to try. With the ache in my middle, I wasn't sure how much I'd be able to eat. I settled for a BLT with fries. Emmitt, as usual, went big and ordered two half-pound burgers. The server thought he was kidding until Grey and Carlos asked for the same.

I waited until the server walked away then asked something I had been wondering since Emmitt had burst into Frank's hotel room.

"So how did you find me?"

"Your blood," Emmitt said softly. His gaze turned troubled again, and I squeezed his hand.

Grey took up the story. "It was on your room's door. We followed the scent trail out the side door. From there, we picked up the scent of the car. They had eyes watching the route, and we ran into a bit of trouble that slowed us down."

"How many?" If Blake had taken men to the Compound, how many had he left here?

"Enough," Grey answered vaguely. "Not too much for Carlos here to handle." Grey nudged the other man with a grin. Carlos didn't answer. Instead, he turned to look at the baseball game on the television.

"Thank you," I said to both of them. Carlos surprised me by meeting my eyes and nodding.

The server brought us our bill just in time for us to pay and walk back for boarding. I sat between Carlos and Emmitt again. In addition to feeling squished, I felt safe.

The flight was short, but the layover at the connecting airport made up for it. Needing to kill three hours, Emmitt suggested we find somewhere to eat, again. Grey agreed and Carlos gave a shrug.

"That's fine with me, but I want to check in with Liam and Aden first."

They waited in a quiet area with me while I made the call. My brothers were having a blast with Henry and Paul and didn't sound like they'd been aware of any attempts.

Content they were safe, I told my brothers I would see them soon.

CHAPTER TWENTY-ONE

Four hours later, we were back in the car Carlos had driven to the airport. Emmitt and I had the backseat to ourselves. We didn't say much. He sat next to me with an arm around my shoulders. I relaxed into him and watched the trees and fields zip by.

I was excited to be going back home. Well, to the Compound, anyway.

When we finally pulled into the long driveway, I leaned forward to watch for the break in the trees. The sight of my brothers, waiting at the door for us, made my throat tight. I'd missed them more than I'd realized. Mary, Gregory, Henry, and Paul stood just behind them, hands on their shoulders to keep them from running toward us as Carlos parked.

I rushed from the car, ignoring Emmitt's soft laugh, and squatted down in front of the boys to hug them tightly. They clasped me in return and started to tell me about their adventures. I encouraged them to head inside as I listened. I didn't like standing out in the open when I didn't know Blake's whereabouts.

Thomas and Charlene waited just inside for us. Emmitt moved to the side to speak to them. I didn't hear everything but did catch Thomas say something about scenting my Claim, and I started to blush. Liam noticed but didn't say anything.

I smiled at Aden as he continued to tell me about the water balloon fight they had with Paul and Henry. He was quick to add that the water fight had been before Mary told them they had to pick inside games. Poor guys.

When the boys stopped to breathe, Paul and Henry asked if Liam and Aden could have another sleepover. All four looked at me with puppy eyes. I was in no shape to disagree. Aden's energetic hug had pulled my hair and tugged at my wound. I did miss them and knew they missed me, too, but another sleepover was a good idea. My still sore stomach needed rest, and I had a lot to discuss with Charlene and Thomas. So I nodded, and my brothers immediately started to tug Paul and Henry away.

As soon as the boys left, both Charlene and Thomas moved toward me with huge smiles on their faces.

"Welcome to the family," Charlene said, excitement lacing her voice. I was glad she refrained from hugging me. I didn't need a visit to the white room at the moment.

"Thank you. Can we talk?"

"Are you sure you don't want to rest first?" Charlene asked. She knew what I'd been through.

"No, there's a lot I need to share, and I don't know how much time..." I didn't want to say too much more in the open but they needed to know what Blake had said and that there was the potential he could return.

"All right," Thomas said. "Nana Wini is already waiting."

As we made our way to the meeting room, Emmitt ran ahead to drop off our bags. When he returned, he had a sweatshirt for me. I didn't know how he'd known I was getting cold but appreciated that he did. He claimed a quick kiss when he handed it to me. Holding hands, we walked into the meeting room.

Nana Wini sat at the table. I eased myself onto the chair beside her and tried not to wince at the tenderness in my stomach, a pointless effort since everyone in the room watched me closely.

"What happened to you? I can smell blood," Nana said, concerned.

"I ran into a door." I smirked at being able to use that line. No one in the room appreciated my humor. I cleared my throat and looked at Thomas.

"Thank you for keeping Liam and Aden safe. Frank admitted Blake attempted to get them back." I glanced at Nana Wini. "I'm guessing Frank followed us here and called Blake. I think Blake was on his way here while we were going to him. Anyway, when we got to Wisconsin," I gently massaged my head, remembering, "I got a visit from Frank. He's the reason I ran into a door. He took me to another hotel and started saying some weird things...like I was just one piece of a huge puzzle and that they would start with me but get all of my sisters."

"You have sisters?" Nana Wini asked.

"No, I don't. I think he means women like me—us." I met Charlene's eyes. "I've been having visions of other women. So far, there seems to be five of us total. I'm guessing each of us has a unique ability. One of the women seemed to have a calming effect on the crowd around her. The other two were harder to tell." I paused, thinking. "Does Gabby have any special abilities?"

"She's told Sam about an unusual pull she has on human men. According to Sam, they appear to be very attracted to her. Yet, our men don't seem any more or less attracted to her because of it," Charlene said.

If I had premonitions, Charlene could control minds, and the redhead could influence people's emotions, I didn't see how being exceptionally attractive qualified as a special ability.

"Hmm. My abilities changed when I met Emmitt and again when I met you. You said yours first changed when you Claimed Thomas. Maybe hers will manifest when she's with her Mate?"

Nana Wini spoke up. "She found her Mate but isn't acknowledging him. We'll have to keep an eye on the situation."

"What happened when you met me?" Charlene asked, circling back to what I'd said.

"Well, it wasn't exactly when we met but when we first touched. Before meeting any of you, my premonitions were about the stock markets. When I met Emmitt, I started to see people. Women. But when I first touched you, I was transported to another place. It was like a white nothing filled with monitors. Each monitor had an image of one of us, women with power. Around us, there were always werewolves. Somehow, we're in the middle of them. I wasn't able to study the images before I was pulled out of that place."

"When I let go," Charlene said, nodding. "It makes sense. I seem to enhance Thomas's ability as pack leader through our mental link. Perhaps I enhance yours when we touch."

"Maybe," I said. "I did notice something else important, I think. The images I've seen played out when touching Emmitt are the same ones in that room. I'm thinking that's my source. And I'm still not clear why I don't see a vision every time I'm with Emmitt." There was a lot I wasn't clear about, actually.

"To be safe, we need to warn Gabby about Blake and his men," I said. "And I think we need to look for the others like us. I don't want any of them to have to deal with Frank or Blake on their own."

Emmitt reached over and clasped my hand. I smiled at him reassuringly, not wanting him to think I was blaming him.

"Did Frank say anything more about the puzzle? What he meant?" Nana Wini asked.

"No. Nothing clear, anyway. He said they were going to stop this cycle so a judgment would be made. He was talking about Urbat, making it sound like it was another type of werewolf."

Everyone sat quietly for a few moments, each lost in their own thoughts.

Finally, Nana Wini spoke up. "I've let Sam know about the possible danger. Gabby has made arrangements for college, which will be starting soon. Sam is working on how to keep her safe." She looked toward Thomas. "We're going to accept Joshua's request. We can use his help."

"Who's Joshua?" I asked.

"He's the candidate for becoming an Elder."

"Isn't he the one you can't read clearly?"

Nana and Sam both nodded. They were taking a risk bringing him over. If he wasn't true with his intent to help the pack, taking the oath could kill him. But if he was, perhaps his unique ability could better protect Gabby.

"It's time to expand," Thomas said. "Tomorrow, you and your family can go back home. We'll be sending six members with you, including Grey. With two elders and eight members, you'll be as safe as here."

I was torn. It felt like he was pushing us out. There'd just been attacks on the Compound, but he didn't seem overly concerned about it. At least, not as much as I was. I wondered why.

"How many came when we were gone?" I asked.

"It was always a solitary man. He was quick to run when we spotted him."

That explained why they thought it safe. One against ten did seem like safe enough odds.

"There are more than that. In the four years Blake kept me, I sat through dinner once a month with ten of his men. I don't remember seeing the same face twice." Charlene looked shocked. "I don't think we should leave. I think this is the safest place, and I think we should get Gabby here, too."

Nana Wini shook her head. "Sam's afraid she'll run if he presses her. She's in denial right now. We'll have to trust him and her Mate to keep her safe. Joshua is willing to move near her, too."

"If you're right about us being targets, wouldn't it be better to split up? We have some money set aside that we can use to add security to the Montana Compound," Charlene offered.

I felt like palm-smacking my forehead. We didn't need to be trapped in one location for protection.

"You're right about the security." I stood up and met four puzzled sets of eyes. "Make plans for us to leave tomorrow. I have some calls to make. Emmitt, tell your parents the good news."

I left the room after he smiled in understanding. His parents had plenty of money to access, and so did I. We wouldn't be going back to a vulnerable home. Time to take the lawyer up on his offer.

WE LEFT EARLY the next morning. Emmitt drove the new SUV we'd picked up. Mary, Gregory, Paul, and Henry had packed their car overnight and now followed us. Nana Wini, Jim, Grey, and Carlos finished out the convoy. It looked like we'd have a full house when we got back. Except this time, the idea of more people excited me.

During the drive, the boys told us everything they planned to do with Paul and Henry once we got home. When they asked where the two older boys would sleep, I knew they were hinting for another sleepover.

Emmitt explained that Mary and Gregory were staying with Nana Wini while we all worked to get an apartment ready for them. Their boys would stay with Jim, and Carlos and Grey would stay in Emmitt's place.

Emmitt gave me puppy eyes and asked if he could sleep on our couch.

I could feel Liam's eyes on me. "What do you two think?" I asked, turning in my seat.

They both nodded without hesitation then started talking about Paul and Henry again. When they ran out of ideas to share, we spent the rest of the ride playing car games.

The familiar mailbox and the crunch of gravel under our tires filled me with as much anxiety as it did relief. But I didn't need to worry. The house looked just the same as we'd left it. I opened my car door with a sigh. Home.

Nana and Jim stood close as the boys jumped out. Aden glanced at the swing set as Emmitt grabbed our bags. After such a long ride, I knew my brothers wanted to play. However, I didn't feel as safe here as I once had. My eyes skimmed over the tree line, remembering how Frank and his friend had stepped out.

I was ready to suggest inside play, but Paul spoke before I said anything.

"Do you think you could show us around again, Liam?"

"Yeah, we didn't spend that much time inside last time we were here," Henry said. "Do you think we'll get the apartment right below yours?"

Aden nodded eagerly and grabbed Henry's hand to start tugging him toward the house, explaining that he wanted to show the two older boys Liam's and his room so they could plan where to sleep in their new apartment. The four raced inside. Crisis diverted, I followed at a normal pace.

When I reached the apartment, I saw Emmitt already had blankets and a pillow on the couch. I walked into my bedroom, saw his bag at the bottom of my closet, and grinned. Since Paul and Henry had my brothers occupied, I went back downstairs to see if Grey and Carlos needed any help moving into Emmitt's place.

That night, the boys and I said good night to Emmitt on the couch and went to our own rooms. After everything that had happened, I had a hard time closing my eyes as I listened to the familiar sounds of the house.

My door silently opened, and I sat up with wide eyes.

"It's just me," Emmitt said softly.

I let out a sigh of relief and pulled back the covers. I should have known staying on the couch would only last until the boys fell asleep.

Before the boys woke, he was back on the couch.

WITHIN A WEEK, the apartment building was fully equipped with state of the art security, including cameras outside each of the apartment doors. Floodlights, installed in the yard, turned on when triggered by any of the new sensors on the property or by a switch within the house. In addition to the latest technology, we also had our resident werewolves' instincts. We wouldn't be taken unaware. I just hoped we wouldn't be outnumbered.

Saturday morning, I woke with a stretch and smiled at Emmitt. He leaned over to give me a kiss, and it dawned on me that I was overdue for a premonition. Pulling back from him, I stared in confusion and tried to think back. I hadn't had one since I'd Claimed him.

"What is it?" he asked watching me.

"I haven't had a stock market premonition since before the trip. Since I Claimed you."

"Does that bother you?"

"I'm glad they're gone, but I can't help but wonder why."

We talked about the different possibilities but really had no clear idea what it meant. I wished I knew how my premonitions worked, but I didn't worry about it too much. I had other things on my mind.

"So, I was thinking..."

He leaned over me to kiss my neck. "About something good, I hope."

"Depends. I was thinking about all this sneaking we're doing. It makes me uncomfortable. I don't want the boys to catch us and start asking questions."

Emmitt pulled back to look at me.

I tugged the hem of his shirt up to slip my hands underneath. "I was wondering if we could set a date."

The wicked grin on his face spoke volumes. "Now's good."

I rolled my eyes, guessing what he'd been referring to.

"Not for that," I said.

"You have me confused. Again."

"That's because you're focused on the physical side of our relationship." I grinned up at him.

"Is there something else?"

"How about a wedding?"

He crushed me in a hug while laughing loudly. "Is that what we're waiting for? How soon can we get married?" He didn't wait for me to answer but kissed me soundly.

"You're still thinking about Mating," I accused after I was breathless.

"No. I'm thinking about forever with you."

EPILOGUE

I SAT ON THE COUCH FOLDING LAST MINUTE LAUNDRY THE DAY before Thanksgiving. Both the boys sat at the kitchen island egging Emmitt on as he flipped pancakes high into the air, just barely missing the ceiling.

"After breakfast, can we go down by Nana?" Aden asked.

Liam and Aden loved being homeschooled by Nana Wini. They usually spent the morning with her and the afternoon at Aunt Mary and Uncle Gregory's to play with Paul and Henry. But I knew he wasn't asking to go down for his lessons. He wanted to find Jim.

"I don't think so, buddy. We need to finish packing so we can see Grandma Char," Emmitt said.

Aden's face fell.

Jim's continued absence from breakfast disappointed the boys. And it wasn't packing that kept the boys from Jim. Earlier in the month, Jim had made a trip to the Compound with Emmitt's bike. While there, it had disappeared. The boys didn't know that Jim stayed away out of guilt for losing Emmitt's motorcycle, even though Emmitt didn't blame him. Well, not much. Jim had borrowed the bike without asking. Again.

"Maybe Uncle Grey can help you pack," I said. My brothers grinned.

The boys now knew all about the other members of our house. Shortly after we'd returned, Grey had taken it upon himself to introduce them to the secret world of furry fun by shifting in front of them and offering werewolf rides.

Neither boy had even flinched. Instead, Aden had called for Jim and insisted he turn into a dog so they could race. Jim willingly obliged and lost to Grey by a lap. Liam had been elated.

Having so many people around to help with the boys freed up my time for wedding planning since Emmitt and I had set the date for just before Christmas. I'd finally managed to book the venue. It was a big place with plenty of room for Emmitt's very extended family—the whole pack.

The phone rang, and I turned away from Emmitt's show to answer. Since it was so early, I thought it might be Emmitt's mom with some final details. We planned to leave later in the day to head up to the Compound. Charlene was organizing a huge Thanksgiving feast, and I couldn't wait to start cooking. Feeding a hungry werewolf was gratifying.

"Hello?" I said, answering.

"Michelle, something's going on with Gabby," Sam said. "We need you to come early. How soon can you be on the road?"

"We're almost finished packing. What's going on, Sam?"

Emmitt glanced at me from across the room, and I shook my head at him. Nothing for him to worry about...yet.

"She's asking questions about having more than one Mate and if there's another werewolf species. I think she's figured out more but isn't saying anything."

I hesitated, recalling my time with Frank. He'd talked about Urbat as if it'd been some other kind of werewolf. Could it be possible? Was there another species out there that Emmitt and his kind were not aware of? If so, how did Gabby play into it?

"Have you asked her about it?"

The line was quiet for several moments. "She's mad at me. I could ask her, but I don't think she'll answer."

I knew why he wanted me, then. It was time to meet the elusive Gabby. From what Emmitt had told me, she sounded like an interesting and determined person.

"We'll be there before dinner."

I hung up the phone and nibbled at my nail. I'd thought our lives were settling down. What did it mean that Gabby was starting to ask these questions now?

"Everything okay, hun?" Emmitt asked.

"Da," Aden interrupted, "Can you cut my pancakes?"

"Everything's just fine, *Da*," I said, stressing his newly acquired title.

It was as if Richard had never been. It saddened me a little that my brothers wouldn't have any happy memories of either parent, but I would make sure they knew how much our mom and Richard had loved them.

"Just a minute, bud," Emmitt said to Aden. Liam reached over to help Aden with his pancake as Emmitt walked over to where I stood, still by the phone. He wrapped me in a huge hug.

A girl—a young woman, really—stood inside an office by the door, head bowed, waiting. Her bleached hair obscured most of her pale face. Still, I felt I knew her.

Her head snapped up, tilted, listening, her gaze unfocused. While her coloring screamed albino, her eyes said something else. The dark irises almost matched her pupils.

"Is he angry?" she whispered.

I looked around the room. We were alone. I tried speaking but couldn't make any noise. Surely, she couldn't see me.

"No, you can go," she said to the room as she smoothed back her hair and walked to the desk, her steps measured. I watched her move and knew she was blind.

The door flew open as she smiled and said, "Welcome home, Papa. Did you find them?"

Blake scowled at the girl but walked up to her and kissed her lightly on the forehead, his actions contradicting his expression.

"Yes. But, your sisters are not as reasonable as you are."

I gasped, pulling myself from the vision.

"Are you sure everything's okay?" Emmitt said, drawing back from me.

"Maybe not."

I laid my head on his shoulder, and he held me close. His hand soothed my back.

Though I no longer received premonitions about the stock market, the visions of the other women like me hadn't stopped. They happened fairly often now, always when I touched Emmitt.

I'd learned a little more about the women, my sisters, but not much. So far, five of us starred in the visions. Some visions were just little snapshots of day-to-day things, like washing dishes or walking somewhere, while a few detailed events that I didn't understand. I shared those with Grey and Nana, hoping they could explain.

This woman was new. A sixth.

"He's got another girl, like me," I said softly so the boys wouldn't hear. "Funny that I get this premonition right after Sam calls to say we need to head to your parent's early." I lifted my head and met his eyes. "I told Sam we'd be there before dinner, but I think we should leave now."

He nodded, gave me a quick kiss, and went to the door. "We're leaving in ten minutes," he called into the hallway. He didn't raise his voice or use a serious tone, but I knew it wouldn't matter. The others would be ready.

Both boys looked up from their plates, and he smiled at them.

"Race time," he said. "You two finish eating. Who do you want to finish packing for you?"

"Grey!" they both called.

I laughed, shook my head, and tried really hard not to feel the gnawing worry in the pit of my stomach.

NOTE TO THE READER

If you recall where we left off on Hope(less), Gabby had just gotten a call from Luke. He has the girl and is in trouble. But how? Why? What happened? Well, you're about to find out!

Bring on the LUKE!!

UNWISE

JUDGEMENT
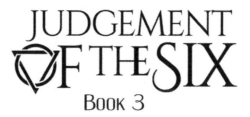
OF THE SIX
BOOK 3

MELISSA HAAG

PROLOGUE

I WOKE WITH A START, THE TERROR OF THE DREAM STILL GRIPPING me. Sweat coated my face, and my soaked shirt clung to my skin. I looked around the room. My room. Safe. I let out a shaky breath and tried to convince myself that the dream had only been a product of my imagination. Nothing more.

The alarm clock next to my bed showed just after five a.m., but it felt like I hadn't slept at all.

Kicking off the covers, I got out of bed. Clothes lay scattered on the floor, shadowy lumps that I stepped over on my way to the bathroom. I turned on the light and scrunched my eyes against its bright glare for a moment.

Scrubbing my hands over my face, I leaned against the sink trying to shake the dream. It just wouldn't fade. I dropped my hands to study myself in the mirror. Dark strands of hair stuck to my glistening pale face, an unnatural flush on my cheeks the only splash of color. Even my lips, usually a warm full pink, matched the surrounding colorless skin. Glassy bloodshot eyes, too wide and filled with lingering panic, stared back at me.

I took a deep, unsteady breath. It wasn't real. I was still me. I let my breath out slowly with a self-deprecating laugh. I looked like crap and needed a shower. Great way to start my senior year.

The details of the dream continued to swirl in my head as I stepped into the shower. The lingering sensation of fur hides brushing against my legs scared me. It made it all seem more like a memory than a dream. A memory from an era long past, seen through the eyes of a woman who wasn't me...yet she was.

She wore animal skins and stood outside her mud and grass hut. Other huts surrounded hers. The heavily clouded sky cast a grey gloom on the primitive village. Fear swelled within her. Her fear filled me as if it were my own. I saw what she saw. I was her...yet not.

People ran past her, sprinting between huts, terror in their eyes. Her stomach turned sour with panic. Her vision suddenly changed. The world disappeared, replaced by nothing but tiny sparks floating in a vast darkness. The sparks moved, flying past her in time with the sound of running feet. After a moment, I understood what she saw.

She had an amazing ability that enabled her to see the locations of people. The sparks shrank in size as the view expanded. Not just the location of those around her, but anywhere in the world. She focused on the immediate area worried about her family, using her gift to try to find them. She ran to check each spark. The tang of smoke drifted in the air. Her despair grew, and she ran faster.

All of the tiny sparks looked the same, making it difficult to find the right ones. Too soon, an orange glow illuminated the dark sky. Smoke burned her eyes and nose.

Close by, a different color appeared in her mind. Panic flared within her when she spotted the blue-grey sparks. She stopped running and stood still for a few seconds, terror squeezing the acrid air from her lungs. One heartbeat. Two. She hesitated. Despairing over her family, she spun away from the unique sparks. Her heart clenched, and tears clogged her throat. She left behind those she loved, hearing their dying screams as she ran.

The smoke masked her direction until the yawning abyss of open air loomed before her. Skidding to a halt at the edge of the cliff near her village, she watched dirt tumble over the ledge. She leaned forward, peering over at the broken rocks below. Hopelessness and despair filled her. There was no escape. Her thoughts filled me. Die as they had or die her own way? She continued to stare at the rocks below as she made up her mind.

I struggled to separate myself from her, to scream at her to stop; but inside her own mind, she couldn't hear me.

She glanced over her shoulder and saw a huge beast running at her. A strange calm filled her.

I finally understood the fear and stopped struggling.

It looked like a wolf on steroids and had blood covering its muzzle. As she watched, it changed midstride from beast to man, never pausing.

She turned and flung herself from the cliff. As she fell, she twisted midair to look back at the fate she'd escaped. The man stood naked at the cliff's edge, blood smeared across his face.

He yelled in a language I couldn't understand, but she did. He cursed her, saying they would never give up. They would wait as many cycles as it took until we were all *theirs.*

I woke before she hit the ground; but the fear, the feeling of freefalling, the willingness to die rather than to fall into the hands of that *thing*...it all stayed with me.

CHAPTER ONE

I NEEDED A FIX, AND I NEEDED IT BAD. STANDING IN THE MALL, I reviewed my options while nervously tugging the long sleeves of my shirt over my wrists to hide the scars there. Since it was a Sunday afternoon, nicely dressed kids trailed behind their equally neat parents in the packed mall. In my worn, dirty clothes from the day before, I stood out. The clerk in the drug store would certainly remember me from yesterday. I'd almost tipped over while waiting in line. When my turn came at the register, he'd looked me over and asked for my ID. His doubtful, long gaze at it had made my palms sweat. When he'd finally glanced up at me, he'd asked, "Are you sure you want these?"

I couldn't go back to the same clerk. My ID was okay at a glance, but it wasn't a great fake ID. And he'd wonder why I was back for more pills when what I'd purchased yesterday should have lasted at least three days.

Shifting from one foot to the other, I chewed on my nail knowing what I needed to do but hating it.

Dani and her friend, Cadence, loitered near the food court, talking. Dani stood six inches taller than me, had multicolored hair (pink and red today), and a cheek piercing to enhance her classic features. She'd get what I needed if I asked. I knew she had a soft spot for me despite her slightly tough appearance. She wouldn't even ask for money though I did have it crumpled in my pocket. No, she was interested in something else as payment.

Everyone knew Dani swung the other way. Just like she knew I didn't. But it didn't stop her from asking for a kiss anyway. She didn't demand a kiss from anyone else. The first time I'd asked for her help, I thought she was doing it to test me. To see if I was really serious about what I wanted her to buy. I'd been desperate. Yeah, I kissed a girl...and I didn't like it.

If I was careful about when I bought, I didn't need to ask her. I'd learned to be careful. I tried to wash up, change my clothes if there were any to change into; and I tried to close my eyes. Not to sleep. No, not that. I just tried to relax so I wouldn't look like a troubled kid strung out on drugs. And I wasn't. Strung out on drugs that is. I was definitely troubled. More troubled than anyone around me would ever guess.

I realized my train of thought had drifted and reined it back in. I needed caffeine, stimulants...whatever I could get my hands on over the counter to stay awake. Not forever. No. I tried to take thirty-minute naps throughout the day and night. If I did that, I could still function. Sort of. Not really. But it was better than the dreams.

Last night I'd finally succumbed. I'd slept twelve hours. I felt like crap today. I'd died again. Several times actually. I hated dying. The last one had been violent. Dogs that looked very human had torn me apart. They'd talked. Well, yelled really. They'd wanted me to choose. I didn't know what.

A shiver ran through me. Just thinking about the dream made me tired. I ran my fingers through my oily, dark hair to comb it out, hoping it looked decent. I couldn't remember my last shower and cringed at the thought of my mom seeing me like this. Thankfully, she worked. A lot. We communicated via notes left on the fridge. Mostly she told me to clean my room. I kept it strategically messy to help hide whatever it was I bought that week, day, hour, whatever... I sighed and rubbed my head. It ached constantly.

My wandering eyes shifted back to Dani. She watched me with a slight smile. She knew. I didn't know how she could stand kissing me. I looked and felt like crap. At least I'd brushed my teeth before leaving the house. Stuffing my hands into the pockets of my faded, ripped jeans, I started making my way to Dani and the next torturous kiss.

"Bethi Pederson," Dani said, flashing her straight white teeth at me. A smile. Friendly, but the sight reminded me of the snarling gleam from my dream. I fought not to cringe.

"I didn't think I'd see you any time soon." Her eyes roved my face, and she angled her head. "You don't look so good, hun. What's up?"

"Same clerk as yesterday. Can you—"

She didn't let me finish.

"Bethi, maybe you'd be better off coming home with me and sleeping for a few hours."

Cadence rolled her eyes at Dani's comment but said nothing. I could just imagine what would happen if I went home with Dani. Though, looking into her soft brown eyes, the concern there made me hesitate. Sure, she'd probably put a move on me, but I knew she'd also try to get me to rest. To help me. I really did like Dani, just not *that* way. If only she knew sleeping was the last thing I needed. I needed peace. Two totally different things. The thought of someone helping me was tempting, but I knew I had to deal with this on my own.

"Thanks, Dani, but I can't." I pulled my hand out of my pocket and tried giving her the money.

She didn't move to take it. "You know the price." Her smile was gone.

"Why?" I partially whined unable to keep the anxious uncertainty from my voice. "You know I like guys, Dani. Plus, I look like hell. Probably smell bad too."

She studied me for a moment. I tried to look confident, but my arms wrapped around me so I hugged myself.

"It's your eyes," she said, taking pity on me but shrugged away any further explanation.

I averted my deep blue eyes, which looked violet in certain light or on days when I got very little sleep. Against my pale skin and dark hair, they startled people with their naturally vivid coloring.

"As far as liking guys goes, I'm hoping you'll change your mind." Her lips curved in a soft smile.

I was glad she didn't mention my smell. It would have hurt. I wanted to shower, but the warm water put me to sleep, and standing tense under a jet of frigid water wasn't worth the pounding headache afterward.

Exhaustion made the floor dip and crest under my feet. Enough playing around. We both knew I didn't have a choice. I closed the distance between us, fisted my hands in her hair, and pulled her down for a kiss. Her lips were soft and warm against mine. My stomach turned sour as memories swamped me.

This wasn't the first life in which I'd kissed a girl. There'd been so many dreams since the start of the school year. In each dream, I starred as the leading lady. I felt what she felt, saw what she saw—her, but not her. After a while, I began to notice similarities. The dreams themselves didn't repeat, but it often felt like I dreamt of the same person even though their appearances changed from one dream to the next. Each time I closed my eyes and dreamed, I had a unique ability. In all the dreams so far, there had been six distinct abilities...six unique women. Learning about them and what they could do was by far the most interesting portion of the dream. If only the dreams ended there. The appearance of the beasts and what they did made me shudder. But worse still were all the deaths I experienced.

Dani misunderstood my shudder and lifted a hand to my cheek as she kissed me sweetly in return. After counting to four in my head, I pulled back hoping it'd been enough.

The dream kiss had been just as chaste. But it'd felt different. I'd been saying goodbye to someone I loved dearly. Maybe a sister or best friend. The girl in my dream hadn't spoken. She'd simply turned and calmly pushed through the fleeing crowd, people running from the beasts who screamed in their guttural voices for me to step forward. In that dream, my life had been spared...for a while. Hers had been taken.

"Kay. I'll get you what you need." She walked away leaving me standing with Cadence.

My hot, gritty eyes tracked her progress. How could I feel this tired after sleeping twelve hours? My life hadn't been like this for long. After the first dream almost three months ago, I'd slept fine for several nights before figuring out the dreams were skipping nights here and there. On the nights I had those dreams, I woke as tired as I'd been when I went to bed. Too soon, I started having them every night. Sometimes several dreams a night if I managed to fall back to sleep. So many dreams. But, I'd learned something.

Without a doubt, each dream played a scene from a past life, an echo of memory. The surety that I was remembering, and not just dreaming made me doubt my sanity. Some *thing* throughout history continued to hunt me...and others like me. Yeah, I wasn't alone. Sometimes the women looked similar to how I appeared now. Sometimes I wasn't me, but a completely different person, one of the other five. Often names repeated in different lifetimes, or we had family members with the same names. But, it was the lingering details of the life after waking that convinced me they were surfacing memories and not just random dreams.

Usually I died young, unaware of the danger. Sometimes, the dreams came and helped me to prepare. To run. Either way, I never lasted long. They could track me by my scent. Back then, though, there hadn't been cars or other ways to travel fast. I hoped this time would be different. I had no doubt...they would come. But maybe I could finally out run them.

I closed my eyes for a second to relieve the hot sting. They stayed closed and wouldn't open no matter how hard I tried. My legs felt weak, and I knew I'd crumple to the ground any moment. In a distant part of my mind, a dream gathered, an angry storm of memories, swirling and gaining speed.

Cadence's voice and rough hold pulled me back from the brink of sleep.

"Geez, Bethi. Get a grip. People are staring."

Paranoia fueled an adrenaline spike. My eyes popped open. My knees kept shaking, but no longer from sleep. Flight or fight mode. I was ready to fly. Controlling my breathing and relaxing my shoulders, I glanced around. A security guard watched me. My relief sprouted a genuine smile on my face. The woman looked confused for a moment, then shook her head and turned away. I could only imagine what she thought of my odd behavior.

"Thanks," I mumbled to Cadence, thinking of the adrenaline rush. Maybe that was the way to go. I fingered the scars on my arms. Pain, though effective, was a pointless method to stay awake. After all, it was the pain in my dreams I wanted to avoid.

Adrenaline might be the answer. I'd watched myself and others do amazing things in my dreams because of it. Although, there were times it didn't work. The phrase "flight or fight" should really be "flight, fight, or freeze." So many times the surrealism of the situation shuts down a person's brain even though the body is pumped full of that magic juice.

Fingers waggled in front of my eyes, and I realized I'd been drifting in my own thoughts. Dani stood in front of me with an amused smile, one that didn't reach her eyes.

"I got you some caffeine pills and a Monster, but rent-a-cop over there is watching us. So how about you tell us what's got you so messed up. And don't say no sleep, we got that."

Dani's eyes pulled me in, encouraging me to let someone help. I'd tried talking to my mom about the dreams, but her answer had been to try sleeping pills. She didn't really hear the problem within my dreams even though she listened to my whole explanation. Since I already questioned my sanity, I hadn't wanted her to start questioning it too so I let it drop. Last thing I wanted was a padded room and an IV cocktail. No, better keep my crazies to myself.

"Haunting memories. Let's leave it at that," I said with a smile I didn't feel.

We were getting too serious, and I needed to break the mood somehow or pretty soon Dani wouldn't be so willing to help me. Not even for a kiss.

Cadence cleared her throat. "Hottie approaching."

Before I could turn to look, I felt a light tap on my shoulder.

"Pardon, do you know where the loo is?"

Loo? I turned to look over the owner of the clipped British accent. Holy, hotness. Shock and awe filled me. My heart stuttered out a beat as my mind went blank. It did that a lot lately.

The man stood well over six feet. Lean and long, his shoulders filled out his worn, brown leather jacket. The mall lights glinted off his bronzed, mussed hair and highlighted the amused twinkle in his hazel eyes. Eyes a girl could lose herself in. Why couldn't I have kissed him instead of Dani? The wayward thought bounced around in my head for a moment as I stared at his dark brown lashes and tried not to sigh. Or drool. I reined myself in not wanting to hurt Dani's feelings. She still had what I needed. I blinked at him while trying to think. His lips twitched as he waited for me. His gaze skimmed me, not settling anywhere, just taking me in the same as I was doing to him.

A sense of familiarity settled over me, and my stomach did a weird little flip. I tried to study him with indifference. Was this someone I knew but my sleep deprived brain had forgotten? Embarrassing.

I closed my mouth, swallowed hard, hoped I wouldn't blush, and tried for cool-sarcastic, "Oh my God, an accent. Take me, I'm yours."

Dani and Cadence sniggered. I curved my lips in a smile as I waited for him to go away. I just wanted to get my stuff and leave.

Something in the man's expression changed. He tilted his head and took a slow deep breath. I thought for a moment he had a witty reply or would say something rude. Instead, he leaned toward me, his eyes locked on mine, and murmured, "You smell amazing."

My insides froze and, for the second time in five minutes, adrenaline spiked through my veins. He pulled back, his intense gaze never leaving mine. I struggled to contain my panic and to think clearly. I did *not* smell amazing.

His pupils dilated as he continued to watch me. A smile tugged at his lips.

A small sound escaped me somewhere between a whimper and a throat clearing. Dani moved beside me. I knew she was trying to figure out my reaction, but I couldn't spare her more than a passing thought.

He caught the noise. Awareness crept into his eyes almost as if he'd emerged from a trance. His smile faded, and he began to look troubled. It didn't matter.

I'd witnessed that concentrated look before and knew what he meant, what he was.

I didn't want to die, but all those dreams had prepared me for what would come next. Dani and Cadence needed to get out of range. Now. Memories of blood and carnage, of the gory ending of past lives, flitted around in my mind. My heart tripled its rhythm at the remembered pain.

"I need a minute," I said to Dani and Cadence. My voice remained calm and steady. Weary acceptance filled my lungs and radiated throughout me.

They nodded and moved a few feet away. I glanced at the rent-a-cop. Her attention once again rested on me. I knew better than to try calling for her help but still felt a small glimmer of hope. Maybe I was safe. Maybe the crowd was enough.

He watched me expectantly, his eyes causing my stomach to do erratic flips of joy. One of their kind always called to me like that. Messing with my insides, my emotions, pulling me to them like a moth to a flame. Just like the poor winged creature, it never ended well for me.

"I do *not* smell amazing," I said softly, trying to keep anyone from overhearing. "I smell like I need a shower. Badly."

He frowned, held up his hands in a placating manner, and said, "No offense, luv. I'm just looking for the loo."

I stared at him for a moment, the wild beat of my heart pounding in my ears as I tried to decide what game he played. Barely lifting my hand, I pointed to the right near the rent-a-cop wondering how long he'd keep up the pretense.

He nodded his thanks, but didn't move. He hesitated. His eyes swept my face. He opened his mouth as if he wanted to say more. Instead, he jammed his hands into his pockets and walked away.

Stunned, I watched him leave. My mind tried to keep up with what my eyes processed. One of them was walking away from me. What did it mean? It meant I wasn't dead. Yet. I knew what I needed to do. Wait...wait for it. He kept walking away. I felt Dani join me as my eyes remained riveted on the man. He didn't glance back, not once, before rounding the corner to the bathrooms.

"Don't come back here," I whispered to Dani.

Then, I ran.

THE OVERGROWN, low border hedges lining the sidewalk of my house loomed ahead. I hurtled them neatly, not knowing I had it in me. Palming the key from my pocket, I slid it into the lock of the front door entering the house only seconds after leaping into the yard. I slammed the door behind me and didn't bother looking out the window to see if I had been followed. Either he would break down the door or not. Looking wouldn't change the outcome, and I couldn't waste time. Not a second.

My bedroom slowed me down a bit as I waded through the ankle-deep clothes swamp. Snatching the grey duffle from under the bed, I crammed in whatever lay nearby until I couldn't fit more. I struggled with the zipper, and the harsh panting of my breath filled the room.

Could he follow my scent even though I had taken the bus most of the way home? Would it slow him down?

I grabbed the dwindling supply of money I'd stashed away for a car and stuffed it in my bra.

Was I taking too long?

Hands shaking, I hefted the duffle. Its heavy weight settled on my shoulder anchoring me to the reality of here and now as I left my room. I needed to catch another bus. This time it would need to take me much further.

Mom's note on the refrigerator caught my eye. I stopped moving and stared at it. My throat tightened. She wouldn't understand why I'd left, and I would never be able to come home. The grief turned into fear when I thought of what she would do after she realized I was gone. She would do *everything* she could to find me again. Police. Newspapers. Radio. If she called too much attention to herself, to me...I shuddered at the possibilities.

I hastily searched for paper and a pen. I had to give her a reason for disappearing. The message hurt to write. My hand shook as I signed it. Then, I pulled out my cell phone and set it on the kitchen table along with the note.

Mom,

School's not for me. I want to see the world. I'm sorry for leaving like this, but hope you'll understand someday.

Bethony

The words screamed at me from the paper. Lies. She'd be hurt and confused, but what else could I say? Tell her about the monsters who would come and threaten her for information? No, she'd go to the police with whatever I wrote. They'd think I just needed a padded room for a while.

But the people looking for me? When they came—and they *would* come—she would probably show them the note hoping they might help find me. If they thought she knew something more, they would hurt her to get it. Keeping her in the dark might help keep her safe. I didn't even want to tell her that I loved her, fearing they'd see it as leverage.

I left my house, jogging toward the bus stop I knew had pickups heading out of town. I didn't turn to look at my house one last time, though I wanted to. I kept focused on what I needed to do.

Several people stood waiting when I got there. After asking, I found the next bus wouldn't arrive for at least another fifteen minutes. Time enough for the adrenaline, which had been keeping me going, to ease out of my system. Time enough for the man with an accent to catch up to me. Time enough for me to give in to the ever-present urge to sleep.

I eyed the people around me. An older crowd, geriatric types. Generally safe. But with that man, that thing, chasing me, I couldn't risk sleeping.

Easing into a squat and leaning back against the pole of the bus stop sign, I struck up a polite conversation with an elderly lady. She introduced herself as Willa Delson and didn't seem to mind when my attention wandered or I slurred a few words between yawns. By the time the bus rolled up, I'd looked at all of the pictures of her grandkids and great grandkids. Very cute, happy kids. I hoped they never learned the truth: monsters were real. If they did, they would never smile at a camera again.

I paid the driver for the farthest stop on his run, a three-hour drive that would take me north. Having found a friend in Willa, I asked to sit next to her. Her ticket took her to the same town, so we settled in for a long ride. She shared the snacks she'd stashed in her handbag and chatted about seeing her newest great grandchild. Six pounds and seven ounces, Joy Marie Delson wailed her way into the world only a week ago. My desperation to stay awake had me absorbing Willa's every word. At the end of three hours, I could have pretended to be a member of the extensive Delson clan. My legs twitched with pre-sleep spasms several times, but I didn't succumb.

The bus dropped us in front of Chris's Cooking Café. A sign in the window advertised CCC's specials at very low prices. My stomach rumbled. I couldn't remember if I'd had anything for dinner. My days blurred.

Willa waved goodbye as she spotted her daughter-in-law, the new grandmother, waiting for her. My stomach growled as I smiled farewell. Tired was bad enough. Tired *and* hungry wouldn't work. I couldn't run—not far anyway—if I didn't eat. I strode to the restaurant. The smell of fryer oil greeted me. Their prices were low, as advertised, but not fast food low. Who knew how long I would need to keep moving. My money wouldn't last. I settled on a plain burger from the kids menu. The waitress gave me a look but let it go.

After devouring my baby burger, I walked to the only motel in town where the waitress said I could find a bus schedule. The posted schedule showed that the same run that had dropped me here would take me back at the same time the following day. *No thanks.* Other than packing before running, I hadn't thought very far ahead. Too tired to concentrate, I decided to sleep a few hours and then think of a plan.

The man behind the desk eyed me when I asked for a room. The need to sleep coated me in a thick film giving the world a surreal quality. I knew I'd fall hard and worried what would happen if I started screaming. I decided to tell him that I suffered from night terrors. The clerk stared at me and took a second look at my fake ID while I tried not to fidget. Finally, he gave me a bill along with the key.

I needed to plan where to go from here, but the bed swallowed me whole as soon as I closed the door. My exhaustion didn't give me a chance to enjoy the feeling. Immediately, images of a dark haired girl surfaced behind my closed eyes. Crap. I didn't want to die again.

She stood panting at the edge of a cliff, staring straight ahead at nothing. The craggy face of the rock dropped steeply to the tree-filled valley below. Moonlight highlighted each rock and scrub brush.

The details soaked into me, and the perspective shifted as usual. I slipped further into the dream, becoming her.

Clutching my hands together, I could imagine each scratch and break my body would suffer. I looked down at a large rip in the forearm of my leather tunic. Dark clotting blood from a vicious bite glistened in the silvery light.

An eerie cry echoed behind me. My panicked heart slowed as I made a decision. I turned from the cliff to watch my pursuers silently emerge from the trees and close the distance. Sleek, furred heads rose to howl together in triumph.

The leader slowly loped forward, shifting forms as he approached. His paws widened and fingers emerged where pads once existed. Black claws shrank and flattened into human nails. Fur receded into skin as bones popped and reshaped giving the forelimbs a human appearance. As soon as his feet developed, he reared back to stand on his morphing legs.

Snuffling through his shrinking snout, he spoke before his tongue fully changed. It garbled his words, but I still understood him.

"Amusing chase, but it is time to choose. We will keep you safe as they couldn't."

Safe? Rage boiled in my heart. One of them had bit me during their attack on my village, a poor example of their care for me. Did he honestly think he could persuade me to go with them? They were unnatural. Evil. The dark glint in his eyes showed it. I saw only one outcome.

"I choose death," I said savagely as I pushed off with my feet doing a backward dive off the cliff's edge. Inside I screamed with fear.

I felt each bounce against the rocky surface until my neck broke bringing dark respite.

Warmth blanketed me, weighing me down comfortably. Something gentle pressed briefly against my forehead. I felt comforted as the dream shifted. I didn't want to witness another death. I tried to surface, but I was in too deep.

Tall stalks of grass and wild flowers swayed in the gentle breeze. To the west, the sun's dying rays painted the sky. A single furrowed dirt track, perhaps made by game, followed the edge of the woods to the east. The air smelled fresh and crisp with no hint of pollution.

In this dream, I drifted as a bodiless bystander without someone else's thoughts or feelings pushing into me as if my own. I observed the area, curious about the change in perspective.

A circle of stones crowned a patch of barren earth in the middle of the wind-ruffled grasses. Seven women stood within. I could see them clearly. One of them had a round, distended stomach, very large with child, and she was dressed better than the rest. Her taupe gown, a thin flowing material, molded itself to her belly in the breeze. The rest knelt in a half circle before her, dressed in rough skins and furs. Dirt dusted their skin and matted hair.

The pregnant one spoke in a guttural tongue. It took a moment for her words to make any sense.

"These I give onto you for your protection."

The speaker motioned for the woman to her right to come to her. The woman stood and approached the one in the taupe gown, her steps hesitant. The woman in taupe gave a small encouraging smile. Her eyes held so many emotions: concern, sadness, hope...

Placing a hand on her swollen belly and the other on the coarse woman's flat stomach, she spoke a single word, "Strength." Immediately, her roundness decreased while a bump formed on the other woman's previously flat stomach.

The woman gave a startled yelp and quickly moved back to her kneeling position, her hand protectively cradling her newly rounded middle. The woman in the gown motioned to the next primitive and repeated the process. It continued until the stomachs of those kneeling were all rounded with child, and hers showed no sign of inflation.

"Go," she said softly to her group. They stood and parted, each heading in separate directions.

CHAPTER TWO

I WOKE FEELING RESTED, BUT CRANKY. I WANTED JUST ONE NIGHT without dreams, not that I wasn't grateful for that last dream. At least no one had died. Struggling out of the bowl my body had created in the mattress, I checked the clock and flew into panic mode. Fourteen hours had passed! Too much time in one spot.

Scrambling to the window, I peeked around the curtain. The sun barely rimmed the horizon. Silence still claimed the morning—but not my thundering heart. My eyes darted around the street, searching for anything out of place. Nothing. I moved away from the window and slid my feet into my shoes.

Grabbing my bag, I eased out the door. The motel office waited a few feet away. Down the road, several trucks stood in front of the restaurant.

I hurried to return the room key. I needed a ride. I needed to move. The man from the night before took the key from me and returned the small cash deposit he'd required since I didn't have a credit card. With a fake smile, I stepped back outside. The bus would bring me back to where I'd started, and I couldn't go back home. I paused looking for options on the very dead street.

An early riser stepped out of the CCC. A dirty green knit cap covered his head and a brown scarf insulated his neck. Grey whiskers protected his cheeks. This far south winter rarely had a bite, but today would be one of those days.

He strode to a late model Chevy truck. Rust and mud speckled the back fender, but I didn't care about that. He was just the option I was looking for.

Waving to catch his attention, I hurried over to ask if he'd give me a ride out of town. He looked me over, eyeing my thin long sleeved shirt and asked me a few questions about where I was headed. Satisfied with my answer, a better paying job in a bigger town, he agreed to give me a lift.

"In the bed, 'course. Can't be too careful. Sorry," he said, getting into the truck cab.

I didn't mind the conditions. A ride was a ride, and I needed it desperately.

Using the bumper, I vaulted into the bed and hunkered down near the cab. As I'd expected, the cold pierced my skin as soon as we started moving. At least, the cold would help keep me awake.

I dug in my bag looking for something warmer. My hand brushed against a zipper. Carefully, I pulled a hooded sweatshirt out of the grey duffle. I frowned at it, puzzled. It didn't look familiar. I turned it in my hands for a moment before deciding I didn't care. Nothing seemed familiar anymore. I pulled it on and zipped it up. It smelled good, clean, unlike most of what I'd crammed into the bag, and it helped a bit against the wind.

The panic and need to move calmed as the driver kept a steady speed heading northwest out of town. It gave me time to think. Fourteen hours was crazy long for only one death dream. Since they had started, they had varied little. Discovery, then death. Like an alarm clock, they woke me to the truth: the beasts were coming, and I needed to run to save those I loved. Unfortunately, like those past lives, I hadn't truly believed the dreams until one of those *things* actually arrived.

I rubbed my nose trying to warm it. At least I'd gotten away...this time.

The second dream about the women puzzled me. It was nothing like the other dreams. What did it mean, and why did I dream it right after that man found me? With a sigh, I leaned my head back and stared at the sky unable to answer my own questions.

I wasn't sure if it was pity or his true destination, but the man drove an hour to the next big town with a bus stop. Discreetly digging in my stash of cash, I offered him a twenty for gas, but he waved it away with a gruff, "Take care."

Looking at the schedule, I studied my options. There were several buses departing within the next hour. Only two general directions, however. North and west. Though I'd tolerated the cold, I didn't want to push any further north in November without a decent jacket. West seemed like a good enough choice.

THE DARK CIRCLES under my eyes, a constant presence for the last few weeks, stood out vibrantly as I stepped off a bus in Springfield, Illinois twenty-four hours later. Wearily, I shuffled away from the drop-off location. The layovers and transfers had helped keep me awake and prevented a screaming fit while traveling, but I knew I needed to crash soon.

A fellow passenger pointed me in the direction of the nearest motel. Just a few blocks. No problem. Money would be an issue, though. This would be the last room I could afford. I wasn't even sure if the fake ID I'd gotten online would work here. Most kids my age got one for drinking. Not me. As soon as I'd started dying in my dreams, I'd planned to run on some level and bought one just for this purpose. Running and hiding. If only I had a destination in mind. But, how could I when I didn't even know where these things came from? For all I knew, I was heading right to them. Hard to plan when you didn't know which direction was safe. Well, I knew home wasn't safe. One found me there. I thought briefly of my mom and felt a pang. *Please let this keep her safe.*

Checking into the cheapest room I could manage, I headed to my room. I wanted sleep. Bad. My stomach cramped. I wanted food, too. However, both food and sleep would need to wait because I just couldn't stand my own smell anymore. I walked to the bathroom as I peeled off my clothes. The money I had stuffed in my bra fell to the floor. The thin fold of bills worried me. I counted my remaining cash. Less than fifty. Enough to buy a few meals, but it wouldn't get me much further, which meant I needed to earn some more. I set the money next to the sink with a sigh. I was tired, hungry, and poor. Could anything else knock me down?

I looked in the mirror, cringed, and added looking like crap to my list. A poster child for runaway teens stared back at me. I didn't even look seventeen. Most of the makeup I'd worn to the mall had rubbed off. The dark circles, sallow complexion, and weight loss just made me look very young and very sick. Shaking my head at the thought, I picked a few items out of the duffle bag to wash. Since most of the clothes on the floor of my bedroom had been dirty, they needed it. The longer I'd traveled, the more strange looks I'd gotten on the bus. I didn't need to call additional attention to myself by looking like a vagrant.

Back home it'd been part of my act to hide the fact I wasn't sleeping. I didn't need to hide that anymore. There wasn't anyone around who'd care. Besides, staying awake seemed stupid now, anyway. I still didn't want to see or feel myself dying in my dreams, but I didn't like the idea of dying in real life because of tired mistakes, either. And if I kept avoiding sleep, that was going to happen.

The high-pressure showerhead made washing quick and easy for my underthings and shirt. The bar soap smelled okay, too. I rinsed until the water ran clear. The jeans were a pain. Waterlogged, they weighed too much to easily maneuver under the spray of water. Giving up, I stepped in and pulled the curtain closed. Standing under the steamy stream and alternating between rinsing the jeans and washing myself kept me awake until I finished.

Thankfully, towels were abundant in the bathroom. After drying off and wrapping my hair, I used another towel for my jeans. I rolled them inside the towel and stomped on the roll. The towel came away soaked. I grabbed a new towel and did it again. The second time the jeans no longer dripped water. I hung them on the rod and trudged to bed.

The pillows called to me. I tossed back the bedspread. Again, a dream wrapped around me as I climbed under the covers.

Glowing embers floated in the air, red stars against the night sky.

A dark haired girl stood before the blazing huts, facing the fire. The heat curled her hair and burned her skin, but she didn't back away. She screamed a name, searching fruitlessly in the shifting orange flames.

Her desperation crowded into me. My heart stuttered as we merged, her every thought and feeling becoming my own.

Turning, I ran into the darkness only to return a second later with a crude clay container filled with water. I tossed the contents toward the flames, but it fell short. Frustration and terror tore at me. I raced away to try again, this time stepping closer. Water hit the burning grass walls but didn't slow the consuming progress. With a hiss and sputter, the moisture evaporated.

Deep, mocking laughter echoed behind me.

"Child! You are not meant for this. Step away."

I spun toward my tormentors. "Help me! If you care as you claimed when you set the fires, help me put them out."

Auburn-hued from the reflection of the flames, a group of men stood watching. Several wore taunting grins.

The leader tilted his head as he studied me.

"Why? They are all dead," he assured me. "There is not one heart left beating, save yours."

A wall of guilt hit me. My family, gone. I screamed my anguish and fell to my knees. The soles of my feet, still so close to the flames, started to blister. My hair curled back from the heat and started to smoke. I fell silent and looked up with dull eyes.

I knew her choice as it settled in her mind. I fought her, wanting to wake up. Falling had been bad; this would be worse.

"*You win. I will choose.*" *I stood, embracing the pain in my feet. It's what my family had all felt while trying to protect me. Searing pain.*

"*You are indeed wise. Who will it be?*" *the leader asked. Several men stood back from the flames waiting eagerly for our choice.*

"*Not who. What.*" *I smiled as his triumphant grin fell.* "*Death.*" *I turned and ran into the flames.*

At first, I felt nothing. Then the pain of every blister and crack as I turned into a human candle consumed me. I opened my mouth to scream but nothing came out. There was only pain, everywhere.

I struggled to escape the pain. My heart thumped heavily as I shifted in my sleep, crying out. A hand soothed a tear from my cheek. Lips pressed against my forehead. A voice whispered, "I'm here." I tried to open my eyes, tried to breathe air that wasn't smoke-filled. My fight was in vain. I sank deeper as the dream shifted.

Hidden in the trees, a mother cradled her child in her arms. Sweat still shone on the woman's skin from her recent labor. Birds sang, and sunlit spots danced on the forest floor.

Still matted and slick from birth, the child suddenly squalled loudly.

The mother smiled at her child. "*I call you Jin, for Strength, as she promised us. I will keep you as safe as I am able and love you always. Protect us with your strength. Keep them at bay.*"

She put the child to her breast and laid her head back against the trunk of the tree.

Before her, the taupe gowned woman appeared. "*There can be no rest. You must run.*"

The startled woman opened her eyes and looked down in concern at the infant. "*She's so fragile,*" *she murmured.*

"*If she dies, she will be reborn as often as necessary each cycle. She will know pain and hardship.*" *The gowned woman knelt to stroke the smooth cheek. She felt compassion and sorrow seeing the fates of the child.* "*Balance must be maintained. The world will burn if they find her.*"

I LINGERED on the edge of sleep for several minutes before opening my eyes. My stomach churned as I remembered the newest death. I curled into a ball under the covers.

Why wouldn't the dreams just stop already? I'd run like the visions showed me. Maybe too late, though. The face of the man from the mall surfaced in my mind. His warm eyes looked gentle and amused, not malicious like the others. But I knew better than to trust them. I wrapped my arms around my knees. There was nothing gentle about the *things* chasing me. Every memory followed the same pattern. I ran from something that terrified me, the "something" exposed itself as a dog, turned man. The dogs—always a group of them— possessed large sleek heads, intelligent eyes, vicious teeth, and claws, which they put to use. After changing forms, they always talked about choosing. Choosing what? The way they acted and spoke, I guessed they wanted me to choose one of them. But to what purpose?

If I didn't kill myself, they tried forcing me to choose. The methods they used...I shuddered. I wasn't sure whose method was worse. Theirs or mine. In all my past lives I died horribly. I thought I understood the messages of the dreams—run. But if that was it, the dreams should have stopped. Instead, they'd changed. Two now had felt like a memory even though I hadn't merged with anyone. The two about babies.

Last night's second dream made my need to run sound like there was more at stake than just my death. Not that my death wasn't important enough to keep my feet moving. That woman made it sound like I didn't really have a choice.

If I hadn't connected with any of the women, why would it feel like a memory? My brows rose as I realized whom I'd overlooked. The infants in the first unique dream. Of course. Six of them just like the six variations of past lives I kept dreaming about. In the first unique dream, they hadn't been born; and in the second, the newborn hadn't yet experienced her gift, the things chasing her, or much of anything, really. Perhaps that was why I hadn't connected.

So, if those two dreams were still memories, then what that woman said scared me. Would the world truly burn if those dog-men caught me? I shuddered remembering the feeling of the flames consuming my flesh. Thankfully, the searing pain had been cut short.

I stopped that thought and with wide eyes froze under the covers. A gentle hand had soothed me. The kiss. Had it been real? I tried to breathe as quietly as possible as I listened for any strange noises in the room. All I could hear was my own heartbeat. Scrunching my eyes for a moment, I braced myself for the worst. I took a deep breath and quickly sat up, looking around the room.

Everything remained as it had when I'd gone to sleep. The outside door remained securely bolted, and the bathroom door still stood open. I let out a large shaky sigh.

That touch, like the dreams, had felt real yet it hadn't been a part of either dream. Rather, it was a fragment of the shift between them. That was one of the difficulties with sleep deprivation. The confused haziness between reality and imagination was hard to figure out. Well, that plus the headaches...

Flopping backwards, I rubbed my hands over my face. Maybe my first inclination to question my sanity had been right. What if all of this was really in my head? I laughed at myself. Of course it was in my head. But what if it was all just my imagination? That guy in the mall might have really just wanted the bathroom. And my physical reaction to him? Well, he was really good looking, and he had an accent. Who wouldn't suffer a little tummy tickle over that?

What did I really have as solid proof that something was out there? I cringed. I didn't have any. That just furthered my insanity theory. My poor Mom. And school. Exams were in a few weeks. I'd skipped so much school my grades were in the gutter. I had enough credits to graduate at the end of the semester if I passed my current class load. If I went back now and asked for help, I could still do it. Maybe. I'd probably still end up in a padded room for a while. But, the details of the dreams, and my ability to recall everything—touch, taste, smell— bothered me. It seemed so real. What if all those feelings *were* memories? If I went back home, would I be setting myself up for another non-choice...where I sacrificed myself?

With a sigh, I flipped back the covers and got out of bed. No matter what I chose, I needed to get dressed first. Padding across the carpet, I stepped into the bathroom to check my clothes. Dry, but stiff.

Dressing slowly, I mulled over my options. Home called to me. I had very little money left and nowhere to go. But, I needed to be sure. I didn't want to go back and bring trouble with me. This was a big enough town. I could find a job and wait out a few weeks. See if the dreams got better.

Gripping my jeans to pull them up, I felt a crinkle in the front pocket. Odd. I hadn't felt anything when I washed them. Something dug into my hip when I tugged them up the rest of the way.

I reached into the pocket, and my fingers brushed something. Hard plastic. I dug deeper. Paper. A chill swept through me as I wrapped my hand around the items and pulled them out. I stared at the five neatly folded hundred dollar bills, a note, and a cell phone lying in my open palm for a moment before I instinctively dropped them on the tan bathroom tile. Nothing was mine.

The hand wiping the tear from my face...

Icy fear pierced my stomach, and I sat heavily on the toilet seat. With shaking fingers, I tentatively picked up the note. Each crackle as I unfolded the hotel stationery sent a shiver down my spine. The paper had nothing on it but a phone number. No. No way! How had he found me again? Could it be the same guy? I crumpled the paper and threw it in the garbage along with the phone.

The dreams. People chasing me. It *wasn't* in my head. I stared at the solid proof that it was real. I couldn't go back home. I needed to keep running. Move. I eyed the money. I wasn't about to use the phone to call that number, but the money...I'll be taking that, thank-you-very-much!

Wasting no time, I gathered my things. At least, I'd showered and slept. Looking around to make sure I wasn't forgetting anything, I spotted stationery on the bedside table. The pen lay beside it. Lifting the pad to the light, I saw the indentations of the phone number that had been in my pocket. Of course, I already knew someone had been in my room but seeing the used pad of paper gave me the shakes again.

Run!

I didn't look back.

CHAPTER THREE

When I stepped outside the hotel, the chilled air slapped some sense into me; and I schooled my terror-filled expression. I couldn't doubt myself any longer. Not even slightly. The dreams had continued after my discovery for a reason. I had lifetimes of wisdom in me. I just needed to remember it all. Remembering would help me survive. But to remember, I needed a safe place to sleep...I needed a lot of it. Where though? A public place would be good. A place where moaning in my sleep wouldn't be too out of the ordinary. Somewhere low cost. A homeless shelter? I'd never been to one in real life and hoped they offered beds like in the movies.

Decided, I hailed a cab. The driver let me know about an overflow shelter where I'd have the best luck in winter months. After showing the cabbie I could pay, he took me there but dropped me off a few blocks away. I didn't think it would look good if I arrived there in a taxi.

I managed two nights before I admitted to myself I'd made the wrong decision. All of the dreams—each memory—depicted hellish nightmares of brutal past deaths, further driving into me the need to run. I still didn't have a destination. I just needed to keep moving. *They* were closing in. I would die.

Though I'd slept every chance I got, it felt like I'd stayed awake since I left the hotel. Hyped up on caffeine, I caught another bus. This time going south. I didn't pay attention to the destination, nor did I make small talk with sweet old ladies.

On the outside, anyone looking at me would see a calm, sleepy girl. Inside, I twitched and jittered; I moaned and cried as I remembered all the slow tiny cuts from the night before. It had taken a week to die. In that dream, they hadn't meant to kill me...her...us...whoever. A past version of one of the others like me had pretended to be more alert and resilient than she had actually been. When they'd realized they'd gone too far, it'd been too late.

THE RIDE LEFT me in a small town with no motel.

I cast my eyes in every direction trying to decide my next move when I spotted an old iron support bridge just down one of the side roads. Its metal skeleton blended with the leafless branches on the banks surrounding it. Trudging in that direction, I kept alert for anyone following me.

Since staying at the shelter, something had changed. The sleep-inducing memories pulled at me even while awake. The pull had an edge to it. It wouldn't be denied for long. I needed a power nap. Thirty minutes tops, I promised myself.

I checked for cars before I stepped off the road and made my way into the ravine that the bridge spanned. The wooden decking provided covering but didn't make a good shelter due to the gaps. Crushed stone had once covered the embankment. Weeds and other growth concealed much of it now. The dry winter vegetation snapped in the quiet as I headed under the bridge and picked a spot where most of the rocks were still exposed.

Peeling off my hoodie, I lay down. The rocks and cold wouldn't allow for a deep sleep. The waiting dream pulled me under before I laid my head on my arm.

I immediately merged with the past.

In this dream, I was myself, or at least a past version of myself, and remembered the man standing before me. He had been responsible for my death twice in the same cycle. He looked much older now.

"This time, we're going to do things a little differently." He motioned for two of his men to step forward. *"Hold her, and open her mouth."*

One man stepped behind me, grasping my already bound arms. Another man gripped my jaw roughly and pressed his fingers inward until I opened my mouth.

My face ached. His fingers left bruises on my skin, but I showed no fear, no pain. I remembered him. I remembered everything. This, however, was new and I wondered what he had in mind.

He motioned for another to join our little group.

This man I'd never seen before. Something about him pulled me, and I felt certain it wasn't good. His eyes roamed over me from head to feet, lingering in any place that caught his interest.

"Her scent is perfect."

"Go then," the leader motioned the man to step toward us.

I braced myself for a brutal Claiming, but the man surprised me by stopping a step away. He tilted his neck to the side. I didn't have time to wonder what it meant. The man holding me shoved my face forward into the man's neck. I pulled my bruised lips back just before the second man holding me moved his hands on my jaw. Instead of forcing it open, he forced it closed so fast and hard that I bit the man's neck. He howled in excitement. I pulled back, stunned and not understanding what had just happened. Both men let go of me and stepped back leaving me with the man I'd just bitten.

He pulled me to him and kissed my mouth passionately. He bruised my lips further. Still, I felt a stirring within me and tentatively responded. His hands tugged at my clothing.

"Stop. You can't mate with her. Not yet."

The man kissing me lifted his head with a feral growl.

The leader didn't back down. Instead, he partially shifted. "She's weak. She's died on us twice already. You need to be in control, not newly Claimed. Wait."

My hands, still bound behind my back, prevented me from catching myself when the man I'd bitten abruptly let go. I fell backward, landing hard on sharp rocks that bit into my thighs and buttocks.

Dream and reality blended in that moment. Rocks still bit into my butt, but they bit through my jeans. I needed to wake up but couldn't open my eyes. The dream still lingered. I hadn't died yet. I always died...except for those dreams with the Taupe Lady. Why hadn't I died?

Something settled over me gently. The physical contact gave me what I needed to pull myself from the dream world. My eyes popped open.

The bronze-haired, hazel-eyed man from the mall swam into focus. He hovered over me. His hands were on my hoodie. We stared at each other for a heartbeat. Then he moved, straightening the hoodie over my shoulder.

I scrambled to my feet. My eyes never left his as he slowly stood from where he'd been crouched on the balls of his feet next to me. How could something so cruel still make my stomach flip in such a toe-tingling way?

We stared at each other for several long moments. His eyes swept over me with a tender look. Concern clouded them when I involuntarily shivered.

He lifted the hoodie still held in his fingertips. "My name is..."

That was as far as he got before I tried to deliver a swift kick to his balls. He dodged smoothly, but his easygoing expression changed to one of wary shock.

I didn't wait for him to recover but turned and scrambled up the embankment to reach the road. It was pointless. I knew he was much faster. Still, I pushed on. Stones slid under my feet. He caught me from behind while I was still scrambling over the loose stones and pinned my arms to my side.

"Easy, luv. Unlike you, I mean no harm," he spoke softly near my ear, sending tingles along my spine. His grip, though firm, wasn't rough. He turned and walked back under the bridge, carrying me easily.

My heart freaked out, going into a very painful overdrive.

He surprised me by letting me go. I spun to face him again with my knees bent and my weight on the balls of my feet, ready to move. His expression seemed more concerned than wary. Probably concerned that someone would hear. We were fairly close to town, no doubt the reason why he'd pulled me back under the bridge.

"As I was saying, my name is Luke Taylor. And you are?"

"Not yours," I answered automatically. "Touch me again and I'll sac tap you so hard you'll be coughing semen for a week. And this time I won't miss."

I felt a moment of pride at my tough words, but that quickly passed as the details of the life I'd just dreamt continued to filter in. I'd survived the fight, but at only fourteen, I hadn't survived long in the hands of my Mate. He'd been rough and brutish but not completely uncaring. As his leader suggested, my fragility hadn't withstood him.

I was older in this life and determined not to be as fragile. I wouldn't be used that way again. They'd wanted to control me to influence a decision. I wasn't sure what decision yet, but I knew it involved the others like me. The ones who had briefly shared the womb of the Taupe Lady with me, the ones I sometimes dreamed of.

In response to my eloquent threat, his lips twitched as if he wanted to smile.

That gave me pause. Something about this was wrong...

The wind rattled through the empty branches while I tried to pinpoint the problem. I risked looking away to scan the bank and trees behind him.

"What are you looking for?"

It wasn't until I looked back at him that I realized what I'd been looking for —what was wrong. "Your pack of murdering dogs."

Surprise flashed in his eyes. "I'm alone."

I snorted in disbelief. They were never alone. Always in a pack. I stayed tense, waiting for his next move. I knew better than to try running again. Who knew how long his humor would last.

He didn't say anything, just continued to study me. After a time listening to the dry rattle of barren tree branches and dead weeds around us, he sighed and sat down on the patch of rocks where we'd started.

I flicked the briefest glance at the trees again, puzzled. "What are you doing?"

"Waiting for you to decide your next move. Keeping up with you is exhausting. I thought giving you money would keep you in one place long enough so you could get the sleep you obviously need." He pulled his knees up and rested his forearms on them in a relaxed pose. "So what are your nightmares about?"

The reminder that he'd been in my room had me narrowing my eyes. "All of the ways I'd rather die than bite the neck of a disgusting werewolf who'd be willing to rape a fourteen year old girl just to have control over her when Judgement comes." The lingering memories of my young past life still haunted me, and the words were out of my mouth without thinking.

He flinched as he looked down at the ground. I didn't know what I meant by it all, but the ring of it sounded so right. Something in what I'd said struck a chord in him, too, because with a clenched jaw, he paled. Satisfaction coursed through me. About time one of them felt guilty about what they did. Just as I had that thought, an angry red flush flooded his face.

"Has someone hurt you?" His softly intense words sounded strained. The veins on the back of his hand stood out. This wasn't a mystery to me. I'd witnessed this many times in my dreams. He struggled to contain the beast.

I recalled the word I'd used. Werewolf. So laughably impossible to me a few short months ago, I embraced the truth of it...him...and of the nightmare of my life.

"Tell me who," he demanded. When he looked up, his eyes were larger in his skull. The pupils dilated as he struggled to maintain control.

I didn't bother wondering why he cared. They were territorial creatures, possessive of their unClaimed women. Even more so of their Mates.

"In this life? No one yet. But it looks like you're about to fix that. In other lives, they've already died." I thought about my dreams and wondered if that was true. Was this my first life in this cycle? I knew I could be born several times in the same cycle, making it possible to meet some of them in more than one life. I'd dreamt that very scenario.

My words seemed to turn off a switch in him. His change receded. "This life?" Confusion laced his voice.

He's good, I thought. The rest had just bullied and beat me. No one had tried acting like they cared.

I narrowed my eyes at him. "Why are you toying with me? We both know what you want."

He shook his head slowly and stood, pulling something from his pocket. Hand outstretched, he offered me the cell phone I'd tossed into the garbage at the last hotel. "Press call. I have a...friend, Gabby. She sent me to look for you. Thought you might be like her."

His words burst a bubble of anger within me. For a moment, I just struggled to breathe. One of my original sisters? This was different. New. Still, I couldn't trust him. They'd talked about the others like me before, but we were never in their control at the same time. Not for very long, anyway. We kept dying on them. The thought made me smile briefly. It faded into a frown. I didn't want to die again.

Looking up at the overcast sky, I decided something felt different this time. Some balance had been tipped. I just wished I knew in whose favor.

Declining to take the phone, I watched him as I gathered my things and put my hoodie back on. In the distance, I heard the rumble of a car starting up. Slowly, I turned away from him and climbed back up to the road. I reached the top. He didn't stop me. I didn't look back but remained focused forward.

Gravel crunched underfoot as I walked back into town. His steps echoed quietly behind me. I hoped it was well behind me. The car turned onto our road. I didn't change my step, my breathing, nothing. No physical signs to give me away. The car increased its speed.

At the last moment, I stepped into the road waving the car down. My pulse jumped and my hands shook. Kill me or stop. Please stop. I didn't want to die; I just wanted a ride. A fast getaway. It was a risk not just for me, but also for the driver of the car if Luke reached the car before I got in.

The two guys in the car didn't hesitate. The car pulled to the side, and I quickly slid into the backseat slamming the door closed with a breathless, "Thanks."

The car didn't move. I glanced at the driver, but he wasn't focused on me. I followed his gaze and met Luke's eyes through the window. My stomach plunged to my toes. He stood on the shoulder of the road, less than a step away, looking down at the car—at me—through the glass. Though his stance was relaxed, he didn't look very happy. I fought not to give into complete panic as his eyes narrowed on the boys in the front seat. Luke looked back at me, studied me for a moment, and arched a brow.

"Is your friend getting in, too?" the driver asked.

I held Luke's gaze and shook my head. Luke's lips twitched again as if he fought not to smile.

"A'right." The kid put the car in drive and slowly pulled away.

I kept my eyes on Luke. I'd seen his kind do incredible things and didn't trust him for a moment. From the front, the driver asked where I was headed.

"Doesn't matter. Next town if you're going that far."

Luke faded into the distance along with his last censoring gaze.

THOUGH I FIRMLY BELIEVED THERE was nothing worse than facing a werewolf, the two boys in the front seat tested me. They suggestively asked about compensation for the ride they provided. Then, when I feigned ignorance of their innuendos, they flat out asked for head.

"Pull over," I said through clenched teeth.

"Oh, come on," the driver said with a laugh. "We're just messing with you."

The warmth of the car and the soft vibrations weren't enough to keep me lucid, so I rolled down the window. With their current line of conversation, I couldn't afford to fall asleep.

"I've been messed with enough. Just get me to the next town or as far as you can take me."

The conversation silenced for almost a minute, and I let out a slow breath. As if it were a signal, the passenger turned in his seat to watch me.

"So do you have a boyfriend?"

Are you freaking kidding me? I'm on the run from sadistic beasts that actually wear fur and run on all fours, and he wanted to know if I had a boyfriend?

"No." I met his gaze. After a few long moments, his smile faded, and he turned forward once more.

The respite from their inane conversation gave me a moment to consider my meeting with Luke. He was the first one ever to offer his name. Sure, I'd learned a few names over my lifetimes but always by listening to the conversation flowing around me. Not only had he offered his name, but he'd also let me go. I had no illusions. He could have stopped me easily by reaching through the glass and pulling me out forcibly. Why hadn't he?

"Can you roll that window up?" The driver reached over and turned up the heat.

I needed the ride. Though it wasn't a good idea, I rolled up the window. Within a minute, the temperature in the car jumped from cool to goodnight. My eyes blinked closed. In my dreams, I could no longer separate my past-self from my present-self. It was just me...

Several of them gathered where I lay broken at the bottom of a ravine. I'd tried jumping over the gap and misjudged the distance. For once, I had not purposely flung myself over the edge of something. My right leg throbbed painfully; and when I tried touching it, my fingers came away wet before I even got to the spot that really hurt. I shook all over. Definitely shock.

Lying on my back, looking up at the overcast sky and the scrub-dotted crumbling edge of the ravine, their faces danced in and out of my line of sight as each of them inspected me. Finally, the leader came close.

"We remember through stories passed down from each generation which of you is most likely to fight or run. Which has succumbed in the past. Who is born first. Who dies too easily. We remember." He reached down and smoothed back a strand of hair that covered part of my face. "You, my wise little girl, have given us plenty of trouble because you remember, too. Let us create some new memories, shall we?"

Their hands tugged at my clothes and grasped my arms. Hurt and bleeding, I fought them as they...

...lifted me.

"Never again," a voice said near my head. "She's crazy!"

A hand fumbled for hold on my flailing arm. I stopped fighting and pried my eyes open. The driver had my legs while the passenger struggled with my arms.

"I'm awake," I said. "Stop!"

The driver dropped me when I met his shocked gaze. The passenger was slower to catch on, and I had to yank my arms from his hold. They both stared at me for a second while I quickly looked around. We were still on a straight stretch of country road. I couldn't have slept more than fifteen minutes. We hadn't put enough distance between us and that *thing*, Luke.

"I have bad dreams," I said as I brought my gaze back to the driver. "Night terrors. The car got too warm, and I fell asleep. It won't happen again. Please, I just need a ride to the next town."

CHAPTER FOUR

THE BANTER SUGGESTING FAVORS CHANGED TO WORRIED, DARTING glances as the driver sped up. I struggled to stay awake—despite my promise— as we drove another twenty minutes in silence. With a sudden jerk of the steering wheel, the driver pulled over to drop me off near a department store. The door had barely closed before the car pulled away. I watched the car shrink in the distance. They were idiots but idiots who may have saved my life. I should be harder to track in a town this size.

Walking a short distance to a sub shop, I ordered food and sat down to plan my next move. I hadn't been eating much since running, so I wolfed the sub down in seconds. People paused in their own eating and stared. Focused on picking the pieces of lettuce off the paper, I stopped paying attention to everyone around me. So, I jumped a little when someone slid into the booth and nudged another sub toward me.

Looking up, I froze with a piece of lettuce still pinched between my fingers. My stomach flipped in a sickeningly pleasant way, and my heart gave an excited beat before I could suppress my reaction.

Luke sat across from me. His hair was windblown, and he had a thread of worry in his eyes.

"Did they take your money?" he asked with a slight growl.

I flicked my eyes around the small seating area. No other men. Well, a few men sat with their families, but they didn't count. He'd come alone again.

"What are you talking about?" I asked quietly, narrowing my eyes. This cat and mouse game made me edgy. When would the others appear?

"The car pulled over halfway here, and you all stood on the side of the road. Why?" He paused and his jaw clenched briefly before he leaned forward slightly. In a quiet, low voice he asked, "Did they hurt you?"

Hurt me? I frowned at him. He was worried they'd pulled over to what? Have a good time with me? My temper flared.

"Why are you doing this?" I said as I tried to keep my voice down.

My dreams had taught me to stay quiet to save lives. Through self-sacrifice, I saved others. Life after life...death after death, I had learned the people who tried helping me always died. I realized I hated my life as much as I wanted to cling to it.

He leaned back and studied me. "Because I want to help you," he said with a slightly confused smile. He lifted a hand as if to reach across the table and touch me.

I jerked back suppressing the urge to punch him in the face. How dare he mock me by feigning ignorance and sympathy.

"If you want to help me, die." My gaze remained locked on him, ready for anything.

His eyes flared slightly, and he dropped his hand. "You are very hostile for someone your age."

I snorted. "Just how many teenagers do you know?" He looked like he'd passed eighteen several years ago. I guessed he had to be in his mid-twenties.

He sighed and scratched his jawline. After a moment he said, "Perhaps we started off poorly. I'm Luke Taylor. My friend, Gabby, sent me to find you. She thinks you may have something in common with her."

I felt a tug of sympathy for Gabby. "How is she?" I murmured before I could stop myself. If they had her, she would already be suffering; and I really didn't want to know the extent of it. It would just hurt more.

"Last time I saw her, she was weak but recovering." He nudged the sub toward me again. "Eat. You're too thin, and you'll need your strength."

Weak? I remembered all the torture his kind had inflicted upon me. He wanted me to be strong enough to endure. "You son of a—"

He cut me off by reaching over the table and gently clapping a hand over my mouth. He looked annoyed for the first time. "Hush," he warned when I would have moved away to keep talking. "The decisions you make and the words you speak influence the people around you. Be aware of your influence."

I scowled at him. What was he talking about?

He sighed and answered my question as if I'd spoken it aloud. "There is an adorable little girl just behind you. She can't be more than two."

When I turned, he dropped his hand. Two seats away, an admittedly cute little girl watched us with curiosity. Taking a calming breath, I turned back toward Luke.

He was gone. The cell phone rested on the table, a number already punched in. I stared at the phone for several heartbeats. What was with this guy? Appearing, disappearing. Letting me go. Giving me money and now food. As much as I wanted to know about Gabby, I wouldn't...couldn't call. They would use her to trap me just like they would use my mom. Besides, she might not even be one of the others I dreamed about.

I ignored the phone but took the sub, shoved it in my duffle, and left. Once outside, I carefully surveyed the light foot traffic around me. Luke seemed to have disappeared, but I didn't believe he had gone far.

Keeping to the populated area, I walked slowly as I tried to figure him out. He had plenty of opportunity to force me to go with him, to hurt me, but he hadn't done either. Instead, he'd found me in the hotels and snuck into the rooms without notice to what? To watch me sleep? To leave me a note and money? But he'd left me alone in the homeless shelter. Why? Probably too many people for whatever he had in mind. My eyes darted around counting as the thought "too many people" stuck in my head.

In all the past lives I'd remembered so far, never had humans gathered in such great numbers. Each time, the dogs had found us in small villages and decimated those around us. No. Not dogs. Werewolves. I needed to face the reality of their existence. The werewolves were vicious and strong, but I'd witnessed them receive injuries. They had weaknesses...and now *we* outnumbered them.

For the first time in days, a smile lit my face. Maybe there was hope after all.

I WORE a new rough woven tunic that my mother and I had dyed with a red and brown pattern. At almost nine, I was glad to have something that made me feel pretty especially when I stepped out of our sod home and saw the stranger.

A boy on the cusp of manhood stood before me. His sudden appearance surprised me.

Winded and shaking, his eyes traced over my tiny frame just as I studied him. His dark hair dripped with sweat and stuck to his olive skin.

My mother and sisters stepped out of our home behind me. I gave the boy a small smile and wondered why he'd come.

The boy fell to his knees before me and brought his face level with mine. His move surprised me, but I didn't budge. I was too curious. My mother made an anxious sound behind me but didn't tell the boy to leave.

His deep brown eyes locked onto mine. "They are coming," he warned with a slight growl in his voice. "Just behind me. They will kill your family. You need to run—as far as you can —to save them."

In this life, I remained unaware of the danger of which he spoke. Perhaps this was one of my sisters' lives where I didn't have the dreams to remember. Or perhaps I was too young for the dreams yet. With the boy's shaking, I knew what was coming even if my dream-self did not.

My mother gasped and tried reaching for me. It proved too much for the struggling boy, and he burst into his fur. My sisters screamed and ran toward the field where my father struggled to turn the hard-packed earth. My mother, sobbing and pleading for mercy, followed them.

I stood frozen, watching the wild creature before me. He struggled with himself, slowly pulling back the beast until he was again in human form.

"I'm sorry. I didn't mean to do that. You must hurry. There are too many of them coming this way." He glanced over his shoulder, looking back at the way he'd come.

He turned back toward me with worry and desperation in his eyes. "Come here," he said.

Heart hammering, I stepped forward. He clasped my hand in his own and looked at me with kindness in his eyes. "I'm going to protect you the only way I know how. After I do, you'll need to run, little one. Go west. Look for my people. We will help you." He tucked a piece of hair behind my ear. "I need you to bite me. It will confuse them and allow you to move away from your family."

It took some convincing, but I did as he asked. He shuddered when I broke the skin, and as I apologized for hurting him, I patted his shoulder.

"Never mind that. Remember, west," he said. He moved back a step, burst into his fur again, and took off at an amazing speed.

By then, my mother and father were running toward me. I waited for them and admitted to biting the boy but forgot about his plea for me to run.

My mother clasped me to her and wouldn't let go. We were still standing like that when a group of men arrived.

I watched as the men attacked my family. Too late, I remembered the boy telling me to run. I screamed my anguish while the leader yelled and cursed.

"Find him. He needs to die so she can Claim another!" the man snarled through his elongating canines.

The dream shifted, but the memory did not fade.

The lady in the taupe gown stood in the circle while watching the women depart. One woman turned back, a worried look in her eyes and her hand resting protectively on her belly.

"What is it, dear one?" the Taupe Lady asked softly.

"I will do as you ask and keep her safe. But, who am I protecting her from?"

The Taupe Lady drifted from the circle, her gossamer skirts flowing as if in a breeze. "Not who, but what. Diversity may have gone too far in the beginning and created creatures your fragile race has no hope to withstand during their evolution and their struggles for dominance."

"I do not understand," the woman murmured in confusion.

The Taupe Lady reached forward and touched the woman's cheek gently. "It is not for you to understand, dear one, but for the child you carry. She is wise, and her knowledge will last through the ages."

I woke with a start as a train rumbled to a halt mere feet from my bench. The air swirled around me...reminding me of the Taupe Lady's dress. I stood on shaky legs and glanced around the shelter. A few other people waited with us as several passengers disembarked, no one I considered suspicious. Still my skin crawled.

A man sitting on the bench a few feet away caught my attention. His focus wasn't on me, but on a figure growing smaller in the distance. My stomach did a crazy flip when I looked.

"Nice of him to see you off," the man said as he stood up to get on the train. "Should have stayed just a few more seconds. Boyfriend?"

Instead of answering, I reached into the pocket of my duffle and found my boarding pass along with more cash. He'd put it there. How much did this guy have on him? Ticket in hand, I climbed aboard and chose a seat away from most of the passengers. The ticket would take me two states west, but I wouldn't actually ride the train that far. When I'd closed my eyes on the bench, I'd anticipated he'd find me. And just as I'd hoped, he'd looked at the ticket.

Leaning my head against the glass, I thought of the two dreams I'd just had. Though I'd only dreamt a portion of a past life in the first dream, I recalled how that life had ended.

The boy's arrival before the rest of his pack had been unique and had spared me from torture. Instead, the men had focused their efforts on finding him. After searching for a day, they carried me east to their settlement. There, they shoved me into a rough half-buried hut already occupied with several other young women.

The women had looked up when I'd arrived but made no move toward me until the door closed. When they did approach, they began sniffing me and asking questions. They were werewolves like the men, but not as vicious. I'd lived with them for five years while the search for the boy who'd run continued.

During that time I had feelings that were not my own. Gradually, based on information from my cohabitants, I'd come to understand that it was the boy I felt.

Finally out of patience, the leader had forced me to bite someone else. It was then that they learned something very significant. The bond created with Claiming could be broken without killing one of the pair. You just needed to Claim another.

That memory, along with the latest one of the Taupe Lady, had me questioning what I thought I knew. The werewolves wanted me to bite one of their own and complete the mating bond. Typically, I didn't live long after that so the purpose behind their insistence to choose still remained a mystery.

Likewise, the boy in the dream confused me. He'd been the only one I'd Claimed who had left me. How ironic that I sat on a train heading west...the same direction he'd told me to run. The thought settled over me for a moment before I realized the potential full message of the dream. It wasn't just the direction. Maybe the werewolves that kept killing me weren't the sum of what they represented. Could there be a few of their kind out there different from the rest? Some who were willing to help? Could Luke be like that boy?

I opened my duffle and ate the sub Luke had purchased for me. The same thing I'd ordered for myself. I thought back to the times we'd met while I was awake and the times I slept. He treated me the same as the boy had. With kindness. Sighing, I watched the scenery as the train rumbled west and fought the ever-increasing pull of sleep.

I STEPPED off the train with blurry eyes and scanned the crowd. Thankfully, I didn't see any familiar faces. I'd stayed on the train as long as possible but hadn't even traveled halfway to my destination. I knew I needed to crash soon and hadn't thought my fellow passengers would understand my thrashing and screaming when I did.

Stumbling forward, I left the station as other passengers boarded. This stop, a decent sized town, had several hotels near the station. I picked one at random, paid for a room, and trudged up a flight of stairs. Sliding the room card through the pad, the door clicked open. I didn't look around as I stepped in and closed the door. The duffle, barely clinging to my weary shoulder, fell to the floor.

I fell face-first into the firm mattress. I bounced once but barely noticed. Sleep had already wrapped its arms around me. Fully dressed and lying on top the covers, I gave in.

Absolute darkness surrounded me. A low distant rumble filled the cool, dank air. Lying on my back, I attempted to stretch out my arms, but they didn't move. Bindings bit into the skin of my biceps and forearms. A small noise escaped me.

"She is awake," a voice rumbled nearby.

"Untie her," another voice responded.

My heart hammered as two large hands lifted me and set me on my feet. A light exploded in the darkness, blinding me.

I could remember dogs trotting into the village. They had rolled onto their backs, vying for father's attention. He had laughed and thrown them some meat scraps. They, in turn, had hunted down two rabbits to set at father's feet. He'd piled straw outside the sheep pen, and the dogs stayed there for three nights. On the fourth night, when father sent me out to feed them, they changed into men. One had scooped me up while the other gagged me. Then, they'd run.

But, something had gone wrong. While running, three dogs crossed our trail. The one carrying me had dropped me to the ground as he shifted and launched at one of the new dogs, tearing into it with deadly force. Then, whirling, he had gone after another while his partner fought the remaining one. The fights had inched closer to me, and I'd scrambled to my feet to try to run, but someone had caught me up from behind. When I'd looked up, the man who held me had a horrible gash where his right eye should have been.

The same man stared at me in the dim light while his partner untied me. Dried blood crusted his face, but I noticed the gash had closed a bit. His eye socket, however, appeared sunken.

"Do not dwell on it, child," he said. "Your life is worth an eye and more."

With the simple thoughts of youth, I didn't understand how I could be worth such an injury but kept quiet.

"My name is Roulf, and I have searched for you these last fifty years."

Since I'd just reached my fifth year, I couldn't understand why he'd looked so long. "Why did you bind me?"

"We could not allow you to run. The cycle ends in a few days. They are still looking for the last one. You. This is your third life in this cycle. My son helped you in the last life," he nodded at the man beside him, "and felt when the bond was broken."

His eyes didn't leave mine as if he waited for me to answer. I shrugged at him, my younger-self not understanding while my older, dream-self did. An ache grew within me. I wanted my father.

"You do not need to understand now, just listen. What I tell you will matter later. They must have all of you alive at once. It does not matter to them if you are Claimed. You saw what they did to me. If they take you, they will do the same to you. They will hurt everyone you have ever loved, and people you never knew. You cannot let them take you," he stressed with a slight growl. He sighed and rolled his shoulders. His son set a comforting hand on him. Roulf reached up and patted it as he turned to smile sadly at his son.

"We will stay here as long as we can. If they find us, you must run that way," he said pointing toward one end of the dark tunnel, "and remember my words."

They extinguished the light then, and I sat isolated in the darkness, my little heart hammering, listening for a threat I didn't understand. I shivered and tried to hold in the whimper that wanted to escape.

Roulf's son, who had already helped me once in his life, sat beside me and wrapped an arm around me.

He whispered, "When you need to feel safe, remember this." He gave my arms a gentle squeeze, much like my father might have if I'd woken with a bad dream. I leaned into him trying not to sniffle.

He remained beside me for two days, holding me in the darkness for hours, keeping me safe with his father not far from us. I slept and didn't complain about hunger when I woke. Roulf's words and their cautious silence impressed upon me the need to stay hidden.

In the dark, I lost all concept of day and night, but they never did. Baen, as I heard his father call him, whispered to me occasionally, telling me when a night animal entered the cave.

When I felt Baen suddenly shift into his wolf form, I knew we had been found.

Roulf pulled me to my feet, spun me to the left, and nudged me forward. I didn't say anything. I knew what he wanted me to do. Sticking my hands out, I groped through the darkness, wanting to run but only managing a slow stumble.

"I am proud to call you son, Baen," Roulf said.

The words struck a deeper fear in me than Baen's abrupt shifting had. I tried moving faster. After his words, nothing but silence rang behind me.

Ahead, the distant roar, which had kept us company during our stay, grew gradually louder. Still, I stumbled forward. The thunderous rumble deafened me. The walls of the cave vibrated beneath my hands. Before me, a dim light glowed, a tiny bit of sight in the nothingness. I hurried toward it. The air grew damp. Running now, heart hammering with a mixture of fear—instilled by Roulf—and excitement for the light, I ignored the pain in my feet as I kept slipping on the sharp wet rock.

When I reached a churning wall of light, I stopped in confusion, not understanding what I saw. Mist coated my eyelashes, and I blinked away the droplets. The way Roulf had told me to go was blocked. I cautiously reached out. Water tore at my small hand, pulling me forward and down. Before it pulled me too far, I tugged my bruised hand back and stared at the rushing water. I couldn't leave this way. Turning, I looked into the darkness behind me. Could I go back to Roulf and Baen?

Something glinted in the black tunnel as I considered going back. Two somethings that slowly grew larger. Eyes. Belonging to a dog. I felt a surge of hope until the dog shifted, and I saw it was neither Roulf nor Baen. Blood coated this man, and my heart ached for my would-be friends. The man stretched an arm forward and motioned for me to come to him.

My little heart hammered as I remembered Roulf's words, "You cannot let them take you." My tears mixed with the mist as I stepped into the falls.

I screamed myself awake and heard someone pounding on the door. Pulling myself off the mattress, I quickly checked the peephole. A member of the hotel staff, along with a police officer, stood outside. I debated not answering the door but ended up pulling it open despite my reservations.

After explaining about a bad dream and letting the officer into my room, the hotel very politely asked me to leave as I had disturbed too many of their guests. Just as politely, I asked for a refund since I hadn't even slept an hour.

DUFFLE once again on my shoulder, I walked away from the hotel feeling the eyes of the police officer on my back. At least the hotel had refunded my money. I stopped a passerby and asked for directions to the nearest bus stop determined to keep heading west.

Still feeling exhausted, I climbed aboard the next bus, eyed the other passengers, and wished I knew what to look for. Werewolves looked just like everyone else until they started transforming.

I sat near the window, looked out with a sigh, and thought of the Taupe Lady. If she had the ability to carry six of us within her and send us into different mothers, why couldn't she help us? Why did I have to die over and over? I thought back to the very first dream of her. She'd sent each of us to our mothers with a word: Strength, Wisdom, Hope, Peace, Prosperity, and Courage. From the way some of those things had talked to each of us in past lives, I knew I was Wisdom. So which sister had Luke and his people already found?

Shifting in my seat, I pulled up my hood so I could block out the world as I thought. My damn dreams. They had shown me that the werewolves would come and that I needed to run. And I had. I'd run from my home, my friends...my mom. But the dreams weren't stopping. They had, however, changed. A little. I wasn't stupid...maybe just a little slow, but hey I was sleep deprived. Twice Baen had helped me...or tried to, anyway. Two dreams showing me that not all werewolves were bad. It gave me a tiny spark of hope, and I knew what I needed to do. West, I thought.

The faint smell of soap tickled my nose. The dreams had just pointed out what I was too afraid to believe; someone had already been helping me. I unzipped the hoodie, pulled it off, and studied it. It wasn't mine as I'd thought when I'd pulled it out of the duffle in the back of the truck. Holding it to my nose, I inhaled deeply. It smelled like Luke. He'd also given me money. Several times. Granted, he'd also snuck into my hotel room—several times—and seemed to be following me like a creeper. It would take more than cash and a hoodie to earn my trust, but I would listen to the dreams. I sighed and shrugged back into the hoodie.

My head ached from the need to sleep. After a few torturous hours, the bus stopped for a refuel. Stepping off the bus into the increasingly frigid air, I chose a road heading out of town and started walking.

CHAPTER FIVE

Several hours later, I heard the loud roar of a motorcycle behind me. I looked back, saw it was Luke, and suppressed the urge to run. It wouldn't do any good. He would just chase me. Besides, I'd already decided to talk to him...to see if he really was like Baen. So I stopped walking and waited.

My stomach tugged and twirled as I watched the bike slow. I forced down my physical reaction—it had been used against me in the past—but that didn't stop me from appreciating how good he looked.

He pulled up beside me and cut the engine. His hair was slightly mussed from the ride, and his eyes sparked with annoyance.

"Are you mental?" He dismounted with grace and pulled off his leather jacket.

Too stunned by the sudden display of beautifully defined pectorals beneath his t-shirt, I couldn't answer. Sure, I'd remembered a few Mates from past lives, but none attracted me like this. He was even more dangerous to me because of it.

He stalked toward me, and I didn't even have a chance to squeak in protest when he pulled the duffle off my shoulder.

"You'll freeze out here." He set the still warm jacket on my shoulders and zipped me in without waiting for me to put my arms in the sleeves.

Every time he found me, he helped me. I tipped my head back and stared into his eyes. He watched me intently. Tiny flecks of green and gold peeked through the soft brown of his eyes. Inside, I gave a little sigh of appreciation. How stupid was I to want to trust this man? I needed to be practical. Squashing my tingling awareness, I recalled what had happened in my last dream. Even my help had set me up to die. Wasn't there a way to live that didn't involve torture or forced servitude?

"Tell me about my sister," I said as I shoved my arms through the sleeves. The jacket was better than the hoodie alone.

"Sister?" he asked completely confused.

"The one who sent you to find me." It came out with more force than I'd intended. I knew better than to provoke his kind. I was tired. Trying again in a softer voice, I said, "You said she was weak. Did you hurt her?"

He snorted. "Not a chance. Her guard dog doesn't let anyone near her." He smirked and added, "Well, he tried to keep us away."

What was that supposed to mean? She was being guarded, and he'd found a way to her. But, which side was guarding and which side was going around the guard?

I eyed him as he stood before me. In just a shirt, he didn't seem bothered by the cold. They never really did. I needed to know his intentions. Did he really want to help me like Baen, or was he like the rest? I couldn't ask him outright. These creatures were never honest. But, they were easy to provoke.

Calming my overly attentive physical awareness, I stepped toward him. He watched me with cautious eyes, no doubt remembering my attempt to knee him. Placing my hands on his shoulders, I stood on my tiptoes stretching to get as close to his height as possible. His heat warmed my palms, and my stomach went crazy. The muscles beneath my fingertips twitched, and a shudder passed through him. His pupils dilated. His attention intensified, and I doubted he heard anything around us. His reactions affirmed what I already knew. We had a connection. But what would he do about it?

I leaned in further and let my cheek touch his jaw. His tremors grew. I knew I was playing a dangerous game. His hands settled on my waist, and the touch spiked my heart rate despite my efforts to control myself. I couldn't be sure whether my reaction was fear or excitement, and it worried me. I needed to stay strong. I knew that a sliver of weakness could bring my downfall.

Against his ear, I whispered, "I will not choose you," as a test—as a statement of truth.

When I pulled back, his eyes were closed and his jaw clenched. As slowly as I'd approached him, I eased away. His hands dropped from my sides without a fight. My throat tightened as I watched him struggle. Fear pooled in me. He inhaled deeply, and I knew he smelled it on me.

After a moment, he calmed and opened his eyes.

"Good," he agreed amicably. "Someone your age shouldn't be choosing."

My age? His words confused me as much as they comforted me. He hadn't grabbed me or insisted I was wrong, and I hadn't died. Still, I'd never met one of them that didn't insist on biting. Even Baen had asked me to bite him the first time I'd met him, and I'd been nine in that life. Things might just be looking up.

He turned away from me and mounted the motorcycle. Then, he held my duffle out toward me. "Coming?"

He'd found me and, apparently, was set on following me. Why not take advantage of it? Stepping forward with lingering reservations, I grabbed the bag and nodded. If he wasn't here to help, I'd find out soon enough. At least sleep wouldn't tempt me so much if the wind battered me as we traveled.

I put the strap across my body and climbed on behind him. As I wrapped my arms around his middle, I noticed his flinch.

"And stay away from my neck," he said as he lifted his feet from the road and eased forward.

I ducked behind him within seconds. The wind bit into me with ferocious insistence, driving me closer to him. He twitched occasionally and told me to hold still several times. I didn't have his ability to stay warm though. Finally, red cheeked, I laid my face against his back. Through his thin shirt, he warmed me. Sighing, I closed my watering eyes.

She stood before me in her taupe gown looking sad and serene at the same time. Nothing surrounded us but the tiny glow of thousands of multi-colored life sparks.

"This was the beginning," she said lifting a pale hand to indicate the sparks. Most had a blue center with a grey halo. Almost as many had a blue center with a green halo. Only a few had a yellow center with a green halo. Among those, I saw six unique colors and knew whom they represented.

"The Judgements must maintain balance," she said. "Only they can decide what that balance may be. Every one thousand years you all return, though only one will remember." *She reached forward and touched me softly on top my head. "Choose wisely, or there may not be a world to return to in another one thousand years."*

"What the hell was that?" Luke shouted in my face.

I blinked my eyes open, trying to pull myself from my dream. Dream? No, it hadn't felt like the past. What the heck was that? Every one thousand years I returned? How many lives would I need to relive? Those dots...I'd seen them before. One of us had the ability to see the sparks of people around us.

"Well?" Luke continued to look down at me with a furious expression.

Understanding dawned. "Crap! Did I fall asleep?"

"While I was flying down the road on a two-wheeled death trap? Yes!"

He held me cradled in his lap while he still straddled the idling bike. The heat from his thighs warmed my backside. How he'd managed the switch, I had no idea.

"Put me down. Please." The last word came out a bit clipped. My stomach was going crazy being so close to him, and it annoyed me.

"Gladly." He surprised me by setting me down gently.

On my own feet, I rubbed my hands over my face. "I'm sorry. I'm tired." When I glanced back at him, I caught a fleeting look of pity in his eyes. "Save your pity. I don't need it," I said. I didn't need pity. I needed decent sleep and an assurance those things wouldn't catch me in this lifetime.

He held up his hands in surrender and took a deep, calming breath. "Are you going to fall asleep again? Because we won't get far this way."

"Yes, I'll most likely fall asleep again. No matter what I've tried, I can't seem to avoid it."

"Maybe you should stop avoiding it," he suggested with an edge of exasperation in his tone.

I didn't bother answering. He wouldn't understand.

He saw something in my face because he sighed and said, "Loosen the strap of your bag as far as it will go, then get on."

He motioned for me to hurry up when I didn't immediately do it. Stifling an eye roll, I did as he asked. Once I sat behind him, he grabbed the strap and lifted it over his head—while it was still around me. Then, he went one step further and tightened the strap so I pressed against his back. He grumbled the whole time, and that was the only silver lining in the whole situation.

"Take both arms out so it's around your waist," he said.

Understanding he meant to strap me to his back so I wouldn't fall, I complied. But I didn't like it.

As soon as he lifted his feet, the dreams pulled me under.

The Taupe Lady once again stood over a new mother. This woman didn't put the babe to her breast. She set the quiet infant aside and hurried to bury the afterbirth not yet noticing the Taupe Lady. Lying on a coarse blanket shivering in the light warm breeze, I watched her with new eyes.

"The men tracking you have crossed the river," the Taupe Lady said.

Fear clouded my mother's eyes, and she spun to face the lady. "Thank you!" My mother scooped me into her arms.

"I did not tell you so you could leave," the lady explained. "You need them. They are her only protection."

"I am her protection," my mother whispered forcefully as she hugged me to her chest to quiet me.

"You protect her from her father, but he will protect her from those who are much worse. For the love you feel for your child, return to him so her life may be spared."

"Who are you?" my mother asked noticing for the first time that the lady's feet didn't quite touch the ground.

"I am a friend. Save your child and return."

"If I return, he will kill me."

The Taupe Lady's eyes filled with sadness. "Yes, he will," she agreed.

"Then, I cannot." My mother ran with me.

I WOKE LYING limply against Luke's back as he braked hard and turned into the parking lot of a small motel.

Instantly alert, I lifted my head. "What are you doing?"

"You keep twitching. You can't ride sleeping. It's not safe," he said over his shoulder as he parked in front of the office.

Not safe? My whole life was not safe. Riding anywhere with one of them was probably not safe. Adding my narcoleptic tendency didn't really decrease my life expectancy that much more.

He loosened the strap as I argued. "Sleeping strapped to you is better than sleeping here. We need to keep moving."

"Believe me, I'm all for hurrying, but I'm not going to risk you falling off." He lifted the strap over his head so we were no longer pressed against each other.

I scrambled to dismount. "I'm not tired anymore." I saw in his eyes he didn't buy it for a second. "I don't want to stay here," I said as I started to panic.

Taking a ride from him was different from locking myself in a room with him. I didn't trust him—us—in a room. There was too much pull going on. My stomach went wild at the idea of a room with a bed and him in it. And my eyes dipped to his snug fitting shirt. Given his reaction when I got close to his neck, I didn't see how this would end well for me.

"Too bad. Inside. Now," he practically growled at me as he pointed to the door marked "Office."

I met his eyes for another moment and then pivoted on my heel intent on walking if I needed to. I took one step toward the road. He stood in front of me before I took the second step. He didn't look happy that I hadn't immediately complied. We scowled at each other. A yawn ruined any hope I had of him taking me seriously. His expression changed to one of concern.

In my crazy, sleep deprived state, all I wanted to do was lean into him. If he happens to kiss me, I thought vaguely, I'll just have to endure. Wait. What? No! No kissing. It led to other things, which led to a life of misery. I shook my head to clear it.

He sighed and tilted his head at me.

"You are so tired, luv. Please. Sleep a few hours," he said.

My stomach went crazy with the pull. Disgusted with myself that a caring tone and a few nice words could cause such a reaction, I snapped at him. "As if sleep is what you really have in mind."

His eyes widened, and he held up his hands. "Sleep. That is all. I can't drive fast with you sleeping. Too many things could happen. I might not be able to catch you in time. If we keep going as we are, snow will cover the roads before we reach the Compound."

"Compound?" I asked, wondering why I was even listening to him.

"It's where Gabby said to bring you. She promised she would be there."

The way he worded it gave me pause. "No one is holding her there?"

"Holding her there? No. She...visits. Honestly, she doesn't seem to like it very much."

I looked down at the faded blacktop. If they didn't hold Gabby as a prisoner and she remained free to wander as she pleased, it probably meant Luke truly wanted to help me get to her. Though, it could all be a lie. Calling the number he had given me wouldn't prove anything. Any woman could answer, and I wouldn't know the difference.

"I don't trust you. But..." I looked at the motel. Sleep tugged at me. I was doing what I thought the dreams wanted me to do. Maybe they would leave me alone, and I would actually get some real sleep. "I'll stay. Just not with you in the same room."

"Fine."

His easy agreement didn't help settle my nerves, but I still followed him into the office. He paid cash for the room and led the way back outside. A sidewalk, protected by the eaves, ran along the building. We didn't follow it far. He stopped at the door marked with a two. Too close to the office for my comfort.

"I got kicked out of one hotel already. He's going to hear me for sure."

"Maybe you won't have bad dreams," Luke said as he unlocked the door and stepped aside so I could enter.

I snorted but didn't bother disagreeing with him. I entered the room, then turned to look at him with an arched brow. He still stood there with his hand on the doorknob.

"I'll sit on the bench outside and wake you in a few hours." He started to close the door.

"The key?" Seriously. Did he really think I would be okay with him keeping it?

He smiled. "I'll hold onto it. Better I wake you when you start getting too loud than the owner."

I scowled and opened my mouth to argue, but he closed the door too fast. I stared at it for a moment. Could I do this? Could I fall asleep with one of them close by? What could he do to me while I was sleeping that he couldn't do while awake? Nothing, really. It just made me feel so vulnerable.

Behind me, the mattress sang its siren song luring me enough to turn toward it. It didn't matter that Luke had a key. He could easily break through the door without it. After all, he'd snuck into one hotel room already.

Kicking off my shoes, I did my usual belly dive into the quilt and closed my eyes with my feet still hanging off the end of the bed. This wouldn't last more than a few...

The dream that claimed me had a new twist. It split into four views of the same thing. I was my current-self, yet at the same time, I was all three of the other girls in the dream. Disoriented by all four viewpoints, I struggled, trying to focus on just one.

I crouched in my pen with three other girls. Branches, thicker than any of our arms, jabbed into the ground to make the walls of our pen. Trees towered around us. Sunlight occasionally speckled the ground as the canopy above shifted.

The stench of our feces and unwashed bodies clogged my nose. We'd been kept in the pen for seven days. The youngest girl, with the strawberry blonde hair, had been first. She paced the earthen floor as she glared at our captors who lounged languidly beyond our pen wall.

Her tiny stature and youth didn't make her very menacing, yet. But when she hit puberty, she would be a force to reckon with.

The most recent captive sobbed softly. Still in her teens but older than all of us, she'd been made to Claim then mate with someone. She kept her eyes fixed on the ground. I sat next to her with an arm around her shoulders. And, like the youngest, I watched our captors.

The fourth member of the party slept and twitched as she did so.

I felt the pain and anguish of the one crying, the rage of the one pacing, the determination of the one holding her sister, and the pure terror of the one dreaming. We were all the same yet different. Sisters of the same womb. Daughters of the Taupe Lady. Pieces in a game we never wanted to play.

The branch door of our pen drifted open in the breeze. None of us moved to run, but it still caught the attention of the men watching us.

"If she is old enough to look at us with hate, she is old enough to mate," one said as he stood. He towered over all of us. A scrap of leather covered his loins. The rest of him remained dusty and bare.

The sister who paced stopped moving and stared at him, her chin tucked close to her chest so she watched him from under her brow. He strode purposefully toward her.

The dream narrowed so I no longer felt the other three. Just her. Just her anger. Her fear. She knew what he wanted. What he intended to do. She would die.

He gripped my arm tightly and pulled me from the pen. The sobbing one flew forward like a wildcat and tried fighting him. It did no good. She sailed back and hit the branches with a hollow thump. The girl next to her tried pulling my arm back. It didn't matter; he swatted her away, too. His big hand reached for me. I bit him hard and felt my teeth hit bone. He hit me; the flat of his palm connected with a crack. I saw stars. My heart beat wildly. I struggled as he lifted me.

The dream faded and restful oblivion cocooned me. I barely registered the gentle kiss pressed against my forehead. I slept.

STRETCHING MY ARMS WIDE, my hand lightly smacked into a face. I stilled and opened my eyes. The white ceiling above greeted me. Cautiously turning my head, I met Luke's amused gaze peeking through the fingers of the hand that still covered his face.

"What do you think you're doing?" I sat up with a scowl. We both lay on top the covers; a line of pillows separated us. I felt rested, but waking with him next to me unsettled me.

"You were having a bad dream. I came in to wake you, but you quieted. So I decided to use my time wisely and sleep, too." I narrowed my eyes at him and he quickly added, "I kept it proper. See?" He gestured to the pillows.

"I don't care if you put a —"

"I'm starving. Let's eat." He rose from the bed with a stretch and moved toward the door. I continued to glare at him.

"Don't think I don't know what you're trying to do. I won't let my guard down. A few moments of kindness will not make me fall into your arms."

He stopped by the door and turned to look at me, his face carefully blank. "I don't want you in my arms."

"Liar." I swung my legs off the bed and stood. Did he think me stupid? I yanked my bag up off the nearby chair.

Luke scratched his jawline as he hesitated by the door. "I don't understand why you're so angry." Frustration laced his words despite his relaxed pose.

I barely understood myself. I didn't really think he wanted to wear me down, but getting angry seemed a better way to keep some distance between us. The idea of someone watching over me just to watch over me...well, that swayed me more than it should have. It also made me miss my mom. She used to do that before my world broke. Before I discovered there were some things she couldn't protect me from. My teeth clenched against my resentment. I hated knowing. I hated the dreams, and at the moment, I hated him, too.

"What's to understand?" I practically screamed at him, angry that he was making me say it. "I'm not safe. I'll never be safe again. I'm so tired, I have no idea how to help myself, and I don't know if I can trust you."

His eyes softened, and he lifted a hand as if he wanted to move toward me. But, he stopped himself, dropped his hand, and sighed softly.

"We can stay here longer so you can rest," he said.

I threw my arms up in the air. "It won't do any good." At his blank look, I said, "I'm reliving all our past lives, mine and my sisters. I've been cut, beaten, starved, raped, drowned, and even blinded."

His eyes hardened at each method of torture I listed, but I barely paid his reaction any attention. Listing the things that I had experienced brought the memories too close to the surface, and there were so many more ways his kind had hurt me that I'd left unsaid.

"Every time I close my eyes, I see more, and there's no rest when that's what

I see. When I wake I'm just as tired as I was when I went to sleep. And I don't just see the past, I feel it. Every injury. Every forced intimate moment. If I let myself dwell on it, I won't ever feel whole again." I gave a pained snort. "I'm not really sure I do now. If I've ever had a happy past life, I don't remember it. Instead, I remember the pain, and death. Always death..." I said, starting to cry in anger and in fear. "I don't want to die again," I whispered brokenly. "But if you're here to try to get me to choose you, you can't have me." I said the words to help remind me, too. He was so...nice. It made the Taupe Lady's warning hard to remember. "Even if it means I have to die again."

He growled, and I saw how what I said had affected him. Jaw clenched, he fought the skin-rippling change trying to consume him. He turned and forcefully yanked open the door. The trim splintered near the latch. When he slammed it shut behind him, a piece fell to the floor.

Stunned, I flopped back down on the bed with a slow sigh. I'd baited him—what? Twice now? Three times?—and I was still unharmed, breathing. A crazy half-sob, half-laugh bubbled from my chest.

The roar of his motorcycle reached me. I hopped off the bed and raced to the door, opening it just in time to see him speed away.

Stupefied, I stood in the doorway for several long moments before my brain kicked in. What an idiot for clarifying who I was when I knew I couldn't trust him. Who knew what he was up to? They always appeared in packs. Maybe he was getting the rest of his pack. Then, I thought of Baen. He'd been alone the first time; but he'd made me bite him before he ran off. So, this was different. And I wasn't a clueless, stupid kid this time. Yet, I still made tired mistakes. I needed to move.

Closing the door, I quickly circled the bed looking for my shoes. They weren't there. I checked the bathroom, using it quickly in the process, and didn't see anything there either. My chest started to tighten. I didn't have time to waste but couldn't just leave without them. My feet were tough, but the temperature was dropping. I wouldn't make it far.

Growling in frustration, I grabbed my bag and dug for as many pairs of socks as I could find. Two. I sat on the bed to pull them on over the ones I wore, but didn't get the chance.

I fell into a dream. Hard.

A SPRINKLING of water on my face woke me before I died. Still caught up in the dream, I looked up at Luke and blinked in confusion at his disgruntled expression.

"You already slept ten hours. How can you still be this tired?"

"I'm not," I said sitting up quickly.

He stood before me with a white paper bag and a large thick paper cup in one hand. The other hand shone wetly.

"The dreams take me over sometimes, no matter how rested I am," I mumbled feeling the need to explain. He held out the cup to me. I didn't move to take it as I remembered how he'd taken off. "I thought you left to get the rest of your men."

He huffed a martyr style sigh and sat beside me on the bed. Too close in my opinion.

"What men?"

Instead of answering, I looked down at my hands while trying to ignore the quick erratic heartbeat his close proximity caused. He misunderstood my move and made a small noise of annoyance.

"Never mind," I mumbled.

"Bethi, I really am here to help you. No strings. I just don't know how," he said softly.

He thought I just didn't trust him. He was right. I didn't. But that wasn't the reason for my hesitancy. I didn't like feeling so dependent on him. Especially since my insides kept going crazy when he was close or when I looked at him or when I smelled him. It was getting ridiculous.

"You are helping me," I said trying for brusque detachment. "If not for you, I'd be walking."

He studied my profile for a moment before handing me the cup. "I thought coffee might help."

My throat dried at the quiet concern laced in with his words, so I accepted the cup and took a hasty swig. It scalded my tongue, and I almost spit it back into the cup. Instead, I swallowed, burning a layer from my throat. Ignoring his concerned frown, I suggested we hit the road. I was uncomfortable just sitting there.

"I brought you something to eat, too," he said opening the bag and pulling out a plastic carton.

He sat there patiently holding out the food, waiting for me to decide.

My mouth watered as a hint of bacony goodness drifted my way. He quirked a slight smile at me as I reached for it, but he willingly handed it over. A stacked breakfast sandwich lay inside. My stomach rumbled as I looked at it. I sat next to him and devoured the offering. He smiled as he watched me. I ignored him.

When I threw the carton in the garbage, he stood, picked up my bag, reached inside his jacket, and pulled out my shoes.

"Gee, thanks," I drawled, reclaiming my missing shoes.

Luke grinned in response and handed me the jacket as well before he shouldered my bag and walked out the door to check us out of the room. I set my almost empty coffee to the side, sat, and peeled off the extra socks.

He'd done it again, helped me without demanding anything in return. Was he just waiting for a moment of weakness before he pounced, or had my dream about Baen pointed me toward help? I wanted to believe Luke was the help I was meant to find. Yet he also did things to make sure I didn't run from him. I mean, come on! He stole my shoes. And did he think I didn't notice him leaving with my bag? I wondered why he did any of it. Was it because he thought I wouldn't be safe if I struck out on my own again or something else? I really wanted the answer to be because he was worried about me. Yet, at the same time, I knew I was being irrational. How many lifetimes had the werewolves shown me that they couldn't be trusted. It far outnumbered the two lifetimes—so far, anyway—that they had tried to keep me safe. Still...I wanted to believe. The thought that he was keeping me captive...well, I needed to believe my life wasn't hopeless.

I beat him to the motorcycle and waited, watching him cross the parking lot. My heart gave a quick stutter as he got closer. He moved with purpose, and his eyes swept over me. I tried to squash any signs of my physical attraction, but I couldn't help watching his long legs clear the seat with ease. To distract myself, I wondered what he'd look like as a dog. Would he have those same menacingly eerie eyes? Would he threaten me with his teeth?

After settling behind him, he motioned to the strap on his shoulder. I grudgingly lifted the bag around my torso. Falling from the back of the bike didn't sound fun.

We pulled away in a hurry. Even with all of the sleep, I felt the tug of the next dream. I tried everything from sticking my face in the wind—versus staying crouched behind Luke—to biting my lip as hard as I could. Eventually, the dream won.

CHAPTER SIX

A HAND TAPPING MY FACE PULLED ME OUT.

"We need help. A car. This isn't working," he said gently.

"No, this is fine," I mumbled, peeling my eyes open. It really wasn't fine. We were pulled over again. Trees lined the sides of the road in both directions. For a second time, I sat in his lap with the bag and strap twisted around us. The bike still idled.

"Can you make it twenty minutes without sleeping?" he asked.

"I don't know," I admitted. "It seems worse with you."

He looked at me in surprise. "When I'm near you, you don't cry out. I thought your dreams calmed when I..." He didn't finish his sentence, but I filled in the missing parts.

He was right. My dreams did calm when I was near him. I dreamed of helpful things like glimpses of explanations from the Taupe Lady, instead of my constant pointless death. In fact, I'd learned so much more after Luke had found me than in the prior months.

My eyes widened as I considered the implications. Was Luke really the key? In my past lives, after claiming a werewolf, the dreams had come less frequently. And when they did appear, their purpose was more focused. So, if I Claimed Luke...

"I changed my mind," I said quickly. "I will Claim you."

"No!" He flinched as if I'd slapped him, but his gaze drifted to my mouth.

He remained motionless, studying me, his eyes filled with barely checked wanting. It wasn't desire as much as it was the ability to call me his own. I'd seen that look before in other lives. They'd coveted me for the power of my knowledge. Why did he want me? I decided it didn't really matter and held myself still, hoping he was reconsidering his answer. So far, he had kept me safe and treated me well. If Claiming him would end my dreams—or at least slow them—did I need any more proof from him that he would take care of me? He had already shown he was infinitely better than the werewolves I'd Claimed in past lives—except maybe Baen. And it didn't hurt that my heart was beating out *yes* like an SOS.

The look in his eyes grew tender as he brushed a stand of hair from my face. His fingers left a trail of warmth where they brushed my skin. I wanted him to do it again. *Touch me.* His breath hitched when I tilted my head slightly. His fingers trembled as he touched my hair. Encouraged, my hand drifted to his bicep.

The contact broke the spell, and he hastily set me on my feet next to the bike. Like cold water splashed in my face, it brought me back to reality. I needed to Claim him for the right reasons—to get rid of the dreams where I died, and not the wrong reason—because he made my insides quiver.

Being connected by the strap didn't give us much room. It pinned us together and brought my face close to his neck. I blinked at the opportunity, and I didn't wait for permission. I darted in with the intent to end the bad dreams, but my teeth didn't reach my intended target.

Luke had shoved his hand between my face and his neck at the first sign of my move. I should have anticipated his speed, I thought. With my face humiliatingly mashed into the palm of his hand, I grew angry.

"What's your problem? I know you feel the pull. This *is* what's supposed to happen." I resisted stomping my foot as he slipped out of the strap. Standing tall and out of his personal space, I glared at him. He looked angry, too.

"No, it is not. Why did you change your mind?"

"I'm tired of dying!" I cried. "It hurts! What don't you understand? Every time I close my damn eyes, I feel every anguished moment of one of our past lives. Claiming you will make the dreams better." I tried to keep the begging tone from my voice, but by the end, that's what I did. Beg. "Please, Luke."

Some of the tension eased out of him, and he looked at the trees, taking a moment before answering.

"I promised I only wanted to help you. And I will. The dreams are better when I sleep near you. We will keep doing that," he said without meeting my eyes. "Climb on."

I felt like throwing a fit, but then I realized the position I would be in if I climbed back on—right by his neck. Keeping the triumphant grin from my face, I slipped behind him.

For the next twenty minutes, he face-palmed me at least fifty times. When I gave up in frustration and leaned my forehead against his back, his heat started lulling me.

"I'm going under," I managed to mumble before my eyes closed.

"Try to hold on. I called for help. There should be a car ahead," he called over his shoulder. He sped up instead of slowing down.

A fear-induced adrenaline spike pushed the dream back, and my eyes popped open. "What do you mean you called for help?"

I barely got the words out when an object flew from the woods beside us. Big, black, and furry, it just missed our back tire. In stunned disbelief, I clung to him as we raced on. He'd really done it. He'd called for the rest of his pack.

Luke twitched before me, and I peeked over his shoulder. In one of the mirrors, I saw the reason. My heart leapt into my throat as I twisted to look behind us.

It ran on all fours. Its paws pounded the pavement as it gained on us. With a sleek head and a vicious snarl, it looked just like the werewolves in my dreams. Seeing it all affirmed, I started shaking.

"Hold on," Luke warned me.

Relief flooded me. Not one of his.

"Faster!" I shouted and hit Luke on the back.

He had already twisted the throttle when another shape flew into our path. Luke leaned far to the left and made a swift deep swerve around the second one. I clung to his back panting in fear. We were both going to die. He'd barely recovered from the swerve when something snagged the bag on my back—the same bag strapping me to Luke—and pulled. My breath left me in a whoosh.

With my arms wrapped around his waist, my shoulders screamed in pain as I struggled to hold on. Then suddenly, the pressure eased. The bike flew forward, riderless, as we stayed in place, hanging in the air. The strap still connected us. Luke whipped an arm back to keep me pressed against him while he severed the strap. We landed with a thud just seconds after being unseated. The bike glided for a distance and then fell onto its side on the gravel shoulder.

Despite my bruised and aching butt, I scrambled to my feet. Luke already stood in a semi-crouch near me, facing off with the two dogs that circled us.

"Go," he said nudging me.

"No, thanks," I whispered. Running through the woods away from the only person who might be willing to protect me didn't seem like a good idea. Besides, I'd been chased through the woods before, and it hadn't ended well.

Luke's skin rippled as he partially changed. My heart thumped painfully seeing the truth of what he was. His nails elongated, and his back hunched a bit. He leapt at the wolf to the right with his upper body, and then he swung his legs to kick the one on the left. He scored a solid hit on both seconds before he fully burst into his fur. I backed up two steps staring at the copper-coated wolf.

The wolf on the right shook his head as if to clear it and spun to attack Luke. The other wolf scrambled to its feet, snarling.

Spinning to meet their attack, Luke savagely ripped into the lead attacker's face with his teeth. Blood colored Luke's muzzle as the wolf tried to shake him off. The second wolf circled the pair watching for an opening. Luke's eyes trailed that wolf's progress as he maintained his gruesome hold. If the second one attacked, he would have to let go to protect himself and would lose the upper hand.

I picked up a heavy rock from the shoulder of the road and chucked it at the stalking wolf. Had it been paying attention to me in the slightest, it would have seen it coming. As it was, the rock hit it square on the right side of its head with a sickening sound, eliciting a yelp of pain.

Luke twisted his hold on the first wolf's muzzle as he dropped his hind legs and rolled. He heaved the wolf into the stunned second wolf, then went for the throat. The first wolf couldn't even manage a yelp. There was just a gurgling wheeze. The second wolf, pinned under the first, struggled for a moment before Luke finished it, too. He turned to me, blinking. I couldn't say anything as I continued to stare wide-eyed at the aftermath of the fighting.

Within seconds, both forms shifted back into their skin. Two dead men on the side of the road with ripped out throats. I didn't flinch at the sight. It was depressingly familiar.

Luke took a few steps toward me, claiming my full attention. The same hazel eyes, but a little bigger, stared back at me. Though he didn't bare his teeth at me, he looked far from friendly with the blood around his mouth. My chest tightened to the point that it hurt to breathe. Still, I managed.

He shook out his fur and trotted over to my bag. With his back to me, he shifted to his skin. Honey-kissed skin exposed to the world did what the fighting hadn't. I felt a little faint. Blood and gore? Not a problem. Luke naked, showing me a perfect backside? I lost my composure, what little I had, and a tiny sound escaped me.

"Turn around," he said not looking at me.

"Ha! No way." A slightly hysterical sigh escaped me.

He scowled over his shoulder at me and reached into my bag for his hoodie and a pair of my pajama pants. It gave me a lovely profile view, just barely hiding the naughty bits. A giggle escaped me as he stepped into what he'd grabbed. His scowl twitched, and I knew he wanted to smile, too.

Covered, he picked up the bag, marched over to me wearing tight, high-water Tinker Bell pajama pants, and handed me the bag.

"We'll need to stop for new clothes," he commented with a wry grin.

I stood frozen, fully seeing his face after his change back, and couldn't make myself answer with either a smile or a nod. Instead, I reached into the bag, grabbed a shirt at random, and used it to wipe the blood from around his mouth. My hand shook. Okay, so maybe the blood did affect me.

He saw the blood and gently took the shirt from my hand. He tucked it back into the bag, then went to pick up the bike.

He waved me over as soon as he had it started again.

I numbly walked past the bodies and put my hand on his shoulder to take my place behind him.

"No falling asleep," he warned, setting the bag in front of him. He used his legs and the broken straps to keep it in place.

I wrapped my hands around him and held on as he took off. Though I felt the dreams calling and the occasional tug of sleep, I didn't close my eyes. I was still wound too tightly from what had just happened.

Apparently, my previous thoughts about using an adrenaline rush were right. It would have been a better method than cutting.

CHAPTER SEVEN

AFTER SEVERAL TURNS, WE MADE OUR WAY INTO A TOWN WHERE WE both used a public restroom to wash. We then picked up some desperately needed clean clothes.

"Who did you call about a car?" I asked after walking out of the bathroom a second time—for changing.

"An Elder. I told him about the attack. He's changed plans with his contacts and suggested we come to a more populated area."

I struggled to remember what an Elder meant, but couldn't. I realized I knew how their kind typically behaved, some of the reasons behind their actions, but nothing about their culture.

"What's an Elder?"

With my Tinker Bell pajamas safely tucked into a new duffle bag, we walked side by side as we slowly made our way to the bike. I noted several long scratches on the once shiny tank and wondered if he cared. He had called the thing a death trap on two wheels after all...

"They are the keepers of our kind. Everything they do, they do in our best interest, unlike pack leaders."

"What do you mean?"

"Pack leaders want to control their members. Elders want to guide them."

"Why have pack leaders, then?"

"Exactly. That's why I don't follow one. The Elders aren't so bad though." He smiled as he mounted the bike.

I climbed on the back and passed him the strap. Once again wearing his jacket, I ducked behind him as he pulled away, but I tried not to lay my head against him. Every time I did, I felt the pull to sleep even more. However, each time I slept against him, the dreams weren't of death.

"Why don't you want to be Claimed?" I asked knowing he'd hear me over the wind.

He turned his head and half-shouted his answer knowing I couldn't hear as well. "I *do* want to be Claimed. Just not now."

That hurt. "I don't get it. Why not? And don't bother denying the pull you feel for me. I know you do."

He shook his head and didn't answer, frustrating me further.

I didn't want to dream about dying anymore and didn't want to spend the rest of this life pressed up against him. Or did I? It wouldn't be the worst fate. But, I truly believed Claiming him would be the key not just to the type of dream I had, but the frequency, too. I could actually go somewhere without worrying about dropping off. Besides, if he felt the pull, he shouldn't have any complaint about me Claiming him. I should be the only one with an issue with Claiming since it gave him a way to keep tabs on me through the link it would establish between us.

I watched the buildings as we snaked our way through town and wondered if there were other men out there waiting for us. When we cleared town, the fields and trees didn't provide any more of a comfort.

The funeral pyre lit the night sky. My friend's mother stood beside me sobbing. The somber faces of neighbors and family, illuminated by the flickering flames, seemed to float in the darkness. One woman stood out. She looked at my friend's mother with compassion as she made her way around the circle of people. A chord of familiarity struck me, but I couldn't place her since my family had recently moved here.

Using the lights in my mind, I searched for my little brother and father. They had remained in our home while my mother accompanied me. Their life sparks comforted me. Grief over the loss of my friend swamped me. She had fallen ill with a sickness that had also taken several others in neighboring homes. I couldn't understand why anyone needed to die in such a way.

"Death always serves a purpose," the woman, who I'd forgotten for a moment, said from just behind us.

My friend's mother and I turned to look at her.

She reached up and touched the mother's face gently. "Often, others die so more may live. Even the most seemingly random death can have the most profound meaning. Your daughter's illness may spark a need in someone's heart to create a cure for the illness, changing the direction of our society for future generations. Try not to mourn. Her death is not meaningless. Celebrate her life. Celebrate your life. To make her memory count, do not squander opportunities."

The woman turned to me. "She felt like a sister to you but did not share your blood. Do not forget her. Do not forget this feeling of loss. You can be the one to change the future, to make the lives of those around you better. Do not squander your chances."

I glanced at my friend's mother, confused. She met my gaze with a stunned tear-filled expression. When we both looked back, the woman had vanished.

"Come on, Bethi!" Luke said, his voice sounding distant and tinny.

I blinked my eyes open to the familiar sight of him looking down at me. We were once again pulled over to the shoulder of the road on an idling bike.

"We're never going to get there at this rate."

"I'm not doing this on purpose!" I said irritably as I struggled to get off his lap.

He sighed. "I know."

I felt his lips brush my hair and stilled. I knew it! He did feel the pull.

Tilting my head back, I met his gaze again. He looked guarded. "Why?" I asked, unable to keep the desperation from my voice. "Why won't you let me Claim you?"

"Because you're afraid and think it's the only way to help yourself."

"And?"

"And nothing. It's not the way to make that kind of decision."

"What *is* the way, then?"

A slight flush crept into his cheeks. "With affection, not fear."

My mouth popped open, and he gently hoisted me off his lap. Woodenly, I took my seat again. He wanted me to like him? How in the hell did I end up finding the only damn werewolf who wanted to take it slow and get to know each other?

"You've been without decent sleep for too long," he said changing the subject. "We need to hole up somewhere so you can get some rest. Then, maybe, driving won't be such a challenge."

I doubted it. The ten hours at the last place hadn't seemed to help much, but I didn't argue. I was busy trying to figure out a way to get him to believe I had feelings for him. I found him physically attractive but knew that wasn't what he meant. Actual feelings for one of them? It would be a stretch.

WE MANAGED to put several miles of traveling time in that day before calling it quits and stopping at another motel. Using some of the money he'd given me, he got a room for us for two nights so I knew he meant business about me catching up on sleep.

As soon as we walked into the room, I claimed the bathroom and got ready for bed not caring about the time of day. Luke didn't comment when I crawled under the covers other than to assure me he would be there keeping an eye on me. Not really what I needed, but I'd take it.

Pain radiated from my legs. My muscles spasmed. Chained to a wall, I couldn't move much to relieve any of the aches. Tears streamed down my face. A tongue licked them away and a low rumble of laughter followed.

I blinked my eyes. Faint shadows danced around me.

"She's nearly useless," a man commented quietly from very close by. The soft sound echoed off the walls.

Damp cool air had me shivering occasionally.

A hand stroked my face.

"Nearly, but not completely," another stated from further away. "Do not touch her. Let her walk once an hour. Whatever ill befalls her, befalls you."

The sound of fading footsteps let me know I was alone with the man who'd touched me. I caught sight of a shadow moving. It was the outline of a person. I turned toward it, trying to focus.

"Stop moving your eyes like you can see. Close them if you want to keep them," he warned with a growl. I closed my eyes while still turned toward the shadow. I knew the threat wasn't idle. However, closing my eyes didn't change what I saw. Even with the lids closed, I watched the shadow approach.

The feeling of a hand on my nonexistent breast distracted me. "You've never lived long enough to Claim," the man whispered.

My stomach flipped in an unpleasant way, and I started to sweat.

His fingers pinched my tender skin, and new tears fell. "This is going to be pleasant."

I sobbed knowing what he intended.

The dream lifted slightly as I was jostled to the side.

"Enough of that," Luke whispered before settling beside me and kissing my forehead.

I wanted to open my eyes, but another dream pulled me under.

The funeral pyre lit the night sky. My friend's mother stood beside me sobbing.

My dream-self looked around at the somber faces of neighbors and family, illuminated by the flickering flames, while my real-self grew angry as one woman's face stood out.

Why would this dream repeat?

The Taupe Lady looked at my friend's mother with compassion as she made her way around the circle of people. A chord of familiarity struck my dream-self.

I wanted to yell at her from across the fire. I willed myself to move but stayed locked in place by my dream-self.

Luke shifted next to me. His movement pulled me from the dream a bit, but not enough that I opened my eyes. I felt him move away for a moment as the dream continued to play out. Then he pulled me back to his side. As soon as my head rested on his warm bare shoulder, the dream faded; and I sank into real sleep.

THE PRESSING need to use the bathroom woke me. Warm and relaxed, I didn't immediately move. I wished the urge would go away because I hadn't slept so well in longer than I could remember.

Snuggling in, I realized why. My head lay cushioned on Luke's chest. Bare chest. My left arm lay slung over his waist. Yep, that was bare too. And my leg...I cringed not wanting to think about it. Wait. If I was draped all over him, it meant his neck was only inches away. My insides somersaulted. I opened my eyes and darted forward.

His palm blocked me, slightly mashing my nose, and I groaned in frustration.

"Fine," I grumbled before scooting off the bed and closing myself in the bathroom. His laughter drifted through the door.

After taking care of business and washing up, I stared at the mirror and tried to see myself through his eyes. I looked a little less waifish but not very healthy. I'd lost a bunch of weight and still had circles under my eyes. Definitely not attractive. I splashed water on my face, trying to wash away my insecurities.

He wanted to stay here for two days. I felt as if I'd slept a long time, but I doubted I'd used all of the time he'd dedicated for me to get the rest he felt I needed. I had time to try to wear him down and convince him of my affection. I dried my face, and I gave my reflection a stern get-to-it look.

Opening the bathroom door, I found the bed made and Luke sitting in the room's one chair.

"Get dressed. We'll grab something to eat and walk around a bit if you're up for it."

Nodding, I moved aside to let him use the bathroom, relieved that I didn't have to try right away. I dug out some clothes and ducked back into the bathroom when he had finished.

How had I let boys know I liked them before the dreams exposed the hot mess that was my life? Long looks, cute clothes, smiling conversation. I didn't think any of that would work with Luke. Trying to trick him was pointless, and I didn't want his hand in my face anymore, either. What did that leave me? Being nice and giving it time? Actually letting myself grow feelings for him? I wanted to throw something. Instead, I opened the door and gave him a halfhearted smile.

A few minutes later, we strolled side by side down the sidewalk in the direction the motel manager had pointed. A small gas station offered premade sandwiches and bags of junk food. My stomach rumbled as I eyed the displays, and his echoed it as if they were having a conversation. He grinned and reached for a bag of chips. I grabbed the sandwiches.

With a bag loaded up with goodies, we headed back. He opened the door for me and stood aside to let me in. After kicking off my shoes, I sat on the bed folding my legs under me. He set the bag next to me, grabbed a sandwich from it, and sat on the chair.

"Thank you for the food," I said reaching for my own sandwich. "And for helping me sleep. And the walk. It was good to get outside and not feel like I needed to run."

He stopped chewing and looked at me suspiciously but nodded his welcome. Crap, was I being that obvious? I took a large bite and chewed slowly. Maybe I shouldn't have mentioned the walk. I was just trying to be nice. And thankful. How else could I ease him into the idea that I cared?

I glanced at him and saw he'd already polished off two sandwiches. I forgot to eat and just stared as he consumed another triangle in two bites. Silently, I popped open a bag of chips and offered it to him. He demolished those and looked at my sandwich which I willingly—and perhaps a little fearfully —surrendered.

"How long was I out?"

"Sixteen hours," he mumbled around a dessert cake.

"Sorry. Maybe we should go back and stockpile some more food in case I crash hard again." And so I had something to eat, I thought as I opened the last bag of chips.

He looked up at me with mixed emotions on his face. First, he appeared happy about my suggestion, then a little disheartened. He finished the cake in another bite and took a drink of water from one of the bottles he'd purchased.

"Do you think you'll sleep that long again?"

"I honestly don't know. I don't feel tired yet, but I can feel another dream calling me."

He leaned back and studied me for a moment. "What do you dream about? And I don't mean you dying. Sometimes, the dreams don't seem to disturb you so much."

"If it's not of death, it's about a lady. I think of her as the Taupe Lady because of the color of the gown she always wears."

"Who is she?"

"I don't know, but from how the people dress in the dreams, I get the feeling she's always been here. Even in my really old dreams, she shows up. She seems like she cares but never really does anything to help me. I mean, she says things that sound like cryptic advice; but if she can show up whenever she wants, why doesn't she show up when I really need her? Why doesn't she step in and stop some of the bad stuff from happening?"

"Maybe she can't," he suggested quietly.

"What do you mean?"

"My kind has rules to follow and laws to obey. Our laws can't be broken even if we wanted to break them. What if she has rules and laws too?"

I thought about it for a moment. "What do you mean you can't break them?"

He sighed and shook his head at me. "Sometimes you seem to know so much about what I am. How did you learn about my kind?"

"My dreams," I answered honestly.

"That's not possible," he said.

"Okay, then how do I know?" He looked at me with a suitably shocked expression, and I continued. "This is what I've figured out. There are dog-men out there that can shift between their dog form and man form."

"I prefer to think of myself as more of a wolf. It's more dignified."

Rolling my eyes, I continued. "They want me and the few women like me for some reason that I haven't yet figured out. We are reborn every one thousand years. There seems to be a period of time within each cycle that we can be reborn several times. Almost every time I'm found, they end up killing me after making me Claim and mate with one of their own." I didn't mention the dreams where I killed myself.

"Almost every time?" he asked tilting his head as his focus intensified.

"Twice I've dreamt of one of your kind trying to *help* me. I still died both times in the end, but someone did try." I thought about those dreams. I'd willingly gone along with their plans to help me and still died. I refused to die again or to go along with someone else's plans in this life. I needed to try something different. But what? Maybe that's what the Taupe Lady meant by every death has a purpose. They all gave me a chance to learn.

He quietly threw away the empty wrappers. I could see his mind turning over what I'd shared.

"Let's get some more food," I said. Seriously, he'd eaten just about everything on his own.

He nodded and walked beside me on our second trip to the gas station.

WHEN WE GOT BACK, I went into the bathroom to change. We'd both been quiet on the walk. I'd mostly debated with myself. Now that he knew I wanted to Claim him in order to avoid a forced Claiming, perhaps he would be reasonable. But seeing his troubled expression after I'd acknowledged I had still died when someone tried to help me had me reconsidering. He truly did seem to want to help me; and if he thought Claiming him would end up getting me killed, I didn't think he'd go for it. Fine. I just needed to convince him that I cared about him and get him to let me Claim him that way. He would eventually forgive me for the deception. I was sure of it.

I stepped out of the bathroom and saw him sitting in the chair, still deep in thought. I wanted to roll my eyes but managed to suppress the urge. I did that a lot I realized. I suppressed urges and feelings because I knew he was too aware of me. It was a habit already. But maybe my reactions to him were the key to all of this. I'd witnessed his reaction to me, but did he really know my reaction to him? In past lives, they'd used it as a means to control me. But I knew better now. I could let the physical reactions show without letting the emotional attraction grow.

Focusing on the flutter I felt every time I looked at him, I let the feeling fill me. The rightness of him, which I usually stomped on with imaginary steel-toed boots, lifted its well-trodden head. My heart somersaulted and stuttered heavily.

Luke's head jerked up in surprise. As he looked at me, a blush spread across my cheeks.

"Would you mind lying down with me? I think you're right. I do seem to sleep better with you."

I didn't miss his quick glance at the door. Frowning, I watched him slowly get to his feet. He looked reluctant.

"Is something wrong?" I asked, truly confused. Was I acting too nice again? Maybe letting him hear my heart stutter hadn't been a good move.

"I, uh, think you should try to sleep on your own for a bit," he muttered.

"I just told you that I—" I rubbed my face and cut off my sharp words. Affection. Show him you care, not that he annoys the crap out of you, I reminded myself. "Okay, fine," I agreed with barely suppressed agitation.

He walked out the door, closing it softly behind him.

Annoyed, I marched to the bed. I wasn't tired, but a dream called. Better to give into it on a bed than try to keep it at bay.

As soon as the blankets covered me, my eyes closed and another past pulled me down.

Perhaps it was still my emotions from before succumbing to the dream, but I felt angry. Rage-filled really. I wanted to rip someone's head off with my own two hands and shove it up their...

"She's awake," a man sighed.

"Thank the skies," someone said contentedly. "I thought that last cut might have gone too deep."

I looked down at myself. I lay naked on a pile of blood-covered straw. A cut ran along one of my lower ribs. The glistening blood indicated its newness. I felt the pain, but the rage overshadowed it. I focused on the men crouched over me who eyed me with peaceful detachment, and I drew more emotion from them. Every bit of anger, resentment, prejudice, fear...anything and everything other than an unresisting peace. My wrath grew. Blood started seeping from my various wounds as if my emotion filled me so much that I had no room to spare for the precious liquid. Soon their eyes began to close. Blood poured from me. Rage consumed me as my last breath drifted from my body in a furious cry.

I woke sitting up wide-eyed and panting. Anger shook my body. A growl started growing until it was a shout of rage. When I realized it came from me, I clamped my mouth shut.

"I'm sorry, Bethi," Luke whispered as he stood up from the chair. He peeled off his shirt and slid under the covers with me.

I barely noticed. I wanted to hurt someone. My hands shook with the need.

"Lay down," he coaxed, leaning on an elbow.

Turning to look down at him, I struggled with my urge to punch him in the face. He'd watched me suffer through that dream just as those men had watched one of my sisters bleed out.

"Let go of the dream," he said. His hazel eyes met mine steadily. "I'm here. I won't leave you. Ever." He reached up, wrapped an arm around me, and gently tugged me toward him. "I'm sorry." His lips pressed against my forehead.

The swell of anger began to recede slightly. The leftover emotions from that dream frightened me. Shaking, I laid my head on his chest.

His fingers ran over my hair, soothing me until the shaking stopped and my eyes drifted closed. I didn't want to sleep ever again. I wanted to stay awake and live forever.

CHAPTER EIGHT

THE ROOM WAS DARK WHEN I WOKE AND FOR A FEW SECONDS I thought a dream still held me. Then Luke's fingers shifted in my hair. I sighed against his skin.

"Had enough?" he whispered.

"I guess so," I said lifting my head. He had a nice chest. Warm. Firm. Warm. I started smiling stupidly and reminded myself to cut it out. I needed to convince him of my affection, not me. "Thanks," I mumbled turning away from his perceptive gaze. Even in the dark, I knew he'd probably caught my grin.

Flipping back the covers, I escaped to the bathroom. When I emerged dressed, everything was already packed and waiting.

"Think you can manage to stay awake for a while?"

I nodded. The only pull I felt was my attraction to him. I walked with him to the office to check out. When we stood beside the bike, I remembered his comment about arranging for a car.

"No car yet?" I asked settling behind him.

"I told my contact we stopped along the way. We're still set to meet." He twisted in his seat to look at me. "Are you trying to tell me you're tired already?"

I shook my head with a smile. He'd sounded almost panicked. I wrapped my arms around him after he tightened the strap on the bag. He wasn't taking any chances.

WE RODE through the remainder of the night and watched the sun rise. We stopped for a quick bite then continued, taking breaks often to stretch and walk so I didn't get tired. Before the sun started hugging the horizon, I could feel the tug of dreams again.

"I think we need to stop for the night," I said, tapping his shoulder.

He nodded and sped up. "We're almost there."

We passed a sketchy looking roadside motel in the middle of nowhere to stop at a nicer small place in the next town. By then, the dreams clung to me like water, coating me with a lethargy that gave me the head bobbles.

"Come on, luv," Luke said lifting the strap and wrapping an arm around me so I wouldn't fall off. "Let's get you to bed."

His phrase made me giggle, and he scowled in response.

All the rooms started to look the same to me. I closed myself into the bathroom no longer caring. When I emerged, I didn't look for Luke. The bed called to me. I fell face-first into the mattress and a nightmare of one of our pasts.

A man knelt unflinchingly before another. The long grey hair hanging over his strong shoulders gave him a regal look. Two sets of hands kept him on his knees. He paid them little attention as his eyes held mine. I stood to the side, held captive by someone I couldn't see. The tip of something sharp pressed into the pulse in my neck.

"Tell the Elders," a man wearing a rough tunic and coarsely woven trousers demanded. He towered before the kneeling man. The ones holding the prisoner sank their nails into the man's flesh at their leader's words. "Tell your leaders we have them all."

I knew the leader lied. He did not have all of my sisters. But he did have me and four others, and I could see where the last one waited; her spark wasn't far away.

"If you have them all, why do I need to tell the Elders?" the kneeling man questioned calmly.

"Do as I say or she dies." The leader waved his hand in my direction.

The captive threw his head back and laughed. A growl rose from the man behind me. No one else made a sound.

"You laugh?" Instead of looking angry, the leader appeared curious.

"You are still trying so hard," the captive said with a pitying smile. "The fight you started is coming. I have told my people you have her, but we know you will not kill her. Not until the balance is turned toward your favor." The man met my eyes, and I caught a glint of

deep sorrow reflected back at me. "But they won't give you what you want. They've discovered their purpose and will die protecting us."

I didn't understand everything the captive said. What purpose? But I did understand the rest of his message. Help would not come in time. I needed to choose. With a sob, I pressed into the sharp object resting on my neck. It pierced my skin with very little pain. My captor grunted in surprise. I quickly twisted around causing irreparable damage. As I collapsed to my knees, the severed head of the man who'd warned me tumbled past. A horrible cry went up through the gathered men, but it didn't drown out their leaders words.

"She will be reborn. There is still time in this cycle. If we fail again, we will kill their Elders so they won't remember in time for the next cycle!" He kicked the head as he spoke.

My heartbeat slowed, and a chill crept along my skin.

The bed dipped as Luke lay next to me. He pulled me into his arms, and I rested my head on his bare chest registering his comfort before sinking into normal dreams. Dreams where I went to school, forgot my locker combination and my pants.

A LOW GROWL pulled me from my sleep. But, it was Luke shoving my head onto a pillow that really woke me.

The mattress bounced as he flew from the bed. I opened my eyes to the sound of splintering wood and bolted upright, blinking stupidly. A large shape filled the demolished doorway. Luke had already almost completely phased into his wolf form and rushed toward the beast coming through the door.

They met with a heavy thud and grappled for each other's throats just inside our room. Vicious snarls and growls filled the air as they both went back on their hind legs. I sat there frozen and gap-jawed watching the fight play out while my chest felt too small for my hammering heart.

The larger one used its weight to push Luke back, unbalancing him. As he fell, he darted in with his sharp teeth. I didn't see if he made contact. A rustle of noise and a shadow of movement from the corner of my eye had me turning in time to watch two shapes fly through the room's wide window.

Still shaking from the first one's arrival, I didn't think, just acted. I rolled from the bed toward the fighting pair and closer to Luke. The newcomers landed crouched on the floor at the foot of the bed while I landed hard on my hip beside the bed. Luke pivoted to face the two newcomers. The original wolf who had struggled with Luke saw me and reached for me. I scrambled away, barely managed to avoid his searching fingers, and bumped into the nightstand as Luke yanked him back.

A yip-howl rent the air. Luke had sunk his teeth into his opponent's right eye. I gagged by reflex and quickly looked away. No time for that!

Snagging the lamp from the table, I held it by the cord and threw it like a mace. Luke lunged at the third attacker while the second batted away my attempt at a weapon. The lamp shattered, and I grabbed a shard of jagged ceramic before wedging myself under the bed. There wasn't much room; the weight of the bed pressed down on me. I inched to the head of the bed where the nightstands created an additional barrier, giving me more protection.

Above me, the snarls increased, and I tried to curl into a ball—as much as the space would allow—to make my legs and arms harder to grab. *Please don't let him die.* Huddled there, I stared at the fake wood grain of the nightstand trying to quiet my harsh breathing so I could hear. My hand tightened around the shard. I didn't want to use it. A grunt of pain preceded several more yips. I didn't want to do this again. Then, silence fell. I stifled the urge to cry as I waited. One heartbeat. Two. No one tried to pull me from under the bed.

I stayed curled up but lifted my head for just a peek. A pair of eyes stared back at me. I jumped hard enough to hit my head on the bed frame and almost curled back up. The eyes didn't blink... Trembling, I struggled to pull in a breath. The man's cheek lay pressed against the carpet, his body relaxed. Dead. It wasn't Luke. I needed to know. Quietly, I uncurled myself. I didn't completely stretch out. Rather, I extended my arms and legs just enough to shift my weight without emerging from under the bed. Three half-formed wolf bodies littered the floor. Whispers of sound invaded the room as their bodies shifted on the carpet, their dog forms slowly receding to show the men beneath. I didn't recognize any of them.

Relief washed over me, and I rested my head on the floor, closing my eyes. Luke hadn't died.

Small noises continued to sound around me while I struggled to regain control of my breathing and my limbs. It took several minutes after the last rustle of movement to register the complete silence. Where was Luke? Was he hurt? Like an idiot, I'd stayed cowering under the bed instead of checking right away.

I lifted my head and frowned at the vacant spot before me. The lifeless eyes were gone. So was the body attached to them.

Creeping from beneath the bed, I surveyed the room. No bodies, no lamp pieces, no glass. No blood. How was there no blood?

The sheets were rumpled and twisted from my quick escape. The curtains, fluttering outward, drew my attention. I edged toward the window and looked at all the glass and lamp pieces scattered artfully on the ground.

Frowning, I turned back to the room. Where had Luke gone? We needed to move fast. I looked down at myself. I wore a long sleeved top and sleep pants. The cold penetrating the room finally penetrated my thoughts. I couldn't go outside like this. I grabbed the bag and dashed to the bathroom. If Luke wasn't back when I stepped out of the bathroom, I promised myself that I would leave without him.

I flew through changing, and when I stepped out, Luke sat waiting on the edge of the bed, his expression filled with concern. I wanted to fly at him and throw myself in his arms but held myself back.

That was twice now that they'd found us. A heaviness settled over me. Was there really only one outcome for me? Hopelessness blanketed my desperation to find an answer where I didn't die.

"Are you all right?" he asked softly, standing.

When he walked toward me, I flinched involuntarily. Apparently, I wasn't all right. Seeing, hearing, and knowing he'd killed five men shook me. It wasn't that I didn't appreciate his defense. I did. But knowing that my life had once again started the death cycle broke me down inside. Two wolves finding us I could try to pass off as a fluke, to deny the inevitability of my death, and to tease myself with maybes. Maybe Luke, one of the good guys, could help me. Maybe I would live this time. Five wasn't a fluke. Those maybes were a fool's dream. I just needed to come to grips with my fate. I would die. Horribly.

He stopped advancing and eyed me sadly.

"It will be okay, Bethi. I left money and an explanation with the manager for the broken window. We should go."

I nodded numbly and watched him pick up the duffle bag. He held a hand out toward me, but I ignored it and walked through the door. My hope to stop the dreams didn't matter anymore. The countdown to the end had started.

SITTING ONCE AGAIN on the back of the bike, the scenery rushed past. I didn't see any of it. I didn't remember getting on the bike. The sight of a gouged eye blinded me to all of it. Instead, I dwelled on the dead of this life and past lives. The loud sound of the battering wind faded as the ticking of the countdown deafened me. I stayed locked behind Luke, feeling him turning occasionally, but not hearing him, not seeing him until he pulled to the shoulder and cut the engine.

"Bethi?" he said turning to look at me. "I am sorry about this morning. Those were not typical challenges. They did not back down. I had no choice."

Challenge? I blinked at him trying to bring myself back. I remembered the fights from past lives where two wolves fought for the right to their Mate. He thought he was fighting for his right to me? Part of me wanted to cry because he hadn't really believed me, or put together what I'd been telling him. Another part wanted to cry because his interest, or lack thereof, was pointless.

"Don't be sorry," I said flatly. "It wasn't a challenge. There will be more wolves. They will come until I choose, or I die."

Luke opened his mouth to say something more but stopped after searching my hopeless gaze. He turned around, told me to hold on tight, and took off from the shoulder. We flew, and this time the tearing wind reminded me I wasn't dead yet.

WOODS AND A CLOUD-LADEN *sky brought an early twilight. The wind picked up as I stood in stunned immobility. On the ground, a man lay gasping. The gurgling wet noise of his inhale told me he wouldn't live long. I stumbled backward and tripped over another prone form.*

Something ran past me too fast to see clearly. Not far away another member of our party cried out and then fell silent. I didn't run. Turning in a circle, I tried identifying who darted around me within the shadows.

A voice, directly behind me, stilled my movement and sent shivers racing over my skin. "So beautiful." A hand stroked my hair. Fear made my heart race.

"Do you still doubt me?" a familiar voice called.

I turned to watch my group's leader emerge from the shadows completely unharmed.

"You were right," the man behind me agreed.

I stared at the approaching man with dawning horror. "You betrayed your people," I gasped looking again at the bodies lying nearby.

"Not my people," the man I thought I knew growled. "My people do not run from a fight, not even to spare a single life."

The man behind me laughed. "Now that we have her, where was she leading you?"

"*She had knowledge of a plant that will bring us wealth. It relieves pain.*" *The betrayer stepped closer.* "*We will need someone to test it,*" *he said.*

I spun and ran, knowing it was useless. They could have outran me, but, instead, made a game of the chase. My sides ached, and my breath came in painful gasps.

"*Enough play time,*" *the betrayer called to his companion.*

Something bumped into me, knocking me to the ground. Pinned by an unyielding mass, I sobbed as the man licked my neck.

"*You will be delicious,*" *he whispered.*

CHAPTER NINE

"BETHI," LUKE CALLED MY NAME AND TAPPED MY FACE.

I opened my eyes with my heart still pounding.

"Why didn't you lean against me? The dreams aren't as bad then," he scolded with a concerned frown.

I blinked at him as the memory of my sister's death continued to cloud my thoughts.

"Betrayer," I whispered.

Luke looked shocked. "I would never betray you," he whispered. Some obscure emotion flicked into his eyes and for a moment he looked so helplessly lost. "Never," he breathed as if talking to himself. Then, determination replaced it and he slowly leaned toward me.

My breath caught as his gaze snared me. Trapped, I watched his eyes drop to my mouth. My heart skipped a beat, but not in fear. I knew he heard it too when his arms tightened fractionally and his fingers feathered over my hair.

"I *will* protect you," he said softly. His lips brushed my top lip, the barest of touches, before he retreated slightly.

My heart struggled painfully as my stomach twisted in anticipation.

"You are everything I am. Without you..."

In his arms, I believed him. A small burst of hope warmed me. What if, instead of worrying about living or dying, I just...lived?

Dropping my eyes to his lips, a shaky breath escaped me; and I lifted my mouth to his. A spark ignited in my stomach. Our lips touched for less than a second before he pulled back quickly.

I wanted to yell and cry. Instead, I took a deep breath and tried to quell my frustration. The stubborn man wouldn't even look at me.

"Why?"

"Why what?" he asked distractedly, eyeing the road ahead.

"Why protect me? I'm not your Mate."

His eyes met mine, and the intensity of his look robbed me of words.

"Do not mistake my patience for disinterest." He gently threaded his fingers through my hair, and I held my breath. His lips lifted in a half smile at my hopeful look, but he dropped his hand.

"I wasn't sure if you wanted to stop yet," he said with a nod toward a building I hadn't noticed. We sat in the parking lot of a hotel.

"No," I said in panic, struggling to get off his lap. I did *not* want to stay at another hotel. I could still see the dead man's eyes from under the bed. A shudder ripped through me.

"Shh," he whispered wrapping his arms around me and pulling me close. "It will be okay."

"No. It won't. They won't give up."

A flush crept into Luke's face. "Have you died in this life? Not this cycle, but this life? No. Do you know why?" He met my eyes and leaned in close. "Because you have me. Because I won't *let* you die. I've already sent a call asking for someone to meet us. We don't need to—"

My head shot up knocking into his jaw as the last two dreams clicked into place. How could I be so stupid?

His mouth closed with a snap, and he grunted but didn't set me aside.

"What did you say?" I demanded trapping his face between my hands. "What did you tell them?"

Surprise colored his eyes as he answered cautiously. "That we would be here and needed an Elder and a few others to help escort you back to the Compound."

"When?" I insisted.

"A few moments before I woke you," he answered, clearly puzzled.

So just a few minutes ago? I dropped my hands and hopped off the bike, scanning the road in both directions. All clear, but the trees around us could hide anything. I wished I could see those sparks like my sister.

"Go get a room. Hurry!" I motioned him toward the main door. He opened his mouth to ask more, but I started power walking.

As soon as I cleared the door, I pasted on my chipper face, the one I'd used so often to hide the fact I wasn't sleeping, and asked for a room. Luke, just a few steps behind me, paid for the room as I filled out the form using my fake ID. I took a moment to write the hotel's phone number on the palm of my hand, too.

I hurried down the hall to the room and opened the door, making sure to touch the handle and the wood. Luke stood watching me with concern. I didn't step further into the room. Instead, I closed the door again and retraced my steps, heading back outside. He followed me without comment.

"What are we doing?" he asked when we reached the bike.

"We're leaving, but you need to keep quiet about it." I motioned for him to get on. He didn't hesitate to settle on the seat. "Don't tell anyone. If I'm right, that room will have visitors soon." He glanced toward the hotel, and I saw he finally understood.

I swung my leg over the seat and slung the strap over his head. He started the engine as he removed the slack. Pressed against him, we pulled out of the parking lot heading west. I tapped his shoulder.

"Go south!"

Taking the next turn, we headed south for the next two hours. I had enough rest that I evaded the dreams calling me. When I thought enough time had passed, I tapped his stomach to get his attention.

"I think we can stop," I said as we sped down a main highway.

He signaled for the next exit, and we took the northern route to the next town.

He turned his head and asked, "Are we getting a room?"

"No, not yet. We just need a pay phone."

He pulled into a gas station, and I quickly ducked out of the strap before hopping off. I moved to the phone and dialed the hotel's number. Pretending to be a reporter, I asked if they would offer a comment regarding their recent break in. The guy on the phone started an exciting tale until his manager cut him off. I hung up the phone and turned to look at Luke. He'd moved from the bike to stand close to me.

"Did you hear most of that?"

He nodded. The muscles in his jaw stood out from clenching it so hard.

"Someone is betraying you," I said softly. "I think we need to be more careful with the route we take to the Compound. They know where we're headed and will be waiting. It should be safe to get a room in the next town. No more communicating. With anyone." I rubbed a hand over my face, tired.

He moved forward, slightly widening his arms as if to hug me. Yeah, right. I quickly stepped away and walked toward the bike. Too much disappointment in one day wasn't good for a girl. Anyway, the countdown to the imminent end of my life still ticked away, and we stood in the open taunting it.

"Bethi," he said with slight exasperation.

I didn't turn back to look at him. "We need to keep moving. The dreams are calling again," I said to explain my hurry.

WE FOUND a room next to a sportsmen outlet before the sun set. I'd managed to stay awake for most of the ride, but exhaustion tugged at me. Once inside the room, I kicked off my shoes and landed on the bed completely ignoring Luke.

The hand hitting my face knocked me off balance. I stumbled but spread my stance to avoid falling.

"Which one are you?" he demanded as he hit me again. Fire lit my face; each strike had created a burning path across my cheek and jaw.

I remained silent. My father and brother stood a short distance away and watched despite their urge to rush forward.

"What is your ability?" he roared, his anger growing.

Smack.

I struggled to maintain my mental hold on my father as the last hit broke skin and a trickle of blood ran down my cheek. My father's anger crawled into me as he yelled at the man to stop. He curled his fist, and I willed my brother to lift a hand and rest it on Father's shoulder. Fear of the group of men surrounding us overshadowed my brother's anger.

"Do you see lights in your mind?" my tormentor growled through his elongating teeth.

I tried again to assert my will over his. Most people's wills felt like a thick sturdy rope, easy to grab and to hold. Once I held someone's will, I easily implanted thoughts into their minds as if the thought were their own. The men around us were different. The slim slick strands of their wills slipped from my grasp. In the half of a second I touched their wills, nothing ever happened.

Smack. I'd waited too long to answer.

"Have you seen things that helped your family become prosperous?"

Several of the men looked at my father's wealthy clothes, a gift from my mother's father and nothing to do with my ability.

"Do you calm those around you?"

My eyes flared slightly before I could stop the reaction. The man hesitated.

"No," he murmured to himself, watching me. "You cannot be her. Her presence is felt by everyone. Her purpose is to calm and prevent fighting." He reached forward and lightly touched the open wound on my cheek. His fingertip came away bloody. "I would not feel so angry right now if you were her," he added with a slight narrowing of his eyes. "Why then did you react to the question? Do you know where she is?"

I kept my gaze locked on his, afraid to give anything further away. I had no idea who he spoke of.

He licked the blood off his finger with an evil smile and glanced at my father and brother. "You are not their Hope or their Prosperity. If you were Wisdom, you would have run when we first appeared. You are not Peace, and Courage always dies young." He turned to me with a bark of laughter. "I smell your loving father's anger and your brother's fear. Yet, they remain here neither running nor fighting. Do you find that odd, my dear?"

I kept my face carefully relaxed as I turned to look at my family.

The man stepped closer to me, his features rippling and contorting. "Asking you questions will result in nothing answered, will it not? Perhaps we need to ask someone else."

Keeping my eyes locked with my father, I said, "I love you. I am sorry." Tears gathered in my father's eyes, and his panic flared within me a moment before I calmed it and pushed the urge to sleep at him and my brother.

The men behind them howled in outrage as my father and brother collapsed to the ground. The man before me laughed. "You will need your Strength," he said a moment before he bent forward and viciously clamped his teeth into my shoulder.

I howled in pain and fought harder to grab his will. As slippery as before, the thread of his will escaped my grasp. He straightened and pulled me up by his teeth. Another scream ripped through me. Giving up on my attempt to hold his will, I imagined my will as a stiff unbreakable rod of metal and jammed it toward him. Fighting for breath and control, I hammered at his thin string of will. The pain in my shoulder grew—

"Bethi! Wake up!" Luke's hand patted my cheek gently.

Pulled out of the dream, I bolted upright and flinched away from Luke's touch. Wide-eyed and panting, I reached for my shoulder where the echo of the bite still throbbed. My gaze darted around the room as the dream continued to haunt me.

Luke held up his hands, looking worried. "It's okay. It's me, Luke."

I swallowed hard and wiped the sweat from my face. "I know it's you," I mumbled as he sat beside me. "Where were you?" His promise never to leave me had only lasted, what? Two days?

He set something on top of the blanket between us. The long wicked blade of a hunting knife caught the light. It had a sturdy handle for a sure grip. It made me nervous. Why was there a knife on the bed?

"It's yours," he said. His gaze trapped mine. For once, he looked unsure. He rubbed a hand on the side of his neck in agitation. "I thought it might help you feel safer. I'll show you how to use it." When I didn't say anything he added, "I want you to feel safe. I want to see the fear fade."

I struggled with my emotions, angry that he'd left me. I was vulnerable not just to my dreams but to anyone looking for me. It annoyed me that he still didn't get it.

"It's not just fear. Imagine discovering you're not who you thought you were, that you belong to a dangerous hidden world. Imagine closing your eyes and seeing yourself and your loved ones die again and again. The fear in your eyes would be eclipsed by your desperation to stop it all." Tearing my gaze from his, I looked at the gleaming steel. "They are coming. They always do." I reached out and touched the knife before standing.

He watched me with sad eyes.

"Thank you for the knife. I already know how to use it," I didn't add that the knowledge wasn't from this life.

A memory tickled my mind but refused to come forward. I had the vague impression of standing in the middle of a large battle, bathed in blood that was not my own, as I tried to defend those who tried to defend me. The moves, agile and sure, filled my mind without the details of who I fought or why. I had no doubt I'd eventually recall all the details, but the vague impression was enough to make me hope that day wouldn't come any time soon.

"The knife might help," I said as I walked to the bathroom forcing my hand from my shoulder. Glancing at the clock, I saw it was just after nine.

In the shower, I let myself cry. I was beyond done with the dreams and feeling so desperate and crazy all the time. Why was I fighting so hard to hold on to a life I hated so much? The answer helped firm my determination. I didn't want to be born again into the same crappy cycle facing the same hopeless situation. With this life, I needed to make a difference. I rinsed away my self-pity and finished washing.

When I stepped back into the main room, Luke waited with my bag at his feet. The knife was still on the bed but now with a holster. His eyes roved my face as I strode to the bed and picked up the knife. I didn't want to see his concern. Instead, I studied his gift to me. I could strap the knife to my bag so it would be easily accessible, but no one would know I had a weapon because I needed to face crazed man-dogs. Well, people didn't know yet anyway. So having it on the outside of the bag would make me look like a troublemaker or worse. Moving closer to Luke, I bent and tucked the knife into the bag. Right along the side so I could find it quickly if needed. Convenient, yet out of sight.

"You all right?"

"Honestly?" I wondered if he really wanted to know. Sometimes people asked, but didn't care. Meeting my eyes, he nodded. "The answer hasn't changed. No, I'm not all right. But the knife gives me—" I took a slow deep breath as I struggled with how to explain what it meant. "A tiny bit of power over my fate." What Luke didn't realize was that if I couldn't use it against my attacker...well, at least I might escape rape and torture this time around.

A glimmer of helplessness shone in his eyes before he looked away. "Are you ready to leave?"

"I think I've slept enough, if that's what you're asking." Shouldering the bag, I followed him out the door.

We stopped at a gas station after several hours to pick up maps so we could plan our route. I wanted to groan when he gave me a general idea of the Compound's location. West wasn't exactly right. Try north. Why Canada? I thought with a shiver. I decided then to start wearing layers of clothing.

Studying the map, I saw the problem right away. We had plenty of options until we neared the Compound. Then our routes narrowed down to three. I had no illusions. They would be waiting for us.

The dreams called to me while we rode that day, but I successfully avoided succumbing to them as we wove an erratic pattern northwest.

Taking a break, we found a restaurant for a real meal. I felt exposed walking into such an open, normal space. I wanted food, but I wanted safety more. Luke held the door for me, and I felt his troubled gaze as I passed him, but he didn't say anything. Picking a booth, I slid in, and he surprised me by sitting next to me.

"Relax," he breathed a moment before the waitress came. She gave us menus and asked for our drink order, barely looking at us in her hurry. When she walked away, Luke turned slightly toward me draping his arm over the back of the bench seat. I met his gaze. He smiled and spoke his next words softly so only I heard them. "Maybe I should have bought you a gun."

The absurdity of his comment struck me, and I laughed as he'd intended. "I don't think it would have made a difference." I hesitated playfully, then said, "Well, maybe it would have."

His grin fell, and he grew serious. "I'd buy you an arsenal if it would help you feel safe." The gruff words and the affection behind them tugged my heart making my stomach twist crazily. His hand moved slightly, so close to the side of my face.

The waitress came with our drinks, and he straightened in his seat leaving me in confused frustration. He ran so hot and cold. He wanted me. I knew he did. But yet, he didn't. Why was he fighting it?

Our waitress asked if we were ready to order. Without looking at the menu, I ordered a burger and fries. She took note of it and looked at Luke. Her smile grew just a bit brighter, and she shifted her stance, cocking her hip in a flirty way. I rolled my eyes.

"He'll have two burgers and an order of fries," I told her before he could speak. She gave me a fake smile, wrote the order on her stupid little pad, collected our menus, and walked away.

"Twat," I mumbled.

He gave me a look.

"What? There aren't any kids around, and I was quiet."

His lips twitched, and he turned toward me once again.

I mimicked his pose careful not to touch him. I didn't want to freak out my stomach or fall asleep. I watched his eyes for a moment, liking the amusement that still danced in them, but decided we needed to address some real issues.

"You know they will be waiting for us, right?"

"Let's talk about something else," he said softly. "I like it better when you have fire or laughter in your eyes instead of what I see now."

"What do you see?"

"Fear."

I narrowed my eyes.

"Pardon. Despair." He spoke softly, his unwavering regard making me feel vulnerable.

I couldn't help the despair. It lived and breathed in me. Sometimes, he helped me forget though. Distracted me. Like when I tried to bite him. A blush crept into my cheeks as I remembered my failed attempts.

His gaze changed. A glimpse of coveting sparked in the depths of it as he lifted his hand from the back of the bench. I dropped my own arm out of the way. He reached forward just a bit and lightly ran the back of his forefinger along my cheek.

I barely felt his slow, soft touch, but my heart stuttered anyway.

He closed his eyes for a moment. "I see your despair and it makes me..." He exhaled slowly before opening his eyes. His intensity pinned me. "I want to hurt whoever put that emotion in your eyes."

"I don't get you. If you feel that strongly about me, why can't I Claim you?"

He abruptly shook his head. "Let's talk about something—"

"Else," I finished for him, annoyed. I paused for a moment, seeing the waitress approach again. "You're a twat, too."

He threw his head back with a laugh just as she stopped by our table. Her eyes glazed over a bit as her eyes swept his face and throat. I briefly considered clawing her eyes out before reining myself in. Whoa, where did that come from? Biting my lip, I quelled my immediate need to freak out over the strong surge of possessiveness that had just rushed me. Nature had set him up as a possibility for me so of course I'd feel that way. It didn't mean anything. I wasn't actually stupid enough to fall for him. But, until we reached his friends at the Compound, if I couldn't bite him, no one else would be allowed to nibble. Because...well, just because.

"Can I get you a refill?" she asked him softly.

"He's fine," I answered, staring her down.

He kept his eyes on me, and they danced with silent laughter. Yeah, I wanted to smack him again.

She walked away to check on her other tables.

"If we can't talk about *them* or *us*, what should we talk about?"

"You. What do you like doing? What are your interests?"

My mouth popped open. "Are you serious?" We were running toward what I considered our impending deaths, and he wanted to get to know me?

He nodded, and I rolled my eyes. "I like breathing and am interested in staying alive."

"Bethi," he practically growled.

Maybe this would help convince him. "Okay, okay. So, interests. Well, before I started losing my mind I—" What had I done? I went to school, hung out with friends, sighed over boys, worried about clothes. "I was self-centered and immature. My interests don't really matter beyond that, do they? Not after everything I've seen."

"I think you're being a little hard on yourself."

"That's just it. I don't think I am. I think the human society lets me be too easy on myself. I have more responsibility to be a better person than what I've been in the past. Sure, I wasn't horrible, but I wasn't great either. Shouldn't we all strive for great?" I thought of the dream with the Taupe Lady and my friend's funeral. "Shouldn't we all strive to make a difference? To impact the lives around us in a positive way? To make our experiences count?"

He watched me with a growing seriousness. "That is a lot of responsibility for someone so young."

"See. That's what I mean. No, it's not. If we held each other to a higher level of accountability, if we raised our children with those expectations and guided them with our own examples of higher achievement, it wouldn't be too much. We would be a better people because of it. Instead, we took a wrong turn somewhere and ended up on Excuses-Are-Like-Assholes Boulevard."

He opened his mouth to comment, but I shifted my attention from him to the waitress carrying our plates. He turned, saw her, and sighed. I read the promise in his eyes to continue our conversation later; and inwardly, I cringed. I went from trying to convince him I cared to stepping up on a soapbox I didn't know I had. And I still felt like I had more to vent. I blamed it on sleep deprivation, bad dreams, and his completely gorgeous hazel eyes.

The waitress set our food on the table and left after our assurances we didn't need anything else. I kept busy with dousing my fries in ketchup, letting the silence build for a moment. "Can I ask why we can't talk about *us*?"

He held out his hand for the ketchup. "It makes me uncomfortable."

I surrendered the bottle and watched him neatly add it to his burger. "Not getting into details, but what part makes you uncomfortable?"

"All of it."

That didn't make any sense. He took a huge bite of his burger while I struggled with my frustration. Stubborn man.

He reached past me for the salt as I leaned forward for the pepper. His hand brushed the curve of my breast, and he jerked back as if scorched. His gaze locked on his hand, and he sat there frozen.

He hadn't bumped into me hard. No damage done. It'd been an accident. So what was his deal? He continued to...just sit there. I ducked my head trying to make eye contact, but he avoided it.

His reaction to the incident was starting to offend me. "It's a boob," I bit out, annoyed. "I have two of them. They don't do much. They just sit there. They definitely don't bite, so stop acting like they're going to come after you. Grow up."

"Please stop talking about them," he said in a stiff strangled voice.

I didn't let up. "You know, sometimes it helps to name the things you fear. Let's call the right one Everest and the left one Fuji. Two mountainous ranges waiting to be...." I never finished. He had cleared the restaurant's door in a few furious strides, leaving me sitting alone.

It felt good to get under his skin, to see him react in a way that wasn't calm and confident. It bothered me that it was at my expense. What was so wrong with me that he freaked out at the slightest touch? Other than the fact that some other werewolves wanted to kill me and I had dreams that made me scream loud enough to shake the nearest window...I mean really, who didn't have some kind of baggage?

He didn't go far. My eyes tracked him as he paced back and forth before the restaurant's front windows. His scowl didn't let up, and I didn't feel so frustrated anymore. Smirking, I shook my head and continued eating my fries. He cast an occasional glance in my direction but didn't appear to calm down.

When I finished my fries and burger, I waited until he glanced at me to take a fry from his plate. His steps hesitated and his scowl changed to a frown as, with a challenging smirk, I ate the fry. I reached for his second burger. He stopped pacing and watched me through the window. His focused stare and complete stillness seemed a little spooky. The other patrons cast nervous glances at him.

Slowly, I lifted the burger to my mouth unable to stop my teasing grin. His eyes narrowed, and he reached for the door. I took a huge bite and hastily set the burger back on his plate.

In just a few steps, he stood by the table looking down at me, his expression carefully blank.

"Well? Did you lose your appetite or not?" I asked.

He slid into the opposite seat and pulled his plate toward him, not saying a word. His avoidance hurt a little. He didn't want to talk about us, he didn't want to talk about the trouble that was out there waiting for us, and he didn't want to talk about my boobs—which was pretty much the same as talking about us. As I watched him eat, I had an idea.

"Tell you what. I'll let you have two closed subjects between us. Two topics we'll keep completely off limits. Three is ridiculous." My tone carried a bit of hostility, but I didn't really care.

He closed his eyes, finished swallowing, and sighed.

"So which one are we going to talk about...our plan to reach the Compound, the reason you won't let me Claim you, or my boobs? You choose."

He set his burger on his plate and took a drink. "They will be waiting for us on all three roads. We could try to leave the bike and take to the woods, but I think they will have scouts ready for that as well. And we'd be slower on foot. Our best bet is to anticipate them and break through before they know when to expect us."

"So the longer we take to get there..."

"The more likely they are to be ready for us," he agreed.

After my stunt at the last hotel room, they'd probably caught onto the fact that we knew they were after us.

"Any word from that Elder?" I asked.

"He asked for an update, but I kept it vague. He's not pushing for anything more. He offered his assistance if we needed anything further."

That sounded non-threatening. Perhaps we were wrong about him. Still, I'd rather not take the chance.

"Okay then, wolf-man, let's get going." I waved the waitress over for the bill as he finished in one huge bite. I waited impatiently as he paid and she flirted. Now that he'd admitted what I already knew—they would be waiting for us—I wanted to get going. With relief, I walked out the restaurant door.

"Tired?" he asked before we reached the bike.

"No," I lied. After a day on the bike, I was ready for bed even without the pull of waiting dreams, but I didn't want to delay getting to the Compound.

He turned to glance at me and only shook his head, not believing me. "We can't go far with you tired."

"And if we take too long to get there, it will only be worse." I'd had enough creatures flying out of the trees at me. I didn't want to give them extra time to gather.

"I could call Gabby and let her know."

"No, we don't know who is betraying us."

"You think she would?" he settled on the bike and fully turned toward me tilting his head to study my expression.

"No, she wouldn't. At least, not purposely. But, who does she believe she can trust? She could say something to the wrong person. If we stayed on our own, we might actually make it to the gates of the Compound." I swung my leg over the back and settled behind him offering the strap. "I'll do my best to stay awake," I promised.

CHAPTER TEN

BIRDSONG AND SUNLIGHT DRIFTED ALONG THE SPRING BREEZE THAT TEASED MY HAIR. MY *hair, not someone else's or a past me.* I recognized where I stood. It was the meadow of my other dreams. Only, the great stone monoliths had aged and weathered to stunted broken pillars. *Was this then a real dream, pointless and meant to be forgotten as soon as I woke? Unsure, I waited for the Taupe Lady to appear.*

Nothing moved in the open field surrounding the stones. I turned in a slow circle. The dream felt empty, a shadow of what it should be if it were a memory. Yet, real dreams, the pointless kind, were so rare now. I couldn't believe this was one of them.

"We need to talk," I called out. *I wanted to shout my questions and make threats, mostly just to vent, but I held it all in hoping she would come to me if I was nice.*

The wind carried her answer to me. "My daughter. Your path is your own to choose. I can *influence it no more than I have already done. Remember,*" she whispered. "Dream."

The dream shifted.

I sat on a bed covered with a light pink quilt and squeezed the teddy bear in my arms as I listened to the footsteps pause outside my door. Using my sight, I checked everyone's location in the house.

Justin had come home for winter break just tonight. I hadn't met him before but had talked to him on the phone. He'd been so nice to me. His mom usually fostered two kids at a time. They had the room, she'd said, in their hearts and in their house. I'd hoped it would be different here. The other foster girl with me didn't really like me, but the other girls usually didn't. Justin, though, had seemed so nice. I'd hoped he would just stay away at school.

When he'd given me a hug in greeting, it had been just a little too tight. When he'd pulled back and looked me in the eye, I knew.

I gently lifted the phone from the receiver with a heavy heart. I'd already disabled the sound so he wouldn't hear me dial from in the hallway. The knob on the door turned, and I quickly set the phone to the side.

"What are you doing, Justin?" I asked calmly as he opened the door.

"I just wanted to check on you," he said with a smile. He stepped in and closed the door behind him.

I clutched the bear tighter. "I'm fine. I think you should leave."

"Don't be like that," he begged softly as he sat on the edge of the bed. "I see you got the bear I sent," he nodded toward the bear I clutched. I'd hoped it would remind him of my age.

"How old are you?" I asked.

"Twenty-one. Why are you asking?" He smiled and reached a hand to smooth over my hair.

"Because I'm twelve, and you shouldn't be touching me. Not even my hair."

He sighed and dropped his hand, his eyes growing puzzled. Then he nodded slowly. "You're right. I'm sorry. Good night, Gabby." He leaned forward with the intent of kissing me. I dodged out of the way, bumping the table that held the phone.

"Don't," I warned. "Justin, I like your mom, but with you here, I can't stay."

The door to my room opened, and Justin's mom looked from me to her son. Her face was white with shock, and she loosely held a phone in her hand. Justin looked at her phone, then the phone on the table by my bed.

"What are you doing in here?"

He scowled. "Nothing."

His mom's eyes shifted to me.

"It's time I leave," I said softly. She nodded and dialed the phone.

The dream shifted.

My foster dad leaned over my chair, his arm brushing against my breast as he served me mashed potatoes. I met the eyes of my foster mom at the end of the table. Her eyes filled with tears, and she looked away. After dinner, I rushed to the phone and dialed a number I knew by heart.

The dream shifted.

Alixe and I had gotten on well for three months before services called asking if she could take on another teen. She assured them I was an angel and that she would have no trouble adding another. When she hung up, she told me that Brandon would be joining our happy home. I tried not to show my disappointment. I asked his age. Fourteen, same as me. Maybe that would make a difference.

We worked together to make the single bed in the third room. She told me to let her know if there was any trouble. Brandon came to the door an hour later. He stood with his head down trying to hide his face. His swollen eye and nose told his story better than his slumped shoulders and dirty clothes.

Alixe coaxed him in and spoke with the officer dropping him off. The boy's abuse was clear. Still, when he risked a look up and met my eyes, I saw a change in him. A small one. He glanced back down quickly, but the slump in his shoulders was gone.

The next morning, I woke with him standing beside my bed, staring at me.

"Why do I feel like this?" he whispered to me, close to tears. His hands shook. I wanted to cry, too. I wished I knew why the men around me acted as they did...why they couldn't just leave me alone.

"If you ignore me, it will help," I whispered back. He nodded but didn't move.

Finally, he sighed, wiped at his tears, and winced when he touched the swollen skin. Then he left.

I sat with Alixe at the breakfast table after he'd eaten and left the room.

"He needs help," I said softly. She nodded, looking sad. "I don't think me being here will help him. He needs you more than I do. Please. Call services. Let them know we talked, and I need a new home so you can focus on Brandon."

The dream shifted.

I sat at the dinner table across from an older man, warily keeping an eye on him as he ate with gusto. It was my third night in his house and so far everything had gone great. I didn't let myself get too hopeful, though. My faith in men hadn't held up well after my experiences with foster care and school.

He forked in the last bite of spaghetti and meat sauce—more sauce than meat—from his plate and sat back with a sigh. He frowned at my plate. "I know it's not much," he said.

I shook my head. "Sam, it's fine. I'm just not that hungry." I eyed the huge mound of noodles on my plate.

He glanced at my plate, too, and grinned. "I'll remember to cut the serving back next time," he promised. I agreed and rose to put the rest into a container and wash my dishes. He stood and waited for his turn at the sink. He kept a respectful distance between us.

When I was about to leave the room with my school bag, he called my name. I glanced back at him. He looked a little lost as he met my gaze. "You'll tell me if you need something, right? Lunch money or a ride to the mall?"

I nodded wondering what he really meant with this unusual line of questioning. He must have sensed my confusion because he sighed and gave a self-deprecating smile. "Cubs are easy. Feed them, give them your time, and they are happy. You don't need much food, and you prefer to be alone. I don't know how to raise a human. A human girl is even more," he waved his hand at me, "confusing."

A tiny smile crept onto my face seeing him so flustered. Living with a werewolf already beat living with any foster family, except maybe the last one. My smile faded, and I felt a tad lonely for Barb.

"If I need anything, I'll let you know." I turned and left the kitchen.

The dreams stopped. Darkness claimed me for a moment before *her* voice floated in.

"Every moment you live offers you a chance to learn. Your experiences and your reactions to them make you who you are. Who are you, daughter? And what have you learned?

The dreams started again. I didn't struggle against them, wanting to know more about what I faced.

My stepfather, Richard, looked pale as Blake suggested I take the children outside to play. At just over a year, my brother couldn't really play outside yet, and the baby shouldn't be in the sun. I knew that from my mom. My eyes watered thinking of her. We'd just had her funeral a few days ago.

Regardless, Richard told me to take them both outside. One of Blake's friends followed us out. Either Blake or one of his associates had been with us since Mom died. I didn't really like any of them. Mostly because Mom hadn't. Aden fussed, and I gently set him against my shoulder, rocking him side to side.

"Shut that kid up," the man with us growled.

I frowned at him but started whispering to the baby, trying anyway.

"Bring the older one back," Blake called from inside.

The man strode over and for a moment, I thought he would grab me. Then he reached down and plucked Liam up by his tiny little arm. Liam screamed and just dangled there not understanding.

"Stop!" I yelled, trying to reach for Liam while still holding Aden. The man held him away and went inside. I raced after him, holding Aden tight.

Richard sat at the table crying, his face in his hands, not even looking at his son.

"Set him down," Blake ordered. His eyes remained on me. I thought he meant Aden, and I clutched him tighter. But his friend set Liam down. "That's not how you carry a child," Blake said to the man. His voice held little censor. He squatted before Liam, who sat in a sobbing heap on the floor.

"You do love your brothers, don't you, Michelle." He patted Liam on the head and stood again. "I'll be helping your father for a while, until he's on his feet again."

I briefly glanced at Richard, not correcting Blake. He wasn't my father, but he'd loved my mom very much. If he felt half the pain I did, I understood how he felt.

"I'm sorry for your loss," Blake said evenly before turning toward Richard. "The contractors will start work this afternoon. We need to keep you all safe."

The dream shifted.

I sat in the boys' room playing quietly with them. The stifling sterile room echoed back even their quietest whispers, but this was the only place in the house that they were allowed to play. The easiest place to monitor us—me.

Richard strode through the door with purpose.

"The last tip did marginally well. Blake would like to thank you and asked me to find out what you would like as a reward."

This was Blake's game. Every time one of my premonitions did well—they all did well —Blake offered a reward. In the beginning, I had used these opportunities to ask for new toys for my brothers or new clothes for us or even to be allowed a few minutes outside. But I'd caught on to what I was doing. Each time I asked for something, I let them know what mattered to me. Last night, Blake had proven my theory correct by threatening to take all outside time away from the boys if I didn't sit down and eat with him and his associates.

"Please tell him I am happy with whatever reward he chooses," I murmured without looking up from our puzzle.

"Michelle, he will insist that you choose," Richard said with worry in his voice. It was the first time in a long time he'd acted human. I glanced up in time to see his fear-filled eyes rest on Liam.

He feared for their safety. So did I. I needed to find a way to escape. Until then, I would pretend to play Blake's game. "A ribbon. For my hair, please."

The dream shifted.

A gag covered my mouth as tears streamed down my cheeks. The gag didn't hurt. The cord tying my hands didn't even hurt. My head though, it throbbed and ached, the pain dull and sharp at the same time, snaking its way through every cell in my brain as the premonition repeated itself.

Blake stood over me smirking.

"I told you, you would be punished if you tried to run." He bent down to where I'd fallen to my side on the floor. The premonition had been running through my mind for almost two days. They'd let me eat and drink in the beginning, unbinding my hands and removing the gag, while they wore earplugs and earmuffs with music. They'd tried getting me to eat and drink a while ago, but I refused. The pain was too much.

I sniffled as my nose started to run. My eyes had been watering for hours now. Blake reached forward and touched the wetness just under my nose. He pulled back and showed me his fingers. It wasn't just a runny nose. Blood smeared his fingertips.

"Do you understand, yet? You need me, Michelle. Who else can you tell this information to?"

I closed my eyes with a sob, wishing the pain would end. Behind the gag, I moved my lips weakly, mumbling the information because I couldn't help myself.

The cord holding my wrists together loosened. Without thought, my shaking hand flew to my mouth to tear away the gag. I sobbed out the information, and the pain immediately stopped. I didn't stop sobbing for a long time.

Luke called my name, and I struggled to wake as I felt the dream try to shift. I didn't want to remember any more. I wanted my own reality back. As crappy as it was. Someone pounded on a door, helping to pull me out of sleep's hold.

I blinked my eyes open, cringing at the cold water hitting my face as I looked up into the spray of the showerhead. It took me a moment to remember what had happened. Tired after a few more hours of riding, we'd found yet another hotel. He said he'd run and get food. I said I would take a shower. I'd kept it cold thinking I'd stay awake. Instead, I'd set myself up for hypothermia.

I shivered uncontrollably and wiped water from my face. My numb legs didn't want to move and my tailbone throbbed painfully.

"She's trying to kill me," I muttered as I struggled to lift myself from the bottom of the tub.

The door flew open with a crack, disturbing the air and making the shower curtain flutter. It stuck to my skin, and I curled my lip. Gross. Hotel shower curtain. Touching me. I frantically batted it away thinking of all the nasty things on it—and once my mind was on the subject, all the nasty things at the bottom of the hotel tub—when the curtain was suddenly torn aside.

Luke stared down at me. Rage and panic filled his eyes.

"What the hell?" I sputtered trying to grab the curtain and cover myself, no longer so picky about it touching me. Red crept up his neck as I watched.

Flustered, he let the curtain go, but he still had the sense to reach around to turn off the water. His eyes raked my face. "You fell asleep again, didn't you?" he asked with soft reproach.

"Of course I did! I *always* fall asleep. Now, get out!" Embarrassment and anger warred for dominance. It was one thing to joke about us, to try to Claim him, and to kid about my boobs. But, to have him actually *see* me? All of me? I wanted to curl up in a ball of shame. I didn't eat right and looked like hell. The scars on my arms still stood out vividly which was why I wore clothes to cover them. And he'd seen *everything*. I'd noted the shock in his eyes before he surrendered the curtain.

"Be out in two minutes, or I'm coming back in," he warned, closing the door behind him.

"If you come back in, you better be naked too," I shouted at the closed door, anger finally winning.

With shaking limbs, I pulled myself from the tub and wrapped myself in a towel. I used the other towel—the one meant for Luke—to dry my hair. Those dreams shook me. The first three had been the same girl. Gabby. No doubt the same Gabby Luke kept talking about. The second set of dreams also involved a single star. Michelle. Their lives sucked just like mine. It didn't make me feel any better.

Taking my time, I brushed my teeth and gradually warmed enough that the blue tint faded from my lips. More than two minutes had passed, and I gave myself a weak smirk in the mirror.

Pulling my bag close, I dug for clean clothes. Not finding any, I settled for the cleanest. I took my time getting dressed.

Finally, I stepped out of the bathroom. I ran my fingers through my damp tangled hair and gave him the barest glance before I moved to the hotel's TV guide, pretending to read it.

"Either we get where we're going tomorrow, or we need to find a laundromat. Everything's dirty," I commented.

Silence greeted me. Stifling the urge to scrunch up my face in annoyance, I took a calming breath and turned to face him.

Luke reclined on the bed, his hands behind his head, as he watched me move around the room. His shirt stretched tight over his chest. I struggled to pull my gaze away. His exposed arms flexed as he moved one out from behind his head. On the inside, I sighed.

"Come on," he said, waving me over. "Get some sleep."

He knew sleeping in a cold shower didn't qualify as rest, but I hadn't expected him to be on the bed waiting for me after my smart remark. I shuffled to the bed in my stocking feet and lay beside him, not too eager to sleep just yet.

He pulled me to his side, slid an arm under my head, and tucked me under his chin. His heat melted away the lingering chill of the shower. His willingness to get so close while I was still awake puzzled me—he usually waited until I was already slipping into a dream. He lightly ran a hand down my covered arm. Right over the cuts I'd once made in desperation. I closed my eyes in shame.

"Don't," he whispered. "Not with me. I'm not here to judge you. I'm here to keep you safe. Always. Even from yourself."

His arm tightened around me. This time I dove for the dream tugging at my consciousness. Anything to escape the little tug at my heart his words caused.

WE LEFT the room several hours later. I didn't think he'd slept at all, but I had five hours of sweet nothing—well, not nothing. I'd woken to my face plastered to his bare chest. Best five hours of sleep ever.

"We should reach the Compound by nightfall."

When we stepped into the parking lot, Luke's stride paused. He tilted his head back, scented the light breeze, grabbed my hand, and pulled me toward the bike. I didn't stop to wonder why. He'd smelled something. I quickly slipped the bag across my body and climbed on behind him as my eyes searched for the cause. Luke started the bike with a roar.

Just then, two men stepped from the office. My heart leapt, and my arms involuntarily tightened around Luke. He took off with a squeal of the back tire. The bike slipped under us a bit, but I risked a look back. Where the men had stood, two large dogs stared after us. They didn't give chase. Instead, they turned and ran into the woods.

"They're not following," I called to Luke.

He nodded and opened the throttle. My stomach rolled at the surge in speed. Thankfully, I hadn't eaten anything.

We merged with an interstate that took us south, not north. I wanted to moan in frustration, but understood his decision. Since we were so close to our goal, they would know our intended direction. Hopping on the interstate would throw them off. Heck, it threw me off. I had no idea which way we intended to come in from.

How had they found us though? We'd been careful, zigzagging all over the place in a non-pattern. I'd been watching the map. Maybe Luke was right. They had sentinels waiting for us. But we were still so many miles away. Could they have so many in their pack as that? I doubted it. Maybe it'd just been luck. Or maybe, he'd told someone again. I rested my head against his back, emotionally drained. I'd fluctuated between "just let me die" and "I don't want to die" too many times to count. I didn't know what I wanted anymore except to be left alone. I had never asked to be in the middle of a werewolf tug of war.

We drove for hours the wrong way and then got off at an exit heading east so we could circle back around. Despite his efforts, I knew it would be pointless.

Like he'd said, they would be waiting—because somehow, they always seemed to know where to expect us. I knew what I needed to do.

When he offered to stop, I pointed to a laundromat. He nodded and pulled in. He loosened the bag, and I slid off, taking the bag with me. His troubled gaze never wavered from me as he followed me into the light airy building.

He used the change machine as I shoved everything in a washer. After adding quarters and dumping in the powder detergent from the packet I'd bought at the vending machine, I finally faced him. He eyed me warily. Apparently his wolfie senses knew something was up. I let out a long, slow breath, calmed myself, and let the beginning of a dream wrap its arms around me—not enough to sleep, just enough to slow my pulse. I had to mask a lie.

"I saw a fast food place a few blocks away. I'll get us something."

He frowned at me. "I'll go with."

"No way. We'll lose our stuff. It's two blocks away and we're in the middle of town," I arched a brow at him and patted the bag I still had slung over my shoulder. "I have protection and can carry everything with this. Two burgers?"

"Three," he grumped reaching into his wallet and giving me a twenty. We'd used all the money he'd given me for rooms along the way.

I plucked it from his fingers with a smile. "Probably a good idea," I agreed. "You may not have fries by the time I walk back."

He smiled at me as he sat down to watch the machine.

I strode out the door, turned right, and didn't look back. Not far away, I flagged down a ride and asked them if they could take me north. Staring out the window, trying to ignore the ache growing in my chest, I watched the mile markers go by.

MY JAW POPPED on my third yawn. The couple had taken me over an hour north. They dropped me off and wished me luck. I smiled and waved as they pulled away. My stomach grumbled, and I thought of the twenty in my pocket. I still had a long way to go; and with no Luke, I needed to save the cash for when I really needed it.

Going into the gas station, I used the restroom and drank from the water fountain. The clerk watched me in the convenience mirror. Apparently my days of looking like a runaway weren't over. I ignored him and headed out the door to begin my long trek—the gas station hadn't had anyone who'd looked willing enough to give me a ride. Plus, the clerk would have probably called it in.

I trudged north for an hour, lost in my thoughts of this life and past lives. Why had the Taupe Lady directed my dreams to Gabby and Michelle's pasts? Why in order? And why couldn't I recall all the details like I could with other past lives? Because they weren't dead yet? It made sense. How could I remember everything when everything hadn't yet occurred? Why direct my dreams at all, though? She claimed she couldn't interfere, but then did just that, hadn't she?

Something had me lifting my head instead of watching my feet. The trees around me had lost their leaves, and I could once again see my breath in the air. I huddled in Luke's jacket and wondered if he'd figured it out yet.

A twig snapped, and a group of three men stepped from the woods onto the shoulder in front of me. Steam rose from their skin. Shorts provided their only covering. Their smiles froze my insides. My feet stopped moving, but my mind whirred with possibilities. Distract and run!

"He went that way," I called pointing to my left. They all turned, and I sprinted to the right, crashing into the trees and ignoring the bite of the branches as they whipped my face.

CHAPTER ELEVEN

I RAN. THEY TOYED WITH ME. WITH THEIR SPEED, I KNEW THEY could catch me at any moment. But what fun would that be, I thought bitterly. The echoes of past lives hit me. Same game, same chase. My anger grew, fueling my legs. I pushed past the pain and kept moving. Just like my dreams, I sought something. A place to jump. A way to die cleanly. They couldn't have me. The price for the world was too high.

A coughing laugh from behind me signaled their full transformation. I dodged around trees gasping for air, not slowing. Was it too much to ask for a random cliff in the woods every now and again?

Fear pooled in my stomach as my leg failed with a cramp. I fell hard but didn't lay in a pathetic heap for more than a heartbeat. I got my knees under me and as I sprang up, I thrust my hand into my bag, which was still slung across my body. My quick moves didn't matter. They were already upon me, their panting louder than my own as they laughed.

Pulling my hand from the bag, I surprised them with my knife. My gift from Luke. I felt a pang thinking of him. Leaving hadn't kept me any safer.

One of the men shifted back enough to speak, but his mouth was still too long for the words to come out clearly. "What do you think to do with that?"

Around us the trees remained quiet. Only the distant chirping of birds reminded me I wasn't alone.

"What did you hope to accomplish by chasing me?" I countered.

"Blake told us you would know. You're the dreamer," he said further shifting into a man.

"Your new leader?" I asked while willing myself to breathe deeply and trying to quell my fear.

They didn't answer but it didn't matter. Their leader changed each cycle, but their goals did not.

"If I'm the dreamer, then we all know the outcome," I said. "Walk away and maybe I'll live for another day."

"I don't think so, little girl," he said as he eyed my knife.

"I'd hoped history wouldn't repeat itself this time. I'm tired of dying." The fear left me. Only sorrow remained as I spun the knife deftly and plunged it toward my soft middle.

The man roared and moved before the tip did more than pierce the surface. I'd underestimated their speed. But, when he batted it out of my hands, he didn't realize he furthered my cause. A thin trail of fire blazed across my middle, superficial at best, but his nostrils flared as he scented my blood. I shifted my stance, bracing myself.

He growled but didn't touch me further. We stood facing each other with me slightly bent holding an arm against the sting on my stomach. The other two stood several paces behind their spokesperson.

"Come with us on your own and spare yourself some pain."

Spare myself pain? He had just acknowledged I remembered my—our—past lives. "Stupid dog," I laughed.

He cuffed me upside the head, knocking me to my side. I staggered but did not fall. It hurt my cut but brought me closer to my knife. I didn't look at the shining blade resting on the decaying leaves. Instead, I straightened and faced him again.

"Your brain mustn't have expanded again with that last shift."

This time he slapped me. It was hard enough to justify a stumble a few more steps to my right.

"See?" I managed on a pain-filled exhale. "Pain is all you know how to give. There won't be any sparing of anything but kindness and mercy."

He snorted. "Mercy is for the weak."

"No. Mercy is for anyone with a big enough vocabulary to —"

I didn't get to finish the insult. He knocked me hard. The side of my face exploded in agony as I went down. This time, right on the knife. I laughed like a madwoman as I lay there. No one moved to touch me again. Were they trying to figure out what was so funny? It didn't matter. I'd reached my goal. They wouldn't have me this time.

Putting my arms under myself, I palmed the handle and stood, hiding my weapon behind my back, trying to angle the blade for my next fall.

"Stupid," I taunted.

Before he could move, something big and dark flew toward one of the beasts, knocking it into a tree. I didn't take my eyes from the man in front of me, but it looked like another one of them, half transformed.

The attention of the one in front of me didn't waver, either. As soon as one of his own hit the tree, he immediately grabbed for me. I slashed out with the knife, taking him by surprise. The wild swing relieved him of a not quite human digit. He screamed as behind him another member of his pack flew at the new attacker.

The wolf before me ignored the blood dripping from his hand and crouched slightly, watching me closely. His injury had wiped his patronizingly amused expression from his face. Tense, he hesitated, unsure how to come at me.

I grinned at him. "Stupid and slow. A bad combination in a fight."

His lip curled back in a silent snarl a moment before he lunged toward me. I swung the knife up and over in a diagonal slash that caught his chest and part of his face when he pulled back. My arm ached from the force I'd used. I knew I wouldn't take him by surprise again. Or could I?

He lunged once more, but this time I did not swing for him. I brought the knife up to my own neck. Seeing the edge poised at my throat, he suddenly flew backwards, away from me. The move gave me a clear view of who'd joined the fight.

Luke, shifted to a mix of more wolf than man, held my tormentor by the throat. The man's flesh bulged between Luke's fingers. The man flailed but didn't make a sound. He couldn't. Luke spun, putting his back to me at the same time his arm twitched. A loud popping crack sounded. The man stilled.

In the silence, I caught a distant sound of drumming feet hitting the ground. My shoulders slumped and the unfurling hope within me quickly withered. Too many this time.

Luke tossed the dead man aside and pivoted toward the sound. His strong back shielded me from the horde racing toward us. For just a moment, I rested my forehead against the solid wall of him. I breathed deeply smelling his sweat and soap. He didn't move. His focus remained on the oncoming pack. He would die for me. My chest tightened, and I struggled with my next inhale. I didn't want that. But I knew he wouldn't leave.

The drumming grew louder. Branches snapped as the wolves forced their way toward us. A howl rent the air.

How had I been so stubbornly stupid? In a way, I still was. Too afraid to admit, even to myself, how much I cared for the man standing in front of me. I'd squandered any chance for happiness—no matter how brief—in this life. I hoped the memory of Luke and how I felt for him would give me more courage in the next one. Courage to trust. Courage to see the truth. He wasn't one of them.

"I will hold the memory of you in my heart forever," I managed to say before a single tear rolled down my cheek. That's all I had time for. I hoped he knew what he meant to me. Straightening, I flipped the knife so the handle was clasped in my hand, but the blade along my forearm angled outward. I hoped it would be harder to knock out of my hand that way.

As the first of them erupted from the underbrush, Luke spun out with his claws, slashing through the wolf's soft underbelly. Its sharp cry pierced the air and signaled the start of madness.

I braced myself, ready for anything, but nothing broke through Luke's guard with the first wave. He knocked body after body back, eviscerating those he could. Blood soaked the ground, but he held firm.

A movement away from the main attack caught my attention. I looked away from the carnage to see several sneaking around us. Turning, I stood with my back to Luke.

I stood in a bloodied field. Bodies littered the ground around me, but still more came. I moved like water, bending and flowing over the mass that would kill me, anger fueling me. I had no claws, but the knives struck them just as well.

The vision slammed into me, then left me as I blinked at the dogs who'd come several steps closer. The echo of that epic battle burrowed into my mind and wouldn't let go. I could *fight*. Loosening my stance, I slightly bent my knees, ready on the balls of my feet. I could do better than a lucky swing that might claim a finger. I could *kill*. Adrenaline surged through me. I looked at the numbers around us and doubted it would be enough.

The first one crept toward me, and I felt Luke shift behind me.

"Focus on your side," I said as I moved like water once again, but for the first time in this life. Wide stance...lean to the side and sweep the arm out as you move, I thought. The blade slid through flesh and bumped bone. I pulled the blade back and shifted my weight to the other side to kick out, knocking the shocked beast to the side.

I grinned. *I got this!* Using my muscles in ways they had never been used in this lifetime, I continued sweeping and slashing my blade. The sharp edge bit into the fur covered flesh of three of them before they partially shifted. They didn't want to kill me so their fangs and claws had less use than opposable thumbs. Still, I had an advantage for a while. Then, I noticed some of the cuts I'd made starting to knit together. I needed to do more than wound. My mind knew the moves, but my untrained body often fell short on delivery.

Soon their anger over my continued slices had them striking harder. Aches formed where they'd managed to sneak through my guard and hit me. Those punishing blows were meant to wear me down. It worked.

An attacker caught my arm and pulled me forward as something bumped into me from behind, off balancing me so I fell toward my attacker's chest. I face planted into the disgustingly wet furred chest then felt a blow vibrate through his body. He jerked oddly. His grip loosened. I pulled back and looked up at his face as he let go. Bile rose to my throat at the sight of the bloody stump of his neck. He fell to the side. I swallowed heavily and looked for the next attacker.

Fewer stood before me than there'd been a moment ago. And those still around me had shifted their attention from me to Luke. Risking a quick glance, I saw why.

Several jumped on him at once, weighing him down as they grappled with his swinging arms. The remaining men joined in, knowing as I did, that if they brought Luke down, they would have me. None of them paid me any attention, now.

Luke's tendons stood out with strain as he continued to struggle. An attacker bit into Luke's neck and held on. Luke didn't have time to shake the man before another attacker flew at him. No one noticed that I had shifted my focus to the wolf still attached to him. I flipped the blade in my hand and threw it. It sank into the biter's side. The man grunted but didn't loosen his hold. Luke gripped another man's head, twisted the man's neck savagely, then turned to the next attacker before the body fell. But Luke's movements were slow and sluggish because of the man whose teeth still pierced him.

I stepped forward and pulled the handle of my knife, now stuck in the man's middle, up until the blade resisted. The man, screaming in pain, let go. Luke continued to fight. I stepped back, flowing into my ready stance, waiting. The sounds of Luke's struggles faded to the background as I maintained my focus.

Rage and retribution filled the man's gaze. His claws elongated, his fingers receding to make room for their full length. With a snarl, he reached for me. But he didn't move far. Luke sent his last attacker flying, then twisted to address the man I faced. He raked the man, gutting him in a spray of blood, from groin to throat.

Looking away, I scanned the area around us, the trees, the undergrowth, searching for more. The thud of the man's body falling to the ground heralded a harsh kind of silence.

Luke's ragged breaths blended with mine, the only noise filling the air. Nothing moved. The animals around us remained silent. Then, a single bird chirped. My eyes flew to Luke's. He too remained partially crouched. But nothing happened.

We'd done it.

I slowly straightened, wincing at the various little pains that tingled into my awareness. My wounds didn't concern me as much as Luke's did. Blood painted his clothes and dotted his half-transformed face. I bent and grabbed a shirt from the bag. With each breath, his features settled back into the man I knew. Except his eyes. They stayed dilated, overly large and completely focused on me. I started shaking from too much adrenaline and nothing to use it on. Or maybe shock. Who knew?

He took two steps forward, plucked the knife from my hand, and dropped it to the ground. Anger remained in his eyes. His jaw muscles twitched rhythmically. His neck bled from the bite, but he didn't seem to notice.

I shrugged out of his jacket and stripped out of the hoodie so I could use it to press against the wound. He jerked slightly at my touch and placed a hand on my waist.

In an unexpected move, he snagged the hem of my shirt with a finger and lifted it high enough to see the slice across my stomach. I'd forgotten about that. His attention brought the pain back into focus. It hurt. He glanced at the cut and then dropped the hem, his eyes devouring me again. His hand stayed on my side, warm and comforting. He stepped close.

He still looked mad, and the lingering signs of his shift unnerved me. Yet, I kept pressure on the bite. I couldn't afford a passed out werewolf. My hand continued to tremble, and he reached up to close his hand around mine. I wondered how much his bite hurt. Still staring at his neck, he surprised me when he leaned forward to rest his forehead against mine. My gaze flew to his, but he had closed his eyes. He breathed deeply, then released my hand. Gently, he wrapped his arms around me and pulled me to him. His mouth brushed my hair. The hug started out light but grew tighter until I squeaked involuntarily in pain.

His arms loosened, and he pulled back enough that I could see his face. His anguish. His frustration.

"Don't," he started saying, but his voice broke and he had to stop. He swallowed hard and briefly closed his eyes. When he opened them again, his look made my heart turnover. Need. Desperate need flooded the hazel beauty of the eyes I'd come to know so well.

He leaned in, lifted a hand, and slid his fingers through my hair. His gaze followed the movement which started at my temple and ended with his fingers cupping the back of my head. Despite the pains, my stomach went crazy and my settling pulse leapt. Then, he did the same with his other hand. He held me gently, studying every inch of my face. He leaned in further, moving closer until his lips hovered over mine. My heartbeat tripled its already exhaustive efforts.

"Don't ever try to tell me goodbye again," he warned in a thick voice. "We're not done yet."

He closed the minute gap separating us, crushing his lips against mine. He set fire to my thoughts and burned away all my pain with his touch. I forgot to breathe. His fingers held me still as he tilted his head and demanded more, needing the affirmation that we were both still alive. The teasing patient man was gone. With his mouth, he claimed me in a way I'd thought he hadn't wanted, a way he'd hidden from me. I lifted my hands to his shoulders holding him in return, not wanting this to stop. I kissed him back, finally sure fate knew what the heck it was doing.

The desperation began to fade, and I felt faint when he tore his lips from mine. He didn't relinquish his hold though. As I gasped for air, he kept my senses spinning wildly with soft kisses to my cheek. My jaw. My neck. Tingles raced over me at the first touch of his lips on my neck. His lips softened and returned to skim my own with small little kisses that started a yearning in me. A yearning I well understood from previous lives.

Too soon he pulled back, leaving me shaking, and my breaths coming out in hot little clouds. Without his attention, the cold wrapped around me, and the pain crept back in. I wrapped an arm protectively over my middle. His pupils shrank while I watched, and a twinge of regret crept in with the change.

"I'm sorry," he apologized gruffly, looking away. I reached out a hand to comfort him and whatever he felt sorry about. None of this was his fault. The burden of guilt laid solely on me. I shouldn't have tried walking away.

"That won't happen again," he spoke slowly, his jaw muscles clenching. Then he looked at me with promise burning in his eyes. "Until you're eighteen."

My mouth popped open, and I made a choking sound while my brain tried to come up with the words to articulate my feelings.

"And don't ever try hurting yourself again," he growled.

"Are you kidding me?" I half-yelled, half-gasped, completely ignoring his reprimand as the shock of finally understanding his standoffish attitude toward me wore off, and my brain started functioning again. "That's the problem? We almost just *died*. We almost lost a chance for an us," I flailed a hand back and forth between us, "and you're worried about how old I am?"

"Bethi."

"Don't Bethi me," I hissed. "First stop, I'm molesting your butt, and you're going to like it!" We both felt the pull, we both had feelings for each other, and I suffered dream after dream because the timing wasn't right for him? What did he think a few months would do for us?

I picked my blade up from the ground before the literal meaning of what I'd just said sank in. Luke's smirk didn't help cool my temper. I stomped off—as much as I could with a gigantic cut decorating my stomach and aches in places I hadn't known I possessed—in the direction I hoped led toward his bike. I slayed small saplings and maimed trees in my wrath. He trailed behind me, wisely remaining quiet.

"How did you find me?" I asked after I cooled down.

"Your scent." After a moment of silence, he asked, "Why did you leave?"

I let out a slow breath. "That's not important anymore. I won't leave again." Not even when he frustrated the heck out of me. Now that I knew his reasons, I'd stick to him like glue. "How long until we reach the Compound? This is only going to get worse."

"Tomorrow."

I glanced at him and met his troubled gaze. I reached out and clasped his hand. He let me, twining his fingers through mine.

WHEN WE REACHED THE BIKE, we both stared at each other. The gore on him was too much to possibly be real. Ugh! I'd kissed that.

He studied me just as intently. Untangling his fingers from mine, he reached up to brush a hand gently along my cheek. "You're pale," he commented. "And you're still bleeding. We need to get that looked at."

I didn't move. "Or you could just take us to a hotel, I could clean up and you could help me with some gauze and tape." He looked like he was about to argue so I added, "We can't afford the questions a hospital would ask."

He reluctantly nodded and moved toward the bike.

"We can't ride around with you looking like that," I said, stopping him.

"What do you suggest?"

I pointed to the nearby marsh, which had a thin layer of ice over the water it offered.

His lips twitched. "You're liking this, aren't you?"

"I'll get Tinker Bell ready. And you better hurry. Who knows what's still headed in this direction."

He snorted, but got back off the bike and pulled his shirt over his head. The muscles in his back rippled as he tossed the shirt aside. I fought not to sigh. I was liking this. Far too much.

CHAPTER TWELVE

FORTUNATELY, THE TINKER BELL PAJAMAS WERE UNNECESSARY. HE had most of our clean laundry—including a pair of pants for himself—in his saddlebags.

He washed while I stood shivering on the gravel shoulder. I pretended the shivers were a reaction to his muscled back flexing each time he bent to rinse away more blood. In reality, exhaustion had claimed its due. The sprint through the trees, the fight, and the blood loss took their toll. Dreams whispered to me, and the insistency of them depressed me. What more could I possibly learn other than more pain and death? And sadly, I didn't have the strength to wrestle Luke down and Claim him, like I'd threatened to, to stop them.

Standing in the cold facing the inevitable, I just wanted to get on the bike, wrap my arms around his waist, and let them have me. I knew he wouldn't like me sleeping while we drove, but I didn't want to delay getting to the Compound by stopping at one more hotel and falling asleep there. It just increased the chances of another run-in with the others.

He doused his hair one more time and turned toward me as he shook the water from it. Sunlight glinted off the droplets that flew. Rivulets ran down his chest. Steam rolled off him. When he turned still dripping water, his eyes roamed over my face for a moment. Concern crept into his eyes as his gaze flicked to the arm I held to my middle. I didn't try to straighten or pull it away.

The cut hurt. I couldn't hide that. But it wouldn't stop my determination to push on.

"If we drive straight through, how long 'til we get there?"

"If nothing happens? Ten to twelve hours depending on the roads we take."

"We need to push through. I can't take another run in," I said. He opened his mouth to argue. "No, Luke," I sighed before he spoke. "I can't. I'm done. Do you get it? Just, *done*." I hurt too much physically, and I had the depressing knowledge that I would hurt more in the near future due to the dreams. I lacked the optimism to fool myself into believing we'd make it through what waited.

He strode over to me with an intense light in his eyes. Both hands gripped my arms lightly. He gave them a gentle squeeze and then pulled me to his chest, hugging me close despite the arm still wrapped protectively around my stomach. His lips grazed my hair, and he laid his cheek on top my head.

"Don't give up," he whispered. "Not now."

He held me for a moment. I soaked up the comfort and the heat he radiated. I really wanted everything to be okay. I just knew we were in too deep for it to be that way.

"We need to get moving," I said. "Every minute we stay in one place, the more likely they are to find us again."

He pulled back and lifted my chin so my eyes met his. We studied each other for several minutes. His eyes expressed more than his words because his worry and fear shone there. "We'll get there," he promised.

He wanted my acknowledgement, but I wouldn't lie. Instead, my gaze drifted down to his lips. The memory of his kiss started my heart thumping in a heavy rhythm. I didn't want to think about the Compound, the journey there, or the men who'd be waiting to attack us. I wanted to lose myself in the way he made me feel just one more time.

My other arm took on a life of its own and drifted from my side to his back. The heat of his skin warmed my cold fingers as I traced the ridges on his muscles.

"Bethi," he begged. "Don't."

His stupid, misguided moral compass was a pain in my butt. "Don't what? Don't think of how that kiss felt? Don't wish that you'd let your guard down enough to let it happen again so I can forget everything else and imagine a world where just you and I exist? A safe place where I can sleep without haunting dreams? A place where men don't chase me down and cut me? Yeah, I better not. Reality and morals are way better, anyway."

I pulled away from him and walked toward the bike. He hesitated a moment and then followed. He didn't leave me waiting long or remind me that I'd technically cut myself. I dug through the bag and handed him a clean shirt without looking at him. I couldn't. I'd start drooling and become more bitter. It didn't matter. The memory of his pecs and his muscled shoulders...I sighed and eased my leg over the bike settling behind him.

I flung the strap of my bag over his head and wrapped my arms around his waist. No air existed between us. My cheek pressed against his back. I closed my eyes even as he warned me not to fall asleep.

"Just get us there before I bleed out. And don't stop because I fall asleep. Just nudge me or something."

He pulled off the gravel shoulder with ease. A chill wind whipped my hair around my face. Even with the layers I wore, I'd freeze by the time we got to our destination. Only a werewolf would bring a motorcycle for a human in November.

We drove north pushing straight toward our destination, forgoing the erratic back road routes. We met up with a group of five other riders on motorcycles. I smiled at one before lying my head back down on Luke's back. We would draw less attention with others.

Penny grabbed the toy from my hand and hit me.

"It's mine," she yelled, her face turning red.

It wasn't her toy. It had been lying on the ground when we'd both arrived at the park. Her mother tried reasoning with Penny, but Penny swung out a hand and hit her mother's face. Her mother, shocked by her daughter's sudden tantrum, didn't move to stop the second swing.

I liked Mrs. Hught and didn't want to see Penny hit her anymore. "Stop." I said it softly, but clearly, pushing the thought and the inaction toward Penny. Penny's arms dropped to her side. Her face grew even redder, and she turned to glare at me.

She knew what I could do and had made me promise never to do it to her. It was a promise I had to break.

"You can't hit your mommy," I tried to explain.

"I can do anything I want," she screeched at me. But we both knew that wasn't true. The hatred in her eyes burned me, and I released her will.

She turned away from me, threw her arms around her mother's neck, and cried. "I want to go home," she sobbed. "I don't want Charlene to have a sleepover anymore."

I emerged from the dream slightly when Luke reached around to push me toward the center of his back. I'd slid to the side, dangerously unbalancing us. Shivering, I sank right back into the next waiting dream.

Sitting at the long black counter in biology class, I tried to ignore Penny's quiet mutterings from the table behind me. We hadn't been friends since first grade, which suited me fine. Middle school had killed any lingering traces of friendship. For two and a half years, she'd tormented me, spread rumors, and caused me nothing but trouble.

I'd been pulled into the counselor's office at least twice a week for the last three months to discuss the malicious relationship we had. The school was just trying to cover themselves in a bullying case, but I had sat there and listened to Penny's pathetic explanations for the rumors she'd started.

Something hit the back of my head. I turned as I reached back to feel my hair. Gum. Penny didn't meet my eyes but looked straight at the teacher as if she'd been paying attention the whole time.

"Ms. Farech. Is there a problem?" Mr. Melski asked from the front of the room.

"Yes." I struggled to keep all the emotion from my voice. "Someone just threw gum in my hair." I stood and picked up my books. "I'll see if someone in the office can help."

His eyes flicked to Penny. The faculty knew. So why in the heck did they let her sit behind me? It was a small school. Because we were in the same grade, we had most of our classes together. Not all, though, because I'd managed to squeak into a few of the advanced ones. Hard classes, but I loved them because she wasn't there.

I kept my pace even as I walked out the door.

The secretary, an older woman who yelled at most kids, made a sympathetic noise when I walked in and showed her the gum. I hadn't touched it much and had walked carefully so it wasn't too embedded.

"Why on earth does Penny dislike you so much?" she asked as she worked.

"Because when we were kids, I told her not to hit her mom." The truth, yet not all of it. Penny was the only one who knew my secret. Never once did I give the rumors she had started any credence. But, she and I both knew I could do what she claimed. I just didn't let her push me to do it openly.

The secretary extracted the gum wad within minutes, only taking a few strands with it.

"Make sure you don't sit near her at the assembly," she warned just before I left.

As if I would purposely do so.

I went to the bathroom to check my hair before heading back to class. Hopefully Penny wasn't chewing more gum in anticipation of my return. The door opened behind me. Penny's eyes met mine in the mirror.

"Why?" I asked, turning. "What do you get from doing this? You were never mean when we were little." She continued to eye me hatefully. I tried again. "We were friends once."

"Ha!" she barked bitterly. "You were never my friend. You never listened to me."

I knew exactly what she meant. She'd wanted me to use my ability to make her mom look away so we could sneak candy when we went to her house. She didn't understand as I did that my ability wasn't meant for that. Somehow I'd always known I shouldn't misuse my power.

"You always asked too much," I said sadly. "Just let this go."

"No. At some point you'll make a mistake, and I want to be there so everyone knows I was right about you." She reached out and slapped the books from my arms. They tumbled to the floor.

"All you're going to prove is how mean you can be," I said glancing down at the books. She didn't answer.

When I bent to pick them up, she pushed me over. I snapped and grabbed hold of her will.

"Stop." She froze poised in a half-crouch ready to come after me. I held her still with my will, but I forced nothing else on her. I felt bad enough for holding her like that. "I'm really sorry, Penny, but this has gone on long enough. Forget your hate. Remember the friendship we once had." I picked up my books and stood. "Don't try to hurt me again."

I walked out the door intending to get a good head start before I released her. From behind, I heard her yell through the door, "I still can't move!"

The dream shifted, but not far. I still wore the same clothes.

Sitting on the gym bleachers surrounded by the entire student body, I looked around warily for Penny. She would hate me even more, now. I should have made her forget. I just couldn't bring myself to mess with someone's head like that. It wasn't like anyone really believed her. Other than the bullying, she wasn't a threat to me. I had no justification for taking the extreme measure of robbing her of her memories.

"As some of you know, there have been cases of bullying. This is a serious matter that this school will not take lightly. We have a short film to help educate you on what steps should be taken if you are bullied, or witness bullying."

The overhead lights dimmed and a beam of light from the AV room near the top of the gym pierced the gloom. The AV room, a recent addition accessed by a set of stairs outside of the gym, was prized by the faculty as a means to broadcast school news.

A shot of the girl's bathroom burst onto the white gym wall we used for projection. My mouth popped open as I saw myself walk into the bathroom and go to the mirror. Some students near me started laughing quietly. The faculty, standing on the gym floor, started conferring in whispers as on screen, Penny walked in and we started talking.

One of the teachers left the gym presumably to reach the AV room and stop the movie. The lights in the gym turned on as Penny knocked the books out of my hand. No one moved. Everyone stayed focused on the projection. My stomach filled with piercing shards of ice.

"The assembly is over. Return to your last hour class. Those with Physical Education should go to the locker rooms and wait there," the principal shouted, unable to use his microphone as the PA had been taken over by my voice, "All you're going to prove is how mean you can be."

No one moved. All eyes remained riveted on Penny as she stared at me, and I moved to retrieve the books. I could taste my panic, the flavor disgustingly reminiscent of vomit. Penny had finally succeeded.

I closed my eyes as the recording of my voice rang out. "Stop." A murmuring rose in the gym, loud enough that others started shushing their neighbors as I gave Penny my little speech and then left the bathroom.

Opening my eyes, I caught the angle of the video change as the cameraman climbed off the toilet and opened the stall door to zoom in on Penny's outraged face. Penny's words, "I still can't move," echoed through the eerily quiet gym. The last image on the wall was of Penny suddenly falling to the floor. The projection shut off.

My face heated unnaturally. Someone next to me whispered to her neighbor, "Holy crap! Penny wasn't lying."

I sat up in the bleachers, surrounded by my peers. All eyes turned to me. A side door opened, and a teacher escorted a beaming Penny into the gym. As I stood, I grabbed everyone's will but hers and planted a seed. My voice rang out. "You just witnessed proof of Penny's dogged determination to expose something extraordinary. Instead, all she did was paint herself as a bully and show she has an amazing ability to act."

Releasing their wills, I nudged my way through my stunned classmates. As I moved, I heard things like, "I can't believe she was so mean," and, "I would have slapped her face instead of walking out."

Penny's smug expression faltered as she noticed the change in everyone. Her mouth popped open as she stared at me. I walked up to Penny while holding the faculty back with simple wait-and-see thoughts. I stopped just in front of her.

"Whoever you had filming did a wonderful job," I said. "If you're this good over a no name nothing like me, I can only imagine how good you'll be when you're reporting on something real. Good luck."

The sudden silence penetrated my dream. I emerged with my heart racing wondering why we'd stopped. I lifted my cheek from the warm spot on Luke's back and, in the gloom around us, took in the shape of an old barn on a slight hill in the distance.

"Why did we stop?" I asked when he loosened the strap.

"I'd rather approach the Compound in daylight," he said quietly.

My determination to push through bowed to his practical reasoning. I didn't really want to face a horde in the dark either. I didn't have their enhanced eyesight.

"How is the cut?"

I pulled the strap from over his head and climbed off the back. My legs ached from sitting so long, but I didn't try stretching them out. The back of his shirt was stained with my blood, but it looked dark and dry. I shrugged in response to his question and asked, "Why here?"

He walked over to me, unzipped the jacket, and once again gently tugged at the hem of my shirt. Only this time, it didn't lift. The blood had dried to the shirt. He frowned as he answered, "They are too used to looking at hotels. I thought this would be safer."

"This" meant sleeping in the barn. He continued to look worriedly at my stomach as if he could see through the fabric. "Some real sleep sounds good," I murmured, trying to reassure him.

He sighed and gently touched my cheek. "You'll tell me if it starts hurting," he ordered softly.

I snorted. "It hasn't stopped hurting."

He smiled at me and dropped his hand. "I imagine not," he commented as he shifted the bike into neutral and began pushing it toward the building. I zipped back up and slowly followed. Patches of snow coated the ground between tufts of long grass. Shivers trembled through me.

The barn leaned heavily to one side. Many of its old boards had rotted at the base. Still, Luke pushed the bike into the gaping door. Any hint of the dusk's fading light disappeared after two steps. Disturbing the layer of dust covering the floor with my steps caused the smell of old, musty hay to fill my nose, and I sneezed once. It killed my stomach.

"I'll look around," he said a moment before he disappeared into the dark. I looked back at the door, just barely outlined now, and stayed where I stood.

"It's empty and untouched. We'll stay here for a few hours."

He took me by the hand and led me further into the black. He flicked on a tiny LED flashlight attached to the bike keys and pointed to an empty stall partitioned by a half wall. I blushed as I understood and quickly grabbed the flashlight and shooed him away. I'd lived many lifetimes without the convenience of a toilet, but that was in the past. I liked flushing and washing.

After I finished, I moved into the hay-filled aisle, clicked off the flashlight, and shuffled toward the front of the building.

"Here," Luke murmured after I'd walked half the length. I paused and felt a tug on the bag. He led me off to the side and gently nudged me down onto some old hay.

"If I wake up to bugs crawling on me, I will not be happy," I whispered waiting for him to settle next to me.

When he lay still, I used my hands to find him. He lay on his back, and I pressed close to his side. His warmth became a halo around me.

"I promise, I will keep them off of you," his low voice rumbled under my ear as I settled my cheek on his chest. Too bad he kept his shirt on. Skin to skin, I tended not to dream at all. I flattened my hand on his shirt and let my fingers thaw.

"I'm glad you're warm," I mumbled, my eyes already closing. At least I wasn't freezing. My stomach hurt, my legs ached from all the kicking and moving I'd done during the fight, and my arms just felt like they would fall off. Dreaming might not be the worst.

"Though she's a pleasure to be around, we've noticed she's very aggressive with others. I wanted to suggest an outlet for her energy." The daycare administrator handed my father a slip of paper. We sat in her office, just the three of us. My legs dangled from the chair, and I idly swung them back and forth. Moving helped. I didn't feel so mad then. I arched my neck to look at the paper. It had a picture of a man kicking and some words. I didn't care about the words, though. I liked the picture. I liked kicking.

The dream shifted.

The other kids congregated around the playground equipment, laughing and chasing each other. I stood back, watching them play with a smile, but not joining. Whenever I tried, they stopped playing to lie around. Sometimes a few of them even took naps. Meanwhile, something inside me grew, tightening my skin to the point of discomfort, to the point I grew angry. So I stood on the outskirts, never really joining, and they let me be though they threw an occasional friendly wave my way. Everybody liked me. They couldn't help it. I made them feel good.

A new boy walked over to one of my classmates and took the ball from her hands. Her lips quivered, but she didn't cry. Instead she walked away. I felt indignant for her and watched the boy stalk away from the group to play sullenly with the ball. I frowned at him.

With most of my classmates further away, I approached him knowing my skin wouldn't tighten too much.

"Why did you do that?" I demanded.

He looked up at me with narrowed eyes. Anger, hurt, and uncertainty flooded me.

"Why are you so mad?" I asked. Usually the people around me were happy. But even happiness, when I soaked up too much, made me feel tight inside.

His eyes opened a little wider before they narrowed again. He balled his fist and swung at me.

I blocked just as my instructor had taught me. The boy dropped the ball to try another swing. I blocked again. He gave a growl of frustration and started swinging wildly. I continued to block the blows, flowing into the different stances and moves, enjoying the movement. The emotions poured off him, and I unwillingly soaked them up, but what we did helped burn them out of me. Soon I could see him tiring and took two quick steps back. I didn't want to drain him. I liked that he didn't lie down like the other kids did. He was different, and playing with him helped me. I felt deflated in a good way. I bowed to him as I'd been taught.

I smiled at his shocked expression. "Do you want me to show you how to block next recess?"

He nodded his mop of sandy blonde hair. I felt the tears hiding behind his grey eyes and reached for his hand, willing to help him again. I took his hurt away as the teacher walked over to us to scold us for fighting.

"We weren't fighting," I explained. "We're training. He's my partner now." I wouldn't need to stand alone anymore.

The teacher shook her head indulgently and shooed us inside.

"What's your name?" the boy asked.

"Isabelle. What's yours?"

"Ethan."

"WE'RE LESS THAN AN HOUR AWAY," Luke called over his shoulder. The move twisted the healing bite on his neck. I hated seeing it, probably as much as he hated the cut on my stomach. His injury, at least, healed faster.

I nodded in response, but otherwise kept scrunched behind Luke. Heavy wet snow blanketed the ground. The wind bit into my skin, chilling it until it stung. I couldn't tell if I felt so cold because of the temperature, which barely hovered above freezing, or because of a fever. My stomach had hurt when I woke, and I worried that the moldy air, or dirty clothes I wore, might have caused an infection.

"Shit," Luke swore and swerved.

I lifted my head from his back, but didn't see anything. Turning, I saw a werewolf running behind us. Before I could panic, Luke opened the throttle, and the bike screamed down the road, distancing us from our pursuer.

"They know," he yelled back at me.

No kidding. I clung to Luke, watching our pursuer. There were only three roads into the pack's territory and ultimately to the Compound. One came in from the north, one from the southwest, and another from the east. We'd abandoned the eastern route when we'd run into them last time. When they'd found me south of here, we'd kept heading north hoping they'd think we'd switch from the obvious. There was no turning around anymore. We were too close. They now knew our direction and would be ready.

The lone wolf stopped running and stood in the middle of the paved lane, no doubt communicating to the rest of the pack. The bike screamed down the road. I didn't dare try peeking around Luke to see how fast we went. If the wind had hurt before, it really tore at me now. We rode for another ten minutes without sighting anything. Then, hell opened its mouth and started spitting at us.

A fully changed werewolf ran in front of us, trying to slow Luke down. Luke didn't let up on the throttle. Somehow, he avoided the beast without dumping the bike. I locked my hands around his waist and carefully looked back. The furry shapes of too many werewolves to count in a glance ran behind us. Determined to gain ground.

Luke used his left hand to dig in his right pocket and pulled out his cell phone. He pressed a few buttons and held it to his ear. Fearing what driving one handed at these speeds could do to us, I wanted to close my eyes but didn't think that was too smart.

"Gabby, I have a problem," he shouted over the roar of the engine.

A problem was a bit of an understatement. We had an army of werewolves following us, a traitor in Luke's band of friends, and he was calling for help while driving at breakneck speeds. I couldn't decide what to freak out over more.

Something flew from the left, hitting the tank with a loud bang and knocking the phone from Luke's hand. As the object had flashed toward us, I'd thought it looked like a chunk of wood but couldn't be sure. The phone hit me in the face and fell between us. A growl erupted uncomfortably close to our right. Maybe a call for help wasn't out of order.

I shimmied an arm between us, snatched the phone up, and tried to redial the number. The first try didn't go through. The second time, it went through, and I was so excited the phone almost slid from my fingers.

"Luke?" a female voice answered after the first ring.

"No. Bethi. We need help," I shouted into the phone. The wind made it almost impossible to hear if she said anything back. "There are too many. They can't take me. If they do, we *all* die. Please!" I shouted which road we raced down. I closed the phone and kept it scrunched in my fist.

More werewolves started pouring from the trees in front of us.

"Don't let go!" Luke shouted as he began swerving. He tilted us so far once, I thought we were going down for sure. But he righted us and opened the throttle again.

The mass of wolves chasing us had gained too much ground when we slowed slightly because of the swerving. One caught my jacket, but I held tight to Luke and heard a tear. Another ran beside the bike, but I caught it—and me—by surprise by kicking out with my foot and connecting with its face. The blow tripped him up more than hurt him, but it knocked him back into his followers causing several of them to fall back.

Ahead of us, a group of six wolves burst from the woods and raced toward us. Now that they knew our direction, they were probably pulling their numbers from the other routes.

"If you get us out of this alive, I swear I'll stop trying to ambush-Claim you," I yelled to Luke.

I braced myself as the oncoming wolves flew at us...and sailed over our heads into the pack of wolves following us. I twisted around in surprise. Help had arrived.

Two moved incredibly fast, taking a chunk out of the mass following us. The other four raced alongside us, keeping most of the wolves out of our way.

Ahead, a bend in the road obscured our view of what lay beyond. Luke eased up on the throttle, and I wondered if he had the same suspicion as I did about what waited ahead. He skidded to a dangerous sideways stop that made my stomach try to crawl out of my mouth, severed the strap connecting us, and leapt from the bike. Already transforming.

The remaining force chasing us collided with our four escorts. Luke joined them, fighting savagely, tearing into anyone who got too close to me. The other werewolves circled us, outnumbering us six to one. I scrambled from the bike too fast and felt the knitting cut on my stomach reopen. Wetness trailed down my stomach, and I cringed. A wave of dizziness washed over me. All of the wolves around me caught the scent, and the rapid movements slowed. Their gazes flew to me as I stumbled and bumped into the bike. It rocked but steadied under me. I bent toward the ground to catch my breath and shake the murk from my head.

No food, no water, and bleeding. Not a good combination.

When I lifted my head, seven wolves circled around me keeping the others at bay. I fumbled in the bag for my knife, relieved when I clasped the handle. An attacking wolf leapt high trying to clear the circle, but one of my defenders jumped up to meet him. The move knocked them both back into the waiting melee and created an opening in my defense. Another of the enemy ran forward to take advantage of the break, but a sleek grey wolf spun from the circle and used a swipe of his claws to rip away the throat of the attacker.

My eyes scanned the forms as I looked for Luke's coppery coat. I found him in a sea of attackers—Luke had been the wolf who'd blocked the attacker's jump. They bit at Luke, tearing into his skin as he swirled, swiped, and savaged those around him. None of the defenders encircling me moved to help Luke. Without thought, I shuffled toward him. My heart hammered, and my palms grew cold and clammy as another line of blood marred Luke's coat.

"No," I whispered as another attacker sunk his teeth into Luke's neck. Luke still hadn't recovered from the last bite he'd received. Possessiveness swelled along with anger.

"I have run," I croaked with an emotion-tight voice. I straightened and dropped the arm protecting my middle. "I have bled." I moved forward, determined. "I have *remembered*." My voice rose and some of those on the outskirts of the fighting angled their heads to watch me. "I am the Wisdom of the Judgements, and I will not fail again!" I screamed at them, flipping the knife in my hand, and throwing hard through the tangle of bodies. The blade flew true, sinking into the eye socket of the one attached to Luke. "Bite him again and I will rip your tongue from your mouth!" I promised.

Two turned from Luke and moved toward me. I touched the hindquarter of the grey wolf in front of me.

"Pick me up," I demanded, not caring that he fought with several wolves. He slashed wildly, spun toward me, shifting so his arms looked more human and capable of throwing, and lifted me.

"Throw me to him," I said, pointing at the screaming wolf clawing at the knife in his eye. I saw the grey wolf's hesitation to throw me into that mess and touched his face.

"Now!"

Catapulted into the air, I tucked into a ball and closed my eyes as I somersaulted toward Luke. *Remember. Remember.* I'd never done this myself. Never my own body. But another of my sisters had. I opened my eyes as I felt the downward pull of gravity. The wolf was just below me. He wasn't paying attention, but others around him were. They moved to try to catch me. Luke looked up, causing an opening for another injury.

I swore again, untucked myself, and twisted to land on the wolf with the knife in his eye, bringing us both to the ground. The impact killed my stomach, ripping me further. I grunted in pain but still managed to pull the knife from his eye. It caught slightly on the bone of his socket. The wolf screamed. I silenced him with a swipe before I stood. A wall of man-wolf bodies leaned in around me. Luke growled and raged just beyond.

"Time to die," I whispered with a slight smile.

Several pairs of eyes widened in surprise as I swiped out in a spinning turn and sliced open their soft underbellies. Yeah, I knew how bad that hurt. Ignoring the grunts of pain, I dodged their attempts to grab at me. I fell to my knees and swiped again, darting the blade behind their knees. Three dropped to my level. Three more crowded in. The handle started to slip in my grip. I swung out again.

A horn blared long and loud. A few of the wolves around me looked up as a white wolf landed on the three new wolves thinking to have at me. Another wolf with a brown coat landed behind me, his growl sent a shiver down my spine. He didn't attack anyone. He partially transformed to lift me, his big hands gentle. Something in his soft brown eyes stayed my knife.

He jumped and brought me back into the circle of six bodies that still surrounded the bike. There he set me on my feet with a firm "stay" and leapt back into the dying fray. Despite the odds, we were winning. Four of the wolves fighting with us moved with such incredible speed and agility that they each faced at least four opponents at once.

Bodies started flying through the air as the wolf who'd saved me started throwing the injured and dead away from the immediate area. The attackers' numbers halved. And then, as one, they turned and fled. No one gave chase. As the road cleared of attackers, two cars sped past and turned the curve in the road that I knew led to the Compound. Several of the wolves turned their heads to watch the vehicles pass, but no one made a move to stop or follow them. In the window of one, I saw a little boy's face.

I bent slightly, curving an arm around my stomach again and was surprised my guts weren't leaking out, yet. Then Luke was beside me, pushing me toward the bike. He bled from several lacerations and no longer wore a shirt. Tinker Bell covered his bottom half. I smiled and sobbed at the same time.

Luke sat on the bike, and someone lifted me up behind him. Everyone moved quickly. We all recognized the need to leave before another bout could begin. I draped against him too hurt and tired to do more. Finding a clean spot near his shoulder blade, I turned my head and gave him a kiss.

Somehow, we'd done it again. Survived. Tears trailed down my cheeks to drip onto his skin.

The wolves ran beside us as we sped to the Compound. I shook and clung to Luke. Blood covered his back, again.

CHAPTER THIRTEEN

ADMITTEDLY, I'D EXPECTED MORE FROM THE COMPOUND THAN what I saw when I lifted my head from Luke's back. A scattering of dilapidated buildings came into view. Someone had put a lot of effort into in an attempt to make them look better. The old wooden structures worried me. I'd watched my family die in flames so many times.

Luke pulled the bike up to the porch, right next to one of the two cars that had sped past us. Wolves surrounded us. Some had helped us during the fight, but a few new ones joined the group. A short brunette woman stepped outside with a robe and tossed it to the white wolf who caught the material with its mouth.

"Come on," Luke said, holding out an arm so I could dismount first.

My stomach cramped with pain as I tried to stand. I hesitated to swing my leg off the bike.

"How badly were you hurt?" a woman asked from behind me.

An older woman with white hair wore the robe the white wolf had caught. The white wolf was gone. I shouldn't have been surprised. Girls could fight, too. I knew that. Yet, I'd foolishly assumed they'd all been male back there.

"Just a nick," I mumbled. I wasn't about to admit any weakness in front of the large group. Who knew which of them might betray me? The woman with the white hair moved to my side and helped me off the bike. She was stronger than she looked.

"Let's get you inside." Still holding my arm, she turned to glance at the brown wolf. "Jim, Emmitt's saying the boys are worried." She herded me toward the door while calling out instructions. "You should go reassure them. Grey and Sam can handle things out here." Everyone did as she said. Since inside was safer than outside, I didn't try to fight her.

A stack of pants waited just inside the door. Made sense.

I shuffled a few more steps before Luke turned and scooped me up in his arms.

"About time," the woman reprimanded.

"Who are you?" I asked, peering over Luke's shoulder at her.

"Winifred Lewis. You can call me Nana Wini," she said with a kind smile. "The woman behind me is Mary, and the man who will be following us shortly, the one who pulled you from that dog pile, is Jim." She looked at me expectantly.

"Oh, I'm Bethi."

"Luke, bring her upstairs. Second door on the right should be open," she said as we neared a set of stairs. "We'll be right up with some bandages."

Luke took the stairs two at a time and had me in a chair in short order.

As soon as he sat me down, he dropped to his knees in front of me and cupped my face between his hands. After everything we'd just gone through, his gentle touch brought tears back to my eyes.

We'd made it. But the place I'd thought would save me was a dump of tinderbox buildings out in the woods. We'd be dead in hours. I already felt dead inside. And tired. All that running. The fighting. Had there been any point to it?

The worry in his eyes tugged at my heart, and I felt a stab of guilt as I thought of everything he'd gone through to get me here.

"Go," I said, reaching up to squeeze one of his hands. "Take a shower and put on your own pants."

He snorted a laugh, then smoothed a thumb over my cheek.

"I'd rather stay with you." His gaze flicked to my very bloodstained shirt.

"There's nothing for you to do right now," I said, crossing an arm over my stomach. I didn't want him to look at it before I could. "They'll fix me up, I'm sure."

Reluctantly, he stood. I arched a brow and shooed him toward the door. Watching him walk away, I couldn't remember Tinker Bell ever looking so good.

When he closed the door behind him, I eased out of the shredded jacket and lifted the shirt. I almost gagged. Pulling it back down, I eyed the blood-soaked fabric. The cut needed stitches. A lot of them, really. I did *not* want to be awake for that. I'd had enough pain for...oh, ever.

The door opened behind me, and an older man with merry grey eyes poked his head in. When he saw me, he smiled and held up my bag. Perfect. I waved him into the room and accepted the bag. He nodded and left without a word, but I caught his worried glance at my stomach.

I tipped the bag onto the floor and found my bottle of pills. I still had two sleeping pills mixed in with the other ones I'd tried.

I swallowed them dry and leaned back into the chair.

"That bad?" Luke asked, startling me.

"What do you mean?"

"Pain pills?" he asked, coming over to take the bottle from me. His shirt showed dark patches from putting it on wet, and it clung to his skin. His hair was still damp too. He couldn't have been gone for more than a few minutes.

A frown settled on his face when he studied the prescription label and the unknown name on it. "How many did you take?"

"Relax. It's just a bottle. I keep other stuff in there. I took two sleeping pills."

His eyes flicked to my blood-soaked shirt. He squatted down near me, balanced on his heels, and lifted the hem of my shirt. His shocked gaze flew to mine.

"I know. It'll need stiches. No hospital though, okay?" I grabbed his hand and begged with my eyes until he nodded. "The dreams will knock me out, and the pills will keep me under." I did a slow blink without trying. Already they called to me.

"Luke," I whispered. "They're not done trying. Tell the others to soak the buildings. I've died by fire before, and it's not fun."

I SUFFERED the same dream duality as I had before, but more. My present-self, my past-self, and the past-selves of four of my sisters. The multiple views disoriented me, and I fought to focus on just one.

Heat flickered over my stomach like tiny flames dancing on my skin. I wanted to look down, but my eyes remained focused on the horde before me.

My fingers gently squeezed the hand wrapped within mine before I looked to my sister.

Through her eyes, I looked back at me. Again, my present-self suffered a wave of vertigo. My stomach twisted with pain, but I couldn't tell from which of us it stemmed.

"All will be well," I promised my sister.

I pushed away the discomfort and tried to focus. My sister squeezed back as her eyes closed.

"What do you see?" I asked.

Concentrating on my sister, I jumped perspectives.

A swarm of glowing lights filled my mind. Blue-green, blue-grey, yellow-green, and then us. The humans were far from us. We'd agreed to leave them out of our fight. The blue-grey almost outnumbered blue-green.

"They will not win. They do not have Courage. Her spark no longer exists," I said on a sob. Knowing they would not win did not soothe the loss of our sister.

"Be strong. They may not win the Judgement, but they may win this fight."

A hand closed over my shoulder and peace flowed through me, taking away fear, hate, worry, even the odd outside feeling of pain in my stomach. I breathed deeply and struggled not to smile. I fought to hold onto my worry.

"Stop, sister. Save yourself for them. We will need you," I begged.

Changing perspectives again, I surged into a mind filled with so much fear, hate, worry, pain, and doubt.

I struggled to breathe. My skin felt too tight as if all the emotion inside of me fought to burst out. Fists clenched, teeth gritted, I growled, "And we need you focused. They will learn to fear me."

"Sisters, join hands," another of us spoke, drawing our attention.

Turning, we clasped hands. Five of us: Strength, Hope, Prosperity, Wisdom, and Peace.

"Courage will always be with us," Strength spoke with confidence as a surge of power flowed through us.

My present-self struggled as what each of the past-selves experienced in that moment flooded me.

The sparks in my mind ignited, glowing brightly...

Emotions surged within me as I had the capacity to drain even more from those around us...

Glimpses of the battle to come floated around in the white infinity of my mind...

Flashes of the past rekindled my purpose.

Our purpose.

"The Urbat have grown too strong. We must reduce their numbers or face a worse fate the next cycle," I, Wisdom, predicted.

"I have no claws, but give me a knife and I will do my part," I, Peace, intoned. Seething rage boiled within me. I itched to pace the field.

"I can only see our fates in this life, not the next. We will stay back and do what we can. Be well and be loved in your next lives," I, Prosperity, said softly, pulling Strength and Hope from the circle.

I looked at my sister, Peace. "I remember how to fight thanks to your past lives, but I don't have the skills you have from this life."

I watched her pull another knife from the leather belt at her waist. She handed it to me hilt first.

"Grip it firmly and don't let go. Swing it around like a wild woman until it feels like your arm will fall off. Then keep swinging. Make them bleed. Make them sorry. Make them see their fate."

An eerie howl rent the air, and it began. The werewolves around us surged forward, meeting the Urbat in the middle of the field. Hand in hand, we ran.

The dream shifted, but not much.

I stood in the center of the red field, the center of the storm, surrounded by a moment of stillness. Bodies lay about me, all reverted to human form. My friends. My adopted family. My protectors. I looked down at the vacant vibrant blue eyes of my sister. She'd fought well with just memories.

A small distance away, the battle continued. Here, I looked around in misery. We'd hoped to decimate their numbers. Instead, they'd succeeded in decimating ours, almost exterminating the Elders, the keepers of knowledge for the werewolves. I glanced around at the Urbat fighters. They didn't believe in Elders. They didn't want any group to hold such power over them. Leaders led. If they were not strong enough to do so, they were challenged and replaced with ones who were stronger.

Their emotions drenched the field. I inhaled slowly and deeply, pulling the stagnant mass toward me. For those closest to me, I siphoned their consuming hate, leaving only traces of fanaticism. Several fell to their opponents during their confusion. I felt bloated and tight. Still I inhaled again, pulling more from them, expanding my reach to pull from every Urbat on the field. Something trickled from my nose, eyes, and ears. I kept breathing in, impossibly filling my lungs, and myself, with everything I could.

Something inside me popped, and a flaring pain seared through my stomach. I knew I needed to let go. I gathered everything I held, everything that made me boil and shake with rage, and released it all at once, killing the still staggering Urbat where they stood. The few friends who remained staggered as well. Blood ran from their ears as they toppled to the ground. I fell to my knees as they fell. The world surrendered to darkness. The time for Judgement faded.

The dream repeated countless times. I absorbed every sight, thought, and feeling from each perspective before I finally floated to the surface. I now understood the war that had raged, since the beginning of time, between the Urbat and Werewolves.

"Bethi," Luke demanded near my ear. Then, not so loud, he asked, "Why isn't she waking up?"

"Go. Away." My lips didn't want to move. My mouth tasted like I'd kissed a skunk's butt, and my stomach hurt. Bad. Still reeling from the graphic dream of death, hate, and pain, I wanted to be left alone. For a long time.

Someone gently touched my head, smoothing a hand over my hair. The touch disappeared a moment before a door opened and closed.

In the silence, I recapped my current life, compared it to past lives, and didn't like the similarities leading up to the finale. I tried licking my lips and instead moaned.

"Do you need a drink?" a new voice asked.

Opening my eyes, I looked at an unfamiliar face. Wait, no. I blinked at her and remembered. I almost smiled at myself. As if I could forget anything. Winifred. Nana Wini. But I stopped the smile because I didn't want her to think I was smiling at her. More than ever, I didn't know who to trust. I needed Hope. I needed to know which of the wolves around me were Urbat and which were Werewolves. Only Hope could tell me that. Knowing the difference between the two wouldn't determine my trust, but it was a start.

I nodded, and she handed me a glass of water. I drank slowly and grimaced.

"Can you help me up? I need a toothbrush."

She nodded.

Setting the glass aside, I gripped her hand and slowly stood. The gash on my stomach felt hot and tight. It pulled a little. I lifted my shirt and looked at it. Neat little stitches ran along my skin where the cut had been.

"I did the best I could. Luke insisted you did not want to go to the hospital."

"Too dangerous," I agreed, moving to my bag and grabbing my toothbrush. The longer I stood, the more I could straighten up. Still, I brushed my teeth, with a slight bend. She stood near watching me closely.

"You really need to change into something clean."

I spit, rinsed, and turned to face her. Her steady gaze met mine. She seemed kind enough, but I couldn't trust anyone.

"Where'd Luke go?" I doubted he'd actually listened to my muttered "go away."

She stepped back to let me out of the tiny bathroom. "He went to get the others. They've been waiting for you."

Just then, the door to the room flew open. Luke strode in followed closely by another man with short dark hair.

"What happened to my bike?" the newcomer demanded, looking ready to strangle Luke.

Two women followed the man. The first one, olive skinned with dark hair, looked worried and the second one, a short blonde pixie, appeared slightly concerned. A second man followed the group in. I couldn't see much of his face due to the dark hair hanging in his eyes and a full beard. Still, his lips twitched as if he shared the amusement of the woman he followed.

"Emmitt," the first woman said, laying a hand on his back. Emmitt stopped his advance and glared at Luke, who ignored them all since his gaze was locked on me. The worry in his eyes told me enough.

"Michelle, he trashed it. It looks like he dumped it," Emmitt said without turning to look at Michelle. "Jim felt guilty enough that it was stolen. He won't even look at me now. You owe me an explanation," he said, pushing Luke's shoulder.

"Ah, there you are," I mumbled. "We were just talking about you. You must be Peter Gibbons." Luke gave me a puzzled look and everyone else ignored me. Obviously, they didn't get the movie reference and had no idea how much I didn't care about their drama at the moment.

Luke tore his gaze from mine. "I don't owe you anything," he said. "But if you ask nice, maybe I'll tell you what happened so you can go running to daddy."

Emmitt moved incredibly fast and grabbed Luke by the throat with a loose hold that allowed Luke to laugh. Michelle paled. I took a step forward. That man's neck was getting way too much attention lately by everyone but me. Before I took another step, a hand clamped down on my shoulder, stopping me.

Luke reached up and knocked Emmitt's hand aside. Both started growling.

I looked back at Nana Wini and with a cold voice said, "Don't touch me."

Her eyes widened in shock, and she immediately released me. Neither Luke nor Emmitt paid me any attention until I stepped up to them and smacked them both in the chest.

"Stop. Both of you."

Luke immediately grew serious and backed up a step, while Emmitt's jaw twitched. He fought not to follow Luke's retreat.

The shaggy man snorted slightly, and I arched a brow at him. "Something to say?"

The woman standing in front of him flicked a glance back at him. "He'd hoped to see Luke get his butt kicked."

"Do you have any friends here?" I said, glancing at Luke.

He grinned at me. "Probably not."

Sighing, I dropped my hand and looked at Emmitt. "He did dump the bike. Several times. Each time it was because we were being attacked." I slanted my head and eyed them all.

Emmitt turned his attention to me, his eyes sweeping me from head to foot. His nostrils flared, and I knew he smelled the blood still very visible on my shirt.

"I would have been a lot worse off without him," I said, acknowledging the truth. If the Urbat would have found me first... I cringed at the thought.

Emmitt sighed and nodded. "It's always *my* bike." The dark haired woman patted his back with a slight smile on her face.

My eyes locked on her, and a memory triggered. "Michelle," I murmured. One of my sisters. The one who had the two brothers she'd tried to protect. I wondered if she'd found a way. She eyed me curiously, obviously wondering how I knew her name. "We need to talk."

My gaze drifted to the other one, her childlike face brought a sad pang. "Thank you for sending him, Gabby." I glanced at Luke sheepishly. "I wasn't very cooperative at first."

She smiled but didn't get a chance to answer.

"Well, Little One, here she is. Now what?" Luke said, impatiently.

My eyes narrowed at him. Little One? She had a pet name?

I looked back at Emmitt. "I changed my mind. Hit him." I turned away and went back to stand by Nana Wini who watched me with a slight tilt to her head. Luke's expression turned slightly pained as his eyes followed my progress.

"Bethi," he said as the shaggy man laughed.

What did he have against Luke?

"Everybody out," I said, then changed my mind. "Except you two." I pointed at Michelle and Gabby.

"Why?" Emmitt asked, casting a glare at Luke.

The shaggy man stepped forward enough to rest his hand on Gabby's back. Good. She was taken. I fought not to scowl at Luke again. It explained why shaggy man didn't like him.

"Because I need to talk to them. In private."

"This isn't the place to do it, then," Gabby said. "Too many sharp ears here."

She was right. I looked thoughtfully at the walls of the room. They would only block so much from werewolf or Urbat ears. I nodded in agreement. She turned and walked out the door. The others followed with Emmitt giving Luke one last look of promised retribution. Luke stayed and eyed me. I wanted to stand straight but knew it would hurt too much, so I didn't bother.

"Do you want me to carry you?" he asked quietly.

I snorted. "No, you can save your heroics for Little One." Idiot. I shuffled past him and heard Nana Wini follow.

The whole group wandered down a set of stairs, turned several corners, and entered a small room. Luke and Nana Wini followed. Everyone stood in the room, waiting around a table that filled the center of the room. I shook my head before Emmitt could close the door.

"Private means the three of us." Instead of looking at him, I looked at Gabby and Michelle. "There are things we need to talk about. Things no one else would believe," I added. Gabby looked a little wary but turned to meet her man's eyes. Shaggy-man's lips turned down in a slight frown. Emmitt didn't look any happier.

"For Pete's sake! What do you think's going to happen in here?"

"She's right," Michelle said with a small smile at Emmitt. "We'll be fine in here. You should check on the boys."

Emmitt leaned forward and kissed her softly on the lips before turning to leave. Her eyes never left him as he walked out the door. The other woman turned to look at the shaggy man. Neither spoke. They just looked at each other. Finally, he sighed, touched her cheek lightly, and exited.

The three of us turned our eyes on the remaining two.

Nana Wini met Michelle's eyes. "She has new stitches and should try not to pull them."

"She's right here," I mumbled, sitting on one of the chairs.

Nana smiled at me and left.

"I'm not leaving," Luke said softly.

Out in the hall I heard, "If he's not leaving..."

"Just shut the door already," I snapped. Luke closed the door on a growl in the hall, his smirk annoying me. He leaned against it, ensuring our privacy.

"I'm Bethi," I said ignoring him.

"I'm Michelle," Michelle said. "How did you know my name?"

Gabby remained quiet. "You're not curious how I knew your name too?" I asked.

She glanced at Luke. "I assumed he told you."

I shook my head. "No. It would be a nice answer though. A normal answer." Gabby's eyes dropped to the table. She knew what I was working up to. Good. "Are you ready for the truth? The truth about your abilities, and why we are the way we are?" Both of their eyes rounded. Michelle slowly sank into a chair. Gabby still stood. "Well, to be honest, I don't know all the details, but I'm pretty sure I know more than you.

"I remember," I said meeting their eyes. "That's my lovely ability. We've existed before and will exist again...and again." The thought of having to keep enduring this made me want to cry. I settled for taking a slow calming breath. "Each life we've lived before, I will eventually remember. Each death. Each emotion," I had to stop again. Maybe it was the pain of the stitches weighing on me, but everything just seemed so hopeless again.

"I can see what will happen with the stock market. Well, I used to, anyway," Michelle admitted.

I nodded. "I know. I saw you. You were curled up in a ball," I tipped my head back looking up at the ceiling as the memory of her pain washed over me. "It felt like your head had already exploded, exposing every nerve ending within you to even more pain." I met her shocked gaze. "I saw a man pick up your little brother by his arm and carry him into the house. The other one was just a baby."

Gabby's gaze flicked to Michelle. I could still see the distrust there.

"I saw you too, Gabby. All those homes. You could never let your guard down."

Finally, she sank into a chair, and I knew they believed me.

"We're not alone. There are six of us. We need to find the others but can't trust anyone. When we do, we die...or worse."

Michelle looked troubled.

"You said you knew why we had our abilities?" Gabby asked.

"Kind of."

"I see lights," she admitted. "I just want to know why."

"Because you're our Hope. But also our biggest weakness. With you, they would be able to find us all."

Her eyes widened in understanding. "Six of us," she whispered.

I gave her a smile. "And you," I said looking at Michelle, "are Prosperity. You always bring fortune to those around you."

"And you know all this because you remember?" Gabby asked.

"It's not simply remembering. I relive our past lives through dreams. Not just my past lives but all of ours. When I wake up, they stay with me—every detail. Our abilities and how we used them in those lives." I tapped my head. "We've died so many times."

"So you know what our abilities are for? Why we are like this?"

"The dreams are still coming. I'm not naive enough to believe I've learned everything. But I do know we exist because something was needed to keep the balance between humans, werewolves, and the dogs of death," I answered tiredly.

"Excuse me?" Michelle glanced at Gabby as if saying "did you hear that too?"

"Urbat. A cousin to Lycan," I explained. "They're close, but not quite the same. They tried to wipe out the werewolves almost a thousand years ago."

"Oh," Michelle said, looking suddenly enlightened. "I think Nana Wini told me something about that. But she didn't mention any cousins. Just that there was a huge fight—they weren't sure of the reason—and that it decimated their numbers."

"Of both sides," I said before turning to Gabby for confirmation. "Right? You can see the difference in their sparks. Are there more werewolves or Urbat?"

Gabby looked slightly stunned. "I knew it," she murmured. "Two different kinds." Her expression grew vacant and then troubled. "There are more Urbat. At least double." Her worried gaze flicked to the door, and she chewed on her lip for a moment. "So what does it mean that I'm Hope?"

"So far, I just know that you're the key to bringing all of us together. You know where the other three are."

Her attention returned to me. "Two," she corrected. "Charlene is one of us, too."

"Who's Charlene?" The name sounded familiar. "Where is she?"

"Here," Michelle said. "She's Emmitt's mother."

"Mother?" Emmitt had to be at least in his twenties. "How old is she?"

Michelle shrugged. "In her forties. I'm not exactly sure."

"What's her ability?" I asked.

"She admitted she could control people."

Of course! The dream starring Penny the bully. I felt like jumping up and down and cheering. "Strength," I sighed with a happy grin. "We are just missing Peace and Courage."

I looked at Gabby. "Where are they?"

Gabby's gaze grew slightly unfocused, and I was glad she didn't ask what I meant. "Both on the East Coast. One is very far north and the other just a little south."

"One is with Blake," Michelle said in a quiet, deeply troubled tone.

"Who's Blake?" I asked a moment before the memory resurfaced. Her stepfather's business partner.

"He kept me prisoner for my premonitions. I thought he was a werewolf, too. But I've heard that word before. Urbat. One of his men was talking about Urbat ruling the world. We have to tell the others that another kind exists," she said, meeting my eyes. Worry filled her gaze. "The Elders have been trying to find Blake through their connection. But they can't. After I met Emmitt, I had a vision of Blake with a tall, blind girl. She called him Father. She seemed okay with him." She shrugged and explained further. "He definitely didn't strike me as a good person when he kept me locked up, but he seemed to treat her well. Kissed her head and everything."

My stomach flipped in a sickening way. One of *them* had one of *us* and treated her well? A cramp started in my chest, and I struggled to keep my face straight as she continued.

"I'm sure she's one of us. The visions I've had so far have all proved to be of us, people with abilities. I saw you in the mall talking to some other girls," she said to me. "And you, sitting on the floor with Clay in wolf form by your side."

Clay. So that was the Shaggy-man's name, I thought absently as I continued to spiral into a dark, depressed place. With their numbers, if they already had one of us, was there any hope?

"You were both reading," she told Gabby. "There's only been five different girls in my visions. The other is a really angry redhead."

That pulled me out of my thoughts for a moment for a harsh, pained laugh.

"That would be Peace." I recalled the dream of the little girl on the playground. Isabelle. But I kept that to myself. "We need her." I felt the tug of a dream coming on and wanted to groan. I'd found them. We were together. Wasn't that enough? "We need her," I repeated. I needed her. Or Luke. If Luke would just let me Claim him, these dreams would stop.

"Are you okay?" Michelle asked.

"No. I'm not," I snapped, sighed, and then apologized. "The dreams I have are less than pleasant, and they won't let up." I changed the subject back to the issues at hand. "Gabby, you pinpointed me enough to send Luke. We need you to do the same for the other two."

She zoned out for a minute. "We can get to one, but not the other. The one in the north is surrounded by the other ones."

If the redhead was Peace that meant...

"The one in the north, the tall blind one that Blake has, must be Courage." If they didn't know Peace's location, we could still get to her. I tried not to dwell on the impossibility of getting Courage. That just left the threat at hand. "Have there been any attacks here since we arrived?" I asked, recalling my warning to Luke. Both women shook their heads. Why hadn't they attacked? What were they waiting for?

"Are there any Urbat here?" I asked Gabby.

She shook her head at me. "But I've seen them before. A few of them attacked us. And then there's Elder Joshua."

An Elder. I looked up at the ceiling and tried to think. We needed to expose the traitors and remove them before we could even consider making a move toward Peace.

"He was the one I contacted."

Luke's voice surprised me. I'd forgotten he was there.

"Someone betrayed us on the way here," I told them. "That's why there were so many attacks." But why not bigger groups of them? If the werewolves already had three, why would they risk me, the fourth, joining them? "There's a lot more to discuss, but I'm about to pass out," I admitted when the dreams nudged me again. My time was almost up.

"Gabby, keep an eye on the Urbat. If they start grouping and heading this way, we need to give everyone a warning." I sighed and tried not to remember what the Urbat had done in the past. "The children should be evacuated, now."

A sharp knock sounded at the door. A moment later it pushed open.

"Time's up," Clay said.

Gabby grinned at him and waved him in. Emmitt followed closely behind, elbowing Luke on his way past. The dream's tug grew more insistent.

"Please keep quiet about all of this," I said, standing. Then, to impress on them the seriousness of our situation, I repeated what I'd told Luke. "You have no idea what's coming our way, but I do. I've been raped, beaten, cut," I lifted my shirt to show them all the stitched gash, "starved, drowned, blinded, burned...you name it, I've lived it. *We've* lived it. You just don't remember. Don't trust anyone with your safety. When we do, we die. And I'll be the one who has to remember."

Turning, I left the silent room. Nana Wini stood just outside the door. Her expression told me she'd heard what I'd said.

Luke stole my opportunity to say anything to her by scooping me up into his arms. I shot him a disgruntled look still upset with his use of a pet name on another girl. But his angry, clenched jaw kept my mouth shut. I'd been too recently abused to have reminded him of all the other abuses I'd suffered. I rested my head against his shoulder and let him carry me.

"It was just a name," he said after a moment.

I didn't answer, keeping my head on his shoulder. But I felt better knowing he understood his mistake.

He gently set me on my feet just inside the tiny apartment's door, and cupped my face in his hands. "There's no room for anyone else in my heart," he said softly. "Only you."

"Then why?" I pleaded. If I was in his heart, then why did I have to wait to Claim him?

"Because I promised I would protect you," he said. His eyes burned with fierce resolve. "Even from myself."

The dream tugged, and my next blink turned into a three-second nap. A fingertip traced my eyebrow.

"You need rest," he said, wrapping an arm around me and guiding me down the hall.

I did. I promised myself I would argue some more about the logic behind letting me Claim him now. But after a nap.

Fully dressed, I crawled up on the mattress, eased onto my side, and curled up protectively around my aching stomach. Stupid idea to cut myself. Didn't work and now the pain lingered. Always pain. With that thought, the dream pulled me as Luke's weight depressed the mattress next to me.

CHAPTER FOURTEEN

I SAT UP, SHAKING FROM THE DETAILS OF THE DREAM. MORE DEATH! Sweat coated my face, not from a fever, but the memory. Why had I dreamed that? I turned and noted the empty cold spot next to me. He'd left me, that's why. After his sweet comment about holding me in his heart, he'd left me. He knew what I suffered. I weakly swiped at my face, removing the moisture and wishing I could remove the memory. Exhaling slowing, I reflected on what I'd learned. My sister Courage always died young.

Light still shone through the room's window. I glanced at the numbers on the digital clock. Less than an hour had passed. Two pills and a glass of water waited on the small lamp stand next to the bed. Without hesitation, I swallowed them down. I could have cared less what they were at that point. I'd have taken anything from painkillers to cyanide. I definitely hadn't gotten the rest I needed.

My stomach ached from sitting up so quickly. I gingerly rolled off the bed and rose to a crouched stand. I hobbled out of the bedroom to look for Luke. I found Michelle waiting on the couch in the living room, but no Luke. She stood when she saw me. Her concern for me was evident on her face.

"Luke asked me to wait here so you wouldn't be alone. I know you said the dreams were bad, but..."

I looked away from her uncomfortably and wondered how much I'd yelled.

"Luke said he left you some pills."

"Yeah, I already took them. What were they?"

"Something for the pain."

Darn.

"Nana and Sam want to talk to you when you're up."

"I'm not up yet," I said as I shuffled toward the bathroom.

Michelle followed me to the door. "They want to know what's going on. Gabby and I haven't said anything. But after you left, Sam tried talking to Gabby and they ended up yelling at each other. Clay looked all bristly like he wanted to hit Sam."

I rolled my eyes, finished up, and opened the door. "And I care why?"

"Sam's an Elder. Gabby's—" The door opened with a bang stopping Michelle's words.

"Gabby's getting annoyed," Gabby said, striding into the room and closing the door behind her. "They let you go because you're hurt, but as soon as you were gone, we were bombarded with questions. They even sent for Luke to grill him."

I couldn't help the panicked look that crept into my eyes. It was too soon to reveal everything. It explained his absence, though.

"We didn't say anything," Gabby assured me again. "Look, I wasn't sure who to trust before you got here, but after talking to you, I don't think we can do this alone. I think we need to talk to the Elders. At least *some* of them."

Michelle nodded her head in agreement.

We were all thinking of Elder Joshua. "I'm sorry I left you. I can't control when the dreams come and go anymore."

"It's okay," Michelle said. "Luke explained that to us."

"Us?"

"Me, Gabby, Clay, and Emmitt. They didn't trust Luke alone with us," Michelle said with an apologetic shrug.

"What did he do to deserve all of this hostility?"

"He stole Emmitt's bike."

"And he and some of his friends ganged up on Clay before I Claimed him," Gabby added. "Luke's your Mate, right?"

"He is a possibility," I agreed.

Her frown grew more pronounced. Her eyes flicked around the room. "I'd really like to talk to you alone, again. I have so many questions."

The door opened. "As do I," Nana said softly. "But I think it would be best if you sat while we discussed this. I don't like how pale you are." She motioned me toward the couch.

"This would be better in the soundproofed room," Gabby said quickly.

"Of course," Nana agreed.

As we walked to the room—at a very slow pace because of me—I contemplated where I wanted to start and what exactly to explain. I couldn't completely trust the Elders with everything I knew. Not yet. I didn't have the right answers to explain our purpose fully. Sure, we were here to maintain balance between the three groups, but how? I wasn't sure I was ready to share the who. At least, not until we weeded out the Urbat hiding in the pack. I believed wholly that the Taupe Lady's warning was serious. The world would burn if we failed. Though I trusted that knowledge, I doubted that anyone else would.

The door to the room stood open. Two other men sat inside. I recognized one. He'd brought up my bag.

Nana made official introductions as we sat. "Bethi, this is Sam and Grey, Elders. People you can trust. Elder Joshua is on his way here. We are missing two others, who are currently assisting in Europe, but we will communicate with them through our link."

I didn't say anything about her trust comment.

"Hello, Sam." So, that was the man who Gabby had argued with. He looked nice enough. Grey hair, neatly dressed. The memory of him eating spaghetti surfaced. He reminded me of my grandpa. I smiled and looked at the other one Nana had indicated. "Grey," I added as an acknowledgement as he shut the door. "Thank you all for your help. I didn't think Luke and I would make it here when they all came on us like that."

Sam cleared his throat, his troubled gaze meeting mine. "We'd never seen anything like that. Our kind...we're peaceful."

I nodded. He seemed so sincere. Could the betrayal go deeper than Joshua?

"We've had instances where we couldn't communicate with a few of our kind in the past, but never so many. Can you tell us why they were attacking you?" Sam asked.

Michelle glanced at me, but I didn't meet her gaze.

"The simple answer is that they were trying to take me back to their leader. There are so many things I don't know. Who their leader is and what they want to do with me when they get me." I rested my hands on the table, took a calming breath, and began my careful tiptoe around explanations that would trip me up and darted to the ones that would get me the result I needed.

"But I think it has to do with what's happening to me. I'm reliving past lives through my dreams. This has been going on for several months. Somehow, those guys learned that I had these dreams and started chasing me. When Luke showed up, I thought he was one. As you know, we were pretty much chased the whole way. Luke kept me safe." I could feel Gabby's eyes on me and struggled not to meet her gaze. "Anyway, he brought me here, thinking you might be able to help me." I couldn't come up with anything better without spilling that there was a definitive difference between the people at the table and the people who'd chased me.

"Why do they care if you are having these dreams?" Nana asked.

"I'm not sure. The dreams seem like pieces to a puzzle. Some of them are fitting together, but I haven't fit enough of them together to figure out the big picture."

"Tell us more about the dreams."

I regretted that Nana had overheard what I'd suffered in them and hoped she'd let me get away with a vague answer. "Mostly they are the same thing. Something is chasing me or comes to my home. Usually it looks like a really large dog. Then it changes into the shape of a man. Those dreams always end with me dying."

"You've dreamt of us killing you?"

No, it was the Urbat. But I couldn't say that.

"Not just me," I said looking at Michelle and Gabby. "I've seen their past lives, too. We all die."

The room was eerily quiet for a moment.

"Why?" Nana asked looking deeply troubled.

I took an easy breath feeling as if I'd just cleared the minefield. "That's why I was willing to come with Luke. Like I said, some things I pieced together, but there are a lot of 'whys' I haven't figured out. I was hoping I'd find help here, that you'd have more answers."

Nana, Grey, and Sam shared a look. "We need some time to speak," Sam said slowly. "Is there anything more you know that could help us?"

He saved me from a complete lie by adding that last bit. There was plenty more that I knew but nothing that would help them. Not until Joshua arrived. Michelle and Gabby watched me shake my head. Neither of them spoke.

"After all of those dreams, I doubted everything I thought I knew," I said with a shrug.

Sam glanced at Nana. The significant pause told me they were communicating silently.

"Michelle, Gabby, help Bethi to the commons for something to eat, please. Your men are waiting there for you," Nana said.

"Sure," Gabby said quickly exiting her chair and moving to open the door. Michelle offered a hand to help me stand. Neither said anything as we left, and I felt relieved. I'd given the Elders enough information to get them off our backs, for now. I just needed to figure out what to do about Joshua. If he had an unusual spark, we couldn't trust him. But what to do about it?

When we entered a huge room filled with tables and chairs, I only caught a glimpse of it before Clay strode toward us. He stopped just in front of Gabby, preventing all of us from moving any further. The heavenly smells of turkey and stuffing drifted to me as his eyes swept over Gabby's face. My stomach cramped. This time from hunger.

"She's fine, big guy, but my stomach's really hurting. Would you mind—" I didn't get to finish the sentence before Clay was jostled aside with a growl from behind.

"Move already," Luke snapped at Clay, scooping me up.

Clay's eyes narrowed as they settled on Luke. Gabby curled her fingers in his hand. He stopped his glaring and gave her his full attention. "I'm fine. Bethi's not. We're supposed to get her something to eat."

I caught Clay's nod before Luke turned, almost bumping us into Emmitt. Two little boys circled around him like satellites. Luke huffed, and I reached up to smack the back of his head lightly. "The decisions you make and the words you speak influence the people around you. Be aware of your influence," I quoted.

His lips twitched, and he looked down at the boys. "Excuse me, please," he said politely.

They scampered out of his way, and Emmitt stepped aside, his eyes on Michelle.

"Didn't you take the pills?" Luke asked softly, carrying me to a cushioned chair.

"I took them." My stomach cramped, and I tried to remember when I'd last eaten. "Nana mentioned something about food." Instead of setting me in the chair, he sat and settled me on his lap.

"I'll get it for you," Michelle called moving toward the kitchen. Emmitt followed closely behind.

Clay moved to the chair across from us and sat, his eyes never leaving Gabby.

Gabby perched on one of his knees and smiled slightly when he set a hand on her waist.

"How long have you two been together?" I asked. I really just wanted to know how safe she was. Claimed was good, but Mated was better.

"Clay has been living with me since the end of August." Her smile widened. "But I just recently Claimed him."

"Not Mated?" I wondered.

She shook her head. Well, crap.

Michelle returned just then with a sandwich. "Here you go."

I accepted the plate with a smile of thanks. "How long have you and Emmitt been together?" Taking a bite of the sandwich, I listened to Michelle say they'd been Claimed for several months and were planning a wedding. Another one not Mated. Dangerous business. I glanced at Emmitt who was watching me closely. We were still all ripe for Urbat picking. I wished again that Luke would just give in and at least let me Claim him.

"What about you two?" Emmitt asked.

I shrugged and took another bite. Everyone continued to wait patiently for my answer. Even Luke, the jerk, was quiet. Fine.

"He has a problem with my boobs." I took another bite of my sandwich.

Luke made a choking noise, and I grinned. "Secretly, I think he's hoping if he waits until I'm eighteen they might grow a bit more."

Emmitt's face betrayed nothing as his gaze flicked between me and Luke. Clay's whiskers split to show two rows of perfect white teeth. His eyes were on Luke. I didn't want to turn around to see why. Michelle looked slightly shocked and worried. Gabby was frowning at Luke.

"They're kinda like the elephant in the room. We're not allowed to talk about them."

Luke stood with me in his arms, turned, dumped me—gently—in the chair, and strode away. I grinned at the group.

"That's usually how he reacts if I do talk about them."

"So you haven't Claimed him yet?" Gabby asked.

I snorted. "Nope. He won't let me. He's pretty quick to protect his precious neck. I got smacked in the face, like, at least fifty times on the trip here." I polished off the sandwich with a sigh. That had to have been the best sandwich ever.

"That makes no sense," Gabby stated. "I was so sure." She looked in the direction that Luke had walked off and moved to stand. The content, happy feeling left my stomach.

Clay wrapped his hand around her wrist to stop her. I took a slow breath and tried to let go of the anxiety filling me. She was my sister. I would need to depend on her. So why was I so jealous of her and her relationship with Luke?

She turned and met Clay's eyes. "It's okay. I'll be right back. I have to know," she said quietly.

Michelle shifted uncomfortably in her seat. See, the restless part of me yelled. Even she sensed that Gabby shouldn't want to go chasing after Luke. I shushed myself.

Clay sighed and let go, but surprised me by following her. She didn't seem to mind.

"Do you want something to drink?" Michelle asked quietly, pulling my attention back to the remaining two.

"Sure." I stood to go with her since I didn't want to sit and dwell on what had just happened.

"The Elders don't have much to go off of," she said quietly.

I smiled at her evasive wording. "No. They don't," I slowly agreed. "Maybe Elder Joshua's arrival will help?" I still wasn't sure what to do about him or how to expose him so he wouldn't tell the other Urbat that I'd figured them out.

She glanced at me with a slight frown, and I could see her making the connections. "I hope so," she murmured.

In the kitchen, I had to pause for a moment to gape in amazement. The heavenly smells that dotted the commons intensified as I stepped through the door. Several ovens lined the walls. The counters and stovetops were spread with numerous ingredients and dishes in various stages of preparation. So much food...

An older woman with long blonde hair came over to us. She smiled at Michelle. "Another sandwich?"

Michelle looked at me.

I watched another woman pull a turkey from the oven. The crisp brown skin called to me. "Turkey," I mumbled in a zombie-like fashion.

The woman laughed and turned to watch the other woman baste the bird. "It'll be another three hours until they're done. Eighteen birds in all," she confided.

Tearing my eyes from the food, I really looked at her for the first time.

"Charlene," I whispered recalling the memory of the girl at school. She didn't look much different. Sure, a little older, but the face was unmistakable.

"Do I know you?"

"Charlene, this is Bethi," Michelle introduced us.

Charlene held out her hand. I looked down at it briefly before meeting her eyes again. "I think it's better if we don't," I said softly. She dropped her hand and eyed me curiously. "You have a lot of food to cook, and I don't want to be responsible for knocking you on your butt. But I'm glad to have met you." Charlene's eyes flared in surprise.

"Same here," she said. "I'll get you something more to snack on. You look like you need it."

"You know how it is when you're on the run. You're so busy moving your feet you forget to shove something in your mouth."

She nodded again—the look in her eyes told me she really did understand what it felt like to be on the run—before turning away to get a plate. She loaded it with two pieces of pumpkin pie covered with a mountain of whipped cream, a large scoop of fluffy stuff hiding mini marshmallows, and an enormous square of bread pudding with cranberries.

"This should help," she said handing over the heavy plate.

Saliva pooled in my mouth. I could only nod as I turned away. My stomach pulled a little as I carried the plate.

"Can I carry that for you?" Emmitt offered. I looked up. Apprehension spread through me. His eyes saw too much.

"Sure," I said with false ease as I surrendered the plate.

The others had returned and sat in our recently abandoned seats. Seeing Luke sitting there calmly, his eyes meeting Gabby's in some sort of silent communication hurt me even as those stupid crazy butterflies took flight in my stomach.

"If you're feeling tired," Emmitt said softly, "you could take this back to your room."

I stopped walking and turned to him, meeting his eyes. "I'm not really tired as much as I just want to be alone for a while," I said honestly, knowing that Luke could hear me. "So going back to my room sounds great. Would you come get me when something interesting happens?"

He nodded and turned to lead the way back.

AFTER EMMITT and Michelle left me in my apartment, I sat on the couch and shoved in a forkful of pumpkin pie. Still warm. I sighed and took another bite. I missed my mom. She made great pumpkin pie when we got together with her side of the family. Cousins, aunts, uncles, my grandpa. I wondered if she was with them. I hoped she was. So many times I had lost the ones I loved. In a way, it helped me now. I still hurt for my mother in this life but also had a numb sort of protection from the hurt. Like scar tissue.

"So you want to be alone, huh?" Luke said as he let himself in and softly closed the door. "A bit rude, don't you think?"

"No more rude than you running off in a drama queen fit so 'Little One' follows you," I said.

He walked around the couch so he stood before me. His expression was slightly amused. "You're jealous."

I wanted to throw my fork at him. "No kidding. Look, either want me or don't, but stop playing the middle ground. I'm tired of waiting for you." That wiped the humor from his expression.

"What do you mean?"

"I mean, I had to suffer through a dream where I was drowned as a baby. If you would have let me Claim you, I'd have more control over the dreams. If you would have stayed by me, I wouldn't have dreamed that at all." Well, maybe not, but he didn't need to know that.

"Bethi, I'm sorry about leaving you. The Elders had questions and wouldn't be ignored."

"I won't be ignored, Luke. Decide."

"There's no decision. We are meant to be together. We just need to be patient for a little while longer. When you turn eighteen—"

"Just stop," I yelled. "Do you hear yourself? Do you even know what you're saying?" I lowered my voice in an imitation of him. "'Bethi, I want to be with you, but first I need you to suffer for three more months. Being killed another ninety times—minimum—isn't asking too much so I can feel virtuous when I allow you to Claim me.'"

He bent down in front of me and plucked the plate from my hands. "Bethi, I swear. I will not leave you again. I won't allow you to suffer another death," he said softly, brushing the loose hair back from my face.

"I already suffered one too many," I said, standing. "If you add up all the years I've lived across all my lives, I celebrated my one thousandth birthday a couple decades ago. You're not cradle robbing, you're grave robbing. Think on that."

He sighed and stood, too. We stayed like that for a moment. Me glaring and him skimming my face with an increasingly tender look. He stepped close and brushed his finger over my skin, tracing my right eyebrow and then feathering into my hair.

"You have the most amazing eyes," he whispered.

"I've heard that before," I said, struggling against the hope building in my chest.

He leaned in and my heart started to hammer. The last time he'd kissed me he'd said it wouldn't happen again. Did it mean he'd actually heard me? Had he changed his mind? My breath caught as I waited for him to close the last inch between us.

"I will do anything for you," he continued. "Even wait." He turned his head and kissed my cheek—my flippin cheek.

I started shaking. "Get out. Before I hurt myself trying to hit you."

He sighed and backed away. "Bethi—"

"No. No more. Go." I turned my head away unable to look at him.

Stupid idiot.

He left the room. I slumped back into my seat, picked up the plate of dessert he'd taken from me, and gorged myself. Pie, good. Luke, bad.

After the last bite, I settled back with a groan. It felt horrible, in a good way, to be so full again; and it put me in a thoughtful mood.

Once Joshua was here, and we eliminated the threat of further information leaking to the Urbat, we could plan our next steps. Until then, I knew Gabby was watching for a sneak attack. I wished I could talk to her about it but couldn't risk raising the suspicion of the Elders by sneaking into the padded room for a private conversation. That meant being patient and waiting. Just like Luke had asked me to.

Screw waiting and screw Luke. I went to my room and strapped on the sheath and knife. I hated waiting, and I hated feeling so defenseless physically and mentally. I knew Claiming wasn't necessarily permanent. I wanted Luke despite his pigheaded hesitation. But maybe I could find someone willing to let me Claim him until Luke was ready. I could care less who I bit. I just wanted the dreaming to stop. At least, the death dreams. And, those would once I Claimed someone. They had in the past. The other dreams were fine, and I could still learn from them.

I left the room and made my way to the commons. On the way there, I heard a lot of laughing and noise coming from another apartment. The door stood open. Inside, Michelle watched as two young boys wrestled with teens just a bit older than me.

"Paul, cheated," one cried.

"Did not," the other little boy shouted back.

"Liam. Aden. If you two are going to fight about this, then play time with Paul and Henry is done," Michelle said.

There was a bunch of whining as the teens stood. I stepped back and waited for them to leave. They noticed me after they closed the door. I smiled. Either would do nicely.

PAUL SAT across from me looking nervous, his gaze darting around the room. Henry had fled as soon as I'd explained the favor I needed.

"He'll kill me just to have you back."

"It won't come to that," I promised.

"Yes, it will. You don't know our ways. He'll challenge me to the death. I really want to help you, but I won't have a chance."

"Please," I begged. As a Judgement, I knew I held a certain level of attraction for all of them. Why was this so hard then? Technically, I'd been rejected three times now, counting Luke as a single rejection. Maybe I needed to stand up on one of the tables and start shouting it out. Take me! I'm yours!

A dream started tugging at me.

"If there wasn't anyone else interested in you, I would agree," he promised me. "But if he doesn't kill me, my mom will."

"Yeah, yeah," I waved away his concern. "If he were really interested, why am I still unClaimed?"

Paul looked unsure. "I'm really sorry, Bethi." His words held a note of finality.

"Whatever," I mumbled and stood. When I turned, I caught Luke watching me from a few seats over. My eyes narrowed. He ignored me and looked at Paul, giving him a quick wink.

The dream hit me upside the head with a frying pan, and I staggered as I took a step toward the kitchen. The dizzy wave passed over me quickly, barely interrupting my slow progress. Still, Luke stood and moved to my side.

"Are you all right?" he asked with concern.

"Peachy," I answered, tugging my arm from his grasp. Whatever dream waited, it waited impatiently. I could only imagine what horrors it wanted to share with me. I met Luke's gaze. He had the power to change the message it bore just with his presence. Why did he continue to hurt me by keeping himself from me?

"I just need something to drink."

He gave me a gentle smile that twisted my stomach with wishful thinking. "I'll get it for you."

He moved off to the kitchen. I moved off toward the doors.

I MEANT to go outside to find someone else to beg to be my valentine. Instead, I collapsed in the hall with a dream tripping my feet.

A thin, bare shell of darkness covered my eyes. I could easily see shapes through it. Swirls of grey floated in and out of my frame of vision. Voices whispered. Some sounded like grating, unintelligible noise. Others spoke in clear tones.

Regardless of the sounds of the voices, the message was clear. "Free us."

Unable to move, blinking but seeing nothing more than shadow, I lay trapped in a hellish unfeeling world.

Then she came. She stood out in vibrant clarity, her taupe grown robbing the surrounding shades of grey of their unique beauty. Her pale face held a kindness I'd never before witnessed.

"Child," she whispered. "You can see me as the others cannot. Stand strong though you lack Strength. Be calm though you lack Peace. Wait for Wisdom. She will find you."

Pain burst in the back of my head. "Move!" someone yelled. I forced my small legs to move, taking steps into the unknown with hands outstretched, hoping I wouldn't fall. Hoping that if I did, someone would catch me.

The dream shifted, pulling me deeper.

I ran through the tall grass, the fronds whipping my face, making tiny cuts as I passed. The dry rustle of the grass behind me marked my pursuers.

I struggled to pull myself from the dream. Why was I always running? Once again, I'd merged with my past-self.

"Come on, little one. Tell us what you saw," a voice laughed.

A claw raked my back, parting flesh. I screamed in pain and terror.

"Bethi, wake up!"

I woke swinging. The flat of my palm connected with Luke's face. He looked surprised and quickly captured my hand in his gentle fingers.

Tears leaked from the corners of my eyes as the residual pain lingered on my back. "Get away from me."

"Bethi, I'm sorry—"

"I'm sorry. I'm sorry... Try being something else for a change. Like on time," I snapped picking myself up off the floor.

Hurt reflected in his eyes as he picked up a glass from the floor and handed it to me. "Here's the drink you asked for."

I took the glass and watched him walk away. He was always doing that. Walking away. But then again, so was I. We were hopeless.

CHAPTER FIFTEEN

I SIPPED THE WATER AND SLOWLY WALKED THE HALLS. AFTER THE
pain had faded from my back, I regretted my words. I roamed, slightly lost, and
hoped to find Luke, but I didn't see him anywhere.

We were at a stalemate. He wanted to wait, and I desperately needed to
Claim him now. Neither of us wanted to bend. Well, I'd been willing to bend by
selecting someone else, *temporarily*. But he didn't like that idea either. I needed a
way to convince him to help me before it was too late. He didn't seem to
understand the risks. The attack on the way here showed the desperation of the
Urbat. What would they do next? I needed to Claim Luke to calm the dreams so
I could focus on their real message. It would also make it easier for him to find
me if they took me. If I were completely honest with myself, I just wanted to
Claim him because he was mine. Done. Forget the Urbat. Forget the whole the-
world-will-burn crap. I just wanted Luke. I sighed. But I couldn't just forget
everything. Elder Joshua concerned me. Having the pack of Urbat pull back
concerned me. Why hadn't they attacked? There had to be something more,
something bigger going on that I hadn't yet figured out. And I needed to, fast.

A few more steps, and I recognized where I was. The door to the padded
room stood before me. Closed, but I didn't care. I needed help. Maybe the Elders
could help me force Luke's hand. I opened it, surprising Nana, Grey, Sam, and a
new guy.

"Oh," I mumbled. "Sorry." I moved to close the door but Nana stopped me.

"It's all right, Bethi. Come in. This is Elder Joshua. We were just discussing you."

The Urbat Elder. He watched me closely, and I made sure to keep my face a blank mask. Having him here was better. We could keep an eye on him. I again wished there was a way to control him.

Inspiration struck. Finally! Luck was on my side.

Closing the door, I smiled pathetically at the group. "Sorry for interrupting. Nana, what's your policy on killing potential Mates?"

Nana looked concerned, Grey amused, and Sam curious. Joshua's reaction was just as I'd hoped. Cautious. Trying to figure me out.

"It's Luke," I said to Nana. "He's being completely stubborn about my age, and I think I'm going to hurt him pretty soon."

Grey actually laughed. Nana smiled in understanding.

"Do you have time to take a break and help me talk some sense into him?" I asked her. I knew there was no talking sense into him. He'd already explained he didn't have a pack leader because he didn't want to be forced to follow rules. Elders only enforced laws. I just needed to talk to her in private, away from the other Elders.

"Certainly," she agreed standing. "I'll return promptly," she assured the rest.

Anticipation made my head spin. I wrapped my arm through Nana's and leaned on her for support as we walked the halls. I'd found a way to stop my dreams, a way to forestall the next Urbat attack, a way to keep tabs on Joshua, and maybe a way to force Luke to hold still so I could Claim him.

I planned to Claim Joshua *temporarily*. Sure there would be risks. Luke would be both furious and hurt with my solution. Joshua would have the ability to find me wherever I went as long as we were Claimed. But the benefits outweighed the risks. Joshua would be driven to protect me. Even from his own kind.

The real problem was getting Joshua to let me bite him. I needed to get him alone, play it carefully, and hope Luke would forgive me afterward.

"Can you tell Luke to meet us in our room?"

"Already done," she assured me.

The door opened before we reached it. Luke stood there waiting.

Nana preceded me. His eyes tracked my progress as I shuffled through the door. My heart beat heavily, and I suffered a moment of doubt. His declaration of what I meant to him, all the times he'd come after me...If I did this, it would do more than hurt him. I wanted to go to him, wrap my arms around his waist, and hold him tight. But I knew he wouldn't let me. His resistance to us as a couple was the whole problem. I'd lived too many short lives. I wasn't about to let any opportunity pass by in this one. I would solve our problem for us. I just hoped he wouldn't hate me afterwards.

"'Bout time you're where you should be," I grumbled struggling with the guilt that filled me. As I passed him, he reached out, his fingers tracing the shell of my ear and tucking back a loose strand of hair. I forced my feet to keep moving.

"Now," Nana started, sitting on the couch and waiting for Luke to close the door and join us. "What is the problem here?"

Luke stood beside my chair, his hands tucked casually in his pockets. He glanced at me with a clear question in his eyes. Oh, the games I played.

"Before we start is it possible for you not to share this with the rest of the Elders? I know you have a special connection with them and everything," I glanced at Luke quickly, playing into my hesitation, "but I really don't want anyone else knowing this. I mean you can tell if someone is close enough to hear, too, right?"

"Of course. For the moment, we have privacy. And I won't share the details of private conversations unless I ask first."

"Do you swear?"

"I do."

"Fine. Nothing is shared from this point forward unless you ask me." I sat across from her. "I lied," I said flatly. "Oh, Luke really is annoying me with his whole Puritan attitude," I assured her when she glanced at him. "I lied about something else. Rather, I didn't tell you everything. But for a very good reason. Now, I need you to trust me." I smiled. "Funny asking for trust after admitting to a lie," I said with a shrug. I took a deep breath, reached for Nana's hand and stared into her eyes so she would see and feel the truth of what I had to say. "Joshua is not one of you. He's an Urbat." Her eyebrows rose in question, but I hurried to explain. "I couldn't say anything before because I hadn't figured out what to do about it, but I have a plan now."

"What's an Urbat?"

"The Urbat are a cousin to the werewolf. Not quite the same, but very close. There's more, but we don't have the time or the privacy to get into it."

She sat quiet for a moment. I knew she had many questions for me, but hoped she wouldn't push for more.

"What do you plan to do?" she asked finally.

I sat back with a slight smile. "That's where I need your trust. I can't tell you yet because it depends on Joshua believing me and you. I'm a great liar to your kind. I know the tricks. Scent. Heart rate. All that stuff. If you can't lie, I need you to stay here. If you can lie, I need you to back me up."

"I don't understand," Nana said slowly.

"We need to go back in that room, tell them Luke won't let me Claim him, which is the truth by the way, and I'll explain to the room why I need to Claim someone. If...when Joshua offers a solution, I want us to go along with it."

"What do you think he'll offer?" she asked.

"Something that will lead me away from here and to my other potential Mate."

Luke growled from behind me.

"No one asked you," I said not looking at him. "I won't go, of course," I said to Nana.

"Will whatever you plan put you or the pack in danger?"

I gave a dry laugh. "I've been in danger since I started having those dreams. What I plan shouldn't make it worse. As far as the pack goes, that's what I'm trying to protect."

Another dream started tugging at me, and I rose to my feet, cringing at the pain in my stomach. "I swear I have the perfect plan, Nana. All I need is your support and trust."

"I would feel more comfortable if you shared your plan first."

"Me too," Luke added. His voice was laced with concern and sprinkled with suspicion.

I was already shaking my head. "Sorry. If I do that, you'll both try talking me out of it because you don't understand everything." She opened her mouth. "And I don't have time to explain it all. We need to start this quickly. Joshua is a huge threat that can't be dealt with through reasoning or a drawn-out fight."

Nana nodded and stood. "I'll give you my support."

Luke made to follow Nana and me, but I stopped him with a raised hand. "No, Luke."

He flicked a glance at Nana. "I will keep her safe," she promised him.

My heart thumped heavily, and I fought to keep a perfectly straight face when his suspicious gaze fell on me again. "What are you planning?" he asked stepping close.

His fingers tangled in my hair, and he leaned in, nuzzling my hair aside so his lips rested near my ear. Shivers ran down my arms, and my eyes closed.

"You smell like sweet pears and cinnamon," he whispered. "The last time you smelled like this you left me at the laundromat waiting for a burger."

My insides froze and my mind told me to push him away. My arms rose to his chest, but not fast enough. Not before he did the unexpected. His tongue darted out, and he lightly licked the edge of my ear. I went stupid. Forgot how to talk. Forgot how to move. I forgot how to breathe. Darn the man.

"Are you running again, Bethi?"

I struggled to gather my wits. His questioning, boyish look helped bring back a little clarity. He was scared, I realized. "I will come back here when I'm done," I managed to say. My internal-self was chanting "more kisses, more kisses!" at the top of its lungs so I couldn't be sure my words came out coherently.

Luke stepped back, his uncertainty clear on his face. "Watch her closely, Winifred. She's up to something."

"Of course I am," I said indignantly. "I already said that."

His lips twitched, and a full smile lit his face. It melted my insides, which made me nervous. He might not forgive me for this.

Containing my doubts, I left the apartment. Nana followed me quietly.

We let ourselves into the padded room, once again stopping conversation.

"Is everything all right?" Sam asked Nana.

She held out a chair for me. "Bethi, sit. You're looking pale again." She turned to Sam. "I'll let Bethi explain."

Clever Nana.

I gave her my best wobbly smile. It wasn't hard. All I had to do was think of Luke's reaction if my plan actually worked.

"Okay," I said with a deep breath. "Like I said, Luke found me a couple of weeks ago. I'd run away from home because of those dreams I mentioned." I met everyone's eyes briefly. Elder Joshua nodded for me to continue, so I guessed the Elders had recapped my last conversation for him. "Anyway, I wanted to run away from Luke, too, after he showed me what he was, but the dreams weren't so bad with Luke around. And he kept me safe, you know?"

They all watched me, waiting for me to get to the point.

"But he only makes the dreams better when he's next to me. And he keeps leaving," I said with true annoyance. I took another deep breath, carefully planning my words as I flattened my palms on the table. "I don't want these dreams anymore. I don't care about puzzles or their stupid pieces. They don't make any sense and they're scary. Terrifying. I think it would help me if I Claimed someone."

I uncurled my fingers with effort. The subject annoyed me to the point that I'd fisted my hands.

"I asked Luke, but he told me I was too young. I almost had Paul convinced to let me Claim him, but Luke showed up and scared him away."

Grey gave me an indulgent smile as if to say "of course, he would scare the boy away."

"If Luke won't Claim me, I'm asking for your help to find me someone who will and to keep Luke out of it." Because I don't want him hurt, I silently added.

No one made a sound. Nana kept her face perfectly straight, but I could still see her surprise. In fact, all of their faces registered different states of shock. Joshua's also held a note of thoughtful concern.

"Does Luke know you've come to us?" he asked.

"Luke knows I'm talking to you guys, but I didn't exactly tell him why."

"I thought you wanted us to help you figure these dreams out," Sam said, finally finding his voice.

"No, I wanted to know why I was having them. After this last one, I don't care anymore. I just want them to stop. Will you help me?" I looked around the table and didn't see much approval. Nana looked like she was having an internal struggle. No doubt she was regretting her promise to support me. "Please."

Nana sighed. "If Luke is denying your Claim, you have a right to request Introductions." She didn't sound happy about it, but she was going along with it.

Silence wrapped around the occupants of the room. I waited, keeping calm, meeting everyone's eyes. I could see the discomfort growing in Grey. Sam looked seriously troubled. Nana looked just a tad angry. I couldn't blame her. She probably felt betrayed on Luke's behalf. Joshua though, kept his eyes on the table, deep in thought.

Finally, he broke the silence. "We should consider this carefully before we move forward with anything."

Good.

"If he is waiting for her to mature," he glanced at me and gave me an apologetic smile, "then it is possible he will challenge whomever she Claims. We don't want to be reduced to chaos when there are so many other elements concerning us."

Meaning the recent attack. I kept my face neutral.

"Joshua's correct," Sam agreed. Grey nodded. They all looked relieved.

"What does that mean for me?" I asked, pushing.

Joshua sighed regretfully. "It means we too are asking for your patience. We need to ensure we are doing what is best for the pack."

Playing my role, I scowled. "Fine. But my patience is limited. I can already feel another dream gathering. I'll give you an hour to decide, or I'm going to jump on the next unMated I see and start biting."

Standing quickly, I fled out the door as if angry and almost ran into Luke. Thankfully, I'd been wearing my I'm-annoyed-and-leaving face and not my ha-ha-you-fool face. He caught my arms so I wouldn't bump into him and pulled back, his eyes searching my face. The hall was empty except for us.

"I thought you were waiting in the room," I said.

"I didn't actually think you'd come back," he commented letting go of my arms.

"I told you I would." How could a man be so annoying yet so endearing?

A corner of his mouth tilted up in a half-smile, and he threaded his fingers through mine. We walked back to the apartment in silence. Though my mouth was quiet, my mind was not. He didn't just hold my hand, he held my heart. I really started to doubt my wisdom. What a joke. Me. Wisdom.

He opened the apartment door for me. I eased onto the couch and closed my eyes.

The cushions next to me dipped as he sat beside me. His arm curved around my shoulders, and he pulled me to his side. "You look tired."

"I'm always tired." Hopefully not much longer though.

Pressed into his warm side, I relaxed and the dreams swirled. Thankfully, less than a minute later, someone knocked on the door.

Luke eased me from his side to answer it. Sam stood in the entry. "Luke, we would like to speak with you." His voice held regret. Luke glanced at me, seeking my permission to leave my side.

"I'll be fine," I assured him.

He walked out with Sam, and I waited for the main player, lightly touching the knife still strapped to my leg. As I anticipated, another knock sounded on the door.

"Come in," I called.

Joshua opened the door with a smile. "Bethi, hello." He closed the door. "We are breaking the news to Luke now. Actually, we are isolating him to give others a fair chance. We called a few candidates to the woods just outside the Compound if you would come with me."

"Perfect," I agreed, not bothering to contain my happiness. Joshua watched me closely as I stood. The stitches pulled when I tried to straighten so a cringe wasn't hard to fake. "I'm not sure I'll make it that far."

He frowned slightly, considering me before stepping close. "If you'll allow me, I'll carry you."

"Thank you."

He bent down, placed an arm behind my knees and my back, and with a quick move, he lifted me into his arms. I settled high with my arm around his shoulders.

"Joshua, I should warn you. There's another dream coming on and I'm not sure how long I'll..." I lightly sighed and dropped my head on his shoulder. I should have been in theater. "I'm not sure how long I'll be able to stay awake."

There was no dream, at least, not one that I couldn't resist. The light scent of his shaving cream filled my nose. Underneath that, I could smell the real Joshua. Woods, sky, and mud. It held no appeal to me whatsoever.

"Don't worry," he assured me, turning toward the door.

I nodded my head, the movement bringing me closer to his neck. All my attempts with Luke had taught me something. Don't dart in until you were sure he couldn't get a hand up fast enough. Joshua didn't see it coming. I ducked in and bit him hard before we made it to the door.

He gasped, a mix of pleasure and fear. I wiped my mouth on his suit jacket. Ew. His taste was worse than his smell.

The arm supporting my legs slackened, and I loosened my arms around his neck, fearing for my stitches. The blade I had strapped to my leg was trapped between us. His eyes met mine as my legs slowly slid to the floor. The arm at my back kept me pinned as he searched my face. Panic flared within me, but it was not my own. I waited patiently for him to sort through what I had just done.

"What did you do?" he finally managed. Apparently, he couldn't sort through it on his own.

"I caused you a mess of trouble," I admitted, keeping control of my emotions. I suppressed my smug joy and my own concern, giving him no indication through our link what I might be thinking. "We both know whoever you had waiting wasn't right for me. Luke would have been right if he'd been willing. I need someone strong enough to protect me. To keep me safe during the storm that's coming this way."

His gaze dipped to my mouth. His hands brushed up and down my arms. The shock of my unexpected Claim was wearing off. The calculated look crept back into his eyes. Desire flared through our link. Dangerous territory. This was the part of the plan that had caused me the most concern. I knew I'd be safe from the other Urbat now, but how did I keep myself safe from him? I'd hoped Nana wouldn't let him out of her sight.

The door burst open, and Luke strode in. Fire lit his eyes as he took in Joshua's hold on my arms. Nana, Sam, and Grey walked in behind him.

"Joshua?" Sam said as he took in the scene.

"I Claimed him," I said softly. The Elders needed to know. All part of the plan. But watching Luke and the pain that flared in his eyes hurt. I couldn't keep the remorse from welling up within me. Joshua growled in response, and dropped his hands so he could stand in front of me.

"As an Elder, you are not permitted to Claim," Grey said with anger in his voice. "You broke your oath to hold the interest of the pack above your own interests." Grey paused, his anger giving way to confusion. "How are you still alive?"

Joshua twitched as if in pain, and his growl grew louder. The tenuous link he'd had to the werewolves had just been irrevocably severed. I held myself still. He was alive because he wasn't one of them, and wasn't bound by their rules. I'd anticipated his reaction going one of two ways. Joshua could go crazy realizing his cover was blown and try to attack the rest, or he could realize the precariousness of his dilemma.

"As you are well aware, we are not able to Claim any of these girls. She Claimed me." A low growl remained in his voice, but I felt a surge of relief that he chose to talk, not attack. "I will hold that Claim."

All eyes in the room swung to me. Luke's pain showed through his gaze.

I gave a quick nod, answering the unspoken question. I would hold my Claim to Joshua as long as he didn't try for more or try to hurt Luke. Not yet ready to get into the whole "why" of it, I eased my hand to the blade at my side. Not drawing it, but ready to as I eyed Joshua's back.

"Joshua, does this mean you are no longer able to communicate with the pack?" I asked innocently.

He turned to look at me over his shoulder, his eyes narrowing on me fractionally.

"He shouldn't even be alive," Grey restated.

"Yes, yes," I said, waving away his concern and keeping my eyes on Joshua. I still saw Grey's surprised reaction and Luke's transformation. He went from wounded ex to suspicious friend. It gave me hope for us.

Joshua's frown grew. He took a slow deep breath. His suspicion flooded me.

"I feel...something from you. Not happiness exactly. You're trying to keep your emotions from me. Why?"

I answered with a small smile. "Have you told your leader what happened? You know he won't let you keep me."

Joshua's eyes flared wide, and he growled. I couldn't quite tell if the growl was at me or at the thought of losing me. I'd counted on his possessive nature and really hoped it was the latter.

"Thomas already knows," Sam's voice rang with authority.

Joshua's hands curled into fists, but I noted his nails elongating.

"Not Thomas," I said with a shake of my head. "His Urbat leader." Nana glanced down for a moment, and I had the feeling she was doing some silent communicating with Sam and Grey.

"So, Joshua, have you told him? We need to know how soon they will be coming to take me and kill you."

He roared a cry of frustration and anguish. I knew he'd just realized his inevitable death sentence from both sides. Only his connection to me kept him safe for the moment.

Luke's skin rippled in response to his outburst.

"We need to take it down a notch, guys," I said raising my hands. "This human's way too easy to break, and neither of you would like that."

Joshua struggled with himself. Grey placed a hand on Luke's shoulder. I could see the two of them having a silent conversation. Luke noticeably calmed, but he still struggled to contain his shift.

"Let's recap for everyone who doesn't know what's going on," I said softly, unsure if Joshua had thought of everything. "By Claiming you, I stripped you of your Elder privileges, blew your cover with this pack, and voided your usefulness here in the eyes of your Urbat leader. In addition, I've made you his target since he will not allow you to keep me. After all, I feel no connection with you that would help sway any decisions that I might need to make. There's really nowhere safe for you right now." Joshua straightened his stance, a sudden seriousness exploding onto his expression.

He took a slow, deep breath. "Why not just have them," he nodded at the Elders, "kill me right away? Why Claim me?"

"If they had killed you, you would have sent one last message to your leader. It probably would have started an attack and cost countless lives."

"What makes you think I didn't already send a message?" he asked softly, his eyes lightly skimming my face.

"To protect me. I'm yours, right?" His eyes softened at my words. "You don't want to lose me. Plus, you'd forfeit your life by doing so. Like I said, they won't let you keep me." I took a step back from Joshua. Luke's tremors hadn't stopped since he'd walked through the door, and I didn't want to ignite that bomb waiting to go off.

Joshua's eyes tracked me. I felt his yearning. He wanted me close. He wanted to touch me. I wondered if Luke felt for me even a fraction of what Joshua felt. If he did, how did he keep saying no?

"He underestimated you," Joshua said softly.

I knew he meant his leader. "Your kind usually does," I agreed. And still I always died.

"So how do you see this ending?"

"That depends on how many are waiting out there to meet me," I said, reminding Joshua of his original intent when he entered the room.

His lips curled. "Three."

I nodded slowly, thinking. Only three. A discreet number easy to slip in and take me. A perfect number to obliterate. I needed to keep the room at peace, and Joshua on my side for a bit longer.

Meeting Nana's eyes I said, "I don't want a Mating challenge."

Luke growled. "It is my right."

"Shush," I said, keeping my eyes on Nana.

She looked troubled by my words. I could see her weighing my safety and the pack's safety. By keeping Joshua linked to me the pack would be safe, but would I? Joshua would soon realize the only way to save himself would be to mate with me and create an unbreakable bond. Hopefully, Nana wouldn't see that just yet. Finally, she reluctantly nodded her agreement.

Luke growled, and Joshua laughed.

"Like Joshua said, I need to think about how this should end. I don't want bloodshed. That's why I Claimed Joshua. To avoid just that." I moved to touch Joshua's arm, tamping down my revulsion.

"Joshua, I'd like to meet with the Elders and figure out how we can leave here without dying."

He purred with satisfaction and in a quick move, wrapped his arms around me in a hug, pressing me tight against his body. My stitches pulled and I made a small noise. Oblivious, he leaned in and nuzzled my neck. I fought not to gag.

"Moron, you're hurting her," Luke growled, taking a step toward me.

Over Joshua's shoulder, I watched Grey clamp down on one of Luke's arms and Sam the other. They held him back as his body flexed in a constant state of shifting. I couldn't tell if his wolf form was coming or going.

"Please, Joshua. He's right. You're hurting me. I was cut recently."

Joshua still didn't pull back. His hot breath warmed my neck a second before his tongue laved it, just below the ear Luke had kissed not long ago. Joshua was marking me, wiping away Luke's scent. Not good. I could feel his desire rising again.

"Nana," I called in a slight panic.

"Joshua," Nana warned. "She is in no shape for what you're thinking. Stop now, or for her safety I will stop you."

He laughed, a rumble I felt in my own chest since we were pressed so close. But he did ease back. "Soon," he whispered, ducking down to meet my gaze. "They can't stop a Claimed pair," he promised, his hand drifting to my belly. His fingers traced the stitches through my shirt. "A few days will see us truly together."

I nodded slowly as if agreeing while trying to keep the tremors from my body. He smiled in return and released me. I couldn't look at Luke. I wanted a shower.

Nana held her hand out to me. I clasped it tightly and left the room with her. I hoped they knew to keep an eye on Joshua. He wouldn't leave without me. I'd ensured that when I Claimed him. But, I didn't want him near Luke.

CHAPTER SIXTEEN

"I DON'T EVEN KNOW WHERE TO START," NANA SAID, SITTING across from me.

The padded room was packed. The Elders, my sisters, and I sat at the table. Emmitt, Thomas, Clay, and Luke stood.

"Who's watching Joshua?" I asked.

"Carlos," Grey answered. "He won't let Joshua leave or let any harm come to him."

I snorted. "I could care less if any harm comes to him."

"Then why did you Claim him?" Luke asked flatly. His regard hadn't left me since he'd entered the room. A glint of hurt still lingered in the depths of his gaze, but something else consumed him. Determination.

I ignored his questions knowing I'd explained myself well enough in the room. "Here's the deal. The world is not just made up of humans and werewolves. There is a third race, the Urbat. They call themselves the dogs of death and are your close cousins."

"They are the ones you can't control," Michelle added, talking to Nana.

I nodded. "Then there's us," I said, looking at Charlene, Gabby, and Michelle. "We don't belong to any of the three groups. Werewolf, Urbat, or human. We are unique."

"Special," Nana agreed.

"We are here to maintain the balance between the three groups." Sam opened his mouth, but I quickly cut him off. "I'm not sure exactly how we're supposed to do that. We have abilities. Mine is to relive past lives—not just my past lives, but all of our past lives—through dreams. Our abilities seem to help the group we are aligned with in some way. Michelle's gift is prosperity. In past lives, she knew the locations of lost treasure, herbs with medicinal properties, how to create things to better lives. Pretty much any knowledge that could be used to create wealth. Charlene strengthens the group she's allied with and so on. I have no idea how that all plays in, but as soon as the Urbat learned of us, they began hunting us."

"If they are hunting you, why did you Claim one?" Luke asked again, maintaining a calm voice. I wondered how angry he really was.

"We return every one thousand years for a period of time. I don't know all the details of that either. But I've recalled enough of those past lives to know we always die." Meeting Luke's eyes, I finally answered him. "I Claimed him to stay alive...to buy us some time to plan."

Nana gave Luke a look before turning to me. "To plan what, dear?"

"An evacuation, to start."

"What do you mean?" Thomas asked.

"When the Urbat come, they will use the people we love to try to sway us. First, they use our families, torturing them until we do what they want. If that doesn't work, they start torturing us."

"What do they want?" Grey asked.

"For each of us to Claim one of them." My eyes darted to my sisters.

"We've already Claimed someone," Gabby pointed out. Clay rested a hand on her shoulder.

"It won't matter. A Claim can be broken by death, or simply by Claiming another. That's why I was willing to Claim Joshua."

Stunned silence held the room. Michelle gave Emmitt a panicked look. Luke's gaze didn't leave me though I refused to look at him.

"The next step is for life," I said. Luke growled a deep warning but I kept going. "Once Mated, we don't Mate again. I mean, they *could* force us to Claim another and mate, but it doesn't do any good. Our hearts stay with the first lost Mate. The new Mate holds no influence."

"Influence for what?" Sam questioned.

"For balance," I explained. "They have been after power ever since they figured out what we are. The Judgements. In the beginning, we always judged in favor of the humans. At least, that's my guess. I haven't dreamed what really happened yet. Since then, as far as I've seen, we haven't made another Judgement. I'm guessing that's why, despite the inferiority of humans in comparison to your races, they have thrived."

Sam looked thoughtful. Everyone else just looked too stunned to think much.

"The Urbat are tired of living in the shadows and want to be the dominant race for a while. The last cycle they almost had it, but one of us died. Without all of us to...do something, things will stay the way they are, with humans maintaining control," I explained. "The cycle doesn't last forever—only fifty years—so they try not to risk our lives. But they will if they must. After all, we can still be reborn again into the same cycle."

"So you're saying we need to clear the Compound because they will come for all of you and use the people here to talk you into surrendering?" Thomas asked, his disbelief evident.

"Don't doubt it. They will come. They always come," I said evenly, trying to contain my building dread. I couldn't afford for Joshua to feel that through our link. Taking a breath to ease the ache in my chest, I added in a low voice, "And death always follows." Those whispered words caught the attention of everyone in the room. Maybe death didn't need to follow this time. I held on to that possibility.

"What then? Where do we go?"

"That's the tricky part. I don't know where the pack should go, but I know where we need to go. We are missing two of our group. We need to find them."

"About this evacuation," Charlene started.

I could see she didn't want to leave. "Out of all of us, you and Michelle are the most vulnerable. Michelle's brothers need to be sent away and protected. Emmitt, if he's taken, will be a risk to both of you. They will want to break the Claim Michelle has as much as they will want to hurt Emmitt to sway you," I said to Charlene.

She glanced at her son, worry in her eyes. Emmitt gave her a smile and squeezed Michelle's hand gently. "Don't worry. We know now so we can make sure it doesn't happen."

Charlene nodded, but her fear remained.

"What are we going to do about Joshua?" Grey asked.

"Nothing. At least not yet. Oh, but I can't be left alone with him. With these stitches," I gently laid a hand over my middle, "I won't be able to fight him off."

"You said you could Claim another to break your Claim," Nana said gently. "Why wait?"

"Because I'm not done with him yet. Until the Compound is clear and we're ready to leave, I have to keep my hold on him. It's the only thing that's keeping him from reporting back to his leader."

"Are you sure about that?" Sam looked troubled.

"No, not really but it's our best chance. Now, there are three Urbat out in the woods waiting for Joshua. Gabby, can you see them?"

All eyes turned to her. She nodded hesitantly, and I reached across the table to lightly touch her hand. "We need to find them and get rid of them before people start leaving. They can't know what we're doing."

"They're not far from here. But, there are ten more scattered in the surrounding area. Nothing close enough for concern though. The rest are regrouping in the east." She paused for a moment, a frown pulling at her brow. "More are coming from the main group. I think you're right, Bethi. They're coming back."

I nodded and patted her hand. "It's good," I reassured her. "I'd be more freaked out if they weren't. Pick an Elder and a team of five to go out and hunt the three Urbat down," I directed. The ones waiting to meet Joshua and me would be the first to question our delay. "Kill them quickly and quietly so they can't communicate back to their leader. Deal with the ten on the outskirts as needed. Closest first."

Nana looked troubled.

"No prisoners, Nana. Think of the families running from here with kids. Those ten prowling the outskirts will track and kill them if they get wind that this is a mass exodus. The three need to be silenced quickly without a chance for them to send word." I held everyone's attention. I could see questions still stirring, but knew we didn't have too much time.

"We need to move," I said standing. "Their leader—"

"Blake," Michelle interjected.

"Blake will be wondering why Joshua hasn't reported by now. Gabby, let us know if you see a change in their direction."

Gabby nodded.

"Nana, will you come with me to talk to Joshua?"

"I'm coming too," Luke said.

I shook my head. "No, Luke. I need him calm. Help Gabby. Clear the field so we can be done with this and I no longer need my Claim on Joshua."

His eyes held mine for a long moment before he nodded and stepped back.

"Please excuse us," Emmitt said pulling Michelle to her feet.

"Where are you going?" Nana asked concerned.

Michelle met Emmitt's gaze, and must have felt something through their link because she suddenly grinned before turning to Nana with a blush. "Cementing my Claim," she murmured.

Charlene chuckled. "If you two could wait just a bit longer, we'll watch the boys for you."

Emmitt gave a curt nod and held out Michelle's chair for her again. Michelle sat, red faced, but happy.

Gabby looked over her shoulder at Clay and shook her head. He laughed and bent to kiss the top of her head.

Seeing the room committed to the direction we needed to take, Nana helped me up from the chair, and we left the rest to plan the evacuation.

WE COULD SEE Joshua pacing the apartment when Carlos opened the door for us. A lamp lay broken in the middle of the floor, and Carlos' lip bled. I wanted to apologize to him but knew how Joshua would take that. Joshua looked worse. His right eye had swollen shut and purple fingerprints decorated the left side of his neck. I didn't feel too badly for him.

"That took much longer than I expected," Joshua said, coming to a stop. His eyes swept over me and held malice as he watched Nana enter behind me.

"I'm sorry about that. Instead of concentrating on the problem of us, they got hung up on the fact that there's another race and that I'm not exactly human."

He barely paid attention to my words. He looked ready to fight again.

Tamping down my aversion, I walked up to him, placed my hands on his shoulders, and stood on my toes to place a chaste kiss on his cheek. The tension in his shoulders eased, and a purr rumbled in his chest.

Crisis averted, I dropped my hands, but his arms came up around me before I could step away. I let out a slow breath trying to keep any panic from welling up. I did *not* want to be in his arms.

"We need to leave here soon," Joshua said. "Our troubles are still waiting. I'm stalling as best I can."

Ah. His agitation made more sense. I could only imagine what his leader was screaming at him through their link. I nodded and tried to wear a concerned look. "I've asked that the Elders help make our troubles go away."

He eyed me for a moment. A surge of possessiveness swept through me, then calculation. I didn't miss the hint of suspicion as he smiled slowly. "That would be ideal."

The suspicion worried me. Perhaps I was playing it up too much. "Would you mind if I took a bit more time to shower? I think I smell like a hot dog." Hot Dog? I kept my face straight while I mentally kicked myself over my random choice of smell comparisons.

He leaned in to inhale deeply. "I smell spiced pears. Delicious."

Crap. I struggled with what to do. I did not want him licking me again.

"Joshua," Nana rumbled a warning.

He reluctantly released me. "Of course. Go bathe. Winifred can fill me in."

"I'll be quick," I promised him. I just needed to wash my neck where I still felt his tongue. Suppressing a shiver, I walked away and closed myself into the bathroom.

Through the door, I heard Joshua's howl of frustration and Nana's calm tones. I stayed in the bathroom, hiding, wondering how long it would take Luke and whoever else to hunt down the three in the woods. Then, how long would it take the wolves living here to pack up and leave? I needed to do something to keep Joshua occupied until we were ready to go. He could send all the messages he wanted after that. The rest of the Urbat would still be too far away to reach us in time. I hoped.

After a few minutes, I emerged with a thoroughly scrubbed neck. Joshua's eyes tracked me as I walked the short distance to him. He'd once again been pacing.

"We're leaving," he growled at me.

"Now?" I forced myself to remain calm. "We still have your friends out there to worry about."

"Not any longer. They've been silenced. He is asking me for information. They are gathering to return. We must leave *now*."

I let out a loud sigh. "Of course. Then we need to leave." Nana sat on the chair watching us. "Is everything ready?"

"Almost," she said.

My stomach gave a sickening lurch, and a wave of dizziness hit me. A dream called, and it almost knocked me out where I stood. I struggled to breathe and stay upright.

Joshua lunged for me, worry in his eyes. Behind him, Nana rose, her expression determined. Joshua's hands gripped my arms as he steadied me. I opened my mouth to reassure them both, but only managed a wide-eyed look as Nana reached for his neck. My shocked expression was the only warning I managed to give Joshua. Nana twisted his head sharply, killing him instantly. Before his body could crumple toward me, she pulled him back.

"What did you do?" I gasped, quickly revising my thoughts that older people were nice.

"We're ready. We don't need him anymore. The families have packed and the last one is leaving. The unMated are following as escorts. Gabby has given the location of the last ten so they can be avoided. We are all that remain."

I stared down at Joshua's lifeless form and felt like crying. His death didn't bother me as much as the timing of it. I'd meant for him to live to pressure Luke to replace the Claim. Now there was no reason for Luke to give up his stubborn determination to keep me at arm's length.

"Come, Bethi," she said, lifting my bag and holding out a hand. Lethal hands, I thought still dazed.

We walked through a quiet Compound. A sense of cold anticipation filled the halls. Doors to apartments stood open. Small things like lamps and blankets were missing. The large pieces of furniture remained. What had I started? They all trusted me. They'd listened. For the first time in all the lives I'd recalled, the people around me had run before it was too late. Did it mean things would change this time around?

Outside, the remaining cars left the parking lot in an orderly fashion. Sam stood on the porch watching it all. Three cars waited nearby with their doors open. Gabby stood near one, her eyes unfocused. Clay stood just behind her, a hand on her shoulder. They both faced the Compound.

"The Urbat have turned," she said when I stepped onto the porch. "A small group, though."

"I'm not surprised," I answered distractedly. I couldn't see Luke.

Nana nudged me aside, and I watched Carlos stride past carrying Joshua. I hadn't even known he'd been following us. He stepped off the porch and headed for the woods.

"Where's he going?" I asked. We didn't have much time if the Urbat were headed toward us.

"Taking him to the woods. Charlene put her heart into this place. Maybe they will leave it be if he's found out there," Nana said, moving past me.

She slid into the backseat of one of the cars, sandwiching two little boys in between her and Jim. Michelle and Emmitt sat in the front. I doubted they'd been given the time they wanted to cement their Claim. Emmitt started the car forward as soon as Nana closed the door.

"Sam," Gabby said, "we need to leave *now*."

Carlos emerged from the woods at a run with Luke at his side. My heart went crazy. Deep down, I'd thought he would leave without me because of what I'd done.

Sam held out his hand and helped me from the porch. He, Clay, and Gabby climbed into his truck while Luke, Carlos, Grey, and I quickly filled the remaining car. Luke kept his distance from me, leaving the space of the middle seat between us. I hugged my arm to my stomach, not so much for the stitches, but for the emotional maelstrom of doubt that lived there. We left in a hurry. Everyone followed the same road heading south. From there, cars in the caravan started taking random turn-offs.

"Does everyone know where to go?" I asked.

Grey answered. "Gabby gave everyone several safe locations where the Urbat population is low. The Urbat are mostly in the northeast so everyone will avoid that area."

"Tell Gabby we need to find somewhere safe enough to stop for a few hours. We need to plan how to get Peace before the Urbat find her."

Grey nodded but said nothing. Hopefully, he was talking to Sam.

I glanced at Luke and found him watching me. It hurt to look at him. My eyes burned, and my lips trembled. I struggled to keep it all in. I didn't think a simple apology would make up for what I'd done to him but said it anyway. He gave the barest of nods and reached across the seat to clasp my hand.

His touch, the light rumble of the tires over the road, and an already long messed up day did me in. My eyes fluttered closed, and a single thought floated to the surface before a dream pulled me under. I hate car rides.

CHAPTER SEVENTEEN

I WOKE WITH A GASP. LUKE'S HAND WAS STROKING MY CHEEK. MY head lay back against the seat.

"You all right?" he asked softly. He'd turned toward me, but he still kept his distance.

The tires still rumbled over the road as I lifted my arms. I flexed my hands and wiggled my fingers as I swallowed hard. "They cut off my fingers. One by one." I let out a shaky breath and closed my eyes again. "Can we stop for an energy drink or something?"

The car remained quiet, and I opened my eyes just in time to see Luke and Grey share a look.

"What?" I demanded looking between the two of them.

Luke picked up one of my hands and started massaging the fingers. After what had just happened to them, it felt great. But, he looked out the window while he did it without answering me.

Grey gave me a wink. "You were only out five minutes. Gabby said the Urbat seem to be tracking us. We're heading for the interstate. She'll let us know as soon as it's safe to stop."

I groaned and dropped my head back to the seat. Even with Luke holding my hand, I'd dreamt of death. It wasn't enough.

Shifting my position often and rolling the window down to let in the cold air helped, but I knew I wouldn't be able to fight off the dreams while sitting still like this.

FIVE DEATHS LATER, we finally pulled into a nice hotel crawling with people. Our four vehicles parked close together. Michelle's brothers tumbled out of the car, climbing over a laughing Jim. Emmitt quickly walked around the front to open the doors for Michelle and Nana. Thomas did the same for Charlene. Clay opened the door and stood aside while Gabby slid out. She looked tired, too.

As soon as Carlos put our car in park, I flung open my door and scrambled out. My skin still crawled from the last dream. Charlene and Thomas walked ahead to book us rooms. I hurried after them.

"No credit cards," I said to Charlene, walking beside her. She nodded and approached the desk.

I waited for Michelle to enter the lobby. "How much cash do you have?"

She looked at Emmitt. "Three hundred," he said.

Shaking my head, I glanced at Gabby who had joined our group. "You said we needed to go east. We need enough cash to make it there. I don't know how deep the Urbat are into the human world. If they have any connections, they could use credit card transactions to track us."

"I have no doubt Blake could," Michelle said, keeping her voice soft. Her eyes followed Jim as he took the boys down a side hall to check out the pool. "I have someone I trust who can wire me some money."

"Good." I turned and almost ran into Luke. He caught my arms before I could walk into him. "Sorry," I mumbled.

Just behind him, Charlene turned away from the desk. "They only had five rooms," she said, joining our group. "One is the honeymoon suite." She handed a key card to Emmitt with a smile. "The others are double queens."

She held up the remaining cards.

"Sam can room with us," Gabby quickly offered. I didn't miss Clay reaching up to soothe her back. She looked over her shoulder to give him a shy smile.

"I thought you and the boys could sleep with us, Nana," Charlene suggested. Nana agreed, and Michelle looked relieved. Her brothers would be well protected.

"Jim can join us," Grey said, looking up at Carlos. "Right, darling?" Grey teased.

Carlos stoically agreed.

Luke grabbed the remaining room card without a word. A room to ourselves. A room with two beds. Yeah, I didn't let my hopes get too high.

"Let's meet in the suite first," I suggested. "If they catch up to us, I want a plan laid out."

Five minutes later, we gathered in the suite minus Jim, the boys, and Nana. They splashed in the pool.

"I've been all over the board with my explanations. So let me be clear with what I'm trying to avoid. Dying. It's not fun," I said. "We need to stop their power trip. I don't mean just in this life and cycle but future lives and cycles, too. We need to rob them of their chance to control us in this life. We need to make their search hard and their goal nearly impossible." I did *not* want to live through another brutal death in my next life. Old age would be a new experience for me.

The thought sparked inspiration. "We need to change the game," I said with a growing smile.

"What do you have in mind?" Sam asked.

Taking a deep breath, I braced myself for the argument that I knew would ensue. "As I mentioned, there are six of us. We represent different things. Prosperity, Hope, Wisdom, Strength, Peace, and Courage. According to Gabby and Michelle, the Urbat already have one of us. Courage. They can't have *any* of us because all of us are needed to make a Judgement this cycle." I knew in my heart I spoke the truth. The world was so unbalanced it wobbled. "We can't get to Courage. There's just no way with our numbers. That's why we need to expose werewolves and Urbat to the humans."

As expected, denial broke out.

"You can't be serious," Thomas said.

"We'll be at their mercy," Sam added. "We don't go to hospitals for a reason."

"I first saw you at one," Gabby pointed out.

"I was visiting a human friend," he said, waving away the reason. "We'll end up in cages."

"No," I said, but no one listened. "Just calm down," I shouted, quieting the room.

"Hear me out. They have the advantage. There are more of them. They know what's going on, and we don't. Not fully...not yet, anyway. They've been building up connections in the human world." I looked to Michelle, and she nodded in agreement. "We need to come into the light before they do. Show the world that werewolves exist, show we're not bad, and then expose the Urbat, too. We need to show that we're different from the Urbat and that they are trying to hurt us.

"If we direct human concern toward the Urbat and not werewolves, we will have less to worry about. The Urbat won't be able to creep around trying to hunt us because the humans will be watching. Urbat won't be safe."

"Neither will we," Sam said.

"Not in your fur, you're right. You'll need to let everyone know to keep it under wraps. And the ones that can't, shouldn't go outside. But we can't expose everything until we have Peace. She takes the panic and anxiety down to almost catatonic. And Charlene can help keep everyone on the same page," I added. "Werewolves are good, Urbat are bad."

Charlene looked uncertain.

"We'll keep the initial group small," I assured her. "We need to find someone at a TV station to take us seriously enough to give us air time. We want this to be recorded at their studio to give it more credibility."

"I might know someone," Michelle offered hesitantly. "She interviewed me once."

"Perfect!" I said, excited and feeling like I was on the right track. "When we're there, Charlene will need to grab everyone in the room and keep them from thinking they should call the National Guard to make us into lab rats. Meanwhile, Peace will keep everyone in the studio from freaking out. The first impression werewolves will give is a calm and kind one. It wouldn't hurt to have a spokesperson who looks sweet and unable to snap someone's neck," I said, knowing the Elders were communicating.

Grey laughed slightly. "Winifred is not comfortable with being the spokesperson and wants me to remind you clothes don't change with us."

"We'll bring a robe," I promised. "By exposing ourselves—no pun intended— we are robbing the Urbat of their advantage. They can't hope to win against humans in an outright war. There are too many. Their technology is too advanced. A bullet in the head would kill any of the three races just the same. If we tell the world we're the good guys, and warn them to watch out for the bad guys, we're more likely to make it harder for the Urbat to win this time around."

"More likely?" Carlos questioned, speaking for the first time.

I blinked at him. "I didn't think you actually talked." He didn't answer, just continued to look at me. "Okay. Well, historically, the Urbat would find as many of the Judgements as they could, and torture us to get our obedience. But one of us always dies too late in the cycle for rebirth and stops them from obtaining their goal. So I can't promise this will work. It's never been done before."

"We agree we should find Peace before the Urbat do," Sam said slowly. "But we will need to further discuss revealing our race before we make a decision. We need to do what's best for the pack."

"Exactly," I stressed. "The pack will die as it is. It can't stay hidden. The Urbat are crazy desperate. The things they've done..." Luke's fingers threaded through mine.

"We have to stop them."

"We agree," Grey said. "We just need to think everything through."

He was right. We had time to discuss the necessity of revealing the Urbat and werewolf races to the humans. I held in a sigh and contented myself with his maybe.

"Fine. But we need to plan our next stop. I'm not sure if traveling together is a good thing or not, but in case we get separated, we should have a place picked ahead of time."

Michelle used her phone to find another hotel a day's drive east of where we were. We all agreed on it, and she made the reservations.

Charlene excused herself and promised to bring back something to eat. When she and Thomas returned, they had one of the turkeys and several containers of the meal they'd been working on before we left the Compound.

Everyone piled food on the plates she brought. I sought her out. "I'm really sorry you didn't get to have your nice meal."

"No, Bethi. What we're doing now is much more important. For years, I've felt a...itch, I guess you'd say. Like I was supposed to be doing something, but I never could figure out what. The itch is gone now. I know what we're doing is right."

She lifted her arms and offered a hug. I went in willingly and fell into the abyss.

"Do you have Courage?" the Taupe Lady whispered from the black.

"No. They have her. But I hope to change that."

"You must have Courage," she answered. A cool hand caressed my face and, for the first time in months, I felt completely at ease and free of the terror and desperation.

"Unite," she whispered. "Before it's too late."

Someone tapped my cheek, and I struggled to stay under, but the Taupe Lady had already faded taking the serenity with her.

I lay on the ground looking up at the bottoms of everyone's plates. "Go. Away," I mumbled. I couldn't even sit up. It would kill my stomach.

"What happened?" Thomas asked. I turned my head and saw Charlene lying next to me.

"She really shouldn't touch any of us too much," I muttered. "We drain her." He frowned at me, but Charlene opened her eyes forestalling whatever he'd been about to say.

"I'm fine," she reassured him. "Just takes me a bit to pull it all back in." She turned and looked at me. "What happens when we do that? Besides draining me."

"Our abilities flare. Gabby's lights ignite with no effort on her part." Gabby's fork hit her plate in shock. "Oh, sorry," I apologized. "The dreams are chaotic and usually painful rather than helpful, but I have actually learned a bit about us. I didn't mean to say something you'd rather I didn't."

"No," she assured me. "It just keeps surprising me how much you know."

"And yet there's so much I don't."

"Do you need help up?" Luke sat on his heels beside me. He already knew the answer, but I liked that he asked first. I nodded, and he slid an arm behind my back.

Luke helped me stand, then walked me to a chair. I felt fine. Gabby followed and sat with me while Luke went to fix me a plate. Nana, Jim, and the two boys stormed the room looking for food. Emmitt caught one of the boys mid-run and lifted him into the air.

"They have a waffle maker," the boy said with a smile, wrapping his arms around Emmitt's neck.

"Really?" Emmitt looked very interested. "We'll have to beat Jim down there, then. Will you come wake us up in the morning?"

The boy nodded and started the put-me-down wiggle.

Gabby distracted me from watching the happy family. "Could we ride together tomorrow?" she asked.

Luke walked over with a heaping plate. My stomach cheered for both of them, plate and man.

"Sure," I said to Gabby. "But I'm not much fun. I tend to fall asleep all the time."

"Maybe conversation will help," she offered.

I shrugged and bit into a forkful of stuffing heaven. But as I tasted it, I thought of home and had a hard time swallowing. I really wanted to call my mom. She had to be beyond crazy with worry by now. But I was too afraid I'd find out they had her, too afraid of what I'd do to try to help her. I knew I should wait until we exposed the Urbat to give her a call. My eyes fell on Nana who was speaking to Charlene. Charlene's color was coming back. She and Thomas sat on the edge of the bed eating together.

"Nana?"

She turned her head to look at me.

"Would you call my mom and let her know I'm okay?" My throat felt tight.

The room grew quiet.

"I ran away to try to save her. I don't know if it worked. I can't know if it worked," I stopped to swallow hard. "At least not until we take away their advantage. But thinking of her alone," I looked down at my Thanksgiving meal. "I just want her to know that I'm okay if she's still there."

Nana moved to me and squeezed my shoulder gently. "Of course, Bethi."

Jim brought over a piece of paper and a pencil. I wrote the number down, hesitated, and then wrote another before I handed it to Nana. "The first one is my mom's. The second one is a friend, Dani, in case my mom doesn't answer. Find out what you can. But don't tell me. Whether you reach her or not, don't tell me."

She nodded slowly, sad understanding filling her eyes. I couldn't know. I had to stay strong. I didn't think I had much left in me.

"I'm not hungry anymore," I said quietly, pushing my plate back.

"Bethi, you need to eat," Luke insisted.

"I just want to go to my room." I stood, and he followed.

He didn't put up too much of a fight about sharing a bed when we got to the room. He even pulled back the covers and took off his shirt.

I ducked into the bathroom to wash my face and brush my teeth. By then, I was ready to sleep. He watched me cross the room and held out an arm to welcome me.

"How are the stitches?" he asked.

"Fine," I murmured closing my eyes.

I woke with a stretch followed by a wince when the stitches reminded me I couldn't stretch too far. Luke's warm hand covered my stomach through my shirt; and I sighed, not opening my eyes. I'd experienced one of the best nights. I'd slept through without interruption for—I lifted my head from his chest to look at the alarm clock—fourteen hours.

"You must be starving," I said, lying back down.

"Your arm was looking good about six hours ago."

"I bet." I wasn't ready to get up yet. I sighed and closed my eyes again.

His stomach growled. I laughed and managed to sit up. "You win. We'll go feed you."

"You, too," he said, sitting up with too much energy. "All you ate yesterday was a sandwich."

"Not true. I had a plate of pie, too."

I picked out clothes while he used the bathroom. He came out showered, fresh, and ready to eat. I shook my head and indulged in a quick shower, careful not to let the scabs around the stitches get too wet. It felt good to be so clean. When I wiped the steam from the mirror, I cringed. I hadn't been paying attention to myself. The circles under my eyes were dark again. I used the hotel hair dryer and brushed my hair until it was dry and then dressed.

Luke sat on a made bed waiting for me when I opened the door.

"Feed me," I begged.

He couldn't hide the worry that passed over his face. Standing, he threaded his fingers through mine and led me out of the room. My bag was slung over his shoulder.

We met everyone in the breakfast area. Michelle and Emmitt couldn't stop looking at or touching each other. Long looks followed by a quick kiss, a hug, or just a shoulder brush. I shook my head. I wasn't the only one. I caught Gabby's look, too. She grinned at me as Luke led me to the counter laid out with food.

He insisted I eat a bagel, eggs, sausage, and a waffle. Then he looked at me and added a bowl of cereal.

"Seriously? I'll be sick if I eat all that," I whispered as he carried the plate to the table Grey and Carlos shared.

"He'll eat what you don't," Grey said with a laugh.

I sat and started eating, asking questions between bites.

"Any news?"

"One of their sentinels must have discovered the Compound empty because they stopped grouping and have fanned out. Gabby said they are creating a net across the states, but there are holes big enough to wind our way through. It just might take a little longer," Grey answered.

Nana came up and asked about the stitches. She insisted on checking them before we left. I reluctantly agreed.

Luke used his fork to stab a piece of sausage from my plate and fed it to me with a soft command to eat.

In no time I was down to just the waffle. I had to push the plate away.

"Too much," I groaned.

Luke had the same meal I did, but twice the serving size. Still, his plate sat empty. He grabbed my waffle and finished that, too.

We shuffled the seating arrangements so Nana, Gabby, and Clay rode with us. Clay sighed when Gabby moved to sit in the backseat with Luke and me. He caught the back of her shirt before she could completely escape him and planted a kiss on her mouth before getting into the front seat.

"How you feeling?" she asked when Nana pulled out of the lot. Since we rode with Gabby, we were the lead car.

"Fine," I acknowledged. Luke's leg pressed against mine, warming me. I would probably be napping before long.

"If it's okay, I have some questions for you..." She glanced at Luke and Nana.

"It's fine with me." I'd relayed everything I thought I knew. If there was some memory lurking, some piece of information I'd failed to mention...well, it wasn't on purpose.

"You've said a lot about our abilities. I thought...I thought I was meant to find pairs."

"What do you mean?"

"When I touch people, if I'm feeling the right things, like empathy, I can transfer my power to them. Then, I get this kind of echo back from it, like ripples. When the ripple hits the right spark, it glows brighter. Does that make sense?"

Though I understood what she was saying, I'd never experienced it. "I haven't lived anything like that yet. I didn't know you could transfer your power. I wonder if the rest of us can," I said, looking out the window for a moment. Who would I want to give these dreams to? It would just be cruel. Well, maybe Luke. Maybe he would finally understand.

"When I transferred my power to Clay, my spark lit brightly. When I transferred it to Luke, your spark lit brightly. That's why I sent him. Well, part of the reason."

"You knew?" he said in a shocked tone.

"I wasn't sure. But I wasn't wrong, was I?" Gabby watched Luke closely.

Luke scowled at her.

"I could pass my power to you," she said.

She'd barely spoken the words when Clay and Luke simultaneously shouted,

"No." Clay turned in his seat to give Gabby a look. It wasn't angry, but I could still see a stubborn warning there.

She and I shared a look. "It drains me," Gabby admitted. "At least, it did before I Claimed Clay." She reached forward and ran her fingers in Clay's hair. "Clay, it probably won't affect me anymore."

He shook his head. "Hands to yourself."

I could see he wouldn't be facing forward again anytime soon. She sighed and sat back.

"What's your reason for not wanting me to try?" she asked Luke.

"She's perfect the way she is," he answered vaguely and looked out the window.

Clay laughed. Gabby looked as confused as I felt, but then understanding lit her eyes.

"Have you felt the other part of my ability? The attraction I have on men?" I nodded recalling the dreams from this life. "I transfer that, too. When I transferred it to Clay," she smiled and her eyes drifted to him. He gave a tiny shake of his head as his teeth made a brilliant appearance. "Well, I Claimed him on the spot," she said.

Ah. So Luke wouldn't be able to resist me? Sign me up!

Gabby and I shared a look, but Clay kept too close of an eye on Gabby.

"I'd guessed about there being another race," Gabby said quietly. She looked at Clay sadly. "We came up here a day early because they tried challenging Clay. The men had a different color spark. While one had Clay distracted, another came in from the back. Clay heard and got there in time. But not before I saw the man." She turned and looked at me, clearly upset. "I felt it. The pull. But it felt so wrong," she whispered.

"Because for you, it was," I said. Then I looked at Clay. "To the death?"

He gave the barest shake of his head. That was a problem. But I didn't say anything more.

CHAPTER EIGHTEEN

A WEEK LATER WE REACHED GEORGIA. WE'D DRIVEN THROUGH A wicked storm and ended up a little further south than where we wanted to be. With Gabby's watchful eye, we'd avoided detection, though we'd experienced a few close calls. We'd woken one morning to a knock on our door and a quick "pack up." We'd left that hotel minutes before the Urbat reached town. They were only scouting Gabby assured us, but no one wanted to take the chance. She said their net was still spread wide. They were still trying to find us.

They had managed to catch a lone werewolf the fourth day after our departure from the Compound. The Elders immediately reached out to the man and remained mute for several hours. I shivered watching their faces and imagined the poor werewolf begging for information to give his captors as they tortured him.

Luke wrapped his arm around my shoulders and whispered words I couldn't remember afterward. He understood that I relived my own tortured pasts while the man remained in the Urbat's hands. When the Elders started speaking again, I knew his torture was over. I struggled to pull myself out of my dark memories. Luke was my anchor. He held my hand through it all, worry etched on his face.

He continued to fuss over what I ate, too. Under his care, I put on a few needed pounds and finally got more than two consecutive nights of good sleep. He started sleeping with a bag of chips next to the bed until I woke with crumbs in my hair and put a stop to his snacking.

We trudged into the lobby of yet another hotel, dripping and tired of being on the road. I was beginning to wonder if anywhere would ever feel like home again. Nana came up to me and pulled me away from Luke.

"I'd like to take out the stitches today. It was a shallow enough cut that it should be fine, but you'll need to take it easy."

I eagerly agreed. They were itching like crazy and uncomfortable. Once we had our rooms, she knocked on our door. Luke held my hand as she cut the first loop. It didn't hurt. Then, she tugged. I suffered a sharp sting on the surface as the stitch broke free from the healing skin. My stomach turned over at the queer feeling of something sliding under my skin.

"That was the easy one," Nana said. "A small one I did as a test to make sure you'd sleep through it. The next few are longer running stitches."

I didn't like the sound of that. More tugging, a little bleeding, and a lot of that under the skin crawling occurred over the next few minutes, but then she was done. I looked down at my stomach unimpressed with the new decoration on my skin. I sighed and moved to tug my shirt down.

"Not yet," she said, reaching down for a bottle. "It needs to be cleaned again." She passed the small bottle of rubbing alcohol to Luke. "I think you can take it from here."

I did not want the alcohol on all the new holes in my skin. Most of them bled like little pinpricks. Luke watched me with a smile when I slowly tugged my shirt down.

"You heard her," he said. "Let's do this quick, and then we can grab dinner."

"I'm too sick for dinner. Let's skip it," I said, referring to the cleaning.

"Bethi, you're tougher than this," Luke said.

His gentle words made me feel like a coward. So, I made a face at him and exposed the cut. "Go on, you sadist. Inflict some more pain on your poor little human." I closed my eyes waiting for the pain, but felt nothing. Then, something brushed my forehead. A soft kiss. I smiled. He did that when he wanted to comfort me. It always worked.

A light touch of something cold on my almost healed cut elicited a gasp from me. Immediately, the antiseptic sting followed. He methodically touched each spot. I knew he had finished when he placed another kiss on my forehead.

Opening my eyes, I caught his tender look as he apologized. "I'm sorry I hurt you."

I gave a little laugh. "You didn't hurt me. I did. I'm good at that."

He helped me sit up. "But not anymore. Never again." He placed gentle fingers under my chin, forcing me to meet his gaze until I nodded.

Satisfied, he moved away from the bed and cleaned up the tissues he'd used. I stood slowly, testing my capabilities. It felt weird. It was probably in my head, but I worried the wound would pop right back open. So, though I stood straight, my movements were slow and easy like Nana had recommended.

"Since we're eating at the hotel's restaurant, it might be better if you leave that here," he commented nodding toward the knife strapped to my thigh.

After leaving the Compound, I'd taken to wearing my knife strapped to my leg. Nana had loaned me a cute peacoat to replace Luke's shredded jacket. The new coat covered the knife whenever we stopped.

Sighing, I bent and released the clasp. I handed the bundle to Luke and watched him tuck it into our bag. When he joined me at the door, he placed another gentle kiss on my forehead. "We'll all be there," he murmured. "You won't need it."

I gave the bag a long wistful glance and left with Luke.

Down in the lobby, the others waited. The boys were being entertained by Grey and Jim doing "up-downs." The term wasn't something I associated with what they did. Each boy held the thumbs of one of the men. The men closed their hands over the boys' wrists and then started lifting and lowering them. It caused fits of giggles, but I didn't see how it could be much fun. To me, it looked like their arms would get sore. The boys', not the werewolves'. I knew the werewolves could lift like that forever.

"All set?" Nana asked.

I wrinkled my nose. "Yes. He got each one."

She smiled. "We'll get you a dessert for putting up with that."

Aden immediately begged to be let down and scampered over to my side. "Can I sit by you?" he asked sweetly. I'd watched how Jim often stole food from Aden's plate, and Aden in turn robbed whomever else sat closest to him. No doubt, he wanted my dessert. Still, I agreed.

The wait staff had already prepared a table for our large party and sat us as soon as we entered the hotel's dining room. Luke sat on one side of me with Aden on the other. Michelle sat on Aden's other side, close to Emmitt. Jim was quick to sit across from Aden. Liam was on his other side.

Gabby claimed the spot directly across from me. Since driving together, she often took every opportunity to talk to me about her gift, trying to figure out all of its possibilities. We even found a moment free of our men where she'd offered to pass her gift to me. I'd been so tempted but knew we couldn't risk her losing her ability to see the sparks and guide our route. So, I'd regretfully declined the offer.

Talk around the table rose as everyone tried to decide what to order. It was nice not having to worry about money. Michelle's lawyer contact helped her get the funds we needed throughout our journey. No one made a fuss about using it, so I didn't either. I had enough to worry about. Besides, that's what she was meant to do.

While eyeing the baked lasagna on the menu, Gabby nudged me under the table. I looked up to see her unfocused gaze. "One of them just changed direction," she mouthed. Both Luke and Clay caught it, but no one else paid it any attention. "Maybe the rain?" she whispered hopefully, her eyes focusing again on the menu. She didn't look up again, but I could tell she monitored the progress of whoever had caught her attention. We ordered, and most of the adults conversed or entertained the children. I kept a close eye on Gabby.

She reached for Clay's hand. He wrapped both of his around hers and tilted his head. That finally caught the attention of Grey.

"What is it?" he asked softly, looking between Clay and Gabby. The table grew quiet, even the boys. Michelle hugged Aden to her side. Jim placed a gentle hand on top Liam's head.

"Someone's changed their direction," I said.

"A complete turn," Gabby added.

"With all this rain, we should be fine," Sam assured the suddenly tense group. But we knew all it took was one of them to catch the scent and send word.

"Have any others changed?" Nana asked.

"I thought the rest looked like the same inconsistencies they've been doing since the beginning. Remember how I said it looked like a net? Several have changed directions moving toward a central point," she frowned. "They are doing that in six areas. We seem to be in the middle of one. The areas are huge though, several states. Big nets to catch little fish."

"Do we need to move?" Grey's eyes lacked their usual humor.

Gabby shook her head slowly. "I'm not as worried about their nets as much as I am the one closest to us. About a mile now."

The Elders shared a look. The waitress came to ask if we needed any refills. Jim asked for a double whiskey and two kiddie cocktails. Aden gave Jim a cautious smile.

"That's close, but with the rain, we don't think they could track us even if they were right outside the door," Nana said. Thunder boomed to punctuate her point. "Gabby, keep us updated. Sam, grab everyone's room keys and gather our things in my room. If they reach the parking lot, we'll all go there."

Sam stood and left. The waitress delivered the whiskey and kids' sodas. Jim pushed the sodas to the boys and the whiskey to Michelle. It was then I saw her pale face and worried looks at the boys.

"Nana," she said. "Call Mary and Gregory. You're right. It's safer."

Nana nodded sadly. I'd wondered when she would send them away and thought her foolish for keeping them with us this long. But I did understand. How could you let go of someone you loved so much?

Michelle took a small sip, and Emmitt commented, "I guess I'm losing another shirt." It did the trick. Some color came back into her cheeks.

She leaned over and kissed the top of Aden's head and asked if they could play tic-tac-toe together. He eagerly turned over his placemat.

I could see the exact moment we were out of danger. Gabby took a deep calming breath and removed her hand from Clay's. "He's close, but stopped moving," Gabby said.

"Probably holing up out of the rain," Clay said. That man's voice did serious things to a girl's insides. Gabby caught my stare and grinned at me knowingly.

"If he clears out before check out tomorrow morning, we'll see if we can book the rooms for another night. It will give Mary and Gregory enough time to reach us," Nana spoke directly to Emmitt. Michelle continued to play with Aden but took another sip of whiskey at the news.

A few minutes later Sam rejoined us just in time for our food. I dug into my meal and looked forward to staying there another day.

STUFFED FROM DINNER even with Aden's help with dessert, I willingly followed everyone back to Nana's room where we all grabbed our things. The Elders agreed it would be best if they spread themselves throughout the rooms in case we needed a quick warning to leave. Grey and Carlos roomed with us, Sam stayed with Gabby and Clay, and Nana with Charlene and Thomas since their room adjoined to Michelle and Emmitt's.

Feeling awkward, I closed myself in the bathroom to get ready for bed. I washed my face, brushed my teeth, then stared at my bag. If we needed to leave in the middle of the night, I wasn't about to run out into the storm wearing sleep pants. I grabbed some clean clothes and changed. When I emerged, I saw the rest had the same idea—except for Luke. When he saw me, he smiled, pulled off his shirt, and lay back with an arm across my pillow. An open invitation to my favorite spot to sleep.

I crawled into bed and gave in to a dreamless night.

THE MORNING BROUGHT BETTER NEWS. Grey greeted me with a smile saying, "We're here for another day." Then he made the news sweeter saying, "Carlos and I are going back into our own room. It's a good thing you're a solid sleeper because he snores." He looked at Luke who grinned and seemed undisturbed by the news.

We went to breakfast and listened to everyone else's plans for the day. Michelle wanted to take the kids to a movie —early showing of course—and Nana wanted to shop for some snacks to pack in the cars for everyone. Grey claimed Carlos just wanted to watch cable all day. Carlos' only reaction to that was a long look at Grey. I had a feeling it was Grey who wanted to watch cable all day. Gabby said she had schoolwork she wanted to focus on for a few hours. I envied her belief that life would continue as normal once we found Peace. I wasn't about to tell her otherwise.

Sam looked at Luke and me. "What about you two?"

"Nothing that involves driving," I said.

Sam smiled. "Well, Grey will be here if you need anything," he said, looking first at Gabby then at me. "I think I'm going to tag along with Winifred."

LUKE and I ended up walking with Emmitt and his family to the movie theater. The kids picked out a new cartoon for everyone to see. Luke and I got our own popcorn to share. It felt weird going to a movie, but Gabby had assured us there was no one close. And there wasn't anything else to do but wait until Mary and Gregory came for the kids.

So, I sat back and enjoyed the show, laughing—really laughing—for the first time since the dreams had started. Luke surprised me by cupping my chin and pulling my attention from the screen. Before I knew what he intended, his lips met mine in a kiss so mind-numbing and brief that I blinked at the screen for several minutes afterward. When I looked back at him, he watched the screen with a tiny image of the movie reflected in his eyes.

Not knowing what to think of the unexpected kiss, I went back to enjoying the movie, as I threaded my fingers through his. Every once in a while his thumb would smooth over the back of my hand.

After the show, we all walked back to the hotel. Everyone else was going to lunch, but the popcorn from the theater ruined my appetite, and I felt the tug of a dream. So, Luke and I walked back to our room.

Instead of giving into the dream, I decided to take a shower and warned Luke it would be a warm one just in case he thought I was taking too long. I hadn't enjoyed the last time I fell asleep in a hotel bathtub.

Stripped down and letting the water run, I looked at myself in the mirror. I still desperately wanted to Claim Luke and wished I was brave enough to walk out there just as I was to try to tempt him. But I wasn't. The scars on my arms bothered me. They were from a desperate time in my life that I really didn't want to think about. The one on my stomach was just stupid. What really bothered me was my weight. I'd gained a little but not enough to look appealing, in my mind. Every time I pictured myself bare in Luke's presence, a scene from *Les Misérables*—the old one, not the new—interposed itself. It was the part where Uma Thurman pulled back the covers to offer herself as payment to her landlord. Thin and sickly, she'd disgusted him. That was what I envisioned. A grand gesture and an epic failure that would leave me crushed.

Covering myself with my arms, I ducked under the spray ready to wash away all my ugliness. It didn't work.

When I stepped out of the shower, I was the same scarred, thin me. I looked around for my bag and started to panic. I hadn't brought it in with me. Was this a self-fulfilling prophecy? I sat on the toilet on the verge of tears with a dream tapping its sharp fingers on my skull.

Why did life have to be so hard?

A knock on the door startled me.

"You all right?" Luke asked from the other side.

I quickly stood and rubbed my yet unshed tears away. "Yeah. I just forgot my bag."

"I'll get it." His voice sounded fainter, and I knew he had already walked away from the door.

Making a quick I-don't-want-to-do-this face, I turned the knob and opened it a few inches to look out. He had his back to me, picking up the bag from one of the beds. When he turned and saw me, he stopped. Shame burned me as I gave him an uncertain smile, closed the door a bit further, and held out a hand, palm up. Only after I did it, did I realize I'd exposed my wrist. My eyes flew to his again. He hadn't moved.

I curled up, died, and was reborn in the fires of my anguish. Yanking the door open, I marched right up to him and pried the bag from his dead fingers.

"Just so you know, I had a boyfriend. Before the dreams started, and I went crazy," I said defensively. "It was pretty serious."

Finally, emotion broke through his shocked expression.

"But I cut ties when I realized what was coming my way. You know I'm old enough in the human world...and I know that by werewolf standards I'm old enough. When you're ready, you let me know," I said boldly, turning away from him.

He stopped me, curling his fingers loosely around my upper arms. The same arms that had a death hold on the towel and my remaining dignity.

"What are you saying?" he asked, his voice laced with a hint of a growl.

I dropped the bag and stepped toward him. "You didn't think a girl willing to cut herself, take drugs, run away from home, and hitch rides from strangers would save herself, did you?"

"Joshua?" he growled.

Giving a small laugh, I touched his jaw, tracing the ridge of it with a fingertip. "No way. He smelled like mud." Then his reaction hit me like a lightning bolt. His tense jaw, his overly focused concentration on my face...nowhere else but my face. He *wanted* to see more. My heart started beating faster, and the angry shame shrank back. Hopeful, I stood on my tiptoes.

"You smell like home," I whispered, brushing my lips against his.

He stood still, keeping his arms at his sides as I reached up and threaded my fingers in his hair. My lips traced his. Tiny tremors shook him. Then, he broke. His arms came alive and gently circled around me. He tilted his head and pressed his lips against mine. Tingles chased up and down my back. His mouth opened slightly as he planted little kisses in a trail down my neck. He nipped the tender skin there before continuing down to my collarbone.

"Tell me this is a yes," I whispered, struggling to keep my focus.

He groaned, but didn't stop. His mouth wandered back up my throat so I had to tilt my head back. He kissed his way to my lips, but before he claimed them, he pulled back to meet my eyes.

"This is a yes." He tilted his head exposing his throat.

I reached up to hold his shoulders and pull him down a bit. The towel fell to the floor. His breathing came in quick pants, matching mine. I kissed him gently, rubbing my lips on the corded muscles of his neck. Then, I bit.

He groaned and held me to him. A surge of love flooded me along with a consuming need to possess. They weren't my feelings. Not all of them, anyway. I moved on, kissing my way up his neck to his jaw. When he pulled back, a bloody smudge remained where I'd bit him, nothing else.

His lips claimed mine in a bruising kiss, and he turned us, backing me toward the bed. My heart started beating so fast I thought it would burst from my chest.

When we reached the bed, he stopped and pulled his shirt off. I knew then that we wouldn't stop at just Claiming. Anticipation flooded me. This time it was all my emotion. I smiled shyly at him and wrapped my arms around his neck.

SNUGGLED AGAINST HIS SIDE, I traced my fingers through the hair on his chest, content and peaceful. No dreams tugged at me. I hadn't looked at him yet. I wasn't sure if he would regret what we'd done.

"You lied," he said quietly, turning to kiss the top of my head.

"The last lie I'll be able to get away with now. Well, with you anyway." I didn't need to ask if he was mad at me. I knew he wasn't. I could feel his contentment blending with mine.

"Was there even a boyfriend?" he asked softly.

"Not a serious one," I admitted. "Still wish we would have waited for the magic eighteen?" I had to know.

He turned on his side to face me, his expression tender. "Yes," he said simply. "You are worth waiting for." His love flooded me, but I felt no regret. I leaned forward to kiss him.

"You're worth waiting for, too," I said softly. "But I didn't want to risk dying without feeling this." The connection between us grew, bursting with love and life. It wasn't just the impressions I had felt with Joshua. It was so much more. There was no room for self-doubt. With Luke, I could endure anything. Be anything. Even a Judgement.

My stomach rumbled, and a thread of concern flowed through our link.

"Let's get dressed and eat," he said. The concern kept growing.

"What's wrong?" The depth of what he felt washed through me.

"You never eat right." He rose from the bed.

I forgot to breathe. I'd seen him in the all-n-all before, but now he was mine. I just wanted to jump on his back and pull him back under the covers with me. I wanted his touch. Needed it. I blinked as I struggled with my feelings and realized with a smile, they weren't just mine, because concern still flavored them.

"If you don't stop, we'll never feed you," he said with a smile as he strode to the bathroom.

WE MET everyone downstairs for dinner. Nana glanced away from her conversation with Charlene to look at us, then did a double take. Her sudden wide smile told me she knew.

"About time he pulled his head from his—" Grey started to mutter, but a nudge from Carlos cut him off.

Four new members had joined our group. Michelle's brothers clung to two faces I recognized. Paul and Henry. They spoke to Gabby with a long time familiarity as they entertained the boys. Michelle and Emmitt spoke off to the side with Gregory and Mary. Michelle's eyes were red from barely restrained tears.

When Paul looked up and saw me hand in hand with Luke, he smiled and nudged his brother. Heat rushed to my face.

Dinner moved slowly, just the way we needed it to. Michelle agreed to let the boys go on a long holiday with Gregory and Mary. Or as the boys thought of it, with Paul and Henry. We spent the time talking about nothing important, though I caught Gabby's unfocused gaze as she constantly monitored the Urbat progress.

After dinner, we all agreed to meet in the lobby early the following morning. The next day's travel would bring us to Peace.

I went to bed eagerly and looked forward to another good night's sleep. But I didn't get what I wanted.

"Daughter," she said, standing beside the bed dressed in her usual taupe gown. "You are so blessed to have finally Claimed a Mate worthy of you."

I stood at the end of the bed, looking at Luke on his side, curled around me, his arm resting over my waist. I looked so small compared to him.

I glanced at the Taupe Lady. "I thought I only dreamt of the past."

She smiled. "This is the past. Just minutes old."

"Why am I dreaming this?"

"I'm bound to the past as much as I'm bound to the present, floating in the shadows in between. This is the only place we may speak. You must hurry to find your sisters. His anger is growing and even she won't be safe much longer. Tread carefully, loved one."

She smiled and reached out to pat Luke's bare arm. He shifted in his sleep. Then, she leaned over him to place a kiss on my sleeping-self's cheek.

I bolted upright, eyes wide, the feeling of her lips lingered on my skin. The place beside the bed was empty, but I couldn't shake the creeped out feeling.

"What is it?" Luke asked, instantly awake and sitting up with me.

I turned worried eyes to him. "I don't think I'm done dreaming, yet."

He kissed me gently, coaxed me back under the covers, and encouraged me to lay my head on his chest. He ran his fingers through my hair and rubbed my back until I relaxed again. Still, I lay awake long after he started snoring.

She was worried about Courage, I was sure of it. If she lived in the past and the present, she had to know what we planned and where we were headed. I bit my lip thinking of what Courage might be enduring despite Michelle's vision of gentle treatment.

Luke inhaled long and loud just then, his fingers twitching in my hair. I smiled at the sound before closing my eyes again. We would never need to share a room with anyone else with the noise he made.

EPILOGUE

THE MORNING BROUGHT HEARTACHE FOR THE GROUP. WE ALL witnessed Michelle hold back tears as she pasted on a bright smile and said goodbye to her brothers.

I glanced at Nana and wondered if she'd reached my mother. She met my gaze briefly, but her expression gave nothing away other than how she felt about the current situation.

Liam gave Emmitt a hug and asked him to watch over Michelle. Everyone heard his loud whisper. "I think she's sad we want to play with Paul and Henry."

Emmitt smiled and hugged the boy until he protested. Then, Emmitt promised to take care of Michelle, always.

"You too, you know," Luke murmured close to my ear.

Puzzled, I turned to him.

His eyes looked slightly green in the morning light. He wrapped his hands around my arms and pulled me close. "I promise to take care of you, always," he whispered just before his lips brushed against mine.

"Always is a long time for a girl who keeps coming back," I said, leaning into him.

"Forever isn't long enough," he said, enfolding me in a warm embrace and taking the kiss to the next level.

Nana cleared her throat. "All right you two. We need to travel today."

Luke pulled back with a sassy grin and clasped my hand. I needed the support after that kiss. My head spun, and my heart stuttered.

WE ARRIVED at the last hotel I hoped we'd need to stay at. Well, in our search for Peace anyway. There was still a lot of traveling and waiting to do when—if—we exposed werewolves. The Elders still hadn't given us their official decision.

"It seems like she's staying in one spot now," Gabby commented sitting on the edge of the bed in Nana's room.

"I think it would be best if just a few of us go," I said. "Gabby, since you can locate her, an Elder, and myself."

Nana looked worried about that but didn't need to comment. Gabby did for her.

"We'll need more than that. There are more Urbat here than there should be," Gabby said.

I wrinkled my nose. It was a big city. We didn't have much of a choice. We needed to be here. I understood the need to protect ourselves but didn't like how it would look to Peace. Having a large group of strangers come up to you and try to convince you to leave with them...I didn't see that going over well with her.

"What do you suggest?"

"Six of us. Grey, Carlos, Clay, you and Luke, and me. It'll give us better protection and still leave enough protection here for the rest," Gabby said.

I knew she was right. "Okay."

"Sam's out driving to see what kind of place she's stopped at. When he gets back we can go." She stood and walked to Clay who waited by the door. "If it's somewhere nicer, Nana promised we can raid her suitcase."

"Absolutely," Nana agreed, hanging some of her things. Most of her wardrobe was a little more mature than I'd ever worn, but she always looked nice.

I looked down at my worn jeans and stained t-shirt. Ugh. Clothes kept you from being naked and cold; I hadn't thought about them any further than that. How had I not noticed? I looked at Luke.

"How can you—"

"What you wear doesn't matter. You are beautiful," he said, leaning in to place a tender kiss on my forehead. "Your clothes just help hide it from all the other guys out there."

Smiling, I shook my head at him. Possessive creatures.

Four hours later, Gabby and I sat in the car with a very mulish Luke, and stoic Clay. To me Clay didn't act much different, but Gabby kept glancing at him and telling him to calm down. When she'd found out Peace was at a club, she'd insisted that we change since we needed to look like we fit in.

Nana agreed and took us both on an impromptu shopping trip that had me twitching. I didn't mind shopping. In fact, I used to love to go clothes shopping. Before the dreams. Before Urbat started hunting us. Before I had a mission to bring us all together. Now, however, the time we spent shopping and being in the open troubled me. When we walked out of the store, I sighed in relief. We had made it through without incident. And I had new clean clothes.

Initially, Nana and Gabby had gravitated toward cute little party dresses that were sure to make a man's eyes melt and his tongue swell, but I'd flat out refused. If we were caught between an Urbat and Peace, I wanted to be able to run. Who ran in heels and a skirt? The movie extras that always died first! I did not want to be an extra. Neither woman could argue with my logic.

In our bags of purchased items, we both had stylish new jeans—mine hugged my thin frame in a sexy way rather than a sickly way—and very gossamer tops to go over low cut camis. Gabby went with pink over a red top, and I went with blue over a green top. My eyes stood out even more with the color combination. I even purchased makeup, surprising both Nana and Gabby that I knew how to use it. To me it was just a depressing reminder that I used to have a frivolous life. Now I had a life worth living.

Luke shifted uncomfortably beside me. He wore his own jeans and a shirt he'd borrowed from Sam. I couldn't believe how trendy Sam dressed.

When I'd stepped out of the bathroom dressed for our encounter with Peace, Luke hadn't said a word. He moved toward me, then did a slow walk around me. He'd whispered words to melt my heart.

"I can't believe you're mine."

However, he ruined it by telling me to go back and change. I squeezed his hand and gave him a quick smile. He frowned at me, his eyes dropped to my top.

"Ready?" I asked the group. Carlos and Grey were up front waiting for Gabby and me to give the word.

"She's still in there," Gabby confirmed.

"Let's go," I said with a deep breath. I struggled to contain my excitement. Five of us together again. My last memory of that was tainted with blood and battle. I hoped for more from this life.

Luke opened the door and extended a hand to help me out. Though I'd won the argument about the dresses, Gabby and I still wore trendy shoes instead of the sneakers I would have preferred. It gave me a few extra inches, which I liked when standing face to face with Luke. I gave him a quick kiss and moved out of the way so he could shut the door.

The neighborhood wasn't the best. A few blocks back we'd passed a burned-out car on the side of the road. There was no parking other than street parking. Bottles littered the sidewalk. Gabby gave me a worried glance. I didn't like it either but stepped forward anyway. I wouldn't leave until we at least met Peace.

Our low heels clicked in unison as we marched toward the club. The red door set in the brick wall of the building marked the entrance. There were no windows on the first level that I could see. I had my fake ID all ready to get in, but the door was unmanned. I began to wonder if the place was even licensed.

Luke made a small sound of disgust as he opened the door. The reek of stale booze and smoke rolled out toward us. Grey, the first one in the group, stepped in with a resigned look. I appreciated that I did not have their heightened senses as I followed. Luke held the door open for a moment longer than necessary trying to let in some fresh air, then followed the rest of us in.

A band played at one end, a mix of emo and rock. A small crowd stood in front of them dancing. The crowded bar stood opposite. The man there kept asking who was next.

Directly across from the entrance a stage sat behind a floor-to-ceiling wall of chain-link fence. Instead of band equipment, which would make sense, there were various fitness bags anchored to the ceiling off to the sides. In the center of the stage, on a huge mat that spread across the floor, a tall redhead faced off with a mountain of a man. The rest of the crowded room focused on the pair. The man's bald head glistened with sweat as they danced around each other. Both wore boxing gloves. It looked as if the fight had been going on for a while.

"That's her," Gabby said unnecessarily.

I knew her at first sight. Her rage boiled in her eyes. I was about to agree and suggest we wait at the bar, but Carlos was already pushing his way toward the fence, his skin rippling dangerously. I didn't care how drunk or high these people were, they were bound to notice.

I heard Grey swear and try to pull Carlos back. Carlos shook him off like it was nothing. That wasn't supposed to happen with an Elder.

On the stage, Peace ducked under a punch and came back with an uppercut to the man's jaw. The crowd groaned, but it was a good-natured groan. The man staggered back and shook his head. Carlos had reached the cage by then and paced back and forth in front of it, barely containing the beast.

Peace caught the movement and glanced at Carlos. Her opponent took that opportunity to swing. It connected hard, snapping her head back with the blow. This time the crowd booed, but I could barely hear it over Carlos' rage filled howl. He burst into his fur—*in front of everyone*—and crashed against the metal.

The wires bent inward, molding to the shape of his head and shoulder. A few of the brackets mounting the fence to the floor gave way. The fight on the stage stopped as the two stared at the huge beast attacking the fence. Peace looked stunned, but her opponent just stood there placidly.

"Clay, Luke," I gasped. "What do we do?" We needed to stop him. He was going to wreck everything. We needed Peace to accept us. We needed our first exposure to her and the world to be nice. "Watch for people taking video or pictures," I shouted.

Clay reached out an arm without moving, or taking his eyes off Carlos, and crushed a phone in someone's hand. Luke did the same but started working his way through the crowd, pulling me with him. People barely noticed us weaving our way through them. They were completely focused on the stage. So was I.

With a roar, Carlos charged again. Brackets popped free from the ceiling with a ping. The fence barely held on.

Peace's eyes rounded, and she took off through a side door behind the fence. Carlos' massive head swung in that direction. He paused for a moment, listened, then he took off with so much force, his claws left trenches in the wood floor.

As if that were the signal, the crowd came alive with panic and fear. Everyone flooded toward the exit. Luke wrapped his arms around me to protect me from being trampled. Clay had Gabby pinned to the wall by the door.

When the bar emptied, and the four of us stood alone with the buzz of an overturned speaker to keep us company, I met Gabby's eyes.

"What the hell was that?" I said in shock.

NOTE TO THE READER

I hope Luke was worth the wait! Keep reading for more information regarding the rest of the series...

AUTHOR'S NOTE

Thank you for reading the first three books in the Judgement of the Six series! As you've noticed, each girl's story overlaps and things are just getting started.

In (Un)bidden, the fourth book in the Judgement of the Six series, you'll find out how Charlene ties into the story so far and how she might have the power to shape their future. (I've included an excerpt, so be sure to keep reading!) Book 5, (Dis)content, will also tie into the scene you just read.

Not ready to move on from the first three leading men? I have just the thing you need. The Companion Series. You can get inside Clay, Emmitt, and Luke's heads and discover for yourself how there really are two different sides to the same story. Check them out here!

Your continued support keeps me writing! Please consider leaving a review or telling a friend about this series. Word of mouth recommendations is the best praise you can give an author.

Want to know about deals, release dates, and giveaways? Sign up for my newsletter at https://melissahaag.com/subscribe.

You can also find me on twitter and Facebook to keep up to date on what I'm working on.

Happy reading!

Melissa

(Un)bidden
Judgment of the Six: Book 4

Now Available!

Exhausted from a day of walking, I was ready to sleep, even without the bed I'd hoped for. Using my bag as a pillow, I made myself comfortable on the floor. As I lay in the moonlight, I wondered what I'd found here. Based on what I'd seen outside, the buildings were definitely not new. Yet, they weren't falling apart either. There were so many rooms, all of varying sizes. I wondered if perhaps this was an old commune or something.

I exhaled slowly and shut my eyes, listening to the night sounds. It didn't take me long to drift off, but I woke often since the hard floor was more uncomfortable than the ground.

By morning light, I stood with a slow stretch. My spine cracked in several spots, and I felt sore.

Shouldering my pack, I began exploring the rest of the building. The empty rooms seemed never ending. Then, I came to a set of heavy double doors.

I pushed them open and stared at the enormous space I'd discovered. Two old stone fireplaces, blackened by soot and age, were the room's source of heat. I frowned, thinking back to the rooms I'd checked, and couldn't recall one outlet or heating vent. How had the people who lived here kept warm in winter?

Along the interior wall to the left of the main doors, a rough counter set with a small stone trough and an old hand pump gave me a good indication of the lifestyle of those who'd once lived here. I stepped into the room and pushed the doors closed behind me. There weren't as many cobwebs in this room, but just as many leaves littered the floor near the room's broken window.

I walked over to the pump and started pumping. A loud, metallic groan filled the air; and though I cringed at the noise, I didn't stop. My arm grew tired by the time any water came out. It ran brown at first, then clear. I scooped a handful and sniffed it. It smelled fine and was cold in my palm. I tried a bit and smiled at the fresh, crisp taste.

As I pulled the water container from my backpack, I heard a distant howl. The sound didn't scare me. I rather liked it. It meant I wasn't alone.

I set the container in the sunken trough and started pumping again. Water splashed the top of it, almost knocking it over. I kept the handle moving with one hand and held the container steady with the other. It took a few minutes, but I filled it.

After the handle fell for the last time and the water stopped splashing, I thought I heard something. As I quietly capped the container and slid it into my pack, I listened. Slight noises reached me. Nothing definite. It could have been the building settling; or because of the racket of the pump, I might have drawn the curious attention of whatever had howled.

It didn't overly concern me. Animals were generally cautious around humans. I slipped my arms through the straps of the backpack.

A noise came from the other side of the double doors. I froze. Perhaps it was a wild critter looking for a nice place to stay, just as I had.

I crossed the large area and pulled the latch of another door I had yet to explore. Sunlight poured through the opening. I stepped outside, gladly leaving whatever it was to roam as it might. The latch fell into place; and a moment later, a loud thud echoed in the empty room. My eyes widened, and I started to back away.

For a moment, there was silence. Then, the faint sound of snuffling carried through the broken window. Something bumped against the other side of the door. I jumped. What was in there? It didn't sound like a little critter. It sounded big.

A howl filled the air.

APPENDIX

The Judgements:

- Hope— Gabby, recently reluctant Mate to Clay [*Book 1: Hope(less)*]
- Prosperity — Michelle, Mate to Emmitt, son of Charlene [*Book 2: (Mis)fortune*]
- Wisdom — Bethi, Mate to Luke [*Book 3: (Un)wise*]
- Strength — Charlene, Emmitt's mother, Mate to the werewolf leader Thomas [*Book 4: (Un)bidden*]
- Peace — Isabelle [*Book 5: (Dis)content*]
- Courage — Olivia [*Book 6: (Sur)real*]

The lights Gabby sees:

- Werewolf — Blue center with a green halo
- Urbat — Blue center with a grey halo
- Human — Yellow center with a green halo
- The Judgements:
- Charlene — Yellow with a red halo
- Gabby — Yellow with an orange halo
- Michelle — Yellow with a blue halo
- Bethi — Yellow with a purple halo
- Isabelle — Yellow with a white halo
- Olivia — Yellow with a brown halo

MORE BOOKS BY MELISSA HAAG

**Judgement of the Six Series
(and Companion Books) in order:**
Hope(less)
Clay's Hope*
(Mis)fortune
Emmitt's Treasure*
(Un)wise
Luke's Dream*
(Un)bidden
Thomas' Treasure*
(Dis)content
Carlos' Peace*
(Sur)real**

*optional companion book
**written in dual point of view

Of Fates and Furies Series
Fury Frayed
Fury Focused
Fury Freed

Other Titles
Touch
Moved
Warwolf
Nephilim

CPSIA information can be obtained
at www.ICGtesting.com
Printed in the USA
FSHW020340080220
66944FS